徐蕾 王守仁 主编

历史·记忆·世界：
新时代现实主义文学研究

History, Memory and the World:
Literary Realism Studies in the New Era

南京大学出版社

第二届新时代现实主义文学研究国际研讨会（2023年10月20-22日）

序

正如埃尔泽(Jens Elze)在近作《现实主义:美学、实验、政治》(*Realism: Aesthetics, Experiments, Politics*, 2022)中所言,"自新千年第一个十年中期以来,现实主义已经强势归来,在更为宽广的文学与文化研究领域获得了重新关注与合法地位"。[①]短短十多年间,对现实主义文学和理论进行系统深入、富有新意研究的专著、论文、专刊相继问世,涌现出不少围绕现实主义文学的新概念:从"情感现实主义"(Thrailkill 2006)、"电报现实主义"(Menke 2008)、"资本主义现实主义"(Fisher 2009)、"现实主义的二律背反"(Jameson 2013)、"转喻式现实主义"(Morris 2013),到晚近的"量子现实主义"(Holland 2020)、"合成现实主义"(Jones 2021)、"现实主义的政治"(Docherty 2022)等等,不一而足。[②] 2012年《现代语言季刊》(*Modern Language Quarterly*)推出"边缘的现实主义"主题专刊时,主持人埃斯蒂(Jed Esty)与莱(Colleen

---

[①] Jens Elze, *Realism: Aesthetics, Experiments, Politics*. Bloomsbury Academic, 2022, p. 1.
[②] 参见 Jane F. Thrailkill, "Emotive Realism," in *Journal of Narrative Theory* 36.3 (2006), pp. 365 – 388. Richard Menke, *Telegraphic Realism: Victorian Fiction and Other Information Systems*. Stanford University Press, 2008. Mark Fisher, *Capitalist Realism*. Zero Books, 2009. Fredric Jameson, *The Antinomies of Realism*. Verso, 2013. Pam Morris, "Making the Case for Metonymic Realism," in *Realisms in Contemporary Culture: Theories, Politics and Media Configurations*, eds. Dorothee Birke and Stella Butter. De Gruyter, 2013, pp. 13 – 32. Mary K. Holland, *The Moral Worlds of Contemporary Realism*. Bloomsbury Academic, 2020. Charlotte Jones, *Synthetic Realism: Realism, Form and Representation in Edwardian Novel*. Oxford University Press, 2021. Thomas Docherty, *The Politics of Realism*. Bloomsbury Academic, 2022.

Lye)将这种文学批评领域研究方法发生的新变化概括为"新现实主义转向"(new realist turn),认为是继"语言学转向""文化转向"之后文学研究发展的新动向。[①] 2021年魏宁格(Robert Weninger)在《现实主义的景观:比较视野下的现实主义文学再思考》(*Landscapes of Realism: Rethinking Literary Realism in Comparative Perspectives*)第一卷中辩证地把这种转向视作一种内涵着双重意义的回归:现实主义的"回归"(return)意味着现实主义文学的复兴,而作为复数的回归(returns)也表征着"某种投资或风险的回报",指向现实主义被重新发现的价值。在他看来,"现实主义从未消失过;它或许被边缘过、驱逐过、嘲讽过、鄙夷过,但——我们今天必须后知后觉地看到——正是因为那些厌恶现实主义的批评家和作家视其无所不在、四处弥散、无孔不入,才会如此坚定地对其进行瓦解与打压"。[②] 显然,现实主义文学的持久影响力远远超过了现代主义者们的想象;甚至依照盖伊(Peter Gay)在《现实主义的报复》(*Savage Reprisals*,2002)一书中的说法,现代主义作家们实乃"各自为政的现实主义者,现实主义小说从未消失",革新者们"只不过是为小说作者更进一步扩展了现实世界的范围而已"。[③]

盖伊的论断与吴元迈等学者在五卷本《20世纪外国文学史》(2004)基于20世纪外国文学整体概况研究而提出的观点几乎不谋而合。吴元迈在《绪论》中指出:"20世纪现实主义文学在形式与手法方面日益丰富多样,包括它对非现实主义诸多流派艺术经验的借鉴,这并不意味着现实主义在非现实主义化,在异化,在离经叛道;恰恰相反,这是现实主

[①] 参见 Jed Esty and Collen Lye, "Peripheral Realisms Now," in *Modern Language Quarterly* 73.3 (2012), pp. 269-288.

[②] Dirk Göttsche, Rosa Mucignat and Robert Weninger, eds., *Landscapes of Realism: Rethinking Literary Realism in Comparative Perspectives. Volume I: Mapping Realism*. John Benjamins Publishing Company, 2021, p. 687.

[③] 彼得·盖伊,《现实主义的报复》,刘森尧译,北京联合出版社,2023年,第23页。

义自身发展的内在需要,也是现实主义的与时俱进。"①中外学者关于20世纪现实主义文学发展走向问题上形成的共识绝非巧合。事实上,这种国内外学术界的同频共振在南京大学当代外国文学与文化研究中心近年来围绕现实主义文学开展的各项研究与国际合作推进下,益发引人瞩目且硕果累累。近五年来,中心出版国家社科基金重大项目研究成果《战后世界进程与外国文学进程研究》第一卷《战后现实主义文学研究》(2019)、论文集《表征与重构:跨越边界的现实主义文学》(2019),在国内外重要学术期刊《外国文学动态研究》(2020)、*Orbis Litterarum*(2022)、《外国语文研究》(2022)、《外国文学研究》(2024)主持现实主义研究专题或专栏,发表系列文章,受到学界的关注和好评。

2018年10月,第一届"新时代现实主义文学研究"国际研讨会在南京大学成功举办。为推进现实主义文学理论、学术观点和研究方法创新,加强国际学术交流,当代外国文学与文化研究中心在相隔五年后再次举办现实主义文学研究国际研讨会,会议主题为"重访现实主义:历史·记忆·世界",有140多位专家学者和年轻学子参会。对于中心而言,新现实主义转向背景下"重访现实主义"的主题还有着另一层更加现实的意义,即借助现实主义文学研究提供的美好学术契机,迎接国内外学术界同行的归来。2023年10月举办的第二届"新时代现实主义文学研究"国际研讨会邀请到诺贝尔文学奖获得者、法国作家勒克莱齐奥(Jean-Marie Gustave Le Clézio)和埃尔诺(Annie Ernaux)参与会议的交流研讨,来自中国、法国、德国、丹麦、克罗地亚、葡萄牙的学者作大会发言,其中一位教授是中国社科院学部委员,两位教授是文科资深教授,两位教授是欧洲科学院院士,他们的积极参与使得本次国际研讨会成为一次高水平、高质量、高层次的学术交流活动。现实主义从历史深

---

① 吴元迈主编,《20世纪外国文学史·第一卷》,译林出版社,2004年,第4页。

处走来,时代经验源自人们对历史的孜孜叩问与深刻反思。当代现实主义文学作品擅长以碎片化、个性化、微观化的个体经验为着眼点,在描摹时代洪流中个人记忆里发现集体记忆,"恢复历史的真实意义"。[①]世界则是我们理解当代现实主义的另一个锚定点。文学作为书写艺术是生活的审美表现、时代的文化表征,无论其最原始还是最现代的不竭源泉始终是现实。研讨会选择"历史""记忆""世界"三个维度展开交流讨论,有助于深化对现实主义文学和知识体系的当代认知与思考。

本论文集收录的二十五篇中英文文章选自第二届"新时代现实主义文学研究"国际研讨会的参会论文,这些文章围绕现实主义文学的经典作品与理论阐释、当代现实主义文学的创作理论、新时代世界文学范畴中的现实主义书写等议题,展开多角度、跨学科、跨文化的辩证分析与比较论证,提出的学术观点和研究方法丰富了现实主义的理论话语与进路,为现实主义文学研究向纵深发展标定了新的出发点。王守仁、刘洋的论文《现实主义的幽灵》("The Specters of Realism")巧妙借用现实主义文学与幽灵的类比关系,高屋建瓴地阐释了当代文学研究重访现实主义的学术价值与实际意义。文章引用《共产党宣言》中"一个幽灵,共产主义的幽灵在欧洲徘徊"的著名论断,指出19世纪中叶欧洲同时徘徊着处于鼎盛时期的现实主义文学"幽灵"。这一幽灵穿越时空,四处弥散,从未离我们而去,在过去与现在、在场与缺席、物质与精神、可见与不可见的阈限边界徘徊,重访现实主义旨在揭示现实主义历久弥新的机制。幽灵不仅作为一种独特的认知方式现身于此次国际研讨会的大会发言上,它也形塑着国内外学者对现实主义文学经典作品与理论阐释的基本策略。奥尔巴赫(Erich Auerbach)的《摹仿论:西方文学中所描绘的现实》(*Mimesis: The Representation of Reality in Western Literature*,1946)无疑是此次国际研讨会上被频频召唤的现

---

① 安妮·埃尔诺,《悠悠岁月》,吴岳添译,人民文学出版社,2010年,第210页。

实主义研究经典论著。德国波茨坦大学埃特（Ottmar Ette）的论文《摹仿论：西方与非西方世界文学中所描绘的现实生活》("Mimesis: The Representation of Lived Reality in Western and Non-Western Literatures of the World")选题直接脱胎于这部现实主义研究史上的里程碑之作，他以曹雪芹的《红楼梦》、中国当代作家残雪的《天堂里的对话》、20世纪上半叶西班牙作家奥布（Max Aub）的《德杰尔法的日记》、诺贝尔奖获得者秘鲁作家略萨（Mario Vargas Llosa）的《凯尔特之梦》为例，考察了被奥尔巴赫归为现代现实主义文学两大源头的《圣经》传统与荷马史诗所分别代表的大陆式书写与群岛式书写在西方与非西方文学作品中纷繁复杂的表现，拓展了现实主义书写的世界文学版图。来自克罗地亚萨格勒布大学的尤基奇（Tatjana Jukic）在《悲剧现实主义》("Tragic Realism")一文中，把《摹仿论》与奥尔巴赫在1941至1942年间发表现实主义主题演讲进行互文式解读，认为奥尔巴赫对现实主义的理解汲取了古希腊经典悲剧的要素，同希腊悲剧一样，现代现实主义介入了世界的激进历时性，而民主的概念体系正是通过这一历史性得以商榷形成。法国图尔大学杜福尔（Philippe Dufour）与蒋承勇不约而同地回到19世纪欧洲现实主义文学作品之中，前者的《现实主义小说或现代讽刺》以司汤达、巴尔扎克、福楼拜等经典法国现实主义作家为例证，认为19世纪现实主义可以被定义为某种"嘲讽"语调，现实主义小说构建了怀疑式讽刺，曾被巴赫金高度赞誉的小说的对话性应理解为他们对社会话语的总体讽刺；后者的《西方文学典型塑造"三模式"论——以现代现实主义为中心的比较辨析》梳理并廓新西方文学"典型"塑造理论，归纳出"观念—性格"、"环境—性格"和"抽象—象征"三种基本模式，指出19世纪现代现实主义注重刻画人物性格与环境之间的关系，更贴近读者且富有人文内涵与审美意蕴。在某种意义上，徐蕾的《全知叙事者的归来：加尔各特的〈诺言〉与维多利亚时代现实主义小说》为现实主义文学幽灵的归来提供了一个有趣的个案研究,文章认为当代南非作家加尔各特(Damon Galgut)2021年布克奖小说《诺言》的叙事者全面复活了英国维多利亚小说中常见的全知叙事运作机制,并借助文本内部的"沉默"或"空白"以召唤读者对南非白人的种族主义无意识进行反动与解构;因此,被挪用的19世纪现实主义叙事传统成为加尔各特面对当代南非文学在现实主义与(后)现代主义之间该何去何从的一种独特选择。

当代现实主义文学的创作理论是本次国际研讨会与会者们关注的核心话题之一,国内外学者们围绕现实主义的本体论、非虚构性、悖论性、道德属性,以及与哥特文学、科幻文学的复杂关系各抒己见,产生了丰硕成果。作为《现实主义的景观》第二卷主编,丹麦奥胡斯大学拉森(Svend Erik Larsen)从本体论视角考察了现实主义在当代全球文化与文学交流背景下,其开放进程所包含的各种冲突及其对中心与边缘的挑战,让"何谓真实"的疑问突破了物质真实的范畴,亟待从更为复杂的全球网络系统中进行重新定位与把握。黄荭对2022年诺贝尔文学奖得主埃尔诺的邮件访谈《"我写作不求'再现现实',而要追寻现实"》引入当代现实主义写作的非虚构维度,揭示了另一种材质的真实。埃尔诺始终如一地书写生活,从自我出发、从个人和集体的记忆出发去揭露和反思现实,通过选择主题和选择处理它的方式介入社会,采用包括日记在内的形式展现现实。现实主义的非虚构性也是葛雅纯文章论证的核心问题,她以华裔美国女作家张纯如的《南京大屠杀》为例,主张打破虚构与非虚构性文类分野,将传记、日记、历史纪实等非虚构类体裁作品纳入现实主义文学的范畴。燕山大学孙立武的文章聚焦现实主义"求真"的悖论性,从哲学层面上回溯了现实主义理论的跨学科旅行,认为可以通过挖掘其悖论性内核,以应对当下现实主义多语症所导致的"失语"。段道余的《论艾丽丝·默多克的现实观》把对现实主义的考察引入了道德的语义场,指出20世纪英国作家默多克笔下的现实承载着个体道德的追寻以及对他人现实的认知,展现了柏拉图哲学思想启迪之下现实主义书写的道德维度。现实主义创作与其他文学风格及类型的交叉融合在刘玉红的《美国南方女性文学的哥特现实主义》、杨湃湃的《从"可能世界"到"实在世界":科幻小说与现实》、林叶的《科幻与现实主义文学的距离与张力》中得到了深入挖掘,充分呈现了现实主义文学的虚构之维及其与哥特文学、科幻文学的暗通之处。

新时代世界文学领域中的现实主义书写研究是本次研讨会上最为突出的议题。有着不同研究语种背景与学术研究专长的中外学者们特别聚焦于20世纪与新千年中外文学作品,范围涵盖亚洲、欧洲、非洲、美洲地区。当代法国现实主义文学研究方面,曹丹红、侯礼颖考察了1970年代末1980年代初法国的新现实主义写作,指出这批身处当代文学转型期的创作者在反摹仿与反小说倾向、文体杂糅与创新,以及自我虚构上具有共性特征。史婷烨与陶沙、高方的研究则分别聚焦新千年以来两位获奖法国作家埃尔诺与迪奥普(David Diop)的现实主义书写:在前者看来,埃尔诺的无人称自传结合了文字与图像的跨媒介手法,最大限度的捕捉了真实;后两位作者认为,获得2021年布克国际奖的塞内加尔、法国混血作家迪奥普通过书写越界人物的身份困境,呈现了格里桑(Édouard Glissant)提出的"世界性"的意义。当代英国现实主义文学研究方面,宋艳芳与刘利平分别考察了当代英国文坛两位重要作家布雷德伯里(Malcolm Bradbury)和诺贝尔文学奖得主石黑一雄(Kazuo Ishiguro)的历史书写,前者借助齐泽克的"歪像"概念剖析了布雷德伯里小说《历史人物》对20世纪60—70年代英国社会景观的曲折再现,后者择取石黑一雄的日本"二战"题材小说,从记忆研究视角探析作家历史书写的个性化风格。陈丽、刘莉的文章分别聚焦了两位新锐英国作家斯图尔特(Douglas Stuart)和卡斯克(Rachel Cusk),前者指出斯图尔特的 2020 年布克奖小说《舒吉·贝恩》以"残酷"为方法,在叙事情节、形式和民族性上构建了格拉斯哥的城市叙事,后者以卡斯克的《转折》为例,揭示了当代英国社会在后真相语境下遭遇的真相与共识的悖论。当代德国现实主义文学研究方面,胡成静、庄玮的论文运用数字人文 BERT 模型解读了 2019 年德国图书奖获奖小说《我从哪里来》(Herkunft)作为德国文学新现实主义时期移民题材小说所呈现的独特情感纹理与日常情感空间。宁宇与王奕红的论文《论中上健次〈十九岁的地图〉动物化书写的现实主义内涵》通过剖析芥川奖作家中上健次的动物化书写策略,展现出 1970 年代初日本社会去历史化、去政治化乃至趋向动物化的时代走向。现实主义书写对于中国现当代文学的发展与繁荣发挥着核心作用。顾宇玥的文章回溯到 20 世纪 20 年代我国左翼文坛对新写实主义的批评话语与创作实践,而周倩的研究立足于新世纪以来中国乡土书写的回归与开拓,提示了复兴现实主义传统对于振兴乡土书写的时代意义。

  若我们将目光投向文学的阅读、接受与评价体系,便不难发现现实主义文学在国内外文学出版市场与大众读者群体中始终占据核心地位,诺贝尔文学奖、英国布克奖(国际布克奖)、法国的龚古尔文学奖等世界级文学奖项对现实主义作品的偏好已毋庸置疑。不仅如此,现实主义文学近年来在外国文学与世界文学研究领域得到的学术关注也呈显著上升趋势。对于中国学者而言,现实主义文学根植于近现代中国深厚的历史资源与肥沃的地域文化土壤,构成中国文学主流主脉,是中国现代文学最鲜明的色泽,相关研究因而有着更加迫切的时代使命与民族责任感,我们须始终牢记的是要回答"何为伟大的现实主义"这一核心和经典问题。这是由于现实主义文学以广阔的社会生活为对象、为依据、为源泉,与社会变革息息相关,是始终把握时代发展脉搏的经典文体。在当今的时代与社会语境中,尤其是在新媒体与新技术的冲击与挑战之下,如何通过文学书写表征真实与虚拟参差渗透的元宇宙或多元宇宙,如何维系与开拓新时代中现实主义文学承载的认知使命和审美价值,以及如何让现实主义在人工智能时代继续引领人类对未来的文学想象,存在许多新的未知领域,有待我们去探索和研究。现实主义文学伴随着时代发展焕发出勃勃生机,开展现实主义研究前景广阔,大有可为。

徐蕾、王守仁

2024 年 4 月于南京大学

目　录

The Specters of Realism ………………… 王守仁　刘洋（1）
A Realism of Conflicting Ontologies …… Svend Erik Larsen（21）
Mimesis: The Representation of Lived Reality in Western and Non-Western Literatures of the World ……………… Ottmar Ette（45）
"我写作不求'再现现实'，而要追寻现实"：安妮·埃尔诺访谈录
　　………………………………… 黄荭 & 安妮·埃尔诺（78）
Tragic Realism ……………………………… Tatjana Jukić（88）
现实主义小说或现代讽刺 ……………… 菲利普·杜福尔（111）
西方文学典型塑造"三模式"论
　　——以现代现实主义为中心的比较辨析 ………… 蒋承勇（131）
哲学的根基与概念的溯源
　　——现实主义"求真"之"悖论性" ……………… 孙立武（156）
论艾丽丝·默多克的现实观 ……………………… 段道余（171）
论法国当代作家的"新现实主义"写作 ……… 曹丹红　侯礼颖（187）
记忆书写的双重载体
　　——试论安妮·埃尔诺作品中的文字与图像 ……… 史烨婷（207）
全知叙事者的归来：加尔各特的《承诺》与维多利亚时代现实主义小说
　　………………………………………………………… 徐蕾（220）

美国南方女性文学的哥特现实主义 ·············· 刘玉红（243）

斜目而视下的英国20世纪60—70年代社会景观
　　——《历史人物》中作为"歪像"的大学校园、现代都市与日常生活空间
　　·························· 宋艳芳（258）

"残酷"作为方法:《舒吉·贝恩》的格拉斯哥城市叙事
　　·························· 陈　丽（276）

卡斯克小说《转折》中的真实与共识 ·············· 刘　莉（290）

战争记忆与历史书写
　　——论石黑一雄日本二战题材小说 ········· 刘利平（306）

数字人文视阈下德国移民家庭小说《我从哪里来》中的情感研究
　　······················ 胡成静　庄　玮（322）

两个世界间的调停者
　　——达维德·迪奥普及其"世界性"书写 ····· 陶　沙　高　方（345）

论中上健次《十九岁的地图》动物化书写的现实主义内涵
　　······················ 宁　宇　王奕红（363）

藏原惟人"新写实主义"理论在中国左翼文坛的译介与运用
　　——以"太阳社"为中心 ················ 顾宇玥（378）

现实主义的回归与开拓
　　——以新时代乡土书写为中心 ············· 周　倩（396）

从"可能世界"到"实在世界":科幻小说与现实 ······· 杨湃湃（415）

科幻与现实主义文学的距离与张力 ··············· 林　叶（436）

论张纯如非虚构类作品《南京大屠杀》的现实主义文学价值
　　·························· 葛雅纯（451）

The Specters of Realism

王守仁 刘 洋

Abstract: This paper explores the critical possibilities of "the specters of realism" as a conceptual metaphor for realism's existence in literary history, its spirit of unfolding truth as well as its approach to reality. Contrary to René Wellek's description of realism as a "period-concept", or a system of norms dominating a specific time with a distinctively traceable trajectory of rise and decline, realism has made recurrent returns to the literary landscape, and, in a spectral gesture, disrupted the linear temporality of a literary history that sees realism as proceeded by romanticism and succeeded by modernism and postmodernism. Behind the acts of mimesis is the realist impulse or desire to pursue truth, which drives realist writers to experiment on various ways to approach reality. Drawing on the "spectral turn" in cultural studies in the past three decades, the paper discusses Yan Lianke's recent critical monograph *The Veils of Liaozhai*. It argues that Yan Lianke's realist practice as both an author and critic of realism, exemplary of the contemporary realist enterprise, is premised on a hauntological epistemology that places the novel on the liminal position between the present and the absent, the material and the immaterial, and the visible and the invisible. The spectral analogy, reforming and innovating the traditional realist theory which regards the writer as the observer/subject and reality as the observed/object, provides a new perspective on realism's resilience and enduring vitality.

Key words: specters; *Liaozhai*; realism; mythorealism; reality

Author: Wang Shouren is a professor at School of Foreign Studies, Nanjing University, China. His research interests are literary history, Anglo-American fiction and realism. Liu Yang is an assistant researcher at School of Foreign Studies, Nanjing University, China. His research interests are early modern English drama and realism.

In 1848, London, at the height of European literary realism, Marx and Engels published their *Manifesto of the Communist Party*, which began with perhaps the world's most famous statement of the ghost: "A specter is haunting Europe, the specter of communism" (Marx and Engels 1). The fortune of realism since the advent of modernism has more or less coincided with that of Communism in the mid-19th century—it was forced to retreat to the realm of the spectral, and relegated to the status of a "nursery tale" (Marx and Engels 1) which affords little, if any, import to a literary academia no longer gullible to the referential illusions after the linguistic turn. The specter, nonetheless, is at the same time evidence of its undeniable existence, however implicit and incorporeal. In fact, writers and critics have in recent years hailed for a "realist turn" in literary studies, and the past decade has witnessed the publications of *The Antinomies of Realism* (Frederic Jameson, 2013), *Realism in Contemporary Culture: Theories, Politics, and Medial Configurations* (Dorothee Birke & Stella Butter, eds., 2013), *Speculative Realism and Science Fiction* (Brian Willems, 2017), *The Moral Worlds of Contemporary Realism* (Mary K. Holland 2020), and *The Politics of Realism* (Thomas Docherty, 2021), to name a few. The resurgence of realist theories and criticism has been further buoyed up by important academic journals such as *MLQ* (2012), *Novel* (2016), and *Orbis Litterarum* (2021) which have published special issues on realism. It is based on such status quo in the literary scholarship that one may suggest some slight alterations be made to the famous quote from the *Manifesto*: "The specters of realism are still haunting the world as we know it." It is also safe to assert that realism has never been away from the academic circle despite the denigrating effort of the alliance between modernism and postmodernism, and that it is a revenant, in every sense of the word, constantly returning to our present world.

In the following paper, we intend to explore the critical possibilities of the "specters of realism" as a conceptual metaphor, that is, not only to use it as a figure of speech or rhetorical device that embellishes what we already know, but to test its potential as "a discourse, a system of procuring knowledge" (Blanco and Peeren 1) in realist theorization and criticism. The first point to be established is that realism did not simply die after the rise of modernism in the 20th century. It exists with us presently rather in the form of a specter.

To illustrate this point, an example is helpful here: "The Luo Cha Country and sea market a mystical story from the classical Chinese tale collection, or as most Chinese have known it since childhood, a ghost story collection, *Strange Stories from a Chinese Studio*, or *Liaozhai*, written by Pu Songling in a period of 40 years since the 1670s to the early 1700s." The story is about how a trader's son, Ma Ji, a youth of astonishing beauty, is carried away by a typhoon in a voyage across the sea and ends up at a country where the people are hideously ugly. Having recovered from the initial shock of seeing a devil-looking stranger, the villagers are much pleased to see him and recollected tales told by their forefathers about a country called China 26,000 *li* to the west of their own, where the people are the most extraordinary in appearance. Ma Ji later learns that everything in this foreign land named Luo Cha depends not on literary talent, as in imperial China, but on beauty—the most beautiful are made ministers of state, the next handsomest are made judges and magistrates, and the third class in looks are employed in the palace of the king. Ma therefore begs the accommodating countrymen to show him the capital. So he departs with the company of the villagers, arriving just about dawn at a city whose walls are made of black stone, as black as ink, and whose city gate-houses are about 100 feet-high. Pu Songling even included a description of detail here: "Redstones were used for tiles, and picking up a broken piece Ma found that it marked his finger-nail like vermilion" (356). Here, Ma gets the chance to catch the first glimpse of the most powerful men in the country. As it turns out, all systems of judgement, all binary oppositions between the beautiful and the ugly, the high and the low are completely inversed in this country. The surpassingly gorgeous young man in China gets a chilly reception and is met with fear and antipathy. Later, in order to have an audience with the kin, Ma has to smear his face all over with coal dust, impersonating Zhang Fei, the fearsome warrior whose roar scares the river to flow backward according to legends. The king is charmed, and at once makes him a privy councilor, giving him a private banquet, and bestowing other marks of royal favor.

  The story continues with Ma Ji visiting a market in the sea, impressing the Dragon King with his literary talent and marrying his daughter. For the purpose of the present discussion, the above excerpt will suffice as a demonstration of Pu Songling's extraordinary style of relating the stories of the strange. Some scholars have noticed the singularity of his narratives as classical tales: "Unlike vernacular stories, which arguably unfold in a space clearly demarcated as fictional, *Liaozhai* tales deliberately straddle the border between fictional and historical discourse and are indeed predicated in part on the ensuing ambiguity" (Zeitlin 5). In the particular case of "The Luo Cha Country and the Sea Market," this ambiguity is unabashedly unveiled to the readers even in the title, for "Luo Cha" in other classical texts, especially in the Qing dynasty, is either the transcription of Russia—reference to an actual land, or the transliterated name of a cannibalistic demon according to Buddhism—allusion to the ghostly and the spectral. Apart from the title, the ambiguity of genre penetrates the entire narration of the story. Take for example this initial moment when Ma Ji arrives at the city wall of the strange country: "picking up a broken piece Ma found that it marked his finger-nail like vermilion" (356). Readers perusing the pages of *Liaozhai* for excitement and sensation, stimulated by tales of the strange and the anomaly, might pause at this description here and wonder: what is the purpose of this detail, which, even in the hindsight of finishing reading the whole piece, has almost nothing to do with the staple of the story? This might remind us of a similar question by Roland Barthes who once mulled over the inclusion of ostensibly irrelevant details in *A Simple Heart* and *History of the Revolution*[①]. Yet Gustave Flaubert and Jules Michelet's novels are widely received as masterpieces of realism; to include Pu Songling's *Liaozhai* in the same category would not only be far-fetched, but also anachronistic and, perhaps, Eurocentric. That a similar realist inquiry might arise from the reading of a strange-story collection tells us a lot about the potential of the spectral as the source of inspiration for the real. With narrative seriousness and arresting descriptions of details, Pu Songling achieves in this short story the paradoxical confluence of the real and the imaginary, the everyday and the strange, the affective and the sarcastic in this short tale.

[①] See Roland Barthes. *The Rustle of Language*. Richard Howard, trans. Berkeley and Los Angeles: University of California Press, 1989.

Also paradoxical are some recent attempts at pursing the real in China which end up in the strange world of *Liaozhai*. A feeling of dissatisfaction is unequivocally registered in these attempts—dissatisfaction with the available and encouraged modes of representing the real in the fiction. As Frank Kermode once pointed out, "we have a loving-hating affair with reality, we 'keep coming back to the real'; and this continually impoverishes us because it is at odds with such concords as we have achieved" (166)—concords here refer to the existing paradigms and structures of story-telling. This emotion of "loving-hating" prompts the more adventurous realist entrepreneurs to conjure up the specter of realism back to a world no longer, it seems, spellbound by its enchantment. In July 2023, Ma Ji's adventures in the Luo Cha country from 300 years ago created a renewed resonance among its contemporary readers, thanks to the eponymous song composed by Dao Lang. Due to the ambiguity of lyrics and its allusion to Pu Songling's equally ambiguous story, volunteered efforts have been made by social media users, who delved into the most infinitesimal details of the song, to discover its referential meanings. Since its release in 2023, the song became immediately an Internet phenomenon, believed by millions to be a cryptic yet unreserved revelation of the hypocrisy and imposture of certain celebrities and fellow singers, as well as an address to our times and to the big philosophical issues, suggested by the reference to Wittgenstein and the last line of the lyrics: "it is the fundamental question of humanity." Whatever Pu Songling's original purpose was, the story of "The Luo Cha Country and the Sea Market" is from now on a symbol for digging out the hidden truth, and unveiling the realities unseeable by the public eye.

When the notion that "the specters of realism are still haunting the world as we know it" is proposed, it is meant to identify a primary impulse of pursuing truth inherent in realist writings. In 2010, Fredric Jameson wrote of a utopian impulse that "is not symbolic but allegorical," which "does not correspond to a plan or to a utopian praxis," and "expresses utopian desire and invests it in a variety if unexpected and disguised, concealed, distorted ways" ("Utopia as Method" 25 - 26). He therefore called for " a hermeneutic, for the detective work of a decipherment and a reading of utopian clues and traces in the landscape of the real; a theorization and interpretation of unconscious utopian investments in realities large or small, which may be far from utopian." ("Utopia as Method" 26) In a similar vein, the realist impulse may be detectable, throughout history, in the most strange and occult stories, deviating from our commonsensical methods of perception fine-tuned by the advancement of modern sciences, as is in the case of "The Luo Cha Country and the Sea Market." Tracing to its Qing-Dynasty context, readers may sense a strong note of political mockery that is aimed at chastising the realities of the imperial court. And adapted as a song in 2023, it still fascinates its audience with the power of truth-telling that it possesses and may unleash.

This enduring vitality of the realist impulse is exactly what reminds one of a specter: a being which should have belonged to the past, yet frequently appears in the present, disrupting the forward flow of time. As Hamlet exclaimed after seeing the ghost of his murdered father:"Time is out of joint," the implication being that a pre-existing temporal sequence has been shattered into bits and pieces. Literary realism in its most restrictive definition is a "period-concept" (Wellek 2) of the 19th century, according to Rene Wellek. In his 1961 essay "The Concept of Realism in Literary Scholarship," he declared that "realism was a regulative concept, a system of norms dominating a specific time, whose rise and eventual decline it would be possible to trace and which we can set clearly apart from the norms of the periods that precede and follow it" (2). Within this 19th century framework, realism was seen as established upon some necessary conditions and criteria: "truth of observation and a depiction of commonplace events, characters and settings" which were "universal in Victorian novel criticism" (4). In short, realism was "the objective representation of contemporary social reality" (11). It is indeed a fact that we often find introductions to realism in literary history textbooks between chapters on Romanticism and Modernism, overlapping with the historical period of the Victorian era, and that we are prone to contemplating realism in terms of the great writers of the 19th century Europe: Balzac, Flaubert, Charles Dickens, etc. After this period, to talk about realism is to be either nostalgic or critical of a distant past, relevant to us now only as a deceased ancestor who provoked the rebellious youths of modernism and postmodernism with their advanced and sober knowledge of what it means to be real. Nonetheless, realism returns, just as Hamlet's dead father, a revenant haunting and disturbing his son while asking for remembrance: "Hamlet, remember me." Robert Weninger once explained the meaning of *return* as in the phrase "the returns of realism":

> The noun *return* has several meanings; it designates among other things an act of coming or going back in return for an investment or risk taken. Reflection on the word "return" in the context of realism reminds us that realism was never really gone; it might have been sidelined or ostracized, ridiculed or demoted, but—as we must conclude in hindsight today—that was only because it was perceived as so omnipresent, pervasive and intrusive that realism-averse critics and writers felt duty-bound to bring it down or put it in its place (687).

And according to the list put together by Mary K. Holland, over twenty different literary realisms have been proposed so far (31 - 32). ① Of course, they vary enormously in narrative techniques, styles and purposes—some of them seem very far from being sub-branches of realism, for example, Postmodern realism, Post-postmodern realism, Poststructural realism, Meta-realism, Metafictive realism, etc.—but they are driven unanimously by the ubiquitous realist impulse.

Let us, for now, return ourselves to the haunted night in Elsinere Castle. Here is another case, from the Renaissance this time, of resorting to the spectral for knowledge and information. It is worth noticing now that the murdered King of Denmark, "unhouseled, disappointed, unaneled" (1.5.77), returns not merely to startle, but more importantly to divulge what has been kept a secret: "Pity me not, but lend thy serious hearing / To what I shall unfold" (1.5.5 - 6). What he indeed unfolded next is the truth of the court of Denmark that unsettled Hamlet's conception of time ("Time is out of joint."). Perhaps not quite unexpectedly, truth was obtained not by the intellectual activities of approaching and scrutinizing—after all, Horatio tried and failed.

MARCELLUS
 Thou art a scholar②—speak to it, Horatio.

---

① To this list we may add with emphasis a Chinese writer's contribution: Mythorealism by Yan Lianke.
② In the 2016 Arden Shakespeare edition of *Hamlet*, the editors mark in the annotation that "Marcellus makes the conventional assumptions that (a) ghost cannot speak until spoken to, and (b) an educated man—perhaps one who speaks Latin—will be better equipped to make this attempt." It may also well be that knowledge of the spectral and the demonic was a prerequisite for being called a scholar in Renaissance England. Consider the description of a scholar in W. Vaughan's *The Golden-groue* (1600): "Now-a-dayes among the common people, he is not adiudged any scholer at all, vnless hee can tell mens Horoscopes, cast out diuels, or hath some skill in southsaying(sig. Y8v.)."

...

BERNARDO

    It would be spoke to.

MARCELLUS   Speak to it, Horatio.

HORATIO

    What art thou that usurp'st this time of night

    Together with that fair and warlike form

    In which the majesty of buried Denmark

    Did sometimes march? By heaven I charge thee speak!

MARCELLUS

    It is offended.

BERNARDO See, it stalks away.

HORATIO

    Stay. speak, speak. I charge thee, speak.

    Exit Ghost (1.1.41, 44 – 50)

The ghost in Hamlet is analogous to "the specters of realism" under discussion in this paper in two important ways. First of all, it returns to the center of focus, once and again, in times of considerable confusion and turbulence, providing a path to truth and reality. Secondly, the ghost is symbolic of the crisis of representation that many reality-oriented writers have felt since the end of the last century and is still experiencing today. The readership, just like Marcellus, would expect the professional ("scholar") to have in their possession the know-hows of approaching reality.[1] They urge their championed scholar to "speak to it," in the hope of some positive response that will bring them one step closer to truth. However, the fact is that the realist writers now often find themselves hesitant with using their representational paraphernalia. Traditionally,

---

[1] Consider, for example, the idea of "reality hunger" by David Shield.

realism assumes the role of the scholarly Horatio who is confident in his intellectual prowess and the efficacy of an investigation. In a famous metaphor made by Stendhal, the realist writer is a mirror walking down the road, reflecting whatever there is along the way. ① Yet the specter, with its response of stalking away, warns us that there is always a part of reality that is evasive to our enquiring minds and observing eyes. The fleeing specter forces us to take a step back and re-evaluate our relationship with the object. Jacques Derrida's *The Specters of Marx*, thought by many to have inaugurated a spectral turn in culture studies, encouraged us to have a refreshed awareness of the specter, not only as an object of exorcism, but also an analogy to the fundamental condition of knowability itself.

> It [specter] is something that one does not know, precisely, and one does not know if precisely it is, if it exists, if it responds to a name and corresponds to an essence. One does not know: not out of ignorance, but because this non-object, this non-present present, this being-there of an absent or departed one no longer belongs to knowledge. At least no longer to that which one thinks one knows by the name of knowledge. One does not know if it is living or if it is dead (5). ②

The second point to be established in this paper is that "the specters of realism" speak to the need for a critical framework that

---

① The mirror is also Hamlet's metaphor for the theatre's relationship with nature.
② A similar message is reiterated in Jameson's explication of Derrida: "Spectrality does not involve the conviction that ghosts exist or that the past (and maybe even the future they offer to prophesy) is still very much alive and at work, within the living present: all it says, if it can be thought to speak, is that the living present is scarcely as self-sufficient as it claims to be; that we would do well not to count on its density and solidity, which might under exceptional circumstances betray us" ("Marx's Purloined Letter" 39).

addresses the not immediately observable reality which may pose a major threat to the conventional notion of literary representation or *mimesis*. The word *specter* rather than *ghost* is deliberately used here precisely for the reason that it implies a liminal position between the visible and the invisible—its Latin etymology *spectrum* means "appearance, vision, apparition." Stendhal's catoptric metaphor is our clue that the traditional realist technique of description hinges primarily on visibility: to see, watch, observe with various methods of scientific inquiry, and to transcribe the data into detailed verbal depictions that would, then, form vivid images in the readers' minds. Critics have already noticed this *modus operandi* of realism's. In the words of Peter Brooks, realism is "a visual inspection of the world of phenomena," and "we tend to believe that sight is the most objective and impartial of our senses" (16), or Nancy Armstrong, "in order to be realistic, literary realism referenced a world of objects that either had been or could be photographed" (7). If this is true, then several questions might be asked. What will happen if reality exceeds the observing capacity of our senses? What if there is more to it than meets the eye? What if the hinges fall apart and everything "is out of joint"?

Answers to these questions will instigate the reconfiguration of realism as not only a style of literature, but also a fundamental method of epistemological exploration. In the more traditionalist view of realism, its primary goal and function are to keep as detailed a record of the world as possible—especially a record of the base and the ugly which were not granted license in literary representations in the classical era—in order to assist human cognition. It is supposed to be, first and foremost, about human, according to Georg Lukács. In an essay titled "Narrate or Describe," he quotes from Marx to highlight the importance of human activity to realist works: "To be radical is to grasp things by the roots. The root of humanity is, however, man himself" (110). It is not surprising then that in this essay, Lukács targets French naturalism, personified by Gustave Flaubert and Emile Zola, as the foil of genuine realism represented by Walter Scott, Honere de Balzac or Leo Tolstoy, and objected the naturalist method of meticulously detailed descriptions. The "descriptive method," in conclusion, "lacks humanity," for the readers are insufficiently informed of the genuinely important social phenomena: the struggle among people and classes, the epic and heroic actions of the central figure, the stages of social change and progression, etc.

There seems to be a common frustration of critics of realism when they are confronted with some parts of the realist work which are elusive to the mechanism of making sense. Lukács' reaction was a verdict of capital sentence: admittedly, he observed, social problems were present in the works of Zola, but they were present in the form of "*caput mortuum*" (113), dead head, eviscerated with the vitalities of life. Roland Barthes was less radical than Lukács, but equally condemning of the inclusion of detailed descriptions which bear no apparent relevance to the entirety of the story. Take for example, his theory of the reality effect. Stumbling upon Gustave Flaubert's barometer in *A Simple Heart* and Jules Michelet's little door in *History of the Revolution*, Barthes tried to contain them in a meaningful framework of explanation by asking the questions: what functions do they perform and what significance do they have? Apparently not satisfied with the speculation that these were meaningless narrative fillers, he came up with a proposition which was linguistic in essence— these details perform the function of signifying the real. They created, therefore, the reality effect, and they were there to make an announcement of their truth-value to the reader. The operation of creating reality effect can be seen as a manifestation of the realist impulse underneath that gravitates towards truth. Teleologically, they operate in a language system of signification that refers not to the outside, but the inside of the text. Elsewhere, Barthes explained this mechanism in more straightforward terms: " The discourse has no responsibility vis-à-vis real: in the most realistic novel the referent has no 'reality'... In short... what we call 'real' (in the theory of the realistic text) is never more than a code of representation (of signification)..." (*S/Z* 80) Yet, *must* we ask the teleological questions about the function and significance of these details and objects? It would probably make more sense if they are understood as objects of Levinasian alterity: the ultimate Other which is beyond the reach of conceptualization and proceeds the foundation of the subject.① One would rather think of these details in terms of the specter: they enter the rooms of Madame Aubain and Charlotte Corday simultaneously with us the readers, yet they remain invisible until the moment when they catch on our eyes and shock us as an inscrutable intruder. And as soon as we start asking questions and demanding them to speak, they stalk away and escape, leaving us to wonder if they come from the limbo, the realm on the borders of the real and the unreal—the world of writings and languages.

To talk about the "specters of realism" is to find a solution for dealing with the dimension of reality that is beyond the reach of our current empiricist paradigms of understanding, be they scientific, linguistic, sociological, or psychoanalytic. As Blanco and Peeran maintained, "what is at stake ultimately is the specter as a figure of absolute alterity, that should not be assimilated or negated, but lived with in an open, welcoming rationality." (33) This new rationality

---

① In 2002, Julian Wolfreys went as far as to state that "any medium through which we seek to communicate today that involves a narrativization of our identities in relation to others not immediately present is inescapably spectral" (2).

is yet to take on an exact critical or philosophical shape,[1] at the same time, a contemporary Chinese realist writer and critic, Yan Lianke, has been working toward a solution. In an epilogue to his own novel, titled "The Non-Existent Existence," Yan recalled that on a posthumous marriage ceremony in a freezing winter, he saw hundreds of red and yellow butterflies sitting on the coffins of his nephew and the bride. To him, the event of the butterflies appearing out of the blue in a winter day was both "true and strange" (*Odes* 352-353), testifying to the existence of certain realities beyond his understanding. Throughout the years, Yan has created a series of oxymorons to call our attention to the discrepancy between what we perceive to be real and the unattainable truth. "The Non-Existent Existence" is a case in point. Another example would be "the real covered up by the real" in his 2011 monograph *Discovering Fiction*. Here, he proposed a variation of realism—mythorealism, by which he means a style of fiction writing as well as a way of thinking not subjected to the logic of raitonality, but rather the souls and spirits of the writer. This new path to reality is through imaginations, allegories, mythologies, legends, dreams, visions, and transformations. Reality is not *reflected* in a mythorealist piece of work, but *created* by the writer.

Mythorealism is different from its magical realist predecessors. The logic of reality in García Márquez's *One Hundred Years of Solitude* is "half-causality," according to Yan, as opposed to the "full-causality" of the traditional realism represented by Tolstoy and the "zero-causality" demonstrated by Kafka. The grotesque story of a man transforming into a giant bug in "Metamorphosis" is "zero-causality," because it is a total violation of the law of nature or society. The 19th century

---

[1] One example might be the recent trend of speculative realism in philosophy, and especially Object-Oriented Ontology.

realism, on the contrary, endeavors to give explanations to every single one of its protagonists, events, and plots so that everything happens with a good cause, mostly rooted in the social milieu in which the characters are immersed. Márquez's narrative is something in between, and therefore "half-causal" in the sense that the events are not explicable following the everyday logic, but not as incredible as a man suddenly transformed into a bug. In Yan Lianke's diagram, "non-causality" and "full-causality" sit at the two ends of the scale, and "half-causality" is forever flowing in-between, occupying the space of "probability" and "likeliness." (*Discovering Fiction* 117 – 118) Yan himself is after something else—to him, the "inner-causality" or the "inner-truth" is the new principle of fiction writing evolved from the whole of the literary experience of the 20th century. Writers are encouraged by Yan's manifesto of mythorealism to perform the task of uncovering this inner-truth, and thus revealing "the real covered up by the real."

A recent invention of oxymoron, "the real of the unreal" (27) is seen in his 2023 monograph, *The Veils of Liaozhai*. Yan declared unequivocally in the Preface this time that "literature is solely committed to the belief in the real" (6) followed by an exclamation mark. He then explained that the real here is not circumscribed by empirically determined facts, realities and possibilities, but also "the real of the unreal," "the real that transcends the real," " the real with no verifiable evidence," or "the real that is counter-real" (31). In this new critical work, Yan extended the view that literature oscillated between the real and the unreal in different historical periods. In the 19th century, the criteria of literary quality were based entirely on its faithfulness to the limitations of experience. From the 20th century onward, the unreal and the impossible reappeared in literature. Specifically, about the Chinese literature, Yan contended that little progress had been made in terms of writing the real since

Lu Xun's 1921 novella "The True Story of Ah Q." In order to push for some progress, Yan proposed not to follow that trail blazed by the 19th century realists, and perhaps not even the modernists and postmodernists, but to return to an age that was pre-modern and pre-Enlightenment—the age of mythologies and folklores. Indeed, China has a *zhiguai* tradition—writing of the strange and supernatural—from *A Search of the Supernatural* in the 4th century to *Old Tales Retold* written by Lu Xun in the height of the New Culture Movement. Yan was confident that there was much to learn from the understandings and dealings of the real in these strange-story writings.

The trick is to make readers believe—not so much demanding a degree of "suspension of disbelief" on the readers' part as providing enough serious evidence of reality as the writers' responsibility. *Liaozhai*, the pinnacle of the *zhiguai* tradition according to Yan, is indeed a strange story collection written in Classical Chinese, but it demonstrated the same narrative seriousness as any realist fiction. It is worth now returning to the story of Ma Ji. As was mentioned, when the young man arrives at the capital, he sees city walls made of black stone, as black as ink, and gate-houses about 100 feet-high. Immediately after this depiction of the wonderous, Pu Songling invited the readers to have an intimate touch with the fantasy world, and commanded Ma to pick up a piece of Redstone. Here, Pu Songling has achieved a displacement effect—the most realistic description is displaced from an expected story of realism, but inserted in a most strange and occult story of the Luo Cha Country. These descriptions serve as the "ocular proof," as was once demanded by Othello, an eye-witness that gives credit to the otherwise incredible beings and happenings. They also serve metaphorically as a bridge—a word used by Yan in an interview explaining the mechanism of mythorealism. It is a bridge that helps us to cross the treacherous river of the superficialities and reach the other shore which is the real. Intentionally or unintentionally, "the other shore" is an allusion to the ultimate Buddhist pursuit of truth, a destination that appeals to us the mortals, with its looming and mythic appeal in the distance.

Specifically, Yan spoke of the specters, in *Liaozhai* as well as in "Pedro Paramo," novella of the Mexican writer Juan Rulfo.[①] Of course there are differences: the boundary between the living and the spectral was unmistakably demarcated in *Liaozhai*, and the line was ambiguously drawn in "Pedro Paramo." Yet the same impulse drives their specters and urges them to visit us, once and again, through 300 years and across two antipodean points on the planet earth: the realist impulse. Like the contemplation of the utopian by Jameson, perhaps what is important about realism is "not what can be positively imagined and proposed, but rather what is not imaginable and not conceivable," the limits of our own perception, and the "lines beyond which" we do not seem able to go in imagining what is real and what is not. This speaks to the necessity and urgency of the contemplation and theorization of the specters of realism today.

As a metaphor, "the specters of realism" has yet another dimension which joins together the past and the present. Blanco and Perran pointed out that the specter was not only a disruption of the chronological flow of time, but also a non-present presence that achieves the effect of synchronization: "For Derrida, the ghost's story is not a puzzle to be solved; it is the structural openness or address directed towards the living by the voices of the past or the not yet formulated possibility of the future... because it cannot (yet)

[①] It might be of some interest to know that the latter was alternatively translated into Chinese as literally "Between the Man and the Specter."

be articulated in the language available to us" (58). Yan Lianke's theorization of "the real of the unreal" is viewed in this light, itself a spectral activity. So not so much different from Dao Lang or Marcellus, Horatio and Hamlet, Yan is also approaching a supposedly dead past for revelation of truth in the here and now. More importantly, Yan's critical effort is based on the activiting of reading Pu Songling's *Liaozhai*, which, according to Blanchot, is fundamentally an act of the resurrectionist.① There have been constantly calls for revisiting realism in literary scholarship in the past decade because realism has been in turn revisiting us all the time, and we have every reason to believe that the specters of realism will not "stalk away", but keep coming back, and perpetuate its visitation to us, now and in the future.

【Works Cited】

Armstrong, Nancy. *Fiction in the Age of Photography: The Legacy of British Realism*. Cambridge: Harvard University Press, 1999.

Barthes, Roland. *S/Z*. Miller, Richard, trans. Oxford: Blackwell Publishing, 2002.

Blanchot, Maurice. *The Space of Literature*. Smock, Ann, trans. Lincoln, London: University of Nebraska Press, 1989.

Blanco, María del Pilar, and Esther Peeren, eds. *The Spectralities Reader: Ghosts and Haunting in Contemporary Cultural Theory*. New York and London: Bloomsbury Academic, 2013.

Brooks, Peter. *Realist Vision*. New Haven: Yale University Press, 2005.

Derrida, Jacques. *Specters of Marx: The State of the Debt, the Work of Mourning and the New International*. Kamuf, Peggy, trans. New York and London:

---

① In *The Space of Literature*, Blanchot compares reading to the resurrection of Lazarus by Jesus Christ: "To roll back the stone, to obliterate it, is certainly something marvelous, but it is something we achieve at every moment in everyday language. At every moment we converse with Lazarus, dead for three days—or dead, perhaps, since always. In his well-woven winding sheet, sustained by the most elegant conventions, he answers us and speaks to us within ourselves" (195).

Routledge, 1994.

Holland, Mary K. *The Moral Worlds of Contemporary Realism*. London: Bloomsbury Academic, 2020.

Jameson, Fredric. "Marx's Purloined Letter," in Sprinker, Michael, ed. *Ghostly Demarcations: A Symposium on Jacques Derrida's Specters of Marx*. London: Verso, 2008.

Jameson, Fredric. "Utopia as Method, or the Uses of the Future," in Gordin, Michael D., et al, eds. *Utopia/Dystopia: Conditions of Historical Possibility*. Princeton and Oxford: Princeton University Press, 2010: 21-44.

Kermode, Frank. *The Sense of an Ending: Studies in the Theory of Fiction*. Oxford: Oxford University Press, 2000.

Lukács, Georg. *Writer and Critic and Other Essays*. Kahn, Arthur, trans. London: Merlin Press, 1970.

Marx, Karl, and Engels, Friedrich. *Manifesto of the Communist Party: A Modern Edition*. London and New York: Verso, 2016.

Pu, Songling. *Strange Stories from a Chinese Studio, Vol. 1*. Giles, Herbert A., trans. London: Thos. De La Rue & Co., 1880.

Wellek, René. "The Concept of Realism in Literary Scholarship." *Neophilologus*, vol. 45, no. 1, 1961: 1-20.

Weninger, Robert. "Straw Man or Profligate Son? Transformations of Literary Realism Since 1900," in Göttsche, Dirk, et al, eds., *Landscapes of Realism Rethinking Literary Realism in Comparative Perspectives Volume I: Mapping Realism*. Amsterdam and Philadelphia: John Benjamins Publishing Company, 2021.

Wolfreys, Julian. *Victorian Hauntings: Spectrality, Gothic the Uncanny and Literature*. New York: Palgrave, 2002.

Yan, Lianke. *Discovering Fiction*. Tianjin: Nankai University Press, 2011.

Yan, Lianke. *The Odes of Songs*. Zhengzhou: Henan Literature and Art Publishing House, 2016.

Yan, Lianke. *The Veils of Liaozhai*. New Taipei City: Linking Publishing Company, 2023.

Zeitlin, Judith T. *Historian of the Strange: Pu Songling and the Chinese Classical Tale*. Stanford, California: Stanford University Press, 1993.

A Realism of Conflicting Ontologies

Svend Erik Larsen

Abstract: As modern realism travelled from Europe to other continents during the nineteenth century, the encounter with literary traditions in foreign places broke the otherwise unquestioned unidirectional trajectory. The encounter shed light on the particularity of European realism but also transformed it by opening writers to more diversified notions of than those discussed by nineteenth-century writers and critics in Europe. From a one-way or maybe a two-way traffic across countries and continents realism became a multi-directional literary and aesthetic enterprise. This process inspired a questioning of the dynamics and the limits of realism which has spurred the continuous evolvement of realism across the world in the twentieth and twenty-first centuries. This has happened in an open global cultural and literary exchange between writers, texts, translations and media that relativized pre-established monolithic ideas about centers and peripheries and showed the existence of more complex global networks. In such cross-cultural and hybrid contexts the conflicting perspectives on what is regarded as real becomes a pressing issue. In this paper I will take issue with this ontological problem through brief readings of a number of novels from different continents. I will argue that realism, old or recent, first of all exposes the ontological uncertainty of the modern social and material world, beyond any

---

① 本文原发于《外国文学研究》2024 年第 1 期。

reference to its material reality.

Key words: ontology; embedment; cross-cultural perspective; realism

Author: Professor Emeritus, School of Communication and Culture, Aarhus University, Denmark; Yangtze River Distinguished Visiting Professor, Sichuan University. His research interests are comparative literature and realism.

Precarious Embedment

One issue stands out in today's cross-cultural context of realist writing which more often than not attracts little or no attention within a local or regional cultural context: what do we regard as real? In local circles, discussions of realism focus on aesthetic strategies pertaining to the local context concerned with characters, narration, imaginary language, intermedia and interart perspectives rather than on the ontological notion of reality itself underpinned by the texts. Revisiting realism today means confronting the ontological question in a world of hybrid localities in which different and conflicting ontologies co-exist. In the following I will do so by exploring the presence of conflicting ontologies in novels by Ahmadou Kourouma: *Allah is Not Obliged* (2007, French 2000), Yi Mun-Yol: *Meeting with My Brother* (2017, Korean 1994), Phaswane Mpe: *Welcome to Our Hillbrow* (2001), Daniel Kehlmann: *Fame: A Novel in Nine Episodes* (2010, German 2009), and Jorge Semprún: *The Long Voyage* (2005, French 1963).

I will first introduce a notion which I find helpful precisely when revisiting realism yet with no intention of reinventing realism or launching yet another program for some kind of neo-realism. I will call the notion *embedment*, a process for which fictional narrative has proven to be a particularly important tool. However, this semiotic process of shaping narratives as scenarios of possible worlds automatically raises questions of the limits of reality and the possibility of moving its boundaries through human agency (see Doležel; Ryan). Since the early days of modern realism a few centuries ago, its products have never approached the ontological question of the real through a discussion of reality in itself, as philosophers would do. Instead, realism has discussed the function of what is regarded as real by human agents, including their doubts, their illusions, their mistakes, their capabilities, their ambitions, their inaction, etc. Embedment is precisely that: *An operation of cultural integration of human subjects as an ongoing attempt that allows them to position themselves through language or other media as agents in a social environment and, simultaneously and self-reflexively, to question both the nature of the reality that grounds their agency and the effects of their agency on that reality.* Without addressing this fundamental problem, embedment would just be a new variant for pure constructivism. To begin with, I want to stress that embedment never approaches reality as such (*ontos*) but the relation between humans and reality through a conceptualization and thus a mediation of reality (*onto-logy*). That is why literature, primarily through its narrative dimension, is an essential driver for cultural embedment (see Larsen 2022).

The most important words in my above characterization are: ongoing and attempt. The narrative tool is no guarantee for a successful cultural embedment, and no embedment lasts forever. It is constantly challenged by the historical changes of the cultural context and the ontology that supports it, a challenge that may be instigated by the narratives themselves. With a series of brief analyses of the five novels listed above I will illustrate how their narratives can be understood as an exercise in a continuous and perilous cultural embedment through human agency in the modern world of hybrid cultural contexts and realities in which different and even irreconcilable ontologies are active. This situation adds pernicious constraints on human agency in a reality the basic features of which are hybridity and fluidity. The novels represent four different approaches to ontologies: reality regarded as material reality, as metaphysical reality, as ideological reality and, finally, as mediated reality. The four approaches cover four dimensions of cultural embedment, calling for different strategies and, ultimately, opening for different views of what is real.

Material Reality—Ahmadou Kourouma: *Allah Is Not Obliged*

Birahima is the protagonist in the Ivory Coast writer Ahmadou Kourouma's novel *Allah Is Not Obliged*, and its unfinished sequel published posthumously as *Quand on refuse on dit non* (2004, *No Means No*). A first-person narrator, the twelve-year-old Birahima explains matter-of-factly and with humor the horrific realities of being a child soldier, always on the run with his *kalash* (Kalashnikov) in various bloody border-crossing conflicts between states, clans and tribes in the general post-colonial turmoil, corruption and looting in West Africa of the early 1990s. The boy is caught between two co-existing realities, one the colonial reality imposed by France, the other the local regional tribal reality, both of which have collapsed but are still present in broken and mixed languages and belief systems, and in the one and only new reality which is defined by war. Birahima is a survivor who, by taking part in the war, tries to be embedded in the new fractured local reality in which local cohesion and colonial dominance no longer define what is real, but only appear as dissolved social constructions. In this context three competing realities or ontological layers are pitted against each other: (1) the colonial reality of suppression and submission imposing a European-based view of what is real, which is now an empty shell leaving only its colonial social hierarchies behind; (2) the indigenous social reality of clans and tribes, supported by local, non-European belief systems that include a spiritual reality whose ontology, Birahima realizes, has now also lost its power; (3) the ontology of a naked material reality of war in which only individual bodily survival counts, for a child as well as for a tribal war lord, one deprived of sustainable cultural and social patterns to guide a cultural embedment.

One embedment strategy that Birahima tries out, though, is his language: both as a local cross-border inhabitant of West Africa and as a narrator. He begins by introducing himself with reference to one of his languages, French, that keeps him locked up in the colonial reality, whose hierarchy has otherwise collapsed:

> My name is Birahima and I'm a little nigger. Not' cos I'm black and I'm a kid. I'm a little nigger because I can't talk French for shit. [...] You might be a grown-up, or old, you might be Arab, or Chinese, or white, or Russian—or even American—if you talk bad French, it's called *parler petit nègre*—little nigger talk—so that makes you a little nigger too. That's the rules of French for you. (Kourouma *Allah* 1)

To narrate the realities of his daily life as if they were self-evident in all their cruel details, Birahima has to be equipped with his copy of the dictionary *Le Petit Robert*. He is imbued with an unflappable survival instinct which makes him a no-nonsense observer with an ethic that makes him care only about the efficient simplicity of

25

action. Language becomes a tool for survival, physically and mentally, in a world of growing chaos. His flexible use of a hybrid, almost personal language protects him from others, and sharpens his ability to maneuver in surroundings of permanent instability, whereas his humor protects himself from insanity.

With his dictionary Birahima translates his coarse slang and the local expressions in his native Malinké into a kind of French, but not in Arabic, except for the modified name of Allah. This linguistic confusion—or synthesis, as the case might be—also characterizes the two contexts, the political and the religious, which together frame his nomadic existence between uncertain places, languages and belief systems. The political context is one of colonial and post-colonial conflicts aggravated by a clash between artificial but fixed national frontiers, tribal conflicts and shifting alliances, amid arms sales and economic interests created by international capitalism and neo-colonial political agendas, constantly kept alive by local warlords (André 166 – 167).

By contrast, the religious or spiritual ideas and values are rooted in the local social and cultural tradition. However, in the post-colonial chaos they do not imply a transcendental ontology anymore but, like language, are tools for physical survival. The local tradition never cared about dogmatic beliefs; instead, it consists of a culturally determined blend of local animism with Islam and Christianity, both imported with colonial migrations. At times, the different warlords who take him in their service ask a local soothsayer to read omens and make prophecies, but only accept them if they suit their personal convictions and warfaring strategies. This "ecumenical" position (47) offers a pragmatic flexibility of tribal affiliations which also helps Birahima to survive under a motto hidden in the title:"The full, final and complete title of my bullshit story is: *Allah is not obliged to be fair about all things he does here* on earth. Okay. Right" (1). So, better do like, for example, the female warlord General Baclay. She was "weird, but she was a good woman and in her own way she was very fair: she shot men and women just the same" (100).

Birahima's linguistic and ideological alacrity reflects this larger political and religious context: his flexible perspicacity helps him to survive and also to express his understanding of reality, but only from moment to moment, situation to situation. He observes how many of his comrades, all of them as flexible as he is, are killed nonetheless when they miscalculate how to adapt to new situations. To understand the entire complexity of the local mess he has to recognize that neither his language nor the traditional norms really help him to overcome his sense of placelessness and vulnerability in a purely physical universe of matter and randomness: " I didn't universe, didn't understand a thing of this bloody world. I couldn't make head or tail of people or society" (118). Even a language user and a survivor as deft as Birahima reaches a barrier that separates him from the "bloody world", the only one the reality of which he recognizes and in which he lives.

Metaphysical Reality: Phaswane Mpe: *Welcome to Our Hillbrow*

The effects of postcolonial social conditions and linguistic challenges also shape the South African Phaswane Mpe's novel *Welcome to Our Hillbrow*. However, the post-colonial situation is of a different kind and so are the linguistic limitations. One might say that South Africa faces post-colonialism 2. 0. Apartheid and post-apartheid realities are domestic phenomena, carried out by descendants of seventeenth-century Dutch and British settlers after the independence of South Africa in the early twentieth century, promoting a suppression entirely based on a hard-core racial ideology, also with regard to language. Yet, the mental and cultural survival of the black population during and after the apartheid regime was underpinned by a loyalty toward the traditional local metaphysics. This local spiritual tradition embraced an ontology different from one condoned by Christian protestantism and its integration in Western materialism. The novel confronts these two ontologies, each complex in its own right and partly irreconcilable with the other.

Mpe's anonymous first-person male narrator addresses a dead childhood friend, Refentše, from the imaginary township of Hillbrow. He blends references to their shared memories with stories of how people they both knew carry on in life after her death, as if assuming that she can follow the ongoings from the ancestral world with no need of too many cohesive details. The storyline winds its way in and out of shared memories and present actions. At the outset, the material present and the metaphysical realm is merged and thus securing the continuous presence of the past through the memories that gives the past a place as a living part of the present. In this way the material and spiritual reality appears as two sides of one and the same reality, as one ontology.

After apartheid, this unity is fractured by the continued presence of the religious moral standards that were established first during the Dutch and, later, confirmed by Victorian colonization. One character in particular, the self-reliant Bohlale, is upset by the constraints imposed on her language as a writer, just finishing a book in her native Sepedi. She is a B.A. student, works in a kitchen and knows enough English, the narrator tells us, to have written it in English, which she should have done, he believes:

She did not know that writing in an African language

in South Africa could be such a curse. She had not anticipated that the publisher's reviewers would brand her novel vulgar. Calling shit and genitalia by their correct names in Sepedi was apparently regarded as vulgar by these reviewers, who had for a long time been reviewing works of fiction for educational publishers [...]. They considered it fine, for instance, to call genitalia by their correct names in English and Afrikaans biology books—even gave these names graphic pictures as escorts—yet in all other languages, they criminalized such linguistic honesty. (Mpe 56)

Bohlale clashes with the linguistic restrictions of the publishing industry and the educational system. Her angry reflections are approved by Mpe's narrator who continues his digressive report from Hillbrow by ruminating on a similar dishonest linguistic power-play with the terms "homeland" or "Bantustan" as his examples, a reflection on the apartheid period. To provide Bantustan with positive connotations, the term is construed by the apartheid regime to allude to the mythical domestic migrations of Bantu peoples for a better life in African pre-history. Yet such terms, the narrator points out, are but "euphemisms" (57) for arid places and for deported native tribes, divided according to language families, real or invented, leaving them with hardly sufficient means of survival (57). The material reality becomes as constructed by the apartheid regime as is the regime's defamation of the reality of traditional African world of ancestral spirits.

This criticism is counterpoised by the narrator's self-defeating irony. The novel is written in English, not in one of the native languages, although in a discourse blending coarse language, descriptive details and a chant-like lyrical prose. The narrator himself also uses clinical euphemisms on genitalia and sex as required by the publishers: "lower hemisphere of the bodies" and "wandering penises" (Mpe 110; 116). At the same time his criticism of publishing with regard to Bohlale's novel, is relativized by Refilwe, another strong female character. She studies at Oxford University and works for some time in publishing in England, though issuing only books "that could get a school prescription" (94). Frustrated, she returns to Hillbrow before she continues to Nigeria, dying from AIDS.

Mpe's linguistic realism reflects the break-up of the ontological unity of the material and spiritual reality of native South Africans, showing how embedment in the post-apartheid reality is impossible equally if based on the traditional synthetical ontology, or on the apartheid view of reality. Characters like Bohlale and Refilwe depend on institutions of education and publishing in English which set up rules against their local language and culture. Ironically, the narrator himself applies the same rules through the two female characters. But he also transcends them by building the novel as a communication with the deceased Refentše, attempting to recreate the past reality through literature (see Knapp). The events of the brutal and fragmented world he describes in jumps and digressions, as if told by the disillusioned and placeless characters themselves, are bridged by passages of lyrical prose which unite the messy Hillbrow, the spiritual world of Refentše and the textual universe of the narrator as a shared space.

With his "linguistic chisel" (122) the narrator has merged the two worlds into shared places that "are flowing into each other [...] in the memories and consciousness of the living" (113). Hence, they can be qualified throughout the novel by the possessive pronoun "our"—for example "our Tiragalong and Alexandra, our Hillbrow and Oxford [...] our Worlds and other Worlds [...] Welcome to our Heaven" (124). With his hands on the linguistic chisel, the narrator is located nowhere and everywhere in the volatile and linguistically hybrid local South African as an international site of forced relocations framed by his worldview that creates social, spiritual and linguistic reality as one, only precariously embedded in the post-apartheid world by his own creative practice.

Ideological Reality: Yi Mun-Yol: *Meeting with My Brother*

Both Birahima and the narrator of Mpe's novel are confronted with the impossibility of living in a context with a shared ontology that frames a workable culture and society in which they can be embedded as active human agents. They are left with their creative language to construct a liveable temporary yet fictional reality. In Yi Mun-Yol's novel *Meeting with My Brother*, this option is not available. The core event is the short encounter of two brothers for each of the two Koreas. The nature of the reality they actually live in is hidden behind the veil of two ideological constructions of reality, and they do not have the language to remove the veil. However, in contrast to the two narrators from West Africa and South Africa, the traditional Korean reality uniting the separated North and South, although denied by both sides, offers them a momentary foothold in a different reality, which is visible only in the cracks of the two ideologically imposed ontological determination of what is real.

The two brothers meet for the first time in a small Korean city in China, Yanji, neither North nor South and certainly not a unified Korea, still separated as it is by the unfinished war between North and South, a place of an almost unreal status. The two half-brothers have never met before and, being as foreign to each other as are the two parts of Korea, they embody the division of their country: the narrator Yi Hyeonseop, about fifty years old, lives in Seoul, and Yi Hyeok, in his forties, in the North. The wider context evoked by the novel is the cultural patterns of the old unified Korea and broader Asian notions of ethics and personal identity based on family, honor and shame. While these values are shared by the brothers, they are also contradicted by the two governing political worldviews on either side of the no-man's land that separates the brothers. The opposing ideologies are both a result of import of European and Western ideas of reality—Marxism and liberalism. The former is now, in the North, adapted to a dynastic Asian tradition; and, in the South, the latter is integrated in a capitalist market economy and a liberal democracy including a Christian minority but situated within a predominantly Buddhist culture.

The brothers' encounter takes place over a couple of days in Yanji. What unites them now is their bereavement over their father recently deceased from cancer, to whose spirit they both want to pay respect by traditional offerings of food and drink from his home in the South. In the 1950s the father defected from the South, leaving his wife and two children behind in poverty, remarried in the North and fathered three younger children. The Southerners felt that their loss was caused by the family in the North who had taken the father away, while the Northerners blamed the Southern family, feeling that the eldest son left behind nevertheless was always first in the mind of the father who, according to Korean tradition, is the head of both families.

At first, the two Yi brothers are hesitant to talk about their own social reality. If they did, they might either appear shamefully unsuccessful or force one brother to lose face because of the other's achievements. Public display of emotions of any kind is shameful according to Buddhist and Confucian ideals that date back much further than the present-day division of Korea, and continues to have a strong presence in people's minds despite outside influence. In fact, in Korea silence and secrecy are more important than public exposure, not just as a pragmatic necessity when dealing with matters of national security, but as a question of honor and shame when it comes to personal failures and lack of self-control, a shame that is shared by individuals and families alike and maybe also the community at large (see Alford; Larsen 2017; in a larger Asian context, see Marks and Ames).

In accordance with old traditions, the family name, Yi, is maintained by both families, and the readers learn that it is a prestigious name dating back to the old united Korea. Being the eldest son, the brother from the South is responsible for the rituals to be carried out, and, appropriately, he has also taken the initiative to organize the encounter and paid for his Northern brother's illegal visit to Yanji. Instead of deciding whether the funeral should be Christian, Buddhist, Confucian or agnostic they have agreed to perform the customary ancestral rites together in Yanji, facing North Korea and sharing the ritual offerings from the South. This balance is a matter of honor for both. Otherwise, the necessary reference to the South, their father's place of birth, would make the ceremony belong to the senior rather than to the junior brother.

To begin with, both brothers are full of stories of pride from their respective homes and past lives. However, it is not the devastating ideologically motivated conflicts that are first in their minds; it is a breach of the family's honor code when the father defected. Gradually, it transpires that the father was not a hero in the North, but was in fact excluded from society as a suspicious renegade from the South, and also that the brother from the South turned out to have earned a great deal of money in dodgy speculations; indeed, the novel ends with him smuggling antiques back to Seoul via a dealer that lurks around him in his hotel in Yanji.

Shortly before the brothers leave China to return home, the clash between language and cultural norms produces a particular communication which breaks the ice between the brothers in the concrete situation and, at the same time, yields the discourse that represents the Korean cultural reality under the ideological Janus-face of the divided country. The situation evolves when the brothers' masks begin to fall, helped by heavy drinking that transports them beyond any sense of shame or fear of losing face in front of each other. However, when they eventually sober up, they cannot verbalize their momentary mutual confidence before they both are about to depart. Their concession has to be indirect:

"Give my regards to our brothers and sisters," I said. Then, as if I'd made a grave decision, I added "To Mother, too."

In the scenario I had choreographed so carefully and for so long after deciding to meet my brother, I had struggled with how I would refer to his mother. "Northern Mother," "New Mother," "Stepmother" [...] Finally, after meeting him, I was able to get by with an added modifier, "your mother," but now all the modifiers had flown away.

In the old days there were also cases in which the taking of a second wife was permissible if certain criteria were met. To my modern rational thinking, it wasn't a problem to consider my brother's mother my mother, too. But I startled myself with how naturally the word "Mother" rolled off my tongue. My brother immediately sensed this, too. He regarded me for a moment, his face now unclouded by drunkenness, and then he bowed his head in acceptance.

"Give our regards to our sister and nephews, too. And

to Mother."

And he did not use a modifier either. (Yi Mun-Yol 131 – 132)

United by old Korean spiritual and cultural traditions that define the limits of what can be said and what has to remain unsaid, language itself takes over from the inebriated brothers' conscious use of language. Before the elder brother has finished his deliberations with himself about the words to use, the right word "rolled off my tongue" spontaneously under the unspoken emotional pressure of the moment, almost as a slip of the tongue but immediately confirmed by his "rational thinking." And with good reason. Taking into account the traditional equivalence between mother, or woman, and nation (see Hübinette), he reaches across the internal national divide as well. The Northern brother accompanies his repetition of the brief linguistic opening with a silent bodily ritual and bows as is customary to his senior brother who is now head of the family. In a short moment of soberness, silence is transformed into language, in conformity with the indirectness required by the old Korean culture in situations with a strong emotional charge.

However, this situation is unsustainable; both brothers have to return each to their own political zone and their home realities veiled in their ideological garments. At the same time, the use of language in this passage of the novel shows that the sense of a shared view of reality is less rigid on the cultural level of a common language and norms than in the petrified and divided political domain. The momentary closing of the abyss between silence and speech in the non-place of Yanji confirms the reality of a latent unity of the two Koreas, notwithstanding their overlapping European and broader Western and Asian overdetermination in contemporary politics, social organization and religion.

Mediated Reality: Daniel Kehlmann: *Fame*

Daniel Kehlmann is a German writer who has discussed the issue of embedment in several novels. In his earlier novel *Measuring the World* (2007) he adopts two approaches to the secularized European worldview with regard to an objective measuring of the world. This mapping turns out rather to be two opposed ways of embedding the human subject actually responsible for the world-mapping into each their own ontological sphere. The novel is set in the first half of the nineteenth century with two protagonists, the restless intercontinental traveler, geographer and explorer Alexander von Humboldt, and the mathematician Carl Friederich Gauss who has no desire for long distance relocations. The latter maps the world in abstract and universal mathematical terms, the former by empirical studies on a global scale, and Kehlmann describes both of them as almost obsessively submerged in their work and hence detached from the larger social and political reality of their time, an ontological detachment as it were. Humboldt and Gauss embody two types of cultural embedding—or rather dis-embedding—framed by the secular European view of reality, whether from the abstract or empirical side, but as a cognitive project, not as a lived reality.

In Kehlmann's more recent novel *Fame*, this disentanglement from the world is taken to a global level with a focus on the role of digital media, which generate a fundamental ontological uncertainty, leaving us with no answer to the question: what is real and what is fiction? (see Arslan and Dag). The novel is composed of nine stories or episodes with no necessary interconnections, but with numerous accidental overlaps. What the stories have in common is a preoccupation and a play with individual identity as it is inscribed in communication via the internet, mobile phones and computer networks in a placeless globalized cyberspace in which communication in a shared natural language cannot undo the communicative alienation produced by the glitches, accidental happenings, deceptions and misunderstandings dictated by the logic of digital technology and its basic encodings, which blurs the boundaries between what is real and what is not.

One of the characters is an IT technician, Ebling, who in the first line of the first story, "Voices", receives a call on his mobile phone. A woman asks for "someone called Raff, Ralf, or Rauff, he couldn't figure out the name" (Kehlmann *Fame* 3). Later in the evening a hoarse voice is on the phone: "'Ralf!' The man's voice was loud and hoarse. 'What gives, what you up to, you old bastard?'" (3–4) and various text messages also seem to address this Ralf. Finally, Ebling calls a help desk to ask them to connect his phone with the correct number. It turns out that digital technology has acquired a power of its own like divine fate, destroying any ontological reliability:

> No, said a woman, they couldn't just give him another number unless he paid for it.
> "But this number already belongs to someone else!"
> Impossible, she said. There were –
> "Security measures, I know! But I keep getting calls for [...] You know, I'm a technician myself. I know you're inundated with calls from people who are absolutely clueless. But this is my area. I know how."
> Nothing she could do, she said. She would pass on his request.
> "And then? What happens next?"
> Then, she said, they'd see. But that wasn't part of her job." (6–8)

The negative result is underlined by the interlocutors' different discourses. They are not in the same communicative space: Ebling's lines are direct speech, hers free indirect discourse. This persistent asymmetry with regard to the kind of reality to which people may belong, gradually pervades his life. Soon he begins to receive calls and messages from unknown people, also from abroad, apparently from places he does not know. Yet, he gradually comes to recognize some of the voices, and begins to engage in conversations with some of them, pretending they are familiar to him, a mistress included, but without telling them that he is not this Ralf. Step by step he develops a sense of Ralf's context and begins to play with his identity, waiting, spell-bound, for the mobile phone to ring again. He makes the fake reality his real one.

Ralf turns out to be Ralf Tanner, a famous actor who has lost grip on the reality of his life-world and only appears in a later episode "The Way Out". He has played too many roles: "In the early summer of his thirty-ninth year, Ralf Tanner the actor began to feel he didn't exist" (66). He corrects his entry in Wikipedia, makes Google searches on sites with his name, finds his films on Imdb.com, checks his name in various theater databases, consults blogs and other fora in several languages where his name and performances are discussed, and he takes a look at some photos of himself as well. Finally, he gets the idea no longer to be Ralf Tanner, but to play and imitate himself instead. He does so in a small venue without being recognized by the owner, who claims that this was not a successful imitation, and later a female fan who has seen all Tanner's films is also sure he is not Tanner. Meanwhile, due to Tanner's fame, another unnamed imitator, known from Youtube, is getting paid to act as a more authentic Ralf Tanner, whereas nobody wants the real Ralf on stage anymore to imitate himself.

An ontological abyss breaks open when he returns to his home without the house key and rings the bell to call his servant Ludwig:

"It's me," he called into the intercom. "I'm back early."
"Who?"
He swallowed. Then, fully aware that this response wasn't a good idea in the circumstances, he repeated, "Me."
[...] Ludwig came out [...]. Leaning against the grill, his weathered face peered through the bars.
"It's me," said Ralf for the third time.
"And who is 'me'?" [...]
"I'm, Ralf Tanner!"
"That'll surprise the boss." (76)

For Ludwig it is not enough that Ralf knows his own name. The man Ludwig observes on the doorstep is not allowed to talk to Ralf Tanner, to the neighbor or to anyone else whom he claims—or rather pretends, as far as Ludwig is concerned—to know. But Ralf is politely offered a glass of water to calm his visibly disturbed mental balance. But as the real Ralf, he is no longer included in the reality of other people.

A little later Ralf sees Ludwig and the neighbor exiting the house together with—Ralf Tanner, who may be Ebling or the imitator; if it is Ebling, he now identifies with Ralf after the accidental mistake with his phone number; if the imitator, then the imitator does the same through his performative perfection. Film, posters and printed media, along with the internet platforms and social media, have sent Ralf Tanner traveling around the world from Germany via Locarno and Valparaiso and further on to the internet, as a virtual migrant in a global digitized cyberspace. This identification is equivalent to a loss of identity. Ebling and the successful imitator may gain a new momentary identity by replacing someone who no longer exists as an individual identity. So, who are they imitating? Are not all three the avatars that embody a non-existing identity, an imagination produced by ongoing imitative actions?

The form of Kehlmann's novel with its recurrent characters who meet by chance, being at the center of one episode, on the periphery of others, is a known narrative device in realist novels, yet here it is implemented with a significant difference. Characters reappear in novels by Honoré de Balzac or John Dos Passos because they have a recognizable identity in each occurrence; in Kehlmann's novel they do so because they play or perform a new identity in a new reality every time they return. In this sense the episodic structure, bound together by the constant reference to and use of communicative media technology, situates all characters in the same globalized cyberspace of chance meetings and mutual lack of recognition, unless they perform a new role and shape it as an identity through ongoing communication. The novel's composition makes it an equivalent of the mediatized personal relations turned into a narrative form. As such, it is a realist representation of today's globalized mediated reality of ontological uncertainty.

Ontological Uncertainty and Fictional Reassurance

The characters in the four novels I have briefly analysed are thrown out into the world of ontological uncertainty. Yet, not the same kind of uncertainty, and never an uncertainty of their own making. The twelve-year old Birahima's sense of reality is reduced to an acknowledgement of the unstable material reality as his only reality, a scene of perilous survival with no guarantee of sustainable cultural embedment. For the characters in Mpe's novel, the new social reality of post-apartheid South Africa is too fractured to offer a stable cultural embedment, unless it merges with the metaphysically grounded ontology of a traditional African life-world, yet one only bound to memories of dead persons. In Yi Mun-Yol's novel the reality that turns out to be a firm ground beneath different ideologically constructed realities is a half-hidden reality of Korean tradition which is only accessible in a brief moment as a cultural embedment, yet out of reach for the two brothers as a shared, sustainable reality. Finally, Kehlmann's scarily funny account of the undistinguishable points to the ontological uncertainty as it is generated by the mediated cyberspace reality of digital media. In order to create, if only momentarily, a human living space they can acknowledge as real, all four novels contain characters or narrators whose use of language bridges the gaps between humans and their realities, and between different and conflicting ontological spheres. Kehlmann balances on the edge of metafictional literature by making construction of reality and identity a key problem but not, like postmodern hyperfiction or some of its neo-realist variants, in the mode of constructivism; rather, the novel makes the loss of ontological certainty a modern tragedy.

To conclude, I will point to Jorge Semprún's belated and reconstructed memories, *The Long Voyage*, to show how fiction as a construction of one's own making may form—paradoxically as it were—a detour necessary to construct ontological reassurance out of uncertainty. The narrative core is the transport from a detention camp in France to the concentration camp in Buchenwald in 1943. During the transport Semprún—or rather his alias, Gérard—is standing in a packed wagon with a young man, called the guy from Semur. They become friends and talk about France, about the passing landscapes, about the resistance and about the traumatic train ride, Semprún being lofty and philosophical, the other down to earth. Before leaving the train to enter the camp, the guy from Semur dies, which some contemporary critics note with sympathetic pity.

However, thirty years later Semprún confesses in *Literature or Life* (1998) and in *Le mort qu'il faut* (2001, *The Dead Man We Needed*), that there is no reason for any pity. The guy from Semur is a fictional character, made up by the author to enable him to tell about the traumatic events he had not been able to touch until 1963 when *The Long Voyage* came out. Only then did he finally find an aesthetic form, in the shape of a fictional friendship, that was strong enough to release the story and integrate his real experiences as an inmate in Buchenwald into his life without forgetting or reducing the factual horrors. "I would invent the guy from Semur to keep me company in the wagon. We did this voyage together, in fiction; thus I have removed my solitude in reality" (Semprún *Long* 187 – 188). To remember the initial situation in the train that defines the rest of Semprún's life requires the creation of a new situation, one of writing about the train ride in a fictional mode (see Olmor). The process of writing as a secondary situation, as it were, has no similarity to the cramped train journey, and can only occur through an invented dialogue based on an equally imagined emotional congruence of friendship. For Semprún, the other person is not real, but nevertheless has to be present, imagined or not, for Semprún's dialogue with himself to be real and allow him to reconstruct his memory as the core memory of his real life. On the cover of the French edition of Semprún, the reader learns that it is about "his own experience", but in fact the central human relation that carries the narrative is invented.

Revisiting realism is in itself a recognition of the fact that any ontology and its historical transformations do not concern reality in itself, but the shared and shareable view of reality across cultures, historical traditions and periods. This recognition underpins any ontology through the media, not least language, and keeps alive the hope that we can share our views of reality, also the ontological uncertainty of our contemporary world. An ongoing revisiting of realism keeps that hope alive and makes—why not?—realism real.

【Works Cited】

Alford, C. Fred. *Think No Evil: Korean Values in the Age of Globalization*. Cornell UP, 1999.

André, Sylvie. *Pour une lecture postcoloniale de la fiction réaliste (XXe - XXIe siècles)*. Honoré Champion, 2018.

Arslan, Muge and Ulfet Dag. "Postmodern Reflections in the Work 'Ruhm' by Daniel Kehlmann." *Academic Journal of Interdisciplinary Studies*, vol. 2, no. 8, 2013, pp. 326 - 32.

Doležel, Lubomir. *Possible Worlds of Fiction and History*. Johns Hopkins UP, 2010.

Hübinette, Tobias. "The Nation Is a Woman: The Korean Nation Embodied as an Overseas Korean Woman in Chang Kil-su's Susanne Brink's Arirang." *Intersections: Gender, History and Culture in the Asian Context* 11, intersections: anu. edu. au/issue11/hubinette. html. Accessed 20 November 2023.

Kehlmann, Daniel. *Fame: A Novel in Nine Episodes*. Pantheon Books, 2010.

---. *Measuring the World*. Quercus, 2007.

Knapp, Adrian, editor. *The Past Coming to Roost in the Present: Historicising History in Four Post-Apartheid South African Novels*. Columbia UP, 2006.

Koné, Amadou. "Discourse in Kourouma's Novels. Writing Two Languages to Translate Two Realities." Research in African Literatures, vol. 38, no. 2, pp. 111 - 33.

Kourouma, Ahmadou. *Allah Is Not Obliged*. Anchor, 2007.

---. *Quand on refuse on dit non*. Seuil, 2004.

Larsen, Svend Erik. "Narratives as cultural embedment." *Chinese Semiotic Studies*, vol. 18, no. 3, 2022, pp. 413 - 25.

---. "The Good Life Lost and Found: East, West, Home's Best." *Cultural Patterns and Neurocognitive Circuits: East-West Connections*, edited by Jan Vassbinder and Balász Gulyás, World Scientific Publishers, 2016, pp. 141 - 68.

Marks, Joel and Roger T. Ames, editors. *Emotions in Asian Thought: A*

Dialogue in Contemporary Philosophy. State of New York UP, 1995.

Mpe, Phaswane. *Welcome to Our Hillbrow*. U of Natal P, 2001.

Olmor, Daniela. *Jorge Semprún: Memory's Long Voyage*. Peter Lang, 2014.

Ryan, Marie-Laure. *Possible Worlds: Artificial Intelligence and Narrative Theory*. Indiana UP, 1991.

Semprún, Jorge. *Le mort qu'il faut*. Gallimard, 2001.

---. *Literature and Life*. Penguin, 1998.

---. *The Long Voyage*. Overlook Press, 2005.

Yi, Mun-Yol. *Meeting with My Brother*. Columbia UP, 2017.

Mimesis: The Representation of Lived Reality in Western and Non-Western Literatures of the World

Ottmar Ette

Abstract: Erich Auerbach's book *Mimesis: The Representation of Reality in Western Literature* is certainly, in the long run, one of the most influential publications in the field of studies on realism. In his book written in exile from Nazi Germany, Auerbach investigates the concept of "mimesis" in a transhistorical series of studies, organized as an archipelagic writing, from Greek and Roman Antiquity through the Middle Ages until the 20th Century. He distinguishes two different modes of representations of reality (dargestellte Wirklichkeit) in Western literatures that we could qualify as continental and archipelagic. This paper aims to study these two modes of writing realism in Western and non-Western literatures, focusing on the representations of lived reality specially in literatures with no fixed Abode from the 18th century until our day. What are the epistemic changes and transformations when we talk about life and lived reality when dealing with realism?

Key words: mimesis; Erich Auerbach; continental vs. archipelagic representations; *Hong Lou Meng*; Can Xué; representations of lived reality

Author: Dr. Ottmar Ette is a professor at the University of

---

① 本文原发于《外国文学研究》2024 年第 3 期。

Potsdam, Germany. His research interests are Romance literatures, travel literature, Alexander von Humboldt, and comparative literature.

In the first chapter of what is certainly the most significant work by a German Romanist of the 20th century, Erich Auerbach's *Mimesis: The Representation of Reality in Western Literature* (1946), composed between May 1942 and April 1945 during his exile in Istanbul, the exiled philologist introduces a fundamental distinction. This distinction not only responds to the question of how the totality of the world can be represented in Western civilization but also touches upon the fundamental dimensions of understanding the concept of realism. This concept is central to the subsequent discussions about the representation of reality in Western literature and the literary depiction of lived reality both within and beyond the Western world.

I deliberately refer to a work that has significantly influenced the discussions about the concept of realism since its publication. The fact that Erich Auerbach, who was already on the trail of his *Philology of World Literature*[1] at that time, understood the Homeric and Old Testament-biblical worlds as two fundamental starting and reference points. These fields of force shape the represented reality in Western literature up to the present, which led the philologist to the realization of a structure that appears paradoxical at first glance.

As a composition, the Old Testament is incomparably less unified than the Homeric poems, it is more obviously pieced together—but the various components all belong to one concept of universal history and its interpretation. If certain elements survived which did not immediately fit in, interpretation took care of them; and so the reader is at every moment aware of the universal religio-historical perspective which gives the individual stories the general meaning and purpose. The greater the separateness and horizontal disconnection of the stories and groups of stories in relation to one another, compared with the Iliad and the Odyssey, the stronger is their general vertical connection, which holds them all together and which is entirely lacking in Homer (Auerbach 17 – 18).

The horizontal and vertical bindings and connections, which could be associated with the distinction between syntagmatic and paradigmatic levels, are reflected not only in their narrative technical possibilities but also in their power and force. This influence is primarily evident in the impact of historical constructions on their readers. The Old Testament narrative model aims for an overall meaning and purpose, to which even the individual lives of the readership must be subjected. Evidently, this embodies a significant narrative force.

In Auerbach's view, the spatially and temporally limited fragmentariness of the Iliad and the Odyssey corresponds to a significant narrative (and narrative technical) coherence. Conversely, the unified historical perspective of the Old Testament is reflected on the textual level in a kind of piecemeal fragmentation. The often-examined dialectic of fragment and totality, as explored in works such as Lucien Dällenbach and Christiaan L. Hart Nibbrig's *Fragment und Totalität*,[2] is complemented in the opening passages of Auerbach's *Mimesis* by an equally influential interplay between spatial-temporal limitation and spatial-temporal delimitation, as well as between a lifeworld-based world of stories and a religiously based world history. In Western tradition, two narrative models of representing reality stand in apparent direct opposition to each other.

For the inquiry into the foundational aspects of a new concept of realism, it is enlightening to consider that the dimension of world history not only aligns with a claim to dominion, endeavoring to relate even the most spatially and temporally distant phenomena to its own narrative of salvation, but also unfolds from an abstraction of concrete spatiotemporal conditions. Moreover, it establishes a direct relationship with the life of Auerbach's readership. This direct connection to the reader and to life is evident from the very first sentence of *Mimesis*. The biographical dimension of Auerbach's reflections becomes immediately apparent through the frequent use of the concept of life in his work (Ette, "Literature" 977 – 93), where he discusses the role of literary studies in the contemporary context. This approach underscores the significance of the life lexeme in Auerbach's work.

On this level, the duplication of the lexeme "life" illustrates the impact and force exerted by the narrative model of the Old Testament within the Jewish-Christian interpretive movement. It becomes clear that, for Auerbach in *Mimesis*, the focus is primarily on the "life of people in Europe," suggesting that, in Auerbach's understanding of the term "the West," the dimension outside Europe holds no real relevance—a point added here descriptively and commentatively, yet not judgmentally. In Dante's *Divine Comedy*, Auerbach discerned the creation of reality through compression, intensification, and diversity. Equally, he recognized the immediate yet artfully intertwined convergence of the two narrative traditions and strands which, from his perspective, are constitutive of all those literary phenomena he termed and understood as "Western literature." These narrative strands fuse in Dante's work, embodying the very essence of the literary elements Auerbach identified as central to Western literature.

I endeavor to recast the distinction of traditions outlined by Auerbach using different terms. For the Old Testament, one might simplistically refer to it as a continental-continuous narrative and writing tradition. This tradition achieves the totality of the world in an encyclopedic manner through incessant additions. In contrast, Homer's narrative model can be described as archipelagic-discontinuous. This model produces reality fractally, in the form of a "modèle réduit" (understood in the sense of Claude Lévi-Strauss) or a "mise en abyme" (outlined by André Gide). The connections to Auerbach's concept of "figura" (Auerbach, "Figura" 55 – 92) are evident. Put differently, one model of narrating reality is continental, while the other is insular or archipelagic.

The masterfully executed interpretation of Dante's epochal work, positing that all existence can only be conceived as historically evolved, and thus must be demonstrated, analyzed, and understood within its historical process of becoming, forms the actual foundation of Erich Auerbach's own philologically grounded understanding of literary representation of reality. Particularly in *Mimesis*, where we encounter the timeless—often in the forms of a transhistorical movement—we are presented with a historical becoming in such a way that in being, not only history but more so life (consequently: experienced, lived, and livable history) becomes discernible. What Auerbach initially referred to as represented reality in Western literature in his title, is already on the path in *Mimesis* to what we today still have to explore and research: the aesthetically thoughtful representation of lived and experienced realities, as we have encountered them from the very beginnings in literatures of the world—across languages, cultures, and millennia—in a polylogical manner.

Mimesis is undoubtedly one of the most influential publications that have significantly shaped various theoretical formations of the understanding of realism, at least in the Western world, up to the present day. Edward Said's intensive engagement with this work highlighted its value for literatures outside of Europe.[③] His insights are discussed in his introduction to the English translation of "Mimesis" and further explored in Martin Vialon's "The Scars of Exile," which examines the relationship between history, literature, and politics, as demonstrated in the examples of Erich Auerbach, Traugott Fuchs, and the Ceercle in Istanbul. In the continuation of this investigation, an attempt will be made to demonstrate Auerbach's central distinction between continental-encyclopedic and archipelagic-fractal traditions. This will be done through the analysis of four exemplary texts that represent not only Western-European cultural traditions but also non-Western contexts. These texts will be used to illustrate the forms and norms of the mutual connections between these two traditions, a dynamic that has been present in Western literature at least since Dante Alighieri.

The aim is not to indiscriminately apply a theory developed by a German Romanist in the mid-20th century at the crossroads of Europe and Asia to non-European subjects. Instead, the objective is to transform this theory, enabling a reanalysis and understanding of literary artifacts under the lens of realism in a new light. The archipelagic writing style of *Mimesis*, divided into individual sample chapters, is particularly well-suited for this task due to its transhistorical orientation. This approach is ideal for the experimental expansion of a concept of the representation of lived reality derived from Auerbach's work. We plan to test this adapted concept first on a "classic" text from Chinese literature, exemplifying how Auerbach's ideas can be applied and evolved in a broader literary context.

*

Cao Xueqin's *The Dream of the Red Chamber*,[4] one of the four great classical novels of Chinese literature, is also one of the most well-known works in Chinese literary history in Europe, where it has been translated into many European languages (Woesler xii). The novel first appeared in German in a shortened edition translated by Franz Kuhn: "Der Traum der roten Kammer," published by Insel in Leipzig in 1932. This abridged translation sold exceptionally well, reaching a circulation of nearly 90,000 copies between 1932 and 1977. There is arguably no better introduction to lived Chinese culture than this expansive yet never tedious novel, spanning well over two thousand pages. Its detailed narrative offers readers a profound insight into the complexity of Chinese society during the transition from the Ming to the Qing Dynasty. It presents what may be considered the Chinese life knowledge of that era, immersing readers in the intricacies of its historical context and societal norms. This novel not only stands as a monumental work in literary history but also serves as a rich source of cultural and historical understanding.⑤

This classic Chinese novel can be somewhat simplistically categorized as a Bildungsroman⑥ that encapsulates a wide spectrum of life forms and norms, particularly under the Qing Dynasty. A distinctive feature of the novel's structure is the paradisiacal Daguanyuan, a vast inner garden. This secluded space, protected from the outside world, forms its own universe and represents the theoretical landscape of the narrative.⑦ *The Dream of the Red Chamber* thus possesses a fractal structure that models the entire world, or the Chinese conception of tian xià (All Under Heaven),⑧ with the Daguanyuan serving as a microcosm of this world.⑨ The totality of Chinese reality is narrated through the literary portrayal of this island-like space, offering a unique perspective on the complexities and intricacies of Chinese society and culture.

The novel *The Dream of the Red Chamber*, which quickly became canonical following its publication at the end of the 18th century, shares similarities with many great works of Western literature in Europe and the Americas. From its island-like microcosm, the novel constructs a world in which significant changes are played out within the inner garden of the narrative world. These changes, though presented on a smaller scale, encapsulate the full complexity of the world it represents. The novel thus offers a comprehensive view of an entire world, showcasing its complexity and the richness of its reduced yet full representation of life. This approach highlights the novel's unique ability to reflect the broader world through a focused, miniature lens, a characteristic it shares with significant Western literary works.

Hóng Lóu Mèng (*The Dream of the Red Chamber*) provides profound insights into various aspects of Chinese society. It delves into the connections between affluent families and the imperial court, contrasts urban and rural lifestyles, and offers glimpses into Chinese gastronomy. Additionally, the novel explores a range of traditional Chinese healing practices, which can be linked to the work of Li Shizhen[1] in Traditional Chinese Medicine. It also touches upon philosophy and religion, as well as myths, legends, poetic writing practices, and painting styles prevalent in China at the time. Published in 1792, *The Dream of the Red Chamber* was primarily written between 1743 and 1753, thus offering a window into Chinese history and culture around the mid-18th century. Without delving into the complex genesis of the novel in detail, it is noteworthy to mention that the novel portrays the transitional period leading to the 19th century. It anticipates and prefigures changes that became more prominent in the subsequent century, serving as both a historical document and a prescient reflection of societal shifts.

Therefore, it is important to recognize that this expansive narrative text represents a pinnacle of Chinese novelistic art. It incorporates autobiographical and autofictional elements—reflecting the author Cao Xueqin's own experience of his family's unjustified decline—as well as historiographical fragments, genealogical considerations, and detailed character studies. The novel also offers intricate analyses of the Chinese language and etymology, and delves into various Chinese games and pastimes. Particularly noteworthy is the novel's artistic and playful approach to the creation of literature, especially poetry, which receives significant attention. The prose is committed to a lyrical density, weaving together narrative and poetic elements seamlessly. This stylistic choice not only enhances the novel's aesthetic appeal but also deepens the reader's engagement with the text's rich thematic tapestry.

In *The Dream of the Red Chamber*, spiritual and transcendent elements are prominently featured. The novel is permeated with Buddhist and Taoist ideas, grounded on a foundation of Confucian thinking,[1] as explored in works like Guo Xiangpeng's *The Confucian Tradition: Between Religion and Humanism*. This amalgamation of philosophies constitutes the novel's fundamental value system and points to a sophisticated life knowledge that is intricately woven into the narrative. The novel repeatedly recontextualizes this knowledge from diverse viewpoints, offering a rich and multifaceted exploration of its themes. The novel incorporates various forms of engagement with spiritual and mythical dimensions, as well as contemplations on the futility of human life and different instances and manifestations of suicide, which play a significant role in the plot. Life in the novel is portrayed as part of ancient cycles of creation and destruction, with love and death, Eros and Thanatos, being fundamental components of human existence and experience. Suicides, often motivated by unfulfilled love, are given substantial structural significance within the narrative. In a parallel to the reception of Goethe's "Werther," the early 19th-century readership of *The Dream of the Red Chamber* experienced several waves of suicides, a phenomenon indicative of the profound impact of the novel. This similarity in the reception of novels in both Asian and European contexts underscores the potential for drawing numerous parallels between the ways novels are engaged with and assimilated across different cultures.

The mythological and ideological context of the Chinese novel *The Dream of the Red Chamber* fundamentally differs from contemporaneous narrative worlds in Europe. The connection of the protagonist, Jia Baoyu, to the mythical repair of the celestial canopy, and thereby to the "Story of the Stone," alluded to in the novel's title, directs us to the ancient Chinese mythological foundation of the entire narrative world. Jia Baoyu, the sheltered and handsome young man born with a jade stone in his mouth, is destined for a unique fate. This connection to the mythological not only situates Baoyu within a broader cosmic narrative but also imbues his character and the novel's events with a deep sense of preordained destiny and symbolism. This aspect of the novel is indicative of the way Chinese literature often intertwines personal narratives with larger mythological and cosmological elements, creating a rich tapestry of interconnected stories and themes.

The dual nature of the world depicted in *The Dream of the Red Chamber* has been aptly described as the coexistence and competition of two realms.[12] There is the world within the Daguanyuan and a wholly different one outside this secluded, isolated island-like area. However, the external world makes its presence felt within the Great Inner Garden, increasingly intruding and impacting it with growing force, akin to how the Orbis tertius invades the everyday world in Jorge Luis Borges's story *Tlön, Uqbar, Orbis Tertius*. In the course of the novel, we observe how history increasingly alters the secluded world of the Inner Garden. This change culminates in a spiritual climax at the end, where the protagonist's transformation defies all the preceding signs of decay. The male protagonist liberates himself from all constraints, choosing a life founded on renunciation after years of idle luxury. This shift represents a significant thematic and character development in the novel, highlighting the intricate interplay between the personal, societal, and spiritual dimensions in the narrative.

The narrative of *The Dream of the Red Chamber* is significantly propelled by evolving romantic relationships, central to which is a passionate[13] love triangle involving the male protagonist Jia Baoyu and the two young women, Lin Daiyu, his paternal cousin, and Xue Baochai, his maternal cousin. The ethereal beauty of Lin Daiyu, marked by a fundamental pallor and an ultimately incurable internal illness exacerbated by her emotional suffering, resonates with the depiction of female characters in Western novels of the late 18th and especially the 19th centuries, both in Europe and Latin America. However, it is striking to observe how such topical parallel structures have developed in largely independent literary traditions. These portrayals of women undoubtedly reflect the patriarchal structures inherent in both societies, where the narrative of beautiful women is often tragically intertwined with their demise.[14] These are parallels of phallocentric origin, characteristic of both cultural systems. The novel, thus, not only tells a story of love and passion but also offers a critical reflection on the societal norms and gender dynamics of the time, drawing attention to the universal themes that transcend cultural boundaries.

The fact that *The Dream of the Red Chamber* has, since its publication, given rise to various schools of thought and entire philological interpretive traditions is noteworthy. It is one of the most extensively researched narrative works in literatures of the world. The fragmentary nature and the unfinished quality of this immense novel have been conducive to the development of a multitude of interpretations and philological theories. It is important to emphasize that Chinese literature and Chinese philology have taken paths quite distinct from the history of philology in the Western world. The extensive and independently evolved "Redology" research dedicated to Cao Xueqin's novel unmistakably points to its polysemy and multivalency. *The Dream of the Red Chamber* intricately combines social chronicle and autofiction, social analysis and exploration of everyday culture, linguistic analysis, and an engrossing delight in storytelling within its complex narrative structure.[15] The novel continues to be extensively studied and is widely read by a broad audience. It has also been adapted into numerous other media formats, from films to graphic novels, testifying to its enduring popularity and significance in both academic and popular cultures.

The various narrative threads woven and reconverged in *The Dream of the Red Chamber* also encompass the expansion of an extensive intertextual network. This network integrates a multitude of Chinese writings, novels, and poems into the plot. As a result, entirely different stories can be thoughtfully incorporated into the novel, both complementarily and contrastively, bringing in realities that could be, or might have been, experienced by the characters. These embedded narratives offer not just thought experiments but also life models, often revolving around the theme of love. This intertextual network is so intricately crafted that it intersects with the main narrative at numerous points, directly influencing the course of events in various ways. Such a complex web of references not only enriches the story's depth but also reflects the novel's profound engagement with the broader corpus of Chinese literary and cultural heritage, showcasing its multifaceted nature and the dynamic interplay between different literary elements.

While I choose not to delve deeply here into the notion that *The

Dream of the Red Chamber can be viewed as a grand laboratory of love, it is a point worth noting. The novel, like a heating, transparent greenhouse, allows us to observe among the initially youthful characters the various forms and norms of love as they were lived and experienced in China at that time. The "Dream," with its interspersed poems acting as a fractal of all passions of love, presciently mirrors the later developments in the narrative. I have addressed this aspect in detail in a lecture in Copenhagen in 2023. It is important to emphasize that the novel owes a significant part of its current multimedia popularity to this facet of a love story that is expressed without explicitly naming love. This subtle approach to depicting love adds layers of complexity and intrigue to the narrative, making it not only a historical and cultural exploration but also a profound exploration of human emotions and relationships.

Undoubtedly, the Chinese authors of *The Dream of the Red Chamber* brilliantly succeeds in creating, through the invention of Daguanyuan, an island from which the totality of a reality can be represented. This island is fashioned in a "continental" manner, as it employs encyclopedic methods that allow the novel's protagonists to experience and live through various layers of narrative. The secluded world of the Great Garden Paradise symbolizes the significant isolation that China experienced relative to the globalizing world at that time, a period when European colonialism, though tentative, was already casting its covetous gaze upon this highly developed empire. European snuff, for instance, presented in a snuffbox adorned with a naked "female" angel, finds its use as medicine (Cao 902 ff.) in the novel (905). However, these external factors play no real role in the fate of the events unfolding within Daguanyuan, in the inner garden of the once wealthy aristocratic family. The novel focuses more on the internal dynamics and societal structures of the time, rather than external influences, providing a deep insight into the isolated yet intricate world of its characters.

The events within Daguanyuan in *The Dream of the Red Chamber* are of an absolutely marginal nature and do not significantly alter the model of reality portrayed in the Great Garden. The eventual permeability and collapse of the garden's walls at the novel's end, leading to the irreversible destruction of the precious garden—as foreshadowed in the novel's "mise en abyme"—marks the culmination of the protagonist's journey from love to renunciation. This journey finds its final expression in the wise silence of Baoyu, who bids farewell to the material world. The island of the Great Garden, a microcosm of a certain way of life and a specific cultural moment, metaphorically disappears into the floods, signifying not just the physical destruction of a place but also the end of an era and a particular social order. The novel thus encapsulates the transient nature of human constructs and the inevitability of change, both in individual lives and broader societal contexts.

* *

My second example comes from the realm of European literatures without a fixed residence.[15] In the preface to his *Diario de Djelfa*, a lyrical diary composed of poems written in the eponymous Algerian concentration and labor camp of the same name, Max Aub reflected on the significance of his writing during his internment. Aub, who was thirty-eight years old at the time, was deported to the camp in November 1941 along with three hundred other inmates. In his writings, he acknowledges the crucial role these poems, penned under the dire circumstances of the camp, played in his survival. Aub's *Diario de Djelfa* stands as a testament to the power of literature as a means of perseverance and resistance in the face of extreme adversity. The act of writing, in this context, becomes more than a creative endeavor; it serves as a lifeline, a way of maintaining humanity, and a form of spiritual and psychological sustenance amidst the dehumanizing conditions of the camp (Aub, *Diario* 93). Aub's experience highlights the transformative and redemptive capacity of literature, especially in situations of extreme hardship and displacement (Aub 93).

For Aub, *Diario de Djelfa* thus becomes an embodiment of both a knowledge of life and a knowledge of survival. Arising from real-life experiences, these poems encapsulate a deep understanding of life, evidencing resistance against its obliteration. Published in 1944 while in exile in Mexico, *Diario de Djelfa* offers poetic testimonies of survival, with poems that navigate themes of life and death in the setting of the concentration camp. These poems represent more than just literary works; they are vital records of human endurance and resilience in the face of extreme suffering. Aub's poetry serves as a bridge between the harrowing experiences of the camp and the outside world, providing a poignant and enduring witness to the human spirit's capacity to find strength and expression even in the darkest of circumstances. This work stands as a poignant reminder of the power of art to transcend, document, and resist inhumane conditions.

Max Aub, born in 1903, survived not just one, but several concentration and labor camps. Consequently, his entire literary oeuvre, from the time he left his last concentration camp in the summer of 1942 until his death in Mexico in the summer of 1972 (Soldevila Durante 43), can be seen as a continuous struggle to find a literary form that expresses the world as a succession of camps. This theme is not incidental; it pervades his narrative work, including novels like *Campo cerrado*, *Campo abierto*, *Campo de sangre*, *Campo del Moro*, *Campo de los almendros*, and *Campo francés*, all of which revolve around the central concept of the camp ("campo"). Aub's writing in the realm of realism, whether in his poems, novels, or many short stories, can be understood as the creation of different narrative "islands." These islands come together to form an archipelago centered around the concept of the camp. In this way, Aub's literary works not only narrate the physical and psychological experiences of life in and after the camps but also metaphorically represent a fragmented world connected by shared experiences of confinement, survival, and resilience. This archipelago of narratives serves as a powerful symbol of the enduring impact of these experiences on human life and history.

At the heart of these many narrative islands crafted by Aub undoubtedly stands *Manuscrito Cuervo: Historia de Jacobo*, a short prose text first published in 1952 in the third and final volume of Aub's self-edited magazine *Sala de espera*. It was later published in a carefully revised final version in 1955, the year Aub acquired Mexican citizenship. *Manuscrito Cuervo* presents the world from the perspective of a raven. The polysemy inherent in the story, suggested by the title's potential as a subjective, objective, or possessive genitive, adds layers of interpretation to the narrative. The raven in *Manuscrito Cuervo* is not just, to modify Umberto Eco's phrase, the raven in the story (a corvus in fabula), but also its author and authority (auctor). This duality positions the raven both as a character within the narrative and as the creator or narrator of the story. This dual role blurs the lines between the storyteller and the story, offering a unique narrative perspective and deepening the thematic exploration of the text. Aub's innovative use of the raven as both a symbol and a narrative voice reflects his ongoing exploration of narrative forms and his commitment to examining the complexities of human experience.

In Max Aub's narrative, a raven observed by many inmates of

the Vernet concentration camp in Southern France—mentioned by individuals like Gustav Regler—is said to have left behind a manuscript. This raven, as we learn at the beginning of the story (Soldevila Durante 46), disappeared forever after its composition. However, this manuscript of the raven was transcribed, translated into Spanish, and published, and it holds significant meaning. The intertextual references to Cervantes' *Don Quixote*, supposedly translated by a fictional editor from Arabic, are apparent. The fictional framework of the story, despite its fantastical elements, emphasizes a claim to utmost realism (Aub, *Manuscrito* 58). This approach addresses the credibility deficit (Arendt 908 f.) in documentary narratives of concentration camp survivors, as highlighted by Hannah Arendt in *The Origins of Totalitarianism*. By enriching the narrative in a world of fiction, Aub overcomes this deficit and asserts the right to a literary representation of lived reality. The text gains credibility not through a strict adherence to factual accuracy but by oscillating between factuality and fictionality, crafting a narrative that engages with reality through the lens of imaginative storytelling. This technique reflects Aub's broader approach to literature as a means of exploring and understanding human experiences, particularly those marked by extreme circumstances.

In Max Aub's narrative, the raven character offers a unique perspective on human life, contrasting it sharply with the qualities attributed to ravens. The raven observes that humans lack the defining features of ravens: wings, feathers, independence, and a sense of togetherness. Instead, humans have arms, crawl like worms on the ground, rely on clothing, divide themselves into genealogies and nationalities, and constantly exclude each other. They fail to coexist in peace and embrace differences. This raven's perspective on human life and social interaction facilitates a shift in viewpoint, allowing a fresh and critical examination of human society. The concentration camp, through the raven's eyes, is seen as a fractal—a miniaturized model of human society. This metaphorical representation highlights the flaws, divisions, and conflicts inherent in human societies. By adopting the perspective of a raven, an outsider and observer, Aub invites readers to reconsider their own perspectives on humanity, society, and the capacity for both unity and division. This narrative device effectively illustrates the profound and often troubling aspects of human nature and social organization.

The literary structures of Aub's *Manuscrito Cuervo* reveal a composition based on discontinuous and archipelagic writing, fragmented into many different parts. This structure is marked by a multitude of discontinuities and breaks, facilitating a constant shifting of the observational perspective. This approach eschews the continuity of a single, definitive viewpoint in favor of highlighting the relationality between various perspectives. Such a structure prefigures a form of experimental writing that spans from the historical avant-gardes to postmodernism, akin to the style Aub would later employ in *Jusep Torres Campalans*, a fictional biography of an invented painter of the Catalan avant-garde, which utilized a cubist, multiperspective approach.[17] In *Manuscrito Cuervo*, the blending of different forms of writing—including poetry, scientific treatise, prologue, factual data compilation, literary narration, and local history—creates a highly heterogeneous text corpus. This corpus, characterized by its constant discontinuities, aims to represent lived realities. The diverse narrative techniques and shifting perspectives employed in the text allow Aub to explore the complexities of human experience and historical reality, crafting a rich and multifaceted portrayal of life within and beyond the confines of the concentration camp. This method not only enhances the narrative's depth but also reflects Aub's commitment to capturing the essence of human existence in all its varied forms.

The raven's perspective on humans and humanity in Max Aub's narrative enables an external, playful examination of the conditions of human life and the mechanisms of confinement and exclusion, inclusion and exclusion. The interplay between discovery and invention, between fictionally generated reality and reality-based fictionality, creates a frictional tension. This friction generates a high energy that allows Max Aub, as homo ludens (the playing human), to explore and blur the boundaries between fiction and reality, and between play and seriousness. This approach leads to an even more intense and, in the sense of Hannah Arendt, a more credible representation of lived reality. Aub's engagement with the totalitarianisms of his time led him to develop elements and origins of total friction. Through the raven's perspective, the concentration camp becomes, in the words of Giorgio Agamben (127), a paradigm of modernity, and with Max Aub, a paradigm of human life itself. The concentration camp island in Le Vernet, Southern France, represents not just a specific place, but all camps where human life is concentrated like in a burning glass. This metaphorical interpretation underscores the camp as a microcosm of broader human experiences and societal dynamics, capturing the essence of human existence in extreme conditions. Aub's narrative thus transcends the specific historical context of the camp, offering universal insights into the human condition.

Max Aub's writing is not a post-Auschwitz writing as Theodor Adorno might conceptualize it, but rather a writing in the face of the camp, emerging from the awareness that humanity is still far from having come to terms with the existence and implications of concentration camps. Yet, it also arises from the understanding that there are forces capable of confronting the reality of the camp: the knowledge of life and survival, the resilience, and the aesthetic power inherent in the literatures of the world. Aub's work embodies the idea that literature serves not only as a reflection of reality but also as a form of resistance and a means of understanding and coping with the most harrowing experiences. His writing encapsulates the belief in the transformative and redemptive potential of literary expression. Through his narratives, Aub demonstrates how literature can confront and challenge the horrors of human history, offering insights into the depths of human experience and the possibility of finding meaning and resilience in the midst of suffering. This perspective affirms the enduring relevance and necessity of literature as a tool for grappling with the complexities of human existence, particularly in the context of extreme adversity.

* * *

My third example focuses on Mario Vargas Llosa, a Nobel Prize-winning author whose literary creations are characterized by a consistent trans-areal[18] expansion of his novelistic worlds, thereby continually broadening the horizon of represented reality. Born in 1936 in Arequipa, Peru, Vargas Llosa's literary journey initially engaged with his Peruvian roots, particularly Lima, the Andes, and the Amazon region of his homeland. Later in his career, he expanded his geographical scope to include other areas of Latin America, as seen in works like *La guerra del fin del mundo* (*The War of the End of the World*), which explores Brazil, and *La fiesta del chivo* (*The Feast of the Goat*), which delves into the Caribbean islands. Vargas Llosa's literary evolution reflects a deepening and widening of thematic and geographical concerns, moving from a focus on Peruvian society and politics to broader issues and settings across Latin America and beyond. His works often explore complex social, political, and historical themes, offering a nuanced and critical examination of Latin American realities. This trans-areal approach not only enriches his narrative scope but also underscores his commitment to capturing the diverse and multifaceted experiences of the Latin American region, making his work an essential contribution to world literature.

In the course of expanding his narrative texts from the trans-local and trans-regional to the trans-national and trans-continental, and finally to the trans-areal level in the broadest sense, Mario Vargas Llosa's 2010 novel *El sueño del celta* (*The Dream of the Celt*), published in the year of his Nobel Prize award in Stockholm, holds particular significance. In this historical novel, the expansive, global diegesis transforms into a complex transtropical landscape that vividly portrays the interdependent realities of America, Africa, and Europe. *The Dream of the Celt* represents a culmination of Vargas Llosa's literary evolution, showcasing his ability to weave together diverse geographical and cultural narratives into a cohesive and immersive story. The novel transcends conventional geographical and cultural boundaries, providing a sensory and vivid representation of interconnected global experiences. This approach reflects Vargas Llosa's skill in creating rich, layered narratives that explore the complexities of human experience across different regions and cultures, making his work a significant contribution to global literature.

In *The Dream of the Celt*, Mario Vargas Llosa employs a highly sophisticated literary structure that is both technically novelistic and reflective of socio-economic and globalization histories. The novel transatlantically interconnects the three continents in such a way that the three "worlds" of America, Africa, and Europe cannot be thought of as separate entities. Instead, they are depicted as components of a system of dependencies, where knowledge of domination and violence is unequally distributed across the globe. *The Dream of the Celt*, as suggested by the title, represents a vision of a world-spanning space where people from the three continents can coexist peacefully and respectfully in their differences. However, this ideal is obstructed by the history and present reality of European colonialism, characterized by its brutality. This narrative underscores the complexities and challenges of achieving harmony and understanding in a world marked by historical injustices and ongoing power imbalances. Vargas Llosa's novel thus engages deeply with the themes of colonialism, cultural interaction, and the enduring impact of historical events on contemporary global relations, offering a poignant critique of the obstacles to realizing a more equitable and respectful global community.

In *The Dream of the Celt*, while the narrative indeed spans three continents, Mario Vargas Llosa's approach to representation is not strictly continental. This is evident even in the novel's cover design by Pep Carrió, which features the contours of Roger Casement's head, the protagonist of the story,[19] superimposed on a world map. The locations central to the narrative, set in the third phase of accelerated globalization, appear as islands in a global archipelago, interconnected by drops of blood. This imagery symbolically represents the interconnectedness of the Congo, the Amazon, Ireland, and England, not through mere geographical proximity or historical coincidence but through a shared history of violence, exploitation, and colonialism. These "blood traces" metaphorically chain these diverse regions together, suggesting that the legacies of colonialism and human rights abuses have left indelible marks linking disparate parts of the world. Vargas Llosa's narrative thus transcends a simple continental depiction, opting instead for a more complex, interconnected, and global perspective that reflects the intertwined histories and destinies of these regions.

The enigmatic historical figure of Roger Casement, born near Dublin in 1864 and executed in London in 1916 for high treason, serves as a pivotal link in *The Dream of the Celt*. He connects his two asymmetric origins, Ireland and England, with the sites of extreme colonial and neocolonial exploitation represented by the Congo and the Putumayo region in the Peruvian Amazon lowlands. Casement's life reflects the era of ruthless expansionist policies among industrial powers vying for the "last" colonies, a paradigm epitomized by the 1884 Berlin Conference on Africa, which is recurrently referenced in the novel. This conference starkly exposed the unvarnished realities of the scramble for Africa. Vargas Llosa's narrative situates itself in a world caught in the crosshairs of many old and some new colonial powers, vividly depicting the specific conditions of the third phase of accelerated globalization in the last third of the 19th century. The novel, through the life and experiences of Casement, powerfully brings to light the complexities and consequences of this period, highlighting the interconnections between various global regions and the impacts of colonialism and global power dynamics.

The tri-continental landscape in *The Dream of the Celt* can indeed be described as an archipelago, not in the geographical sense of isolated islands, but as interconnected regions within the vast expanses of the global capitalist system. While the mighty rivers of the Congo and Amazon may signify vast continental expanses, Mario Vargas Llosa's narrative skillfully illustrates that these regions are "islands" in terms of their roles within a globalized, capitalist, and division-of-labor world economy. The novel's writing style is tailored to unfold these relational and interdependent elements. It becomes clear throughout the plot that these regions, while geographically part of large continents, function as isolated spheres within the global economic system, each subjected to its forces and influences. Vargas Llosa's novel acknowledges and addresses this reality, offering a nuanced exploration of the impacts of colonialism, exploitation, and global interconnectedness. This approach allows the novel to transcend traditional geographic boundaries and delve into the complexities of a world shaped by global economic and political dynamics.

The continental "islands" depicted in *The Dream of the Celt* find themselves in a state of extreme lack of freedom and dependence, much like the geographical island of Ireland in relation to England. They are subject to the centers of global trade and politics that ruthlessly and remorselessly drive the surge of globalization in the late 19th century, often with a total disregard for the loss of human life in the colonies. The world portrayed in the novel is one of slavery and exploitation of man by man, where, with few exceptions, those aligned with Western "civilization" commit heinous crimes against those they often label as "barbarians." Mario Vargas Llosa's narrative exposes the dark underbelly of colonialism and the global expansion of Western powers, highlighting the gross human rights violations and the moral bankruptcy accompanying this period of history. The novel underscores the stark contrast between the rhetoric of civilization and the brutal realities of colonial exploitation, shedding light on the dehumanizing aspects of imperialist endeavors and the far-reaching impacts of these actions on both the colonized and the colonizers. This critical examination challenges the reader to confront and reconsider the narratives surrounding colonialism and its legacy in the modern world.

The Peruvian author Mario Vargas Llosa made a wise choice in centering his novel *The Dream of the Celt* around the figure of Roger Casement. This character—a highly decorated British diplomat elevated to nobility for his services to the Empire, and later a rebellious Irish national hero—epitomizes the various landscapes, asymmetries, and forms of exploitation that connect the Congo, the Upper Putumayo region, and ultimately Ireland, despite their differences. In Casement's life and actions, the novel transarchipelagically interweaves the narratives of these diverse regions, bound together in prosperity and ruin. Vargas Llosa presents a complex story, far from the simplistic transfer narrative that the young Roger Casement might have believed in, shaped by his Christian and Western upbringing. The novel poses profound questions about the underlying colonial and imperial interests driving political and economic actions. It suggests that the exploitative conditions observed in the Congo and Putumayo are not unique to these regions but are a global phenomenon. *The Dream of the Celt* thus transcends the story of one man to comment on the pervasive nature of colonialism and imperialism, questioning whether places like the Congo and Putumayo represent broader global realities. This narrative approach encourages readers to reflect on the universality of these issues and their relevance in various contexts, underscoring the interconnectedness of historical and contemporary global dynamics.

The aforementioned passage illustrates the cross-examination, through which a commission appointed by the British government and dispatched to the Putumayo region in Amazonia seeks to shed light on what is undoubtedly one of the darkest and most barbaric facets of Western expansion history. All those participating in this cross-examination are ultimately deeply convinced of the moral and material superiority of the West, even and especially those whose hands are instrumental in implementing the most barbaric forms of exploitation (Vargas Llosa, *El sueño del celta* 174). Consequently, their own wrongdoing remains in the blind spot of their perspective. We are witnessing an unrelenting critique of an exploitative Western civilization model.

The passionately idealistic British diplomat gains a profound understanding, as advocated by Wilhelm Dilthey (139), of the colonial and neo-colonial situations in Africa and America. Through this deep understanding, he not only becomes aware of the inhuman ruthlessness of the self-proclaimed "civilized" colonial powers but also recognizes that his own Irish homeland is subject to the same principles of British power politics and is rendered powerless. For Roger Casement, the situation of his green home island of Ireland, becomes newly comprehensible, writable, and experiential in the light of rubber extraction in the Putumayo and Congo regions—and thereby transformable. Consequently, he resolves to oppose the United Kingdom, which he had diplomatically represented for many years, and to confront the unquestionably powerful protagonist of the third phase of accelerated globalization, the British Empire.

The Dream of the Celt offers a critique of colonialism, but it goes far beyond that: it provides a shocking portrayal of lived slavery and dependency. The transareal relationality created in the third phase of accelerated globalization binds all dependent regions together as islands in a worldwide archipelago, characterized by a hierarchy and radical asymmetry of power. Roger Casement's historical publications revealed that, under the guise of Christian missionary work and civilization, entire peoples were driven into disguised forms of enslavement or death, simultaneous to the deportations of labor slaves in the Pacific region. This was a process of extreme brutality, one that *The Dream of the Celt* seeks to meticulously depict in all its details of human cruelty and, even more so, make sensually comprehensible.

Mario Vargas Llosa's novel successfully manages to aesthetically portray the entire veneer of civilization masking a barbaric violence in such a way that, in accordance with the author's theory of the novel, the brutal violence can be transformed into the fictional power of realistic representation. As he explained in his foundational essay *Cervantes y la ficción*, this narrative force succeeds in freeing itself from the "cárcel de la historia" (19), the prison of history, and unfold a realism that extends far beyond all historiographical depiction.

*　*　*　*

With my final example, I return to Asia to examine the orientations that varieties of realism take in contemporary Chinese literature. I am certain of the fact that Chinese literature, as we saw in our first example, possesses within its own traditions[②] long-term and comparable to Western models of various realistic writing and representational forms.

The Chinese writer Can Xue, born in Changsha in 1953, undoubtedly ranks among the prominent voices of Chinese literature at the turn of the 21st century. Her prose texts, such as *Dialogues in Paradise*, which were written in the 1980s and first translated into English in 1989, garnered worldwide attention. However, she did not achieve the same level of recognition as the later Nobel laureate Mo Yan within the heterogeneous group of young Chinese authors, where she stood as the only female voice. Nonetheless, in the same way that Mo Yan's *écriture* is committed to the evolution of realistic modes of representation, exploring Can Xue's literary forms of writing is highly rewarding.

The writer, who is well-versed in both Chinese tradition and Western modern and postmodern authors like Franz Kafka and Jorge Luis Borges, has chosen a setting in her *Dialogues in Paradise* that corresponds autobiographically to the long periods she lived in the Hunan province until her move to Beijing in 2001 (Baus 7 – 14). The placement of the first prose text "at the foot of the Yuelu Mountain" (15) selects a highly specific space within Chinese traditions. This is because the sacred mountain of Yuelu, amidst a landscape filled with countless graves of intellectual luminaries, is where the famous Yuelu Academy is located. The Yuelu Academy is one of China's oldest and most prestigious educational institutions, founded on that very spot in the year 976. Yuelu forms a mountainous island within the surrounding flat river landscape, serving as the backdrop for the events from the very beginning.

Within this island-like diegesis, the first prose text does not describe a cityscape but rather portrays the forms of poverty that constitute the daily struggle for survival of a young girl and her disgraced family. In this diegesis on the west bank of the Xiang Jiang River, one gains insights into a knowledge of survival that relies on the utilization of even the most minimal opportunities for the most frugal sustenance, both in terms of food and drink. The slopes of Yuelu Mountain are certainly not a paradise.

In this regard, the Chinese writer undoubtedly draws from literary predecessors who lead us into the realm of "Magical Realism," a style often associated with Latin American Boom authors. At the same time, she crafts modes of representation that depict lived and autobiographically experienced reality within a well-defined diegesis, akin to the works of authors like Gabriel García Márquez and William Faulkner. Similar to these mentioned authors, one of the great merits of this outstanding Chinese writer is her ability to address and overcome traumas of Chinese history.[①] In the workshop of this author, who once worked as a tailor, she creates cuts and patterns that present reality in a garment that the reading audience continually assembles anew before their eyes.

The metaphor of paradise is ironically projected onto a lush and densely forested mountain landscape, deeply rooted in a continental setting yet reminiscent of the island worlds of the Caribbean where Christopher Columbus sought the Earthly Paradise. Repeatedly, and as already suggested by the title "Dialogues," rapid shifts in perspective are incorporated, illuminating the depicted realities of 20th-century Chinese history from various angles. Different narrative voices come into play, each presenting its own viewpoint on the matters at hand.

Many of these autofiction-based voices that engage in an intense dialogue or polylogue exhibit a characteristic focus on the smallest details of everyday objects and their use by human characters. Many of Can Xue's characters are in search of affection and love,[②] but more importantly, they seek other forms of coexistence on both an individual and collective level, with other people as well as with the animate nature.

Our fourth example teaches us, firstly, that since the second half of the 20th century, there has been a clear shift in Chinese literature (as well as in literatures of the world) regarding the two lines of tradition that Erich Auerbach differentiated in the portrayal of reality. Can Xue's prose represents a clear preference for insular and archipelagic structures of reality perception and representation, as can be readily observed in her writing since the 1980s.

Certainly, this preference for the insular is marked by creative appropriation of the literatures of the West and, in particular, literatures of Latin America, with which the writer from Changsha also engaged deeply from a literary-critical perspective. However, as my first example already demonstrated, the island-like structures of realistic mimesis are fundamental components of the Chinese literary tradition. These traditions have significantly influenced the forms of development in realistic writing in China, both in the case of Can Xue and authors like Mo Yan.

The expansion of the concept of realism to encompass forms and norms of lived reality, as briefly explored through this discussion of literatures of the world, will be of paramount importance in the future. This is because literatures of the world unfold a practical knowledge that manifests in polylogical, island-like discontinuities of lived reality. It will be intriguing to observe how these forms of realistic engagement with reality will influence other literatures in China in the future, once it becomes known in Western countries how the forms of literary representation of lived reality in China have evolved into polylogical writing.

【Notes】

① For further reference, see Ette, "Toward." The derivation of the term "literatures of the world," which is used below, can also be found there.

② Cf. among others, Dällenbach and Nibbrig.

③ Refer to Edward Said's introduction to the English translation of *Mimesis*, as well as Vialon.

④ In the following, I quote from the only complete German translation by Tsau and Gau E; the novel was first published in German in an abridged edition translated by Kuhn. This abridged translation sold remarkably well and reached a circulation of nearly 90,000 copies between 1932 and 1977.

⑤ For the concept of "Lebenswissen" (knowledge for life), see also Ette's trilogy *ÜberLebensWissen I-III*.

⑥ Martin Woesler has pointed out the astonishing parallels between Chinese and European literary genres and demonstrated the similarities with the European Bildungsroman (coming-of-age novel; "Der Traum" xvii).

⑦ Regarding the concept of the "Landschaft der Theorie" (landscape of theory), see Ette, *Roland Barthes*.

⑧ Cf. Zhao.

⑨ Cf. Ette, *WeltFraktale*.

⑩ Cf. the valuable German edition by Uschuld.

⑪ Cf. Peng.

⑫ This is the central thesis in Yü.

⑬ See also Woesler, "Things."

⑭ Cf. Bronfen.

⑮ Cf. Wei.

⑯ For more on this topic, see Ette, *Writing*.

⑰ For further information on this topic, see Ette, "Vanguardia."

⑱ For more on this topic, see Ette, *TransArea*.

⑲ For further exploration of this topic from a travel literature perspective, see Carr.

⑳ Cf. Part V, Chapter 2.2, Part VI, Chapter 3, and the Excursus Chapter 6 in Pohl.

㉑ For further insight into this undeniable aspect of Chinese history, refer to the insightful book by Unschuld.

㉒ Cf. Can Xue.

【Works Cited】

Agamben, Giorgio. *Homo sacer: Die souveräne Macht und das nackte Leben*. Translated from Italian by Hubert Thüring, Suhrkamp, 2002.

Arendt, Hannah. *Elemente und Ursprünge totaler Herrschaft. Antisemitismus, Imperialismus, Totalitarismus*. Piper, 2001.

Auerbach, Erich. *Mimesis: The Representation of Reality in Western Literature*. Translated by Willard Trask, Princeton UP, 1995.

---. "Figura." *Gesammelte Aufsätze zur romanischen Philologie*, edited by Fritz Schalk and Gustav Konrad, Francke, 1967, pp. 55–92.

---. *Mimesis: The Representation of Reality in Western Literature*. A. Francke, 1946.

Aub, Max. *Diario de Djelfa. Obras completes, vol. 1: Obra poética completas*, edited by Joan Oleza Simó, critical edition, introductory study, and notes by Arcadio López Casanova et al., Biblioteca Valenciana, 2001, pp. 49–112.

---. *Manuscrito Cuervo. Historia de Jacobo*. Introducción, edición y notas de José Antonio Pérez Bowie con un Epílogo de José María Naharro-Calderón. Segorbe—Alcalá de Henares: Fundación Max Aub—Universidad de Alcalá de Henares 1999.

Baus, Wolf. "Can Xues Berichte aus der Wildnis." *Dialoge im Paradies. Erzählungen aus der Volksrepublik China*, by Can Xue, translated from Chinese and with a preface by Wolf Baus, Projekt, 1996, pp. 7–14.

Bronfen, Elisabeth. *Nur über ihre Leiche: Tod, Weiblichkeit und Ästhetik*. Beck, 1994.

Can Xue. *Liebe im neuen Jahrtausend: Roman*. Translated by Karin Betz, with an afterword by Eileen Myles, Matthes and Seitz, 2021.

Carr, Helen. "Roger Casement in the Amazon, the Congo, and Ireland." *Writing Travel, and Empire: In the Margins of Anthropology*, by Peter Hulme and Russell McDougall, I. B. Tauris, 2007, pp. 169–94.

Dällenbach, Lucien, and Christiaan L. Hart Nibbrig, editors. *Fragment and

Totality. Suhrkamp, 1984.

Dilthey, Wilhelm. "Goethe und die dichterische Phantasie." *Das Erlebnis und die Dichtung. Lessing—Goethe—Novalis—Hölderlin*. Göttingen: Vandenhoeck & Ruprecht 1985, pp. 129 – 159.

Ette, Ottmar. *WeltFraktale. Wege durch die Literaturen der Welt*. J. B. Metzler, 2017.

---. "Literature as Knowledge for Living, Literary Studies as Science for Living." Edited, translated, and with an introduction by Vera M. Kutzinski, *Special Topic: Literary Criticism for the Twenty-First Century*, coordinated by Cathy Caruth and Jonathan Culler, *PMLA. Publications of the Modern Language Association of America*, vol. CXXV, no. 4, Oct. 2010, pp. 977 – 93.

---. "Toward a Polylogical Philology of the Literatures of the World." *Modern Language Quarterly*, vol. LXXVII, no. 2, June 2016, pp. 143 – 73.

---. *TransArea: A Literary History of Globalization*. Translated by Mark W. Person, Walter de Gruyter, 2016.

---. *Writing Between Worlds: TransArea Studies and the Literatures Without a Fixed Abode*. Translated by Vera M. Kutzinski, Walter de Gruyter, 2016

---. *Roland Barthes: Landschaften der Theorie*. Konstanz UP, 2013.

---. *ÜberLebensWissen I-III*. Drei Bände im Schuber. Kulturverlag Kadmos 2004 – 2010.

---. " Vanguardia, Postvanguardia, Posmodernidad. Max Aub, Jusep Torres Campalans y la vacunación vanguardista." *Revista de Indias* (Madrid), vol. LXII, no. 226, Sept.-Dec. 2002, pp. 675 – 708.

Kuhn, Franz, translator. *Der Traum der roten Kammer*. Insel, 1932.

Peng, Guoxiang. *The Confucian Tradition: Between Religion and Humanism*. Bridge, 2023.

Pohl, Karl-Heinz. *Ästhetik und Literaturtheorie in China. Von der Tradition bis zur Moderne*. K. G. Saur, 2007.

Soldevila Durante, Ignacio. *El compromiso de la imaginación. Vida y obra de Max Aub*. Fundación Max Aub, 1999.

Tsau, Hsüä-tjin, and Gau E (Cao, Xueqin, and Gao E). *Der Traum der Roten Kammer oder Die Geschichte vom Stein*. Translated from Chinese by Rainer Schwarz and Martin Woesler, edited and with a preface by Martin Woesler, Europäischer Universitätsverlag, 2010.

Unschuld, Paul U. *Chinas Trauma—Chinas Stärke: Niedergang und Wiederaufstieg des Reichs der Mitte*. With a foreword by Ulrich Sendler, Springer Vieweg, 2016

Vargas Llosa, Mario. *El sueño del celta*. Santillana-Alfaguara, 2010.

---. *Cervantes y la ficción: Cervantes and the Craft of Fiction*. Schwabe, 2001.

Vialon, Martin. "The Scars of Exile: Paralipomena Concerning the Relationship Between History, Literature, and Politics: Demonstrated in the Examples of Erich Auerbach, Traugott Fuchs and the Cercle in Istanbul." *Yeditepe Defteri* (Istanbul), no. 2, July 2003, pp. 191–246.

Wei, Ling. *Der Traum der roten Kammer. Die erzählerische Komplexität eines chinesischen Meisterwerks*. Harrassowitz, 2019.

Woesler, Martin. "Things Unspoken in the Red Chamber Dreams. Connecting Readers Across Boundaries of Time and Culture Through Human Emotions." *EJSin*, no. 10, 2019, pp. 95–111.

---. "Der Traum der Roten Kammer in deutscher Übersetzung—Ein Generations—und Entwicklungsroman als paradiesische Zuflucht verklärter Jugenderinnerungen in schwieriger Zeit." *Der Traum der Roten Kammer oder Die Geschichte vom Stein*, by Tsau and Gao, pp. 11–25.

Yü, Ying-shin. "The Two Worlds of *Honglou meng* (*Dream of the Red Chamber*)." *Chinese History and Culture: Seventeenth Century Through Twentieth Century*, edited by Michael S. Duke, Columbia UP, 2016, pp. 134–51.

Zhao, Tingyang. *Alles unter dem Himmel Vergangenheit und Zukunft der Weltordnung*. Translated from Chinese by Michael Kahn-Ackermann, Suhrkamp, 2020.

"我写作不求'再现现实',而要追寻现实":安妮·埃尔诺访谈录[①]

黄荭 & 安妮·埃尔诺

内容摘要:2022 年诺贝尔文学奖得主安妮·埃尔诺一直强调她写作的"非虚构"之维,她始终如一地书写生活,尽可能地贴近现实,从自我出发、从个人和集体的记忆出发去揭露和反思现实种种。现实主义之于她就是求实抵真,开创新的语言、新的文体,塑造新的文学形象,在阶级和女性这两大领域表达她强烈的社会介入和现实关怀。

关键词:安妮·埃尔诺 现实主义 文学介入

作者简介:黄荭,南京大学法语系教授,主要研究方向为法国文学和比较文学;安妮·埃尔诺,法国作家,2022 年诺贝尔文学奖得主。

Title: "No to 'Represent Reality' but to Pursue Reality": An Interview with Annie Ernaux

Abstract: Annie Ernaux, the 2022 Nobel Prize laureate in Literature, has consistently emphasized her "non-fiction" writing style. She consistently writes about life, trying to align the writing with reality. From the self and from personal and collective memories, she exposes and contemplates various aspects of reality. For Ernaux, realism involves the pursuit of truth, the innovation of new language and literary styles, and the shaping of new literary images, through which she expresses a strong societal engagement and concern for reality especially in the realms of class and gender.

Key words: Annie Ernaux; realism; literary engagement

Author: Huang Hong is a professor at French Department,

---

① 本文原发于《外国文学研究》2024 年第 1 期。

Nanjing University (Nanjing 210023, China), specializing in French Literature and Comparative Literature. Email: hhermite@126.com; Annie Ernaux is a French writer, the 2022 Nobel Prize laureate in Literature. Email: annie.ernaux@gmail.com.

黄荭:安妮·埃尔诺,非常感谢您接受我的邮件访谈。2023 年 10 月在南京大学召开的第二届现实主义文学研究国际研讨会的主题是"重访现实主义:历史、记忆、世界",可以说历史、记忆和外面的世界也是您写作的关键词,这一契合也是此次访谈的缘起。您写作的内容和形式都非常独特,是否有一个决定性的时刻,让您的文学观念发生了转变?您在《写作是一把刀》(*L'Écriture comme un couteau*,2003)中说"我不再想写那种一看就很美的东西,而是想写一看就很真实的东西。写作就是揭露现实的工作"(77)。您一直强调非虚构之维,反对评论界将您的作品归入"自我虚构"之列,这种对虚构和自我虚构的拒斥,是否可以被看作一种现实主义的回归,一种新现实主义,一种更当下、更直白也更尖锐的现实主义?

埃尔诺:我想,和所有热爱文学的人一样,我首先肯定是把美的概念和文学连在一起。但我一开始并没有好好琢磨文学之美是由什么造就的。事实上,从我的第一本书开始,我就力求言说现实。这一目的从来没有改变,改变的,只是我对言说现实的方式的看法。我并没有质疑小说和虚构,我最初的作品就是见证。我当时也迷信一种近乎表现主义的写作手法:找到让读者身临其境、感同身受的表达方式。因此我采用了一种极富表现力的暴力写作,但始终没有迷失创作目的:现实。我最早的三部作品,《空衣橱》(*Les Armoires vides*,1974)、《如他们所说的,或什么都不是》(*Ce qu'ils disent ou rien*,1977)及《冻住的女人》(*La Femme gelée*,1981)都是这样写的。转折点发生在我想写父亲的一生的时候,父亲先是工人,后来做了小商贩,我想写他质朴的一生,我想探究自从我上学开始就突然横亘在我和他之间的距离,社会文化意义上的差距。这让我思考自己作为"阶级变节者"(transfuge de classe)在写作中的位置,还有如何在文学中表现平民阶层的世界的问题。就这样,我转向一种简洁朴素,只讲述事实,和资产阶级读者保持距离,不会招致他们的评判。我不知道自己全身心投入的这种真实的、实事求是的写作是否可以称之为新现实主义,我的写作不求"再现现实",而要追寻现实。我承认,我对把我的创作手法理论化并不感兴趣。

黄荭:从写父亲的《一个男人的位置》(*La Place*, 1983)之后,您的创作就转向某种"介于文学、社会学和历史学之间"的东西,您希望"颠覆有关文学和社会的等级秩序",去书写"那些被认为'不配'进入文学的'物'"(Annie Ernaux, *L'Écriture comme un couteau* 80 - 81)。在诺奖演说中您说写作是"为我的出身和我的性别复仇"(Venger ma race et venger mon sexe),阶级区隔和女性处境是您作品的两大主题,您如何看待现实社会中被统治阶级和女性的境遇呢?比如您在1974年出版的处女作《空衣橱》中已经写到了堕胎问题,是什么促使您在2000年又写了《事件》(*L'Événement*, 2000)旧事重提?虽然在过去的半个世纪里,不管在法国还是在世界各地,社会政治环境和女性生存状况都发生了很大变化,但您书中针对的一些问题至今仍是热议的现实问题。

埃尔诺:要区分男女都遭受的社会统治和女性遭受的性别统治,二者是可以叠加的。别忘了还有种族统治。在2023年,在法国,在世界各地,还有一部分女性在遭受这三种统治的压迫。我可以给您举那些从非洲出来的母亲的例子,独自带着几个孩子,每天四点起床坐火车去巴黎,在酒店、办公室或医院打扫卫生。总的说来,50年里,产生了一个中产阶级,有钱去消费、去坐飞机、去度假,但如今这个中产阶级变穷了,他们孩子的日子就可能过得"不如他们好"。

50年里,女性生活发生了巨大的、闻所未闻的变化:通过避孕和医疗性流产自由,女性掌握了生育权。在20世纪末,因为我意识到这一段女性曾经遭受暴力的历史被淡忘了,所以我又回到了自己23岁时堕胎的经历,而这也是我第一部作品《空衣橱》的创作背景,当初写的时候堕胎还是被法律禁止的。当《事件》2000年出版时,很难想象有一些国家会再次回到这个女性根本的自由问题上。说到自由,没有任何自由是一旦得到就一劳永逸的,尤其是对女性而言。

黄荭:在您给上海人民出版社写的丛书中文版序言中,您说自己20岁开始写作,您的第一部作品被出版商拒绝了。后来您有试图重写这部作品吗?还是以后会重写?抑或是彻底放弃了?但最初的写作就算是青涩的、造作的,往往令人难以割舍。

埃尔诺:我20岁开始写第一个文本,改了又改,22岁时写完,先取名为《树》(*L'arbre*),之后改为《五点的阳光》(*Du soleil à cinq heures*)。它和我下一个文本《空衣橱》的写作相隔十年之久,这十年彻底改变了我对写作的看法。我和现实艰难缠斗,我意识到"为我的出身复仇"不可能是诗意的。我想要言说的不再是和以前相同的东西。我从来没有想过重写,以后也不会重写最初的那个文本。《树》想要写的,是我在《一个女孩的记忆》(*Mémoire de fille*, 2016)中讲述的,和H在夏令营相识,性和疯狂的爱,以及随之而来被全世界抛弃的感觉。我强调是"想要写的",因为所有这一切在文中始终都没有被描述出来。结构很复杂:梦中的意象,童年的回忆,对未来、对当下的遐想交替闪现。那是新小说的时代,我当时以为要先确定形式,然后让内容适应形式。而事实上,形式是从内容里诞生的。

黄荭:说到形式,我们都注意到从《一个男人的位置》开始您在写作语言层面的明显变化,您可以谈一谈家乡或者童年的生活环境对您创作的影响吗?

埃尔诺：法语是我的写作语言，但使用它总让我感到不真实。有些东西如果不用方言——用最初的"母语"表达，就无法再现视觉、嗅觉、触觉等感官的强烈程度，所以我的作品保留了一些方言的特色表达。诺曼底方言与我儿时那么多的东西息息相关，周遭的环境、各种熟悉的声音腔调、母亲的笑容，它们是无法翻译成规范的法语的。"母语"是和我们融为一体的，有一种特别的力量。

这种力量来自我的家乡、我的原生家庭、我生活的街区。这也是为什么我说写作需要一种"浸润"。这种浸润，从我的童年到现实世界，不断扩散。为了捕捉现实，我需要让文字可触可感。一切都发生在我的记忆中，我的肉体记忆，它不同于书本上的历史，不是一种习得的记忆，而是一种完全感性的记忆。

黄荭：您把自己的写作分为两种：一种是日记，属于私人领域；另一种是其他文本——也包括《外部日记》（*Journal du dehors*, 1993）和《外面的生活》（*La Vie extérieure*, 2000）——属于公共领域。您说"我在私人日记中大概是在享受，而在其他文本中是在加工。比起享受，我更需要去加工"（Annie Ernaux, *L'Écriture comme un couteau* 24）。您在出版私人日记《我走不出我的黑夜》（*Je ne suis pas sortie de ma nuit*, 1997）和《迷失》（*Se perdre*, 2001）时，是把日记原封不动拿出来发表，还是也做了删节和修改（难免做一点小小的"加工"）？因为私人日记会揭露出某些和已经发表的书中不一样的"真实"，您是否打算发表其他私人日记？发表您经历人生那些"严重的时刻"时写的日记，是为了给出人生拼图所需的所有拼片，提供一种平行的阅读？给写作的"黑色工作室"提供更多的光亮？

埃尔诺：您提到的《我走不出我的黑夜》和《迷失》是公开发表的，因为二者都有与之对应的、精心创作的文学文本，分别是《一个女人的故事》（*Une femme*, 1987）和《简单的激情》（*Passion simple*, 1991）。对我而言，日记是展现另一种真实的方式，更直接，更粗暴，因为是在事情发生的过程中及时记录下来的。在《迷失》中,我只做了非常小的改动,把一些可能会被人认出来的人名只保留了首字母。《我走不出我的黑夜》起初是我在1983—1986年母亲生病期间写的一堆纸片,某种探访日记。大概是在1995年,我把这些纸片打在电脑上——当时我刚有了一台电脑,但用得还不是很习惯,或许做了几处形式上的修改,对此我记得不是很真切了,因为我一边写到电脑上,一边就把那些纸片扔了。但我当时一点都没有发表的打算。1996年底,写完《羞耻》(*La Honte*,1997),我想到那些关于我母亲患阿尔茨海默症的文字,我计划把它们和书稿一起拿给我的出版商,因为重读那些文字让我大受震撼。于是我写了序,选了书名,用的是我母亲没有写完的一封信开头的句子。我不打算在我活着的时候出版其他私人日记。但在我死后,我的全部私人日记会出版。

黄荭:当上海人民出版社找我翻译您的作品时,我第一时间就选了《我走不出我的黑夜》,当然我有很重要的个人原因。2012年夏天,我参加了一个魁北克的文化项目,之后计划去温哥华看朋友,也约了去岛上采访作家应晨。没想到刚到温哥华三天就接到国内传来的噩耗:母亲突发心梗,抢救无效!我改签了当天的机票回国,而一切发生得太快,赶回去还是为时已晚……母亲去世后的三四个月里,我几乎每天凌晨两三点钟都会醒来,再无法入眠,黑暗中睁着眼睛盯着无边的沉默和永远的缺席。母亲依然活在我的梦里,仿佛一个平行世界,但每次醒来我都要面对残酷的现实:她已经不在这个世界。"我经常梦见她,就像在她生病前一样。她还活着,但已经死了。当我从梦中醒来,那一刹那,我确信她真的以这种双重形式存在,既生又死,就像那些两次越过冥河的希腊神话中的人物一样。"(Annie Ernaux, *Je ne suis pas sortie de ma nuit* 14)您的文字抚慰了我,尽管它充满了泪水。

从某种意义上说,我把翻译《我走出不出我的黑夜》当作一场错过的告别礼,我多么希望可以看着母亲老去,缓慢而宁静地死亡,尽管对于父母的离世我们永远都不可能做好思想准备,永远都太过突然。翻译的时光对我而言也是一段重现的时光,仿佛穿过岁月的黑水,我又看到她从前的模样,和她慢慢地挥手,告别。

埃尔诺: 您母亲骤然离世的故事深深打动了我,丧母之恸让您对我的文字感到那么亲近。当我写我母亲时,我感受到了写作的这种不可思议的可能性,与其说是文字让她重生,倒不如说是在挽回。挽回她的人生,一个女人的人生。在那之前我从未感受到,更从未如此清晰地感受到我在写作时所做的一切就是在挽回。我相信我所经历的事情在别人身上也曾发生过。如果人们写下发生在自己身上的事情,写下自己的经历,那同样也会为别人挽回某些东西。

黄荭: 您在《我走不出我的黑夜》中直白地描写了老年人的生存状况,在翻译您的这部作品时,我也重读了西蒙娜·德·波伏瓦的《安详辞世》(*Une mort très douce*, 1964)和《老年》(*La Vieillesse*, 1970),还有日本女性主义社会学家上野千鹤子的《一个人最后的旅程》,这本书可能还没译成法语。不管是在法国、日本还是中国,我们都越来越步入一个"老龄化社会",书写老年的作品却很少,或许是"耻于谈论",但"年老"是每个个体和社会都要面临的问题。您如何看待这个问题,就这个主题您是否会再写一本书?写作,也是揭露羞耻感并克服它?

埃尔诺: 上野千鹤子的书的确在法国还没有翻译。我不知道这位日本女性主义社会学家。慢慢地,但越来越明显地,老年会成为作家、社会学家和历史学家关注的主题。很简单:我们,老年人,越来越多了!10月,我将参加老年问题全国委员会(CNAV)的开幕式,并接受米歇尔·佩罗(Michelle Perrot)的采访。老年在我的写作计划之列,但写到何种程度,目前还没有确定。它本身就是一个大陆。

黄荭: 您多次提到您在1959年发现了马克思主义、存在主义和西蒙娜·德·波伏瓦(Simone de Beauvoir)的《第二性》(*Le Deuxième* sexe, 1949)。发现这三者是否改变了您的文学观？而皮埃尔·布尔迪厄(Pierre Bourdieu)、乔治·佩雷克(George Perec)等人的作品让您的内心更加坚定？

埃尔诺：1958—1959年，在高三毕业班，哲学老师让我发现了马克思主义和存在主义，我也偶然地发现了《第二性》，一个女友邀请我去她家，我在她家发现了这本书。说实话，这些阅读并没有改变我的文学观，当时我的文学观还非常模糊。那一时期，我完全沉浸在哲学里，因为我最想寻找的是活着的意义，一种思考和生活的方式。如果说《第二性》给我留下了深刻的烙印，那是因为它让我能解释之前那个夏天和一个男人发生的种种情感纠葛，西蒙娜·德·波伏瓦就像我人生路上的一个导师。这是一次真正的觉醒。但那时候，我并没有将自己所受的非典型教育与波伏瓦写的东西联系起来。我就这样一头扎进了一个巨大的、到那时为止对我而言还是未知的领域，那就是女性的历史和女性的处境。

我已经说过，在1960年我20岁之前，我都没有动过写作的念头。我对文学的思考是从新小说派的作家开始的，不是萨特，也不是波伏瓦。是乔治·佩雷克，同样还有克莱尔·埃切雷利(Claire Etcherelli)让我跳出了新小说的框框，之后是阅读布尔迪厄和帕斯隆(J.C. Passeron)的《继承人》(*Les Héritiers*, 1964)[①]，这本书我也是偶然读到的，我把所有这些与我意识到自己是个"阶层变节者"这件事联系在一起。

黄荭：您的文学创作有很明显的政治维度，反思男性统治、关注象征暴力和集体记忆，表现出对底层、边缘民众的深切关怀。文学介入是否需要保持一个距离才能更好地去观察和分析，还是作家也要像一个

---

① 皮埃尔·布尔迪厄、J. C. 帕斯隆，《继承人：大学生与文化》，邢克超译，商务印书馆，2021年。

斗士一样积极投身社会运动、政治地介入？

埃尔诺：在写作中，我通过选择主题和选择处理它的方式政治地介入。社会、文化、种族统治和男性统治的形式是我作品的核心。我在写作中的介入在于寻找现实并赋予它一种能让人感受到它的形式。比如，《悠悠岁月》(*Les Années*, 2008)的目的是让人感受到时间的流逝、历史的变迁。我有一种所谓"形式的责任"，最明显的例子是写我父亲的书《一个男人的位置》，在这本书里，我拒绝虚构，并质疑用来谈论被统治阶级的语言。《简单的激情》刻意采用了反浪漫、反"爱情小说"的写作手法。

但用书、用作品介入，不能取代直接参与、公开表明立场，例如和罢工者站在一起。对我来说，这种形式的介入是我写作的延伸。

黄荭：您强调自传写作中的"我"(«je» autobiographique)和所讲述之事的"集体价值"(la valeur collective)，可以看出《第二性》对您的重要影响。还有哪些女性主义论著和作品让您印象深刻？您是否可以给我们推荐一些这方面的书单？

埃尔诺：15年前，维尔吉妮·德庞特(Virginie Despentes)的《金刚理论》(*King Kong théorie*)[1]让我印象深刻。近期的有莫娜·肖莱(Mona Chollet)的《女巫》(*Sorcières*)[2]和《重塑爱情》(*Réinventer l'amour*)[3]。

黄荭：您对中国有什么印象？通过书籍、电影、纪录片、报纸杂志得到的印象跟您自己来中国旅行时的所见所闻吻合吗？您在旅行期间有写点儿什么吗？日记或游记？如果健康允许，您是否还想再来中国看看？

---

[1] 维吉妮·德庞特2006年出版的作品，在这本书里，她回忆自己的青年时代，从亲身经历出发，讨论强奸、性工作、色情片等诸多与性别密切相关的话题，犀利地剖析女性气质和男性气质的社会化生成。

[2] 莫娜·肖莱，《"女巫"：不可战胜的女性》，崔月玲译，上海社会科学院出版社，2022年。

[3] 莫娜·肖莱，《重塑爱情：如何摆脱父权制对两性关系的影响》，吴筱航译，北京联合出版公司，2023年。

埃尔诺：我只去过一次中国，2006年，在北京和上海待了一周。因此，体验非常有限。但我依然记得那次旅行给我留下了几个很深的印象，比如大，虽然我去过纽约、芝加哥等城市，但中国给我的第一印象是大，甚至可以说是太大了，北京的天安门广场和上海高耸入云、消失在雾气中的高楼大厦让我惊讶不已。比如活跃，城市的飞速变化，当时北京是一个热火朝天的大工地，正紧锣密鼓地为奥运会做准备。

关于那次旅行，我写得很少，当时我一门心思在写《悠悠岁月》。我想再去中国，看看长城、九寨沟、云南……

黄荭：写作是您"真正的地方"，或者说真正的归宿，我很喜欢您谈论写作的书，我也正在翻译您和米歇尔·波尔特（Michelle Porte）的访谈录《真正的归宿》（*Le Vrai lieu*，2014），还有您的创作日记《黑色工作室》，对您而言，写作的意义究竟是什么呢？

埃尔诺：我觉得写作之于我的意义，是深入社会现实、女性现实和历史现实，是通过我的个人经历深入我们的集体经历。

【Works Cited】

Ernaux, Annie, and Frédéric-Yves Jeannet. *L'Écriture comme un couteau*. Stock, 2003.

Ernaux, Annie, «Venger ma race et venger mon sexe», le discours de la Prix Nobel de littérature. https://www.politis.fr/articles/2022/12/annie-ernaux-venger-ma-race-et-venger-mon-sexe/2022-12-30.

---. «*Je ne suis pas sortie de ma nuit*». Gallimard, 1997.

Tragic Realism

Tatjana Jukić

Abstract: Tragic realism is a concept outlined by Erich Auerbach; in many ways, it summarizes his understanding of mimesis and, by extension, his understanding of philology. While Auerbach employs it mainly to describe the intellectual stakes of the novel in the nineteenth century, what it captures is no less than the imperative of nineteenth-century modernity, in the wake of the French Revolution, to sustain and investigate the radical historicity of the world; hence Auerbach's emphatic concern with the everyday in *Mimesis* (1946). By then, however, tragic realism has already dominated Auerbach's thinking, most pointedly perhaps in his Istanbul lecture on realism in 1941 – 1942: "tragic" suggesting that modern realism entails the intelligence of Greek tragedy, invested as Greek tragedy was in engaging the world's radical historicity, against which the conceptual apparatus of democracy was negotiated. With this in mind and a focus on the Istanbul lecture, I propose to discuss tragic realism against three points that Auerbach makes, but does not pursue: first, that tragic realism serves to explain history as a structure of catastrophe, as evidenced by the Second World War; second, that the nineteenth-century English novel sidesteps realism; and third, that cinema takes over as a

---

① 本文原发于《外国文学研究》2024 年第 1 期。

foothold of realism in the twentieth century. Taken together, these three claims seem to chart a tacit theory of tragic realism that supplements *Mimesis* and invites a general theory of modernity.

Key words: tragic realism; Erich Auerbach; war; tragedy; the novel; China; atomism; world literature

Author: Tatjana Jukić is a professor at University of Zagreb, Croatia. Her research interests are Victorian literature and realism.

Introduction: War

In perhaps the single most important book of Western philology in the twentieth century—Erich Auerbach's *Mimesis*, written in Turkey during the Second World War and first published in 1946—tragic realism surfaces in Chapter Eighteen (458) as a concept that describes not merely the intellectual stakes of the novel in the nineteenth century but the rationale of nineteenth-century modernity. In the wake of the French Revolution, Auerbach suggests, the novel is tasked with sustaining the terms of the radical investigation of the world against a sense of historical complacency, and realism references the fact that the world remains targeted for investigation; hence Auerbach's concern with concepts like the everyday, the common and the ordinary when he speaks about realism. The French Revolution was when the "process of temporal concentration" began in Europe, he writes, "both of historical events themselves and of everyone's knowledge of them," resulting in "modern tragic realism based on the contemporary" to which forceful "modern consciousness of reality" was key (*Mimesis* 458, 459). It is an argument voiced emphatically in his lecture "Realism in Europe in the Nineteenth Century," delivered in Istanbul in 1941 – 1942, in which tragic realism is pervasive: "tragic" implying that realism should be explained against the intelligence of tragedy, and that nineteenth-century modernity may well depend for its self-definition on acknowledging this fact.

That tragic realism entails a general theory of modernity, not only in the nineteenth century, can be inferred from a point that Auerbach makes at the end of the Istanbul lecture, but does not pursue: in his view, realism is a position from which to "understand ... the tragic events occurring today"—in the Second World War— that contribute to a history "manifested through catastrophic events and ruptures" ("Realism in Europe" 193). Clearly, tragic realism in Auerbach's view proceeds from the French Revolution but accommodates the idea of world war, so much so that realism receives its rationale from a world which is wholly engaged in war; it is in this sense that world war is as much about war as it is about the modern world, whose totality coincides with warfare. In another Istanbul lecture, on literature and war, delivered at about the same time, in 1940 – 1941, Auerbach states that "[w]orld war puts forth the world problem" ("Literature and War" 204); or rather, he says that "[w]orld war is how the world problem is clarified" (*Kultur als Politlk* 48).[1] This means that the underlying condition of the modern world is revealed to be one of fundamentally interrupted identification and substitution. If that is the case, then tragic realism begins as a language of interrupted identification and substitution— say, a language in which metaphor is suspended—but one whose world persists, even prevails, as a sustained, relentless demand to think transformation, so much so that a failure to think transformation manifests as catastrophe and rupture.

These early lectures constitute in many ways a preamble or supplement to *Mimesis*. Like *Mimesis*, they were written in Turkey during the war, a document to Auerbach's sojourn there as an exile from Nazi Germany.[2] Unlike *Mimesis*, they point emphatically to world war as an intellectual stake of realism, and suggest that realism is instrumental to understanding the Second World War, specifically as a structure of repetition. Repetition turns out to be a trajectory of rupture and catastrophe in modernity and an index of failed attempts to think transformation; for the same reason, repetition is an index of failed attempts at realism. Without realism, Auerbach implies, the Second World War is likely to remain underanalyzed and misunderstood, and contribute a less than tragic flaw to modern humanity—it is not for nothing that Auerbach, a preeminent philologist, should call the Second World War a plural *tragic* event. Indeed, in the conclusion of his lecture on realism in Europe in the nineteenth century, Auerbach says, "That which is being prepared today, that which has been in preparation for a century, is the tragic realism I have discussed, modern realism, the life shared in common which grants the possibility of life to all people on earth" ("Realism in Europe" 193).

Tragedy

That last sentence is particularly revealing, and it entails another argument which is formative to realism: apparently, realism relates to the reason of tragedy, because its task, like the task of tragedy in fifth-century Athens, is to negotiate a political rationality—an understanding of life which is shared in common, one comparable to the invention of democracy in ancient Greece.

There is a theory of realism in that one sentence, and it relies on aligning tragic realism with modern realism into a single thought. It is not only that modern rationality, as Auerbach understands it, is informed by the intelligence of Greek tragedy and, by extension, of democracy; it is also that the true extent of this contact—indeed, of this in-formation—cannot be known except in terms of realism, or as realism. It is in this sense that realism constitutes the truth of modernity. After all, Auerbach's understanding of war, too, is a fit for the role which was assigned to war in the imaginary of Greek antiquity. According to Nicole Loraux, war and politics were "the experiences basic to the Greek city" and "the starting point for deciphering the fantasies of the Athenian imaginary," and "understanding citizenship in its origins also implies an appreciation of the armed warrior in Athena, 'the goddess-woman armed with every weapon'" (*The Children of Athena* 17 – 18).

That realism thus imagined is implicitly political can be inferred from Auerbach's claim that realism professes no less than "the life shared in common," whose promise is one of "life to all people on earth." As noted, *the life shared in common* spells out the concept of democracy, whose invention in fifth-century Athens coincides with the language of tragedy. Tragedy, as Jean-Pierre Vernant points out, was invented in the fifth century BC so as to address and engage the transformation, of language too, that ultimately brought about the conceptual apparatus of democracy in ancient Greece. Once the process of shaping the democratic polis is finished, not even Aristotle can know, says Vernant, "the tragic consciousness or tragic man": because tragedy "is born, flourishes, and disappears in Athens within the space of a hundred years" (89).

What realism captures as tragic, that is, seems to be a radical, overwhelming historicity of the world, one that, while feeding into the concept of democracy, remains excessive to it. Hence Auerbach's interest in the everyday: when he speaks about the life shared in common, which is implicit to tragic realism, Auerbach insists on defining realism as a sustained investment of language in the everyday, so much so that the relentlessness of the everyday is synonymous with realism in his work. For Auerbach, the everyday points to the acute historical conditions of participation in the affairs of world—to the life shared in common—and, as such, paves the way to the idea of democracy. Without taking the everyday into account, democracy is void of radical historicity, which is given up for bland historicism. For Auerbach, it is only when the common is translated into the everyday, and the ordinary into the contemporary, that tragic realism is truly in operation: "the topic could be ordinary only when it was contemporary" ("Realism in Europe" 182), says Auerbach in his discussion of tragic realism in the nineteenth century. Also, this is why tragic realism, while proceeding from the French Revolution, is still *in preparation*: Auerbach argues that the world keeps pressing on the conceptual apparatus of modern European democracy, which is why the language of modern democracy keeps revisiting the very terms of its formation, as or into literature. For Vernant, tragedy is about a language being forged without which the conceptual apparatus of early democracy would have been impossible; for Auerbach, modern realism is about feeding that conceptual apparatus back to the conditions of tragedy.

That is also how Auerbach revisits his own philological formation. For him, the invocation of tragic realism is always also a reference to Dante Alighieri, with whom modernity begins as *figural* realism: figural pointing to "the maintenance of the basic historical reality of figures, against all attempts at spiritually allegorical interpretation" that prevail in the European Middle Ages (*Mimesis* 196). This, in Auerbach's view, explains Dante's decision to call his *Commedia* just that, a comedy, because figural realism allows for bringing together historical reality and allegory into "a mixed style" (*Mimesis* 198) by which the concept of comedy is decided in the first place. It follows that Dante's *Commedia*, precisely because a comedy, "had compassed... tragic realism" too, destroying in the process Christian-figural realism—yet Auerbach is quick to add that

"that tragic realism had immediately been lost again" (*Mimesis* 231). Tellingly, this constitutes an astute hint at ancient Greek comedy, which in many ways began as a comment on tragedy, or as paratragedy, so that Athenian "comedy is always, and *by definition*, ready to criticize democracy" (Loraux, *Divided City* 229, emphasis added). Or, in the words of Froma Zeitlin, "[a]long with the parody of other serious forms of discourse within the city (judicial, ritual, political, poetic), *paratragōdia*, or the parody of tragedy, is a consistent feature of Aristophanic comedy" (378). Pierre Vidal-Naquet goes so far as to say that "Aristophanes was a better reader of Aeschylus than many of our twentieth-century critics" (253).

To sum up: what Auerbach's Dante captures is the loss of tragedy to modernity except as genre, whose best chance at truth is in the mixed style of comedy. It therefore comes as no surprise that, in his discussion of Jean Racine and the seventeenth-century French classicist tragedy, Auerbach should hold that "[t]he classic tragedy of the French represents the ultimate extreme in the separation of styles, in the severance of the tragic from the everyday and real" (*Mimesis* 387)—a comment the historian Roger Chartier identifies as being germane to the intellectual groundwork of the French Revolution (10). Tragic realism is retrieved when tragedy as literary archive is unpacked into a language of radical historicity—of the everyday—in which substitution (allegory, metaphor) is sidestepped for contiguity and proximity (metonymy), just as identification is sidestepped for relations of intimacy. This also means that democracy is functional only when its conceptual apparatus is unpacked into metonymy.

The Novel

This unpacking, according to Auerbach, happens in the novel, and realism is how the nineteenth-century novel is betrayed to entail the function and conditions of Greek tragedy. The novel cultivates the language of radical historicity in which the French Revolution is inflected, now as tragic excess in the nineteenth century, and realism names precisely the excess of historicity that tragedy, or the revolution for that matter, forgot on its way to being archived. In fact, the intellectual constitution of nineteenth-century modernity seems decided in this excess, insofar as the nineteenth century is the century of the novel. It follows that the novel is as historical as the Greek tragedy (which, in Vernant's words, is born, flourishes, and disappears in Athens within the space of a hundred years); hence Auerbach's claim that "the realist novel would have a brighter future in times to come if it were not for the art of cinema, which rivals it in the field of realism" ("Realism in Europe" 185). Hence, also, Auerbach's claim that "[r]ealism as we understand it today, whether in the novel, the cinema, or something else, could not have emerged prior to the nineteenth century, for there was no readership that could understand it" ("Realism in Europe" 185).

Auerbach voices these concerns as early as "Romanticism and Realism" (1933), when he writes that only realism impacted by "the French Revolution and its aftermath" embedded, consistently, "the tragic within the everyday" and "discovered the sphere of the tragic within a realm that had until then been home only to the base and the comic" (*TLH* 145 – 146). In nineteenth-century realism, he adds, "everydayness does not merely interrupt tragedy" but "is the very home of the tragic itself" (*Time, History and Literature* 147). That, as well, seems to spell out the distinction between figural and tragic realisms: figural realism appears to be pre-revolutionary, whereas tragic realism surfaces as revolutionary language, whereby revolution is revealed as an essentially realist function. If film is how this tragic excess is rehearsed in the twentieth century, then film does to the twentieth century what the novel did to the nineteenth; put otherwise, film may be how the twentieth century comes closest to the radical conditions of tragedy. Once again, this is a claim put forward as early as 1933, Auerbach observing that, "[w]hile not undermining all prior aesthetic traditions in their entirety, the cinema does, in my opinion, shake them to their foundations and forces upon them a complete transformation" (*Time, History and Literature* 155). This in many ways anticipates Stanley Cavell's philosophy of film, for instance, Cavell's claim that the creation of film "was as if meant for philosophy—meant to reorient everything philosophy has said about reality and its representation, about art and imitation, about greatness and conventionality, about judgement and pleasure, about skepticism and transcendence, about language and expression" (vii, xii)—not least because it is only in film, or as film, that Cavell can fully think a coming together of tragedy and the ordinary, his two philosophical lynchpins. [3]

Auerbach repeatedly cites Stendhal's *The Red and the Black* (*Le Rouge et le Noir*, 1830) as an exemplifying instance of tragic realism (*Time, Literature and History* 146, 152; Realism in Europe 189 - 190; *Mimesis* 466). Repeatedly, Stendhal's Julien Sorel is advertised as the first self to exact the modern outline of the tragic consciousness or tragic man, as Vernant would put it: like Stendhal, Sorel is above all a relation of susceptibility to the world (he is *ombrageux*, *Mimesis* 466) against which a self is asserted. "[T]his," says Auerbach, "explains the fact that the stylistic level of his [Stendhal's] great realistic novels is much closer to the old great and heroic concept of tragedy than is that of most later realists—Julien Sorel is much more a 'hero' than the characters of Balzac, to say nothing of Flaubert" (*Mimesis* 466). This, then, is why Stendhal's novel is revolutionary in the final analysis and Balzac's is not, or not quite—realism itself being a tragic hero in the history of the novel.[4]

To Auerbach, the French Revolution is instrumental to tragic realism in the Stendhal novel, and in the novel as such, because the revolution engages a self essentially as a relation of susceptibility. Compared to Stendhal, Balzac fails at tragic realism because he "was sixteen years younger than Stendhal and had not seen the old society or the revolution" ("Realism in Europe" 189). The same may be the reason why Auerbach dismisses the English novel, even though "many would have me give place to Thackeray and Dickens beside Balzac and Stendhal" ("Realism in Europe" 191). "I do not find in them the best understanding of the political and economic entities which characterize the new forms of tragic realism," says Auerbach, and adds: "Although everyday life in England is very modern, the vantage point on life is very backward" ("Realism in Europe" 191).[5]

Yet the new form of tragic realism, in which a self is claimed for radical susceptibility to historical transformation, seems to have been invented precisely in the nineteenth-century English novel, by Jane Austen—so much so that a self falls prey to the novel as an instance of relentless education. It is for this reason that Austen's narrative selves, her focalizing consciousnesses, cannot coincide with the narrator even though they are engaged for radical narrative intimacy; in each of her six finished novels, they are consistently metonymic to the narrator but never identical to it. For the same reason, Austen does not subscribe to the idea of the Bildungsroman. While it is true that Thackeray and Dickens do not come across as Austenites, or not easily, Elizabeth Gaskell does, as does Henry James. Moreover, to Gaskell the focalizing consciousness is a trajectory to the industrial novel, whereby the Industrial Revolution becomes a format of understanding and Manchester a Victorian Athens, especially in *North and South* (1854–1855).

Austen's first published novel, *Sense and Sensibility* (1811), is already a summary of this process. Elinor Dashwood, Austen's first focalizing consciousness, begins by becoming fatherless and dispossessed, stripped down to being the poor relation: to being merely a relation and the poorer for it. While her widowed mother and orphaned sister Marianne overplay being *ombrageuses* into selfishness (Austen mockingly calls it "romantic delicacy" [63]), Elinor is strict in acknowledging a sense of self only as it is subject to dire historical contingency of the everyday. If that in itself constitutes her realism as tragic, it is also how the constitution of the focalizing consciousness in the nineteenth-century novel is shown to proceed from tragic realism. Elinor is prey to language in the same way: by strenuously keeping her word to those who do not keep theirs (Lucy Steele), she educates her narrative self into a bare, vulnerable linguistic relation—into a tragic speech act. That is why sense and sensibility in Austen's novel are not opposite but relate exactly as they sound: they make for an alliteration and a sustained metonymy, their intimacy ultimately a syntactic one of the narrator and the focalizing consciousness. When Fredric Jameson identifies Auerbach's realism, repeatedly, as "a syntactic conquest" (3, 163 – 164), what this brings to mind is precisely Austen's radical narrative syntax.⑥

That Austen's novel was also a shorthand for an economic understanding that went into the making of tragic realism is suggested by the economist Thomas Piketty. Piketty takes Austen and Balzac to be no less than the specimen stories of capital in nineteenth-century Europe; additionally, Piketty suggests that realism was instrumental to this understanding when he notes that Austen "[i]n particular... minutely describes daily life in the early nineteenth century" (415). To Piketty, Elinor Dashwood's destitution may be exemplary insofar as Norland, the parental estate in Sussex from which Elinor is banished, is "the pinnacle of wealth in

Jane Austen's novels" (413). This makes Elinor a revolutionary figure, because the focalizing consciousness in the Austen novel is shown to begin as the conceptual purity of wealth is being dismantled into relations of impoverishment. By *Mansfield Park* (1814), "being honest and rich has become impossible" (85) in an Austen novel, as Terry Eagleton astutely remarks.

If that is how the focalizing consciousness begins in the Austen novel, it is certainly symptomatic that it ends once the novel takes for its subject the immediate aftermath of the Napoleonic Wars, in *Persuasion* (1818), Austen's last finished work. It is thus the Austen novel that the historian Peter Fritzsche references when he writes that, between 1806 and 1815, "the revolutionary wars killed as many soldiers and civilians, proportionately, as did World War I," and also that "the revolutionary wars mobilized and garrisoned and ultimately killed more men than had any other previous war" (34). Taken together, Austen's novels seem to imply that the French Revolution is indeed the trajectory of tragic realism in the nineteenth century, as Auerbach argues, but one whose rationale derives from an understanding of modern revolutions as they go back to the English Revolution, and anticipates world war, which is why the French Revolution fails to contain it. That Auerbach, too, is open to this line of thought can be evinced from his remark, in "Literature and War," that in nineteenth-century "Britain the democratic state was bound to an unshakable tradition," Britain being "the most democratic of all" nations at the time ("Literature and War" 202). Auerbach seems to associate nineteenth-century Britain with democratic excess here, precisely the excess in which tragic realism is decided—which is why his decision to dismiss the (pre-)Victorian novel from tragic realism, on the evidence of Dickens and Thackeray, could be explained as a failure to take into account the radical format of the focalizing consciousness in the English novel at the time, just as Dickens and Thackeray themselves were reluctant to engage it.

The fact that Auerbach concludes *Mimesis* with a chapter on Virginia Woolf's *To the Lighthouse* (1927) and a close reading of Woolf's "middle voicedness" (*Figural Realism* 40), as Hayden White calls it, seems to compensate precisely for this failure—it is only that Woolf already coincides with cinema taking over as a domain of tragic realism. In the words of Laura Marcus, Woolf, while critical of cinema, "undoubtedly saw or found in film a relationship to reality that gave visible form to her own world-view, and her fascination with 'the thing that exists when we aren't there', the phrase linked, at one point in her diaries, to the concept of images and ideas 'shoulder[ing] each other out across the screen of my brain'" (115).

China

It is a line of thought whose historical climax is a reference to China, China constituting for Auerbach the present tense—the tense present?—of tragic realism and the democratic project in 1946. In the last paragraph of *Mimesis*, Auerbach indexes "Pearl Buck's Chinese peasants" for "a common life of mankind on earth" (*Mimesis* 552): a claim that echoes Auerbach's earlier remark, in the Istanbul lecture on realism, that "[w]e rightly consider the wonderful Chinese novels of Madame Pearl Buck to be realist novels" ("Realism in Europe" 182). Historically, this coincides with Chinese culture itself negotiating the concept of realism into an operable relation. Wang Shouren notes that "etymologically, the term 'realism' (现实主义) ... originated from other languages, and literary realism is an imported idea" (75 - 76); likewise, "the word 'reality' (现实) ... did not appear in the Chinese vocabulary until the late 19th century when it was first coined in the Japanese language and then travelled to China " (76). Lydia H. Liu speaks emphatically about transformation when she observes that "[t]he huge influx of translated European literature into China in the first few decades of the twentieth century so radically transformed the nature of written vernacular Chinese that subsequent translations between modern Chinese and English assume a whole different character" (106).

What appeals to Auerbach about Pearl Buck's Chinese novels in the 1940s, that is, is not their presumption to authenticity, but their ambition to investigate the life "shared in common" outside of modern Europe, one whose formative intelligence, while not identical to modern Europe's, allows for metonymic closeness. Also, in this brief comment, the constitution of Auerbach's own language, and of his philology, is again revealed as one staunchly based in metonymy—and, by extension, in realism—insofar as metonymy serves to explore relations of proximity and contiguity, of intimacy past identification. For this reason, Auerbach could well be a sinologist in the making, Chinese being a culture in which the metonymic limit of Europe's modern intelligence is decided. And this is why I would argue that tragic realism, as Auerbach understands it, takes Chinese culture to be its intellectual perimeter. For the same reason, I take tragic to indicate the condition of realism in which relations of intimacy and susceptibility take over from the concepts of identification and substitution, language itself becoming *ombrageux*.⑦

Auerbach's understanding of historicity, too, finds an important inflection in his concluding reference to China in *Mimesis*, because China at the time was how revolution peaked in the present tense and, with it, the conditions of tragic realism. When Auerbach speaks of "Pearl Buck's Chinese peasants," he in fact speaks of humanity being claimed for revolutionary urgency, revolution essentially a realist function in the American novel which is thus being confronted with its own revolutionary buildup. It is an argument I propose to understand against a point made by the historian Jürgen Osterhammel (265 - 267), that revolution was a concept modern Europe forged while also describing historical shifts of authority in Asian cultures, notably in China. This means that a decision to write about the English, American or French Revolutions—or about the novel, or, finally, about realism—has been prearranged as it were by the language Europe had forged in order to relate to Asia.⑧

Atomism

There is nothing imprecise about Auerbach's philology here; in fact, tragic realism is how Auerbach negotiates a point of contact between the languages of philology, political theory and philosophy.

Once again, one turns to the Istanbul lectures for confirmation. In a telling example, almost a parable, Auerbach argues that an ordinary baker engaged for a heroic act would not constitute a realist figure, because heroism is not of the order of the everyday and therefore fails to count as realism. A baker who does what he does every day, however, and is, say, "mixed up in an important court case," does constitute realism, because it is as the everyday and in the everyday that that baker partakes of the world together with and alongside exceptional figures like "Atatürk, Roosevelt, or Einstein" ("Realism in Europe" 183).

In political terms, this is the language of democracy, whose modern theory harks back to the philosophy of David Hume and an empiricist appreciation of proximity, in a world in which Atatürk, Roosevelt, Einstein, and an ordinary baker are decided by a network of relationships that brings them together. In the words of Gilles

Deleuze, it is a language decided not by the verb *is*, but by *and*, a conjunction: "Thinking with AND, instead of thinking IS, instead of thinking for IS: empiricism has never had another secret" (57). The focus may well be on Hume in this particular context, because, while "every history of philosophy has its chapter on empiricism: Locke and Berkeley have their place there," it is in Hume that "there is something very strange which completely displaces empiricism, giving it a new power, a theory and practice of relations, of the AND" (Deleuze and Parnet 15). In philological terms, this is metonymic language, insofar as metonymy, unlike metaphor, is exhausted by negotiating the relations of proximity and contiguity (to which the conjunctions *and* and *with* are instrumental), over and above the relations of substitution and identification (the verb *is*). In terms of modern science, this is a language which points to atomic physics, the physics of subatomic particles, whose emphasis is on understanding the extreme relations of proximity; it is certainly telling that Auerbach should reference specifically Albert Einstein in his discussion of realism.

That Auerbach should engage physics for realism is in character with his philology, and one could argue that Auerbach's own grasp of the everyday—of the radical historicity of the world that goes into the making of tragic realism—is consistently atomistic. In "Figura," his 1938 essay on figural language, he remarks that hardly anyone understood figural language better than ancient atomist poets/philosophers, notably Lucretius, which is to say Epicurean physics; one should add that Epicurean physics is in many ways a precursor to modern atomic physics. Lucretius, says Auerbach, "espoused a cosmogony indebted to Democritus and Epicurus, in which the world consists of atoms ... bodies whose clashings, motions, order, positions, [and] shapes create all things," which is why Lucretius often refers to atoms "as 'shapes' (*figurae*), and..., conversely, one can often translate *figurae* with 'atoms'" (*Time, History and Literature* 70). When Auerbach describes this to constitute a contribution to philology that is "without a doubt the most individually brilliant, if not the historically most important one" (*Time, History and Literature* 70), he actually claims Epicurean atomism for a bedrock of mimesis, mimesis naming the world precisely in terms of relentless transformation, whose physics is available to philology as a relation of radical historicity. That radical historicity is how physics absorbs this relation can be evinced from the fact that Einstein, in June 1924, contributed a foreword to the very Hermann Diels edition of Lucretius that Auerbach emphatically references in "Figura"; Einstein praised Lucretius for a "geometric-mechanical" presentation of atoms that nonetheless adumbrates the conceptual outline of quantum mechanics, which "must make a profound impression" (255). Einstein's biography supplies further, narrative clues: he attended Diels's funeral in 1922 (398) and, during his Berlin years, was a colleague of Hans Reichenbach, a physicist/philosopher who later "served on the search committee for Auerbach's position and chaired the department of philosophy at Istanbul University" (Konuk 50). This, then, is how to read Auerbach's claim, in 1952, that "our philological home *is* the earth" (*Time, History and Literature* 264); Geoffrey Hartman rightly observes that Auerbach's chosen authors are "*irdisch*" and that, to Auerbach, "'Wirklichkeit' is a favorite word, better translated as 'actuality' or 'world actualization' than as 'reality'" (171). Insofar as tragic realism best captures this particular condition of mimesis, Auerbach seems to suggest that Epicurean atomism, not Aristotle's philosophy, is a truly apt summary of Attic tragedy, and an equally true anticipation of the novel and film.⑨

What is also interesting about the Epicurean take on atomism, as it departs from Democritus, is that the movement of atoms is explained as a metonymic trajectory, atoms moving in response to the relations of proximity whose closest philological equivalent is metonymy. Lucretius calls this movement *clinamen* or 'the swerve', the relation Stephen Greenblatt finds instrumental to the impact of Lucretius on the formation of modernity, not least on the reinvention of democracy, when he remarks that Thomas Jefferson "owned at least five Latin editions of *On the Nature of Things*, along with translations of the poem into English, Italian, and French," and that "[t] he atoms of Lucretius had left their traces on the Declaration of Independence" (262 - 263). There is a historical swerve here in its own right, leading from Jefferson's impassioned reception and rejection of Hume's *The History of England* to the fact that Karl Marx's doctoral dissertation, in 1841, was on the difference between the Democritean and Epicurean atomism: a case could be made that realism as Auerbach understands it had left its traces on Marx's earliest philosophical formation.⑩

When a few years after "Figura" Auerbach engages Einstein for the everyday from which realism receives its (tragic, metonymic) formation, his reference is therefore also to the Epicurean swerve of Einstein's physics. And there is further philological evidence for this in the Istanbul lectures: as Einstein is claimed for a figure of realism, Stendhal, Auerbach's epitome of tragic realism, is described, explicitly, as "Epicurean" ("Realism in Europe" 189). After that, the equation, if an equation it is, is fairly simple: if Stendhal, whose constitution is Epicurean, comes closest to tragic realism, and Epicurean atomism comes closest to the truth of philology, then Auerbach's philology is, in its entirety, inflected in tragic realism, just as tragic realism, by this equation, entails a theory of modernity.

World Literature

The everyday, while accommodated in metonymy, clearly falls short of a concept and, by extension, of philosophy, insofar as concepts are the building blocks of philosophy. Yet, for Auerbach, it is exactly the everyday that indexes a radical proximity to the world of the modern man, so much so that this proximity—this metonymy—constitutes the modern human condition. Put otherwise, what realism spells out for modernity is metonymic humanity, which may well be philological rather than philosophical, just as Auerbach's understanding of realism is philological rather than philosophical. In short, modernity for Auerbach seems to be just short of philosophy, just short of concepts, and realism addresses and explains this philosophical shortcoming of the modern man. For the same reason, modern humanity seems decided in a literary excess, realism being the true name of this excess, one that philosophy cannot but register as a shortcoming.

Auerbach's view of world literature in "The Philology of World Literature" may be his conclusive response to this problem. In this essay, first published in 1952, some years after the Second World War, Auerbach, now in America, argues that world literature is not about the man's being at home everywhere in the world, but about the man's being at home nowhere in the world. Quoting Hugh of Saint Victor, he concludes by saying that "he to whom every soil is as his native one is already strong; but he is perfect to whom the entire world is as a foreign land" (*Time, Literature and History* 264–265). It follows that world literature, or *Weltliteratur*, is not about the world which is domesticated by literature, and perhaps only by literature, into a concept upon which philosophy then proceeds to think thinking itself. Instead, world literature, like realism, seems to be about the world in which home as concept is given up for thinking the everyday: not because the everyday is a substitute for home or domicile, but precisely because, once confronted with the everyday, home is undone into a radical historicity of the world in which no domicile can be sustained, and no concept.

That would be my conclusion, too, for now: if realism charts metonymic humanity whose philosophical condition is one of shortcoming, but whose notation is one of literary excess, then world literature, in Auerbach's view, follows the same reasoning, insofar as the world from which world literature receives its rationale is the world of tragic realism. This may be why Auerbach's philology is radical, also perhaps in the sense in which radicalism is captured by Hayden White in *Metahistory*, a book precisely about the intersections of the French Revolution and the historical imagination in nineteenth-century Europe. According to White, radical histories of the French Revolution tend to favor metonymic thinking, and their "historical realism" (*Mimesis* 191) is one of tragedy.

【Notes】

① Kader Konuk dates "Literature and War" to 1941 – 1942 (204), Christian Rivoletti to 1940 – 1941 (189). Auerbach's lectures collected in *KP* were translated from Turkish into German, by Christoph Neumann; English translations from *KP* are mine. The lectures had originally been published in Turkish as translations from either French or German, and were previously not available in any other language; see Konuk (150 – 151).

② James I. Porter reports that "Auerbach began composing *Mimesis* as early as 1942, and he dated its completion to April of 1945, only weeks before the Germans finally surrendered to the Allies," adding that the "conception for the book itself goes back to around 1940" (98). See also Konuk (135 – 138, 141 – 143).

③ Auerbach's grasp of tragedy in relation to realism implies a critique of the positions outlined, in different ways, by Walter Benjamin in his *Trauerspiel* book, and by György Lukács in *The Theory of the Novel*, insofar as Auerbach, while implicitly acknowledging the historicity of tragedy, proceeds to analyze historicity *as* tragedy, this being the modern condition. See, also, Orr (3 - 19) for a comparative reading of Auerbach, Lukács and Benjamin. See Barck and Auerbach (STE) for the extant Auerbach—Benjamin correspondence.

④ This is why tragic realism is not an oxymoron as Terry Eagleton calls it, when he writes that "[i]t is in the great post-revolutionary realist novel above all, in the writing of Stendhal and Balzac, that the apparent oxymoron of *tragic realism* is fully achieved" (190); see also Nixon (75).

⑤ See also *Time, History and Literature* 145.

⑥ The narrative procedure instrumental to inventing the focalizing consciousness is one of free indirect style or free indirect discourse; Dietrich Schwanitz (175) identifies Austen as the first author to employ it consciously and extensively. See also Jukić(16 - 17).

⑦ Ortwin de Graef (317 - 318) rightly observes that Woolf's repeated reference to Lily Briscoe's "Chinese eyes" in *To the Lighthouse* is how Auerbach's own language in *Mimesis* is readied for the concluding remark about Pearl Buck. While de Graef understands this to be essentially a relation of sympathy in which humanity is then inadequately theorized, what seems to be at stake is, rather, the fact that Briscoe, a painter, self-identifies as a machine, "the human apparatus for painting or for feeling" (158), not far from Woolf's—or indeed Auerbach's—perspective on cinema. What paves the way to Auerbach's Chinese conclusion, in other words, appears to be cinema, already addressed in the Istanbul lectures and in "Romanticism and Realism" as a new footing of tragic realism.

⑧ See Rachum for the history of the concept of revolution; I am grateful to Svend Erik Larsen for a detailed discussion of the issue at Nanjing University in October 2023.

⑨ See Bachelard for Epicurus, and Lucretius, in terms of "realist atomism" (27).

⑩ See Nial for a comparative reading of Lucretius in Marx *and* Woolf, Auerbach's closing literary figure in *Mimesis*, and for a remark that " [t] oday, Lucretius' legacy continues, to some degree, among quantum physicists who explicitly credit him as the philosophical precursor to Einstein's kinetic theory of matter and to quantum indeterminacy" (5).

【**Works Cited**】

Auerbach, Erich. *Kultur als Politik. Aufsätze aus dem Exil zur Geschichte und Zukunft Europas* (1838 - 1947). Ed. Christian Rivoletti, Konstanz UP, 2014.

---. "Literature and War." *East West Mimesis. Auerbach in Turkey*, ed. Kader

Konuk, Stanford UP, 2010, 194-207.

---. *Mimesis. The Representation of Reality in Western Literature*. Fiftieth-Anniversary Edition, Princeton UP, 2003.

---. "Realism in Europe in the Nineteenth Century." *East West Mimesis. Auerbach in Turkey*, ed. Kader Konuk, Stanford UP, 2010, 181-193.

---. "Scholarship in the Times of Extremes: Letters of Erich Auerbach (1933-1946), on the Fiftieth Anniversary of His Death." *PMLA*, vol. 122, no. 3, 2007, 742-762.

---. *Time, History, and Literature. Selected Essays*. Ed. James I. Porter, Princeton UP, 2014.

Austen, Jane. *Sense and Sensibility*. Ed. Claudia L. Johnson, W. W. Norton & Company, 2002.

Bachelard, Gaston. *Atomistic Intuitions. An Essay on Classification*. State U of New York P, 2018.

Barck, Karlheinz. "Walter Benjamin and Erich Auerbach: Fragments of a Correspondence." *Diacritics*, vol. 22, no. 3/4, 1992, 81-83.

Cavell, Stanley. *Contesting Tears. The Hollywood Melodrama of the Unknown Woman*. The U of Chicago P, 1996.

Chartier, Roger. *The Cultural Origins of the French Revolution*. Duke UP, 1991.

Deleuze, Gilles and Claire Parnet. *Dialogues II*. Columbia UP, 2007.

Eagleton, Terry. *Sweet Violence. The Idea of the Tragic*. Blackwell, 2003.

Einstein, Albert. *The Collected Papers. Volume 14. The Berlin Years: Writings and Correspondence, April* 1923-*May* 1925. Eds. Diana Kormos Buchwald et al, Princeton UP, 2015.

Fritzsche, Peter. *Stranded in the Present. Modern Time and the Melancholy of History*. Harvard UP, 2004.

Graef, Ortwin de. "Shaft which Ran: Chinese Whispers with Auerbach, Buck, Woolf and De Quincey." *Fear and Fantasy in a Global World*. Eds. Susana Araújo, Marta Pacheco Pinto, Sandra Bettencourt, Brill, Rodopi, 2015, 303-322.

Greenblatt, Stephen. *The Swerve. How the Renaissance Began*. Vintage, 2012.

Hartman, Geoffrey. *A Scholar's Tale. Intellectual Journey of a Displaced Child of Europe*. Fordham UP, 2007.

Jameson, Fredric. *The Antinomies of Realism*. Verso, 2013.

Jukić, Tatjana. "Jane Austen i roman 19. stoljeća: obrazovanje fokalizacijske svijesti." *Književna smotra*, vol. 52, no. 152(1), 2020, 11-19.

Konuk, Kader. *East West Mimesis. Auerbach in Turkey*. Stanford UP, 2010.

Liu, Lydia H. *Translingual Practice. Literature, National Culture, and Translated Modernity – China, 1900 – 1937*. Stanford UP, 1995.

Loraux, Nicole. *The Children of Athena. Athenian Ideas About Citizenship and the Division Between the Sexes*. Princeton UP, 1993.

---. *The Divided City. On Memory and Forgetting in Ancient Athens*. Zone Books, 2006.

Marcus, Laura. *The Tenth Muse. Writing About Cinema in the Modernist Period*. Oxford UP, 2007.

Nial, Thomas. *Matter and Motion. A Brief History of Kinetic Materialism*. Edinburgh UP, 2024.

Nixon, Jon. *Erich Auerbach and the Secular World. Literary History, Historiography, Post-Colonial Theory and Beyond*. Routledge, 2022.

Orr, John. *Tragic Realism and Modern Society. Studies in the Sociology of the Modern Novel*. Macmillan, 1977.

Osterhammel, Jürgen. *Unfabling the East. The Enlightenment's Encounter with Asia*. Princeton UP, 2018.

Piketty, Thomas. *Capital in the Twenty-First Century*. Harvard UP, 2014.

Porter, James I. "Disfigurations: Erich Auerbach's Theory of *Figura*." *Critical Inquiry*, vol. 44, no. 1, 2017, pp. 80 – 113.

Rachum, Ilan. "The Meaning of 'Revolution' in the English Revolution (1648 – 1660)." *Journal of the History of Ideas*, vol. 56, no. 2, 1995, pp. 195 – 215.

Schwanitz, Dietrich. *Systemtheorie und Literatur. Ein neues Paradigma*. Springer Fachmedien Wiesbaden, 1990.

Vernant, Jean-Pierre and Pierre Vidal-Naquet. *Myth and Tragedy in Ancient Greece*. Zone Books, 1993.

Wang, Shouren. "Manifesting Reality in the Context of China's Cross-Cultural Encounter with Realism." *Representation and Reproduction: Literary Realisms Across the Boundaries*. Eds. Shouren Wang, Lei Xu, Nanjing UP, 2019, 75 – 98.

White, Hayden. *Figural Realism. Studies in the Mimesis Effect*. The Johns Hopkins UP, 1999.

---. *Metahistory. The Historical Imagination in Nineteenth-Century Europe*. The Johns Hopkins UP, 1973.

Woolf, Virginia. *To the Lighthouse*. Ed. David Bradshaw, Oxford UP, 2006.

Zeitlin, Froma L. *Playing the Other. Gender and Society in Classical Greek Literature*. The U of Chicago P, 1996.

现实主义小说或现代讽刺

菲利普·杜福尔

内容摘要：19世纪法国现实主义可以被定义为某种语调：嘲讽。巴尔扎克认为这种语调是历史的要求。现实主义作家并不将自己视作启发读者、描画未来蓝图的先知。1830年革命后，当资产阶级自由主义民主试图强加自己的模型时，现实主义作家指出了现实的困境。现实主义式嘲讽与启蒙时代伏尔泰的反讽有根本差别，后者奠基于真理与谎言的截然区分之上，是好战的，以确定性的名义行事，为进步而斗争。前者则属于某种彻底的怀疑主义。小说的对话性不应理解为对民主精神（通过视角的多元化来关注多样性）的赞扬，而应理解为对社会话语的总体讽刺，这一社会话语是种巨大的众声喧哗。本论文意图界定的，正是这一"抽离"美学。

关键词：巴尔扎克 司汤达 福楼拜 讽刺 复调 民主

作者简介：菲利普·杜福尔，法国图尔大学教授，主要从事19世纪法国小说研究。

Title: Realistic Novels or Modern Satire

Abstract: The French realism of the 19th century could be defined by one tone: mockery. According to Balzac, it was determined by history. The realist writer did not see himself as a romantic mage destined to enlighten his reader or chart the paths of the future. Instead, he pointed out the dead ends of the present,

---

① 本文原发于《外国文学研究》2024年第3期。

while the bourgeois liberal democracy sought to impose its model after the revolution of 1830. This mockery differs greatly from Voltaire's irony during the Enlightenment, which was combative, exercised in the name of certainties, with a clear distinction between truth and lies, and militant for progress. Realist mockery is paired with radical skepticism. The very dialogism of the novel is not to be understood as a celebration of democratic spirit (acknowledging plurality through diverse points of view), but as a global satire of social discourse, a vast cacophony. This aesthetic of disengagement is what we seek to characterize.

Key words: Balzac; Stendhal; Flaubert; satire; polyphony; democracy

Author: Philippe Dufour is a professor at the University of Tours, France. His research interests are French novel in the 19th century.

黑格尔在《美学》中指出了艺术史上的三大节点以及三者间的一个共同点：象征艺术、古典艺术和浪漫艺术是构想绝对性的三种方式。这位哲学家还预见了专属于现代的第四个时间节点：在幻想破灭的时代，艺术再也无法表达神秘、传递启示或颂扬理想。黑格尔顺势承认，"我们缺乏的是心灵深处的信仰"(Hegel 739)。艺术家再也无法坚持某种轻易便可以凝聚起一个共同体的世界观。艺术家不再与自己时代的精神和谐一致，而是将远距离地展现自己所处的时代。黑格尔承认这种混乱局面也有积极的一面：墨守成规的态度消失，艺术家自视是自由意识的化身。艺术进入了一个批判性思考的时代。作品变成了一张白纸："对于当今艺术家来说，被某一种特定的观念以及适合它的表现方式所束缚，这一切已成过去。"(同上)在这个新阶段，艺术的任务不再是再现时代所公认的理想，而是揭穿理想化现实的假想。

历史根源

霍乱让黑格尔没有机会阅读到巴尔扎克和司汤达的作品,但当他谈到浪漫主义艺术的消亡时,我们总模糊地感觉黑格尔是在说这二人。他的话在大革命后的法国历史背景下产生了回响,当时《红与黑》和《驴皮记》相继问世,资产阶级自由派刚在1830年七月革命中夺取政权,这场革命与1789年法国大革命一脉相承,彻底推翻了传统的君主制。值得注意的是,这场世界之变并没有被当作充满希望的新开端,也没有被视为旧世界的悲剧(旧政权复辟的失败),时代似乎进入了一个巨大的空白。在被清除的过去和不确定的未来之间,作家看到的是一个再无参照模式,也无基础信仰的社会。黑格尔曾言:"我们缺乏的是心灵深处的信仰。"巴尔扎克回应道:"世界在向我们索要美丽的画作吗?那原型何在?你们的褴褛衣衫、你们的失败革命、你们的高谈阔论的资产阶级、你们的死气沉沉的宗教、你们的已然消亡的权力、你们的名存实亡的国王,这些东西难道诗意盎然到要你们去一番美化吗?"(Balzac, "Préface à *La Peau de chagrin*" 57)

巴尔扎克盘点了这个世纪,但他在罗列时,嘲讽地把糟糕的着装品位和上帝之死放在一起,把革命的失败和君主制的垮台混为一谈。文学脱离了美(那些"美丽的画作")和理想:它不再是美化(transfigurer),而是反讽地展现(figurer)当时社会彻头彻尾的平庸。这是新的美学要求,是艺术的转变:"现在我们只能嘲讽。嘲讽是垂死的社会的全部文学……"(同上)1830年的七月革命推翻了国王查理十世的统治,并声称最终实现了法国大革命的精神。巴尔扎克并没有嗅到大革命的新气息,反倒是从中察觉到某种呼唤颓废主义文学的苦闷:"走向衰亡的社会的文学。"巴尔扎克混杂的罗列既非并列,也无等级(穿着、革命、资产阶级、宗教、国王),表达了社会分裂、无法统一的思想。在《全球报》的一篇匿名文章中,一位记者在评论《红与黑》时,认为在司汤达的小说中也看到了这种颓废主义文学,这是某个时代所特有的文学,"在这个时代,大家不再认同社会制度,并在制度之外行事,没有团结,也没有共同情感"(Anon., "*Le Rouge et le Noir, chronique du XIXe siècle* par M. de Stendhal" 4)。远距离嘲讽这种形式象征着个体无法融入一个共同体之中。人人各自为政:行走在巴黎街头的年轻人,这种现实主义小说中的典型场景,便是个体孤独之旅的写照,例如《情感教育》中漫步在巴黎街头的弗雷德里克,《贪欲的角逐》中徘徊在午夜巴黎的阿里斯第德·鲁贡。年轻人想要进入一个以自我为中心、没有社会规划的世界(近两个世纪后,这种现实主义场景仍在当今欧洲民主国家引起强烈反响)。当理想不复存在,剩下的便只有野心。

现实主义作家并不认为自己是浪漫主义魔术师,肩负启迪读者并描绘未来道路的责任。社会浪漫主义正是在1830年七月革命后出现的:曾经退回自身的美丽灵魂(比如夏多布里昂的《勒内》)融入城市。另一个美学要求,是雨果在浪漫主义第二阶段——这一阶段最终走向失败——所定义的诗人的使命:

> 诗人在渎神的日子
> 就为更美好的时代操劳。
> 他是乌托邦的战士;
> 立足当下,憧憬明朝。
> 正是他,该在每个人的头脑里,
> 在任何时候,像先知一样,
> 在他那掌握一切的手上,
> 不管人们对他是辱骂还是赞美,
> 让未来大放光芒!(雨果,596 – 597)

浪漫主义诗歌和现实主义小说：两种同时代的美学，两种体验历史的方式。浪漫主义诗歌始终是有关理想的体裁，展望未来（那时，会出现有待揭开的新秘密，有待宣告的新启示，也就是进步的启示录），而现实主义小说则用嘲讽的口吻描述了当下的绝境。脱离了浪漫主义的现实主义是怪诞而非崇高的。它能颂扬什么呢？

讽刺精神

嘲讽并不局限于对某一特定政权的批判：现实主义小说提供了一种新的讽刺类型，其对象不像传统讽刺那样局限（有时针对个人，通常针对某个群体或机构，例如医生、神职人员、司法机构）。现实主义讽刺针对的是整个社会。这里又体现出现实主义与雨果的差异。作为进步力量的代言人，他在《惩罚集》（1853）中针对当时的社会环境（路易-拿破仑·波拿巴发动政变，推翻共和国并建立第二帝国），抨击了官场、政客和投机商人，并试图唤醒人们的良心。但现实主义讽刺中，读者成为被攻击的对象，无论其意识形态如何（你们的革命、你们的宗教、你们的国王，巴尔扎克如是说）。除了故事发生的时间（巴尔扎克的小说时而以复辟时期为背景，时而又以七月王朝为背景），小说家还考虑到了精神史的漫长周期、社会基础以及司汤达口中的"十九世纪文明"。司汤达起初把《红与黑》的副标题定为"1830年纪事"（这部小说在1830年七月革命之前就已写成，但因革命而推迟了出版），后来他认为这个日期会导致误解，可能会让人把这部作品与历史事件联系在一起，便采用了一个新的副标题："十九世纪纪事"。于连·索雷尔的故事虽然发生在复辟时期，但在七月革命后仍具现实意义。现实主义小说的时间是风俗史的时间，而非事件史的时间。

因此，现实主义小说偏爱传记形式，而非紧扣某场风波的危机小说：一个年轻人渐渐衰老。巴尔扎克和左拉让自己笔下的人物在小说各卷中反复出场并刻画其各个年龄段，以此来凸显这种生命的延续。在现实主义小说中，政治历史只是一个背景，却赋予讽刺以全部力量，而讽刺攻击的是一个彻底腐朽的社会。

愤怒的读者

面对这种尖锐讽刺的攻击，最初的各方读者，不论是保皇派、自由派还是进步派，都同样感觉自己遭到了针对，并意识到现实主义小说是一种讽刺。这个标签成为该流派的决定性特征。《红与黑》的一位评论家称这部作品为"讽刺小说"，另一位评论家则明确指出这是"对当代风尚的讽刺"[①]。巴尔扎克逝世后，圣伯夫将他比作拉伯雷，另一位来自都兰的作家，称他具有"拉伯雷式的都兰人的讽刺精神与坦率做派"（Sainte-Beuve 2）。福楼拜尽管鼓吹无人称小说（roman impersonnel），评论家还是在他身上看到了上述精神，并说《包法利夫人》是"对一个平庸社会的强烈而冷酷的讽刺"（Calmels）。但评论家也指出了这种讽刺的独特性：它针对多个目标，并非为了某一方的利益发声。现实主义者属于怀疑论者这一哲学大家庭。关于司汤达，儒勒·雅宁写道："他是一个冷静的观察者，一个残忍的嘲讽者，一个刻薄的怀疑论者。他喜欢怀疑一切，因为怀疑让他有权不尊重一切，有权谴责他所接触的一切"（Janin）。伊波利特·卡斯蒂利亚拒绝相信巴尔扎克在《人间喜剧》前言中所说的，以"永恒的真理：宗教和君权"（Balzac, *La Comédie humaine I* 3）之名写作。他顶多承认巴尔扎克的天主教信仰是虔诚的，但除此之外，卡斯蒂利亚在圣伯夫之前就已经将巴尔扎克比作拉伯雷了："现在，在拉伯雷的直接影响下，巴尔扎克先生已经达成了纯粹的怀疑主义，不是怀疑宗教原则，而是怀疑人和社会。"（Castille）受巴尔扎克影响，左拉也承认人的保守思想和作品中漩涡般的讽刺间的差距，这种讽刺不仅嘲讽自由主义模式，也嘲讽从前的社会。讽刺作家甚至把自己的理想都当作了讽刺的对象！"讽刺贵族和资产阶级,描绘当时的纷争场面,戏剧化地展示夹在永远尘封的过去与开放的未来之间的现状:这就是《人间喜剧》"［Zola, "Balzac (édition complète et définitive)" 3］。现实主义小说不是论题小说(roman à thèse)。评论家们在阅读《情感教育》时惊讶地发现,尽管福楼拜这部小说的核心是1848年,一个发生法国二月革命和"六月天"的年份,当时所有的社会模式都彼此对立,但这部小说对所有保守主义与共和主义进行了多重讽刺。因为无法被界定,福楼拜遭到了三个读者群体的反对:君主主义者、自由主义者和社会主义者,这就注定他的小说在商业上的失败。库维利尔-弗勒里谴责《情感教育》是部"没有任何发自内心的呐喊,没有任何情感,没有任何教益的现实主义讽刺"(Cuvillier-Fleury 3)。自由派天主教徒圣勒内·塔扬迪耶也为现实主义小说中缺乏作为传统讽刺基础的人文主义观点而感到遗憾:"最刻薄的讽刺诗人在揭示人类苦难时,内心也还是怀有对更美好的人性的理想;厌世的、不人道的讽刺是一种不自然的行为,是一种不合逻辑的畸形情况。"(Taillandier 1004)维克多·雨果的《惩罚集》以《黑夜》(*Nox*)开头,以《光明》(*Lux*)结尾。相比之下,现实主义小说里看不到希望。②只有害怕屈服于幻觉的恐惧:"我,我嘲笑一切,甚至是我最喜欢的东西。［……］这是个好方法。""然后看看还剩下些什么",福楼拜在给路易丝·科莱的信中写道。(Flaubert, *Œuvres Complètes II* 387)

现实主义讽刺拒绝了明天会改变或欢唱的幻想。共和主义者乔治·桑也批评福楼拜的小说冷漠无情、无动于衷,为讽刺而讽刺,其实读者希望看到一个真实的世界:"艺术不仅仅是绘画。另外,真正的绘画充满了舞动画笔的灵魂。艺术不仅仅是批评和讽刺。批评和讽刺只描绘了真相的一面。我想看到人的本来面目。他不好也不坏。他既好又坏。"(Sand, *Correspondance* 368)乔治·桑的小说努力尝试在皮埃尔·勒鲁和费利西泰·德·拉梅内之间开辟一条新思路,它们是一位道德教化家的小说,这位道德教化家相信人可以日臻完善,理想也终将实现。乔治·桑与福楼拜各执己见的对话无疑体现了两种文学观念的冲突:"当然了,你会让人悲痛,我会让人宽慰。"(同上)

现在,让我们来看看构建这种怀疑式讽刺用到的美学手法。

小说的复调

人们之所以感觉讽刺针对的是当时整个世界,主要是因为小说对话。除了常见的功能外,对话还承担了一项新的使命:记录社会话语,表达一个时代的各种社会方言。福楼拜在《情感教育》中特别喜欢那些被远处的主人公偶然间听到的辩驳:一句响亮的话浓缩了一种意识形态。例如,在当布勒兹公馆举办的晚会上,保守派的人说:"我真希望设几个军事法庭,堵住记者们的嘴! 一有不逊,就把他们拖到军事法庭去!"(福楼拜 159)在智慧俱乐部里召开的共和党会议也是如此:"工人是教士,正如[……]我主耶稣·基督一样!"(Flaubert, *L'Éducation sentimentale* 409)在这两个例子中,人物都没有名字:他们只是发言人。这种手法并不局限于保守派社会方言和共和派社会方言的对峙,因为每种语言又被细分为不同的立场,体现在小说众多的次要人物身上(例如塞内卡尔的布朗基主义、杜萨迪埃的人道主义乌托邦、瓦特纳兹的女权主义或上述共和派人士的基督教社会主义)。叙事让大家听到了当时的各种语言,但没有区分等级,也没有确立一种代表真理的语言,结果就让人感到各种声音嘈杂乱耳。巴尔扎克在写于复辟末期的一篇文章中提到"十五年来我们一直在说巴别塔的语言"(Balzac, "Complaintes satiriques sur les mœurs du temps présent" 744)。通过小说人物视点的多样性,叙事反映了思想的多元。但小说并没有通过这一多样性来颂扬民主精神。语言的分散反映了社会的分裂。这个世纪已与过去一刀两断,但又无法就未来达成共识,无法孕育一个新人。

理想的微弱声音

但我们可以在对话中找出两三种典型的陈述方式。在次要部分中,我们会听到理想主义人物一丝微弱的声音。这些声音几乎弱不可闻,因为这种价值观言论并非出自主人公之口。这些主人公都是不道德的,适应世风日下的社会(从这个意义上来说也算是典范了!),为了功成名就,他们接受了社会的规则。这种情况下,如何理想化当今的年轻人?巴尔扎克问道。"今天,社会把所有孩子请去共赴同一场宴会,让他们年纪轻轻就野心勃勃。社会剥夺了年轻人的风度,让他们失去仁厚之心,变得精于算计。诗歌渴望另一种样貌,但现实往往与人们想要相信的虚构格格不入,让人只能如实描绘十九世纪的年轻人"(巴尔扎克,《幻灭》54)。巴尔扎克笔下众多的主人公中,就只剩欧也妮能够作为某种理想的诗性代表。巴尔扎克为这个特别的人物创造了一个新词,看上去充满拟古风,像是属于另一个时代:欧也妮是"compatissance"(Balzac, Honoré de. *Eugénie Grandet* 140)③的女主角。仿佛"compassion"这个词已无法再使用,太简短了些!欧也妮、她的母亲以及女佣纳侬一起体现了人性的观点——"三个充满怜悯的女人"(146),仿佛在雄心勃勃的男性社会,怜悯也被性别化了——"女子的怜悯"(158)。关于欧也妮,巴尔扎克进一步明确道:"她那满腔的怜悯,是女子胜过男子的崇高德行之一。"(161)在《人间喜剧》中,很少有女人能与这位女主人公相媲美。在被社会达尔文主义腐蚀的世界里,怜悯不再是卢梭所说的那种自然情感。另外,这种只存在于苦难背景之下的团结又是什么呢?难道革命的博爱理想,人人都能过上更好生活的承诺,就只剩共同受苦、相互怜悯吗?

在《人间喜剧》中,理想主义人物都是次要角色,甚至是插曲式的角色,比如无能为力的见证人。笨嘴拙舌的埃斯巴侯爵就是一个典型象征："他说话不清晰，不仅咬字听起来像是个口吃的人，而且思想也表达得不清不楚，让听的人觉得他翻来覆去、想东想西[……]"（巴尔扎克，《傅雷译巴尔扎克作品集1》76）。巴尔扎克在一封信中承认，美丽的灵魂在审美上比不过主宰社会的不道德的野心家："这让我感到绝望。夏娃·查尔顿和大卫·塞夏（《幻灭》中的人物）纯粹的美永远无法与巴黎的图景相媲美。"④文本趣味与道德观念背道而驰。实际上，在《幻灭》第三部中，天才发明家大卫变成了一个小资产阶级的食利者，终日无所事事，一心研究昆虫。看到这里的读者又怎会被塞夏夫妇所吸引呢？现实主义叙事背离了浪漫幻想，展示了平庸面前的人人平等。

    福楼拜的作品则更进一步。在他那里，评论家们再也找不到依然萦绕在巴尔扎克小说中的理想主义人物的苍白身影。乔治·桑在为《包法利夫人》写的书评中强调了这一点："巴尔扎克肯定很乐意在其中几页上署名。但或许他免不了要在这生动又荒凉的现实描写中安排一个善良的人物或温馨的场景。"(Sand,"Le réalisme")没有一个可以代入或倾听的人物。在《情感教育》中，杜萨迪埃这个人物怀揣着博大的情怀和普世共和的梦想，但艾米莉·博斯凯认为他太平凡了，并在他身上看到了另一种嘲讽："杜萨迪尔被塞内卡尔剑杀，但他死得像个英雄，为共和而战。他被安排在这儿是在为人性平反吗？唉！渺小而无用，他似乎是被特意创造出来，以证明献身精神只属于精神匮乏之人。"(Bosquet)在福楼拜的小说中寻找理想的残余，注定会无功而返。现实主义从根本上说就是书写荒凉。

愤世嫉俗的声音

    理想主义人物的声音弱不可闻，嘲讽者的声音却清晰响亮，并道出了历史谎言的真相。巴尔扎克把嘲讽者塑造成了小说中的一类典型，这种人物以不同的身份反复出现，例如《莫黛斯特·米尼翁》中被视作

"嘲讽者"(Balzac, *La Comédie humaine I* 531)的勃隆台、《搅水女人》中"厌世的嘲讽者"(Balzac, *La Comédie humaine IV* 531)皮可西沃，当然还有《高老头》中有着"嘲讽的声音"(Balzac, *La Comédie humaine III* 237, 158)的伏脱冷。愤世嫉俗，玩世不恭：这些词在小说中经常被用来形容伏脱冷。愤世嫉俗者是说真话的人。在现实主义小说中，真相就是揭穿假象。现实主义所能提供的唯一的积极内容就是：不要再上当受骗。通过塑造嘲讽者这一人物形象，巴尔扎克解决了他在1832年皈依天主教并接受正统主义后所面临的意识形态上的矛盾：作为叙述者，他装成"永恒的真理：宗教和君权"的捍卫者；作为小说家，他把历史真相置于愤世嫉俗者的口中。他们延续了《驴皮记》序言中的话："现在我们只能嘲讽。"他们是以第三人称嘲讽的巴尔扎克的面具。

巴尔扎克笔下的嘲讽者就现代社会的动力都发表了相同的言论，社会的实用道德取代了无私道德：成功就是一切。这就是推动个人超越意识形态差异的社会引擎。这就是《人间喜剧》中一再强调的最高准则。伏脱冷作为讽刺的主力军（他不是被比作拉丁诗人尤维纳利斯吗？[⑤]），不厌其烦地对拉斯蒂涅和吕西安·德·鲁邦普莱重复着这句话。他为这部作品定下了基调："因为你们早已没有了道德。如今，在你们那里，成功是所有行为的最高理由，不论何种行为。"(Balzac, *Illusions perdues* 593)德·鲍赛昂子爵夫人这位贵妇人也同意这个罪犯的观点，她告诉自己的表弟拉斯蒂涅："在巴黎，成功就是万事亨通，就是权势的宝钥。"（巴尔扎克，《傅雷译巴尔扎克作品集2》152）生活经历也证实了这一准则："'伏脱冷说得对，财富即美德！'拉斯蒂涅自言自语道。"(137)于连·索雷尔在去世前夕还将其奉为现代社会之法则："不，大家尊敬的人，不过是群侥幸没有在犯罪时被抓现行的无赖。"(Stendhal, *Le Rouge et le Noir* 649)在巴尔扎克的作品中，他的观点与司汤达或左拉的观点相互印证："成功是净化一切的金色火焰"，阿里斯第德·萨加尔无耻地宣称道(Zola, *La Curée* 108)。成功的美德，这就是现实主义讽刺的要旨。

  除了理想人物微弱的声音以及嘲讽者雷鸣般的声音外，我们还能在不经意间分辨出愤世嫉俗者的声音。作为次要人物，他们在直接引语中突兀地承认自己的思想观点，毫无愧疚之意，甚至坚信自己是对的。但在读者听来，这就是一套空话。这些人自得其乐地表达着他们群体的语言及其预设。乔治·桑从中看出了《情感教育》里的对话的原始印记："[……]每类典型人物都与自己的同伙或受骗者一起，伴着自己的兴趣、激情和本能行事。他们匆匆忙忙登台又下场，但每次都会在自己行进的道路上再迈出去一步，并抛出一个有力的总结、一段简短的对话，有时是一句话、一个词，这个词带着某种可怕的天真，浓缩了他们脑子里的所思所想。"（Sand, "*L'Éducation sentimentale, Histoire d'un jeune homme* par Gustave Flaubert" 3）马蒂侬的反驳就是一个很好的例子，他的反驳看起来像在背课文，通过将贫困归咎于穷人来回避社会问题："'不过，'马蒂侬反驳道，'我们得承认，贫困是存在的！但治愈它的良方既不是科学，也不是政权。这纯粹是个人的问题。当下层阶级愿意摒弃他们的恶习时，他们就可以从需求中解脱出来。人民的道德越高尚，就越不贫穷！'"（福楼拜 240）极端自由主义者马蒂侬摆出一副道德家的姿态，对这一成见坚信不疑。让我们再举一例来看看这些身不由己的嘲讽者，他们表达又解构了一整门社会方言。《贪欲的角逐》中，在萨加尔家举办的晚会上，商人和政客纷纷称赞奥斯曼男爵的伟大工程，说这项工程美化了巴黎，振兴了经济，并创造了就业机会。这些论点强调的都是大众利益。但企业家米尼翁毫不掩饰且并无恶意地把房地产投机带来的个人财富也纳入奥斯曼改造巴黎的好处中："我知道不止一个人发家致富了。你看吧，当你赚钱时，一切都是美好的。"（Zola, *La Curée* 66）刚说完，米尼翁身边那群发了不义之财的人就陷入了尴尬的沉默，他们原本可能会对自己说出的话信以为真。

叙述声音

现实主义小说不是论题小说。叙述者的话里并没有呈现出对未来的展望。福楼拜在创作《包法利夫人》时，在写给路易丝·科莱的两封信中对这种新文学进行了理论探讨。这两封信应该放在一起对比着看。在第一封信中，他谴责了论证文学（试图证明的文学）："有关论证文学，那可有的好写了。""你一证明，就说谎。上帝知道开头和结尾；人类只知道中间"(Flaubert, *Œuvres Complètes II* 379)。福楼拜反对这种有失偏颇的文学，他梦想着一种中性的小说创作，此时醒世作家化身为科学观察者："文学会越来越像科学；它首先是陈述性的，但这并不意味着说教。我们确实要描绘画面，要展现自然原貌，但要描绘的是完整的画面，刻画上上下下。"(Flaubert, *Œuvres Complètes III* 158)对完整性的诉求胜过了论证的欲望。巴尔扎克也站在陈述文学这边，这类文章中的论题泛滥成灾，多到失去效力。只需查阅有关《高老头》的资料剪报，就能发现试图从中找到一个论题的评论家们的错乱。巴尔扎克先生的书中缺乏一个中心思想。一位评论家说，他随即又补充："要是在读完后提出这个问题：'这证明了什么？'[……]几乎总是会得出这样的结论：尽管作者本想要证明些什么，但他什么都没有证明得了。"(Anon., "*Le Père Goriot* par M. Balzac" 1)巴尔扎克的小说中有很多论题，却没有一个中心思想，真相碎片之间也没有联系。偶尔的介入构成了碎片化的话语，比如理想人物的微弱声音。巴尔扎克的道德准则变成虔诚愿望，因为这与当下的道德相冲突（"财富即美德"）。巴尔扎克没有在《人间喜剧》中提出论题：论证文学被稀释为陈述文学。叙述者的声音不再具有权威性："这样的构思有何用意？这样的描写有何寓意？"《高老头》的另一位评论家问道(Monnais)。作品并没有传递出清晰的信息。小说家放弃了道德家的雄心，转而深耕一种回避式写作。

巴尔扎克的结尾

对于这种回避式写作，人人有各自的风格。我们仅以巴尔扎克和福楼拜二人为例。

巴尔扎克的长篇大论在叙事面前黯然失色，比不过所讲述的故事。我们可以说，巴尔扎克用反例叙事代替了典范叙事。巴尔扎克式小说正是由某种错位构成，错位的一方是情节上的悲观主义，另一方是小说家的肯定语气，后者声称自己是以永恒的真理——宗教和君权之名写作的。巴尔扎克本人也意识到了这一点。他有时会在叙事的结尾处表现出论述的崩溃。这一点在《幻灭》（巴尔扎克将其称为"作品中的首要作品"）的结尾表现得十分明显。叙述者向我们讲述了不同人物的命运。面对流氓得逞，并没有愤愤不平，只有一种观察的语气。最后这一页是陈述文学之典范。例如，谈到通过抢占大卫·赛夏的发明而致富的企业家戈安得："他有几百万钱财，当上了议员，不久又进贵族院，传闻他可能会在下一届内阁中担任商业部长。1842年，他娶了包比诺小姐，她的父亲安赛末·包比诺先生是七月王朝最有势力的政治家之一，巴黎选区的国会议员，兼某区区长。"（巴尔扎克，《傅雷译巴尔扎克作品集6》280）事实不言自明。了不起的达官贵人戈安得的故事证实了嘲讽者的格言："伏脱冷说得对，财富即美德！"巴尔扎克中性的语调让人对未来感到绝望：一切都结束了。巴尔扎克的这种沉默在《邦斯舅舅》的结尾处得到了重现，《邦斯舅舅》最后一章名为"结论"，但在这一章中，叙述者的声音被人物的声音淹没。这一章实际上由两个场景组成：一个是在公证处的对话，另一个是在包比诺伯爵家中的对话（了不起的戈安得迎娶的正是包比诺伯爵的女儿，包比诺最初是凯撒-比罗托的出纳员，他是白手起家神话的化身），此处，那些骗取了邦斯舅舅遗产的人虚情假意地对这位故人大唱赞歌,钱到手后,他们开始高扬家族精神。还有很多人生轨迹都证实了伏脱冷的法则!叙述者没有评价这种虚伪。《邦斯舅舅》是巴尔扎克最后一部小说,可以作为《人间喜剧》的结尾。我们在此目睹了"永恒的真理"的终结:在这本人物众多的书中,没有与生俱来的贵族;邦斯和施穆克这两位信奉天主教的主人公都死了,成为那个时代的牺牲品,甚至他们的死也被人利用。故事省略了邦斯舅舅临终的场面,他的葬礼变成了一场纯粹的金钱交易和一大堆繁文缛节。巴尔扎克最后一部小说终结了过去,展现了一个再无根基的世界。

从风格上看,巴尔扎克放弃了任何形式的激进主义,《邦斯舅舅》中没有出现小说家惯用的大段离题的政治评论。巴尔扎克叙事中惯常出现的名言警句被一些空洞的格言所取代:"长胡子的女看门人是业主秩序和安全的最大保障之一。"(Balzac, *Le Cousin Pons* 383)风俗史学家诙谐的社会学取代了道德家的愤慨。叙述者用这种不入流的知识打破了自己的权威。准则与成见难分彼此。终极的嘲讽:当时的世界不值得被认真对待。小说家不会折磨自己。比起对历史的意义进行哲学思考,小说家更倾向提供一些不可靠的统计数据,比如这种民族心理学:"犹太人,诺曼地人,奥凡涅人,萨瓦人这四个民族,天性相同,用同样的方式发家致富。一个小钱都不花,一个小钱都要挣,利上滚利的积聚:这就是他们的章程。"(巴尔扎克,《傅雷译巴尔扎克作品集8》101)《人间喜剧》结尾所呈现的普遍真理听起来空洞无物。

福楼拜的无人称反讽

福楼拜继承了巴尔扎克作品中声音的消失。他的无人称风格把回避式写作发挥到了极致。从《包法利夫人》的评论文章,再到《情感教育》的资料剪报,"无人称"这个形容词一直与福楼拜的风格联系在一起。但评论家们都理解错了,无人称并没有被当作一种中立的态度,或一种近乎科学的客观严谨，因为它看起来似乎是一种轻蔑的冷漠。其实无人称是嘴上一言不发但心中不断思考的人的嘲讽。它预设任何评论都没有意义。在《情感教育》问世时，福楼拜的沉默尤为引人注目：作者在叙述政治激情迸发的1848年，怎能不表明自己的立场呢？无人称是嘲讽，是一种没什么要证明的反讽的最高形式。它标志着拒绝参与、拒绝加入多元化的民主游戏的态度。与浪漫主义魔术师大为不同的是，无人称作家表明了自己与社会的疏离。这就是福楼拜深刻的无政府主义。

第一批读者将这种无人称风格与福楼拜的描述性风格联系在一起。有评论家批评福楼拜在《情感教育》(第二部，四)中，在描写弗雷德里克和罗莎内特在香榭丽舍大街上骑马的场景时，对不同类型的马车进行了描述："当我掌握了阳光照耀下的马车拉杆、马具、马鞍、车环、车门、车轮、车窗和轮圈的一整套统计信息后，我能前进得更快些吗？"(Chasles 3)叙事停顿处的啰唆废话让叙述者在1848年这样关键的年份里的沉默变得更加明显。巴尔扎克同时代的评论家们已批评过作家对建筑、家具和服装的冗长烦琐的描述，小说风格让位于百科全书式的汇编：作者于是隐身，让人感觉他是在为后人记录自己时代的物质文明信息。我们期待的是一位思想家，等到的却是一个道具工。巴尔扎克和福楼拜的描述性风格是不是对"十九世纪文明"的一种嘲讽？没有精神价值，唯一的理想就是舒适。在小说中，物品堆积如山。与巴尔扎克同时代的托克维尔在《论美国的民主》一书中说道，民主社会沦为对物质财富的狂热。无论如何，在福楼拜的无人称叙事中，风景的秀丽取代了作者的话语。我们期待的是富有启发的评论，得到的却是多余的细节。事实上，在这段跟随着弗雷德里克的脚步（他那天早上起得有点晚）来描写1848年革命的叙述中，我们发现事情总来得不是时候。当我们进入杜伊勒里宫时，路易·菲利普的政权已经垮台："楼下的一个小房间里，一杯杯拿铁咖啡被端了上来。"(Flaubert, *L'Éducation* sentimentale 389）这种描述性的风格取代了基于因果叙事的事件史，而只有因果叙事才能还原1848年的时局（马克思在六月革命中看到了阶级斗争轰动壮观且不容忽视的表现⑥，这一点直至那时一直被自由主义的人道言论掩盖）。"一杯杯拿铁咖啡"，在福楼拜那里，泛滥的现实就是在控诉意义的缺失。

法国现实主义缺乏仁爱精神，这是十九世纪下半叶保守派评论家们给出的诊断，他们拿法国小说家与英国和俄国现实主义作家进行对比，从狄更斯到艾略特，从果戈理到托尔斯泰，他们无论是否真的信教，都保留了基督教根基中的共情能力［把俄国小说引入法国的沃盖在1886年说道，"心灵的宗教品质"（Vogüé 107）］。因此，症结不在于，或者说不再在于叙述的故事，而在于叙述的声音，在于其道德和宗教上的冷漠。"但如果作者不是基督教徒，那就不要指望他会奇迹般地有同情心；他不会劳心费力地走进灵魂深处，他在同情之前会先嘲讽，他会去观察而不是去爱，他会因此而拘泥于外在的表象，他只会去描绘这些表象。"（Montégut 877）蒙特古在赞美乔治·艾略特的作品时这样说。他在1859年写下这几行字时，心里想的显然是《包法利夫人》的作者，但他并没有指名道姓，而是不动声色地展现了福楼拜的描述性风格。这就是法国古典现实主义小说的转变：巴尔扎克、司汤达、福楼拜开创了一种去道德化的、令人气馁的叙事！

注解【Notes】

① 这两篇文章分别见于 Anon. "Le musicien italien." *Mercure de France au XIXe siècle*, no. 17, 1830, pp. 458–463. 以及 Anon. " *Le Rouge et le Noir, chronique du XIXe siècle*, par M. de Stendhal." *Revue de Paris*, t. XX, 1830, pp. 258–262.

② 但请注意，左拉的《萌芽》以夜晚的到来开始，以黎明的离去结束（左拉意识到了自己的浪漫主义，尽管他自己……）。

③ 但这个词最早见于1792年。［文中的"compatissance"和"compassion"都表示"同情"，但后者更为常用（译者注）。］

④ 参见 Balzac, Honoré de. *Lettres à Madame Hanska*. TOME 2. Le Delta. 1968, pp.198.《外省大人物在巴黎》是《幻灭》第二部分的标题。
⑤ 通常是一个尤维纳利斯式的俏皮话,参见 Balzac, Honoré de. *Le Père Goriot*, Le Livre de Poche, 2008, pp.65。
⑥ 与二月革命不同的是,二月革命是第三等级最后一次在自由、平等、博爱的旗帜下团结奋战。

引用文献【Works Cited】

Anon. "Le musicien italien." *Mercure de France au XIXe siècle*, no.17, 1830, pp. 458–463.

---. "*Le Père Goriot* par M. Balzac." *Le Constitutionnel*, no.82, 1835–03023, pp.1.

---. "*Le Rouge et le Noir, chronique du XIXe siècle*, par M. de Stendhal." *Le Globe*, no.279, 1830, pp.4.

---. "*Le Rouge et le Noir, chronique du XIXe siècle*, par M. de Stendhal." *Revue de Paris*, t. XX, 1830, pp.258–262.

奥诺雷・德・巴尔扎克:《傅雷译巴尔扎克作品集1》,傅雷译,北京日报出版社,2017年。

[Balzac, Honoré de. *Collected Works of Honoré de Balzac Translated by Fu Lei I*. Translated by Fu Lei, Beijing Daily Press, 2017.]

——:《傅雷译巴尔扎克作品集2》,傅雷译,北京日报出版社,2017年。

[---. *Collected Works of Honoré de Balzac Translated by Fu Lei II*. Translated by Fu Lei, Beijing Daily Press, 2017.]

——:《傅雷译巴尔扎克作品集6》,傅雷译,北京日报出版社,2017年。

[---. *Collected Works of Honoré de Balzac Translated by Fu Lei VI*. Translated by Fu Lei, Beijing Daily Press, 2017.]

——:《傅雷译巴尔扎克作品集8》,傅雷译,北京日报出版社,2017年。

[---. *Collected Works of Honoré de Balzac Translated by Fu Lei VIII*. Translated by Fu Lei, Beijing Daily Press, 2017.]

——:《幻灭》,傅雷译,台海出版社,2016年。

[---. *Illusions perdues*. Translated by Fu Lei, Taihai Publishing House, 2016.]

Balzac, Honoré de. "Complaintes satiriques sur les mœurs du temps présent." *La Mode*, 1830–02–20, *OD*, t. II, pp.744.

---. *Eugénie Grandet*. Le Livre de Poche, 2008.

---. *Illusions perdues*. Garnier-Flammarion, 1990.

---. *La Comédie humaine*, t. I. Gallimard, «Bibliothèque de la Pléiade», 1976.

---. *La Comédie humaine*, *t. III*. Gallimard, «Bibliothèque de la Pléiade», 1976.

---. *La Comédie humaine*, *t. IV*. Gallimard, «Bibliothèque de la Pléiade», 1976.

---. *Le Cousin Pons*. Garnier-Flammarion, 2015.

---. *Le Père Goriot*. Le Livre de Poche, 2008.

---. Préface à *La Peau de chagrin* (1831). Le Livre de Poche, 2004.

Bosquet, Amélie. "Gustave Flaubert, *L'Éducation sentimentale*." *Le Droit des femmes*, 1869-12-18.

Castille, Hippolyte. "Critique littéraire. Romanciers contemporains. I. M. H. de Balzac." *La Semaine*, no. 49, 1846-10-04.

Chasles, Philarète. "La vérité dans le roman—M. Flaubert." *Le Siècle*, no. 12645, 1869-12-14, pp. 3.

Cuvillier-Fleury, Alfred. *Journal des débats*, 1869-11-02, pp. 3.

Flaubert, Gustave. *L'Éducation sentimentale*, Garnier-Flammarion, 2013.

---. *Œuvres Complètes. Correspondance. II.* 1847-1852, Louis Conard, 1926.

---. *Œuvres Complètes. Correspondance. III.* 1852-1854, Louis Conard, 1927.

Calmels, Fortuné. "Salammbô, par Gustave Flaubert." *Le Boulevard*, no. 49, 1862-12-07.

Hegel, Friedrich. *Esthétique*, tome I. Livre de Poche, 1997.

古斯塔夫·福楼拜:《福楼拜文集2》,艾珉主编,王文融译,人民文学出版社,2014年。

[Flaubert, Gustave. *Collected Works of Flaubert* II. Edited by Ai Ming. Translated by Wang Wenrong, People's Literature Publishing House, 2014.]

Janin, Jules. "*Le Rouge et le Noir, chronique du XIXe siècle* par M. de Stendhal." *Journal des débats*, 1830-12-26, pp. 2-4.

Monnais, Édouard. *Le Courrier français*, no. 102, 1835-04-13.

Montégut, Émile. "Le roman réaliste en Angleterre, *Adam Bede*." *Revue des Deux Mondes*, t. XXI, 1859. pp. 867-897.

Sainte-Beuve, "M. de Balzac." *Le Constitutionnel*, col. 6, 1850, pp. 2.

Sand, George. "L'Éducation sentimentale, Histoire d'un jeune homme par Gustave Flaubert." *La Liberté*, 1869-12-21, pp. 3.

---. "Le réalisme." *Le Courrier de Paris*, 1857-07-08.

---. *Correspondance:* 1812-1876. *VI*. Calmann Lévy, 1884.

Stendhal. *Le Rouge et le Noir*, Gallimard, coll. «Folio», 2000.

Taillandier, Saint-René. "Le roman misanthropique. *L'Éducation sentimentale, histoire d'un jeune homme* par M. Gustave Flaubert." *Revue des Deux Mondes*, vol. 84, no. 4, 1869-12-15, pp. 987-1004.

维克多·雨果:《雨果诗歌集 第1卷》,张秋红译,河北教育出版社,1999年。
[Hugo, Victor. *Collected Poems of Hugo*. Translated by Zhang Qiuhong, Hebei Education Publicating House, 1999.]

Vogüé, Eugène-Melchior de. *Le Roman russe* (1886). Classiques Garnier, 2010.

Zola, Émile. "Balzac (édition complète et définitive)." *Le Rappel*, 1870-05-13, pp.3.

---. *La Curée*, Gallimard, coll. «Folio», 2015.

西方文学典型塑造"三模式"论

——以现代现实主义为中心的比较辨析[①]

蒋承勇

内容摘要：19世纪以前，西方文学中的人物形象通常是某种观念的承载者，其性格非环境之产物，属"观念—性格"模式的典型。19世纪现代现实主义注重刻画人物性格，性格与环境密切关联，环境描写服务于丰富复杂性格的展示，其人物形象属"环境—性格"模式的典型。20世纪现代主义反叛性地消解人物性格，淡化人物与环境之关系，其人物形象属"抽象—象征"模式的典型。相较而言，"观念—性格"和"环境—性格"模式的典型更贴近读者，尤其是后者因其更注重性格、环境和历史之演变的立体化互动而更富有人文内涵和审美意蕴。对不同"模式"典型的体认旨在深化对丰富繁杂之典型人物的深度理解，并在开放性接纳人类文学之人物描写优长基础上促进本土文学研究、文学创作与文学鉴赏。

关键词：西方文学　典型人物　模式　现代现实主义　现代主义
作者简介：蒋承勇，浙江工商大学文科资深教授，主要研究西方文学思潮、西方文学人文传统。

Title: On the "Three Patterns" of Typical Characterization in Western Literature: A Comparative and Discriminative Analysis Centered on Modern Realism

Abstract: Before the 19th century, literary figures in Western

---

① 本文原发于《外国文学研究》2024年第1期。

literature were usually the carriers of certain ideas, with their personalities not being products of their environment, adhering to the "idea-character" pattern. In 19th-century modern realism, there was an emphasis on depicting character traits closely linked to the environment, with the portrayal of the environment serving to enrich the display of complex personalities, thus falling under the "environment-character" pattern. In 20th-century modernism, characters were rebelliously dissolved, with their traits and their relationship with the environment being downplayed, rendering them as typical examples of the "abstract-symbol" pattern. Relatively, typical characters in the "idea-character" pattern and the "environment-character" pattern are more relatable to readers, especially the latter, which possesses richer humanistic implications and aesthetic connotations due to its emphasis on the three-dimensional interaction of characters, environment, and historical evolution. Recognizing the characteristics of different " patterns" aims to deepen the understanding of the rich and diverse typical characters and to promote the study, creative writing, and appreciation of local literature on the basis of embracing the strengths of character portrayal in open-ended acceptance of human literature.

Key words: Western literature; typical characters; pattern; modern realism; modernism

Author: Jiang Chengyong is a Senior Professor of Liberal Arts, Zhejiang Gongshang University. His research interests are the ideological trends and humanistic traditions of Western literature.

文学典型主要是指叙事作品中塑造的富有性格特征、具有艺术魅力的人物形象；人物形象是叙事文学的重要构成元素。"典型""指能够反映现实生活中某些方面的本质而又具有极其鲜明生动的个性特征的艺术形象"(《中国大百科全书·中国文学》113)。在19世纪现代现实主义文学①中,塑造典型人物是文学创作的根本性任务,而且这种创作理念与原则影响极为深远,迄今依然有重要的理论与实践意义与价值。有鉴于此,本文以19世纪现代现实主义文学典型人物塑造为中心展开比较式讨论与辨析。

一、"典型"观念的渊源与流变

"典型"这一概念来自西方文学,在我国,鲁迅和成仿吾最早于20世纪20年代初将其从西方文学介绍到本土学界。不过,典型作为一种理论真正对中国产生影响,则始于瞿秋白对马克思主义典型学说的译介。在西方文学史上,传统文学的理论基石之一是"典型论"。这种研究人物性格"典型化"的文学理论来自于西方文学史上源远流长的"性格类型"说。早在古希腊时代,苏格拉底便意识到"类型化"的问题,亚里斯多德则从理论上提出了"性格类型"的创造原则,要求人物性格具有普遍性和必然性(亚里斯多德49)。罗马时代的贺拉斯与古典时代的布瓦洛,提出了按人物年龄(贺拉斯146)写出他们的性格区别的类型说(布瓦洛301—302),一定程度上接触到了典型的个性特征问题。18世纪以前,西方文学的典型观念基本上是类型说。到了18世纪,狄德罗强调性格与环境的关系,与狄德罗同时代的德国美学家莱辛第一次提出了人物性格是创作中心的主张。狄德罗认为一个作家"把人物性格刻划好了,他怎么会不获得成功? 可是,人物的性格要根据他们的处境来决定","真正的对比乃性格与处境的对比"。(363)莱辛则要求性格既具有一致性和目的性而又有内在历史真实,要注重环境对性格的影响。(428)狄德罗和莱辛的观点进一步丰富了典型理论的内容,也说明了叙事文学应该把人物形象的塑造摆在更重要的位置,且重视环境与性格的关联。在黑格尔那里,"典型论"趋于成熟,他提出了具有经典意义的"这一个"的著名论断,揭示了典型性格的根本特征:丰富性、明确性和坚定性。(296—297)黑格尔为典型理论打下了坚实基础。19世纪西方现代现实主义作家注重在深入观察现实生活的基础上对客观事物加以典型化,强调塑造典型环境中的典型人物,人物形象的塑造成为文学创作的首要任务,并且将典型化人物形象的塑造作为衡量一部叙事文学作品成败与否的基本标准。对现代现实主义小说来说,"一部小说的特殊发现常常浓缩在典型人物身上,尽管表现为单个的个体"(Terras 192)。因为,"正是通过这些典型人物,社会生活更深层的力量和实际的活生生的呼吸的人物之间得以建立相互的联系,正是通过这些联系,确保了小说的现实主义"(Dentith 44)。

马克思恩格斯的现实主义文艺思想对我国文论话语体系的构建起了重要作用,其中,塑造典型环境中的典型人物的论断是这种文艺思想的重要组成部分。马克思恩格斯文艺思想的一个重要来源就是19世纪欧洲文学,尤其是现代现实主义文学。恩格斯强调现实主义要塑造"典型环境中的典型人物"(《马克思恩格斯选集》第4卷578),把典型人物的塑造和典型环境的描写辩证地结合起来,这一论断已成为文学现实主义的一个基本创作原则和审美原则。恩格斯强调的环境和人物的典型性,指的是环境和人物都要体现生活和历史发展的某些本质内容,能够表现一定的规律性;真正优秀的现实主义作品,首先要能够展现真实的、具有典型意义的社会环境,然后才能塑造具有典型意义的人物形象。因为,正如马克思所说,"人的本质并不是单个人所固有的抽象物,在其现实性上,它是一切社会关系的总和"(《马克思恩格斯选集》第1卷60);要从体现环境之典型性的"社会关系的总和"中揭示人物性格的本质特征与丰富内涵,从而使人物具有典型性。"也就是说,典型环境与典型人物,是相互依存的,一旦割裂,就不能写出既有生动个性又富有社会内涵的人物形象了"(杨守森8)。恩格斯的"典型说"和

"典型环境中的典型人物"理论,无疑是在继承了西方数千年有关典型理论的基础上提出的,尤其是在研究与总结19世纪现代现实主义经典作家创作实践基础上提出的,这一理论本身有其经典性和普适性,对我国现实主义文论与创作都产生了深远影响,不同时期我国学界对恩格斯论断的诸多阐释虽然有差异,但迄今总体形成共识。

近一百年来,现实主义文学及其理论也在不断遭遇诟病和攻击中发展演变着,迄今为止,文学现实主义不仅在继续而且势头强劲,但是,轻视、藐视乃至否定现实主义现象也依然存在,其典型人物塑造理论也不时在不同程度上被忽视。在20世纪现代主义作家那里,典型理论被忽略,在"非典型化"口号之下,人物性格的整体性、有机性被消解了。这当然不是说现代主义在人的表现和人物形象描写上毫无可取之处,事实上,这类作品的人物形象在象征隐喻和抽象晦涩中也不无深刻之处。但是,站在人类文学发展的高度和大视野去看,面对现代主义的颠覆性理论与实践,典型理论和典型人物塑造到底还有无现实价值与意义呢?鉴于此,梳理并廓新"典型"理论,重新认识叙事文学创作中典型人物塑造之内涵,归纳与总结不同时期西方文学关于典型形象塑造的理论精华与实践经验,汲取其中的合理养分,无论对重构文学研究的话语体系还是推进新时代文学创作健康发展,都是十分必要且极为重要的。为此,笔者把西方文学典型人物塑造归纳为三种基本模式:"观念—性格"模式、"性格—环境"模式和"抽象—象征"模式,并以现代现实主义文学为中心展开比较论析。

二、"观念—性格"模式

与"典型"理论在西方文学史上古已有之一样,"典型人物"塑造的创作实践也古已有之。阿喀琉斯、赫克托尔、俄狄浦斯、美狄亚、哈姆雷特、堂吉诃德、浮士德、冉·阿让等都是不朽的典型形象。不过,从人物形象塑造的角度看,古希腊神话和史诗中的典型人物性格比较简单、纯粹,它们虽然有某种个性特征,但往往只是某种人类情感或思想观念的化身,通常不具备丰富的性格内涵,尤其是,它们的性格形成通常不构成与社会环境的关联,多少有点"横空出世"的意味。这种叙事文本从口头文学演变而来,以故事的叙述为主,性格描写的意识薄弱,这正是人类"童年时期"文学的标志性特征之一:以叙述生动的故事和曲折的情节打动和吸引读者或听众(口头文学),人物形象的塑造是相对次要的。《荷马史诗》中作为古典英雄的阿喀琉斯或者赫克托尔,勇武之共性特征多于个性特征。尤其是,人物的环境是相对虚化的,因此他们的个性与共性主要随着情节的演进而不是具体环境的变化得以显现。阿喀琉斯勇武善战、嗜血成性且骄傲任性,赫克托尔勇武善战且沉稳自律、善良宽厚,他们的这种共性与个性似乎皆为神所赋予,故而几乎无文学意义上的"环境"依据。在这方面,普罗米修斯、俄狄浦斯、美狄亚等形象皆大同小异。普罗米修斯就是一个反抗和自我牺牲观念的符号;俄狄浦斯被"命运"确定为"弑父娶母",其反抗"命运"本身就是"命运"赋予他的既定性格;美狄亚的刚烈及其弑子的冷酷,似乎也是神赋予的,既不合乎性格逻辑,也缺乏环境依据。这类人物通常都是某种观念的承载者,其性格与某种观念直接关联却疏离于具体的环境,因此,笔者认为它们大致上可指称为"观念—性格型"模式的典型人物。这种观念的赋予者貌似是神格化的"命运"或者人格化的神本身,而实质上是这种特定文学文本的口头传叙者。由于历史之遥远和口口相传的繁复交替,口头传叙者也就消隐在时间的幕后,文本内容及观念的历史具体性和时代性也在传叙过程中被消磨得依稀模糊,人物的思想与性格也通常缺乏现实性及具体的时代和历史的印记。因此,此类"观念—性格"模式的典型人物不无概念化特征。

人们通常说堂吉诃德是一个不朽的艺术典型,这是无可争议的。塞万提斯在《堂吉诃德》的创作中已经有了较为鲜明的人物塑造和性格刻画的意识,堂吉诃德和桑丘可以说性格分明。堂吉诃德这个人物是喜剧性和悲剧性的矛盾统一,这不仅造成了其性格的两重性,也反映了这个人物思想上的复杂性;他是一个不识时务的荒唐的行侠者,又是一个见义勇为、匡扶正义的理想主义者。然而,他的性格也不过是作者观念的产物,而不是环境的产物。作者宣称:他写这部作品是为了攻击骑士小说,把骑士小说的那一套扫除干净。塞万提斯仿效骑士小说的形式创作出了《堂吉诃德》,而且,堂吉诃德形象的精神面貌全然不同于当时流行的骑士小说中的骑士形象。这里,人物之"观念"的赋予者是作者塞万提斯自己,这种"观念"有明确的现实针对性,因此,《堂吉诃德》的时代性和当下性较强,这样的作品不无时代的和现实的意义。但是,堂吉诃德的性格也几乎是一成不变的,与环境没有必然联系。他最终唯一变化的是,经过反复的失败冒险游侠之后,认识到了骑士小说的危害,最后终止了冒险游侠生活。这种观念的变化恰恰是塞万提斯创作这部小说所要达成的目标——抛弃骑士小说。所以,尽管中外学界通常将这部小说称为西方文学史上早期的现实主义作品,其实,那也只不过是指宽泛意义上具有一定真实性的创作风格而言,而决不属于相对成熟意义上的"现实主义"范畴。显然,从人物塑造角度看,堂吉诃德不是典型环境中生成的典型人物,而是作者观念统摄下的"观念—性格"模式的典型人物;《堂吉诃德》显然也不属于真正的现实主义文学小说,而是既有传奇性又不乏现实性的新形态的"流浪汉小说"。

与之相仿,作为人类文学史上不朽典型的哈姆雷特,其性格虽然有从忧郁、延宕到行动的变化过程,但是也不构成性格与环境的互动关系和必然联系。哈姆雷特性格的核心元素是"忧郁"和"延宕","忧郁的王子"是他的别称。作者从剧本一开始就已经赋予了哈姆雷特的核心性格元素,剧情发展与人物的行动,都只不过在"展示"这种性格元素。哈姆雷特最后的复仇"行动"——杀死新国王克劳狄斯,也不过是情节发展对人物行为的一种短暂的终极性激发,却并未在整体上改变人物性格的核心元素。因此,莎士比亚致力于描写的是剧情的推进和场景的变化,而并不是在描写环境如何构成对性格的演变或改造。事实上,剧本也并未描写一个与人物性格相应的环境,而最多只不过描写了人物活动的场景或情境而已。虽然,哈姆雷特确实因其象征性地表现了人在特定历史时期的迷惘与困惑(蒋承勇,《哈姆莱特:人类自身迷惘的艺术象征》97),使剧本也有反映特定社会状况的历史意蕴,但全剧不构成典型人物性格与具体现实环境的互动关系。在整个作品中,矛盾、迷惘,"思想的巨人、行动的矮子"几乎成了作者赋予人物的既定观念,情节描写为演绎这种观念服务。因此,哈姆雷特形象实际上也就成了这种观念的化身和象征,他总体上也属于"观念—性格"模式的典型。歌德笔下的浮士德也是如此,他是人类不断追求之欲望与意志的显现,也属于"观念—性格"模式的典型形象。(117)

　　即使是被称为"现实主义小说"的18世纪英国小说,其中的人物也未曾达到"典型环境中的典型人物"的塑造高度。伊恩·瓦特(Ian Watt)在《小说的兴起》一书中指出:在18世纪,古老的叙事文学发展成现代意义上的"小说",笛福、理查逊和菲尔丁等人的作品采用"现实主义"的表现手法。(11)丹尼尔·笛福的创作标志着英国长篇小说的成形或形成,所以他被称为"英国和欧洲小说之父"(Richetti 26)。他的创作涉及了小说"真正的真实"问题(23),他以亲身的实践赋予真实以具体的时代内涵和意义(41)。笛福所主张的"真实"是指小说与现实生活层面的一致性,他强调的是一种"真正的真实"(26)、"历史的真实"(28)。他将创作对象确定在个体的人所经历的具体事件上,让个体经验成为关注的焦点。看起来,笛福的小说理念和创作风格在追求真实性这一点上似乎已经接近于19世纪现代现实主义,然而,实际上这种关于"真实"的追求仅仅停留在题材的真实和故事同现实生活有关联的层面上,尚未指涉对生活本质真实的追求,尤其是在人物塑造上不属于在典型环境中塑造典型人物的范畴。《鲁滨逊漂流记》的故事来源于一个富有传奇色彩的事件,笛福受这一事件的启发,经过自己的再创作形成了小说《鲁滨逊漂流记》。笛福说,"一个社会应该坚定地相信,聪明、智慧、勤劳、勇敢的人,必定取得不同凡响的成就"(Novak 106)。鲁滨逊身上无疑表现了这种富于新教精神的现代个人主义思想,鲁滨逊式的英雄主义也成了"体现西方人精神品格的基本因素之一"(Tournier 183)。从人物形象塑造来看,鲁滨逊身上的这种现代个人主义思想,正是作者要传达的观念。鲁滨逊所处的那个荒岛不具备生成其思想观念的社会依据,他与自然环境抗争的精神是人的抽象意志和精神的表现。小说表达的是一种资本主义时代资产者的开拓精神。伊恩·瓦特说,"小说的时间尺度常常自相矛盾,并且与书中所假设的历史背景不协调"(Watt 24)。这恰恰说明了笛福这部小说的"现实主义"更多地体现为题材的现实性和第一人称叙事个人经历的真实感,以及所表达的主题思想具有一定的时代性,这相对于热衷于想象、虚幻、抒情的浪漫主义小说来说,自然更富于"现实主义"精神,但还不属于19世纪成熟的现代现实主义文学的观念范畴,鲁滨逊也不具备性格塑造的丰富性和内涵的深刻性。因此,鲁滨逊依然属于"观念—性格"模式的典型人物。

19世纪浪漫主义小说家维克多·雨果的作品塑造了一系列人物形象:卡西莫多、爱斯梅拉尔达、克罗德·弗洛诺、冉·阿让等。就这些人物形象所表达的思想意义而言,显然具有现实性以及社会批判性,就某些人物的艺术感染力之经久强盛而言,它们无疑是西方文学史上难得的典型人物;但是,这些人物也依然属于"观念—性格"模式的典型。《悲惨世界》是雨果小说中最具现实主义色彩的,冉·阿让这一人物也极具艺术感染力。然而,他是一个寄寓了雨果人道主义理想的传奇人物,在创作技巧上体现了雨果式浪漫主义的想象与夸张。初始,冉·阿让的性格从善良到阴冷的转变,起因于他为饥饿中的外甥偷面包而被判监禁，其一再出逃又被逮回监狱并屡受增加刑期的处罚，他被那个社会的法律及持有某种社会偏见的人认定为社会的"破坏者"。作者借此演绎证明了法律和社会偏见的不合理、非人道。后来，卞福汝主教对他施之以博大的爱与宽容，这种道德感化奇迹般地改变了冉•阿让的思想与性格，从此他成了博爱的化身，又传奇般地做了许多拯救他人的高尚、感人的善行，最终这种善行战胜了铁石心肠的法律与社会偏见之化身的沙威警官。小说故事的叙述和情节的演进，无不在演绎博爱、慈悲、宽容战胜冷酷、偏见和狭隘的人道理想，而不是通过描写环境去揭示人物性格形成与演变的依据，进而塑造性格丰满的典型人物；人物的思想、情感和个性特征无不是作者一厢情愿的赋予，而极少有现实生活环境和性格生成与演变的逻辑互动依据。于是，冉•阿让形象神圣高大且感人肺腑，人物性格却是凌空蹈虚，丰富性、生动性、深刻性皆无从谈起。由此，我们当然地认定《悲惨世界》是浪漫主义的小说，而非有的研究者说的现实主义小说。雨果笔下的冉•阿让无疑也属于"观念—性格"模式的典型形象。

总之，19世纪现代现实主义之前的西方文学，纵然有许多不同和不朽的典型人物，但是总体上都是转达作者思想与观念的符号化、类型化人物，故事的展开与情节的推进主要是演绎作者的某种思想、观念抑或哲理，因此，这类人物大致上都属于"观念—性格"模式的典型，与现代现实主义文学"典型环境中的典型人物"理念意义上的"环境—性格"模式的典型人物有迥然之异。

三、"环境—性格"模式

到了19世纪现代现实主义文学中，典型人物的塑造有了崭新的面貌与内涵。现代现实主义作家总体上反对人物塑造的主观性与概念化倾向，格外重视客观真实的人物形象塑造，追求人物性格刻画的独特性

("这一个")和丰富性("普遍性"),使之富于深刻的社会历史内涵和审美意蕴。这类作品通过塑造生动的人物形象,从而具有道德伦理的功能(Harvey 31)。现代现实主义小说家普遍强调并致力于塑造典型环境中的典型人物,他们不满于浪漫派将人物过分理想化而忽视环境影响的主观主义创作方法,强调人是社会环境的产物,主张从人物所处的社会历史环境和现实情势中刻画人物性格,真实地揭示人物和事件的本质特征及其发展趋势,体现文学"写实""求真"的实证性原则,从而达成文学文本与现实生活之间高度密切的同构关系。正如德国文学批评家奥尔巴赫(Erich Auerbach)所说,较之于之前的文学,现代现实主义的作品"与当时的政治、社会、经济结合的更加密切,显得更为重要,更有自觉意识,描写得也更加具体"(458)。英国作家 J. A. 卡登(J. A. Cuddon)则认为:"根据现实主义者的说法,艺术家应当关切此时此地,应当关切日常的事件以及本人所在的环境和所处时代的各种(政治和社会等)运动。"(591)可见,现代现实主义在典型人物的塑造上特别强调人物与环境的关系。出于对社会问题的特别关注,现代现实主义作家对人的关注视点主要集中在人的社会性、阶级(阶层)性上,也就特别关注人物与现实社会之关系;人物性格的形成与发展,都有其生活和社会环境的逻辑依据;不同作家和作品笔下的人物,就像处于社会网络的不同方位的聚焦点上,可以折射社会的不同状况。"大多数现实主义作家都不会描写出性格完全不连贯、不完整的人物"(Taillis 69)。从作品的底蕴上来说,现代现实主义文学基本上可以被看作对社会及生活于其间的人所进行的伦理学、政治学和经济学的研究。与此相应,现实的社会现象也就合乎逻辑地成了现代现实主义作家为揭示社会不完善之基本主题所通用的和决定性的题材。理性书写原则让现代现实主义作家不愿再将笔下的人物像以往的文学那样神圣化、情感化和理想化以及时空的虚化,而是最大限度地将其生活化、历史化、时代化和"人化",写出特定现实、特定时空中人的内心世界的丰富性与生动性,并努力把这种丰富性通过性格的复杂性展示出来。这是现代现实主义文学在人物形象塑造上的一种总体价值取向与美学追求。巴尔扎克在《人间喜剧》导言中说："不仅仅是人物,就是生活上的主要事件,也用典型表达出来。"(176)别林斯基更把人物塑造的典型化提到了事关艺术创作是否具有独创性的高度,他认为,"典型性是创作的基本法则之一,没有典型性,就没有创作"(《别林斯基选集》第2卷25)。并且,"创作的独创性,或者更确切地说,创作本身的显著标志之一,就是典型性","在一位具有真正才能的人写来,每一个人物都是典型"(《别林斯基选集》第1卷191)。也就是说,作家塑造出了典型人物,就说明其创作有了独创性,其创作也就有了艺术的生命力。由于现代现实主义的"典型人物"必然地生成、生存于"典型环境",与其所处的现实社会达成密切关联,因此,这种人物除了具有"典型性"之外,其性格必然地带有现实环境的深刻印记,是特定时代、特定社会的产物。于是,塑造"典型环境中的典型人物"成了现代现实主义文学在人物塑造上的一条基本准则,也是检验现实主义文学本质特征的重要原则。循着这条原则,我们可以梳理和罗列一系列类似的人物形象:于连、拉斯蒂涅、高老头、葛朗台、爱玛、培基·夏泼、简·爱、大卫·科波菲尔、苔丝、泼留希金、安娜·卡列尼娜、聂赫留朵夫、娜拉、汤姆·索耶安等,他们的性格内涵的形成或展现都离不开所处的环境,环境的描写服务于人物性格的铸造与展示。为此,笔者把这类人物形象称之为"环境—性格"模式的典型人物。通过这种模式的典型人物塑造,现代现实主义把叙事文学之人物形象塑造艺术推向了西方文学史上的历史新刻度,这是现代现实主义文学对西方文学乃至整个人类文学的重要贡献。

司汤达《红与黑》塑造了于连这个光彩夺目的典型人物;可以说,于连世界文学之典型形象塑造的经典案例,也是现代现实主义文学之美学和艺术成就的重要标示。于连无疑是一个个人奋斗者的形象。强烈的自我意识是其性格之核心元素,这种自我意识生发于那个张扬自由主义、个人主义的19世纪初的法国社会,它在特定的环境外力作用下,又生出自由平等观念、自我反抗意识和强烈的个人野心。在环境与性格之张力的作用下,于连的性格内涵得以形成和展示。司汤达"一心一意地倾注于社会现象的每一个细枝末节,高度准确地塑造每一个环境的特定结构"(Auerbach 463)。从典型人物与典型环境之关系角度看,《红与黑》十分典型地体现了"典型环境中的典型人物"塑造的准则。于连一生的奋斗,主要在维立叶尔城、贝尚松神学院和巴黎木尔侯爵府这三个典型环境中。小说通过对现实环境变迁与人物性格展示的互动关系的描写,揭示性格的丰富性、复杂性及其形成与演变的社会原因。"在司汤达的现实主义作品中,所描写的都是他在生活中遭遇的现实本身"(462);"所有的人物形象和人物的行为都是在社会和政治的变化中得以展示的"(463)。《红与黑》经典性地体现了现代现实主义"环境—性格"模式的典型人物塑造的特点。

　　巴尔扎克提出了环境乃"人物和他们的思想的物质表现"(166)这一著名论断,把典型人物的塑造作为再现社会历史真实风貌的重要途径。而且,在他的理解中,"典型人物"是许多同类性格特点的人的高度概括,是"类的样本",因而在描写时不可能"包括着所有那些在某种程度跟它相似的人们的最鲜明的性格特征"(童庆炳、马新国 1280);塑造典型的材料必须是生活"事实";于是,通过这种"典型人物"的塑造就可以达到再现现实社会"风俗史"的总目标。巴尔扎克的小说极为重视事实之"实证";在他笔下,人的生存环境——无论是物质环境还是社会环境,对人的性格都起着决定性的作用。"在巴尔扎克所有的作品中,环境随处可见,那简直是一种生物和魔力的合二为一、千姿百态的环境,而且它们总是力图让读者感受到这种环境的存在"(Auerbach 473)。因为在巴尔扎克看来,"社会环境是社会加自然"(166),所以他以一种类比的思维来描写人物与环境:"动物是这样一种元素,它的外形,或者说得更恰当些,它的形式的种种差异,取决于它必须在那里长大的环境"(164);"在这一点上,社会和自然相似。社会不是按照人类展开活动的环境,把人类陶冶成无数不同的人,如同动物之有千殊万类么?"(165)正是这种类比的方法与理念,使巴尔扎克的人物塑造格外重视性格与环境的联系。"人与环境一致的观念对巴尔扎克产生了巨大的影响,因为对他而言,构成环境的物对于人通常有第二种意义,这是一种既不同于理性,又比理性更加重要的意义"(472)。他笔下的主人公,几乎始终处于物质环境和社会环境的重重包围与"压迫"之中,他们与环境搏斗,但又无法高于环境和超越环境,而往往被环境所战胜、改造和重塑。他们与环境搏斗的过程,在终极意义上成了向环境学习并顺应环境的过程,于是,性格的形成、发展与演变依赖于、受制于环境,最终达成了环境对人物性格的铸造。长篇小说《高老头》中的拉斯蒂涅便是一个典型代表。他就是在巴黎上流社会那灯红酒绿、金钱支配一切的环境的诱惑与"铸造"下完成了野心家性格的发展历程的,环境对人物性格的形成与展示起着决定性作用。巴尔扎克对拉斯蒂涅这一人物形象的塑造,其着力点不像司汤达那样重在展示性格的复杂性、多面性及性格对环境的抗拒,而是重在展示环境和金钱(它其实也是客观上的"环境")对人性的腐蚀作用。巴尔扎克的这些描写应该说不无艺术夸张的成分,但在艺术性的集中和夸张中把握了金钱时代人性异化的本质特征。作为西方文学史上又一个个人奋斗者的典型形象,拉斯蒂涅与司汤达笔下的于连形象不同,他不具备于连那种对环境的强烈的抗争力,而更突出的是对环境的顺应和接纳,因此,这个人物也就没有于连性格的矛盾性、复杂性以及由此而生的心理与情感冲突的张力。这恰恰体现了巴尔扎克在人物塑造上的科学类比思维与实证理性特点:人与物质环境的关系就像动物和环境的关系,人的思想源于所处的物质环境。"巴尔扎克对环境的真实描写的风格是他所生活的那个时代的产物"(Auerbach 473)。"巴尔扎克在自己的作品中感受到了那种姿态万千的生物与魔法的力量交混在一起的环境,他总是力图把这种对环境的感受传达给读者"(473)。巴尔扎克自己说,"在形形式式的生活中表现出来的处境,有典型的阶段,而这就是我刻意追求的一种准确"(176)。在巴尔扎克的创作中,典型环境与典型人物的关系集中体现为人物对环境的依存性,环境是性格形成与展现的物质前提与依据。这正是巴尔扎克式"环境—性格"模式的典型人物铸造的现代现实主义风格。巴尔扎克通过这种人物描写方法,表达了他对物欲横流、人被普遍"物化"的现实世界的深刻洞察与理解,体现其观察和揭示人性及社会的深邃性与真实性,他笔下的人物形象也因此承载了独特的艺术魅力和思想魅力。

安娜·卡列尼娜是19世纪现实主义文学中又一个光彩夺目的典型人物。在小说的最初构思中,安娜是一个堕落的女人。显然,托尔斯泰原先心目中的安娜是一个否定性人物,她是《战争与和平》中那个爱伦式放荡女人的重现。若此,安娜就成了一个情欲的化身,一个精神和灵魂匮乏的"动物的人"(也即"肉体的人")——这是托尔斯泰予以极力否定并在创作中反复表现的关于"人"的理解的一种观念。但是,在实际创作过程中,托尔斯泰却赋予安娜以精神和灵魂的内涵,使其由"动物的人"向"精神的人"(也即灵魂的人)提升,但"动物的人"同时仍以一种强烈的生命欲求和生命活力的形式存活于其间,其性格底蕴表现为尖锐的双重矛盾,人物的性格内涵和精神—情感世界就得以拓展并充满了张力,而且人物的行为也因此与她所处的环境发生了尖锐的冲突——生命力的欲求与庸俗环境的冲突。小说在多重矛盾的碰撞中最终把安娜塑造成了一个激荡着生命活力、坚定地追求新生活、具有个性解放特点的贵族妇女形象,她的悲剧是她的性格与社会环境发生尖锐冲突的必然结果,也是其性格之内在双重矛盾尖锐冲突的结果。可以说,安娜形象的审美奥秘主要生发于其以强劲生命力为底蕴的叛逆性格。在托尔斯泰看来,安娜的追求尽管有合乎人性之善的一面,但是,距离善与人道的最高形式——爱他人,为他人而活着——却还有很大的距离。这就是作者对安娜态度矛盾的根本原因，也是安娜内心矛盾和性格冲突的根本原因。而从典型人物塑造的角度看，正是这种矛盾因素提升了人物形象的生活气息和真实性以及审美的张力，既使小说对人性的开掘大大地深化，又使人物形象的艺术魅力显著提升。

　　需要进一步辨析的是，如果说司汤达笔下的于连表现了性格与环境的互动关系，巴尔扎克笔下的拉斯蒂涅表现了性格对环境被动接纳，那么，托尔斯泰笔下的安娜则表现了性格对环境的强力抵御和抗争。《红与黑》中于连性格与环境的关系是双向互动的辩证关系，性格与环境之间富有张力。于连性格中的这种对环境的抵抗力和自我调节能力，造成了于连在与社会搏斗过程中复杂多变的心理世界，使这一形象的性格演变显得丰富多彩，也使这个人物深深打上了时代的印记。从典型人物塑造的角度看，体现出了现代现实主义"写实"与"求真"的基本宗旨。在托尔斯泰笔下，虽然安娜的性格是在同环境不断的冲突、碰撞中得以彰显的，但是，她对平庸与伪善的现实环境始终表现了奋力的抵御和抗争，环境和性格始终处于对立的状态，环境并不构成对性格的再造和重塑；安娜的性格与环境的关系不表现为前者对后者的生成性依存，而是对抗性展示。由是，人物的精神品格与平庸而险恶的环境形成了善与恶的鲜明对照，安娜也就成了污浊环境中的"异类"——一个令人同情和惋惜的正面形象。这就体现了作为俄罗斯作家的托尔斯泰——其实也包括其他的俄罗斯现实主义作家——在"典型环境中的典型人物"塑造方面体现的基本风格，其间淡化了巴尔扎克式法国作家的那种环境决定人的思想与性格的物质主义和环境主义特点，而强化了人物之主体意识和主观能动性。这样的人物形象富于情感的和精神、心灵的润泽，具有别一种艺术和思想的魅力，也足见托尔斯泰在典型人物塑造上独特的现代现实主义风格。

　　现代现实主义这种"环境—性格"模式的典型人物，因其带有不可磨灭的时代和社会历史的印记，其性格内蕴也必然透射出特定时代之社会历史和生活的本质特征,于是,人物塑造本身也就是"再现"或"反映"现实生活的重要途径,读者也可以通过这样的人物形象认识现实生活。正如英国作家特罗洛普所说,19世纪现代现实主义小说家通过塑造真实的人物形象感动读者、"引发泪水",最终揭示"关于人的真理"(Allott 68)。在某种意义上,现代现实主义文学的典型人物既是作品思想内容的载体,也是某个时代与社会的形象化符号;它们都必然地存活于某个"典型环境"——某个特定的时代与社会,而不是一个超时代、超时空的形象。

四、"抽象—象征"模式

经过19世纪末非现实主义文学思潮和流派的过度,历史发展到20世纪,大部分现代主义者既不屑于"观念—性格"模式的人物塑造,更不屑于现代现实主义式的人物塑造,而是反叛性地消解人物的性格,淡化人物与现实环境之间的逻辑关系。新小说派代表罗伯-格里耶说,"以人物形象为中心的小说完全已经成为过去"(Robber-Grillet 28),人物的真实性已经成为"远古的神话"(23);博尔赫斯则认为"我的小说里根本没有人物"(Newman and Kinzie 399)。当然,他们这么说,并不意味着其作品真的就不塑造人物或没有人物,而只是关于人物塑造的观念有所不同而已。不过,不可否认的是,在现代主义倾向的作品中,人物的典型性、形象性和现实性被消解以后确实趋于抽象化、隐喻性、象征性和超现实性;人物的崇高美也被"以丑为美"所取代,"英雄"成了"反英雄""非英雄";人物的塑造也趋于"非典型化"。"20世纪的创新作家,包括从詹姆斯·乔伊斯到法国的新小说家,以及荒诞戏剧、小说及实验各种不同形式的作家,常常在作品中以违反常规的手法塑造人物,即他们不是通过展示人物个性特征的一致性来塑造逼真的人物形象"(艾布拉姆斯47)。有鉴于此,笔者认为现代主义倾向的文学的典型人物属于"象征—抽象"模式。

詹姆斯·乔伊斯的《尤利西斯》是意识流小说的代表作之一，其中的核心人物布鲁姆是一个极为普通的现代人。他既非天使又非恶魔，既不是超凡脱俗的英雄又不是卑鄙无耻的小人；他的意识和行为既表现了一切时代最普通的人的本性，又显示出典型的现代特征和个体特征。乔伊斯在塑造布鲁姆形象时所采取的是一种超然的态度，写他的平庸并无讽刺意味，写他的挫折并无感伤之情，甚至在描写他最富于吸引力的同情心和人情味时也绝无颂扬的语气。乔伊斯对布鲁姆所作的不是价值的评判，而是对现实存在的认同并客观地描述。小说给我们展示的布鲁姆就是这样一个失去了传统文学人物的崇高性，精神空虚、人格分裂、人性处处受到伤害而又无力自救的"非英雄"或"反英雄"，更是一个失去性格的丰富性和完整性的"非典型"人物，一个与环境失去有机逻辑联系的抽象类型。布鲁姆是现代人的某种精神状态的象征或隐喻，是一个典型的非性格化的象征性人物形象，也即"抽象—象征"模式的典型。奥尼尔《毛猿》作为表现主义戏剧的代表作之一，其中的人物更具有抽象和象征的特性。主人公扬克与其说是一个有血有肉、鲜明生动的典型人物，不如说是一个含蓄抽象的观念与意志的象征符号。扬克是一艘邮轮上的火炉工，在整个剧本中，邮轮、监狱、动物园的铁笼是他有形的物质生活环境，但是这些环境物只是现代社会的抽象化象征——人赖以生存的抽象意义上的"笼子"，它不构成与人物性格的互动关系，因此不是展现人物性格的"典型环境"。这种抽象化的环境不具备表现人物性格的功能，而主要是人物精神意象的外化。扬克的抗争过程实际上是从一个"笼子"到另一个"笼子"的过程，象征性地表现了现代人难以摆脱异己力量的悲剧命运。与之相仿，卡夫卡笔下的土地测量员 K 和大甲虫、加缪《局外人》中的莫尔索、萨特《恶心》中的洛根丁、海勒《第二十二条军规》中的尤索林等，皆属"抽象—象征"模式的典型。

"抽象—象征"模式的人物作为20世纪现代主义文学中反传统、实验性的典型,标志着西方文学在典型人物塑造方面从观念到方法上的演变。它们通常不属于某个具体社会环境——典型环境——中具有特定现实意义的"这一个",而是某个超现实"情境"中具有普遍性意义的"这一个"。相较而言,"抽象—象征"模式的典型与"观念—性格"模式的典型相类似,偏于观念的表达而虚于性格刻画。就思想观念的表达方式而言,前者是作者隐逸后的象征性表达,后者是一种作者直陈式表达。相较而言,"环境—性格"模式的典型人物也有作者思想与观念的表达,但这种表达是十分隐晦、含蓄的,是在生动、鲜明、丰富的性格刻画中自然而然地流露出来的,性格大于思想,形象大于观念,从而体现出文学现实主义所追求的客观性与真实性特质。

五、"模式"体认与去"模式化"

　　上述对三种典型人物塑造模式的归类,在宏观上梳理了西方文学中人物形象塑造的历史演进过程。既然是"宏观"的归类,就难免挂一漏万甚至削足适履。因为任何一种归类分析都有因其边界的模糊性以及类与类之间的交叉重叠,导致这种归类不可能绝对准确,而仅仅是一种大致上的区分与概括,因而无法一一解说难以数计和丰富多彩的个体事物的独特性。不过,对任何事物做相对抽象化与理论性的归纳研究都是必须的,因为这有助于对事物的复杂现象作分门别类、条分细缕基础上的概括而抽象化的理解与把握,进而从个别性和一般性中把握普遍性与特殊性。笔者对西方文学典型人物塑造的模式作上述归类与辨析,其宗旨是为了宏观上把握西方文学在典型人物塑造的理论观念与创作实践上的演变过程,体悟不同历史时期和社会背景下作家与文学对人的洞察、理解与表现方法之差异,尤其是力图在比较辨析的基础上更集中、突出地界定现代现实主义文学在典型人物塑造上的突出特点、历史贡献与现实价值。

必须说明的是,就文学史意义与价值而言,不同类型的典型人物生成于不同时代与不同文化土壤,各自标示着西方文学的特定文化内涵与历史进程,却很难似乎也没必要区分彼此在艺术水平上的高下与优劣。只要体认这些典型人物作为文学经典的基本元素,体认其永久的文学史价值与艺术魅力,因而不可互相替代即可。正如马克思在论及古希腊神话时所说的那样,"人类童年时代"的艺术是"永不复返"和"高不可及"的"范本",具有"永久的魅力"(《马克思恩格斯选集》第 2 卷 32)。在这种意义上,阿喀琉斯、堂吉诃德、哈姆雷特、浮士德等形象都是代表了不同时代的文学典型,不可或缺,彼此不可替代;后来的于连、拉斯蒂涅、安娜·卡列尼娜等也不可替代前者。从读者接受的角度看,正是这些不同时代的典型人物形象,给不同读者以丰富多彩、各取所需的审美资源,人们可以在经典性人物形象的历史长廊中反复流连、不断品味,领略其无穷的人文意蕴和恒久之艺术魅力。不过,就这"三模式"典型人物而言,"观念—性格"模式和"环境—性格"模式的人物形象显然更有其通俗性与可鉴赏性,而"抽象—象征"模式典型虽有其实验性创新及独特之审美价值和文学史贡献,却因其特有的抽象性艰涩和审美趣味的"颠覆性"从而增加了读者理解、接受与鉴赏的难度,由此也与读者拉开了心理距离。所以,"抽象—象征"模式的典型人物的通俗性与可鉴赏性程度偏低。就此而论,"抽象—象征"模式的典型人物虽有其对前两种类型的人物塑造的创新与超越,但并不意味着就是最完善和最先进从而更受读者欢迎的。文学艺术之价值并不以"新"与"旧"作为衡量标准,"新"的不一定意味着超越"旧",传统的作品不意味着"落后"于新兴作品;文学艺术强调传承中的延续与发展,"旧"在"新"中的延续,"新"者只能代表自己而不能取代和覆盖"旧"者,而是各有其审美价值、文学史价值和艺术生命力。总体而言,"观念—性格"模式的典型和"环境—性格"模式的典型倒是更受当下读者的欢迎与接受,其经典的意义和现实价值也就更高。尤其是现代现实主义文学的"环境—性格"模式的典型人物,因其对人性和人类本质的揭示而表现其深刻性的一面,又因其生动形象、贴近生活而表现其更切合读者审美期待视野的一面。就叙事性文学的人物性格描写而言,无论较之"观念—性格"模式还是较之"抽象—象征"模式的典型,都相对更注重人物性格、现实环境和历史演变三者的立体化互动关系,这种典型人物的人文内涵和审美内涵通常也相对更加丰富。

众所周知,文学是人学,关注"人"是任何时代的文学之共同而本质的特征,描写人及其生存状态是人类文学"艺术地掌握世界的方式"(《马克思恩格斯选集》第2卷104)的根本任务。而人是一切社会关系的总和,把人物的描写置于现实环境及历史演变密切结合的立体互动关系之中,这种典型形象之性格形成于特殊的社会历史环境中,这种性格有深刻的内涵——其间隐含了复杂而丰富的社会历史信息和时代氛围。这也正是现代现实主义塑造"典型环境中的典型人物"原则具有普遍性意义与价值的根本原因,也是现代现实主义永久生命力产生缘由之一。英国作家特罗洛普说,19世纪现代现实主义小说家通过塑造真实的人物形象感动读者、"引发泪水",最终揭示"关于人的真理"(Allott 68)。对此,卢卡契的阐释更具经典意味:"现实主义的主要范畴和标准乃典型,这是将人物和环境两者中间的一般和特殊加以有机结合的一种综合。使典型成为典型的并不是它的一般的性质(无论想象得如何深刻),使典型成为典型的乃它身上一切人和社会所不可缺少的决定因素都是在它们最高的发展水平上,在它们潜在的可能性彻底的暴露中,在它们那些使人和时代的顶峰和界限具体化的极端的全面表现中呈现出来。"(卢卡契48)从马克思主义文艺观看,只有那些时代与历史蕴含丰富,揭示了社会历史发展趋势性格和环境才算得上"典型环境中的典型人物"。正是在这方面,现代现实主义文学表现出了其突出的成就,也是在这种意义上,"环境—性格"模式的典型至今依旧特别具有艺术魅力。这样说并不意味着让我们在典型观念和典型人物塑造上走入"模式化"的狭隘境地,而旨在通过"模式"的归类与体认对文学中丰富繁杂的典型人物有一种自觉而深度的理解与把握,进而在接纳人类文学中关于人的描写与表现以及人物形象塑造的各种模式之优长基础上,让我们的文学创作更深刻而艺术地揭示变动不居的社会环境中人的生存状况,塑造更具时代特色的典型人物现象。因此,通过模式化的归类辨析,其根本目的是让我们在获得对丰富复杂的人物形象相对深入又更清晰的辨识与体认的基础上,最终超越"模式"的阈限,达成去"模式化"。我们肯定现代现实主义的独特个性与价值,但我们倡导的是开放包容、更具人类情怀和世界意识的文学现实主义精神。无论从文学创作、文学研究还是文学鉴赏角度看,我们都要打破"模式"或"主义"之类的既有框定与限制,总结并接纳不同模式与类型的文学在典型人物塑造方面的成功经验,借以繁荣新时代本土之文学创作,推进文学研究话语体系的建设,提升读者的人文素养与艺术情操。就此而论,从典型人物塑造的"模式"体认到去"模式化"的思考,旨在追求弘扬传统与突破传统基础上的创新。

注解【Note】

① 笔者指称19世纪现实主义文学为"现代现实主义",是因为这种文学相较于之前的"写实"倾向的文学,表现出了"现代性"特征。请参阅蒋承勇《现代现实主义及其"现代性"内涵考论》,《文艺研究》2022年第1期,第69—79页。

引用文献【Works Cited】

艾布拉姆斯等:《文学术语词典》,吴松江等编译,北京大学出版社,2014年。
[Abrams, M. H., et al. *A Glossary of Literary Terms*. Edited and translated by Wu Songjiang, et al, Peking UP, 2014.]
Allott, Miriam. *Novelists on the Novel*. Routledge & Kegan Paul, 1959.
亚里斯多德:《诗学》,罗念生译,人民文学出版社,1988年。
[Aristotle. *Poetics*. Translated by Luo Niansheng, People's Literature Publishing

House, 1988.]

Auerbach, Erich. *Mimesis: The Representation of Reality in Western Literature*. Princeton UP, 2003.

巴尔扎克:《〈人间喜剧〉前言》,陈占元译,《西方文论选》(下卷),伍蠡甫主编,上海译文出版社,1979年,第164—177页。

[Balzac, Honoré de. "The Preface of *La comédie humaine*." Translated by Chen Zhanyuan, *The Selection of Western Literary Theories*, vol. 2, edited by Wu Lifu, Shanghai Translation Publishing House, 1979, pp. 164 – 77.]

别林斯基:《别林斯基选集》(第1卷),满涛译,上海译文出版社,1979年。

[Belinsky, Vissarion Grigoryevich. *Selected Works of Belinsky*. Vol. 1, translated by Man Tao, Shanghai Translation Publishing House, 1979.]

别林斯基:《别林斯基选集》(第2卷),满涛译,上海译文出版社,1963年。

[---. *Selected Works of Belinsky*. Vol. 2, translated by Man Tao, Shanghai Translation Publishing House, 1963.]

布瓦洛:《诗的艺术》,《西方文论选》(上卷),伍蠡甫主编,上海译文出版社,1979年,第289—303页。

[Boileau, Nicolas. *L'Art poetique*. *The Selection of Western Literary Theories*, vol. 1, edited by Wu Lifu, Shanghai Translation Publishing House, 1979, pp. 289 – 303.]

马克思恩格斯列宁斯大林著作中共中央编译局编译:《马克思恩格斯选集》(第1卷),人民出版社,1995年。

[Central Compilation and Translation Bureau of Works of Marx, Engels, Lenin and Stalin. *The Selected Works of Marx and Engels*. Vol. 1, People's Publishing House, 1995.]

——:《马克思恩格斯选集》(第2卷),人民出版社,1972年。

[---. *The Selected Works of Marx and Engels*. Vol. 2, People's Publishing House, 1972.]

——:《马克思恩格斯选集》(第4卷),人民出版社,2012年。

[---. *The Selected Works of Marx and Engels*. Vol. 4, People's Publishing House, 2012.]

Cuddon, J. A. *A Dictionary of Literary Terms and Literary Theory*. 5th ed., Wiley-Blackwell, 2013.

Dentith, Simon. "Realist Synthesis in the Nineteenth-Century Novel: 'That Unity Which Lies in the Selection of Our Keenest Consciousnesses'." *Adventures in Realism*, edited by Matthew Beaumont, Blackwell Publishing Ltd., 2007, pp. 33 - 49.

狄德罗:《论戏剧艺术》,《西方文论选》(上卷),伍蠡甫主编,上海译文出版社,1979年,第347—395页。

[Diderot, Denis. *De la poésie dramatique*. *The Selection of Western Literary Theories*, vol.1, edited by Wu Lifu, Shanghai Translation Publishing House, 1979, pp.347‐95.]

《中国大百科全书·中国文学》(第1卷),中国大百科全书出版社,1986年。

[*Encyclopedia of China: Chinese Literature*. Vol. 1, edited and published by Encyclopedia of China Publishing House, 1986.]

Harvey, W. J. *Character and Novel*. Chatto & Windus, 1965.

黑格尔:《美学》,《西方文论选》(下卷),伍蠡甫主编,上海译文出版社,1979年,第292—317页。

[Hegel, G. W. F. *Vortesungenueber die Aesthetik*. *The Selection of Western Literary Theories*, vol.2, edited by Wu Lifu, Shanghai Translation Publishing House, 1979, pp.292‐317.]

贺拉斯:《诗艺》,杨周翰译,人民文学出版社,1988年。

[Horatius. *Ars Poetica*. Translated by Yang Zhouhan, People's Literature Publishing House, 1988.]

蒋承勇:《浮士德与欧洲"近代人"文化价值核心》,《外国文学评论》第2期,2007年5月,第115—123页。

[Jiang, Chengyong. "Faust and The Core of 'Modern People's' Cultural Values in Europe." Foreign Literature Review, no.2, May 2007, pp.115‐23.]

——:《哈姆莱特:人类自身迷惘的艺术象征》,《上海师范大学学报》第4期,1994年11月,第97—102页。

[---. "Hamlet: The Artistic Symbol of Human Confusion." *Journal of Shanghai Normal University*, no.4, Nov. 1994, pp.97‐102.]

莱辛:《汉堡剧评》,《西方文论选》(上卷),伍蠡甫主编,上海译文出版社,1979年,第424—438页。

[Lessing, G. F. *Hamburgische Dramaturgie*. *The Selection of Western Literary Theories*, vol.1, edited by Wu Lifu, Shanghai Translation Publishing House, 1979, pp.424‐38.]

卢卡契:《卢卡契文学论文集》(二),刘若端编译,中国社会科学出版社,1980年。

[Lukács, György. *Collected Essays of György Lukács*. Vol. 2, edited and translated by Liu Ruoduan, China Social Sciences Press, 1980.]

Newman, Charles and Marie Kinzie. *Prose for Borges*. Northwestern UP, 1974.

Novak, Maximillian E. *Daneiel Defoe: Master of the Fiction*. Oxford UP, 1996.

Richetti, John. *The Columbia History of the British Novel*. Columbia UP, 2002.

Robber-Grillet, Allain. *For a New Novel: Essays on Fiction*. Translated by Richard Howard, Grove Press, 1966.

Taillis, Raymond. *In Defence of Realism*. Hodder & Stoughton, 1988.

Terras, Victor. "The Realist Tradition." *The Cambridge Companion to the Classic Russian Novel*, edited by Malcolm V. Jones and Robin Feuer Miller, Cambridge UP, 1998, pp. 98–122.

童庆炳、马新国编:《文学理论学习参考资料新编》(中),北京师范大学出版社,2005年。

[Tong, Qingbing and Ma Xinguo, editors. *Literary Theories: New Edition of Reference Materials*. Vol. 2, Beijing Normal UP, 2005.]

Tournier, Michel. *The Wind Spirit: An Autobiography*. Translated by Arthur Goldhammer, Beacon Press, 1988.

Watt, Ian. *The Rise of the Novel: Studies in Defoe, Richardson and Fielding*. U of California P, 1967.

杨守森:《马克思主义文艺理论在中国》,《齐鲁艺苑(山东艺术学院学报)》第3期,2018年6月,第4—10页。

[Yang, Shousen. "Marxist Literary Theory in China." *Qilu Realm of Arts*, no. 3, June 2018, pp. 4–10.]

哲学的根基与概念的溯源
——现实主义"求真"之"悖论性"

孙立武

内容摘要：19世纪以前，现实主义这一经典概念与文学思潮、流派、创作方法无关，它最早作为一个纯粹的哲学名词意指一种与唯名论相对的"现实性信仰"。从当下的现实主义热回溯到哲学根基，既是历史的回溯，也是概念内部的回退。回溯是解读现实主义之"求真"奥秘的一种基本视角和理论方法，同时也会复现现实主义这一"累积型概念"在不同话语谱系下的"求真"坐标。"悖论性"作为现实主义被忽视的特质之一，是回溯视角中一个隐在的让现实得以发生的推动力。"溯源"与"求真"的遭遇，恰好解答了现实主义是如何从哲学概念转向了思潮流派又转向了话语符号这一问题。哲学溯源虽在一定程度上削减了现实主义作为一个文学概念的丰富性，但是也为现实主义的"失语"或"泛化"提供了可供参考的解读视角。

关键词：哲学 现实主义 求真 回溯 悖论性
作者简介：孙立武，燕山大学文法学院讲师，主要从事文艺理论与大众文化批评研究。

Title: Philosophical Roots and Conceptual Retroactivity: The "Paradoxical Nature" of Realism's "Search for Truth"

Abstract: Before the 19th century, the classical concept of realism had nothing to do with literary trends, genres, or creative methods, and it was first used as a purely philosophical term to refer to a kind of "belief in reality" as opposed to nominalism. Going back to the philosophical roots of realism from the current craze for realism is not only a historical retrospection, but also a retrogression within the concept. Retrospection is a basic perspective and theoretical method for deciphering the mystery of realism's "truth-seeking," and at the same time, it will also revitalize the "cumulative concept" of realism, which is the "concept of accumulation." At the same time, it will also reproduce the coordinates of "truth-seeking" under different discursive spectrums of realism, which is a "cumulative concept." Paradoxicality, as one of the neglected qualities of realism, is an implicit driving force in the retrospective perspective that allows reality to happen. The encounter between "retrospection" and "truth-seeking" is an answer to the question of how realism shifted from philosophical concepts to ideological genres and then to discursive symbols. Although the philosophical traceability cuts down the richness of realism as a literary concept to a certain extent, it also provides an interpretative perspective for the "loss of words" or "generalization" of realism.

Key words: philosophy; realism; truth-seeking; retrospection; paradoxicality

Author: Sun Liwu is a lecturer at School of Humanities and Law, Yanshan University, China. His research interests are literary theory and popular culture criticism.

现实主义一直是创作界和理论界所共同关注的一个核心概念。虽然进入21世纪以来关于现实主义的讨论已经褪去了20世纪80年代的激情,也没有了90年代的那种带有"消逝感"的繁荣,但是随着现实主义题材和类型的不断推新,近几年又掀起了一股反思现实主义的热潮。为什么现实主义文学经久不衰? 现实主义的内在特质是什么？现实主义的理论根源有何特别之处？许多发问是基于时代语境或话语秩序的发问，正是因为受时代语境和话语的干预，所以对现实主义的深度反思会越来越模糊。或者囿于历史的局限性，搁置对概念本身的发问，陷于一种无力的阐释循环，在陈旧的话语逻辑里，不厌其烦地谈论作为一种方法、一种理念的现实主义。实际上现实主义不是一个纯粹的文学概念。它发轫于哲学，建基于人类认识世界和把握世界的方式；它更是一种主体意识，随着知识形态的演进而更新和凸显；它还是一个话语秩序的核心载体，随着时代语境的变化而为不同主体所用。

一、回溯作为"求真"历史脉络的视角与方法

"回溯"在这里有两重意义：其一是指现实主义的考察需要溯流而上，回顾其所来之路，此重是一个基于时间概念的回溯；其二是指作为一个理论概念，它是意义发生的隐秘逻辑，只有当意涵穿透能指链上的某个点，能指才得以回溯性地固定，意义才得以确定。在拉康看来，"相对于能指而言，意涵效应（effect of signification）具有回溯性；相对于能指链的行进而言，意涵效应处于所指之后"（齐泽克 143）。既然意涵效应处于所指之后，那么意义的获得也就成了"漂浮"中的偶发结果，也就是拉康所认为的意义产生过程具有强烈的偶然性。但是当人类进入开启智慧的时代，这种意义的偶然愈发地变成了主体参与的不偶然。如果单纯地把现实主义作为一个能指链条上的"漂浮"，那么意义的获得就有了无数可确定但又悬在空中的坐标点，还有那么多的所指意涵亟需回溯性地建构。

在现实主义的"理论旅行"中，其意义是被建构出来的。阿兰·米勒曾延续拉康的理论把"缝合"发展为一个哲学概念，在其看来，"能指结构与意指客体就是一种缝合关系。缝合建基于能指链的主体生产"

(雷晶晶57)。有鉴于能指链条的滑动和不确定性,当"约定俗成"的那些"缝合点"显现的时候,也就是能指链的主体化之坐标点显露之时,我们便获得了不同的现实观。如此之回溯的理论谱系为我们重新认识现实主义所来之路提供了可能,这样它就不再是一个单纯的文学概念的编写,而是进入了一个有着哲学推演的"理论旅行"之中。在萨义德看来:"相似的人和批评流派、观念和理论从这个人向那个人、从一个情境向另一情境、从此时向彼时旅行。"(赛义德.赛义德自选集138)此时向彼时的旅行,既是时空的迁移,又是情景作为决定性因素的体现。"所谓理论的旅行'由此到彼',最根本的变化是情景,它是时间、空间和历史文化诸因素在生活世界的具体整合。"(吴兴明114)从比较的视角出发,现代意义上的现实主义从西方进入中国也就百年的历史,但是其理论的旅行不限于一国之"变异",这也是为什么要回溯性地建构其"理论旅行"脉络的出发点之一。

韦勒克认为早期经由绘画领域兴起现实主义在为一些作家所使用之后形成了现实主义文学流派的早期雏形。"艺术应该忠实地表现这个真实的世界,因此,它应该通过精微的观察和仔细的辨析来研究当代的生活和风俗。它应该不动感情地、非个人地、客观地表现现实。从前一直被广泛运用于对自然的忠实表现的这个术语现在就同一批特定的作家联系起来,并被作为一个团体或一个运动的口号。"(韦勒克220)"现实主义选择了文学"还是"文学选择了现实主义",这是一个难以厘清的问题,但不可否认的是现实主义进入文学中是由作为主体的作家把这一术语主体化的过程。这也就是为什么历来的现实主义文学研究总会把现实主义文学的源头追溯到法国现实主义流派的原因之一,但是这仅仅是完成了回溯的第一重意涵。回溯的目的还在于在把现实主义主体化之前,也就是现实主义被文学绑缚其意义形成一个具体坐标点之前的逻辑架构呈现出来。这就需要打破文学史脉络视角的局限性,真正地回溯到一个术语的跨学科"旅行"。

回溯的一个重要原因还在于现实主义问题尤其是在进入"复数现实主义"阶段后面临着走向"泛化""空壳化"的处境。批评家罗斯认为："由于语言的表征本性,多种复数的现实主义的出现是不可避免的。"(Brooke-Rose 6)无论从跨国别的视角还是从一国之文学史流变的视角出发,现实主义都已经超出了其单一的形态,现实主义文学不再局限于经典现实主义理论的范畴,也不再是狭义的法国现实主义文学概念,而是呈现多元的发展趋势。"'现实主义'惊人的繁殖力,所表征的正是其作为文学传统之'写实''变数'基础上的'主义'的'复数',这些'主义'的'复数'形式则不应冠之以'文学思潮'的概念,而仅仅是现实主义或写实主义创作方法、创作原则的变体。"(蒋承勇 271)就在各领域都充斥现实主义,人人都在谈论现实主义的时刻,现实主义的概念也就迷失于"多语"的语境中,一种"多语症失语症"便出现在这一经典概念的话语场中。所以回溯的目的之一就是去繁就简,尽可能地回溯到"单数"的现实主义,去建构现实主义的由来之路,厘清泛化和多元语境所不能厘清的概念内涵问题。这不是退回到某一中心主义的视角去追溯概念的发生,而是在承认差异的基础上尝试构建一个经典概念的内在逻辑体系。

二、知识形态与"求真"——现实主义"实"之理念的演进

近年来,关于现实主义文学的研究围绕"现实""摹仿""真实"等核心概念展开。无论是文学史的溯源,还是原理学的构建,都有一个历史坐标点的追溯。从史料考察的角度,人们一般将"现实主义"这一概念追溯到席勒的《论素朴的诗与感伤的诗》,席勒在该文中将现实主义与理想主义者进行了比较,他认为："在天然单纯的状态中,人仍然全力以赴,起着一个和谐的统一体的作用……他整个天性的那种和谐共事不

过是一种想法而已,造就诗人的必然是将现实提升为理想,或(其结果一样)对于理想的描绘。"(席勒102)从理论的渊源上,一般将其追溯至"镜子说",甚至是柏拉图的"摹仿论",这是一个文学和现实关系问题的考证,"奥尔巴赫、托多罗夫、利科、沃尔什、多勒泽尔等现当代学者将这一美学基本问题重新演绎为文体论、象征符号学、认识论、可能世界理论的多种命题,在与传统摹仿论的对话中不断发掘新的诠释空间。"(刘洋、王守仁17)总体看,文学史的脉络是基于文学创作实践的溯源,而理论的溯源则复杂的多,尤其是围绕着"真实"的考察呈现为多样化的理论观。现实主义之"实"的不确定性,在方法上造就了多重可能性,原理学的建构、概念史的发问,都试图深入现实主义的内部,构建一个以"实"为核心的理论体系。从实际效果看,多元并没有让不确定性走向更为明晰,反而让概念变得更加模糊,进而呈现出"去中心化"之势。

现实主义之"实"的考察切中了这一概念的内核,需要把文体论和哲学认识论结合起来,只有这样才能消弭现实主义理论批评和文本实践的错位,具备厘清这一概念发生逻辑的可能性。"文化论转向""语言论转向""认识论转向""神学""本质论"等知识形态统摄下的世界,人类所表现出的认识世界和表达世界的方式也会呈现出不同的形态。这里有必要回溯西方知识形态演进逻辑中现实主义之"实"的基本视角。

"文化论转向"以来,"文化"成为人类的符号表意行为,以语言论为基础,但更注重语言的社会文化意义。人们对于"实"的关注也就不在于其本身,而是关注其是什么,为什么如此,其文化语境如何造就了"实"等问题。现实主义在此成为一种话语形态,而不是独立的语言词汇或文学概念,它是一个多种文化力量交互作用并由特定的社会文化语境造就的产物。"实"之内涵被淡化,其形式和外在语境被凸显。"语言论转向"以来,语言和符号取代理性而成为学术研究的中心问题,"主体——语言/符号——现实世界"这样的架构中,符号和现实世界得以分离,人们所认识的世界的"真实"是通过符号这一载体所捕获的。

"意义不仅是某种以语言'表达'或'反映'的东西；意义其实是被语言创造出来的。"(伊戈尔顿76)如此一来，现实主义之"实"的符号地位要远远高于其内涵和意义。"认识论转向"以来，人的理性觉醒，逐渐从宗教神学中解放出来。与之相对应的认识世界的方式发生了改变，人们认识到人类可以通过理性把握所面对的世界。随着科学的发展，人们开始从数字、图像、微观世界中寻求确定性，经典物理学到量子物理学蕴含了确定性到不确定性的转变，人们对现实世界的把握有了对于确定性的质疑。在"认识论转向"之前，人类在一段时间内一直相信上帝是世间万物的创造者，在神学论的统摄下，现实之"实"指向了唯一的造物主——上帝。回到"本质论"的追问。西方知识形态最早就是对于事物本质的追问，现实主义的研究回到概念本身去研究其发生机制会更有助于理解这一经典概念。

在这样一个大的知识形态谱系中，现实主义之"实"的考察抵达了一个核心问题——世界观与创作方法的关系问题，更进一步讲是二者的关系与真实性之间的辩证逻辑问题。这就使得现实主义之"实"与整个西方哲学关于真实的认识论结合在一起，"西方哲学视外部世界的客观本质为'真实'或真理的认识论由来已久，其中柏拉图的理式说与亚里士多德的可然律为人们把握形而上真实定下基于唯心和唯物的两个方向，并分别在黑格尔以绝对理念为真理之根本的客观唯心主义和马克思以实践为获得真理唯一方法的辩证唯物主义中发展到极致"(刘洋、王守仁18)。在现实主义的学术史溯源中，学界习惯于搬出柏拉图、亚里士多德、康德、黑格尔等哲人的论述；在现实主义的文学批评脉络中，也是不断地谈论奥尔巴赫、韦勒克、马克思、恩格斯等人的著述。不可否认，柏拉图的理念论为我们探索本原问题提供了较早的可靠范例，黑格尔唯实和唯名的论证为我们把握"实在"问题提供了借鉴，奥尔巴赫的摹仿论在文体上为我们理解现实主义提供了帮助，马克思的典型论则一直被文学创作者奉为典范。这些学说都指向了现实主义的一个核心特质——悖论性,唯物和唯心共同建构了现实主义,二者在不同知识形态下的混合构成了不同的现实主义观。"现实主义一方面应当依循唯物主义的思维路线,具有关注现实事物,通过事物特殊性揭示其普遍性的思想特征;一方面又应当同时依循唯心主义的思维路线,具有重视观念、理性和抽象,运用直觉、象征与隐喻,把思维和存在整合为同一体的思想特征。"(张连营 85)现实主义的"混沌状态"源于人类认识世界方式的两种对立,唯物和唯心对立之下的争论,恰好将现实主义之"实"的思考从复杂的逻辑中解救出来。

现实主义的"悖论性"特质决定了它需要不同话语主体的介入才能保证"实"之形态的存续,也就是主体的介入使得"实"的悖论性得到压制,这在创作方法上就呈现为概念化、公式化。"世界观与创作方法的关系或倾向性(思想性)与真实性(艺术性)的关系是理论方面的命题,在创作上则表现为公式化、概念化等问题。"(陈顺馨 408)假设没有主体的介入,知识形态的构建也就没有可能,现实主义之"实"的悖论性将不会让现实的"实"在话语体系中显现,它只能是一个矛盾体,换言之,"实"乃一种主体意识的建构。这种压抑悖论性的必然走向就是"实"的概念化和公式化,所以说现实主义之"实"是一个哲学意义上的主体意识问题,其本质是悖论性的内在冲突作为动因的系统,主体意识的介入使得这一矛盾系统外在地显现为名为"现实主义"的概念。

三、现实主义的悖论性内核与"史前史"中的"求真"坐标

"摹仿说"作为现实主义较早的理论阐释一直以来为批评者所重视,其最早可追溯至古希腊时期,在柏拉图和亚里士多德的论述中,已经窥见了艺术之于现实的辩证关系。柏拉图的三一式结构理念使其成为古希腊摹仿说的集大成者,他认为绘画等艺术创作,"在进行自己的

工作时是在创造远离真实的作品,是在和我们心灵里的那个远离理性的部分交往,不以健康与真理为目的地在向它学习"(柏拉图401)。摹仿者只是形象的创造者并没有抵达实在,宇宙是造物者按照理念的范型所仿制的作品,而艺术则成了对次一级的摹本的再制造。亚里士多德进一步对摹仿说进行了阐释并使之定型,他主张将"照事物本来的样子去摹仿"作为现实主义创作原则的最基本的要求。但是,"《诗学》中的'摹仿'既不指恶意的扭曲和丑化,也不是照搬生活和对原型的生吞活剥,而是一种经过精心组织的、以表现人物的行动为中心的艺术活动。艺术源于生活,但不必拘泥于生活"(亚里士多德213)。《诗学》中的"摹仿"可以说是现实主义作为创作方法的最早的提法,"按照生活的样子"但并非对原型的照搬。在亚氏的"摹仿"中,人的主体性并非完全从属于客观,客体和主体在文本中的互动构成了"摹仿"的实质,即艺术的摹仿是基于理性原则的指导,在主动精神的引导下,去对客体对象进行书写,现象因其客观性也非完全被动的一方。亚里士多德在《诗学》文本所详察的摹仿对象的位置是为了表明:"摹仿并不是'复制'现实世界,而是按照可然律进行的创造;亦不是对所谓现实'原本'的仿制,而是在诗中对目的的追寻。"(徐平88)在此,亚氏突出了主体之于材料的中介作用,即艺术家按照可然律或必然律赋予"物因"以"形式",从而促成新事物的"实现"。

相较于柏拉图的基于理念论的摹仿说,亚里士多德将摹仿说进一步推进到悲剧、喜剧等艺术创作之中。二者在"真"的认知上有着传承关系:"在柏拉图那里,真是摹仿的理念境界,在亚里士多德这里,真仍摹仿的极致。"(李珺平19)柏拉图的"摹本的摹本""影子的影子"否认了模仿艺术创造的现实形象的"真",而亚里士多德则相反,他肯定了现实世界的真实性,从而肯定了摹仿艺术的真实性。但是亚氏也呈现了真实之实现条件,那就是艺术创作者遵照事物之可然律或必然律,赋予形式于材料,上升至艺术的真实。这就凸显了主体之于真实的不可回避性。

尔后中世纪唯实论和唯名论的争锋，呈现了西方哲学史上两种截然不同的思潮，这两种思潮贯穿了整个中世纪甚至是近现代哲学。在16世纪的时候，"realist"（"现实的"或"现实主义的"）这一形容词，用以指中世纪中与唯名论相对的唯实论，认为概念是独立于思想和客体对象之外的客观存在。简单讲，唯名论指向的是概念，唯实论指向的是真实存在，"波尔菲思在他的《导论》中把这个问题表述为：一般概念（类和种）是不是实在的实体，或者是否只存在于人心中；如果它们是实在的，到底是物质的，还是非物质的；它们是脱离具体的可感觉的事物而存在，还是存在于它们之中"（梯利183）。唯名论和唯实论论争的核心则是概念和事物之间的关系孰先孰后、孰是真。柏拉图的理念论、亚里士多德的形式质料说、洛色林对三位一体说的反对以及后来经院哲学中的各种争论，都为现实主义的"史前史"提供了一个牢固的根基，也就有了如下的认识："现实主义这一术语最早出现于哲学中，意指一种与唯名论相对立的对于观念的现实性的信仰。"（张秉真413）

在唯实论和唯名论的对立之中，可以发现，最初的唯实论与我们今天的实在论是一个截然相反的概念，"凡主张共相在思维的主体之外，区别于个别事物，是一个存在着的实在，并认为只有理念才是事物本质的人，就叫作唯实论者"（黑格尔336）。唯实论所主张共相居于思维主体之外，是区别于个别事物的实在，这种依托"共相""理念""普遍者或类"的唯实论，后来发展为"事物像它们直接地那样就具有真实的存在"，这里有一个翻转式的转变，也可以说是唯心和唯物的悖论。

而唯名论则认为："这些共相仅仅是名字、形式、一个由心灵构造出的主观的东西，是为我们的、被我们所造成的表象——因此只有个别的东西才是实在。"（黑格尔336）二者对于"实在"内核的认知，一个指向了"独立于思维主体的共相"，一个指向了"个别具体事物"，很显然"共相"之主张的理念论、经院哲学的唯实论等唯实论相关的学说指向的是对于观念或概念的信仰，它是一种唯心主义，而我们今天的现实主义沿着唯实论那条翻转式的谱系脉络，则比较坚定地指向了唯物主义。这种悖论性并不影响我们追溯现实主义的概念流变，恰好为我们思考现实主义提供了哲学维度上的深度内涵。

现实主义在哲学的溯源指向了一种唯心与唯物交汇的"浑沌状态"，这种状态并不是把我们对于现实主义的思考引向一种始于中国传统中庸之维的调和观点，而是在理解现实主义之哲学原初意义的基础上，去把现实主义的演变视作一个与人类认知方式、科学理性推进等勾连在一起的辩证概念。认识现实主义的发生和演变逻辑要求我们重新审视这样一个概念与哲学的关联性，它在哲学上的演进也并不是单一的洛色林、奥康、布里丹等人的共相与个性的争论，也不能把现实主义的产生直接归于托马斯·阿奎那以及19世纪新托马斯主义哲学的唯物与唯心兼容的哲学思想。文学之中的现实主义延续或继承的是实在论之确定性的内涵，借助于主体经验之认知，来达到描述世界再现世界之真实的效果，从原始的这种悖论性回到当下现实主义理论批评和文本实践的发生场域，是为了沿着柏拉图、亚里士多德、洛色林、托马斯·阿奎那、康德、黑格尔、马克思等人的脚步，去重新发现现实主义的由来和变迁，悖论性始终是这一经典概念的内在动因。

主客体共同建构的现实主义始终呈现出悖论性：一方面真实是客观的，一方面又是主观参与的。"悖论性"时刻发生的一个基础在于现实主义与现实要素紧密关联在一起，但是现实主义文本存在于现有的语言系统中，"真实"将意义寄托于文本之上，文本并不能阐释自身所蕴含的显在和隐在的多重意义。西方知识形态是催化剂，中国当下的文学实践是阐释基础。现实主义自始至终都是围绕着"主体——标志物——现实世界——哲学本质"几者之间的关系而展开的研究，不同的侧重视角会形成不同的现实主义观。现实主义所具有的"悖论性"特质，正在召唤新的批评方法和新的理论观。

四、"概念源"与"真内核"遭遇的可能与局限

萨义德在《开端:意图与方法》一书中区分了"开端"和"起源",在其看来"起源"具有天赐、神话及特权的性质,而"开端"则完全是一个由凡人创造的世俗概念。开端是历史性的,而"起源"是神圣的;"开端"是复数的,"起源"是单数的。"开端"不同于起源,它不仅仅是一个简单的点,"开端意味着开始了某段与一个指定的出发点相连的过程"(15)。在某种意义上讲,现实主义"概念源"的追溯更多的是一种现实主义开端的研究,它从本质上是对属神的起源的违反,"起源处于一种必然消失的地方,即事物的真理与可信的话语相对应之处,也处于话语所遮蔽并最终要消失的偶然结合处"(鲍尔德温 211)。在起源之上孕生的是一种不断生成的状态,这一状态之中就包含了以悖论性特质为核心的话语秩序的更迭,现实主义之"求真"被赋予了图谋新意义的各种意图。一个复数的现实主义概念再采用传统的起源的追溯已经不足以厘清这一经典概念所承载的多重表征,现实主义的"概念源"不仅仅占据着一个可以成为"开端"的临时坐标点,而且引导着意图与方法在特定的历史语境中孕生一个相对确定的意义。

从某种意义上讲,正是有了悖论性这一特质,现实主义的"概念源"才有了一个基于历史语境和话语秩序的历史谱系,而非由某一个体或某一流派所创生的固定不变的概念,它是一个话语问题、一个历史性问题,还是一个主体意识问题?有学者指出,"'复数'现实主义的发展潮流推动了现实主义文学写作主体的多样化进程,也使得曾经不被纳入现实主义文学题材的社会现实进入了其表征的范畴之中,从另一个角度将现实推向了无边"(刘洋、王守仁 22)。事实上随着后现代主义思潮的风靡和退潮,文学和真实之间的关系也在"失语"和"多语"两种语境之间徘徊。在 21 世纪的今天,现实主义的无边更多的是一个从"失语"

到"多语"转变过程中的盲从。现实主义所表现的"复数"或者说"泛化",并不是因为"复数"的潮流涌动催生了写作主体创作的多样化,而是在一个"文本大爆发"的时代,写作主体创作的多样化构成了"复数"的潮流,这一"复数"进一步推动了文学与真实关系的重新审视。加洛蒂在《无边的现实主义》中所提到的"无边"是指:"没有非现实主义的,即不参照在它之外并独立于它的现实的艺术。"(167)现实主义的"无边"并非这一概念独有的特征,当下"复数"潮流中的"无边"更多的是写作主体的多样化,真实之内核悖论性的暴露,才是与"无边"形态的动因,换言之,悖论性内核赋予现实主义形态以无限的可能。

在"开端"而非"起源"的维度上,现实主义不再是单一的题材、方法或精神,它是文类、语体、风格等要素融合在一起的文体系统,"文体是指一定的话语秩序所形成的文本体式"(童庆炳1)。特定的精神结构、体验方式、思维方式、文化精神等作用于"现实主义"这一文体使之呈现为不同的表征形态,其所内在的悖论性特质作为哲学意义上的张力成了文体得以发生和实现的动因。如格兰特所说:"现实主义曾经分别效忠于唯心主义和唯物主义(但两种态度冷热不均),似乎忘记了对于现实本身应负的职责。"(格兰特6)一个重要的原因就是现实主义由哲学进入文学领域之后,无论是创作者还是理论者都不愿承认现实主义之"现实"概念本身就是一个充满矛盾的概念,尤其是与特定话语秩序结合在一起的时候,它就完全褪去了哲学色彩,在世俗的维度上完全与唯物主义联姻,成为一个易掌控的单一概念。以至于一段时间内出现了人人都在谈论现实主义,人人都不关心现实是什么的境遇。

五、余 论

把现实主义回溯到一个哲学式的"概念源"的发生,虽然有可能使得这一"确定了的""内容清晰"的经典概念陷于昏暗不明,但是从另一个角度讲,现实主义之"现实"虽然在形式上褪去了悖论性内涵达成了单一的确定性,但是恰好是长久以来对于"现实"之重心的偏离,忽视了对现实本身的关注。现实主义之"现实"与客观世界有着一层反映的关系,或许还以其固有的悖论性内涵孕育了现实本身的昏暗不明。早在20世纪80年代,王蒙和王干的谈话中就论及了反映现实并不等于现实主义;"李陀曾提出一种观点,认为中国应该用另外的一套概念体系,就像中国未必有真正的现代主义一样,中国也未必有严格意义上的现实主义"(王蒙、王干 45)。现实主义在历史进程中扮演了太多本不属于这一概念本身内涵的角色,概念的溯源只是为了厘清这一概念自身内部所具有的"悖论性"特质,而"求真"的哲学溯源也仅仅是厘清这一概念之动力源的一种尝试。与其让现实主义在"文本大爆发"的时代陷于多语症的失语,不如唤起"求真"的悖论性内核,让现实得以发生的内在逻辑在以开端为名的孕生体系中显现。

引用文献【Works Cited】

[齐泽克:《意识形态的崇高客体》,季广茂译,北京:中央编译出版社,2017年。]

[雷晶晶:《论"缝合":一个电影概念的梳理》,《当代电影》2015年第4期,第56—60页。]

[爱德华·W.赛义德:《赛义德自选集》,谢少波、韩刚等译,北京:中国社会科学出版社,1999年。]

[吴兴明:《"理论旅行"与"变异学"——对一个研究领域的立场或视角的考察》,《江汉论坛》2006年第7期,第114—118页。]

[韦勒克:《文学思潮和文学运动的概念》,高建为译,北京:中国社会科学出版社,1989年。]

C. Brooke-Rose, A Rhetoric of the Unreal, Studies in Narrative and Structure, Especially of the Fantastic, Cambridge: Cambridge University Press, 1981.

[蒋承勇:《19世纪西方文学思潮研究.第二卷,现实主义》,北京:北京大学出版社,2022年。]

[席勒:《席勒文集(6),理论卷》,张佳珏、张玉书、孙凤城译,北京:人民出版社,2005年。]

[刘洋、王守仁:《论现实主义文学原理的构建》,《上海交通大学学报(哲学社会科学

〔版）》2023年第1期,第14—24页。〕

〔伊戈尔顿:《二十世纪西方文学理论》,伍晓明译,西安:陕西师范大学出版社, 1986。〕

〔张连营:《现实主义的哲学背景探源》,《河北师范大学学报(哲学社会科学版)》 2000年第3期,第85—88页。〕

〔陈顺馨:《社会主义现实主义理论在中国的接受与转换》,合肥:安徽教育出版社, 2000年。〕

〔柏拉图:《理想国》,郭斌和、张竹明译,北京:商务印书馆,1986年。〕

〔亚里士多德:《诗学》,陈中梅译注,北京:商务印书馆,1996年。〕

〔徐平:《亚里士多德"摹仿说"再考察》,《云南大学学报(社会科学版)》2009年第1期,第88—93页。〕

〔李珺平:《寻绎摹仿说在古希腊起承转合的哲学轨迹》,《外国文学评论》1999年第4期,第16—21页。〕

〔梯利:《西方哲学史》,北京:商务印书馆,1995年。〕

〔张秉真:《西方文艺理论史》,北京:中国人民大学出版社,1994年。〕

〔黑格尔:《哲学讲演录(第三卷)》,贺麟、王太庆译,北京:商务印书馆,2017年。〕

〔萨义德:《开端:意图与方法》,章乐天译,北京:生活·读书·新知三联书店,2014年。〕

〔阿雷恩·鲍尔德温:《文化研究导论》,陶东风等译,北京:高等教育出版社,2004年。〕

〔罗杰·加洛蒂:《论无边的现实主义》,吴岳添译,上海:上海文艺出版社,1986年。〕

〔童庆炳:《文体与文体的创造》,昆明:云南人民出版社,1994年。〕

〔达米安·格兰特:《现实主义》,周发祥译,北京:昆仑出版社,1989年。〕

〔王蒙、王干:《文学这个魔方:王蒙王干对话录》,北京:北京联合出版公司,2016年。〕

论艾丽丝·默多克的现实观

段道余

内容摘要：小说家与哲学家艾丽丝·默多克在著作中对现实多有思考。本文聚焦默多克的哲学，通过分析默多克对当代哲学秉持的现实观、道德与现实、艺术与现实的论述，探讨默多克的哲学呈现的现实思想。在其哲学著作中，默多克不仅批判了当代哲学的现实观，更挑战了当代哲学基于其现实观建构的道德哲学。不满于当代道德哲学，默多克立足柏拉图的哲学思想构建了自己的道德现实主义。默多克的道德现实主义不仅将个体的道德追寻与个体对现实的认知密切关联，而且将道德中的善演绎为完美的现实知识，将自由阐释为对他人现实的认知。此外，默多克的道德现实主义也将艺术与现实链接，既揭示了艺术对现实的呈现与遮蔽，也指出艺术家的责任在于真实地呈现现实。

关键词：艾丽丝·默多克　现实　道德　艺术

作者简介：段道余，南京农业大学外国语学院讲师，主要从事英国文学和当代英语文学研究。

Title: On Iris Murdoch's Idea of Reality

Abstract: Novelist and philosopher Iris Murdoch stresses the issue of reality in her writings. Focusing on Murdoch's philosophy, this paper explores Murdoch's idea of reality by examining her critique of contemporary philosophy's idea of reality, her elaboration of morality and reality, and her discussion of art and reality. In her philosophy, Murdoch not only criticizes the idea of reality followed by contemporary philosophy but also challenges the moral philosophy constructed by contemporary philosophy. Dissatisfied with contemporary moral philosophy, Murdoch develops her own moral realism by resorting to Plato's philosophy. Murdoch's moral realism not only relates the individual's moral pursuit to their cognition of reality but also ties the Good with the perfect knowledge of reality and connects freedom with the cognition of the others' reality. Moreover, Murdoch's moral realism relates art to reality, exploring art's revelation and distortion of reality, and artist's responsibility to truly represent reality.

Key words: Iris Murdoch; reality; morality; art

Author: Duan Daoyu is a lecturer at the college of foreign studies, Nanjing Agricultural University, China. His research interests are British literature and contemporary English literature.

作为英国战后著名的小说家与哲学家,艾丽丝·默多克(Iris Murdoch, 1919—1999)在其创作中对"现实"(reality)与"真实"(truth)议题多有思考。不论在其哲学还是小说中,现实与真实都是默多克论述的核心思想之一,贯穿作品前后。在哲学著作中,默多克不仅论述了柏拉图、康德与叔本华等人的哲学对现实与真实的演绎,而且批判了存在主义、行为主义与结构主义等当代哲学流派秉持的现实观。不仅如此,默多克还在自己的道德哲学中演绎了自身对道德与现实、艺术与现实的哲学思考。在小说创作中,默多克不仅对狄更斯、托尔斯泰和普鲁斯特等19世纪现实主义大家的创作颇为青睐,而且试图在其传统下展开小说创作。不仅如此,默多克在小说创作中也将现实与真实作为小说的重要主题,呈现了小说人物从"臆想"(fantasy)经由"关注"(attention)最终抵达"善的现实"(the reality of Good)的道德提升与寻真历程。纵观默多克的26部小说，这一历程反复出现，构成默多克的小说呈现的一种主要加入情节模式。可以说，不论是默多克的哲学著作，还是其文学创作都与现实以及真理议题密不可分。前者构成默多克的"文学现实主义"（literary realism）思想，而后者则构成其"伦理现实主义"（ethical realism）的主要内容。

在以往的研究中，尽管学界对默多克的小说创作体裁多有争论，但是学界对其文学现实主义已有较多研究。迪普尔（Elizabeth Dipple）、休赛尔（Barbara Stevens Heusel）和尼科尔（Bran Nicol）等人在其著作和文章中都对默多克的文学现实主义多有论述。与学者对默多克的文学现实主义的研究相比，学界对默多克的伦理现实主义的探讨相对欠缺。这与学界对默多克哲学思想的研究起步较晚不无关联。随着学界开始重新审视默多克的哲学，学界对默多克的哲学思想的研究日趋增多。默多克在哲学著作中呈现的伦理现实主义也引起了越来越多学者的关注。

目前，学界对默多克哲学中的现实主义、真理和"道德现实主义"（moral realism）已多有思考。菲德斯（Paul S. Fiddes）在其著作《艾丽丝·默多克与其他作家：一位与神学对话的作家》（*Iris Murdoch and the Others: A Writer in Dialogue with Theology*，2022）中就曾专辟一章"艾丽丝·默多克和对真实的热爱"（"Iris Murdoch and love of the truth"）探讨了默多克的哲学对真实的追寻。罗宾特（David Robjant）、彭斯（Elizabeth Burns）与乔丹（Jessy E. G. Jordan）也都撰文探讨或重审了默多克哲学中的现实议题，譬如默多克与柏拉图的"世俗现实主义"（earthy realism）、默多克对道德与现实以及宗教与现实的思考。除此之外，默多克的哲学对当代哲学的现实观、艺术与现实的关系也多有论述。然而，目前的研究对此并未进行全面地探讨。因此，本文将立足默多克的哲学著作，从默多克对当代哲学的现实观、道德与现实以及艺术与现实的论述出发，系统探讨默多克在哲学中呈现的现实思想。

一、当代哲学的现实观

在默多克开启创作生涯之际,英国本土的两大学术重镇剑桥与牛津正被分析哲学笼罩。然而,作为哲学家与小说家,默多克对行为主义、功利主义与分析哲学等占主导地位的当代哲学都颇为不满。这从其哲学著作对当代哲学的批判可见一斑。在这些著作中,默多克不仅点出了当代哲学的弊病,更反思了造成这一弊病的缘由。在默多克看来,以行为主义、功利主义与分析哲学为代表的当代哲学都过于强调人的外在"行动"(action),忽略了人的"内在生活"(inner life),而当代哲学之所以看重人的行动而轻视人的内在生活与其秉持的现实观脱不了干系。

对于何为现实,行为主义、功利主义与分析哲学等当代哲学流派都认为,"'现实的'事物能够向不同的观察者敞开"(Murdoch, SG 5)。换言之,如果人可以直接或间接地观察到事物及其外在的变化,那么该事物便现实存在。否则,该事物便是虚幻。基于此种现实观,行为主义、功利主义与分析哲学等当代哲学流派将人的行动与内在生活作了区分。在它们看来,由于人的行动可以"引发可见的变化"(Murdoch, SG 5),人的行动便是现实之物。而与人的行动相比,由于人的内心世界隐晦难察(Murdoch, SG 5),人的内在生活则是虚幻之物。在当代哲学看来,除非人的内在生活被引向人的外在行动,即内在生活能够外显于人的外在行动之中,人的内在生活才能被视为现实之物,否则,人的内在生活只能是"无内容的梦"(Murdoch, SG 7),即虚幻不实之物。

深受这一现实观的影响,当代哲学在界定人的本质时将人与人的行动而非人的内在生活关联起来,因为人的行动是真实的,而人的内在生活则是虚幻的。在当代哲学家看来,由于人是运动着的物体,总是"不断地将意图转化为行动的洪流"(Murdoch, SG 4),人的存在则是一种

"外在选择意愿的运动"(Murdoch,"Idea" 304)。因此,对当代哲学而言,与静态的"视域"(vision)相比,"运动"(movement)更宜用来隐喻人的存在(Murdoch, SG 5)。而人的运动则主要体现为外在可察的行动。在此意义上,当代哲学可谓"将现实的人与空无的选择意愿等同",强调人的"行动而非视域"(Murdoch, SG 34)。

对于当代哲学勾勒的人,默多克颇有微词。在她看来,当代哲学呈现的人"并不现实"(Murdoch, SG 9)。对此,默多克从经验、哲学与道德三方面作了解释。对默多克而言,就经验而谈,"人必然或本质上并不'如此'"(SG 9)。换言之,就默多克对人的理解而言,当代哲学对人的本质的呈现并不符合现实的人。从哲学上来看,默多克则指出,当代哲学呈现的人并不令人信服。而从道德上来说,默多克则认为,人不应这样刻画自身(SG 9)。

默多克之所以有此论断与其对人的内在生活的再审视不无关联。在默多克看来,在当代哲学呈现的人中,"某种重要的东西丢失了"(SG 9)。这便是人的精神活动构成的内在生活。与当代哲学轻视人的内在生活不同,默多克认为人的内在生活也有其"自身的内容与价值"(MGM 153)。不仅如此,在默多克看来,人的内在生活也构成人物人格的内容(SG 21)。尽管它并不总是见于人的外在行动,但是它并非"'不现实'的虚幻"(Lazenby 60)。相反,它也"有现实的内容"(Lazenby 60),构成人的内在现实。因此,如果哲学要对人的本质做出现实的界定便无法否认人的内在生活。而如果否认了人的内在生活,哲学也就"否认了个体的现实"(Widdows 21)。

为了进一步说明人的内在生活真实不虚,默多克援引一位母亲对儿媳妇的认知转变事例做了说明。她假设有这样一位母亲 M 对儿媳妇 D 颇为不满。不过,M 是"一位非常'体面'的人,始终与女孩相处甚欢,丝毫不流露她的真实想法"(Murdoch, SG 17)。在默多克看来,如果 M 是"一位明智、心眼好的人,善于自我批评,能够认真和公正地关注她所面对的对象"(SG 17),那么随着时间的流逝,她会重新审视自己对 D 的看法,并改正她先前的成见。纵观 M 对 D 的认知转变过程,默多克指出 M 对 D 的认知前后经历的转变实际上"完全发生在 M 的脑海中"(SG 17),并无任何外在可见的变化。

对此,默多克进一步指出,若依照当代哲学秉持的现实观来看,M 在整个认知转变过程中没有任何变化,因为她的认知转变没有引发任何可见的外在行动。不过,在默多克看来,情况并非如此。实际上,M"在此期间一直很活跃"(Murdoch, SG 19),因为她的精神世界在此期间一直思绪万千。尽管这些变化并不见于 M 的外在行动,但它并非虚无,而是真实存在过。它不仅属于 M,而且构成了她不断生成的存在的一部分(Murdoch, SG 21)。

通过反思当代哲学对人的内在生活的贬抑,默多克重新审视了人的内在生活,不仅赋予人的内在生活以现实,而且将之演绎为人存在的重要组成部分。在此意义上,默多克可谓修正了当代哲学只注重人的外部现实忽略人的内在现实的现实观。

除了反思当代哲学对人的内在生活的忽视,默多克也批判了当代哲学勾勒的"理想的理性的人"。在默多克看来,当代哲学呈现的理性的人过于理想化,因为这一理性的人不仅"能够意识到他所有作为记忆的记忆","能把他现在的情况与过去无意识的记忆区分开来",而且"能在满足他本能的需求中发现自身的行动动机"(转引自"Idea" 303)。在默多克看来,这一"理想的理性的人"不仅见于当代哲学,也"被许多作家理所当然地接受",甚至"几乎每一本当代小说的主人公都是如此"("Idea" 304)。

对于当代哲学与文学呈现的理想化的理性的人,默多克并不认同。在她看来,这一理想的理性的人并不存在,因为人的性格具有多重维度,很难捉摸(Murdoch, SG 6)。不仅如此,默多克还认为,这样一种理想的理性的人也不可能存在,因为倘若这样一种人真的存在,我们将

"没有艺术,没有梦想或想象,没有与本能需要不相关的喜好或厌恶"("Idea" 304)。而现实的情况是,艺术、梦想与想象普遍存在。默多克的言外之意显然表明,当代哲学勾勒的理想的理性的人并不存在。这与默多克对人的现实处境的认识分不开。受弗洛伊德的心理机制思想的影响,默多克认为人总是倾向寻求"想象性慰藉"(imaginary consolation),避免直面痛苦的现实。在默多克看来,"我们对自己的描述已经变得过于宏大,我们已经疏离并将自身与一个不现实的意愿概念认同,我们已经失去了与我们自身分离的现实的视域,我们也没有充足的原罪概念"(SG 46)。不仅如此,在默多克看来:"我们并非疏离的自由选择者和巡视一切的君主,而是陷入一种现实的愚钝生物,我们不断且无法抗拒地倾向用臆想扭曲现实的本质。我们当前的自由图景鼓励了一种梦幻般的才能;而我们所需要的是一种对道德生活的难度和复杂性以及人的不透明性的崭新认知。"("Dryness" 293)

此外,默多克也批判了当代哲学领域弥漫的乐观与浪漫气息。在默多克看来,自康德以降的经验主义、行为主义以及包含海德格尔和萨特等哲学大家在内的存在主义无一不带有一种乐观主义与浪漫主义色彩。这是一种并不现实且"没有抱负的乐观主义"(Murdoch, SG 49),难以真正解决战后社会中的个体面临的困境。

正是基于这样的现实观、人的本质观与乐观主义气质,当代哲学在思索道德时更多地聚焦人的选择与行动。在当代哲学看来,人的选择与行动构成道德的重要组成部分,而人的内在生活则不然。因此,个体的内在生活被当代哲学踢出了道德的范畴。于是,在当代哲学演绎的道德哲学中,人的"道德成为事前思考清楚,然后前去与其他人进行外在交往的一件事情"(Murdoch, "Idea" 305)。在默多克看来,当代哲学的这种道德就如同人们"去商店购物"的行为:"在拥有完全负责的自由的情况下,我进入商店,客观地评估商品的特点,然后做出选择。"("Idea" 305)默多克并不看好这种道德观。在她看来,人的道德实际上既"复杂又难以分析"(Murdoch, "Idea" 306),而当代道德哲学显然将人的道德活动简单化。也正是因此,默多克指出,当前的道德哲学既不充分,也不正确(SG 74)。

可以说,默多克对内在生活、理想的理性的人以及当代哲学的浪漫气息的反思,不仅批判了当代哲学秉持的现实观,更挑战了当代哲学基于科学主义的现实观建立的道德哲学。通过重新审视个体内在生活的重要性,默多克将个体的道德与个体的意识重新关联。被当代哲学排斥出道德领域的意识,由此重新获得了道德重要性。

二、道德与现实

作为哲学家,默多克不仅批判了当代哲学秉持的现实观及其基于这一现实观建立的道德哲学,而且立足柏拉图的哲学思想,发展了自己的道德哲学,探讨了道德与现实的关系。纵观默多克的道德哲学,现实或真实构成其核心关键词之一。在默多克看来,"道德哲学是对所有人类活动中最重要活动的考察"(SG 76)。这一考察需要两个因素,其中之一便是"这一考察应该是现实的"(Murdoch, SG 76)。默多克不仅主张道德哲学探索本身应遵循现实原则,避免当代哲学的乐观浪漫倾向,更思考了个体的道德追求、重要的道德概念,如善和自由同现实的紧密关联。通过论述个体的道德追求、善、自由与现实的重要关系,默多克构建了一种道德现实主义。

恰如前文所述,通过反思当代哲学秉持的现实观,默多克将被当代哲学忽视的个体的内在生活重新与道德关联。不仅如此,默多克更是在其道德哲学中将个体的内在生活,尤其是个体的意识,发展为个体道德追寻的重要组成部分。这从默多克在哲学中对意识的论述可见一斑。在其出版的最后一本哲学著作《作为道德指南的形而上学》(*Metaphysics as a Guide to Morals*, 1992)中,默多克就专辟两章讨论了意识与思想。不仅如此,默多克更是指出,"意识或自我存在是道德存在的根本模式或形式"(*MGM* 171)。在此意义上,默多克实则将当代哲学基于人的行动建立的道德哲学发展为基于人的意识的道德哲学。

鉴于对意识与道德关系的思考,与当代道德哲学将个体的道德与个体的行动关联不同,默多克在其道德哲学中将个体的道德与个体的"视域"(vision)即个体对事物现实的认知联系起来。在默多克看来,视域的清晰度即个体对事物现实的认知程度决定了个体道德追寻的层次。在个体的道德追寻中存在不同的视域,既有清晰的视域,也有扭曲的视域(Murdoch, *SG* 36)。前者展现了个体在道德追寻中对事物现实的充分认知,而后者则呈现了个体对事物现实的偏颇认知。由于清晰的视域揭示了个体对事物现实的充分认知,清晰的视域也就真实地呈现了事物的本来面貌。也正是在此意义上,默多克指出,"清晰的视域与对现实的尊重分不开"(*SG* 88)。换言之,在个体的道德追寻中,清晰的视域并不歪曲或遮盖事物的现实,而是如其所是地呈现事物的现实。对此,默多克在其后的哲学著作《作为道德指南的形而上学》中就表明,在个体的道德追寻中,"现实作为真实视域的对象出现"(39)。言外之意,清晰的视域揭示了现实。与清晰的视域相比,扭曲的视域则歪曲事物的现实。

在默多克的道德哲学中,扭曲的视域展现了个体道德追寻中的臆想状态,阻止个体看清自身之外的现实,而清晰的视域则将个体引向了"善"(the Good)。对默多克而言,善代表了一种"完美的道德视域或者无虚幻的现实知识"(Antonaccio 182)。在此意义上,默多克实则将善与现实联系起来。

在其哲学著作中,默多克对善与现实的关系也多有思考。恰如以往的哲学家柏拉图与康德,默多克也将善视为一种知识。在她看来:"在一个严肃的常识层面和关于道德本质的普通而非哲学的反思方面,善很明显与知识相关;不是与非人的近似科学的、关于普通世界的知识有关,不论它是什么,而是与对现实情况精确而如实地理解有关,与耐心和公正地观察并探索人所面对的事物有关,它不仅仅是睁开眼看的问题,而是一种特定的、完美的、熟悉的道德规训。"(Murdoch, *SG* 37)在其后的哲学著作中,默多克更是清晰地指出,"善包含探索真理的知识和对欲望的规训"(*MGM* 39)。

默多克之所以将善与现实知识关联与其对善的认识分不开。在默多克看来,"道德的主要敌人是个体的臆想:自我膨胀的机理以及令人慰藉的愿望和梦想阻止人看清自身之外的事物"(*SG* 57)。臆想使个体陷入自我中心主义的泥淖,阻止个体看清自身之外的世界与他人的现实。而道德生活或向善历程则意味着将个体从臆想中解救,使之看清自身之外的世界与他人的现实。在此意义上,个体的道德提升与向善同个体对世界与他人的现实认知密切相关。对此,默多克就指出,现实是道德追求的"理想终点",而"这也是善的概念所在的地方"(*SG* 41)。换言之,在默多克看来,善与现实密切相关(*SG* 41),而"至善就是至真"(*MGM* 398)。也正是因此,默多克得出结论"道德与善是现实主义的一种形式"(*SG* 57)。在默多克看来,"善要求的现实主义(感知现实的能力)是一种感知现实的思想能力,它同时也是一种自我的压制"(*SG* 64)。鉴于善与现实的关系,默多克指出,"一个真正善的人生活在一个私人的梦幻世界的观点看似不可接受",他"必然知道他周围的特定事物,最明显的就是他人的存在和他们的宣称"(*SG* 57)。

默多克不仅论述了道德、善与现实的关系,更对这种关系作了进一步思考。在默多克看来,"如果理解善即是理解个体和现实,那么善便介入了现实无限逃逸的特点"(*SG* 41)。言外之意,善代表的现实总是逃离个体,无法被个体捕捉。对此,有学者就指出,在默多克的哲学中,善所代表的现实是一种"无法触及的现实"(Forsberg 124)。对此,默多克在其哲学中也作了详细论述。在她看来,的确"存在一种道德现实,一种尽管无限遥远却现实的标准"(Murdoch, *SG* 30)。然而,这一现实很难实现,因为对这一现实的"理解和模仿依然不乏困难"

（Murdoch，*SG* 30）。不仅如此，在默多克看来，"理解一个具有吸引力，却无法穷尽的现实的任务具有无限的困难"（*SG* 41）。原因就在于，在道德追寻中，个体的心智总是倾向陷入自我中心主义的臆想，从而看不清自身之外的现实。

在默多克看来，道德追寻中的个体可以通过"关注"（attention）行为抵达善的现实。默多克的关注一词借自法国哲学家薇依（Simone Weil）。在默多克的笔下，关注指"公正和有爱地凝视个体的现实"（*SG* 33）。它是一种"无私的关注行为"（Conradi，*SA* 107），并不展现个体的意志。此外，默多克认为"关注的任务一直在发生，并见于我们正在'看'的看似空无和日常的时刻"（*SG* 42）。对默多克而言，这些时刻的关注虽只是无足轻重的观看尝试，却可以"通过累积显现出十分重要的效果"（*SG* 42）。换言之，关注行为不仅无时不有，持续不断，而且也见于日常生活中看似无意义与平淡的观看时刻。这些时刻的关注虽然对个体的道德提升影响甚微，却可以通过累积的方式使个体寻求道德提升的努力发生质变。恰如默多克所言，善与现实密切相关，而"关注则被赋予了现实的知识"（*SG* 87）。

此外，默多克也思索了自由与现实的关系。与当代哲学如存在主义和行为主义不同，默多克并不认为自由是意愿的施展。相反，她认为自由是"远离臆想的自由"（Murdoch，*SG* 65）。在默多克的哲学中，臆想展现了扭曲的视域，"远离臆想的自由"则是"对正确视域的体验"（*SG* 65）。由于视域呈现了个体对事物的认知，展现了正确视域的自由则呈现了个体对事物现实的真实呈现。也正是在此意义上，默多克指出，自由是一种关乎"同情的现实主义"（*SG* 65）。

三、艺术与现实

在默多克的道德哲学中，道德与艺术密切关联。恰如默多克所言，她的道德心理学的最大优势是"它并不将艺术与道德对立"(*SG* 39)。相反,在默多克看来,道德与艺术是"同一抗争的两个方面"(*SG* 39 - 40)。在《崇高与善》("The Sublime and the Good")一文中,默多克更是指出,在特定条件下,艺术和道德是一体的,因为"它们两者的本质都是爱"(215)。鉴于爱是"对个体的理解",是"极其艰难地认识到自我之外的事物是真实的",默多克于是指出"爱、艺术和道德都是发现现实"("Sublime" 215)。

对默多克而言,她关于艺术与道德关系的论述"不仅适用于文学艺术,而且适用于所有艺术"("Sublime" 218)。在她看来,"对一种现实而非自我充满爱意的尊重概念"既与文学艺术譬如"写一部小说"有关,也与非文学的其他艺术形式有关,譬如"做花瓶"的艺术。此外,这一论述也"不仅仅适用于在明显意义上与模仿有关的艺术"(Murdoch, "Sublime" 218)。

鉴于艺术与道德的紧密关联,默多克在其道德哲学中论述道德与现实的同时,也对艺术与现实的关系作了较多思考。概括来看,默多克对艺术与现实的论述主要包含以下三个方面:艺术与现实、伟大的艺术与现实以及艺术家与现实。

在默多克看来,艺术与现实密切相关。一方面,默多克指出,"艺术揭示现实"(*SG* 94)。从默多克的著作来看,她此处所说的艺术指向"好的艺术"(good art)。对默多克而言,"好的艺术,不论其风格如何,都有坚硬、坚定、现实主义、清晰、疏离、公正和真理的品质"(*MGM* 226)。它不仅呈现了人拒绝寻求慰藉的努力,而且通过揭示我们普通而枯燥的意识无法看到的世界(Murdoch, *SG* 86),向人展现了一种现实的视域(Murdoch, *SG* 63)。对此,有评论者就指出,对默多克而言,"好的艺术使人更接近现实"(Fine 116)。另一方面,默多克也反思了艺术对现实的遮蔽。在此,默多克主要思考了"糟糕的艺术"(bad art)对现实呈现的影响。在默多克看来,与好的艺术不同,糟糕的艺术掩盖现实。

不仅如此,默多克也以具体的艺术形式,尤其是小说为例,思考了艺术与现实的关系。在她看来,小说的功能是"去强调通常被掩盖的真理"(Bellamy & Murdoch 53),而"好的小说关注善与恶之间的斗争以及从表象到真实的历程"(Murdoch, *MGM* 97)。

除了论述好的艺术、糟糕的艺术与现实的关系,默多克也论述了伟大的艺术与现实的关系。在默多克看来,伟大的艺术扮演着双重角色。它既揭示现实,也教导人如何观看现实。恰如默多克所言,"伟大的艺术扮演了教育者和揭示者的角色"(*SG* 63)。

在其著作中,默多克对伟大的艺术对现实的揭示多有论述。在《用词拯救》(*Salvation by Words*)中,默多克就指出,伟大的艺术通过将自我批评式的准确性引入其模仿和用试图完整却不完整的形式呈现世界"激发了真实性和谦卑"(240)。不仅如此,默多克还认为,"伟大的艺术可以以一种比科学或者甚至是哲学更加准确的方式展示和讨论我们的现实、我们真实意识的核心领域"("Salvation" 240)。

此外,默多克更以伟大的作家如莎士比亚和托尔斯泰为例思考了伟大的艺术与现实的关系。尽管默多克承认"伟大的艺术家有'个性',拥有独特的风格",而即便莎士比亚有时也在其著作中呈现了他自己感兴趣的东西,尽管这种情况十分少有,但是默多克仍认为,"伟大的艺术是'非个人的',因为它清晰地向我们展示了世界,我们的世界而不是另一个世界"(*SG* 63)。言外之意,在默多克看来,伟大的艺术揭示了真实的世界,"教导了一种现实感"(*MGM* 430)。为此,默多克以莎士比亚和托尔斯泰的文学为例作了具体说明。她写道:"考虑一下我们从思考莎士比亚或托尔斯泰的人物又或维拉斯凯兹或提香的绘画学到了什么。我们从此处学到的是人性的真实品质,它们被画家用公正和富有同情的视域展望。"(Murdoch, *SG* 63-64)

在其后的著作《重访崇高与美》(*The Sublime and the Beautiful Revisited*)一文中,默多克又以莎士比亚和托尔斯泰为例做了进一步说明。在此，默多克提出了"伟大的文学作品的特点是什么？"("Beautiful" 275)。随后，她解释道，这一问题可以这样提出，即"是什么使托尔斯泰成为最伟大的小说家和莎士比亚成为最伟大的作家？"("Beautiful" 275)在默多克看来，这主要在于他们的人物塑造，即他们的作品呈现了人物的现实。以莎士比亚的作品为例，默多克指出，"莎士比亚的著作充满了自由和奇特的人格，莎士比亚理解这些人格的现实，并将这些现实展示为与自身十分不同的事物"("Beautiful" 275)。换言之，莎士比亚在其创作中真实地呈现了人物的现实。

在默多克看来，伟大的艺术不仅揭示现实，而且教育观者如何观看现实。对默多克而言，"伟大的艺术教导我们如何观看和爱现实之物"，而非"被吸收进自我的贪婪机制中"(*SG* 64)，因为观看和爱现实之物需要"准确性和好的视域"，而这些准确性与好的视域则确保了艺术家和观者可以做到"非感伤、疏离、无私和客观的关注"(*SG* 64)。

除了艺术与现实、伟大的艺术与现实，默多克也论述了艺术家与现实的关系。在默多克看来，"艺术家的责任是艺术，是用自己的媒介讲述真理"(*EM* 18)。换言之，一个艺术家的职责在于利用艺术讲述真理。不过，对默多克而言，这并非易事。在主张艺术家职责的同时，默多克也意识到艺术家讲述真理的困难。在她看来，"几乎所有的艺术都是一种形式的臆想式慰藉，而少有艺术家获得了关于现实的视域"(Murdoch, *SG* 63)。对默多克而言，情况之所以如此在于艺术家的才能很容易就会被用来呈现艺术家自己的慰藉和自大，而其艺术作品也很容易被投射了艺术家自己的关注点和愿望(*SG* 63)。然而，"去压制和消除自我，去思考和用清晰的视野描述自然并不容易，它需要一种道德训练"(Murdoch, *SG* 63)。默多克所说的道德训练指向了艺术家所需的"公正的判断"品质(*MGM* 134)，即艺术家对自身之外的事物与他人现实如其所是地呈现。具体而言，它指艺术家在创作中并不从自己的视角思考和扭曲所要呈现的事物与他人的现实。也正是在此意义上，默多克指出，"伟大的艺术家展现的现实主义不是'照相式'的现实主义，它本质上是同情和公正"(*SG* 93)。

此外，默多克也以小说家为例进一步论述了艺术家与现实的关系。在默多克看来，在小说创作中，作家应创作现实的人物，而非使人物成为作家的传声筒。这就要求小说作家应努力"理解他们的现实"(Murdoch, "Beautiful" 284)，并在人物创作中秉持自然主义的人物观(Murdoch, "Dryness" 294)，即创造现实的人物。只有如此，作家创作的小说才能成为"一间适合自由的人物生活的房子"(Murdoch, "Beautiful" 286)，才能规避小说创作中采用的形式对现实的遮蔽，因为"现实的人对神话具有破坏性"(Murdoch, "Dryness" 294)。

四、结　论

总而言之，对现实的思考贯穿默多克的哲学著作。作为哲学家，默多克不仅反思了当代哲学秉持的现实观及其在此基础上构建的道德哲学，而且基于柏拉图的哲学思想发展了有别于当代道德哲学的道德现实主义思想。默多克的道德现实主义不仅将个体的道德生活与个体对现实的认知密切关联，而且将道德中的善演绎为完美的现实知识，将自由阐释为对他人现实的认知。此外，默多克的道德现实主义也将与道德密切相关的艺术与现实链接，既揭示了艺术对现实的呈现与遮蔽，也指出艺术家的责任在于真实地呈现现实。

【Works Cited】

Antonaccio, Maria. *Picturing the Human: The Moral Thought of Iris Murdoch*. Oxford: Oxford UP, 2000.

Bellamy, M. O. and Iris Murdoch. "An Interview with Iris Murdoch." *From a Tiny Corner in the House of Fiction: Conversations with Iris Murdoch*. Ed. Gillian Dooley. Columbia: U of South Carolina, 2003. 44–55.

Conradi, Peter J. *Iris Murdoch: The Saint and the Artist*. Basingstoke: Macmillan, 1986.

Fine, David J. "Disciplines of Attention: Iris Murdoch on Consciousness, Criticism, and Thought (*MGM* Chapters 6 – 8)." *Reading Iris Murdoch's Metaphysics as a Guide to Morals*. Ed. Nora Hämäläinen and Gillian Dooley. Cham: Palgrave Macmillan, 2019. 107 – 123.

Forsberg, N. "'Taking the Linguistic Method Seriously': On Iris Murdoch on Language and Linguistic Philosophy." *Murdoch on Truth and Love*. Ed. Gary Browning. Cham: Palgrave Macmillan, 2018. 109 – 132.

Lazenby, Donna J. *A Mystical Philosophy: Transcendence and Immanence in the Works of Virginia Woolf and Iris Murdoch*. London: Bloomsbury, 2014.

Murdoch, I. "Against Dryness." *Existentialists and Mystics: Writings on Philosophy and Literature*. Ed. Peter J. Conradi. New York: Penguin, 1997. 287 – 295.

---. "The Idea of Perfection." *Existentialists and Mystics: Writings on Philosophy and Literature*. Ed. Peter J. Conradi. New York: Penguin, 1997. 299 – 336.

---. *Metaphysics as a Guide to Morals*. London: Penguin, 1993.

---. "Salvation by Words." *Existentialists and Mystics: Writings on Philosophy and Literature*. Ed. Peter J. Conradi. New York: Penguin, 1997. 235 – 242.

---. *The Sovereignty of Good*. London: Routledge, 2001.

---. "The Sublime and the Beautiful Revisited." *Existentialists and Mystics: Writings on Philosophy and Literature*. Ed. Peter J. Conradi. New York: Penguin, 1997. 261 – 286.

---. "The Sublime and the Good." *Existentialists and Mystics: Writings on Philosophy and Literature*. Ed. Peter J. Conradi. New York: Penguin, 1997. 205 – 220.

Widdows, Heather. *The Moral Vision of Iris Murdoch*. Hampshire: Ashgate, 2005.

论法国当代作家的"新现实主义"写作

曹丹红　侯礼颖

内容摘要：1970年代末1980年代初是法国当代文学的转型期，这一期间不少法国作家抛弃上一阶段的形式游戏，逐渐回归"及物的写作"，关注变动不居的现实世界，创作了大量被热方等研究者称为"新现实主义"的作品。法国当代"新现实主义"并非一个统一的流派，根据热方、维亚尔等学者的研究，可知"新现实主义"大致包括邦、施维亚尔、古·拉诺迪、瓦赛、菲利佩蒂等作家以及重要文学团体"无知者"。这批作家的创作尤其具备反摹仿与反小说倾向、不断实践文体的杂糅与创新、对"自我虚构"这一写作形式青睐有加等特征，在继承19世纪批判现实主义传统的同时也体现了法国当代文学在题材与形式上的创新。

关键词：新现实主义　法国当代文学　反摹仿　文体创新　自我虚构

作者简介：曹丹红，南京大学外国语学院法语系教授、博士生导师，主要从事翻译学、法国诗学与文论研究；侯礼颖，南京大学外国语学院法语系硕士研究生，主要从事当代法国文学与文论研究。

Title: On the "New Realism" Writing of Contemporary French Writers

Abstract: The late 1970s and early 1980s marked a period of transition in contemporary French literature. During this time, numerous French writers moved away from the formal games of the previous phase and gradually returned to "transitive writing". They turned their attention to the ever-changing real world, producing a significant body of works referred to as "New Realism" by scholars such as Alexandre Gefen. Contemporary French "New Realism" is not a unified literary school. According to scholars like Alexandre Gefen and Dominique Viart, the "New Realism" roughly includes writers like François Bon, Éric Chevillard, Jean-Paul Goux, Mathieu Larnaudie, Philippe Vasset, Aurélie Filippetti and the important literary group "Inculte". Their creations are characterized by anti-mimesis and anti-novel tendency, continuous practice of genre hybridization and innovation, and a preference for autofiction. While inheriting the critical realism tradition of the 19th century, these works also reflect the innovation of contemporary French literature in terms of themes and forms.

Key words: New Realism; contemporary French literature; anti-mimesis; genre innovation; autofiction

Author: Cao Danhong is a professor at School of Foreign Studies, Nanjing University, China. Her research interests are translation studies, French poetics and literary theory. Hou Liying is a MA student at School of Foreign Studies, Nanjing University, China. Her research interests are contemporary French literature and literary theory.

提到现实主义,我们似乎会认为,这一诞生于 19 世纪的文艺思潮已成过去。不过,比利时法语语言文学皇家学院院士布里克斯(Michel Brix)在近著《从古典主义到现实主义:17—21 世纪法国文学史》[*Du classicisme au réalisme: Une histoire de la littérature française (XVIIe-XXIe siècles)*, 2021]中指出,19—20 世纪占据主流地位的现实主义在今天,也就是 21 世纪初,始终在文学场域中拥有一席之地。①

实际上，在20世纪末，法国文坛确实涌现出某种可以称之为"新现实主义"(Nouveau Réalisme)的写作倾向，值得我们关注。

"新现实主义"并非一个全新的表述，英语世界已有不少研究者关注到近年来现实主义在文艺领域的复兴。在艺术领域，美国当代艺术批评家与历史学家哈尔·福斯特(Hal Foster)针对世纪末的前卫艺术提出了著名的"实在的回归"(Return of the real)的论断。无独有偶，英国学者马尔科姆·布拉德伯里(Malcolm Bradbury)也在文学创作中关注到类似趋势，并使用了"新现实主义"(Neorealism)这一名称，认为在战后几十年的发展中，后现代主义逐渐走向终结，现实主义的潮流却愈发明显，"无论是创作实践上，还是理论阐释上，随处可见现实主义的强烈复兴"(Bradbury 19)。

不少法国当代文学研究者，如热方(Alexandre Gefen)、格勒努耶(Corinne Grenouillet)等人，以及聚焦法国文学的重要期刊《法国文学电子杂志》(*Revue électronique de littérature française*，简称 *Relief*)也不约而同地采用了"新现实主义"的标签[2]，他们从不同的侧面出发，试图定义、描述这股处在不停发展中的"新现实主义"潮流。另一些学者虽没有采用"新现实主义"这一标签，但同样认为现实主义并未在19世纪以后偃旗息鼓，而是历经20世纪各种文学思潮的洗礼后，在不同作家的笔下不断流变。[3]除此之外，研究者还在艾什诺兹(Jean Echenoz)、邦(François Bon)、埃尔诺(Annie Ernaux)、盖兰嘉尔(Maylis de Kerangal)等当代重要作家身上发现某种对现实的关切，有时会启用"现实主义"这一旧标签[4]去探讨这些作家的写作。当代文学研究专家维亚尔(Dominique Viart)多次涉及该论题，认为对现实的关注、书写、介入是法国当代文学的一个突出特点。在《今日法国文学：继承、现代性、转变》(*La littérature française au présent: héritage, modernité, mutations*, 2008)中，维亚尔将"书写世界/现实"列为法国当代文学最重要的三大命题之一[5]，并辟专章进行论述。其为在线的"法国环球百科全书"(Encyclopædia Universalis)撰写的"当代法国文学""小说(当代法国小说)"等词条中也将"书写现实"作为主要特征之一。⑥在与儒比诺(Gianfranco Rubino)合编的《书写现时》(*Écrire le présent*，2012)中，维亚尔在引言中给出了对当下如何书写现实的总体性思考："谈论现时，从其定义而言，就是谈论现实，谈论文本之外发生的事件。"(Viart and Rubino 19)那么，哪些作家可以称得上"新现实主义"作家？法国当代作家的"新现实主义"写作具有哪些特征？下文我们将尝试对这些问题进行回答。

一、"新现实主义"与"批判性虚构"

要回答哪些作家属于"新现实主义"这个问题并非易事。法国并无自称属于"新现实主义"的作家。虽然不少作家被认为可以属于"新现实主义"或其他各色现实主义团体，但他们的创作特点各异，表面看来缺乏统一性。尽管如此，借助已有研究，我们仍能圈定几位能代表"新现实主义"创作潮流的作家：多位研究者均提到的邦，不少研究者提到的贝蒂纳(Arno Bertina)、施维亚尔(Éric Chevillard)、古(Jean-Paul Goux)、拉诺迪(Mathieu Larnaudie)、瓦赛(Philippe Vasset)、菲利佩蒂(Aurélie Filippetti)等作家。此外，热方还提到当代重要文学团体"无知者"(Inculte)，包括贝戈多(François Bégaudeau)、埃纳尔(Mathias Énard)、盖兰嘉尔等十余位作家；维亚尔还提到埃尔诺、维勒贝克(Michel Houellebecq)、卡莱尔(Emmanuel Carrère)、莫维尼埃(Laurent Mauvignier)等当代重要作家。下面我们将借助他们的创作，来探讨"新现实主义"写作的基本特征。

顾名思义，"新现实主义"这一标签包含两个部分——"新"与"现实主义"。换言之，"新现实主义"与"现实主义"之间既存在某种关联，又存在差异。"新现实主义"与19世纪现实主义写作存在差别，这一点不言而喻。我们首先可以通过维亚尔提出的一个重要理论术语"批判性虚构"(fiction critique)来管窥这种差别。这一术语最早被维亚尔用来描述当代作家米雄(Pierre Michon)的作品,维亚尔指出后者"确实是一项批评性的工作,尽管它没有遵照这一体裁的惯例"(Viart, "Les 'fictions critiques' de Pierre Michon" 204)。维亚尔之后进一步发展了"批判性虚构"概念,指出:"我建议将一些书称作'批判性虚构',这些书重新沉浸于世界中,对某种文学的死胡同有清醒的认识,并努力避免它们。它们是虚构并知道自己是虚构,因为它们永远不会将自己简化为纪录片或新闻报道,也不声称是某种客观现实的真实反映。"(Viart, "Les 'fictions critiques' de la littérature contemporaine" 10)反观19世纪现实主义小说,巴尔扎克(Honoré de Balzac)的很多作品自称是"社会研究""哲学研究",《人间喜剧》(*La Comédie humaine*, 1829 - 1848)更是自诩"风俗研究"。《红与黑》(*Le Rouge et le noir*, 1830)的副标题是"十九世纪纪事",在书中又将小说比作"沿途拿在手里的镜子"(Stendhal 133),这都强调了现实主义小说事实性、客观性甚至科学性的一面。换言之,自1980年代初以来,作家又重新关注世界、关注人这一主体,"但这个人已失去一切幻觉,而这个世界也已抛开企图改变它的话语"(Viart, "Les 'fictions critiques' de la littérature contemporaine" 10)。"当代作家继承了'怀疑'",面对现实,他们的责任与其说是"再现",不如说是"调查"(investigation)(Viart, "Les 'fictions critiques' de la littérature contemporaine" 10)。因此,即使19世纪与当代的现实主义作品会使用同样的写作素材,如社会新闻,邦的《一则社会新闻》(*Un fait divers*, 1994)与《红与黑》或《包法利夫人》(*Madame Bovary*, 1856)在写法与效果上完全不同。就如学者阿玛尔(Ruth Amar)所说,19世纪现实主义小说将读者置于被动地位,而在当代作品中,作者是见证者、调查者,读者在阅读中也必须跟着不断地转换位置、产生困惑与思考(Amar 49)。观念层面的差别也导致了书写形式的差异：相比19世纪现实主义小说，"新现实主义"写作具备了一些全新的特征，其中反摹仿与反小说倾向、不断实践文体的杂糅与创新、对"自我虚构"这一写作形式青睐有加这三方面可以说构成了"新现实主义"的基本特征。

二、反摹仿与反小说

这里所说的"摹仿"是亚里士多德意义上的，即文学作品讲述"某个有机整一的行动"（曹丹红 170）。与标榜真实、反映现实的传统小说相反，"新现实主义"写作明显体现出对摹仿的有意拒绝[⑦]。正如维亚尔所言，"批判性虚构几乎不再关心如何讲好故事，也不再追求叙事那令人安心的线性顺序"（Viart, "Les 'fictions critiques' de la littérature contemporaine" 10）。

在作家中，邦与贝古尼乌（Pierre Bergounioux）两人对"小说"这一标签的批判尤为激烈。早在1980年代，邦就曾表示过对这一提法的不满，因为它太容易令人联想到《红与黑》《包法利夫人》等传统小说。到了1990年代，他的作品几乎都弃用了"小说"这一标签。他在《急躁》（*Impatience*, 1998）中写道："再也没有小说，只有从硬壳中溢出又逃逸的闪光，不，没有故事，只有这些似乎承载着无法摆脱的痛苦的、晃动着的碎片，再也没有收集、整合一切的图景。"（Bon, *Impatience* 67）贝古尼乌对小说的声讨有过之而无不及，他借助黑格尔（小说是资产阶级的史诗）和卢卡奇（小说是那些不寻求真理的人的语言）的言论，指出小说之所以有过黄金时期，"主要因为有两样东西没有进入舞台，第一样是社会科学，第二样是政治批判"（Bergounioux and Alphant）。在贝古尼乌看来，小说这一形式在提供知识方面不及社会科学，在政治批判力度上不及其他形式，因此他认为，"小说已无法满足我们这个时代的期待。我们比我们的前辈更有学识。我们接受了长时间、大规模的教育。我们至少已失去前辈们的一部分天真。不应再给我们讲故事了"(Jeannet and Bergounioux)。在两位作家看来,"小说"属于某种以取悦人为主的方便文学,已和新的内容、新的形式不相兼容,是一种已过时的、应被超越的类型。

我们尝试从邦的作品来理解当代"新现实主义"作品的反摹仿倾向。从写作技法上看,除了采用去情节化、意识流式的书写,使用泛指人称代词以及支离破碎的句式,"新现实主义"写作还采取了其他反摹仿技法,例如多视点讲述同一个故事、将空间而非时间作为结构原则等。这些技法往往令新现实主义写作呈现出"碎片化"特征。邦的《工厂出口》(*Sortie d'usine*, 1982)中有一段对咖啡厅的描写:

> 幸亏到处都有挂钟。这里的钟挂在吧台上,是做广告的。地下咖啡店。在这一亩三分地不需要戴表,他那块表从签定上一个租约起就不走了,可他照样过得很好。他周围尽是顾客,奶油咖啡或不带奶油,小杯黑咖啡或速蒸咖啡,他们说,一杯速蒸,一杯,外加小瓶饮料,苏维农面包或羊角包,柜台里面三条汉子穿梭来往,这个时候够他们忙的。他们的嘴也没闲着,嘴巴有它们的忙闲周期,有它们的时尚,来吧孩子们吃了喝了付钱,要不就叫一声大夫,一边在你鼻子底下晃动杯子,总要洒出一点。也躲不开那个从背后偷看他那份《锁鸭报》的家伙,对这种事他总是不习惯。拿开报纸,做出不高兴的样子。三个侍者中有一个尤其忙得不亦乐乎,只听见他的声音,他的奥维涅口音,我们这些移民,他说,他那副圆眼镜,吧台新鲜的橙色,塑料瓶。(邦 12)

这并不是一段传统的描写,它不服务于作品情节的发展。实际上,虽然此时的邦并没有放弃"小说"标签,但《工厂出口》已经属于"没有情节的小说"(roman sans romanesque)。这段描写接近于速写,读者跟随匿名主人公的视角快速移动,叙述者对事物精确命名,句子简短,甚至是只有半截、名词性的句子,具象的人物、声音、事物一闪而过,近似于佩雷克(Georges Perec)在巴黎街头试图穷尽眼前一切的写作实践:"63号公交开往犬舍门。86号开往圣日耳曼德普雷。清扫,保持地面清洁,这样很好。一辆德国汽车。"(Perec 15)维亚尔这样评价《工厂出口》的写作特征:"现实只能通过片段、通过瞬间的形象呈现",作家能够记忆、描绘某个画面,但后者"始终没有发展成为'小说'的素材[……]它始终处于一种原始的、基本的状态"(Viart and Vercier 216)。邦自己也曾谈论过这种碎片化写作的必要性或者说强制性:"最开始并没有人物,只有一些图像。我无法抓住它们,它们仅通过某种执念、某种恐惧与我关联[……]在很多年的努力无果后,对我来说唯一可能的突破,正是强迫自己严格遵从这些现实碎片的召唤,只借助这些不经意间发现的图像,这些在大街上听到的只言片语来写作,严格遵从这一切的贫瘠本身。之后,在书中,通过它们的匮乏、它们的无力来记录它们。"(Bon, *Impatience* 76)

不过,以邦和贝古尼乌这两位作家为代表的对小说的声讨与1980年代以市场营利为导向的大众文学泛滥有关,他们反对的并不是小说体裁,而是某种庸俗化的小说,尤其是滥用虚构、编造故事情节的"小说"。总体而言,虽然维勒贝克、恩迪亚耶(Marie NDiaye)等书写现实的当代作家并没有放弃小说体裁,甚至会采用虚构甚至奇幻的写作曲折反映现实,但创造摹仿式小说,通过想象构筑令读者沉浸其中的虚构世界,这一做法已越来越遭到部分当代作家的质疑。

三、文体的杂糅与创新

对传统摹仿式小说形式的抛弃意味着作家需要寻找新的形式来讲述现实,这便推动了当代作家对其他文体的借鉴、吸收与混用。以邦的

《大宇》(*Daewoo*, 2004)为例。21世纪初,韩国大宇集团开办在法国东部小城的工厂全部关闭,大批工人失业,邦对此进行了"调查"。从形式来看,《大宇》可以说是"大杂烩",由10出戏剧、10个虚构的访谈以及作家的调查日记等内容构成。其中,数个"虚构访谈"章节与"见证"章节交错进行,并且均将"火灾、暴力、反抗"作为标题,旨在形成某种对照。有趣的是,该作品2004年在法雅尔(Fayard)出版社出版时,封面上只标记了"小说"。而在2014年的新版中,作品封面标记了"戏剧/小说/日记",三种体裁的并置有意识地强调了作品的文体杂糅性。

类似的文体实验在邦的作品中数见不鲜。《停车场》(*Parking*, 1996)涉及一起停车场看守抛妻弃子致妻子自杀的悲剧事件。该作品由独立的三部分组成,第一部分是长达二十多页的独白,发话者是自杀女子的母亲,这些独白是她前往停车场对看守的责问;第二部分可以说是邦的创作手记,记录了将此事件作为题材进行创作的缘由、创作灵感,以及由创作引发的思考;第三部分作者又基于同一事件,以戏剧的形式分别构想了证人、母亲、自杀的女子三个角色的台词。《噪声》(*Bruit*, 2000)由邦与四位无家可归者的8组访谈以及4组虚构的人物独白构成,前8组对话都发生在四位访谈者非法占据的房屋中,每当时间与参与者发生变化便另起一组,表现出某种戏剧的形式。

从这些例子不难看出,邦有意识地在叙事中融入戏剧的文体形式,通过一种"齐唱式的""众声齐发的""无限接近于戏剧的小说"(Viart, "François Bon, la convocation au théâtre" 99),让读者听到小人物的内心呼声,从不同角度的诉说中寻找某一事件或某种处境的真相,并从对不同声音,甚至是不同文学形式的反思中理解"话语"对"真相"的制造。这些各自独立的声音虽然并不直接对话,彼此之间却不断关联、产生意义,"以独立的声音所组成的整体促成一种批判性的、反对单一的话语"(Viart, "François Bon, la convocation au théâtre" 99)。在邦之后,这种将戏剧、访谈等文体融入创作的"多声部"写作还体现在塞雷纳

(Jacques Serena)、沃洛迪纳(Antoine Volodine)、莫维尼埃、罗森塔尔(Olivia Rosenthal)等"新现实主义"作家的创作中。

在热方看来,邦等作家对不同文体的混用体现出某种不连贯性(incohérence),甚至有逐渐走向"异质化"(hétérogène)的倾向。这种改变的原因在于法国当代作家,尤其是书写现实的新一代作家对现实的存在方式、文学的任务等问题有了新的认识:"文学所见证的,正是这个世界的不连贯性,它的众声喧哗,以及它充斥着不协调的异质性。"(Gefen)此外,文体杂糅性还由一个事实导致,那便是当代文学与人文科学、工人阶级历史和社会学等学科与知识之间愈发紧密的联系。上文贝古尼乌的言论已涉及社会科学的影响。另一些具有"新现实主义"写作倾向的当代作家,例如埃尔诺、米雄、维勒贝克、路易(Édouard Louis)等人也都表现出类似特点。以路易《谁杀死了我的父亲》(*Qui a tué mon père?*, 2018)的开头为例:

> 当被问及种族主义这个词对她意味着什么时,美国知识分子露丝·吉尔摩回答说,种族主义是某些人群向提前死亡状态的暴露。
> 这个定义同样适用于男性霸权、对同性恋或变性者的仇恨、阶级压迫,也就是一切社会和政治压迫现象。如果将政治视为一些群体对另一些群体的统治,以及个体生存于他们没有主动选择的社区,那么政治就是对一些生活得到支持、鼓励、保护的人群和另一些暴露于死亡、迫害和谋杀的人群的区隔。
> 上个月,我到你现在居住的北方小城来看你。[……]

(Louis 11)

我们注意到,这个开头可以分为两部分:第一、二段是一个部分,涉及对

"种族主义"的定义,采取的是社会科学的话语,体现出知识性、思辨性与客观性;第三段开始引入事件,符合文学叙事的文类要求,体现出故事性、主观性与某种诗意。实际上,"新现实主义"的很多作家从政治社会科学理论,尤其是从布尔迪厄(Pierre Bourdieu)的社会学著作中汲取了不少养分,不仅可能在书写形式上戏仿这些学科的理论话语,甚至可能在作品中直接引用理论文献,造成作品杂糅程度的加深,同时也促使文类的界限进一步模糊。

这种对于不同文学形式、不同学科的开放性还催生了鼓励文体创新与实验的创作出版生态,热方提到的"无知者"文学团体以及垂直出版社(Éditions Verticales)尤为典型。"无知者"是一个始于2004年的文学团体,由十几位作家、哲学家、翻译家共同发起,试图用"无知者"这一具有幽默色彩的名称"消解过于封闭、严肃、固化的作者形象"(Pluvinet)。团体的作家们以"无知者"为名共同创作了一系列形式多样的集体作品,包括小说、著作、文集等。在创作上,如团体所出版的集体作品《小说的未来(卷二):写作与实在》(*Devenirs du roman II: écriture et matériaux*, 2014)封底所言,他们主张囊括"多样化、异质性的知识、社会事件,声名显赫或默默无闻的各色人物的生活","以同样的方式运用形形色色的素材"。他们还鼓励团体内的作家随心所欲地"试验其野心勃勃的写作计划,将自己的写作与那些由于专业性或通俗性而被认为是非文学的素材相融合"(Baud)。团体还创办了一本同名文学杂志、一个同名出版社,为实践文学理念提供了场所。成立于1997年的垂直出版社更是以"垂直是对抗标准化的一种方式""分歧的集结点"(Escola)作为宣言,对大众语言、媒体语言、非虚构写作等均持开放态度。

四、自我虚构倾向

在当代法国文学中,"自我的回归"也是一大趋势,当代作家对个体记忆、生命历程、父辈与家族历史乃至个人与所处社会及时代的关联产生好奇，由此衍生出许多与自我书写相关的文学标签，如自我虚构（autofiction）、亲子小说（récit de filiation）、虚构传记（fiction biographique）等。其中，杜布罗夫斯基（Serge Doubrovsky）以其所提出的"自我虚构"概念挑战了遵循线性叙述、将虚构与事实对立的传统自传观念，更新了自我书写的范式。

个体经验的回归与自我书写在对当代现实的书写中也起到了独特的作用。当代法国文学"主体"的回归不仅体现在日益扩展的自我书写实践中，也表现为一种"以作者感知到的世界来重构现实的倾向"，将主体视作"地震仪"，以一种现象学式的方式记录"面对某一社会情境时的真实感受"（Amar 41）。法国当代作家德莱姆（Philippe Delerm）以对细微事物的描写著称，通过对日常生活中司空见惯的事物的描写唤起读者对生活空间的关注以及与之相关的美好记忆。同样是去情节化、碎片化，德莱姆的描写与邦对场景中性甚至冷峻的描写不同，体现出叙述者的主观性对描写对象的影响，使读者得以窥见叙述者的心理状态与内心情感，甚至邀请读者进入其隐秘的记忆宫殿。以德莱姆对夜间高速公路的描写为例：

> 你在穿过黑夜。间隔一定距离而立的路牌——未来景观城、普瓦捷北郊、普瓦捷南郊、下一个出口是普瓦特万沼泽——都是些标准的法语名称，让人觉得是在上地理课。但这是一种抽象的趣事，是你以旧日偷懒取巧的背景心态在淡化的一种模糊现实：你一脚踩着油门，一只眼睛看着里程表，你所不顾及的这个潜在的法兰西，也是你不会去学习的一课书。
>
> 大型便餐店就在十公里处。你将在那里停下来。你已经看到了远处教堂的一抹淡淡的灯光，随着灯光越来越宽，你感觉就像乘船旅行之末港口在向前迎接那样。九十八号高级汽

油。风是凉爽的。输油嘴在机械地顺从,计油器在轰轰地作响。接着,去了大型便餐店,里边充满了有点黏稠的浓烈气味,就像所有车站和所有夜间避风港那样。一杯意式咖啡——加点糖。重要的是喝咖啡的念头,而不是味道。一阵热烈,一阵苦涩。脚步僵硬,两眼浑浊,几个人影交错,但都无话而过。接着,又是先前的星体船,又是把你紧紧地包住的车壳。(德莱姆 27)

这种"自我虚构"式的书写甚至使作者能够以一种自我暴露的私人化表达介入现实,令写作成为体现作者伦理立场的手段。以德庞特(Virginie Despentes)的《金刚理论》(King Kong Theory, 2006)为例:"我作为丑女人中的一员,为丑女人、老女人、男人婆、冷淡的女人、让人提不起兴趣的女人、恶心的女人、疯女人、有毛病的女人、所有被排除在好女人的市场之外的女人而写。"(Despentes 9)德庞特以一个边缘女性的视角,列举了在现实生活中听到的对所谓"坏女人"的负面评价,以一种融合客观陈述与私人体验的形式"回敬"了对女性进行凝视与评判的目光,巧妙地对评价行为的主客体进行了置换,并以此表达了对女性歧视以及性别规训的态度与立场。

除此之外,自我虚构流行的原因还在于新技术的影响。一些"新现实主义"作家在网络博客、个人网站等平台进行创作,潜移默化中促成了当代文学创作体裁的转变。以网络博客这一大众传媒手段为例,法国媒介研究学者泰朗蒂(Marie-Ève Thérenty)基于对邦和施维亚尔的博客写作的研究,提出了"博客效应"(effet-blog)概念,指出博客写作实践的是"一项自我虚构写作的独创性工作以及一种书写日常的尝试"(Thérenty)。对日常生活的碎片化纪事"是某种观看现实的方式,换言之,它邀请作者去书写重复的动作(习惯),书写平凡的事物(平庸与普通),书写细节(微小与私密)"(Thérenty)。从这种意义上说,采取博客写作的作家"参与到了社会斗争中"(Thérenty)，因为通过不断书写、无限放大存在于社会各个角度的原本不起眼的事件，作家一方面令现实的某种荒诞性得以呈现，另一方面也像朗西埃(Jacques Rancière)所说的那样，赋予底层人民与事物以话语权，在重新分配感性的过程中，为某种更为公平正义的社会而斗争。

当然，类似博客写作的行为在19世纪也是存在的，巴尔扎克的小说就常常先在报纸上连载，最后结集出版。区别在于，博客写作往往采用第一人称视角，在题材方面没有任何禁忌，这促使文类界限不断瓦解，同时令作品的杂糅程度进一步加深。在这方面，邦的《喧嚣》(*Tumulte*，2006)特别具有代表性。《喧嚣》最初是在网络博客上创作的，如作品封底所言，邦在创作之初就希望这是一部"通篇混杂虚构故事与真实回忆的作品，记录日常经验与城市经验中那些让人摇摆不定的时刻，不作预先准备的写作，直接写在网上"。在一年的时间里，邦每天在自己创建的一个文学爱好者网站(Remue. net)上写作。2006年，他将三百多篇博文集结出版。这部在出版后被贴上"小说"标签的作品内容包罗万象，且极为碎片化，内容涉及火车与车站、酒店房间、人间惨剧、一系列自传性质的博文、大量梦境、其他作家等等，内容之间的唯一关联就是叙述者"我"，这也令事实笼罩上虚构的色彩。

五、"新现实主义"的社会批判精神

反摹仿、反小说、文体杂糅与创新、自我虚构……"新现实主义"写作在形式创新方面的这些特征均会令我们联想到"新小说"(Nouveau Roman)或后现代小说。此外，很多"新现实主义"作家确实都受西蒙(Claude Simon)、萨洛特(Nathalie Sarraute)尤其是福克纳(William Faulkner)的影响。那么当代的"新现实主义"写作与"新小说"或后现代小说有什么区别？这一点可能要从"新现实主义"与19世纪现实主义文学之间的关联入手进行思考。从关联来看,21世纪的"新现实主义"写作是对19世纪现实主义的继承。这种继承主要体现在两个方面。首先是主题方面的继承。"新现实主义"写作往往被认为与法国当代文学的转型发生于同一时期。维亚尔等学者认为,在1970年代末1980年代初,法国文学内部进行了更新。这种更新首先是文学面对全球经济形势与政治气候的显著变化所做出的反应。在种种"世界的压力"下,法国文学逐渐抛弃结构主义与新小说实验时期围绕语言和形式游戏展开的"不及物"写作,重新开始关注现实、关注社会、关注世界(Viart, "Introduction" 15-18)。1970年代末1980年代初出版的三部工厂题材的作品——林纳尔(Robert Linhart)的《工作台》(*L'Établi*, 1978)、邦的《工厂出口》、卡普兰(Leslie Kaplan)的《过剩-工厂》(*L'Excès-l'usine*, 1982)反映了这一转型。

对"工厂"与"工作"题材的关注确实是当代"新现实主义"写作的重要内容。对"工作"问题的聚焦延续了左拉(Émile Zola)、于勒·罗曼(Jules Romains)等经典作家对无产者、底层人民的工作环境以及生存处境的关注。不少"新现实主义"作品尤其关注当下工作环境的新变化及其对人际关系、人的精神状态的影响,例如班斯坦热尔(Thierry Beinstingel)在《总部》(*Central*, 2000)、《简历小说》(*CV roman*, 2007)等作品中刻画了工作环境的冷漠以及工作任务的反人性本质,发人深思。此外,"新现实主义"对移民问题、城乡冲突、阶级压迫、性别歧视、失业贫困、老龄化与代际冲突等重大社会问题,以及科技伦理、生态环境、当代人的内心困境等时时涌现的新议题均有所涉及。

其次,"新现实主义"还继承了19世纪现实主义的社会批判精神。上文我们已提到维亚尔提出的"批判性虚构"概念,维亚尔认为:"这些虚构从双重理由来说是具有批判性的事业,一方面,它们抓住了问题,例如人存在于世以及人的命运问题,历史以及具有歪曲性的历史话语问题,记忆及其不确定的干扰问题[……]另一方面,这些虚构朝它们自己的文学方式投去了毫不留情的目光。"(Viart,"Les'fictions critiques'de la littérature contemporaine"10)这或许是当代的"新现实主义"写作与1950—1960年代的"新小说"最大的区别。另外,在热方看来,当今"新现实主义"写作的目的不再是对文学经典的破坏或反思:"近年来,文学内部进行的令人精疲力竭的对抗与战争似乎已经止息,为一种新的、'热烈的'(米歇尔·塞尔语)唯物主义让出了位置:一种'物的文学',在物中间是人类与动物,一种'活跃的'、有形的文学,一种'颤动的''具身的美学',然而与一个扁平的、没有等级的世界相连,既是一种资料的文学,也是一种语言激荡的文学,毫无顾忌地融合两者,将人纳入整体的生态人类世界,一个可能有关甚至中心偏移至后人类问题的世界。"(Gefen)

对19世纪现实主义文学的继承令当代"新现实主义"区别于1950—1960年代的"新小说"。然而,我们能不能像谈论19世纪现实主义文学那样理直气壮地谈论当代"新现实主义"文学？很多人指出,科学领域的范式转换是不可逆的,但人文社会学科允许多种范式并存,共同为一个问题提供解决之道。然而,实际上,人文社会学科同样存在某种程度上的不可逆现象。在利奥塔(Jean-François Lyotard)出版《后现代状况》(*La Condition postmoderne*, 1979)之后,我们在阅读过去时代的"宏大叙事"(grand récit)时都会带上反思的目光,而自从加洛蒂(Roger Garaudy)提出"无边的现实主义"(réalisme sans rivages)后,我们在看到"现实主义"一词时难免想到它兼容并包,甚至自相矛盾的内涵。从这个意义上说,"新现实主义"这一术语的提出与其说是要框定一个流派,不如说是评论家试图理解当代法国文学写作中的某种共同倾向,以便更好地把握当下的文学与时代、与社会的关系。

在这样的目光之下,我们发现一种共同倾向的存在应该说是毋庸置疑的。对于这种写作倾向出现的原因,维亚尔准确地总结道:"面对一种双重的要求——文学应逃离封闭的唯我论并回应社会语境的压力,叙事文学重审了其关键问题,同时改变了其实践。"⑧

无论我们如何命名这种叙事文学,这些写作实践的现实介入姿态是不容忽视的,也应该得到我们的肯定。正如比利时著名社会学家杜布瓦(Jacques Dubois)所言:"纵使现实主义几乎不复存在,其最重要的目标却留存下来。它们关乎某种定义文学社会功能的方式,关乎以历史视角来观照文学的方式,更简单地说,甚至关乎我们阅读与实践文学的方式。也就是说,我们亟须建构或者说重构'现实'对象,这将是以批评的方式来延续某场今日仍在进行中的辩论,辩论的主题是文学与世界表征之间的关联。"(Dubois 10 - 11)

注解【Notes】

① 法国基梅出版社(Éditions Kimé)网站介绍了该专著的核心观点,布里克斯认为从17世纪至今,法国文学的主流美学范式先后被古典主义与现实主义主导,从19世纪开始,古典主义最终让位于现实主义,后者的主导地位延续至今,详见 "Du classicisme au réalisme. Une histoire de la littérature française (XVIIe-XXIe siècles)", *Éditions Kimé*, 2021, https://editionskime.fr/produit/du-classicisme-au-realisme-une-histoire-de-la-litterature-francaise-xviie-xxie-siecles/。

② 热方的文章《世界不存在,当代法国文学中的"新现实主义"》(Alexandre Gefen, "Le monde n'existe pas, le 'nouveau réalisme' de la littérature française contemporaine." *L'incoerenza creativa nella narrativa francese contemporanea*, edited by Matteo Majorano, Quodlibet, 2018, books.openedition.org/quodlibet/824)、格勒努耶的文章《面对社会与工人问题的当代法国文学:'新'现实主义的发明(弗朗索瓦·邦、让-保尔·古)》(Corinne Grenouillet, "La littérature française contemporaine face à la question sociale et ouvrière: l'invention d'un 'nouveau' réalisme (François Bon, Jean-Paul Goux)." *Raison publique*, no.15, 2011, p. 83 - 99),以及贝尔纳的博士论文《20世纪末法国小说中的新知识与新现实主义:施维亚尔、德维尔、艾什诺兹、图森》(Isabelle Bernard, *Nouveaux savoirs et nouveau réalisme dans le roman français à la fin du XXe siècle: Éric Chevillard, Patrick Deville, Jean Echenoz, Jean-Philippe Toussaint*. Université Paris III, 2000)等均提及"新现实主义",《法国文学电子杂志》2019年第13辑第1期在介绍中提到,该期杂志主要从政治角度谈论"文学中各种各样的新现实主义"(Olivier Sécardin, dir., *Relief—Revue électronique de littérature française*, vol. 13, no. 1, 2019, revue-relief.org/issue/view/292)。

③ 可从数部专著的书名管窥,如《书写现实的小说家:从巴尔扎克到西默农》(Jacques Dubois, *Les Romanciers du réel: de Balzac à Simenon*. Seuil, 2000),

《现实主义：从巴尔扎克到普鲁斯特》(Philippe Dufour, *Le Réalisme: de Balzac à Proust*. PUF, 1998)，《真实的回音：从巴尔扎克到基尼亚尔》(Chantal Lapeyre-Desmaison, *Résonances du réel: de Balzac à Pascal Quignard*. L'Harmattan, 2011)。

④ 例如哈米迪的专著《让·艾什诺兹与弗朗索瓦·邦：一种介入现实主义》(Chaïmaa El Hamidi, *Jean Echenoz et François Bon: un réalisme engagé*. Éditions universitaires européennes, 2016)、麦吉尔瓦尼的文章《安妮·埃尔诺：一位遵循现实主义传统的作家》(Slobhán McIlvanney, "Annie Ernaux: un écrivain dans la tradition du réalisme." *Revue d'Histoire littéraire de la France*, vol.98, no.2, 1998, p. 247-266)、热方的文章《弗朗索瓦·邦的现实主义》(Alexandre Gefen, "Réalisme de François Bon." *François Bon, éclats de réalité*. Edited by Jean-Bernard Vray and Dominique Viart, Presses universitaires de Saint-Étienne, 2010, p. 93-104)、德蒙克的文章《抓取现实、撼动文本：盖兰嘉尔作品中的吊诡现实主义》(Jean De Munck, "Capter le réel, faire vibrer le texte. Le réalisme paradoxal de Maylis de Kerangal." *La Revue générale*, no.3, 2021, p.131-149)。

⑤ 专著第三章题为"书写世界"(Écrire le monde)，此处"书写世界"基本等同于"书写现实"，维亚尔在章首介绍便开门见山地指出，"在重归'及物'的文学所书写的'对象'中，对'现实'(réel)的书写是一个重要部分"，专著中论述的另外两大主题是自我书写以及历史书写，详见 Dominique Viart, *La littérature française au présent: héritage, modernité, mutations*. 2nd ed., Bordas, 2008, p. 27, 129, 211。

⑥ "法国当代文学"词条中表述为"对现实的书写"(L'écriture du réel)，见 Dominique Viart, "Littérature française contemporaine." *Encyclopædia Universalis*, https://www.universalis.fr/encyclopedie/litterature-francaise-contemporaine/；"小说(当代法国小说)"词条中表述为"书写现实"(Écrire le réel)，详见 Dominique Viart, "Roman. Le roman français contemporain." *Encyclopædia Universalis*, www.universalis.fr/encyclopedie/roman-le-roman-francais-contemporain/。

⑦ 法国当代文学批评家亨利·戈达尔(Henri Godard)在《小说使用说明》(*Le roman modes d'emploi*, 2006)论及法国反摹仿的小说传统，详见亨利·戈达尔，《小说使用说明》，顾秋艳、陈岩岩、张正怡译，北京联合出版公司，2023年。

⑧ 引自维亚尔为"法国环球百科全书"撰写的"小说(当代法国小说)"词条，详见 Dominique Viart, "Roman. Le roman français contemporain." *Encyclopædia Universalis*, www.universalis.fr/encyclopedie/roman-le-roman-francais-contemporain/。

引用文献【Works Cited】

Amar, Ruth. "De l'évolution du Réalisme: les aspects du roman français contemporain." *Synergies Mexique*, no. 10, 2020, pp. 39 - 52.

Baud, Jean-Marc. "Les camaraderies contemporaines du collectif Inculte." *La littérature contemporaine au collectif*, edited by Anthony Glinoer and Michel Lacroix, 2020, www. fabula. org/colloques/document6683. php.

Bergounioux, Pierre and François Bon. "Du réalisme." *Centre Pompidou*, 9 Dec. 2005. www. centrepompidou. fr/fr/ressources/media/P6c4Pmu.

弗朗索瓦·邦:《工厂出口》,施康强、程静、康勤译,湖南文艺出版社,1999年。

[Bon, François. *Sortie d'usine*. Translated by Shi Kangqiang, Cheng Jing and Kang Qin, Hunan Literature and Art Publishing House, 1999.]

---. *Impatience*. Minuit, 1998.

---. "Interview avec François Bon." *L'Infini*, no. 27, 1989, pp. 70 - 78.

Bradbury, Malcolm. "Writing Fiction in the 90s." *Neo-Realism in Contemporary American Fiction*. Edited by Kristiaan Versluys, Rodopi, 1992, pp. 13 - 25.

曹丹红:《试论朗西埃的现代虚构观》,《文艺理论研究》第5期,2019年9月,第170—177页。

[Cao, Danhong. "On Rancière's Concept of Modern Fiction." *Theoretical Studies in Literature and Art*, no. 5, Sep. 2019, pp. 170 - 177.]

菲利普·德莱姆:《第一口啤酒》,怀宇、郭昌京译,上海文艺出版社,2014年。

[Delerm, Philippe. *La première gorgée de bière et autres plaisirs minuscules*. Translated by Huai Yu and Guo Changjing, Hunan Literature and Art Publishing House, 2014.]

Despentes, Virginie. *King Kong Théorie*. Grasset, 2006.

Dubois, Jacques. *Les romanciers du réel: de Balzac à Simenon*. Seuil, 2000.

Escola, Marc. "Éditions Verticales 1997 - 2017: éditer et écrire debout (Poitiers & Paris)." *Fabula/Actualité*, 6 Jan. 2017, www. fabula. org/actualites/75861/colloque-editions-verticales-1997 - 2017 - editer-et-ecrire-debout. html.

Gefen, Alexandre. "Le monde n'existe pas: le 'nouveau réalisme' de la littérature française contemporaine." *L'incoerenza creativa nella narrativa francese contemporanea*, edited by Matteo Majorano, 2018, books. openedition. org/quodlibet/824.

Jeannet, Frédéric-Yves and Bergounioux, Pierre. "Entretien Frédéric-Yves Jeannet / Pierre Bergounioux." *Diacritik*, 21 Feb. 2017, diacritik. com/2017/02/21/entretien-frederic-yves-jeannet-pierre-bergounioux/.

Louis, Édouard. *Qui a tué mon père?*. Seuil, 2018.

Perec, Georges. *Tentative d'épuisement d'un lieu parisien*. Christian Bourgois, 1983.

Pluvinet, Charline. "Décloisonnements auctoriaux: signer 'Collectif inculte'."

 Auctorialité multiple, Inculte: pratiques éditoriales, gestes collectifs et inflexions esthétiques, edited by Alexandre Gefen et al., 2023, www.fabula. org/colloques/document9825.php.

Stendhal. *Le Rouge et le noir: chronique du dix-neuvième siècle*. Le Divan, 1927.

Thérenty, Marie-Ève. " L'effet-blog en littérature. Sur *L'Autofictif* d'Éric Chevillard et *Tumulte* de François Bon." *Itinéraires*, no. 2, 2010, journals. openedition.org/itineraires/1964.

Viart, Dominique. "François Bon, la convocation au théâtre." *Études théâtrales*, no. 33, 2005, pp. 91 – 101.

---. " Introduction." *Écrire le présent*, edited by Gianfranco Rubino and Dominique Viart, Armand Colin, 2012, pp. 17 – 36.

---. *La littérature française au présent: héritage, modernité, mutations*. 2nd ed., Bordas, 2008.

---. "Les 'fictions critiques' de la littérature contemporaine." *Spirale*, no. 201, 2005, pp. 10 – 11.

---. "Les 'fictions critiques' de Pierre Michon." *Pierre Michon, l'écriture absolue*, edited by Agnès Castiglione, PU de Saint-Étienne, 2002, pp. 206 – 216.

记忆书写的双重载体
——试论安妮·埃尔诺作品中的文字与图像

史烨婷

内容摘要:法国作家、诺贝尔文学奖得主安妮·埃尔诺(Annie Ernaux)以融合了社会学和历史学的创作理念开辟了"无人称自传"(或社会自传),不倦书写着融合了个人记忆、集体记忆的现实生活,以求打破阶层、映证时代。在这一过程中,埃尔诺的记忆书写呈现出明显的跨媒介性。一方面以精准文字描绘图像(照片),将现实与记忆的物性诉诸笔端,依据福柯"物的秩序"原则,以语词将世界纳入话语的主权之中,再现表象。另一方面,埃尔诺作品中的文字与图像亦有差距,埃尔诺认为照片是痕迹,而文字必须"致幻"。她利用文字与图像在时间上的间离,构建特有的创作空间,以求捕捉人类心理世界的现实。图像反映现实,文字映照内心,在文字与图像的双重作用下实践了"镜与灯"的隐喻。安妮·埃尔诺结合了文字与图像的跨媒介手法,最大限度地捕捉真实,反映了时代洪流中个人之于社会留下的印记。

关键词:安妮·埃尔诺 跨媒介 文字与图像 记忆

作者简介:史烨婷,浙江大学外国语学院高级讲师,主要从事法国当代文学、文学的跨媒介研究。

Title: The Dual Vehicle of Memory Writing—Text and Image in the Works of Annie Ernaux

Abstract: Annie Ernaux, a French writer and Nobel Prize laureate in literature, introduced the concept of "Impersonal autobiography" (or social autobiography) by creatively integrating sociology and history. She tirelessly wrote about real life, which integrates personal and collective memory, to break down hierarchies and reflect the times. Ernaux's memory writing exhibits transmediality. On one hand, the author describes images (photographs) with precise language, capturing the physicality of reality and memory. In accordance with Foucault's principle of "the order of things", the author brings the world under the sovereignty of discourse and reproduces representations with words. On the other hand, there is a gap between the text and the image in Ernaux's works. For Ernaux, photographs are traces, while words must be "hallucinogenic". Annie Ernaux utilises the temporal separation between words and images to create a distinctive creative space that captures the essence of the human psychological world. The image reflects reality, while the text reflects emotions. The metaphor of the mirror and the lamp is realised through the dual role of text and image. By combining transmedia techniques, Annie Ernaux captures the truth and reflects the impact of individual on society in the current era.

Key words: Annie Ernaux; transmedia; text and image; memory

Author: Shi Yeting is an associate professor at School of International Studies, Zhejiang University, Hangzhou, China (310058), specializing in comtemporary French literautre and transmedia studies in literature.

法国作家安妮·埃尔诺于2022年获得诺贝尔文学奖,评奖词有言"她以勇气和手术刀般的精确,通过个人记忆揭露根源、异化和集体层面的限制"。埃尔诺的创作手法抛却传统规范,以勇气和信念践行自己的创作理想,开创了"无人称自传"(或称社会自传,auto-socio-biographie)的写法。而在这一过程中,作家的书写带有明显的跨媒介性,时常出现文字与图像的交错叠映。她曾清晰表达自己对于这两种媒介的偏爱和倚重:"我偏爱两种私人材料的联合,影集和日记:一种照片日记。"(*Ecrire la vie* 8)从形式上就能直接看出两种媒介的作品主要有《照片的用途》(*L'Usage de la photo*,2005)、《悠悠岁月》(*Les Années*,2008)和《书写生活》(*Ecrire la vie*,2011)的第一部分,当然,在作家的其他作品中,这种文字、图像的杂糅现象也并不陌生。法国学者、莫迪亚诺和埃尔诺研究专家布鲁诺·布朗克曼(Bruno Blanckman)将《悠悠岁月》视为安妮·埃尔诺所有作品的"元小说",认为"(它)是作品中的作品,一生的作品"(78),看重其核心地位,也因此变向肯定了埃尔诺的跨媒介创作思维在理解作家创作过程中的重要性。虽然文字和图像分属不同的艺术媒介,但它们之间的关联显而易见,像在进行着一种相互呼应的游戏。因此,两种媒介在艺术表现手法和效果上的差异性成为学者们关注的重点,这种差异性很大程度上,表现为某种间离(intervalle),被描述为一种"时差、不协调、含糊不清、争议、矛盾"(Montémont 54)。法兰西学院院士、文学理论家、批评家孔帕尼翁(Antoine Compagnon)曾评价《悠悠岁月》最令他喜欢的地方在于:她叙述自己一生时的距离感,评述家庭照片时不断匿名化的运动及其自我隐私在共同时间——世代、时代和大众文化中的融入。"距离感"——无论是纵向时间上,还是个人相对于大时代——成为理解埃尔诺作品的一个关键点。

埃尔诺习惯用文字极其精确地描绘照片,《悠悠岁月》中并没有照片,但读者几乎不用看照片便能想象出照片的样子,以及它所呈现的画面。《照片的用途》中有照片,但埃尔诺依然执着地对照片进行细致描写,相比之下,M描述照片的部分则仅是一种对照片的补足,简省、粗略得多。那么,埃尔诺以文字复写图像有何意义?这是否真的只是一种重复?《书写生活》中的文字和图像依然可见精准复写的特点,但同时又呈现出另一种时间上的间离关系,照片的拍摄时间与节选日记的时间往往存在差距,其表达效果何在、意义何在?

我们试图从文字对图像的精准呈现、文字与图像的贯通,以及文字与图像的间离三个方面来看埃尔诺在创作过程中对两种媒介的运用,从而探知作家在捕捉现实、反映人类在时代洪流中的个人记忆与集体记忆时想要达到的效果,以及所传达的思考。作家在访谈录《书写如刀》(*L'écriture comme couteau*, 2003)中将书写比作"给日常的、城市的、集体的事实拍摄照片。[……]但无论是潜在的,还是真实存在的照片,摄影全然成了普鲁斯特笔下的小玛德莲娜蛋糕,扮演着叙述和记忆流程的转承角色"(让内特 60)。埃尔诺的记忆书写因而在文字与图像的双重载体中成为别具一格的存在。

一、复写图像的文字

《悠悠岁月》开篇第一句话是"所有的图像都将消失"(*Les Années* 1)。整部作品没有古典的叙事,而由许多零碎的记忆片段连缀而成,行进的过程中,我们仿佛看见一幅幅照片呈现在眼前。作品由十四张照片划分成十五个段落,每段的时间跨度大约是四至七年,总是从照片的细致描述开始,不同年代、不同人物固定在瞬间捕捉的画面中,成就了小说最为牢靠的结构,一路从 1940 年写到 2006 年。作者对于每张照片的相框、装饰、拍摄时间地点都有详细描述,照片中的人物更是被从样貌、穿着、神态、动作,以及拍摄场景等诸多方面进行了细致描写。全书没有任何图片,十四张照片全靠文字描摹。在西方的文学与艺术传统中,狭义上以文字详细描述绘画、雕塑或其他视觉艺术作品的文学手段被称为"艺格敷词"(ekphrasis),可追溯至古希腊,荷马史诗《伊利亚特》中对阿喀琉斯盾牌的长篇描述被视为最早的实例。埃尔诺以语词媒介(文学)来描述视觉艺术作品及其总体面貌(照片),唤起读者的视觉想象,居于传统的文学范畴,凭借语词的力量进行表达。但埃尔诺的创作实践显然不仅仅局限于此，她尝试在文学与图像的互涉领域进行更为深入的尝试。

《照片的用途》就是这种探索性质的实践。该书由安妮·埃尔诺和他的爱侣马克·马力（Marc Marie）分头书写，每一段落都始于一张呈现在书中的照片，两人基于同一照片各自生产文字，写作期间不互通消息。因此有关图像的书写方式立即呈现出了差异性：马力的文字明显因为图像的存在而简省了许多，而埃尔诺依然坚持以艺格敷词手法进行书写。但实体照片的存在已经使其创作方法跳脱了"艺格敷词"。埃尔诺曾在访谈中提及《照片的用途》的创作方法，认为这部作品是"[……]危险的文字，因为我自己提议从可见的照片出发"（Ernaux and Schwerdtner 759）。如若照片真实出现在作品中，则使文字的描述居于一种自反性的视角下，接受图像的检验，并同时强化了文学与视觉艺术之间的媒介差异性及竞争关系，"危险"在于照片的可见性，因为"可见的照片"是我们更易理解的"物证"。罗兰·巴特在《明室》中谈道："照片具有证明力，[……]从现象学的观点来看，摄影的证明力胜过其表现力。"（118）并认为，相较于文字，图片的这种肯定性，任何文字的东西都无法给出。巴特认为"自己不能证实自己，是语言的不幸运（但也可能是语言的乐趣所在）。语言的本质可能就是这种无能为力。语言从本质上说是虚幻的；[……]但摄影对任何中介物都不感兴趣：它不创造什么；它就是证明的化身"（115）。法国摄影理论家、美学学者弗朗索瓦·苏拉热也将照片的功能归结为："[……]不仅仅是一个目击者，更是我们生命的一个证明[……]因为这种生活成了'客观'再现的对象。"（15）可见埃尔诺意识到了这种图文并置超越了文学修辞，跨出了纯文学范畴，进入艺术间的跨媒介领域，构成了不同艺术门类间的"互文关系"，直面语词与图像的竞争，对于作家来说，成为一种文学创作上的全新挑战。她一方面执着于图像的实证效果，一方面继续以文字的物性，追求对现实的记录。

埃尔诺自年轻时代起就深受社会学和哲学的影响,福柯的《词与物》(*Les Mots et les Choses*, 1966)提出以语词将世界纳入话语的主权之中,这种话语有力量去再现其表象;加之同时期的一些实验性文学实践,如佩雷克(Georges Perec)的《物》(*Les Choses*, 1964)、《我记得……》(*Je me souviens*, 1978),运用的清单式写作手法,倚重实证。埃尔诺逐渐认同文学具备社会学调查的特质,以外部视角捕捉日常生活的细节,进行记录,重新审视出生的社会阶层,保持距离、保持真诚。正是在写作中对实证的不断探索,促使埃尔诺不断对文字与图像的关系进行思索。在纪录片《石头般的语词》(*Les Mots comme des pierres*, 2013)中,作家坦言,"我的语言是物质性的,我很难做到抽象,我脑海中是实际的场景。词对我而言,就是物","我要通过字词去捕捉的'物'"(让内特 76)。而这种文字的物性成了她极为重视的创作基础,对她来说具有重要意义:以语词为武器,精准刻画一切,借助这种方式让记忆、社会生活、情感关系尽可能地脱离巴特所认为的"虚幻",变得如图像般切实可见,"以最贴近现实(réalité)的方式书写生活,不虚构,不改头换面[……]"(*Ecrire la vie* 8),追求并成就"实证"。

二、贯通图像的文字

埃尔诺曾表示:"记忆是物质性的[……]记忆把看到的东西、听到的东西(得益于一闪而过的碎言断语)、姿态、场景,最精准地带回给我。这些不断的'灵显'是我写书的素材,也是现实的'证明'。"(让内特 64)而这些"灵显"如何起作用?除了基于文字的物性带来的实证,"带回"还必然涉及时间的维度。如果对图像(照片)本质进行更为深入的思考,除了作为"物",与文字叠加除强化了实证效果外,时间同样也是不可忽略的维度,如巴特所说:"照片的证明针对的不是物体而是时间。"(118)"这个存在过"才是照片真正想说的,一个真实的东西在镜头前摆过,才会有照片。因此"这里存在着双重的互相关联着的肯定:一个是真实,一个是过去"(103)。同样在时间的向度上,福柯认为:"语言向时间的永久性中断提供了空间的连续性,并且,正是就语言分析、表达和划分表象而言,语言才具有在时间的跨度上把我们关于物的认识连接起来的力量。凭着语言,空间之模糊的单调性被打破了,而时间连续性的多样性却被统一起来了。"(福柯 155)因此面向照片进行书写,埃尔诺抓住图像与文字共有的物性,进入更深层的时间维度,图像打破时间连续性的实证需要文字将其贯通,在她看来,"它们[照片]是时间最纯粹的形式。[……]我书里描写的照片自然都是属于我的照片,它们会首先出现在我的眼前"(让内特 65)。然后作家所做的不再仅仅是艺格敷词,而是创造性地运用照片和文字的并存践行跨媒介书写,找寻接近记忆的最直接路径,以求捕捉她眼中记忆的真相——存于时间之中的物证。

罗兰·巴特认为:"在照片里,时间的静止不动只以一种极端的、畸形的形式出现:时间被卡住了脖子,停滞了。"(121)在时间这一维度上,照片与文字媒介有着极大差别,照片是对于静止画面瞬间的抓取,语词段落呈现的、让读者感知的文字所叙述的内容"是时间里的一个过程,在时间里流动"(桑塔格 82),即使埃尔诺习惯于针对碎片化的时间进行写作,她笔下捕捉的现实也无法避免的是一种"流动的过程"。在《外部日记》(*Journal du dehors*, 1993)中,虽然作者的写作目的是用文字捕捉外部世界的瞬间,但这种捕捉更多的是运动中的画面,包含人物的动作和语言,更加贴近活动的影像或真实世界。即使在《照片的用途》中,她以语词精准描述照片,也总是以空间为序,先后描述着窗前、桌上、床上、地上的各个物件,更像观众跟着电影镜头扫视房间,而非一张照片。因为"生命不是关于一些意味深长的细节,被一道闪光照亮,永远地凝固。照片却是"(82)。因此在本质上,摄影不直接是记忆,而是阻断了的、抽象了的关于记忆的"刺点"(punctum)[①]。照片与真实生活的关系,或者它所提供的记忆,在时间层面上,是"使现在和未来与过去保持联系。摄影提供的不只是对过去的一种记录,而是与现在打交道的一种新方式[……]"(桑塔格 161),于是照片变成了连接过去与现在、记忆与感知的中间事物(medium),依照巴特的描述,就是"一种新形式的幻觉:在感觉层面上是假的,在时间层面上是真的。这是一种有节制、有分寸的幻觉,是介乎两种事物之间的幻觉(一方面是'这个不在那里了',另一方面又是'这个确实存在过'"(154)。

埃尔诺在写作中也有类似的"刺点",因为她坚信,总有一个细节会让记忆"痉挛",从而导致"定格"、触发感觉及一切,比如一个物件——父亲去世时我母亲手里拿着的餐巾。小说《位置》(*La Place*, 1983)中,她写道:"我母亲出现在楼梯上。她用手里的餐巾擦着眼睛。那条餐巾一定是午餐后她上楼去房间时顺手拿着的。[……]我不记得接下来的几分钟里发生的事了[……]"(*La Place* 13-14)这个令作者印象深刻、回忆起来依旧占据脑海的小细节(母亲手中的抹布)正是"刺点",是安妮·埃尔诺对照片刺点的文字性借鉴。

因此在埃尔诺的创作中,作为两种不同的媒介,文字与图像在大多数情况下并不是完全重叠的,她对两种媒介也有着不同的诉求。她需要图像作为书写的起点,但更需要在文字中享受自由、进行表达。"我看照片,但什么也没得到,是通过记忆和书写,我才找回些什么,照片展现的是我的样子,而不是我的所感所想,它告诉大家在别人眼里我是谁,仅此而已"(*Ecrire la vie* 37)。图像与文本在埃尔诺的创作中逐渐间离开来。

三、与图像间离的文字

使用照片和日记作为素材是埃尔诺感兴趣的创作方式,在《书写生活》的第一部分,埃尔诺对这两种素材的排布明显制造了时间上的距离。埃尔诺根据照片来挑选日记片段,有的片段写于照片同一时期,更多的时候,日记滞后于照片。如 1949 年拍摄于海边的一张照片,埃尔诺选择了一段写于 1998 年 6 月的日记:"所有的少年时光都在那里,在外省一个个孤独下午的大风里。"(*Ecrire la vie* 23)又如里尔博小城的照片配着 1994 年 7 月的日记:"[……]这个炎热的周日,炎热。所有其他的周日都包含在这个周日里"(14)。在她看来,这样的文字才能"揭示在时间长河中记忆的波动,在我生命中的种种事情上撒上不停变换的光辉"(9)。照片、日记和当下的书写联合了三重时间——经历过的时间、觉察到的时间和此刻真实的时间——从固定下来的过去直至现在。

相对于固定下来的照片时间,文字媒介享受着"流动的时间",有着更大的自由度,时间上的间离成为作家的创作空间。布朗克曼在评价《悠悠岁月》时提道:"为了在时光中保存画面,记忆并不满足于被动存储,而是将之同步适应于生命中的不同年岁。"(Blanckeman 74)这种同步针对时间差,也因为在时间差中生发的感受、想象、回忆、评论等内心活动才得以完成同步。因此这样的时间差所造就的文学空间对埃尔诺来说必不可少。在她其他类型的作品中,我们甚至能见到刻意创造时间差的做法。如在小说《事件》(*L'événement*,2000)中,作家直接使用括号,添加内容,有时是她当时写在随身手账本上的简短字句,如电报一般:"(手账本里'尽管在码头和 T。问题堆积起来'。)"(*Ecrire la vie* 282)此时主人公见了朋友让·T,他给意外怀孕的女主人公提供了一些信息,但显然不愿意帮更多的忙。括号里的短句像一条叠加在主线叙事上的轨道,以另一种方式补足了主人公的内心活动。有时括号里是多年以后自己对当时情形的回顾、感受和想法,甚至可以长达一页,讲的是与故事主线并无直接关系的时事评论。

而在另一个例子里,我们看到了完全打乱了的时间线,和一种跳出时间的目光:"我真真切切地看见了自己,以我 8—12 岁时的目光:一位成熟女性,优雅,非常'有教养',正要去巴黎的一家电影院在公众面前发言,巴黎的电影院,一个陌生的地方,这位女士距我的母亲十万八千里远[……]"(*Ecrire la vie* 20)。所配之图,是幼年的作家和母亲的合影。无论在时间上,还是在主题上,文字与图像都产生了间离。作家走了与回忆相反的方向,回忆往往从成年回望幼年,而她从幼年眺望成年。为了在自己和母亲之间形成对比,不同阶层、不同生活的对立甚至包含些许敌对的对比。埃尔诺完全脱离照片给予的实际图像,转而书写自己的感想,她避开了照片在这里带来的物性而想要抓住内心世界的真实,在文字媒介的描述中,她"不只是想要回到另一个时间中,去重新审视自己,审视周围的世界,也想要记得自己的记忆,与现在的记忆可能并不相同的记忆"(*Ecrire la vie* 36)。"与现在的记忆并不相同的记忆"正是过去无数个时间平面上对当下的感知,是柏格森式的时间模型[2]在起作用。返回头去再看照片,观者无法避免地开始想象母亲当时的生活,以及年幼女儿对母亲的感情。如桑塔格所说:"照片既是一片薄薄的空间,也是时间。[……]否认互相联系和延续性,但赋予每一时刻某种神秘特质。任何一张照片都具有多重意义;[……]照片本身不能解释任何事物,却不倦地邀请你去推论、猜测和幻想"(21)。文字与图片所拉开的距离中,作者填充了诸多感觉和想象,拉开了与现实的距离,却成就了所捕捉的记忆本身。文字因此在感受和想象的层面成了记忆的载体。

在谈及《悠悠岁月》的创作时,埃尔诺说:"我想要让人感觉到时间的流淌,同时我自己是在消弭时间,寻找一切永恒之物。"(Ernaux and Schwerdtner 767)这样才能形成记忆,个体的记忆,集体的记忆,时代的记忆。而在书写中所形成的记忆,必然与现实保持着一定的距离,这才是作家得以回望的空间。至于图像,它同样在视觉感知中带我们落入另一重空间、另一重时间。照片本身即一道痕迹[3],对现实进行着发散的记录,这道痕迹让人幻想、让人提出疑问、令人着迷并使人忧虑,每每看到就触发想象,"然而[……]想象力是曲解由感知提供的图像的能力。[……]它尤其使我们从原初图像中解放出来[……]"(苏拉热 229)。而在埃尔诺兼具图文的写作中,这种曲解由感知提供的图像的能力正是文字带来的:埃尔诺承认自己的写作离不开"看到"或"听到",或者更确切地说应该是"再次看到"和"再次听到",因此她的创作绝非原样照搬图像或对话,不是描述或引用它们。可见埃尔诺将照片这种图像当作触发想象的出发点,它们除了是证据,更是去往想象的通路,如安妮·埃尔诺所说:"我必须使它们'致幻'。"(让内特 64)

结 论

语词与图像两者都拥有留下痕迹和激发幻想的双重功能。

埃尔诺以作家的本能用艺格敷词的手法复写图像,探索文字的物性带来的实证效果,以语词塑造图像,使文字发挥社会纪实的效果,作为坚实基础捕捉记忆。同时,埃尔诺对照片本身相当重视,将其视为记忆的激发点,基于图像发散开来,进一步创作,利用文字贯通图像中凝固的时间,达成书写生活与记忆的目标。而文字与图像之间存在的时间差才是埃尔诺遨游其间的创作空间,填充着大量内心世界的真实(感受、思考、评论、幻梦……),抽离现实、成就致幻。

正如文论领域时常提及的"镜与灯"的隐喻,图像如镜,侧重模拟现实,具备完美的映证和模仿的能力;文字如灯,重在映照内心,通过对内心世界的细致描摹,引发读者内心的共鸣,从而达到影响读者的目的。普鲁斯特擅长用潜意识激发出模糊的记忆,而埃尔诺利用照片,从图像出发寻找记忆,并利用两种媒介各自的特点进行跨媒介书写。在她的作品中,文字与图像的关系从外在到内在,从具体到抽象,从紧密到疏离。埃尔诺从她对过往岁月的越来越长的记忆来写,从不断承载着他人影像和话语的现在来写。使自己参与或目睹的人和事不被遗忘,不湮没在社会和时代的洪流中。这是她写作的巨大动力,也是属于她的自我拯救。

2022年,埃尔诺与自己的儿子一起通过剪辑家庭录像推出了纪录片《速8岁月》(*Les Années super 8*)。图像,更确切地说是活动的影像再次与文字完美结合,在成就了记忆的书写和表达的同时,牵扯出了另一种图像与文字的关系,等待我们的挖掘。

注解【Notes】

① 罗兰·巴特在《明室》中提出的术语,指照片内影响观看者,使其被触动的细节。"刺点来自最意想不到之处……并且会在最适当的时机直抵观众的内心,激发出一种远远超出语言和含义的情绪。刺点是一种无法领会但可感知的现象;我们可以准确地描述,但无法正确地指定。这是一件不可言传之事,令观众既神往又困扰。"参见罗兰·巴特,《明室》,赵克非译,北京:中国人民大学出版社,2011年第33、56和58页。

② 柏格森提出的过去现在未来并存的时间椎体模型是一个倒立的圆锥形,S是圆锥的定点,AB是圆锥的底面。S与平面P接触。平面P代表当前,AB平面表示过去。P平面无尽延伸,S点在其上不断运动。人的精神生活在AB与S间不断往返。SAB存储了我们全部的记忆。参见 Henri Bergson, *Matière et mémoire: Essai sur la relation du corps à l'esprit* [1896]. Paris: Quadrige/PUF, 2012。

③ 参见[法]弗朗索瓦·苏拉热,《摄影美学:遗留与留存》,陈庆、张慧译,上海:上海人民美术出版社,2021年。另外,苏珊·桑塔格也在《论摄影》中提及"一张照片首先不仅是一个影像,不仅是对现实的一次解释,而且是一条痕迹,直接从现实拓印下来"。[美]苏珊·桑塔格,《论摄影》,黄灿然译,上海:上海译文出版社,2022年第148页。

引用文献【Works Cited】

Barthes, Roland. *La Chambre claire*. trans. Zhao Kefei. Beijing: China Renmin University Press, 2011.

[罗兰·巴特:《明室》,赵克非译,北京:中国人民大学出版社,2011年。]

Bergson, Henri. *Matière et mémoire*. Paris: PUF, 2012.

Blanckeman, Bruno. "Du romanesque dans *Les Années*." *Littérature*, N° 206, 2022 (2), 72-78. https://www.cairn.info/revue-litterature-2022-2-page-72.htm (consulté le 20 mai 2023).

Char, René. "Les compagnons dans le jardin." *Les Matinaux* (*suivi de la Parole en archipel*), Paris: Gallimard/poesie, n°38, 1974.

Ernaux, Annie. *Ecrire la vie*. Paris: Gallimard, 2011.

---. *La Place*, Paris, Gallimard, 1983.

---. *L'événement*, dans *Ecrire la vie*, Paris, Gallimard, 2011.

---. *Ecriture comme couteau: Entretien avec Frédéric-Yves Jeannet*, Paris, Gallimard, 2003.

---. *Les Années*, Paris, Gallimard, 2008.

Ernaux, Annie, and Karin Schwerdtner. "Le 'dur désir d'écrire': entretien avec Annie Ernaux." *The French Review*, Vol. 86, No. 4, 2013(3), 758 - 771. https://www.justor.org/stable/23511244 (consulté le 20 mai 2023).

Foucault, Michel. *Les Mots et les Choses. Une archéologie des sciences humaines*. trans. Mo Weimin. Shanghai: SDX Joint Publishing Company, 2001.

［米歇尔·福柯:《词与物——人文科学考古学》,莫伟民译,上海:上海三联书店,2001年。］

Jeannet, Frédéric-Yves, and Annie Ernaux. "L'Ecrire comme un couteau (extrait)." Trans. Wang Xiuhui. *World Literature*, 2023(2), 58 - 76.

［弗雷德里克-伊夫·让内特,安妮·埃尔诺:《利刃般的写作(节选)》,王秀慧译,《世界文学》2023年第2期第58—76页。］

Mauriac, François. *Mémoires intérieurs suivi de Nouveaux mémoires intérieurs*, Paris, Flammarion, 1985.

Montémont, Véronique. "Vous et moi: usages autobiographiqes du matériau documentaire." *Littérature*, n°166, 2012(2), 40—54. https://www.cairn.info/revue-litterature-2012-2-page-40.htm (consulté le 20 mai 2023).

Sontag, Susan. *On Photography*. trans. Huang Canran. Shanghai: Shanghai Translation Publishing House, 2012.

［苏珊·桑塔格:《论摄影》,黄灿然译,上海:上海译文出版社,2012年。］

Soulage, François. *Esthétique de la Photographie*. trans. Chen Qing, Zhang Hui. Shanghai: Shanghai People's Fine Arts Publishing House, 2021.

［弗朗索瓦·苏拉热:《摄影美学:遗失与留存》,陈庆、张慧译,上海:上海人民美术出版社,2021年。］

全知叙事者的归来:加尔各特的《承诺》与维多利亚时代现实主义小说[①]

徐 蕾

内容摘要:当代南非作家达蒙·加尔各特的布克奖获小说《承诺》的叙事者充分发挥了维多利亚时代现实主义小说中全知叙事者作为历史代言人和内窥镜的作用,既能基于外叙事层——异叙事者的立场呈现南非从种族隔离时代向"彩虹之国"转型的历史变迁,又可以借助自由间接引语如内窥镜般切入人物或施事者的内心世界。更具鲜明特色的是,加尔各特的全知叙事者具有高度的自反性,即一面摹仿维多利亚小说全知叙事对中产阶级群体意识的表征,一面借助文本内部的"沉默"或"空白"以召唤读者对南非白人的种族主义无意识进行反动与解构。因此,全知叙事者在《承诺》中的归来与其说是"南非对福克纳的回应",不如说是加尔各特面对当代南非文学在现实主义与(后)现代主义之间该何去何从的独特回答。

关键词:加尔各特 《承诺》 全知叙事者 现实主义 维多利亚小说

作者简介:徐蕾,南京大学外国语学院教授,主要研究英语文学、现实主义文学。

Title: The Return of the Omniscient Narrator: Damon Galgut's *The Promise* and Victorian Realism

Abstract: Contemporary South African writer Damon Galgut's

[①] 本文原发于《外国文学研究》2024年第3期,有改动。

Booker-winning novel *The Promise* fully taps into the realist convention of omniscience in the Victorian novel and creates an extradiegetic-heterodiegetic narrator to chart out the transformation of South Africa from Apartheid to the Rainbow Nation as well as to cut into the inner worlds of characters and agents via free indirect discourse. What is stylistically striking about the highly self-reflexive omniscient narrator is that on the one hand, it sets out to imitate the collective mind of the white South Africans in the typical vein of the Victorian novel while on the other hand, it calls upon the reader to react to and deconstruct the racist unconscious laid bare by way of a purposeful silence or blank within the text. Therefore, the return of the omniscient narrator in *The Promise* is more of the author's individualistic response to the call of contemporary South African literature at the crossroads of realism and (post)modernism rather than a South African answer to William Faulkner.

Key words: Damon Galgut; *The Promise*; Omniscient narrator; Realism; the Victorian novel

Author: Xu Lei is a professor at the School of Foreign Studies, Nanjing University (Nanjing 210023, China), specializing in English literature and literary realism.

西方媒体把2021年称为非洲文学的"奇迹年"(annus mirabilis)——在短短一年间,非洲作家获得了五项国际重要文学奖项[①],其中南非作家达蒙·加尔各特(Damon Galgut,1965—)凭借小说《承诺》(*The Promise*,2021)斩获英国文坛最具影响力的布克小说奖(Man Booker Prize)。尽管此前,加尔各特及其作品较少得到国内学界的关注,这位17岁便初登文坛的资深作家其实曾两度(2003,2010)入围布克奖的决选名单。《承诺》让他成为继纳丁·戈迪默(Nadine

Gordimer)、J. M. 库切(J. M. Coetzee)之后,第三位获得布克奖的南非作家。

作为南非后种族隔离时代(post-Apartheid)的重要作家,加尔各特深切关注南非进入民主化时代以来"彩虹之国"(Rainbow Nation)②多种族社会面临的历史遗留问题与难以弥合的新矛盾。同时在文学创作风格上,他不愿拘泥于戈迪默为20世纪南非文学树立的批判现实主义的传统再现模式,认为"把政治色彩鲜明的小说视作唯一可以反映社会现实的文学作品是错误的"("Reality and the Novel" 53);或者说,尽管"小说完全、绝对有关真实"(51),但他更加关注"扩展风格与文体选择,从而实现可以容纳非现实主义的表意模式的'讲述真实'"(Kostelac 17)。加尔各特的个性化写作风格也在不少学者的评价中得到了印证,如2010年入围布克奖的小说《在一个陌生房间》(*In a Strange Room*)被认为回应了德勒兹块茎思想的跨现代运动(transmodern motion)(Yebra 509),是当代"自我虚构小说"(autofiction)的代表(van den Akker et al 48);还有书评人发现,即便表面遵循现实主义框架特征的《良医》(*The Good Doctor*)也不能简单归入现实主义旗下——作品将种族时代的文学转喻投射到对后种族隔离社会的表征中,造成"有意的年代错误"(Barris 28),因而"不能算作后种族隔离时代的文本"(26)。

某种程度上,西方评论界对《承诺》的总体评价延续了对这位作家的一贯认知。2021年布克奖评审团主席、哈佛大学历史系教授马娅·亚桑诺夫(Maya Jasanoff)高度评价作品"在结构与文学风格上的匠心独运"(qtd. in Scharper),评审团一致认为该作"非同凡响的叙事风格平衡了福克纳的饱满与纳布科夫的精准"("The 2021 Booker Prize Press Release")。詹姆斯·伍德(James Wood)在《纽约客》(*The New Yorker*)书评中指出,小说"采用了一系列现代主义技巧,在叙事风格上与前辈作家如乔伊斯、伍尔夫非常相似"("A Family at Odds Reveals a

Nation in the Throes")。美国当代作家加斯·格林维尔(Garth Greenwell)高度赞誉作品的形式创新与道德严肃性,认为"《承诺》令人想起现代主义以意象派的光芒、摧枯拉朽的祛魅以及对人性无情探索所获得的伟大成就"(qtd. in Verity)。还有英美评论家把该小说概括为"一节令人愉快的现代主义大师课"(Mesure),或看到小说在情节设置上借鉴了福克纳的《我弥留之际》,称之为"南非对福克纳的回应"(Scharper)。

值得注意的是,评论者们无一例外地都注意到这部小说令人印象深刻的自由流动的视点。伍德称小说"自由漂浮"的叙事者"融合了自由间接文体(free indirect style)和或许可以称之为'不确认的自由间接文体'(unidentified free indirect style)",前者表现为跟随某具体人物的第三人称叙事,后者则体现在跟随一个身份不明的叙事者或某个模糊乡村合唱团的第三人称叙事。这一自由流动的叙事者带来"令人头晕目眩的效果",使读者可以最大限度地寓居他人视角(Mesure),人物与意识之间的切换"有时出现在一个段落中,甚至在一个句子里"(Boehmer 5)。根据加尔各特的个人解释,这一灵感来自他 2019 年为一部电影撰写分镜头剧本时的发现——通过宛如镜头切换般的视角转换,他找到了在人物与合唱团之间迅速移动的方法(Verity)。2022 年 3 月在和伍德的线上访谈中,加尔各特再次提及从电影镜头语言中汲取的创作灵感:"我本能地不想被任何声音所束缚,即便全知叙事者也有其局限,我可以在场景中从一个视角转移到另一个,再调转角度,超然、冷静地观察某个事件或对话或聚焦一个全新的具体细节。"("Damon Galgut in Conversation with James Wood")加尔各特认为,自己在小说中付诸实践的叙事视角超越了传统的全知视角,展现出收放自如、无限自由的特征。然而,也有评论者认定小说里的叙事者具有全知叙事的基本属性(Scharper),展现了"全知叙事的权威"(Wood),甚至可以称之为"超全知叙事"(hyper-omniscience)(Skidelsky 9)。如此看来,至少全知叙事与加尔各特追求的类似电影艺术中镜头任意切换的自由并不冲突。如果我们回归到全知叙事作为19世纪英国现实主义文学的一般叙事规约来看，可以发现小说《承诺》采用的叙事手法实际上充分发挥了传统全知叙事既能全面展示外部社会和自然环境，又可探究人物内心世界的权威性与空间灵活性。维多利亚小说所著称的全知叙事非但没有限制加尔各特寻求自我突破的叙事风格，反而为这位当代南非作家提供了更具文学张力的表达方式：一方面，全知叙事者对全书关键人物黑人女仆的"无视"让南非白人社会对黑人底层民众的集体沉默暴露无遗；另一方面，在接受美学层面上，叙事者的人物留白所激发的召唤结构最终引导读者走向对南非白人中产阶级种族主义无意识的否定与批判。

一、全知叙事与维多利亚时代现实主义小说

全知叙事（omniscience）又称"全知视角""第三人称全知叙事"，可以出现在不同类型的叙事作品中。M. H. 艾伯拉姆斯（M. H. Abrams）在《文学术语辞典》（*A Glossary of Literary Terms*，1999）中阐明全知叙事者具备如下两个特征：其一，"叙事者知晓有关施事者、行动、事件的所有必要信息，有知晓人物思想、情感与动机的特权"；其二，"叙事者可以随心所欲地在时空中自由运动，从一个人物转移到另一个人物，并且汇报（或隐藏）他们的言语、行为和意识状态"。（232）杰拉德·普林斯（Gerald Prince）在《叙事学字典》（*A Dictionary of Narratology*，2003）里给出的定义也突出了全知视点中叙事者"知晓（几乎）一切情形与事件"的能力（68），类似于吉拉尔·热奈特（Gérard Genette）在《叙事话语》（*Narrative Discourse*，1972）中提出的没有固定观察角度的零聚焦（zero focalization），常见于传统的经典叙事作品，如《亚当·贝德》《汤姆·琼斯》《名利场》（69）。

普林斯举例的三部作品中,《亚当·贝德》与《名利场》都是维多利亚时期英国现实主义小说,前者出自乔治·爱略特,后者是威廉·萨克雷的代表作。实际上,在许多维多利亚时代小说研究者看来,这一时期的经典英国作家几乎都是全知视角的最佳践行者。乔纳森·卡勒在《全知叙事》("Omniscience",2004)一文中特别指出,"从乔治·爱略特到安东尼·特罗洛普,他们笔下呈现仿佛历史学家的外叙事层-异叙事者(extradiegetic-heterodiegetic narrator)是全知叙事概念的最佳例证"(Culler 31),他们是历史的权威代言人,能够审慎地拣选有效信息,知晓人物的内心秘密,也可以就人类的愚蠢进行智者的反思。伊莲·弗里格特(Elaine Freegood)在近作《足以世界:维多利亚小说开创的现实主义》(*Worlds Enough: The Invention of Realism in the Victorian Novel*,2019)中为梳理有关维多利亚小说现实主义传统的学术话语,特别选取了包括全知叙事在内的五个层面,并具体考察了这一叙事特征在盖斯凯尔夫人作品《玛丽·巴顿》中的呈现方式。有趣的是,卡勒与弗里格特在各自研究中不约而同地都提到了 J. 希利斯·米勒(J. Hillis Miller)早在 20 个世纪 60 年代对维多利亚小说全知叙事提出的重要观点。

米勒在《维多利亚小说形式》(*The Form of Victorian Fiction*,1968)一书中以 19 世纪英国作家萨克雷、狄更斯、特罗洛普、爱略特、梅瑞迪斯、哈代的多部小说为研究基础,指出全知叙事是 19 世纪英国小说"形式的决定性原则","当这些小说家不充当第一人称叙事者、扮演戏剧中某个角色,甚至拒绝做代表个人意识的匿名的故事讲述者,而选择扮演某个集体心灵时(a collective mind),他们每个人的典型性作品就诞生了"(Miller 63)。因而全知叙事者不是超越的(transcendent),而是内在的(immanent)(64)。米勒将叙事者之于小说世界的内在性比喻为"无所不在的大海或气味四散的香水,可以穿透最为隐秘的内在,自由进出任何地方"(65 - 66);作者拥有的全部知识基于他们对独立存在世界的信念,当他们走到镜子的后面,把自己放在叙事者的位置上时,"他们在想象中也把自己置身于集体的心灵中或至少最令他们感兴趣的那群人的心灵之中"(67)。米勒认为,这个集体的心灵对于大多数维多利亚时代小说家来说,意味着中产或上层阶级。维多利亚时代小说家们倾向于相信这种集体心灵伴随着每个人的成长,"从第一天出生到死亡,环绕着他、拥抱着他、弥漫在他的身上"(67)。维多利亚时代小说家进行创作的目的就是认同这种群体意识,或者实现一种集体参与。另一方面,维多利亚小说的读者也会在叙事者召唤下进入一种先于小说即已存在的集体心灵。米勒对维多利亚小说中全知叙事者所承担的群体意识功能在伊丽莎白·埃尔玛斯(Elizabeth Ermarth)的研究中得到了进一步支持,后者认为19世纪英国小说的叙事视点无论是否具有全知属性,一般都统一于完整、统一的世界观。小说中没有面部特征、没有确定身份或特定位置的"无名氏叙事者"实乃"集体的结果,共识的具象化,……并不能作为个体被理解"(65-66)。实际上,当现实主义小说叙事形式对中产阶级集体意识的召唤与规训渐渐取得学界共识时,该特征也成为凯瑟琳·贝尔西(Catherine Belsey)、D. A. 米勒(D. A. Miller)等学者解构与批判的19世纪英国现实主义文学作为中产阶级意识形态工具的核心依据。[③]

二、《承诺》的全知叙事者:历史代言人与施事者内窥镜

回到以南非社会近三十年变迁为时代大背景的《承诺》,作为一部当代小说,它与这种无所不知、行动自由且代表着中产阶级集体心灵与群体意识的全知视角有着怎样的共振与关联?

从《承诺》的整体叙事框架上来看,存在着一个外叙事层-异叙事者的声音,稳定地从小说开篇发声到结束,几乎贯穿始终。值得一提的是,尽管有评论家指出《承诺》借鉴了福克纳小说《我弥留之际》的基本故事情节(美国南方小镇农民本德伦一家人按照母亲生前遗愿,将遗体

送回其故乡安葬的故事),加尔各特用南非行政首都比勒陀利亚附近一户白人农场之家自1986年到2018年间举办的四场葬礼串起了整部小说的主线,这部小说的叙事声音显然镌刻着作家自己的独特印记;具体而言,他并没有延用福克纳以59个章节的不同人物独白而搭建起的多重视点叙述,而是塑造了一个位于叙事层之外、面目模糊的叙事者来充当历史代言人与施事者内窥镜。

《承诺》的叙事者在宏观上洞悉南非社会三十多年来的时代变化,微观上可以轻松切入人物内心乃至动物世界的叙事者。在宏观层面上,故事主线中斯瓦特一家的四场葬礼被安排在1986年、1995年、2004年、2018年,充分的时间间隔有利于叙事者以点带面地记叙南非从种族隔离时代走向国家民主化进程中的阶段性变化。第一场葬礼是斯瓦特家母亲蕾切尔的,发生在南非国内种族矛盾异常尖锐的1986年,彼时南非城镇黑人群众开展罢工、罢课、抗租、抗税等各种形式的斗争,南非非洲人国民大会(African National Congress)不断进行斗争,给南非当局沉重打击,为了遏制南非人民斗争,南非白人政权于6月实行全国紧急状态,大肆逮捕拘留反种族主义领导人和积极分子,疯狂镇压黑人群众的反抗活动。虽然故事第一部分围绕着私人葬礼展开,但国家与小家的关联在叙事者看来是斯瓦特家庭的每一个成员以及读者必须知晓的现实。当家中妹妹阿莫尔质问从约翰内斯堡兵役站匆匆赶来参加葬礼的哥哥安东,为什么父亲曼尼不能兑现对母亲的承诺——把家里黑佣萨洛米住了一辈子的房子赠送给她时,哥哥惊讶地反问她:"你不知道你生活在一个什么样的国家吗?"(123)叙事者紧随哥哥的话语,将妹妹的懵懂无知引向了少女看得见却参不透的整个社会的动荡不安,将矛头指向了南非根深蒂固且在20世纪80年代日渐激化的种族矛盾:

> 阿莫尔才十三岁,历史还没有将她踩在脚下。她不知道自己生活在一个什么样的国家。她曾见过黑人因为没有携带

身份证，一看到警察便跑得远远的，也曾听到成年人急迫地小声谈论着黑人居住区里发生地暴乱；就在上周，他们还不得不在学校里接受了一场培训，学习如何在遭遇袭击时躲到桌子下面，可她依旧不知道自己生活在一个什么样的国家。眼下正处于紧急状态，人们未经审判就被逮捕和拘留，谣言满天飞，但没有确凿的证据，因为新闻被封锁了，出现媒体上的，净是喜讯或虚假消息……（123－124）

毫无疑问，相较于人物角色，故事叙事者显然拥有对种族隔离制度时期的南非更加清晰的认知和批判性眼光，这份超越人物的睿智与成熟以及对社会的整体性解读能力也是维多利亚小说中全知叙事者们不吝向读者展示的特质，比如《米德尔马契》中自比历史学者的叙事者，"我们这些后起的历史学家……有许多人生的悲欢离合需要铺叙，看它们怎样纵横交错，编成一张大网"（爱略特137），以烘托他们屹立于历史长河的叙事权威。

第二场葬礼是斯瓦特家父亲曼尼的，在1995年6月17日举行，这个时间点对于在两年前刚刚结束种族隔离制度、由第一位多种族民主大选获胜者纳尔逊·曼德拉（Nelson Mandela）领导的非国大治国阶段的新南非意义重大。因为葬礼前一天恰好是为纪念1976年索韦托起义（Soweto uprising）④的南非青年节，而葬礼当天又赶上了在约翰内斯堡举行的橄榄球世界杯赛的半决赛，南非队历史性地打败了法国队，整个国家为这场被寄予厚望的胜利而欢呼雀跃。叙事者的视角仿佛长镜头般扫过约翰内斯堡的街道、餐厅、酒吧、公共广场，在每个南非普通家庭的客厅、厨房、后院，当然也包括斯瓦特农场上的劳工小屋、主人居住的大屋里，人们都在关注着电视直播的画面，而整个赛程、众人的反应以及曼德拉与代表南非参赛的荷兰裔白人运动员的握手，也被叙事者以热情洋溢的笔触记叙下来：

比赛非常紧张刺激,足以让你抓挠家具。我方的小伙子们严防死守,没让那个壮得跟山似的乔纳·罗姆过去,不过我们也没能触地得分,一直在踢落地球,比分咬得很紧,胜负只在毫厘之间。……而就在这时,乔尔·斯特兰斯基挺身而出!我们赢了!这一刻是最最幸福的时刻,每个人都跳了起来,互相拥抱,陌生人在街上庆祝,按响汽车喇叭,车灯闪个不停。……曼德拉身着绿色的跳羚队橄榄球衫,将奖杯授予了弗朗索瓦·纳皮尔,哟,这可不得了。堪比宗教仪式。强壮的布尔人和年迈的恐怖分子握起了手。谁能料到呢。天哪。不止一人回想起几年前曼德拉出狱时挥舞着拳头的那一幕,那时,没人知道他以后会是怎么样。如今,他的脸随处可见。(220-221)

叙事者见微知著地从一场将南非白人与黑人团结在一起的球赛中揭示了这个国家在结束近半个世纪之久的种族隔离制度后,普通大众对重塑国家凝聚力和自信心的渴望;然而,这份来自大众的殷切期待随着南非政治腐败与执政党非国大党的分裂而被无限搁浅。九年后,斯瓦特家姐姐阿斯特里德在购物中心停车场遭遇暴徒打劫后被枪杀、家人为其举办葬礼(即故事里的第三场葬礼)便浓缩了南非政府在转型期奉行自由主义经济政策而导致经济下滑、大面积人口失业、全社会动荡不安的恶果。颇具讽刺意义的是,阿斯特丽德的意外死亡设定在2004年总统姆贝基(Thabo Mbeki)的连任就职典礼后不久,她因丈夫与某政客的生意合作关系,刚刚受邀参加了安排在南非民主化十周年当天的总统就职典礼,并视之为"这辈子最激动人心的一天"(239)。可令人始料未及的是,不但民主化进程中的南非难以保障公民的人身安全,就连她的丈夫——一位自黑人接管这个国家之后,为无数政客与富人提供私人安保服务而发了大财,也为自家提供了"最高级别的保护"(251)的商人,也只能接受自己的妻子被一个"居无定所、食无常处的"(252)黑人劫车贼和瘾君子为了一辆青灰色的宝马车,取了卿卿性命。警方派来的两位探员甚至对这桩谋杀案见怪不怪,而叙事者适时的插入性解说也进一步勾勒出非国大党接管南非十年后的社会乱象:"南非人有时候自相残杀,似乎只是为了找乐子,或是为了一点小钱,一些小小的分歧。把人射死、捅死、勒死、烧死、毒死、闷死、淹死,用棍棒打死/妻子和丈夫互相残害/父母杀死孩子,或是孩子杀死父母/陌生人杀害陌生人。尸体被随意扔在一旁,就像没有任何实际用途的皱巴巴的包装纸。"(264-265)

如果说南非社会在21世纪初已然陷入了暴力丛生、道德崩坏的怪圈,那么这个国家的国运在十多年后似乎每况愈下。叙事者结合哥哥安东的葬礼——最后一场葬礼——的时机,亦即祖马(Jacob Zuma)总统因深陷贪腐丑闻被非国大党逼迫辞职的2018年初,直击南非人民日常生活面临的空前危机,"水坝几乎空了,水只能限量供应……电网正在崩溃,无人维护,资金断流,总统的朋友们已经带着现金跑了。没有电,没有水,富饶之地正处于困难时期"(372),普通人连洗澡都成为难题,更不必说人们精神上的巨大失落——"在人行道上、桥梁下、红绿灯前聚集了越来越多的憔悴、枯竭、受伤之人,正在不断挥舞着伤口"(373),甚至安东的自杀在某种意义上也是这个时代的尘埃落在个人头上的结果。

《承诺》的叙事者将一个家庭的四次葬礼编入南非三十多年国运变迁的时间轴,俨然承担了卡勒指出的维多利亚小说全知叙事者的历史代言人功能。与此同时,这位自由漂浮的叙事者还展现了全知叙事者独有的穿透人物以及非人类内心世界的超能力,通过直接引语(direct discourse)、间接引语(indirect discourse)、自由间接引语(free indirect discourse)穿梭于包括斯瓦特一家父母兄妹在内的一众人物群体的思想与感情世界。其中最为典型的片段莫过于母亲蕾切尔因病去世之后的当夜,斯瓦特一家终于进入梦乡,叙事者则如同运动中的全景镜头,依次聚焦了服用镇静剂后终于睡去的爸爸——他在梦中看到变了模样的妻子倍感羞愧难当,刚刚开始与异性交往而沉浸在春梦中的大女儿阿斯特丽德,与丈夫同床异梦的玛丽娜姑妈,梦中抽搐得"像只跳舞的熊"(49)的姑父奥吉,以及不断复盘白天遭遇而难以入睡的小女儿阿莫尔。紧接着叙事者话锋一转,"也许所有这些梦融合在一起,化作一个单独的梦,一个单独的梦,一个属于全家人的梦,又有谁能说得准呢?但有个人不在"(50),这个人便是斯瓦特家的独子——在约翰内斯堡附近参加两年义务兵役的安东。于是叙事者又转而聚焦他在母亲逝世当天过失杀死一位黑人妇女后的内疚、自责以及得知母亲死讯后的双倍痛苦。在这段宛如长镜头的全知叙事中,除了叙事者对不同人物思绪与情感的间接引用("他服用了拉夫医生开的镇静剂,这会让他一直刚好沉在水下面")、直接引用("他冲她喊道,你已经死了"),还有不少自由间接引语出现在不同人物的梦境或内心世界里。

普林斯将自由间接引语定义为在人称和时态上保留间接引语特征,但"没有引述句(如'他说''她想')来介绍和修饰所呈现话语与思想(Prince 34)。申丹教授认为自由间接引语通常会保留体现人物主体意识的语言成分,如疑问句式或感叹句式、不完整的句子、口语化或带感情色彩的语言成分,以及原话中的事件、地点状语等(290)。值得注意的是,尽管自由间接引语在以乔伊斯为代表的 20 世纪现代主义小说创作中得到了广泛运用(Toolan 241),但这种叙事风格早在 19 世纪现实主义小说中已得到充分发展。弗里格特曾表明自由间接引语是维多利亚小说全知叙事的关键技巧(55),欧美学者近年合作研究现实主义文学的一项最新成果——两卷本《现实主义的风景》的第一卷(*Landscapes of Realism: Rethinking Literary Realism in Comparative Perspectives*, 2021)也把自由间接引语视作 19 世纪英法现实主义文学最突出的风格与技巧。不同于现代主义作品通过自由间接引语呈现出人物"多元的、经常是相互矛盾甚至是无意义的信息",从而将"文本从作者的专制中解放出来"(吕国庆 81–82)。19世纪英国现实主义小说的自由间接引语表面上促进了人物主体性的呈现,但是人物其实并没有超越叙事者(Freegood 71),人物与叙事者之间的视角差异"可以用于反讽效果和提示人物意识的局限性"(Göttsche et al. 168)。《承诺》大量使用的自由间接引语更接近于其在19世纪现实主义小说中的模态与功能,即便在全知叙事者从外在型向内在型偏移时[5],脱离了引述句的人物语言、思想、冲动依然在叙事者的调度与评判之中。回到蕾切尔去世当晚斯瓦特家中这一幕,难以入睡的阿莫尔因白天发生的一切心神不宁、痛苦万分,"她手臂上的痛处(她姑妈将满腔怒火注入手指,猛掐了她那里),那痛处向宇宙发出怀着痛意的小小脉冲,看这里,我,阿莫尔·斯瓦特,在这儿呢,现在是一九八六年。愿明天永不到来"(50)。刚刚失去母亲的阿莫尔在家中无人关心或慰藉,姑妈因为她的短暂失踪——独自跑到小山坡哀悼母亲逝世,把自己的各种不满以肉体惩罚的方式转嫁给侄女。阿莫尔当然不是因为肉体的痛苦辗转难眠,她甚至希望借助这份痛苦而祈求得到世界的一点关注与垂怜——让时间停止,与母亲不再分离。此处自由间接引语的运用无疑让我们听到了一位失恃少女直抒胸臆的真诚祈祷,引发读者同情;但也没有人会相信,这份天真稚嫩的祈祷能够实现,第二天如约而至的葬礼立刻打破了少女的幻想。

  自由间接引语在全知叙事调度下产生的微妙反讽作用同样参与了小说对许多人物的塑造。安东作为家中的独子兼浪子,他的一生充满了叛逆与失败,他先因不满在军队中服役充当种族隔离制度的帮凶而逃亡至独立的黑人家园特兰斯凯(Transkei),又在父亲意外身亡后回归家园,继承农场、娶妻成家后,却迟迟不肯兑现母亲临终前的承诺——把女仆萨洛米住了一辈子的房子赠予她,人到中年酗酒、赌博、债台高筑、夫妻关系破裂,终于在某天深夜被幻听声吸引,携枪到农场上逡巡,试图驱赶假想入侵者,不料在半醉半醒中扣动扳机自杀身亡。加尔各特在记叙安东自杀一幕时,采用了全知叙事与自由间接引语反复切换的方式,一方面便于读者从外部视角,看到这位酗酒成性、自我麻痹的中年男人的狼狈与可笑:"他一直在走,不知道在找什么……天刚亮,安东跌跌撞撞地穿过自家院子,他半醉半醒,还有些难受,衣服敞着,扣子都没扣,仿佛他身上有一些接缝,被撕开了,填料都跑出来了。"(360)另一方面,通过自由间接引语的内部视角,读者直接看到人物自我质疑时的痛苦:"你怎么受得了呢? 你这个老荡妇,一遍又一遍上演着一模一样的演出,晚上演,白天也演,而你周围的剧场都在坍塌,剧本里的台词却已成不变,更不用说化妆、服装和夸张的动作了……"(361)然而叙事者并不愿读者被安东自编自导的悲剧所牵动,反而以戏谑的口吻对人物开起了玩笑,"安东啊!你的那些填料,会是些什么呢? 噢,都是些常见的圣诞礼物,一些糖果,一块幸运饼干,一点炸药"(360-361),毫不含糊地暗示了这位人物内心极度空虚和咎由自取的下场。

　　除了运用自由间接引语展现人物的内心世界,叙事者甚至借此捕捉动物的心理活动。父亲曼尼的葬礼过后,有一只野鸽子撞击斯瓦特家宅毙命,被人们埋在房屋附近,死亡的气味引来在附近生活的一只胡狼和它的同伴。全知叙事者追随两只胡狼的行踪,看它们穿过漆黑的风景,发出嚎叫的信号,一路向北。而叙事者的画外音也在某一刻被胡狼的内心声音所取代:"离公路还有很远的时候,它们便在它们的领地的边界外缘处听了下来。有必要更新一下记号,用自己的体验来划定界限。过了这里,就是我们的地盘了。"(191)主语从"它们"到"我们"的变化提示了全知叙事者声音转为自由间接引语指向的施事者声音。

三、当代全知叙事者的"沉默"与召唤结构

　　事实上,上文提及的胡狼桥段被不少评论者(Wood, Scharper,

Mesure，Skidelsky）视为小说叙事者可以自由进入人物或施事者头脑中的最佳例证；仅就这一点而言，19世纪现实主义全知叙事者著称的上帝视角和对人物的外察内透在这部小说中的确得到了典型体现。然而，尽管这位全知叙事者既能在宏观上把握南非三十多年来的社会变迁，又可无孔不入地走进上至政客、牧师、企业家、农场主、律师、警察、家庭主妇，下至抢劫犯、流浪汉、掘墓人的内心世界，却唯独对小说的核心人物黑人女仆萨洛米保持着一种特殊的沉默，没有给小说标题直指的"承诺"所包含的财产馈赠受益人一次表达心声的机会。所谓承诺，原为斯瓦特家母亲蕾切尔临终前要求丈夫作出承诺，即允许老仆萨洛米拥有她住了一辈子的一幢老屋和宅基地，但人走茶凉，这份承诺直到斯瓦特一家四口逝世，只剩下小女儿阿莫尔时，才在阿莫尔的斡旋下得以兑现。作为推动小说故事情节发展的核心矛盾一方，被形容为"仿佛戴着面具，如同雕像一般"(26)的萨洛米的反应、诉求、心态却被全知叙事者完全搁置，用伍德的话来说，"全书最重要的人物萨洛米的视角几乎完全没有被小说凸显的无往不至的叙事者所覆盖"(Wood)，这种安排究竟是作者刻意为之，还是结构上的漏洞，甚或是为了应对南非国内文坛身份政治危机的一种策略？

  对此，加尔各特在小说出版当年的采访中便作出了明确回应，"我想努力澄清一点，这不是向身份政治投降……我着意让萨洛米保持沉默，是为了让读者感到不安，而她的存在就会得到增强而不是削弱"(Studemann)。值得一提的是，身份政治的问题在南非国内文坛一直是敏感话题，白人作家是否有资格代表黑人发声的命题长期困扰着包括戈迪默在内的许多白人南非作家，但在加尔各特看来，这并不应该构成对文学创作的干扰，毕竟"虚构文学的全部前提就是要想象变成其他人的感觉"(Studemann)。两年后，在回应《非洲英语研究》(*English Studies in Africa*)杂志刊登的围绕一组关于《承诺》的专栏文章时，他再一次重申了自己让萨洛米成为不可见者的文学立场：

> 我的视而不见是一种选择。我在看她——或者说,没有看见她——就如同一个南非中产阶级的普通白人可能看不见她一样……我希望这种空白,这种无视成为画面的一部分,从而确保读者因此感到困扰。或者换个稍稍不同的说法,当在现实世界中,即便是在2023年,仍然有成百万的人们像萨洛米一样没有声音,无权无势,几乎没有存在感,那么赋予萨洛米这个人物全部的人性特征又有什么用呢?这会让我觉得是一种刻意抚慰读者的举动……更有用的做法当然是让读者在阅读结束后,对她的沉默感到不自在、困惑不解、牵涉其中、惴惴不安。(42)

从某种程度上看,加尔各特为萨洛米刻意保持的沉默暗中践行了萨特在《文学是什么》一文中高举的散文的"介入"(engaged)使命,后者认为作家应通过揭露而行动,特别是"向其他人揭露人,以便其他人面对赤裸向他们呈现的客体负起他们的全部责任"(20),而这种揭露也包含着沉默,因为沉默也可以是一种谈话、揭示和行动的方式,"就像音乐中的休止符从它周围那几组音符取得意义一样。……沉默不是不会说话,而是拒绝说话,所以仍在说话"(20)。萨洛米的无声或者说叙事者对萨洛米的沉默指向的无疑是作为特权阶层的南非白人长期以来对被压迫在底层的黑人群体话语权的剥夺和习而不察的残酷无视,而成就这部小说对南非后种族隔离时代种族主义问题进行深刻揭露并引导读者(尤其是白人读者)走向自我反思的密码恰恰在于加尔各特对全知叙事这一在现实主义文学中臻至颠峰的传统叙事声音之吊诡般的运用,亦即叙事者愈是对南非三十多年间的变迁洞若观火,对小说中其他所有人物或施事者的内心世界明察秋毫,他对萨洛米的沉默便愈加触目惊心、震聋发聩。

从接受美学的角度来看,萨洛米的"沉默"也类似于沃尔夫冈·伊瑟尔（Wolfgang Iser）提出的文本"空白"（blank），作为文本内容选择与视角安排的结果，是塑造现象学意义上隐含读者（implied reader）的"召唤结构"（response-inviting structure）的重要手段（Iser 35）。根据伊瑟尔的阅读理论，召唤结构由两部分构成，即文本的"保留内容"（repertoire）与文本"策略"（strategy），前者指取材于现实的社会文化现象，尤其是"在社会中站主导地位的思想体系、道德标准、行为规范，以便对它们的合法性提出质疑，'召唤'读者对此语义否定"，后者是作品对其保留内容进行艺术加工，"即安排文本视角，以便更好地吸引读者"（朱刚 156-157）。在《承诺》中，无论是文本的"保留内容"还是"策略"，都与全知叙事者的运用紧密相关：它既是被文本精心安排以吸引白人中产阶级读者的策略，又是呈现"保留内容"以召唤更多读者进行否定的窗口。

具体而言，如果说全知叙事者对萨洛米的留白激活了《承诺》的召唤结构，那么奠定其运作基础的便是全知叙事者切入第二人称时与读者进行的直接交流。该交流模式可以在罗宾·沃霍尔（Robyn Warhol）基于19世纪英美女性作家小说中叙事者共性特征而提出的"吸引型叙事者"（engaging narrator）理论中找到一定程度的关联。沃霍尔指出在盖斯凯尔夫人、斯托夫人、爱略特的作品中有一种鼓励读者认同的叙事者声音，叙事者通过频频运用第二人称的 you，直接召唤受述人（narratee）的记忆、情感，"意在激发持书阅读者的识别与认同"（811）。实际上，加尔各特笔下的叙事者在大多数时候也颇具吸引型叙事者的风范，通过频频切入第二人称叙事，激发读者对叙事者身份与立场的认同，同时将读者引向对南非社会现实的关注。值得注意的是，这位吸引型叙事者特别模拟了前文提到的承载着群体心灵的维多利亚小说叙事者的姿态，从故事伊始就不断彰显其代表南非白人中产阶级的身份特征；当他亲切地向读者发出集体记忆的召唤，他所试图代言的目标人群已经有了清晰的轮廓。斯瓦特家农场首次出现在读者眼前的时候,在一段淡红色的墙砖、平房的铁皮屋顶、晒得褪了色的花园、大草坪上轮胎秋千的直接描写后,叙事者突然转向读者,"也许,你也是在那里长大的。所有这一切,都始于那里"(8),出生并成长在农场上的白人读者被唤醒了童年的记忆。又或者当叙事者第一次向读者介绍萨洛米,细数她在女主人重病期间任劳任怨、尽忠职守的工作内容时,一句"但有些事情你确实知道,因为你亲眼见过"(26)立刻拉近了与那些目睹过、享受过黑人家仆贴身服务的白人读者的距离。叙事者进一步告诉读者,萨洛米做的活"都是些自家人不愿意干的活,要么太脏,要么太私密,让萨洛米去做吧,花钱雇她,就是让她做这些事的,不是吗?"(26-27)叙事者居高临下的口吻无疑提示了他此刻对白人中产阶级身份的认同。

不过,加尔各特并没有让叙事者稳定地寓居在白人中产阶级的身份之中,随着斯瓦特一家——"没什么独特或非凡之处"(321)的南非白人家庭——历经四场葬礼,最终走上了穷途末路,叙事者刻意与白人读者拉近的亲切感也渐渐淡去。第四次葬礼结束后,叙事者对萨洛米的三缄其口终于走到了"不在沉默中爆发,就在沉默中灭亡"的时刻。当斯瓦特家最后一位在世成员阿莫尔终于向垂垂老矣的萨洛米拿出了赠与房产的可行方案,叙事者借由第三人称道出了这位早已放弃继承希望的老妇对未来的打算:"她近年来一直在想,回到家乡,在那座小村庄安度晚年,也许是个不错的选择。就在梅富根之外,离这里只有三百二十公里;如果之前没有提到过萨洛米的家乡,那是因为你没有问过,也不屑于知道。"(414)这是叙事者第一次,也是最后一次为萨洛米的沉默而直接与读者对话,此时的第二人称"你"依然如故,是从没有问过,也不屑于知道萨洛米个人故事的"你",是对底层黑人群体视而不见的"你"——南非的普通白人。这个珍贵的瞬间见证了叙事者终于放弃了吸引型叙事者的口吻,转向更接近于菲尔丁、萨克雷塑造的疏离型叙事者(distancing narrator)的立场,后者往往以"向读者提供具有反讽或喜剧效果的评论"(Warhol 817)为主要特征。叙事者把对萨洛米的异常沉默直接归咎于白人读者的种族主义无意识，而这一针见血的尖锐批评也宣告了他与普通白人读者的立场差距以及同白人群体意识形态的决裂。不难看出，如果说第二人称是叙事者用以吸引白人读者并推动身份认同的策略，该策略同时也实践着对文本"保留内容"的复现，即通过充分暴露白人群体对南非社会种族主义与主导价值观的长期内化而形成的认知盲区与褊狭自私，从而进一步质疑种族主义制度及其思想的合法性并"召唤"读者对此进行否定与批判。

小说《承诺》对全知叙事模式的运用在当代英语小说中并非个案。早在十年前，有研究者就曾指出当代英语文坛出现了一股全知叙事的回归之势，从青年作家扎迪·史密斯（Zadie Smith）、亚当·瑟尔维尔（Adam Thirlwell），资深作家乔纳森·弗兰岑（Jonathan Franzen）、戴维·福斯特·华莱士（David Forster Wallace），到文学大师萨尔曼·拉什迪（Salman Rushdie）、马丁·艾米斯（Martin Amis）、唐·德里罗（Don Dellilo），他们的作品中都不约而同地出现了一位"知晓一切的权威叙事者，可以直接向读者说话，对讲述的事件进行插入性的点评，自由穿梭于时空中，提供进入人物意识的路径，并经常凸显其在虚构世界中的存在感"（Dawson 1）。曾几何时被后现代小说频频挑战的经典现实主义，其形式特征——全知叙事——却被当代英语文坛的主流文学作品广泛吸纳，研究者将这种变化归因于当代作家面对小说的文化权威日渐衰落时的一种回应（5）。

该研究者的分析具有一定的普遍意义。不过，全知叙事之于《承诺》的意义还不仅在于作家可以藉此在虚构世界中确立一种叙事的权威：一方面基于外叙事层-异叙事者的立场担任历史代言人，从而徐徐展开南非社会自种族隔离阶段末期向彩虹之国转型的历史概貌；另一方面自由回旋于公共与私密场景之间，借助自由间接引语如内窥镜般地深入人物或施事者的内心世界。更具鲜明特色的是，全知叙事为作家揭露与批判南非社会白人群体根深蒂固的种族主义无意识提供了一面自我映射的反光镜和一套召唤读者反思乃至否定白人群体意识形态的文本策略。因此,《承诺》的全知叙事者具有高度的自反性:叙事者一面摹仿了维多利亚小说全知叙事模式所表征的群体意识,一面通过文本内部的"沉默"或"空白"展开对这种群体意识的反动与解构;频频吸引白人读者对南非种族主义立场的识别、认同,是为了向种族主义无意识发出致命一击。

自20世纪60代初南非获得独立以来,曾经塑型着南非英语文学史的现实主义传统因其欧洲文学的渊源以及同大英帝国殖民扩张史的交织,与当代南非英语文学之间存在着相当复杂的关联,在20世纪80年代甚至引发过南非文化界的激烈论辩。作为"第一个将现代主义和后现代主义引入南非的作家"(蔡圣勤145),库切1987年接受耶路撒冷文学奖(Jerusalem Prize)时的演讲揭示了南非文学彼时遭遇的现实主义陷阱,指出南非文学是"被束缚的文学"(98),因为"在南非,艺术要承载的真相太多了,那些大量的真相使得每个想象的举动都难以承受"(99)。然而,在三十多年后的当代南非文坛,现实主义的冲动或许可以被重新定义为"一种现象学意义上的铭刻于文本的意向性,可以或突出或低调地表现为任何一部作品在风格和叙事上的倾向性"(Helgesson 101)。如是,小说《承诺》与其说是"南非对福克纳的回应"(Scharper),不如说是加尔各特面对当代南非文学在现实主义与(后)现代主义之间该何去何从这一时代命题的独特回答。

注解【Notes】

① 除了加尔各特凭借《承诺》在2021年获得布克奖,当年其他四位获奖的非洲作家分别是:塞内加尔的大卫·迪奥普(David Diop)拿下了国际布克奖(International Booker Prize),旅居英国的坦桑尼亚裔作家阿卜杜尔拉扎克·古尔纳(Abdulrazak Gurnah)折桂诺贝尔文学奖(Nobel Prize in Literature),塞内加尔作家默罕默德·萨尔(Mohamed Sarr)摘取代表法语文学最高奖项的龚古尔奖(Prix Goncourt),莫桑比克作家宝琳娜·齐兹阿尼(Paulina

Chizane)获葡萄牙语文坛最高奖卡蒙斯文学奖(Cameos Prize for literature)。

② "彩虹之国"是1994年南非宣布废除种族隔离制度之后由南非大主教德斯蒙德·图图(Desmond Tutu)提议的别称,寄托着南非人民对各色人种和谐相处,如同彩虹各种颜色和谐共存的美好愿景。

③ 贝尔西和米勒对19世纪现实主义小说全知叙事的解构与批判详见Catherine Belsey, *Critical Practice* (Methuen, 1980)和D. A. Miller, *The Novel and the Police* (U of California P, 1988)。

④ 索韦托起义是南非历史上的重大事件,20世纪70年代南非当局强迫黑人学生学习南非荷兰语,遭到学生们的强烈抗议,警察向在索韦托举行和平示威游行的学生开枪,"动乱"蔓延到其他城市,直至扩大为反抗白人政府压迫的政治性起义。

⑤ 根据申丹的梳理,叙事学家把全知叙事看作"外在型视点",强调观察位置在故事之外;文体学家把全知叙事看作"内在型视点",因为全知叙事者可以像第一人称叙事者那样报道人物的内心活动。详见申丹,《跨学科视野下对Point of View的重新界定》,《上海交通大学学报(哲学社会科学版)》2023年第1期,第4页。本文基于两种不同观点,认为全知叙事者可以在两种位置之间移动。

引用文献【Works Cited】

Abrams, M. H. *A Glossary of Literary Terms*. Thomson Learning, 1999.

蔡圣勤:《库切小说〈耻〉中的人性形式解读》,《西南民族大学学报(人文社科版)》第26卷第11期,2005年11月,第145—147页。

Barris, Ken. "Realism, Absence and the Man Booker Shortlist: Damon Galgut's The Good Doctor." *Current Writing: Text and Reception in South Africa*, vol. 17, no. 2, June 2011, pp. 24-41.

Boehmer, Elleke. "Brand Recognition: Damon Galgut's The Promise as National Allegory Plus." *English Studies in Africa*, vol. 66, no. 2, Oct. 2023, pp. 5-10.

[Cai, Shengqin. "A Reading of the Form of Humanity in J. M. Coetzee's *Disgrace*." *Journal of Southwest University for Nationalities* (Philosophy and Social Sciences), vol. 26, no. 11, Nov. 2005, pp. 145-147.]

Coetzee, J. M. *Doubling the Point: Essays and Interviews*. Edited by David Attwell. Harvard UP, 1992.

Culler, Jonathan. "Omniscience." *Narrative*, vol. 12, no. 1, Jan. 2004, pp. 22-34.

Dawson, Paul. *The Return of the Omniscient Narrator*. The Ohio State UP, 2013.

乔治·爱略特:《米德尔马契》(下),项耀星译,人民文学出版社,1987年。

[Eliot, George. *Middlemarch*. Translated by Xiang Xingyao, People's Literature Publishing House, 1987.]

Ermarth, Elizabeth. *Realism and Consensus in the English Novel*. Princeton UP, 1983.

Freegood, Elaine. *Worlds Enough: The Invention of Realism in the Victorian Novel*. Princeton UP, 2019.

Galgut, Damon. "Damon Galgut in Conversation with James Wood." 22 Mar. 2022, africa.harvard.edu/event/damon-galgut-conversation-james-wood.

---. "Reality and the Novel." *New Contrast*, vol. 18, no. 1, Jan. 1990, pp. 51 - 55.

达蒙·加尔各特:《承诺》,黄建树译,广西师范大学出版社,2022年。

[---. *The Promise*. Translated by Huang Jianshu, Guangxi Normal UP, 2022.]

---. "A Response." *English Studies in Africa*, vol. 66, no. 2, Oct. 2023, pp. 39 - 43.

Göttsche, Dirk, et al. *Landscapes of Realism: Rethinking Literary Realism in Comparative Perspectives. Vol. I: Mapping Realism*. John Benjamins Publishing Company, 2021.

Helgesson, Stefan. *Transnationalism in Southern African Literature: Modernists, Realists, and the Inequality of Print Culture*. Routledge, 2009.

Kostelac, Sophia Lucy. *Damon Galgut and the Critical Reception of South African Literature*. Doctoral dissertation. University of the Witwatersrand, 2014.

吕国庆:《论自由间接引语与乔伊斯的小说构造》,《外国文学评论》,第26卷第3期,2010年8月,第72—83页。

[Lü, Guoqing. "An Analysis of James Joyce's Use of Free Indirect Speech." *Foreign Literature Review*, vol. 26, no. 3, Aug. 2010, pp. 72 - 83.]

Mesure, Susie. "Damon Galgut: I'm Not Ungrateful for My Booker Win." 3 Mar. 2022, inews.co.uk/culture/damon-galgut-interview-the-promise-im-not-ungrateful-for-my-booker-win-but-it-creates-an-artificial-popularity-1494935.

Miller, J. Hillis. *The Form of Victorian Fiction: Thackeray, Dickens, Trollop, George Eliot, Meredith and Hardy*. Arete Press, 1968.

Iser, Wolfgang. *The Act of Reading: A Theory of Aesthetic Response*. The John Hopkins UP, 1978.

Prince, Gerald. *A Dictionary of Narratology*. U of Nebraska P, 2003.

让-保尔·萨特:《什么是文学?》,施康强译,人民文学出版社,2018年。

[Sartre, Jean-Paul. *What Is Literature?* Translated by Shi Kangqiang, People's Literature Publishing House, 2018.]

Scharper, Diana. "Review: South Africa's Answer to William Faulkner." 31 Mar. 2022, www.americamagazine.org/arts-culture/2022/03/31/review-damon-galgut-promise-242711.

申丹:《叙述学与小说文体学研究》,北京大学出版社,2007年。

[Shen, Dan. *Narratology and the Stylistics of Fiction*. Peking UP, 2007.]

Skidelsky, William. "A Poisonous Legacy." *Financial Times*, 19 June 2021, p. 9.

Studemann, Frederick. "Damon Galgut on His Booker Winner *The Promise*: 'Death Sets Things Off'." *Financial Times*, 08 Nov. 2021, p. 20.

"The 2021 Booker Prize Press Release." 03 Nov. 2021, thebookerprizes.com/media-centre/press-releases/the-promise-wins-2021-booker-prize.

Toolan, Michael. "Language." *The Cambridge Companion to Narrative*, edited by David Herman, Cambridge UP, 2007, pp. 231–244.

van den Akker, Robin, et al. "Metamodernism: Period, Structure of Feeling, and Cultural Logic—A Case Study of Contemporary Autofiction." *New Directions in Philosophy and Literature*, edited by David Rudrum et al., Edinburgh UP, 2019.

Verity, Michalea. "Cover Story: The Methods of Damon Galgut." 12 Feb. 2022, opencountrymag.com/cover-story-the-methods-of-damon-galgut/.

Warhol, Robyn R. "Toward a Theory of the Engaging Narrator: Earnest Interventions in Gaskell, Stowe, and Eliot." *PMLA*, vol. 101, no. 5, Oct. 1986, pp. 811–818.

Wood, James. "A Family at Odds Reveals a Nation in the Throes." 12 Apr. 2021, www.newyorker.com/magazine/2021/04/19/a-family-at-odds-reveals-a-nation-in-the-throes.

Yebra, José María. "Transmodern Motion or the Rhizomatic Updated in *In a Strange Room*, 'Take me to Church' and *Babel*." *Anglia*, vol. 106, no. 3, Sept. 2018, pp. 508–529.

朱刚:《论沃·伊瑟尔的"隐含的读者"》,《当代外国文学》,第19卷第3期,1998年8月,第152—157页。

[Zhu, Gang. "On Wolfgang Iser's 'Implied Reader'." *Contemporary Foreign Literature*, vol. 19, no. 3, Aug. 1998, pp. 152–157.]

美国南方女性文学的哥特现实主义

刘玉红

内容摘要：内战后的美国南方艰难走向工业化和城市化,社会矛盾尖锐,混乱和失序是常态,为文学的现实书写有效融入哥特性提供良机。长篇小说《飘》《铁脉》和短篇小说《难民》的哥特现实主义以多感官叙事和丰富的哥特化意象分别表征19世纪下半叶和20世纪上半叶南方社会转型中城市空间的阈限化、怪诞人物的生存困境,以及"南方骄傲"的毁灭力量,在写景、写人、写事中表现出南方文艺复兴时期女作家对南方不同时期思想症结和社会问题的深刻洞察。

关键词：美国南方 女性文学 哥特现实主义 社会转型

作者简介：刘玉红,广西师范大学教授,从事美国文学研究。

Title: Gothic Realism in American Southern Female Literature

Abstract: American south moved painfully to industrialization and urbanization after the Civil War, during which the society was besieged by intensified contradictions, chaos and disorder. And this provided writers with a good opportunity to fuse Gothic style in their realist writings. Characterized with the multi-sensory narrative and rich gothic images in their Gothic realism, the novel *Gone with the Wind* and *Vein of Iron*, and the short story "The Displaced Person" represent respectively liminality of the urban space, the living predicament of the so-called grotesque people as well as the destructive power of the "Southern pride". In narrating urban landscape, characters and events, the works reflect the women writers' insightful observations of the south's ideological and social problems in the latter half of the 19th century and the first half of the 20th century.

Key words: American south; female literature; Gothic realism; social changes

Author: Liu Yuhong is a professor at the College of Foreign Studies, Guangxi Normal University, China. Her research interest is American literature.

哥特性是美国南方文学的显性标识。南方哥特小说最早出现于19世纪30年代，内战前的西姆斯(William Gilmore Simms)写独立战争，爱伦·坡(Edgar Allan Poe)展现人类心理的阴暗面，由此形成美国哥特写实和写心两条主脉。南方女性写哥特小说起步于40年代，一开始便表现出写实意识：聚焦家庭生活，超自然现象极少或得到合理解释，女主人公是道德标干。道德标干这一形象虽理想化，却基于作者的现实焦虑：社会邪恶多由男性造成，女性是"维护南方家庭和社区的核心力量，肩负在道德上改造'坏男人'的使命"(Smith 54)。20世纪上半叶的南方文艺复兴挞伐奴隶制，揭露旧道德，同时又徘徊于田园和工业化之间，对战后重建和新秩序满怀忧虑，而哥特风格尤其适用表达这种复杂矛盾的现实情感，从而形成"哥特现实主义"(Gothic realism)，它指征用哥特技巧，淡化其超自然因素，以南方时空为背景，通过典型人物和事件来表征和探究南方的历史创伤和社会问题，强调可读性和叙事张力，以获得强烈的叙事移情效果。借此认识，本文以南方文艺复兴时期玛格丽特·米切尔(Margaret Mitchell)的《飘》(*Gone with the Wind*, 1936)、埃伦·格拉斯哥(Ellen Glasgow)的《铁脉》(*Vein of Iron*, 1936)和弗兰纳里·奥康纳(Flannery O'Connor)的《难民》("The

Displaced Person", 1954)三部/篇作品中的代表性场景或主情节为对象,从小说的故事背景、人物塑造、情节架构三要素出发,分别探讨南方女作家如何以视觉、听觉等多感官叙事和丰富的哥特化意象来表征南方社会转型中城市空间的阈限化,经济和社会重压下怪诞折射出的生活困境,以及"南方骄傲"的毁灭力量,以此理解作者"在真实描写'现实关系'时,经常揭露现实中存在的种种问题"(王守仁 47-48)的文学创作使命感。

一、故事背景:社会剧变与空间阈限化

空间的异质性是哥特小说的第一体裁要素。在传统哥特里,内空间的阴暗迷乱与外空间的明朗有序这一对立关系暗示理性与非理性、善与恶、非我与自我界线分明。哥特小说在美国的本土化,首先表现为空间的现实性,"家居、工业化和城市化背景成了神秘恐怖的场所。……城市黑暗的街巷取代阴暗森林和迷宫般的地下通道"(Botting 123)。这种糅和日常生活和哥特氛围的空间因而具有阈限特征。阈限源自拉丁语"limen",意为门槛(threshold),原指成长仪式中的过渡阶段,后从人类学扩展到文学、文化领域,影响渐盛,产生了居间诗学、门槛诗学等提法。阈限的基本特征是过渡性、杂糅性、不确定性和无限的可能性(Mukherji xvii)。阈限模糊边界,解构辖域化、科层化的条纹空间,创造出一个不同力量或要素对话或对撞的场域,能有效检视美国南方现代转型中复杂的社会形态。

《飘》中的亚特兰大融合了哥特性和阈限性。无论是作品篇幅还是时间跨度,《飘》都堪称南方"史诗般叙事"(epic narrative)(Taylor 261)。从1861年到1886年,故事几乎覆盖了南方现代历史上所有重大变化:脱离联邦、内战、奴隶制解体、庄园文化衰落,以及重建时期(the Reconstruction, 1863-1877)。在社会变迁中,新旧力量的对抗、

历史与当下的矛盾、"瞻前顾后"的焦虑和未来的不确定性使南方成为一个时空阈限场,生动地具象化在1886年春天一个夜晚亚特兰大的街景中:

> 整个城市在吼叫(roaring)——它像边境村庄一样门户大开,丝毫不掩饰它的邪恶和罪过。酒馆遍地开花,一条街就有两、三家酒馆,彻夜喧闹。夜幕降临,满街都是醉汉,有黑人,也有白人,晃晃悠悠(reeling),从墙壁撞到马路牙子,又撞回去。暴徒、小偷、妓女躲藏在没有灯光的巷子和阴暗的街上。赌(Gambling)场闹哄哄如炸弹轰鸣,夜夜都少不了动刀动枪(cutting and shooting)。体面的市民惊骇地发现,亚特兰大有了红灯区,竟比战时还大,还要兴旺(thriving),从拉下的窗帘后面通宵达旦飘出钢琴声、吵闹的歌声和笑声,时而插入尖叫声和手枪的劈啪声。(米切尔,《飘》666)

在这里,城市的喧嚣和失序契合哥特小说的"极端书写"(writing of excess),即以对抗性叙事(counter-narrative)使理性和道德蒙上阴影,展现人性价值的阴暗面(Botting 1-2),如威廉·贝克福德(William Beckford)的"东方哥特"《瓦赛克》(*Vathek*,1786)中哈里发宫廷里醉生梦死的欢闹、坡《红死鬼面具》("The Mask of Red Death",1842)中的末日狂欢。亚特兰大街头的混乱和狂欢与之不无相似之处。这一片断聚焦酒馆、赌场和红灯区这三个处于文明社会边缘地带的公共场所,以声(吼叫)赋景、赋人、赋行,为整个场景定下异于常态的基调。夜晚是一天中违法乱纪的高发时段,是哥特小说常见的隐喻性时间背景。在这个阴暗与光亮斑驳错杂的时空里,摇晃的醉汉、嘈杂的声响、碰撞打斗富有动感,形成视觉、听觉、触觉多感官冲击,从而营造出迷失自我的氛围。多个-ing词汇交织的声景在正常和非正常之间激荡,而行走于这一躁动空间里的是居于法律边缘的"非正常人"：暴徒、酒鬼、妓女、小偷。如此，声、景、人"和谐地"融入一个既真实又异化、既欢乐又暴力的城市空间中。这样的亚特兰大生动体现了"城市哥特"（Urban Gothic）的特质："城市是一个废墟，既常在常新，又总是走向衰败。"（Mulvey-Roberts 288－289）这里的"废墟"类似艾略特的"荒原"：物质生活在发展，道德人性却在退化。南方"重建的魔爪"（米切尔，《飘》665）既塑造出这个充满活力、"飞速前进的城市"（665），也使思嘉这些有财产的白人焦虑不已，"无视法律的黑人和北方士兵到处都有，这种威胁使她惴惴不安，而财产充公的危险挥之不去，连做梦也不得安宁。她还担心发生更恐怖的事"（664）。这个"更恐怖的事"指当时对妇女的暴行不时发生。亚特兰大由此成了一个哥特式阈限：经济发展，社会混乱；既是思嘉的发财福地，又是她嫌恶的罪恶之场。

亚特兰大的阈限性进而在城乡对比和思嘉的矛盾情感中得到强化。思嘉返回老家塔拉种植园参加父亲的葬礼，看到"开着沟的红土路两边，忍冬彼此缠结，垂挂下来，郁郁葱葱，芳香扑鼻，雨后的忍冬向来如此，这是世界上最甜美的香味"（699）。思嘉沉醉于田园静美，不禁自问，"她怎么在亚特兰大待了这么久？"（699）然而，思嘉终究没有回归乡下，她仍是"亚特兰大人"。即便在故事结尾，她打算回种植园想出办法重新赢回丈夫瑞德的心，这也只是"明天"的计划，是否实施，不得而知。可以说，种植园既真实又虚幻，既落后又美丽，成了与亚特兰大对位的另一个阈限存在，突显了思嘉纠结于生活现实和情感反差，这种矛盾情感微妙地流露在亚特兰大的"邪恶和罪过"和塔拉种植园散发出"世界上最甜美的香味"这一抽象与具象的对比中，这正是米切尔阈限情感在文本中的符码化。

米切尔成长于20世纪上半叶，这一代人已经抛弃对旧南方的过度浪漫化，他们"呼唤的不是梦想和幻想，而是现实主义和社会学……不是骑士精神，而是中产阶级价值观"（Pyron 242）。时代背景在一定程度上形塑了她的现实主义创作思想,她要"真实地"写出佐治亚州北部地区的生活原态(Mitchell, "Mitchell to Virginlus Dabney, 23 July 1942" 359)。在《飘》中,她"以更为真实的北佐治亚州人物形象取代传统的弗吉尼亚绅士和南方淑女,前者出身自耕农,或是转为地主的冒险家,不久前晋升为中产阶级,他们更关心如何获取财富而非如何维护传统文化"(Bryant 37)。然而,"文学描绘的不是别的什么,就是'我'所体验到的东西,是'我'对世界的看法"(周宪 23)。米切尔和同时代不少南方女作家一样,虽不像重农派那么固执地怀旧,但多少保有旧日田园梦想,她视自己为"南方宝贵传统的守护者"(Tylor 260)。这种浪漫过去与纷乱现实的卷缠不仅是对重建后南方社会的真实写照,也为作品注入了叙事的内在张力,这或许是《飘》长久畅销的一个原因。

二、人物塑造:生活困境与怪诞对位

怪诞(the grotesque)是哥特小说独特的人物范式。传统哥特的怪诞多为超自然或通灵书写,与"不可视为崇高的恐怖、令人不安的、丑恶的物体或体验密切相关"(Llyod-Smith 174)。在南方女性文学中,怪诞已走进日常生活,通常指"畸形或反常的人物,居于特点鲜明的南方背景中,他或她形体有缺陷,精神有问题,行为异于常人,因而在阅读反应中持续形成张力"(Haar 210)。如卡森·麦卡勒斯(Carson McCullers)《心是孤独的猎手》(*The Heart Is a Lonely Hunter*, 1940)的米克和《婚礼的成员》(*The Member of the Wedding*, 1946)的弗兰淇两个女孩都为自己的中性身体而烦恼,折射出女性在成长过程中对身体变化的体验、认知和接受或拒绝。在奥康纳笔下,残疾人、智障人、自残的杀人犯等畸形人传达出她的宗教信念:生活充满原罪,精神扭曲投射于身体畸形中,只有通过暴力,人才可能获得拯救。评论界讨论南方怪诞多提麦卡勒斯和奥康纳,却忽视了早于她们的格拉斯哥。

格拉斯哥被誉为"打开南方文艺复兴的闸门"(Skaggs 336)。她的作品多以真实的地点、人物和事件为原型,聚焦内战后南方社会文化、家庭关系、道德意识的变迁。长篇小说《铁脉》被认为是她"最成功的小说"(Skaggs 339),讲述了19世纪下半叶到20世纪初弗吉尼亚一家四代以爱和坚强应对生活困境的故事。作品的怪诞书写采用"双层对位"叙事模式:故事前半部分为铁边村芬卡瑟家和沃特斯家的共时空对位,体现旧南方"文化共同体"对异己的迫害和驱逐;后半部分为大萧条时期昆伯勒市贫民的"身死"与富人的"心死"这一隐喻性反向对位,复现了经济危机和人情冷漠对城市"穷白人"的致命打击。

芬家和沃家社会地位高低不同,却都因"怪诞"而陷入生存困境。故事以怪诞开篇,"一群小孩在追打一个傻小子"(Glasgow, *Vein of Iron* 3)。这个傻小子就是沃太太的儿子托比,他"脸上的嘴巴不过是一个弯洞,眼睛小而斜视,目光呆滞,眼睑红肿"(3)。与儿子长相之怪相配的是母亲身份之"坏":她年轻时是个妓女。19世纪下半叶的南方性观念极为保守,虽然沃太太出卖身体是为了养家糊口,但村里长老会的"牧师和长辈们"(69)认定"她就是个坏女人"(54),将母子赶出村外,他们只能栖身于恐怖荒地,"穿过田野,经过墓园里最后一个塌陷的坟墓,休耕地尽头突然出现一条旱沟,它原先是河道,一百年多前这里埋了一个被吊死的人,故称'谋杀者之墓'……旱沟边有一间茅舍,里面住着傻子托比·沃特斯和他母亲"(3-4)。人是社会动物,让活"死人"与真死人比邻而居,这样的流放无疑是一种极端孤立。当年那个人被吊死原因不明,现在沃家遭受"谋杀"的结果却是清楚的:母子靠养猪为生,孤苦无助,备受欺凌。与"贱民"沃家相比,芬家是"体面的":祖辈是建村元老,祖母当过村医,德高望重,父亲芬卡瑟本是牧师,收入不错。然而,他在出版第二部哲学著作后,公开承认自己的哲学思想与教会不和,并坚持已见。在19世纪"80年代,人们比这个新世纪要严格得多"(38),于是他被剥夺教职,转为教书,收入微薄,连给女儿买布娃娃的钱都不够,"他给毁了,他完了,他给忘了"(38)。

格里夫斯认为,格拉斯哥通过《铁脉》和其他作品"探究了普通白人常遭遇到的社会问题,在这一点上,她早于福克纳、厄斯金·考德威尔或其他南方哥特式作家几十年"(Graves 357)。但他没有具体分析《铁脉》探究了什么社会问题。笔者认为,无论是沃家母子的身体流放,还是芬卡瑟的精神放逐,他们的生活困境都是占据主流地位的宗教话语规训和惩罚的结果,而这是有现实依据的。同在19世纪80年代,詹姆斯·伍德罗(James Woodrow)博士在南卡一个神学院讲了达尔文的《人类起源》,"南方长老会宣判他犯有异端罪,剥夺了他的神学院职位"(Cash 139)。

如果说乡村怪诞以"流放"造成的生活窘境透视出旧南方社会伦理和宗教思想的自我隔离,那么城市怪诞则聚焦于经济危机中贫富对比的寓指召唤。1929年10月,股市崩盘,经济大萧条席卷欧美,1930年夏,南方又"遭遇严重干旱,农村地区大受影响,庄稼被毁,牲畜死亡,失业恶化"(Scott 401-402)。已定居昆伯勒市桑树街的芬家和很多人一样,存款归零,一夜返贫,勉强度日。为帮助更困难的邻居,芬卡瑟的女儿艾达决定向富有的娘家亲戚寻求帮助。贫与富仅隔三条街,景象却是天壤之别,这生动反映在空间氛围和身体观感中。亲戚家"屋里灯光闪耀……乐声不断……酒香入鼻"(Glasgow, *Vein of Iron* 341-42)。而桑树街"似乎所有的窗户、门,甚至被遗弃的地下室都呼出恐惧的气息,像是一支送葬队伍或一场瘟疫刚刚经过"(333)。亲戚家正在举行生日派对,人们"衣着鲜艳,头饰如花,身影摇摆"(341)。两个年轻人在拥抱调情,女的"身材苗条,那张脸像人工画出的康乃馨",男的"索然无味,年纪尚轻,神气活现"(342)。桑树街则有"这么多稻草人般的身影,枯瘦胳膊从破烂衣袖里伸出来!这么多肮脏粗糙的手在乞讨!这么多张脸面色干黄、神情憔悴、恐惧万分!"(317)排队领救济餐的人们"眼神空洞,不洗澡,不刮胡子……他(芬卡瑟)看着他们排好队,如同看漫画里阴森的鬼魂"(355)。从"稻草人"到"鬼魂",哥特式隐喻强化了怪诞:稻草人虽扭曲人的形貌,但尚有实体感,而鬼魂已失去实体感,暗合人饿极之虚,形容惨淡,稻草人是怪异的"非人",而鬼魂已是恐怖的"非人"。在强烈的视觉冲击中,富人的美酒欢宴与"路有冻死骨"的惨状形成鲜明的主题性对位。

生活方式是价值观的一面镜子。对亲戚家的歌舞升平和欢声笑语,艾达尖锐地评论道,"他们不可能知道苦难是什么,他们不知道生活是什么"(341)。她失望而归并不令人奇怪。不久,她想帮助的哈伯伦夫妇不愿去救济院,打开煤气自尽,靠邻居凑钱才得以下葬。八十岁的芬卡瑟为能用自己的保险金帮助家人度日,挣扎回到乡下,死在老屋前。作品暗示,他们的死与富人的冷漠不无关系。两个年轻人不太正常的面貌和气质表明,同情心是人基本的道德情感,人一旦失去同情心,就会成为另一种"非人"。哈尔说南方作家写怪诞时"通常对这样的人物寄予同情"(Haar 210)。《铁脉》不但体现了对受苦民众的同情,更通过讽刺无良富人增加了怪诞书写的宽度和厚度。

"双重放逐"和"求富济贫"这两个对位叙事的社会批判内涵指向小说名"铁脉"的多义性。目前的评论基本认为"铁脉"彰显了芬家代代相传的坚强精神,这忽略了"铁"和"脉"兼有正反义:iron 既表坚强,也表冷硬;vein 既刻画了芬家坚韧的传统,也暗示了南方"自然和文明的毁灭力量"(Glasgow, "Preface" ix)一直都在。书名的内涵对位丰富了怪诞的政治意涵。

三、情节架构:旧南方的执着与多重暴力

暴力是哥特小说最具标识性的情节。早期哥特打造了暴力全景图:超自然凶杀和真实暴力、个人施暴和群体施暴、肉体暴力和心理暴力、他杀和自杀,应有尽有。在南方女性文学中,暴力传达的是现实主

义批判态度:女性奴隶叙事控诉奴隶制的身心迫害,家庭小说揭露父权、男权的性别暴力,战争小说质疑国家暴力的正统叙事,等等。在女作家的暴力书写中,奥康纳独树一帜,其作多以现代南方乡下为场景,充满凶杀、溺水、纵火,在这些杀戮中,人际关系充满敌视,鸿沟般的隔阂似乎只能消弭于死亡中。短篇小说《难民》是奥康纳"最好的作品之一"(Orvell 152)。学界讨论其暴力主题多集中于波兰难民古扎克的受害者形象,对小说的多重暴力书写及其关联性意涵挖掘不够。从古扎克远渡重洋来到美国南方农场做帮工到他被杀,文本以三重暴力构筑起情节主干:"二战"是现实背景,诉诸言语暴力和"心里"暴力的"南方骄傲"是红线,个体暴力是高潮。暴力的因果关系和彼此叠加暗嵌了作者焦虑:南方的"骄傲之罪"具有毁灭力,而南方是否因暴力而获得拯救,则是存疑的。

小说名"The Displaced Person"(D. P.)是"二战"官方术语,指战争结束后因种种原因不能回国的民众,他们或集中住在原地,或流落到其他国家。古扎克就是这样的难民,他携妻女来到麦克英特尔太太的农场讨生活。从他出场开始,欧洲大屠杀的"尸体"意象数次出现,与接下来发生在农场内外的猝死、谋杀、疾病形成暗线呼应,因此,战争既是故事背景,也是重要的叙事铺垫。

布鲁姆指出,"在奥康纳笔下众多怪诞又不值得同情的世俗人物中,骄傲是主要罪过。只有通过预言式暴力,世人的骄傲才得以纠正"(Bloom 9)。在《难民》中,骄傲由表及里,渗透于麦太太和她的管事肖特利太太两个人物形象中,主要有三类表征——具身的、言语的和心理的,它们与暴力息息相关,互为因果。

"南方骄傲"首先体现在两人身体的象征性描写中。肖太太"两腿粗壮,昂然直立,满怀高山的雄伟自信……两道冰蓝色的目光直刺前方"(O'Connor, "The Displaced Person" 194)。她看难民一家的目光"如同秃鹰在空中滑翔,发现尸体残骸,才盘旋下降"(197)。和肖太太的"高大"相比,矮小的麦太太以"尖利"见长。她"眼睛睁大时颇为温和,一旦眯眼检查牛奶罐,目光如钢铁或花岗岩一般"(197)。当黑人帮工萨尔克告诉她古扎克要把表妹嫁给他时,她尖叫起来,"阳光落下,她的眼睛像蓝色花岗岩"(220)。两人虽身形有别,但"山脉""冰""花岗岩"和俯视"尸骸"等物化隐喻彰显了她们的共性:身为南方白人,自视甚高,个性冷硬。由此折射出两个当权者思想僵化和情感冷漠,暗示她们取代了传统哥特的暴君/男性形象。

麦太太的骄傲,其内核是种族隔离,表现为言语暴力。追求利润的她起先很欣赏古扎克会操作机器,干活利索,不抽烟喝酒,称他为"我的救世主"(203)。可一旦得知他想把自己的表妹嫁给萨尔克,借此帮她来到美国,她便痛骂他让一个白人嫁给"一个成天偷东西、臭哄哄的白痴黑鬼,你真是个魔鬼!"(222)她强调,"这太蠢了"(222)。骄傲的另一面是冷漠。古扎克告诉麦太太他表妹的悲惨遭遇:双亲死于集中营,"她在集中营里待了三年"(154)。麦太太回答:"我不用为世上的苦难负责。"(223)当麦太太的传统思想战胜经济利益时,古扎克自然成了"多余的人"(225),他的死亡也就成了必然。这与肖太太看到他就想起欧洲大屠杀的尸体堆形成呼应,引出讽刺性悲剧:难民逃过了残酷的战争,却死在代表他们美国梦的南方农场里。

肖太太"和麦太太一样骄傲,对他人缺乏同情心"(Kirk 56)。肖太太权力有限,地域偏见和种族歧视主要体现在她的"内心图景"(200)中。她"自认为有真正的信仰,且坚如磐石,而其他人:黑人、穷人、欧洲人,不过是上天惩罚的牺牲品"(Orvell 145)。在她眼里,欧洲"神秘,邪恶,就是恶魔的试验场"(O'Connor, "The Displaced Person" 205)。欧洲极度落后,"看不出这些人信仰什么,因为愚昧还未消灭"(198)。她认为古扎克一家就是"带着伤寒病毒的老鼠,远渡重洋,把这些杀人的东西带到这里"(196)。她的歧视还蔓延到语言上,古扎克女儿的名字听上去"像虫子的名字"(197)。波兰语是"肮脏的""未革新的",而英语是"干净的"(209)。

如果说麦太太和肖太太的软暴力是坚守南方种族隔离思想的表现，那么肖特利谋杀古扎克的硬暴力则是出于现实的报复心理。肖特利经常消极怠工，还偷售私酒，肖太太一直焦虑古扎克抢走丈夫的工作，她偷听到麦太太打算赶走肖特利，大受打击，为维护尊严，率家人半夜离开，却在路上中风而死。不久肖特利重返农场，他制造谣言，煽动麦太太解雇古扎克，看到她因经济利益犹豫不决，便决定自己动手。他趁古扎克躺在地上修机器，故意不刹拖拉机，麦太太和萨尔克看到了，却没有提醒古扎克，看着"拖拉机的轮子压断波兰人的脊椎骨"（234）。这一"共谋"使个人暴力上升为群体暴力。

奥康纳的创作离不开其天主教信仰，但这并非意味着她疏离现实，相反，她强调，"我觉得每个作家谈到自己写小说的方法时，总希望他是一个现实主义者，他的作品具有重要而深刻的现实意义"（O'Connor, *Mystery and Manners* 37）。在她眼里，社会问题与宗教是彼此勾连的：暴力与骄傲这一原罪互为因果，又与现实焦虑相关。南方在"20世纪上半期是美国最贫穷落后的地区"，种植园"工人多为非技术工人"（高红卫109，111）。古扎克会操作、修理农业机械，这冲击了农场仍以手工劳作为主的生产模式，他所代表的工业化在为农场带来经济效益的同时，构成了一种外来威胁，而三个主要人物的反应展现了南方的复杂心态：麦太太在经济利益和种族偏见中纠结而至崩溃，肖太太在南方骄傲遭受重击时愤怒而亡，肖特利在丧妻之痛和失业焦虑中诉诸人身报复。可以说，古扎克之死和麦家农场没落是20世纪上半叶南方仍在艰难转型的缩影。

古扎克之死和农场没落都是暴力的结果，因此，有人认为他的死象征"上帝之死，为的是拯救全人类"（Hyman 42）。故事结尾，老神父每周来探望困于病榻的麦太太，"为她讲解教会教义"（168），这表明麦太太获得了精神拯救（Hyman 18），如是，那么文本又自我消解了这两点。古扎克之死没能拯救任何人：肖特利未受惩罚，他和萨尔克不辞而别，农场丢荒。结尾只说神父苦口婆心，却没提麦太太是否心有所悟。其实,这种开放式结尾正是奥康纳的风格,她的作品的"共同点就是它们没有为读者提供解决方案"(Cofer 129)。旧南方的思想痼疾如此根深蒂固,她并不乐观,认为她身为作家,只能通过书写暴力来"促使读者思考作为一个肤浅而危险的物质世界之基础的精神现实"(Fitzgerald 257),并提供"有限的启示,但总算是启示"(O'Connor, *Mystery and Manners* 34)。

结　语

　　20世纪的现实主义文学追求表达作者"看到的"的深层真实,"摹仿冲动和对外界现实的关注是现实主义诗学的根本,但是这种摹仿并非简单的复制,现实主义文学是作者主观意识参与的创造性再现的结果"(王守仁、刘洋 7)。内战后直到20世纪上半叶,南方在彷徨中走向工业化和城市化,思想游离,矛盾激荡,情感和认知失调。在南方文艺复兴时期崛起的格拉斯哥、米切尔、奥康纳等女作家有着深切的现实主义情怀,她们意识到"哥特性最合适用来书写当下经验,那就是悠久而控制一切的体系,社会机制的异化和毁灭力,以及至今仍在延续的兽性"(Lloyd-Smith 62)。在她们笔下,哥特技巧是行之有效的陌生化手法,她们的哥特现实主义在写景、写人、写事中深刻揭示了南方社会不同时期的思想症结和社会矛盾,对哈珀·李(Harper Lee)、多萝西·艾莉森(Dorothy Allison)、鲍比·安·梅森(Bobbie Ann Mason)等当代名家影响深刻。

注解【Notes】
① 本文引用的《飘》出自李美华所译,译文有所修改。
② 作品引文首次标注作者,之后只标页码。

引用文献【Works Cited】

Barkley, Danielle. No Happy Loves: Desire, Nostalgia, and Failure in Margaret Mitchell's *Gone with the Wind*. The Southern Literary Journal, 47.1(2014): 54 - 67.

Bloom, Harold. "Introduction". Ed. Harold Bloom. *Bloom's Major Short Story Writers: Flannery O'Connor*. Chelsea House Publishers, 1999.

Botting, Fred. *Gothic*. London and New York: Routledge, 1996.

Bryant, J. A. Jr. *Twentieth-century Southern Literature New Perspectives on the South*. University Press of Kentucky, Kentucky: The University Press of Kentucky, 1997.

Cash, W.J. *The Mind of the South*. New York: Vintage Books, 1991.

Cofer, Jordan. *The Gospel According to Flannery O'Connor: Examining the Role of the Bible in Flannery O'Connor's Fiction*. New York: Bloomsbury, 2014.

Fitzgerald, Sally. "Flannery O'Connor." *The History of Southern Women's Literature*. Ed. Carolyn Perry and Mary Louise Weaks. Baton Rouge: Louisiana State UP, 2022. 404 - 12.

Gao, Hongwei. *A Study of American Southern Culture in the First Half of 20th Century*. Shenyang: Liaoning People's Publishing House, 2015.

[高红卫:《20世纪上半期美国南方文化研究》,沈阳:辽宁人民出版社,2015年。]

Glasgow, Ellen. "Preface." *Vein of Iron*. Charlottesville and London: University Press of Virginia, 1995.

Graves, Mark A. "Ellen Glasgow's Gothic Heroes and Monsters." *The Palgrave Handbook of the Southern Gothic*. Eds. S. C. Street, C. L. Crow. 2016. 351 - 363.

Haar, Maria. *The Phenomenon of the Grotesque in Modern Southern Fiction: Some Aspects of Its Form and Function*. Stockholm, Sweden: Umea University, 1983.

Hyman, Stanley Edgar. *Flannery O'Connor*. Minneapolis: University of Minnesota Press, 1966.

Kirk, Connie Ann. *Critical Companion to Flannery O'Connor: A Literary Reference to Her Life and Work*. New York: Facts On File, Inc., 2008.

Lloyd-Smith, Alan. *American Gothic Fiction: An Introduction*. Shanghai Foreign Language Education Press, 2009.

Mitchell, Margaret. *Gone with the Wind*. New York: The Macmillan Company, 1936.

[玛格丽特·米切尔:《飘》,李美华译,南京:译林出版社,2017年。]

---. "Mitchell to Virginius Dabney, 23 July 1942," in *Margaret Mitchell's "Gone* with the Wind": Letters, 1936‑1949. Ed. Richard Harwell. London: Collier Macmillan, 1986.

Mukherji, Subha. *Thinking on Threshold: The Poetics of Transitive Spaces*. New York: Anthem Press, 2013.

Mulvey-Roberts, Marie, ed. *The Handbook to Gothic Literature*. London: Macmillan Press, 1998.

O'Connor, Flannery. *Mystery and Manners*. Ed. Sally and Robert Fitzgerald. New York: The Noonday Press, 1969.

---. *The Complete Stories of Flannery O'Connor*. New York: Farrar, Straus and Giroux, 1989.

Orvell, Miles. *Flannery O'Connor: An Introduction*. Jackson & London: University Press of Mississippi, 1991.

Pyron, Darden Asbury. *Southern Daughter: The Life of Margaret Mitchell*. Oxford: Oxford University Press, 1991.

Scott, Anne Firor. "Afterword." *Vein of Iron*, Ellen Glasgow. Charlottesville and London: University Press of Virginia, 1995.

Skaggs, Merrill Maguire. "Ellen Glasgow." *The History of Southern Women's Literature*. Ed. Carolyn Perry and Mary Louise Weaks. Baton Rouge: Louisiana State UP, 2022. 336‑42.

Smith, Karen Manners. "The Novel." *The History of Southern Women's Literature*. Ed. Carolyn Perry and Mary Louise Weaks. Baton Rouge: Louisiana State UP, 2022. 48‑58.

Taylor, Helen. "*Gone with the Wind* and Its Influence." *The History of Southern Women's Literature*. Ed. Carolyn Perry and Mary Louise Weaks. Baton Rouge: Louisiana State UP, 2022. 258‑67.

Wang, Shouren. "Realism in the Twentieth Century." *Foreign Literature Review* 4 (1998): 45‑49.

［王守仁:《谈二十世纪的现实主义》,《外国文学评论》1998年第4期,第45—49页。］

Wang, Shouren, Liu Yang. "'The Realist Turn' and Others—An Interview with Wang Shouren." *New Perspectives on World Literature* 6(2020): 6‑13.

［王守仁、刘洋:《"现实主义转向"及其他——王守仁教授访谈录》,《外国文学动态研究》2020年第6期,第6—13页。］

Zhou, Xian. "Realism in the Twentieth Century: Perspectives from Philosophy and Psychology." Ed. Liu Mingjiu. *Realism in the Twentieth Century*. Beijing: China Social Sciences Press, 1992. 15‑40.

［周宪:《二十世纪的现实主义:从哲学和心理学看》,《二十世纪现实主义》,柳鸣九主编,北京:中国社会科学出版社,1992年,第15—40页。］

斜目而视下的英国 20 世纪 60—70 年代社会景观
——《历史人物》中作为"歪像"的大学校园、现代都市与日常生活空间

宋艳芳

内容摘要: 马尔科姆·布雷德伯里的学院派小说《历史人物》所描述的文化空间——大学校园、现代城镇和人们的日常生活空间——提供了一系列"歪像",让读者得以从不同侧面审视 20 世纪 60—70 年代英国的社会景观,探察其背后的现实。虚构的大学校园反映了现实中英国的"新大学运动"及遍布国内外的激进主义潮流;沿海的南方城镇影射了英国区域间的发展差距以及人们意识形态的发展变化;日常生活空间里上演着女权主义运动的戏剧性故事,同时也揭示了女性抗争所受到的局限。小说以小见大,以戏仿反映现实,虚实之间既关照了历史,也彰显了空间与文化的关联与互动。

关键词:《历史人物》 歪像 空间 文化
作者简介: 宋艳芳,苏州大学外国语学院教授,主要从事英美文学研究。

Title: Spectacle of 1960 - 70s British Society When Looked Awry—Campus, Modern City and Domestic Spaces as "Anamorphosis" in *The History Man*

Abstract: The cultural spaces depicted in Malcolm Bradbury's academic novel *The History Man*—university campuses, modern towns and domestic spaces—offer a series of "anamorphosis" that enable readers to scrutinize the social spectacle of Britain in the 1960s and 1970s from multiple perspectives, so as to delve into its underlying reality. The fictional university campus serves as a reflection of the "New University Movement" and the radicalism prevalent in Britain and the world; the coastal town in the south symbolically reflects regional disparities in development and ideological progress of individuals; the domestic spaces where dramatic feminist stories are on show expose the inherent limitations of women's struggles. By employing parody, this novel puts individual stories in a bigger picture of social conflicts and reflects reality through parody, providing an insightful examination of historical relevance between imagination and reality while emphasizing the interplay between space and culture.

Key Words: *The History Man*, anamorphosis, space, culture

Author: Song Yanfang is a professor at School of Foreign Languages, Soochow University, China. Her research interest is British and American literature.

马尔科姆·布雷德伯里的学院派小说《历史人物》反映了20世纪60年代末至70年代初英国的社会状况,具有强烈的时代感。梅里特·莫斯利曾表示:"虽然他的大多数小说,正如他所宣称的那样,可以被认为是'关于它们的时代,它们的主题、思想、情感、虚伪、知识风尚和当务之急',但《历史人物》最充分地再现了其特定的历史背景。"(Moseley 58)

《历史人物》的故事发生在1972年10月初至12月初,围绕主人公霍华德·柯克和妻子芭芭拉所举办的两次家庭聚会展开,描述了他们在不同时空的成长、成熟、变化及其相关的社会历史与文化。相较于布雷德伯里的前两部小说,这部小说吸引了较多的评价和分析。理查德·托德在《马尔科姆·布雷德伯里的〈历史人物〉:作为不情愿的指挥家的小说家》一文中分析了小说中的"小说家"这一人物跟作者布雷德伯里之间的联系(Todd 162 - 182);詹姆斯·艾奇逊在《马尔科姆·布雷德伯里的〈历史人物〉中的正题和反题》中分析了小说中作为"反题"的现代马克思主义社会和作为"正题"的中产阶级社会对人们的影响(Acheson 41 - 53);罗伯特·莫拉斯在他的专著中分析了小说形式上的实验性、语言和内容的对话性、人物的符号性(Morace 60 - 85)。2020 年,史蒂夫·莫里斯的一篇小文章回顾了 20 世纪 70 年代的英国历史,分析了布雷德伯里的创作意图和深意,指出:"这本书为读者提供了 1972 年特定时刻的一副快照,背景设在南海岸某处一所新式大学,其中时髦人物、马基雅维利式情节一应俱全。"(Morris 29)《历史人物》在中国也得到较多关注:管南异曾于 2005 年发文探析小说的叙述语言,揭示作者"在英国社会经历剧烈观念变革的 20 世纪 60—70 年代所捕捉到的极其矛盾和焦虑的心态"(管南异 29)。近年来的研究注重探讨这部小说中的人物形象(知识分子形象、女性角色等)和叙事艺术,对于小说中所揭示的空间、历史和文化的互动以及现实主义因素缺乏细致分析。

  在此基础上,本文借鉴齐泽克针对"歪像"的阐述,结合文化地理学有关空间与历史、文化关系的论述,探讨《历史人物》通过大学校园、城市景观、居家环境等表象所揭示的 20 世纪中期英国社会景观及其背后所隐藏的深层现实,特别是当时激进主义、马克思主义、女权主义的流行及其对人们的影响。齐泽克借用绘画领域来自荷尔拜因的名画《大使们》的一个隐喻,提出"歪像"(anamorphosis,亦译为"变形")的概念,说:"'正眼望去',即直接望去,绘画的细节显得模糊不清;一旦我们从某个角度'斜目而视',这些细节就会变得十分清晰,人们可以一目了然。"(齐泽克 18)本文从空间的角度"斜目而视"《历史人物》中所描述的社会现象,试图挖掘其背后的历史现实。

一、沃特茅斯大学:激进主义潮流下的新大学运动

《历史人物》以沃特茅斯大学(Watermouth Univeristy)[①]这样一所虚构的大学给读者提供了第一个"歪像",展现了 20 世纪 50—70 年代初的激进主义、新大学运动及其对大学校园、师生的影响,同时也从一个侧面反映了当时英国和世界范围的激进主义潮流。布雷德伯里本人也表达了他对这种激进潮流的担忧、愤怒和对秩序的渴望。

在《再看〈历史人物〉》中,莫里斯提到,布雷德伯里的朋友克里斯托弗·比格斯比(Christopher Bigsby)曾告诉他,"布雷德伯里对东安格利亚大学(University of East Anglia)的学生静坐感到愤怒,随后写了《历史人物》"(Morris 31)。布雷德伯里本人也曾表示,这部小说"完全是对现实主义的戏仿、对历史的嘲弄……"(Bradbury, *No Not Bloomsbury* 17) 换言之,《历史人物》既基于现实又超越现实。在 80 年代的一场访谈中,布雷德伯里也提到他小说中的现实主义因素问题,指出:"所有的艺术都是模仿,所有的模仿都是欺骗。因此,作为持续不断的人类探究之作,艺术的价值恰恰处于模棱两可的模仿领域:所有模仿都必须诉诸某种真实的观念——如果使用'模仿'这个词,就必须有一个被模仿的东西——同时宣称自己是一种欺骗。"(Haffenden 33)他在 1983 年出版的《兑换率》(*Rates of Exchange*)中以戏谑的口吻再次重申了这一点:

> 语言也只是被发明出来的交换系统,试图把文字(word)变成世界(world),把符号(sign)变成价值,把讲稿变成货币,把符码(code)变成现实。当然,在任何地方,甚至在斯拉卡,都有政治家和牧师,阿亚图拉(ayatollahs 伊斯兰教什叶派宗教领袖)和经济学家,他们会试图解释现实就是他们所说的那

样。永远不要相信他们；只相信小说家，那些更有深度的银行家，他们花时间试图把一张张印刷的纸变成价值，但从不讳言结果只是一个有用的虚构。(Bradbury, *Rates of Exchange* 8)

这跟齐泽克有关现实的阐释有异曲同工之妙。齐泽克在阐释拉康的"实在界"(the Real)这一概念时反复强调，我们日常生活中所谓的"现实"不过是一种幻象(fantasy)，经过了符号界的歪曲和变形。"如果我们所经历的'现实'(reality)是由幻象构成的，如果幻象是保护我们不被原始的实在界直接淹没的屏障，那么现实本身就可以作为逃避实在界的工具。"(Zizek, "Psychoanalysis and the Lacanian Real" 222)简言之，"我们日常所见、身处其中的，不过是幻象和符号界的现实，实在界一直在场却难以窥视，绝对的真实不可捕捉"(宋艳芳 29)。那么，艺术家的责任就是通过模仿来尽力拨开符号界的迷雾，去探询其背后未被歪曲的真实。

布雷德伯里在《历史人物》中试图通过语言符号来模仿他所经历、窥探到的现实。细读可见，这部小说基于作者真实的体验，反映了英国从20世纪50年代的保守主义逐渐走向20世纪60—70年代的激进主义的历史进程以及新型大学校园中的激进主义运动给师生们带来的影响。多林在他纪念布雷德伯里的文章中提到，"《历史人物》出色地唤起了英国'新'大学校园的激进氛围：沃特茅斯大学为信奉马基雅维利主义的社会学家霍华德·柯克提供了完美的伪装，因为他在追求伟大的过程中摧毁了婚姻和事业"(Doering 160)。

英国早在19世纪就开始了新大学运动，这场运动的影响持续到了20世纪中期并得到新的发展。在《新大学运动与英国高等教育的近代化》一文中，邓云清梳理了英国新大学运动的来龙去脉，探讨了英国高等教育从19世纪到20世纪初的发展历程，指出："新大学以功利主义为导向，取消教派限制，提供职业教育与科学教育，力图面向全社会培养实用人才。"(邓云清 85)以 1827 年伦敦大学(University of London)的建立为开端,英国高等教育经过半个多世纪的发展,从注重职业化教育到重新重视人文学科的基础性功能,开展综合教育,形成一批"人文学科与理工学科兼备、教育与科研并重的综合性大学"(邓云清 89)。这场新大学运动"基本实现了英国高等教育的世俗化、平民化与泛智化"(邓云清 90)。到 20 世纪 50 年代,这种新型大学发展日趋稳定,受到人们的欢迎,并吸引了大批学生入学。

在《历史人物》中,叙述者花了较大篇幅描述了柯克夫妇从保守主义到激进主义的转变,也揭示了英国大学从 20 世纪 50 年代到 70 年代初的发展状况。布雷德伯里本人分别在英国的莱斯特大学(University of Leicester)、伦敦大学玛丽王后学院(Queen Mary College, University of London)和曼彻斯特大学(University of Manchester)获得本科、硕士和博士学位,从广义上来讲,三座大学均属于与牛津大学、剑桥大学等古典大学相对的"红砖大学"(Redbrick University)。其中,曼彻斯特大学是六所著名"红砖大学"之一[②];莱斯特大学是新晋红砖大学[③];伦敦大学虽然不是典型的"红砖大学",但按照"文化百科"上的说法,"红砖"一词也被更广泛地用于指代任何非古典大学,《旁观者》(Spectator)将包括伦敦大学、苏塞克斯大学(University of Sussex)、诺丁汉大学(University of Nottingham)在内的多所大学也归入红砖大学。("Red Brick University" at Culture Wikia)因此,布雷德伯里是红砖大学的亲历者和拥护者,他自己的小说也基本上以这类新型大学为背景,展现其中的新风气、革命精神和激进主义氛围。这在《历史人物》中尤其突出。正如科恩在他的一篇书评中所说,小说中虚构的沃特茅斯镇,在某种程度上就是布莱顿(Brighton)的化身,沃特茅斯大学校园是"埃塞克斯大学、肯特大学、约克大学和东安格利亚大学(布雷德伯里任教的地方)的糟糕混合体"(Cohen 533)。因此,布雷德伯里将自己在各个大学校园的体验混杂在一起,完成了这部小说。

小说用两章(第二、第三章)的内容回顾了柯克夫妇在世界性的激进主义浪潮下的成长和改变,这种成长和改变与他们所接受的大学教育紧密相关,也从一个侧面反映了当时英国大学的开放环境、新大学运动以及大学里研究方向和学科的创新与融合。小说第二章的开头就给了柯克夫妇一个明确的定位:"毫无疑问,柯克夫妇属于新人类。然而,有些人生来如此:天生与变化和历史相熟,而柯克夫妇达到这种状态却经历了更为艰辛的过程,是通过努力、不断的改变和痛苦的经历达到的。"(*The History Man* 18)他们于20世纪50年代进入大学,1960年毕业,随后结婚。霍华德继续攻读研究生学位,芭芭拉成为家庭主妇。在经历过20世纪50年代的保守主义之后,他们感觉环境压抑,心情沉重,试图做出一定的改变:"历史环境在改变。正经历着一场革命的整个世界也在改变。"(24)芭芭拉寻求改变的方式是出轨;而霍华德则试图通过申请其他新大学的职位来做出改变:"整个研究方向正处于不断扩张的状态,并因为众多新大学的影响而发生了许多变化。他们中的许多学校把社会学当成了新的学术框架的主体。"(34)他到南方的沃特茅斯大学参加了面试,"大学里交叉式的学科设置、新颖的教学模式让霍华德在经历了利兹大学之后感到兴奋不已"(34)。这一点反映了新大学其中的一个特点:跨学科研究的兴起。阿萨·布里格斯曾以苏塞克斯大学为例,指出,该校大二、大三的一些课程和讲座"将会以研讨会的方式予以加强,其中一些研讨会将会是'跨学科的'"(Briggs 65)。

此类描述在《历史人物》中不胜枚举,展现了英国新型大学的革新及其大学生们的开放和激进。这与20世纪60年代的社会大环境也息息相关。1968年的"巴黎五月风暴"引发了欧洲各个国家的高等教育改革,英国也不例外。《历史人物》以此为大背景,以柯克夫妇为典型,反映了这一时期校园内外的激进主义风潮。实际上,叙述者表示,1968年这激进的一年把柯克夫妇彻底改造成了激进主义者。那一年,沃特茅斯大学的学生在"巴黎五月风暴"的影响下,在校园里静坐,要求副校长"宣布大学是一个自由的组织、一个革命的机构,与过时的资本主义划清界限"(48)。学校里的革命分子们在崭新的剧院里的混凝土墙壁上写上"烧毁一切""立即革命"等字眼(49)。在这样的社会风潮之下,"憎恨与革命的热情不断高涨。……城市的中心广场上,人们举行着游行示威。最大的百货商店里,许多窗户被砸了。学院里的员工分成了两派,一派支持激进的学生,一派却发表声明,呼吁学生回到他们的学业之中"(49)。霍华德·柯克显然属于激进派,他参加了静坐,到工人组织和工会大会上进行演讲,利用这个激进的时代,加入战斗,试图推翻原有的组织和体系,准备迎接一个崭新的时代,一个新的大学体系和世界体系。

因此,透过沃特茅斯大学这一"歪像",读者可以窥见20世纪60—70年代英国的新大学运动和这一运动所反映的教育发展、英国社会历史进展与当时的文化潮流。布雷德伯里以虚构的大学和故事揭示了隐藏其后的真实社会景观。

二、沃特茅斯镇:马克思主义思潮下的现代都市景观

沃特茅斯大学所在的沃特茅斯镇可以看作小说提供的第二个"歪像"。透过这一歪像可见这一时期马克思主义的复苏、流行及其在现代都市中的体现。作为一个沿海的现代化城镇,沃特茅斯与柯克夫妇原来所在的内陆城市形成对比,表现了英国城镇发展的区域差别以及人们在迁徙过程中的意识形态变化。

邓肯等学者在《文化地理学指南》中曾提到20世纪60年代的激进主义、马克思主义与文化地理学之间的关系,认为马克思主义正是通过这一时期激进学者们的积极参与才进入了地理学研究。"在这方面,转向马克思主义是更广泛的地理学激进变革的一部分——包括无政府主

义、女权主义、生态学和人文主义的发展,因为地理学家试图在理论上为自己日益增长的激进主义奠定基础。"(Duncan et al. 60)《历史人物》通过描述沃特茅斯这一虚构城市,表现了马克思主义在英国现代城市中的发展和流行。主人公霍华德·柯克这样一位激进主义者、行为主义者的人物形象更是为此提供了便利。他自己是一位马克思主义者;他和妻子奉行马克思主义的行事原则;现代城镇沃特茅斯提供了他们践行马克思主义理论原则的沃土。从芭芭拉的视角来看,沃特茅斯"有一种乐观的、令人振奋的气息,四处都能找到一种亲切的激进主义。这种不断奋进的现代式风格比利兹城里那个阴暗而严酷的世界要先进好几个光年"(34-35)。

在沃特茅斯,激进分子霍华德不满于资产阶级小资化的、舒适的生活环境,也不赞同他的朋友比米什在郊外找田园式住宅的做法,而是特意寻找了一所灰泥粉刷的老房子,这所房子"位于市中心贫民窟拆迁后的一块空地上"。因为,"对于柯克夫妇而言,这是一处理想的境地。这里靠近真正的社会问题,周围还有沙滩、激进派书店、计划生育诊所、长寿食品商店、福利办公室以及高耸入云的市建居民楼和九十分钟就能到达伦敦的快速电力火车。总而言之,就是靠近不断运转的生活"(4)。这也意味着,作为马克思主义者,柯克试图靠近鲜活、真实的生活,参与阶级斗争。

这一点戏仿了马克思和恩格斯对于社会阶级斗争的描述。布雷斯勒对此有过这样的总结:

> 马克思认为,所有社会都在向共产主义迈进。马克思认为进步是反动的或革命的,他断言,随着一个社会的经济生产方式从封建制度向更加市场化的经济发展,生产、分配和消费商品的实际过程变得更加复杂。因此,人们在经济体系中的职能变得不同。这种差异不可避免地将人们划分为不同的社

会阶层。最终,各个社会阶层的愿望和期望发生冲突。这种冲突或阶级矛盾导致社会经济基础从基于继承财富和地位的封建权力制度向基于私有财产所有权的资本主义制度发生根本性变化。这种转变需要社会的法律、习俗和宗教发生无数变化。(Bressler 193)

在《历史人物》中,柯克本人通过努力从工人阶级跻身中产阶级,试图挑战资产阶级,以自己的亲身经历实践着马克思主义的信条。

小说叙述者在第二章曾经交代过,柯克夫妇是经过了艰苦的过程,通过努力、改变和痛苦的经历变成了如今的"新人类"。因为"他们并不是出生在拥有各种机会和控制权的中产阶级家庭,也没有生长在这个明亮的海边城市,这个拥有码头、沙滩和体面的住宅,拥有到伦敦的便捷条件以及与潮流和财富紧密接触的地方"(18)。相反,柯克夫妇"都生长在更为严肃、纪律更为严明的北方,出生在可敬的工人阶级上层-中产阶级下层这样的背景中"(18)。因此,他们试图通过自己的努力获得阶级上的爬升。霍华德·柯克1957年凭借学业上的努力进入利兹大学,三年后以优等生的身份毕业,继续攻读研究生学位。再后来还通过长期的努力完成了博士论文,获得了博士学位,成功在利兹大学的社会学系扎稳脚跟,跻身中产阶级,实现了自己的梦想。芭芭拉作为女性,通过嫁给霍华德也获得了阶级的进一步提升。

叙述者刻意以地理空间的变化反映了柯克夫妇阶级的变化、经济状况的变化给他们带来的意识和思想的改变。柯克夫妇通过自己的努力从北方城市一路向英国中部和南部进发,实现了地理空间的变迁,也摆脱了原生家庭清规戒律的束缚。从北方到了利兹,"他们开始变得口若悬河,一切都有了一种新的味道。他们长期居住其内的墙壁突然打开,他们开始因为新的欲望和期待而变得骚动不安起来。……通过自己的努力和别人的帮助,他们的举止、风格以及性情都焕然一新"(22)。这契合了马克思主义的一些基本原理:经济基础决定上层建筑,你是什么样的人取决于你所拥有的东西。叙述者以调侃的语气解释柯克夫妇的这些变化:

> 要理解这个,就像霍华德作为一个热情的解释者说的那样,你需要知道一点儿马克思,一点儿弗洛伊德,还有一点儿社会历史。……你要知道时间、地点、环境、微观结构和宏观结构、意识的状态和决定因素以及人类意识的扩展能力和爆发能力。如果你理解了这些,你就明白了为什么老的柯克夫妇慢慢退出了视线,而新的柯克夫妇得以形成。(22-23)

这是作为学院派作家的布雷德伯里对马克思主义决定论的一种具象化的阐释。脱离了父辈和出生环境的影响,柯克夫妇也脱离了原来的意识形态,形成了新的价值观,有了更高的物质和精神追求。从物质上来说,"借助工作的优势,柯克夫妇住进了一个稍大的单元房,有了一张小一点儿的床,而且能够安装新的厨具、购买电视并举行一些小型聚会"(27)。从精神上来说,"在其他的研究生以及现在的同事中间,他们结识了一些新的、更加激进的朋友。他已不再被人评价,而是可以去评价他人,这一事实把他拖出了长期生存其中的、以卑躬屈膝的方式获得成绩的精神荒原"(27)。

地理空间的变化、物质的进步、精神的解放也让他们愈来愈激进。柯克在利兹大学也逐渐心生不满,继续往南进发,在沃特茅斯找到新的教职,准备开始新的征程。他们一家于1967年举家南迁,在越南战争形势不断升温的社会大背景下穿过英格兰中部、伯明翰南端,进入了一个新的、更加现代化的区域。布林利·托马斯(Brinley Thomas)曾指出,在英国,自维多利亚时代与爱德华时代以来,人们就喜欢向南迁徙(Thomas 296):"在1951—1966年间,英国南方吸引了1 059 000的移民,北方则失去了815 000的人口,其中苏格兰地区流失人口将近500 000。西南、东南、东安格利亚和中部地区在制造业扩张率和净移民率方面排名靠前。北部地区和苏格兰的制造业发展速度相对较低,净外迁人口较多。"(Thomas 297)这说明,英国南方意味着发展的潜力。

在脱离原生家庭之后,1967年的南迁是柯克一家又一次地理上的迁徙和精神上的解放。从原生家庭到利兹,他们并没有经历过于激烈的震荡;但到沃特茅斯,他们开始自我怀疑,不知道如何面对新的环境、新的状况、新的意识。"利兹是工人阶级,人们依靠工作生存;沃特茅斯是资产阶级,这里依靠旅游业、财产、退休金、法国大厨而繁荣。"(38)柯克夫妇并不想如他们的老朋友比米什夫妇那样融入资产阶级,停止战斗。他把亨利·比米什追求享乐的生活方式称为"推脱责任的寂静主义"(40)。而他和芭芭拉,则逃离比米什夫妇在郊外田园式的生活场所,"逃到沃特茅斯去重新感受城市生活的气息,去再次融入基本的现实。这里有房屋、垃圾桶、污秽和犯罪"(40-41)。霍华德决定去拜访沃特茅斯城的社会安全部。"他需要首先鼓足自己的士气,确保在这个自己要扎根命运的地方确实有社会学——有社会张力,有是非之地,有种族政治,有阶级斗争,还有政府与群众的斗争、被孤立的区域、素材资料,总而言之,有真实的生活。"(41)于是,他在沃特茅斯镇找到了一处贫民拆迁区,准备亲历激进派、嬉皮士、失业者、酒鬼、醉汉、吸毒者们的生活,将自己的社会学理论和生活实际结合起来。

透过沃特茅斯镇这一歪像,读者可以管窥英国20世纪中期以后城镇发展的区域差别:南方城镇的开放、激进与北方城镇的闭塞与保守形成鲜明的对比;开放的城镇环境也带来人们意识形态的变化,展现了空间与政治、文化之间的关联。

三、日常生活空间:女权主义运动的
文化场所及其局限

  小说提供的另一个"歪像"是日常生活空间,透过这些看似不起眼的空间,读者可见20世纪中期以后女权主义运动对英国女性的影响:19世纪以来的女权主义运动确实给现当代女性带来了一定的权力,但也带来新的问题。她们并不能完全挣脱宗教、道德、男权社会施加于女性的束缚,从而在激进中保守,在开放之余懊悔。

  《历史人物》中体现女权主义运动和思想的文化空间与众不同,不是在常见的公共空间,如工作场所、咖啡厅等,而主要是在日常生活空间或私密场景中:厨房、卧室、起居室。正如邓肯等学者所说,如果谈到马克思主义、女权主义等社会理论与地理空间的关系,只关注生产空间、工作场所是不够的,"家庭、邻里、学校和商店都是针对资本主义及其社会形态进行谈判和斗争的关键场所"(Duncan et al. 62)。《历史人物》通过芭芭拉·柯克、弗洛拉·本尼弗姆、安妮·卡伦德以及其他相关女性人物展现了他们在各自的日常生活空间中针对男权主义所进行的斗争以及这些斗争的结果。

  在《历史人物》中的所有女性人物中,芭芭拉显然占据了最为重要的位置。布雷德伯里本人在访谈中承认,芭芭拉是整部小说隐藏的中心人物,是悲剧女主角。"但问题是,她的故事没有得到完整展现。直到你把书放下,回头细想,才可能发现她的故事本来会是怎样的。我认为她实际上是非常重要的。尽管她刻意地没有被前置,这并不意味着这本书本质上不是她的故事。"(Haffenden 41)按照作者提供的这条暗示,回头从芭芭拉的视角来看事态的发展,我们会发现,芭芭拉的故事确实体现了一位女性艰难成长的过程和最终的绝望。正如弗吉尼亚·伍尔夫在《自己的一间屋》(*A Room of One's Own*)中提到的那个著名假设一样,如果莎士比亚有一个跟他一样才华横溢的妹妹,这个妹妹在成长过程中会经历很多的阻碍——比如父母不重视她的才能发展、不提供受教育机会,长大后可能被骗失身、怀孕,最终不仅难以像莎士比亚那样功成名就,还可能名誉尽毁、陷入绝望、自杀身亡。(Woolf 45 - 46)在《历史人物》中,芭芭拉被描述为一个比霍华德还聪明的女性,然而,同虚构的莎士比亚的妹妹一样,在男性主导的社会中,她不仅不能发挥自己的才能,反而陷入婚姻的牢笼,最终绝望自杀。

当然,《历史人物》的时代背景是20世纪50—70年代,较之于莎士比亚所处的文艺复兴时期,人们对女性已经有了更多的宽容。然而,即便是在这样的情况下,即便芭芭拉积极地参与女权主义运动,维护自己的利益,她仍然陷入了死胡同。小说从各个侧面展现了芭芭拉的斗争和失败。提到霍华德和芭芭拉考进大学的情况,叙述者提到,霍华德是靠拼命努力考上大学的。对照而言,"芭芭拉天生更加聪明,她必须如此才行,因为那种家庭背景对女孩的学业没有太过严厉的要求。她是从女子中学考上的大学,但她并不像霍华德那样是通过强大的动力,而是因为一位有同情心并倾向社会主义的英语老师的鼓励和建议。这位老师曾嘲笑过她多情的居家抱负"(19)。然而,到1960年毕业的时候,霍华德获得了一等荣誉学位,"而芭芭拉因为不太喜欢她的英语专业课程,而且花费过多的时间帮霍华德复习,只拿到了二等下荣誉学位[④]"(19 - 20)。

从这些描述我们可以看出芭芭拉成长的困境和可能的未来走向。她从小得到的教育让她像很多传统女性一样,最大的梦想就是做家庭主妇,囿于厨房、卧室等方寸之地;她之所以能考上大学不是靠家庭的推动,而是因为一位英语教师的嘲讽。但由于她那"多情的居家抱负"和客观条件的限制,上大学并没有真正改变她的命运。同霍华德结婚后,芭芭拉成了一名家庭主妇,深陷于家庭琐事,他们的婚姻也"成了一个监狱,其功能是检验成长,而不是打开成长的渠道"(24)。她大学毕业后就成了"一位标准女性,一个一心操持家务的人,其结果是性冷淡、压抑性歇斯底里和肉体羞耻感的典型性综合病症,最终是肉体上和社会上的自我厌烦"(24)。后来,在第二次女权运动的影响下,芭芭拉出轨,打破了他们婚姻的平静和稳定。随后两人复合,芭芭拉怀孕生子。这让芭芭拉的情况雪上加霜。尽管孩子出生后霍华德"恪守职责"(30),承担起很多照顾孩子的事情,但"芭芭拉依然抱怨说自己为母亲的角色所束缚,这种角色既否定又满足她的自我价值。于是,她让他为自己作为妻子和母亲的社会角色付工资,以证明自己不是二等公民"(30)。做了两个月的全职妈妈之后,芭芭拉想要经济独立,找邻居帮忙照顾孩子,自己开始兼职做一些公共意见调查和市场调研,获得了心理上的满足。

在婚姻中,在日常生活空间中,芭芭拉作为一位"现代女性",竭尽全力地追求自由、独立和自我价值的实现。她试图摆脱"二等公民"的地位,与霍华德平分家务、平起平坐;她率先出轨,宣布自己的自由;她通过兼职试图获得经济独立,实现自己的价值。然而,最终,她仍然面临各种困境:当霍华德在大学校园里参与各种激进主义活动时,她的斗争舞台仍然主要局限于居家环境。她不得不清洗家庭聚会后的盘子,照顾孩子;她自己有一个情人,却只能偷偷摸摸到伦敦私会。因此,当她的情人里昂准备离开伦敦,当她发现自己完全没有从自己所谓的开放式婚姻中得到幸福,当她发现有些人认为保守的亨利才是"唯一一个表现得体的人"(218),她意识到自己在现代婚姻中,在激进主义社会中并没有实现自我的价值,反而违背了传统的道德原则,因此选择了自杀。

除了芭芭拉·柯克,《历史人物》中还有几位女性人物同样在女权主义运动的影响下对男权社会做出了自己的抗争,这些抗争也并不是发生在公共空间,而是在日常生活的私人空间。其中,弗洛拉·本尼弗姆是一位年近40岁的社会心理学家,在卧室展开研究和斗争:"她喜欢跟那些婚姻出问题的男人睡觉;他们身上有更多的话题可以讨论,并因为来自家庭中的微妙政治而具有吸引力。这是弗洛拉的研究领域。"

(53)与传统女性不同,她大胆前卫,在与霍华德·柯克的婚外情中占据主导地位,引导霍华德讨论他与芭芭拉婚姻中的问题,以此作为她研究的素材。作为一位女学者,她冷静机智,能够理性地处理感情问题,细致入微地分析现代婚姻的本质,显然是一个现代女强人的代言人,但布雷德伯里字里行间的调侃也不言而喻:如果一位现代女性走到如此激进的地步,显然会为社会所不容。

透过小说提供的日常生活空间这一歪像,读者可见20世纪60—70年代英国的女权主义浪潮以及女性的各种反抗,小说中的这种反抗主要发生在日常生活领域,更加彰显了这一时期女权主义运动的普遍性和局限性:经过长期的斗争,任何空间都可能成为女性斗争的舞台,但最终,她们并不能挣脱空间、生理、心理上的限制,在激进与保守之间进退维谷。

结　语

《历史人物》中的大学校园、现代城市、日常生活空间为读者提供了一个个的"歪像"。透过这些"歪像",读者可见作者布雷德伯里的良苦用心和他对20世纪60—70年代英国社会发展、历史进程、文化潮流的关注、思考和再现。通过展现大学校园内外的激进主义浪潮、现代城镇中的马克思主义复苏、日常生活场景中的女权主义运动给人们带来的影响,小说现实主义地再现了英国那个时代的思想与文化,勾勒了时代发展的痕迹。同时,小说也以英国的新大学运动、城市发展差距以及日常生活场景中的政治斗争等揭示了空间与文化之间的关联。这对读者来说提供了两点启发:其一,真正的"实在界"或者绝对的现实也许无法百分之百还原或再现,文学艺术却总是在以各种方式挖掘现实,使之符号化,让读者通过这些符号来尽量靠近其背后的现实;其二,空间与文化之间有着紧密而微妙的联系,培养空间感和空间意识对于了解特定时代、国家的文学与文化也大有裨益。

注解【Notes】

① 英国有多所大学有类似名称：普利茅斯大学（University of Plymouth）、朴茨茅斯大学（University of Portsmouth）、伯恩茅斯大学（Bournemouth University）等，可见布雷德伯里对现实的戏仿。

② 这六所"红砖大学"包括：伯明翰大学（The University of Birmingham）、利物浦大学（The University of Liverpool）、利兹大学（The University of Leeds）、谢菲尔德大学（The University of Sheffield）、布里斯托大学（The University of Bristol）、曼彻斯特大学（The University of Manchester）。

③ 杰克·西蒙斯的《新大学》专门讲述了莱斯特大学作为新大学的兴起和发展。见 Simmons, Jack. *New University*. Leicester: Leicester University Press, 1958。

④ 英国大学本科毕业证书有四个等级：一等荣誉学士学位（First Class Honours）、二等上荣誉学士学位（Upper-second Class Honours）、二等下荣誉学士学位（Lower-second Class Honours）、三等学士学位（Third Class Honours）。

引用文献【Works Cited】

Acheson, James. "Thesis and Antithesis in Malcolm Bradbury's *The History Man*," *Journal of European Studies* 33.1 (Mar. 2003): 41 – 53.

Bradbury, Malcolm. *The History Man*. New York: Penguin, 1975.

---. *Rates of Exchange*. London: Secker & Warburg, 1983.

---. *No, not Bloomsbury*. London: Deutsch, 1987: 17.

Bressler, Charles E. *Literary Criticism: An Introduction to Theory and Practice*. (4th ed.) New Jersey: Pearson Education, Inc. 1994.

Briggs, Asa. "Drawing a New Map of Leaning." *The Idea of a New University: An Experiment in Sussex*. Ed. David Daiches. London: Deutsch, 1964: 60 – 80.

Cohen, Stan. "Sociologists, History and the Literary Men." *Sociology* 11.3 (Sept. 1977): 533 – 47.

Deng, Yunqing. "The New University Movement and the Modernization of Higher Education in England." *Journal of Higher Education* 01 (2008): 85 – 91.

［邓云清：《新大学运动与英国高等教育的近代化》，高等教育研究 01（2008）：85 – 91。］

Doering, Jonathan W. "Malcolm Bradbury: A History Man for Our Times." *Contemporary Review* 278. 1622 (Mar. 2001): 159 – 163.

Duncan, James S., Nuala C. Johnson and Richard H. Schein (eds.), *A Companion to Cultural Geography*, Oxford: Blackwell Publishing, 2004.

Guan, Nanyi. "Where Will You Go—On Malcolm Bradbury's Novel *The History

Man. *Foreign Literature* 02 (2005): 29 - 34.

［管南异:《你往何处去——评马尔科姆·布拉德伯里的长篇小说〈历史人〉》,《外国文学》2(2005):29 - 34.］

Haffenden, John. *Novelists in Interview*, London: Methuen & co. Ltd., 1985.

李西祥:《社会现实的解构:幻象、现实、实在界》,《现代哲学》4(2012):22 - 28。

［Li, Xixiang. "The Deconstructed Reality: Fantasy, Reality and the Real." *Modern Philosophy* 4 (2012): 22 - 28.］

Morace, Robert A. *The Dialogic Novels of Malcolm Bradbury and David Lodge*, Carbondale and Edwardsville: Southern Illinois University Press, 1989.

Morris, Steve. "Another Look at 'The History Man'." *New Criterion*, vol. 38, no. 10, June 2020, pp. 29 - 31.

Moseley, Merritt. "Malcolm Bradbury." *Dictionary of Literary Biography* (*DLB*) *Vol. 207: British Novelists Since 1960*, 3rd series. Ed Merritt Moseley. Detroit: Gales Group, 1999: 51 - 65.

"Red Brick University." at https://culture.fandom.com/wiki/Red_brick_university. Accessed on Jan. 4, 2024.

Simmons, Jack. *New University*. Leicester: Leicester University Press, 1958.

Song, Yanfang. "A Critical Analysis of Zizek's and Eagleton's Notions of the 'Real', Reality and Realism." *New Perspectives on World Literature* 6 (2020): 25 - 34.

［宋艳芳:《齐泽克与伊格尔顿笔下的"实在界"、现实与现实主义考辨》,载《外国文学动态研究》6(2020):25 - 34。］

Thomas, Brinley. *Migration and Economic Growth: A Study of Great Britain and Atlantic Economy*. 2nd ed. London: Cambridge University Press, 1973.

Todd, Richard. "Malcolm Bradbury's 'The History Man': The Novelist as Reluctant Impressario." *Dutch Quarterly Review of Anglo-American Letters* 11.3 (1981): 162 - 82.

Woolf, Virginia. *A Room of One's Own and Three Guineas*. London: William Collins, 2014.

Zizek, Slavoj. "Psychoanalysis and the Lacanian Real: 'Strange Shapes of the Unwarped Primal World'." *Adventures in Realism*. Ed. Matthew Beaumont. Malden & Oxford: Blackwell Publishing, 2007: 207 - 223.

Zizek, Slavoj. *Looking Awry: An Introduction to Jacques Lacan Through Popular Culture*. Trans. Ji Guangmao. Hangzhou: Zhejiang University Press, 2011.

［斯拉沃热·齐泽克:《斜目而视:透过通俗文化看拉康》,季光茂译。杭州:浙江大学出版社,2011年。］

"残酷"作为方法：
《舒吉·贝恩》的格拉斯哥城市叙事

陈 丽

内容摘要：在2020年布克奖获奖小说《舒吉·贝恩》中，道格拉斯·斯图尔特将"残酷"视为一种方法论的关键词，在叙事情节、形式和民族性三个方面建构格拉斯哥城市叙事的新趋向。"残酷"既是去工业化浪潮下城市底层生活状况的真实写照，也是斯图亚特为格拉斯哥小说确立的新现实主义美学立场。通过描绘底层女性在日常生活中遭遇的"残酷"现实，斯图亚特传达出当代苏格兰性就是个体残酷感知的理解。

关键词：《舒吉·贝恩》 残酷 苏格兰性

作者简介：陈丽，安徽师范大学外国语学院副教授，主要从事当代英国小说研究。

Title: Urban Writing of Glasgow in Douglas Stuart's *Shuggie Bain*

Abstract: Douglas Stuart considers "cruelty" as a key concept with methodological significance in his 2020 Booker Prize winning novel *Shuggie Bain*, which constructing a new approach in Glasgow urban narrative in terms of narrative plot, narrative form and ethnic identity. "Cruelty" is not only the portrait of the living conditions of the underclass under the wave of deindustrialization, but also an aesthetic stance in Stuart's Glasgow novel writing. By depicting the "cruel" reality faced by underclass women in their daily lives, Stuart conveys his understanding of contemporary Scottishness that is the individual's perception of cruelty.

Key words: *Shuggie Bain*; cruelty; Scottishness

Author: Chen Li is an associate professor at the School of Foreign Studies, Anhui Normal University, China. Her research interest is contemporary British fiction.

2020年的布克奖是道格拉斯·斯图尔特（Douglas Stuart, 1976—）开启作家身份的一份褒奖。他的首部小说《舒吉·贝恩》（*Shuggie Bain*, 2020）出版不久就摘得这个当代英语小说界最重要的奖项，之后还进入了当年美国国家图书奖的决选，获得广泛赞誉。斯图亚特成为继詹姆斯·凯尔曼（James Kelman）之后第二位获此殊荣的苏格兰作家。然而，相对于"后分权"时代涌现出的苏格兰叙事作品而言，《舒吉·贝恩》的获奖更像是当代苏格兰文学的一次事件性宣言。此前登顶的凯尔曼小说《这是多么晚，多么晚》（*How Late it was Late, How Late*, 1994）引发的批评话语生动地展示了英国文化内部不同阵营对苏格兰性问题的激烈争辩。此外，阿莉·史密斯（Ali Smith）曾四次入围布克奖，其"脱欧"小说《秋》（*Autumn*, 2016）呼声最高却止步于布克奖短名单提名。甚至有苏格兰学者认为"只有加深对苏格兰民族认同复杂性的理解之后，才能充分体验苏格兰文学的独特性"（Wolfreys 6）。

那么，在苏格兰分离主义趋势加剧的今天，为什么关于苏格兰城市题材的作品获得这一权威性的文学肯定？评论者不约而同地聚焦于该小说的两个特点。其一是"一部宏大的社会小说"（Jordan），它精心绘制了当代苏格兰城市边缘空间的残酷景图。这个观点并不陌生，得出了相似的结论：工作和意义被剥夺，"充斥着贫困、孤独和无助，弥漫着一股颓败和绝望的气氛"（吕洪灵 194）。这一评价流露的局外人视角提醒我们：苏格兰性的解读不必拘泥于本质性，也可以放置于文学与社会的同构关系中。其二是小说叙事风格的矛盾性：残酷且幽默，布克奖评委会主席玛格丽特·巴斯比（Magaret Busby）将这一阅读体验称为"令人心碎"和"感动"，"让人又哭又笑"等，认为小说的"联结"主题使其"注定是一部经典之作"。上述论述点明了"残酷"是这部小说不言而喻的叙事艺术，却并未进一步阐述"残酷"在小说中被赋予的方法论意义。本文将结合小说的自传色彩，从叙事情节、形式和民族性隐喻三个方面入手串联小说"残酷"书写，阐明新生代苏格兰作家对民族性问题的认知转变。

一、"残酷"作为叙事情节

"残酷"作为一种小说创作的方法论，首先指向了作家继承了再现小市民精神颓废、酗酒乱性且暴力犯罪等恶习的格拉斯哥小说传统，以及与之相关联的"残酷"叙事程式。《舒吉·贝恩》便是以"残酷"作为小说的叙事表层风格得以呈现。实际上，这一"残酷"情节写作正是作家受到经典性肯定的重要基础，也是成就他独特地方性风格的有效叙事手法。《舒吉·贝恩》是作家斯图亚特经过十年创作，遭遇三十余次拒稿之后，在"残酷"的文学市场中获得出版，赢得了为苏格兰底层群体发声的机会。

残酷本身就是一种言语行为，它在词源学上源于古法语"cruelte"，意指"对众生痛苦或漠不关心，或以之取乐"。"漠不关心"，抑或"以之取乐"，皆是人性之"恶"的复杂表现。在后现代状况下，"残酷"的社会意义引起文化批评界的关注。法国戏剧家安托南·阿尔托（Antonin Artaud）在《残酷戏剧》（*Le Théâtre et son Double*，2015）一书中将"残酷"（cruelty）概念归纳为个体无法回避的必然性，须直面的痛苦，却借此获得延续生命的希望（81）。在《舒吉·贝恩》中，"残酷"的悖论内涵可以解释主要人物阿格尼斯令人费解的悲剧命运，同时也为评论者对小说赋予经典性论断提供一种较为合理的解释。一般而言，格拉斯哥底层女性的酗酒恶习无疑受到家庭婚姻压力，或是生活极度贫困的影响。但长期以来，宗教文化和父权制思想的交叠影响，她们的酒精上瘾症状并未得到善意的关注，因此令人厌恶而受到暴力对待。围绕着阿格尼斯"酗酒"母亲的形象，斯图亚特展开了以"酗酒——戒酒——再酗酒死亡"为叙事程式的"残酷"故事，塑造了努力挣扎却无力逃脱死亡命运的底层女性形象。

如果说小说的前两章基本延续了格拉斯哥小说女性创伤叙事的传统，那么在随后的第三章矿区生活中，斯图亚特则悄然颠覆了这一传统形式呈现的残酷情节。《舒吉·贝恩》中，作家有意无意弱化城市消费异化的心理包袱，将叙事重心转移至笔下人与物的互动关系，在其中探索定义主体价值的可能。格拉斯哥去工业化的集体记忆虽然贯穿于全书背景，但却不再仅仅投射于酗酒、贫困和绝望的社会悲剧，还被重新想象为底层女性在消费之物中"保持紧密联结，坚守价值观的故事"（Busby 2020）。阿格尼斯试图以酗酒抚慰婚姻失败带来的创伤，最终被丈夫舒格抛弃在格拉斯哥城市边缘的矿区，独自抚养三个孩子，几乎处于自生自灭的危险境地。可喜的是，阿格尼丝应聘了煤矿加油站的工作，开始远离酗酒，她用这份微薄的薪水在弗里曼邮购目录中重新定义物质生活世界。家中的冰箱、吸尘器、时髦的服装无一不代表着她的"清醒"，以及"这份清醒带来的平静生活"（斯图亚特 268）。舒吉一家的公租房成为矿区街道里最整洁、充满生活气息的住所，"光鲜亮丽的玫瑰园，对于破败的煤矿小镇来说过于招眼了。门上刷了一层红色漆，和别家的颜色都不一样，看起来很自信"（333）。消费之物隐喻出她所向往的生活和精神的改善，也正是这种消费主义意识支撑着阿格尼斯开始重新塑造自我，主动加入格拉斯哥的各类戒酒会，寻求新的社会联结。

与此同时，孤独感成为一种写作残酷情节的新美学形式。在《舒吉·贝恩》中，"孤独"（loneliness）一词多次出现在阿格尼斯酒醒之后的生活中。虽然她试图用加油站的夜班工作、电话本、酒友的毒友谊等诸多方式保持与外部联系,但孤独感犹如阴影一般伴随着她短暂的一生。小说不惜用大量细节描述她日常生活中的孤独,譬如阿格尼斯翻阅电话簿,用打电话的方式宣泄孤独的桥段,她的疯癫表演足以投射出残酷生活对其生存状况的挤压程度。"她在电话桌前坐到天黑,又在一篇漆黑中坐到深夜。烟头上的火是她唯一的光亮……"(255)此类孤独场景在小说中频繁出现,共同指向了1980年代格拉斯哥工人阶层所经历的城市转型之痛。蓝领家庭在童年时期被灌输的阶层价值观和工人阶级身份不复存在。原本子承父业的工人阶层产生断裂,遭遇"恐惧、失落、羞耻等"孤独情感病症(艾伯蒂9)。这一共同记忆使得读者对《舒吉·贝恩》的故事产生强烈的共情,足以调动起有过孤独体验的读者的阅读欲望。

更进一步说,这种孤独感不仅是格拉斯哥人的独特体验,还是全球化趋势下贫困和失业人士的共同经验。尤其在全球疫情大流行期间,英国封城模式中的"自我隔离"已经将新自由主义带来的社会和经济矛盾暴露无遗。《舒吉·贝恩》中无处不在的孤独感突显出作为有血有肉的人的共通性,因而颠覆了传统格拉斯哥创伤叙事中"我们"与"他们"之间的二元对立。同时被质疑的还有新自由主义的神话。新自由主义对缓解"英国病"发挥了不可忽视的作用,但它的核心话语——自由——并非一剂良药,反倒更像是一种离间苏格兰民众的团结感、加剧社会贫富分化的催化剂。以造船业为代表的苏格兰实体工业体系就在这场市场自由化经济转型中轰然坍塌。经济金融化、虚拟化迫使曾经处于优势的苏格兰实体工业转移至发展中国家,小说中舒吉的姐姐凯瑟琳和新婚丈夫远赴南非谋求生计就是一个例证。尽管两人分属天主教和新教,但共同的求生目标让他们抛开彼此的宗教信仰差异,一起筹划着婚后飞到南非从事打小就熟悉的父辈行业。

这一看似自由选择的背后隐含数十万苏格兰青年背井离乡的痛苦

和难以消磨的孤独。凯瑟琳每次从南非打电话给舒吉哥哥利克,都叮嘱他绝不能在阿格尼斯面前提到她的现状。孤独的意象还被用来描绘那些留守苏格兰的家人的落寞凄苦。故事中搭乘舒格出租车的老妇人,无法理解格拉斯哥青年们为谋生计选择踏上南非之旅,哀叹这座巨人城市的衰败给工人家庭带来的灾难,"整整二十五年。就在达尔马诺克钢铁厂。走的时候只领了三周的薪水"(斯图亚特49)。可以说,格拉斯哥人陷入越自由,越贫困,越孤独的怪圈。孤独感构成了一种反复重述的共通感,成为苏格兰内部群体之间的情感纽带,颠覆了以往苏格兰文学中常见的宗派对立关系。与去工业化相关的历史叙事和政治影响被淡化,沉重的、挥之不去的孤独感却被前景化,成为格拉斯哥城市叙事风格的新标识。对于斯图亚特来说,"残酷"作为格拉斯哥叙事的情节,不只是一个个格拉斯哥底层家庭故事,还是每一个普通人在身处绝望困境中顽强扎根的写照:贫病相侵、善恶较量、抵抗孤独、亲历灾难后的心理重建。讲述"残酷"故事,也让斯图亚特的这部处女作小说出版不久就占据了一个独特的文坛位置。事实上,他对过去经验的再现和凝练正是作品能够经典化的重要因素,而文学奖对这一历史经验的承认又印证了能够成为经典的重要依据:"能够呈现民族主义、被发明的传统和独特的文化认同。"(Kolbas 139)

二、"残酷"作为叙事形式

作为小说叙事形式的"残酷",指的是作家在格拉斯哥小说形式革新的探索。"残酷"是一种棘手又重要的叙述对象。作家如何在书写残酷场景的同时,避免落入道德合法性的陷阱,这无疑是一个考量作者文学能力的问题。在叙事形式方面,让读者跟随叙述者视角观看残酷场景,检视作者的伦理立场,这是斯图亚特"残酷"故事获得经典性肯定的重要叙事形式。作为一部自传小说,斯图亚特似乎总是在搭建"解释"

与"真实"之间的关联性(杨正润139),一方面强调小说的真实性,蓝本源自他和母亲在格拉斯哥生活写照。这段真实经历的书写,"对于成长在1980年代的格拉斯哥男孩而言,获奖是做梦都没想过的"(Simpson)。同时在行文中,斯图亚特保持着自反性的内在冲动,却又对自传文本规约保持着高度自觉。可以说,斯图亚特选择的是在真实经历基础上的虚构,他所运用的叙事技法显然不同于传统格拉斯哥小说的虚构性。斯图亚特曾在访谈中向凯尔曼为代表的格拉斯哥小说致敬,深刻理解其再现艺术所透露的绝望感。正是在这个意义上,作家所追求的真实感在于,小说借用视角的切换,有效制造了真实的多重面向,逼迫读者去反思这段格拉斯哥残酷记忆的真实效度,引导读者见证以阿格尼斯为代表的底层群体的人性悖论。

  小说中,阿格尼斯作为一位单亲母亲在贫困中挣扎求生,婚姻阴影让她染上酗酒恶习,被遗弃矿区后她主动戒酒,试图重新开启爱心母亲的角色,却屡屡遭受社区醉酒汉们的身体侵害。阿格尼斯也由此成为小说中最受争议的人物。那么,斯图亚特为何要让读者见证阿格尼斯所遭遇的残酷暴力?小说大多以第三人称视角回忆讲述,第一人称视角和第二人称视角穿插分布于全书中,几种视角的交叠使用用意何在?这其实展现的是作者向读者传递潜在意图的文学能力。换言之,作者如何将读者角色迁移到文本结构之中,赋予真实读者依据"历史语境和个人情景",以"不同介入方式"展开阅读进程(Iser 36-38)。斯图亚特的意图绝非仅仅是让读者去哀其不幸怒其不争那么简单,更是在冲击读者固有的伦理立场的同时,去亲近、反思自己所不曾面对的人性悖论。

  阿格尼斯的孤独和受害者形象在社区邻里的集体想象中被扭曲和被污名化。随着两次婚姻的解体,阿格尼斯带着三个子女先后搬迁到观景山社区和英国政府废弃的格拉斯哥煤矿区。每一次邻里环境的转移,阿格尼斯与当地邻居的关系便日渐紧密,人性中的坚韧、狡诈和疯癫就越来越明显,而她也从一个明艳、爱情脑的女子变为一个被鄙视、被羞辱的女酒鬼。社区邻里的闲聊中,这些邻居是在阿格尼斯每次酗酒断片曝光之后才聚集议论的,但故事的第三人称叙述者在故事的第二部分就已经向读者描述过她醉酒之后的窘态。如果不是因为婚姻变迁,阿格尼斯或许就像一个普通酒鬼那样消失在人们的话题中,正是她每次清醒后表现的羞耻感和悔过行动,再次得到邻里们的关注。然而,当邻居们再次看到阿格尼斯的门厅布置和孩子们的着装打扮时,却发现自己的无知。这些叙述者要么是观景山社区的邻居,要么是矿区街道的居民,在叙事过程中重复出现的"时髦""英国女王"之类的描绘语,充分说明这些邻里对阿格尼斯印象:孤傲、清丽和格格不入;同时也对其行为感到不解,都试图靠近去观察这样的时尚女性为何进入贫民窟生活。"女人们上下打量这位新邻居:细细高跟鞋,高高梳起的黑发,华丽的貂皮大衣。阿格尼斯盯着冷清的大街,任她们肆意审视。"(斯图亚特128)不仅如此,她们对阿格尼斯酒鬼形象的评价还要隐藏在日常的闲言碎语中。阿格尼斯的男友尤金为了验证这一流言,特意在她的生日宴中加入饮酒环节,让已经戒酒的阿格尼斯再次陷入灾难。"干杯!你太让我骄傲了。我就知道我妹妹说的不是真的。"对"我妹妹说的",也就是说不止我一个人觉得你就应该是个女酒鬼。这是对阿格尼斯的集体性污名化。也就是在这样一次次的邻里交往中,社区邻里们并没有伸出援手帮助阿格尼斯,反而是积极去验证邻居口中"一个酗酒的婊子"的形象描述是否真实(283)。而污名化的结果便是将阿格尼斯异化为妖魔一般的存在,在邻里共同体内部被边缘化,不得不开始又一次搬迁。

然而,故事中不时出现的直接评论有意提醒读者的介入,去反思作者在叙述邻里残酷生存状况时所采取的伦理立场。"这些陌生叔叔固然令人讨厌,但他们的目标仅仅是阿格尼斯。对舒吉来说,各类阿姨婆婆则要坏得多。"(258)第三人称叙述者的这些直接点评,拉开读者对文本中那些残酷场景的欣赏,也提醒读者从这一混乱、暴力的体验中及时抽身,警醒读者对这种残酷现实的批判,并反省自身的阅读趣味。同时,作家还启用第二人称"你"的模糊指涉,逼迫读者与人物、叙述者进行直接交流。在理查德森看来,第二人称视角表示"这种叙述将读者作为其话语的对象"(Richardson 33)。面对邻里对自己的污名化攻击,阿格尼斯在男友尤金面前羞耻心爆满,无法回答尤金的质问。此时第二人称叙事"你"的出现,意味着作家在传记中调用"非我"的称呼,直接邀请读者来介入这一场景,"多年的酗酒会打乱你的记忆"。"旁人的重复询问会让你失去对事实的感应。"(斯图亚特 285)这表明斯图亚特有意突显自传中的反身指涉,意在与另一个阅读主体发生关联,进而将个人的残酷生活状况纳入与社会的互动关系中。

三、"残酷"作为小说叙事的民族性隐喻

"残酷"作为小说叙事的民族性隐喻,指的是作家斯图亚特对小说是否能够针砭时弊,能否再现当代苏格兰残酷现实的限度测试。在 2020 年布克奖颁奖词中,《舒吉·贝恩》叙事艺术的魅力被认为与构建的"苏格兰价值观"密切相关(Busby)。有关当代苏格兰性的讨论在学界并未形成一致的看法。在《理解苏格兰》(*Understanding Scotland*, 1992)一书中,卡鲁瑟斯(David Carruthers)的观点是,历史上苏格兰民族性在"妥协"和"协商"中构建的(200)。然而事实并非完全如此。征用叙事的力量进行诗学"抵抗",发出苏格兰地方的声音也未尝不是一种选择。

《舒吉·贝恩》获奖不久,斯图亚特在访谈中阐明自己的诗学主张,他笔下人物对话中的格拉斯哥方言并非只是刻画人物本身,更是再现方言在当代英国文学中集聚的能动性。斯图亚特坚信作为能指的方言的力量,足以能够弥合文学作品中词与物的裂隙,让他的作品

呈现苏格兰人的"同理心、幽默、爱和斗争"(Simpson)。这一诗学主张与此前凯尔曼对苏格兰方言的辩护一脉相承。彼时评论者眼中粗鄙的格拉斯哥言辞和底层书写让凯尔曼发出愤怒的呐喊,"我的文化和语言拥有存在的权利","文学中脏话的合理性辩论"会陷入"我们"和"你们"的价值观区隔(McGlynn 20)。这里颇有意味的是,斯图尔特认为正是凯尔曼让他看到了苏格兰人及其方言的创造性,而写作帮助他以中产阶级的视角真正理解底层民众的那种绝望感(Simpson)。可以说,斯图尔特延续了凯尔曼对于苏格兰文化地方性的辩护立场,却更倾向利用方言的特质来引导读者重新理解1980年代格拉斯哥城市历史的残酷性。

有趣的是,为了突显这一民族性记忆的残酷性,斯图亚特在《舒吉·贝恩》中十分青睐幽默叙事手法。残酷与幽默——这一矛盾的阅读体验与近年来格拉斯哥小说日常生活叙事转向不谋而合,曾以苏格兰高地历史为主体的宏大叙事让位于寻常百姓的微小叙事。对小市民精神面貌、社区暴力和亲密关系的探讨构成了当代格拉斯哥小说一个显著的日常主题。而这一转变与近年来后后现代主义文学中强烈的喜剧意识相结合,更加自觉地展示了底层小人物在日常生活中的生命质感。这主要体现在方言和身体表演两个方面。

首先,格拉斯哥方言口音具有能动性,构成了一种言语行为,把阿格尼斯塑造成一位爱慕虚荣却勇于抵抗残酷现实的格拉斯哥时尚女性形象。方言口音因其所蕴含的社会阶层属性,成为阿格尼斯想象社会交往的重要方式,具有能动性。"传统的文学现实主义不能让人物'用他们的方言说话',所以会失败;方言能提供一种幻觉,日常现实在其中既听不见,又看不见。"(Craig 76)作家在人物对白中运用格拉斯哥不同社区的口音搭配与句法构造,营造专属于格拉斯哥特殊阶层的滑稽性方言,将方言的有机地渗透到叙事层面。故事中,阿格尼斯为了生计打算去当铺卖掉那件气场十足的紫色貂皮大衣,因避雨躲进一间出租车行,意图借用"最标准的米尔盖口音"掩盖当下狼狈形状,却不想被车行伙计当场戳穿。他倒是给阿格尼斯一句忠告,也促成她决心戒酒的关键,"过好自己的日子,你他妈就得给她看看……那个傻逼见不得你好,你偏偏就好,气死他"(斯图亚特 155)。格拉斯哥方言以人物对话形式频繁出现,不单表现出浓厚的方言在底层民众意识中积聚的认同感,更是突显了语言在纾解底层残酷生活状况的能动性。方言对白的氛围突出了格拉斯哥地方性色彩,也在更深层次上映射出地方民众对底层残酷生活的独特认知。方言的能动性本身是一种地方文化力量,必然体现着由苏格兰文化观念和价值所塑造的行为之中,彰显出斯图亚特对格拉斯哥小说现实主义美学立场的坚守。

其次,身体表演也成为斯图亚特制造幽默叙事的重要手法,意在表达一种明确的意图:重审当代苏格兰民族性,尤其注重运用模棱两可的喜剧形式描绘小人物在残酷日常生活中的无力感,"将'苏格兰性'视为每个苏格兰人的处境,这从根本上定义了苏格兰人"(Schoene 15)。可以说,个人在日常生活中的残酷感知就是当代苏格兰性最典型的特征。故事中,阿格尼斯为改变这一残酷生存状态,完成了人生中的两次逃离:一次从天主教婚姻中逃离,转嫁舒格生下小男孩舒吉;另一次从父母家中离开,被舒格丢弃在危险的废旧矿区生活。每一次离开带来的情感创伤,阿格尼斯都借助酗酒来抚慰自我,她的主体意识从未被真正表达,也从未得到善意的倾听。她的无力感和身不由己的选择是格拉斯哥底层女性共通的创伤。然而,斯图亚特在沿袭再现传统格拉斯哥小说底层女性形象的同时,又赋予了阿格尼斯命运多舛之外的喜剧形象。

具体而言,斯图亚特挪用卓别林式"闹剧"(slapstick)的形式,塑造了一个多重面向的格拉斯哥底层女性形象,展现其脆弱和顺从之下强烈的主体意识,并通过形象反差来展示母性之美,引导读者在笑声中思索残酷和痛苦的根源。身体表演成为彰显主体意识的有效手法。喜剧因素在人物阿格尼丝身上主要体现在夺子大战。在这起事件里，人性的真相成为一个被不断重新定义的对象，它被残酷和温柔交替改写，也逼迫读者进入身体表演的世界中，打破了对"言说"的依赖。身体表演给悲惨的阿格尼丝渲染上了滑稽的色彩。在夺子大战中，阿格尼丝听闻小儿子舒吉被送到了前夫情妇琼妮那里，她不顾自己刚从死神手上挣脱出来，颤颤巍巍地抱起垃圾桶，本想砸开琼妮家大门，却不偏不倚地飞入客厅窗户砸烂了大电视。虽然此时在全知叙述者视角下，琼妮家屋内弥漫着浓厚的复仇情绪，但舒吉不紧不慢地翻过客厅窗户扑向阿格尼丝的怀中。在这一滑稽性场景，人物阿格尼丝完成了倔强母亲形象的建构，也在不经意间完成了用具有强悍、自省和反抗意识的"酗酒"女性意识来挑战"社会对女性社会角色的限定和对女性叙述传统的压制"（何宁 25），反拨 1980 年代以来格拉斯哥城市叙事中女性"有意识的现实分离感"（Bell 24）。因此，在作家道格拉斯这里，以底层母亲形象的名义，残酷的格拉斯哥故事被重新讲述，但这一地方文化的重新复兴却仍然在延宕。在这个意义上，我们理解作家的自传性书写，大概是注重服务于一种对残酷生活经验产生共情的叙事模式，意在表现"作为生活经验的苏格兰性必须始终先于并战胜作为不变、限定的苏格兰性，即使存在和本质将永远密不可分"（Schoene 15）。

结　语

"残酷"在《舒吉·贝恩》的格拉斯哥城市叙事中构成了一种方法论意义上的关键词。首先，作为小说叙事外层的"残酷"故事，斯图亚特以底层人物阿格尼斯的悲剧命运转喻去工业化记忆的残酷性，让我们看到了在自传与虚构、地方与民族性意义等多重关系中定位这位苏格兰文坛新秀的小说创作实践。其次，作为小说叙事形式的"残酷"视角，引导读者关注自传小说中虚构与真实之间的交融关系，审慎阅读残恶叙事的道德合法性。而作为小说叙事民族性隐喻的"残酷",则是召唤读者参与建构当代苏格兰性的活动中,表明个人日常生活中的残酷感知就是当代苏格兰性最典型的特征,体现了作家在苏格兰性问题上现实主义诗学立场。这其实构成了由表及里、由残酷到感动的文学阅读功能。在此过程中,"残酷"作为一种文学方法,体现了作家对格拉斯哥叙事策略的认知转变,也显示出自传文类所具有"时代精神的表征"(杨正润 61)。

引用文献【Works Cited】

费伊·邦德·艾伯蒂:《孤独传:一种现代情感的历史》,张畅译,译林出版社,2021年。

[Alberti, Fay Bound. *A Biography of Loneliness: The History of an Emotion*. Translated by Zhang Chang, Yilin Press, 2021.]

安托南·阿尔托:《残酷戏剧——戏剧及其重影》,桂裕芳译,商务印书馆,2015年。

[Artaud, Antonin. *Le Théâtre et son Double*. Translated by Gui Yufang, The Commercial Press, 2015.]

Bell, Eleanor. *Questioning Scotland: Literature, Nationalism, Postmodernism*. Palgrave Macmillan, 2004.

Busby, Magaret. "*Shuggie Bain* wins 2020 Booker Prize." 19 Nov. 2020, 21 Dec. 2020, www. thebookerprizes. com/booker-prize/news/shuggie-bain-wins-2020-booker-prize.

Carruthers, David. *Understanding Scotland*. Routledge, 1992.

Craig, Cairns. "Kelman's Glasgow Sentence." *The Edinburgh Companion to James Kelman*, edited by Scott Hames, Edinburgh UP, 2010, pp. 75-85.

何宁:《论丽兹·洛克海德诗歌中的女性声音》,《外国文学》第4期,2022年7月,第21-28页。

[He, Ning. "Women's Voices in Liz Lochhead's Poetry." *Journal of Foreign Literature*, no. 4, Jul. 2022, pp: 21-28.]

Iser, Wolfgang. *The Act of Reading: A Theory of Aesthetic Response*. Johns Hopkins UP, 1978.

Jordan, Justin. "Douglas Stuart's Booker win heralds arrival of a fully formed voice." *The Guardian*, 20 Dec. 2020, 21 Dec. 2020, www. theguardian. com/books/2020/nov/19/douglas-stuart-booker-voice-shuggie-bain.

Kolbas, E. Dean. *Critical Theory and the Literary Canon*. Westview Press, 2001.

吕洪灵:《当代苏格兰小说研究》,人民出版社,2019 年。

[Lv, Hongling. *Studies on Contemporary Scottish Novels*. Renmin Press, 2019.]

McGlynn, Mary. "*How late it was, how late* and Literary Value." *The Edinburgh Companion to James Kelman*, edited by Scott Hames, Edinburgh UP, 2010, pp. 20–30.

Richardson, Brian. *Unnatural Voices: Extreme Narration in Modern and Contemporary Fiction*. Ohio State UP, 2006.

Schoene, Berthold. "Going Cosmopolitan: Reconstituting 'Scottishness' in Post-devolution Criticism." *The Edinburgh Companion to Contemporary Scottish Literature*, edited by Berthold Schoene, Edinburgh UP, 2007, pp. 7–16.

Simpson, Craig. "Booker Prize: Douglas Stuart becomes only the second Scot to win prestigious book award with *Shuggie Bain*." *The Telegraph*, 19 Nov. 2020, 21 Dec. 2020, www.telegraph.co.uk/news/2020/11/19/booker-prize-douglas-stuart-becomes-second-scot-win-prestigious/.

道格拉斯·斯图尔特:《舒吉·贝恩》,席小丹、钟宜吟译,译林出版社,2022 年。

[Stuart, Douglas. *Shuggie Bain*. Translated by Xi Xiaodan and Zhong Yiyin, Yilin Press, 2022.]

Wolfreys, Julian. *The Poetics of Space and Place in Scottish Literature*. Macmillan Press, 2019.

杨正润:《现代传记学》,南京大学出版社,2009 年。

[Yang, Zhengrun. *Studies on Modern Biography*. Nanjing UP, 2009.]

卡斯克小说《转折》中的真实与共识

刘 莉

内容摘要：当代英国小说在回望与实验中不断反思现实主义书写的价值。《转折》是作家蕾切尔·卡斯克探索叙述与现实关系的三部曲之一。本文将小说置于当代英国"后真相"的语境中加以解读，考察作家如何将目光投向公共生活，揭示真实与共识的关系。小说以独特的文学策略审视了共识瓦解的社会空间和心理空间，揭示出真相的流转过程。小说摒弃追问共识的伤感主义倾向，以"去情节化"演绎新的共识路向，彰显个体叙事的不可化约性，还表达了文学叙述的认识与疗愈价值。小说借助美学形式的探索呈现出对英国社会共识问题的新思考，体现了当代现实主义书写的潜能。

关键词：蕾切尔·卡斯克 《转折》真实 共识 现实主义

作者简介：刘莉，山东师范大学外国语学院讲师，主要研究方向为英国文学、文化研究。

Title: Truth and Consensus in Rachel Cusk's *Transit*

Abstract: The use of realism is the critical concerns of twenty-first century British novel writing, in its retrospection and experimentation. *Transit*, one of Rachel Cusk's Trilogy, explores the entanglements between narration and truth. By interpreting the novel within the context of "post-truth" in contemporary Britain, it can be found that the author raises questions about truth and consensus in public life. Through innovative narrative modes, the novel reworks the social and psychological spaces with disintegrated consensus and reveals the path of dynamic truth. Turning away from the sentimentalism in pursuing consensus, the novel dramatize an alternative approach by rejecting "emplotment". It celebrates the irreducibility of individual narrative, as well as the heuristic and therapeutic value of literary narrative. This novel expands the discussion of consensus in contemporary Britain with aesthetic innovation, demonstrating the vitality of realistic writing.

Key words: Rachel Cusk; *Transit*; truth; consensus; realism

Author: Liu Li is a lecturer at the School of Foreign Languages, Shandong Normal University, China. Her research interests are English literature and cultural studies.

蕾切尔·卡斯克(1967—)以作品对家庭、社会问题的敏锐观察而多次获得英国文学奖项,并两次入围布克奖提名。她的成名作《纲要》(*Outline*, 2014)三部曲毫不掩饰对现实主义创作美学的挑战,受到评论界的热切关注。卡斯克曾大胆表达自己的创作观,提出"对塑造人物不感兴趣","维多利亚时代的小说写作模板中,人物才至关重要",她"试图从侧面(lateral)而不是人物中去看待经验"(Schwartz, "A Conversation" 2018)。现实主义书写的发展在当代英国一直是评论家与作家论辩的焦点。2008年,扎迪·史密斯(Zadie Smith)在《纽约书评》上对"小说的两条道路"的探讨广为评论界所知。她批评"抒情现实主义"(lyrical realism)的作品"一直占据着(小说发展)的高速路,而其他出口都被拦截";她认为虽然自己也曾沿着这一传统进行创作,但这类作品过于堆砌细节,对"形式的超然价值、语言揭示真相的魔力和本质上完整延续的个体"过于自信,对这些美学特征的逐项拆解在她看来才预示着小说的未来(71, 73)。2014年,研究者以"元现代主义"(metamodernism)来命名当代英国小说的探索风格，认为包括扎迪·史密斯、伊恩·麦克尤恩等在内的作家开始直接以现代主义为源泉，以推动当代小说的创新。即这些作品不仅在形式上推崇"间断、非线性、内在性和时序游戏的实验美学"，而且在主题上探讨的也是现代主义那种"社会政治、历史和哲学情境"（James and Seshagiri 89，93）。本文探讨的卡斯克三部曲之一《转折》（Transit，2016）也处于这样一个抉择和交叉的文学创作图景中。作家既热衷从语言层面对小说叙事方法进行尝试，也对"本原"问题抱有兴趣，热衷探讨真相在个体和公共生活中的流转和生成。

《转折》设定叙述者为带着两个孩子的离异女作家，匆忙迁入伦敦某社区，一面亟待装修房屋整饬环境，一面维系日常工作，为混乱的环境确立起秩序。沿着她的生活轨迹，作品总体由主人公每天的会面来快速推进叙事，每一章聚焦于一个独立的场景，装修现场、理发店、咖啡馆、读书见面会、朋友重聚、家庭聚会。在各场景中，主人公或与人对谈、或默默倾听他们的独白。小说保持着三部曲的整体基调，彷佛都是一些"谈话片段，未解决的旋律"（Garner，"With 'Kudos'" 2018）。所有事件看似前后相继，实际并无因果关联。众多人物只会出场一次便谢幕隐去。这一叙事方式被认为很大程度上"撕掉了写作指导手册"（Ali，"On Rachel Cusk's" 2017）。值得关注的是，主人公每次会面都平静而执着地叩问；而人物虽社会地位、生活状况各异，但在交谈中大多都会与"当时究竟是怎样"这一问题相遇。他们措不及防，有时感到很残酷，但都逐渐展开了各自的叙述。小说中场景不断叠加，就像同一声音反复登场，对相似的问题持续追问，使这部形式简单的小说呈现出象征化、寓言化的多重维度。

小说体察到当代个体所处的不确定性窘境，更同时聚焦于社会整体意义上真实感消逝的缘由和回归的途径。《转折》对变化中公共秩序的美学回应构成了一个审视当代英国现实主义创作的入口。将小说置于当代英国"后真相"的语境下，可以更好观察作品如何以美学形式演绎出社会意识的误区和共识生成的新的情境。正如我国学者所说，现实主义的研究需要"在坚持文本与世界各自独立的同时寻找与过去机械反映论不同的现实主义新模式,并挖掘具有动态内涵的模仿观",以观察当代现实主义文学"如何调和外部指涉与自觉建构的难题"(王守仁等 49)。

一、真相的危机

这部小说前后相继的事件都发生在大都市伦敦及其郊区,而人物所处的空间被挤压到趋于扁平,文中从开始就充斥着模糊迟疑的氛围。主人公倾尽所有在伦敦购得一处住房,房子风格古旧破败亟待维修,邻居们也是形形色色。叙事进展了很久,主人公与装修工头商谈完出门,在街上从整体环视,此时才让共享同一视角的读者如释重负:终于获得了一点对整个住宅区立体架构确定的样貌。这种难以捉摸的基调就像街区衰败花园里成片的鸽子,"聚在一起、歇脚等待的样子,确实有些邪恶的意味"(Transit 37)[①],令人感到隐隐的威胁。倪迢雁(Sianne Nagi)以"负面情感"(ugly feelings)来描述一种主体失去方向感的存在状况,即缺乏明确客体,"对自己的感觉感到混沌","能动性被悬置""矛盾不定"(14),小说将这种失真的感受呈现为当代人的普遍日常存在状态:小说家成名后坐上奢华的椅子,感觉身体里好像有新的部分生长出来很陌生;家庭主妇总有昨日重现的感觉,觉得有些事是自己经历过,实际都是自己读过的小说……如果情感可以视为"标示物","将(形式、意识形态、社会历史)不同领域的问题表现出来,还以独特的方式将这些问题结合起来"(Nagi 3),那么这部小说在描绘当代人自我危机的同时,就借助这个模糊而复杂的社区空间呈现了一种共通的困境。主人公要彻底翻修房屋,与住在地下室将近 40 年的老夫妇产生了激烈矛盾。他们是这片社区最后的公租房住户,屋子如"洞穴"一般,生活极度贫困,重病在身,午饭时间家里传出的味道是"花园中的某种动物"

(139)。主人公背负沉重的贷款,只求尽快完成装修把两个孩子从前夫那里接回。矛盾因噪音而起,但远不仅于此。在这部不依赖情节推动的小说中,一些简单勾勒出的冲突打破了自我的界限,传达出小说的社会关注。

主人公曾进到老妇人家中,一眼就看到桌上身材高挑的女子在海边的照片,她认出正是眼前满身污垢佝偻的老妇人,可以说她对楼下邻居的境遇并非无动于衷。可在若干回合的对抗后,小说并未为主人公安排一种由共情而起的内在超越,却使她在这些经验基础上直接确认了对立的正当性,甚至觉得"邪恶不是意志的结果,而是相反,是投降的结果"(196)。小说断断续续讲述了双方的对立,但令人有些费解地逆转了通常公共生活中对弱势群体的道德话语。甚至小说还一定程度肯定主人公的立场,借题发挥铺叙了一场以邪恶、愤怒与宽恕为主题的对谈。从主人公口中可以得知,老妇人不断向其唾骂,甚至向邻居控诉其私生活的"劣迹";从老妇人口中可以得知,主人公夜半时分仍不管不顾楼下安宁、逾越道德边界。就这些事实的视角而言,或许可以说,小说淡化道德话语、以模糊的叙述悬置道德判断,相当于把社区中的中下阶层放到了相似的位置——贫病交加的困境、单亲母亲的养育焦虑,行动者受制于"无法控制的事件","丧失了过一种繁盛的人类生活所必需的某些伦理上的重要的要素"(纳斯鲍姆 3)。更重要的是,小说为这种相似的脆弱性赋予了一层认识论的意味。即不同阶层都陷入了意识的误区,犹如洞穴寓言中的人物,分不清真实与折射,就采取敌对彼此的行动。主人公被刻画为具有相当的反思能力,她看出老妇人在反抗的愤怒中"面目扭曲",真正的根源跟她一样,都是想在反抗噪音和愤怒中"想要证明她依然自由"(159)。但她在自己生活濒临崩溃的情势下,无法客观面对老妇人的困境,拒绝共情让步。这意味着即使条件较好的阶层,日常有机会可以任意出入"洞穴"内外,能涉足城市更广阔的空间,但同样会受困在自己的精神空间之中。

如果按照真理的符合论(correspondence theory),"真"在于与事实相符合、与实在相一致"(Audi 930)。这个场景中的事实显然已经主观化、个体化。事实的地位"取决于人们想相信什么——有些事实比其他更重要(McIntyre 10)。按主人公的表述,对方的阻挠已经具有"非人"的色彩,构成了展开生活的最大障碍(195)。换言之,这个冲突源起于噪声问题,却体现着双方对生存环境的挣扎,是各自对社会境遇感到无奈甚至绝望的声讨。这个日常居住空间的矛盾成为社会中下层生存焦虑的缩影,在小说中进一步转化为公共生活中的认识论问题。

2016年6月英国举行公投,脱欧阵营以52%的结果意外获胜,英国社会长久以来隐藏的诸多矛盾在这个进程中不断发酵,"中产阶级的自由派、进步派和激进派都突然要正视这个粗俗而分裂的国家"(McGarvey 148)。虽然欧洲怀疑论、抵触全球化、移民劳工等是脱欧阵营胜出的重要原因,但公众意见的分裂还有一个不可忽视的源头,那就是英国传统"共识政治"(consensus politics)的破裂导致社会正义失衡。"共识"通常指的是"二战"以后英国各政党在内外政策方面的趋同,它们虽意识形态色彩不同,但在充分就业、福利国家、混合经济、工会政策、外交防务等层面取向基本一致(刘杰 94,99)。而本应更多体现社会中下层利益的工党,在"共识"中已经彻底倒向全球化与新自由主义经济的政策逻辑,"凡有益于经济的举措都被认为有益于英国"(Evans 114)。这种"精英的共识"不可避免将社会正义置于岌岌可危的地位,不同阶层对社会现实的解读日趋"部落化",埋下更多社会隐患。"后真相"(post-truth)这一命名就是揭示客观事实对当代公共意见的影响力衰落,而情感和个人信念的影响更显著(McIntyre 5)。《转折》洞察到个体生活混沌、彷徨的表象之下经济、社会结构的深刻变化,而公共意见的撕裂又往往源于中下阶层在生存和认识的双重脆弱位置上相互伤害。这也正是我国学者所指出的,"后真相"本质其实是"后共识"。当"经济发展失去了必要的互惠和共享性","认知者的认识意愿和真理程序"将必然受到破坏(汪行福 15)。那么这种认识与生存之间的断裂在公共生活中又是如何产生？

二、可疑的"替代物"

在小说开端部分"犹如剧院一般"的理发店里，"镜子反射着各种表面"(74)。理发师言语间充满象征意味，他觉得对衰老等人生真实面貌的恐惧犹如屋里的"庞然大物"，但大家对此往往视而不见。人们都好似孩童，自欺欺人地以不同方式遮掩，实则失去了做出不同选择的能力。无论是生活中以沉溺娱乐逃避独处，还是到理发店遮盖白发，在他看来本质都等于从此被单一的选择所束缚，恰恰是与追求真正自主生活目标背道而驰。这些观点呈现出一种萨特意义上的存在论意味，即将欲望视为自为的自我否定与自我超越，与此同时，欲望也成为"存在之缺失的体现和证据"(卢毅 121)。从这个视角会更容易理解，当初主人公看清老妇人的阻挠时，为何会把一个日常矛盾界定为"一种与创造力相关、具有原始否定性的力量"(195)。因为当中蕴含了彼此都要弥补的生存缺失，都在以否定性的欲望形式伸张新的生存可能。存在的缺失是欲望的基础，但小说指出，这种追求也会走向另一极端，杰勒德感情受挫后竟砸掉屋里所有的墙壁，仿佛借助一览无余的空间才能理清思绪；少年时的伯姬德在厨房安置录音机，悄悄录下几百个小时父母的谈话，只为从中解读他们的情感是否真的平静如水。正如大卫·希尔兹(David. Shields)在《渴望现实》(*Reality Hunger: A Manifesto*)中提到，不知道寻找什么，"于是就抓住任何看上去实在、有机一体和真实的内容"(90)。这种癫狂的状态犹如拉康所分析的欲望的"换喻过程"，"总是指向或被推给下一个能指，总是'对他物的欲望'"(卢毅 123)。不过小说并不认为这种"倒置"是无意识所为，而是人们常带有想要确定下来的盲目感(blindness of fixation)(6)，想找到救生筏

(132)。于是在恐惧支配下受制于某种人与物、人与人关系的确定性,以为这就替代了真实缺失。

但小说更关注的是,在既定的现实中,能否辨别出一个事件究竟是自由意志的选择,还是被动依赖滑动的能指的后果?小说认为这并不容易。就像主人公准备购置房屋时陷入绝望,她的归因是手头极度拮据,因而后续不得不选择恶劣的住房地段,自己的选择带有无法逃避的色彩。小说指出,"早有定论"这类想法虽古怪却很有诱惑力。但可怕的问题在于,如果始终被动地去作为他人行为的"回响"(reverberation)而存在,以此当作真实,那在公共生活中就有可能掩盖一些人的"破坏力"(198),导致那些本应负有道德责任的人脱逃,他们会被视为无辜的"生活中的角色";甚至在一些冲突当中,错置的命定论会使一些"代理人"有机可乘,危及对公共秩序的认识。

小说开头曾收到星座家的电子邮件,寄希望于星图恢复一种宇宙意义上对生活的全景把控。就在邮件预示将会导向"转折"的那天,主人公遭遇了被"代理"讨还公道这一事件。装修工托尼为继续展开拆除工作,自告奋勇到楼下与老妇人交涉噪音问题。令人意外的是,他竟胜利而归,"现在他们对我像儿子一般"(186)。开始他执意不愿告诉主人公,到底怎样平息了老妇人的怨气。后来在追问下才说出,他告诉老妇人,主人公对待他们跟"奴隶主"一样,他们也是"受害者"。尽管托尼辩解,这不过是个说辞把戏,但他躲闪的表情刺痛了主人公,因为这半真半假中不乏真意,原本以为存在的友善和信任都是表象而已。更无法挽回的是,托尼强调自己与主人公雇佣关系中的对立,这样就与老妇人站在同样"受剥削"的位置,赢得后者的共鸣。他既代理着双方的欲望,又代理着双方的正义,缓解了眼前的局面,达成了暂时的共识。但激起仇恨之后,主人公"得跟孩子们在这里继续生活"(186)。托尼的抱怨强化了老妇人心中原来的"真实"认识,是激化而不是消解了她对主人公的憎恨,加剧了主人公的道德危机。小说中,主人公与前男友多年后重逢，指出城市中当人们相遇"还不确定彼此的立场时，那先停留在中立的位置，由公共的地标来导引"(18)。如果代理了公共情感的地标已经位置扭曲，后果会怎样？

英国脱欧公投的结果与此前多数专业调研的预测相差悬殊，公众投票支持的对象最终都是那些貌似言之凿凿的政客。麦克尤恩(Ian McEwan)在小说中《蟑螂》(Cockroach, 2019)曾嘲弄英国脱欧进程中各个利益群体都受到利用操纵：年迈的老人把脱欧派的反转主义(reversalism)理解为让时光倒流，怀旧情愫被调动；社会底层和老人又都受到民族主义狂热情绪的鼓动。脱欧派媒体自我美化为奉行爱国主义，承诺会带来"民族复兴和净化"(29)。卡斯克虽未这样铺叙过脱欧事件，但也曾描写支持脱欧的公众"有点像火鸡们在给圣诞节投票"(Cusk, Kudos, 165)，暗示他们做出的选择趋于盲目，被现实的"中介"操纵认知时等于束手就擒。小说中主人公被"代理"协商的过程与脱欧公投的相似之处在于都显示出一种强烈的现实悖论：人们恐惧真实的缺席才会找寻"替代物"，反而与现实更加疏离；尤其在公共生活中，认识的"中介"许诺了具有诱惑力的前景，结果对人们的认知和判断能力提出了更高的要求。《转折》呈现了真相在公共生活中隐匿的机制，也暗示了后真相时代公众处于幻想、惶惑状态的社会心理。然而无论是个体还是整个社会，小说并不认为找寻替代物是可以无休止延异下去的过程。理发店的旋转门被小说视为人们逃避面对真相的另一个隐喻，转来转去"总停留在门中并不现实"(76)。独身的阿曼达与设计师产生了亲近感确立了关系，最终感情破裂，发现不过是想弥补幼年一直居无定所缺憾；劳伦斯严苛地控制自己和孩子的饮食，美其名曰走出舒适区、建立欲望的边界，实际却是再婚后对重组家庭的秩序感到应对无力。小说不停揭露人们在社会生活中对"替代"判断失误，也是在不断强调某种本原性的"缺席"。由此，小说在叙述层面的实验或许可以视为作家尝试提出的美学解决方案。

三、被动与超越

艺术的特性是'使我们看到','使我们觉察到','使我们感觉到'某种暗指现实的东西"(阿尔都塞 665)。对于卡斯克三部曲很大程度上"去情节化"的手法,有学者认为除了文本意义之外,也对叙事哲学提出了挑战。即过度编织的叙事排斥了偶然和意外的出现,而去情节化则使得叙事和人生都得以向一种被动而具观察力的态度敞开(Warren 173,176)。诚然,卡斯克曾坦言并不想创造那种具有明显自我形象,"会引发读者共鸣、认同"的人物。但要看到她同时强调,作品中叙事者被动的位置是出于个体的自主选择,是想在选择了任由生活摆布之后去发现究竟会怎样(Schwartz)。这里更侧重的显然还是人的主体作用,而非现代主义作品那种濒临绝境后的疏离或解体。《转折》用一帧帧场景拼装起叙述结构,将不同事件叠加,对真相反复追问,呈现出的是人们无论何种选择之后依然渴望寻求经验与情感的真实解读。因此本文还是更赞同艾拉·奥非拉(Ella Ophir)的观点,即包括《转折》在内,三部曲都"保持了社会小说那种对人群和人际关系的热衷(devotion)"(355)。以此为前提,才会更清晰看到作家对探索公共生活真相的期许。

小说中的女摄影师准备为某画家写传记,积攒了30万字的资料却迟迟不知如何动笔。她描述当初偶然冲进画廊以后受到强烈的触动,从画作中看到了同病相怜的慰藉和希望。在一对一的写作课上,主人公层层推进向她提出不下十个问题,专门去看画吗?平常拍什么照片?其中一个提问让摄影师无法回答:如果那天早上画廊展出的是其他画家,她现在会不会(对自己的感触)有另外一种说法?或者虽然说法跟现在一样,但"用不同的方式组合相同的元素"(142)?主人公提出这个商榷,是因为之前谈话中已涉及,摄影师实际只想为童年被职业画家的母亲忽略、食不果腹的创伤找到出口。主人公觉得她在"竭力加工一种既熟悉又有些不和谐的感受"(136)。

伊丽莎白·迪兹·艾尔玛斯(Elizabeth Deeds Ermarth)在讨论英国十八、十九世纪现实主义作品时提出,那些小说中的叙事往往在表层与深层之间存在极大的张力,表层呈现出一种具有"共识"意味的提炼、概括,而个体的经历被归入"次要层面",潜在被认为是"不重要的事情"(adiaphora)(47)。在上文的场景中,主人公建议摄影师放弃书写传记,实际是在提示,她是否一直被外在的逻辑所束缚?只为制造某种人生"情节",反而更加忽略了应直面的真实。换言之,卡斯克通过去情节化强调个体叙述应确立自身合理自主的地位,偶然性如果显现的不过是背后的必然性,那么就失去了存在的意义。事实上,小说中的人物无论处于人生境遇的哪个阶段,他们各自的叙述走向都保留了最大程度的开放,作家并未设计让人物改变彼此,更未对他们的经验做强行归纳。可见作家并不赞成将个体叙述纳入必然的时间逻辑,也不赞成以外在的叙事向度对其进行整合。小说终局一章让我们可以更清晰地观察到作家对共识生成形态的理解。

小说发展至倒数第二章,人们日常生活中对真实的各种焦虑已尽数呈现,所有场景可以说完整结束。但终局一章进行了略显突兀的空间转换,浓雾中主人公"驶出了伦敦",来到表兄的乡村大宅,与劳伦斯再婚的一家、三位女客聚在一起聊天,开始梳理各自与现实之间断裂的关系。小说之前呈现的很多事件中,人物都是在主人公引领下开始叙述,逐渐获得了更清晰的认识。如果说这一章与之前的场景有何不同,那就是交流的环境更纷乱、在同一空间中的干扰更多:孩子们的喧闹、争吵、哭泣,对父母的各种要求穿插在聊天中,失控的局面中"仿佛他们在燃烧"(249)。身处这片混乱的空间,随机的阻碍让人应接不暇,探求真实过程更加曲折难料。然而人物们还是一次次重拾起叙事的线索,卸掉面具,旁观自己的生活,摸索无法面对的真实到底是什么。正如主人公开车踏上这趟旅程时的那种心理感受:"这条路缓慢、枯燥似乎没有尽头","好像随时会炸裂";但是"这种恐惧中又夹杂愉悦的期待,彷佛某种障碍将被挪走,某种疆界将被打破,通向释放之路"(211)。在这片混乱里,多数时候隐藏在叙事边缘的主人公也开始讲述个人生活,从"我告诉她""我询问",到"我发觉自己告诉她……"(233)。小说以去情节化拒绝了时间的必然性,也释放出了人的能动作用。众人一起在叙述中不断构造出的"当下"时刻,从具体细微的经验中促成真实生成的情境。这正如卡斯克在谈到作品《纲要》时所说,其作品的"全部基础就是一种'群体讲述'(communal storytelling)","犹如《奥德赛》一般",这种形式"是关于叙述的根本观念,是叙述与疗愈的关系——是伤害发生之后的讲述,逐渐成为一种基本的疗愈方式,也激发出共通的经历"(Schwartz)。

  需要看到,尽管小说人物常在回溯往事中获得洞见,但叙述价值的实现并非通过一味的怀旧感伤,不是强行到历史时间中寻找"过去未完成的现实",以备将来能够实现(Boym 351)。小说曾指出人们往往有一种错觉,以为向前发展就意味着转变。而现实中"时间可能会改变一切,而没有改变需要改变的内容"(109),而"命运就是真相处于自然状态"(256)。小说中,叙述就被视为一系列事件,讲故事的人牵涉程度或多或少,但并未刻意预测未来,或对叙述走向施加影响。这些叙述中蕴含了人们面对生活形形色色的基本价值、认识意愿与表达形式。通过"去情节化"和拒绝将历史时间感伤化,《转折》展现出"后真相"语境下"共识"强烈的社会属性,"公共意见的普遍化表达已经成为真理显现的必要条件","'一'的真理性内涵只有在'多'当中才能获得表达"(夏莹70)。

  "共识"政治是"二战"后英国社会经济发展、政治稳定的重要基础。在脱欧事件暴露出英国内外交困的危机之后,"盎格鲁文化圈"(Anglosphere)等类似话语继续试图在不满的民众中营造和维系"共识"的幻象(Wellings 368)。《转折》对公共生活中共识的生成语境并不抱有天真的想法。作家曾提到,当主人公处于人生困境、彷佛失去了所有社会身份之后,好像也失去了参与对话、参与群体叙述的资格(Schwartz)。这意味着只要固有的社会逻辑还在侵蚀人们认知真实的情境,小说标题所示的"转折"就很难显现。这也是研究者为何指出,虽然《转折》中叙述的力量向所有人物敞开,但真正意义的对谈往往只发生在相似社会地位的成员之间,而那是身处社会底层的老妇人无法进入的"故事讲述空间"(Ophir 360)。

结　语

《转折》剖析了城市生活中人们渴望真实的无奈和困窘,房产经纪人、装修工、生活优裕的职业人士、公租房的老人、未成年的孩子……都被纳入作家的叙述空间,呈现了生存意义上相似的命题。丹尼尔·李曾指出,21世纪的英国小说表现出对于主体真实存在状态的强烈焦虑。他观察到,当代作品往往陷入"表现主义的伦理与后解构主义主体的前景之间悬而未决的张力"(Lea 461)。《转折》对真相的关注亦体现出他所分析的那种"抗争性质(combative)"的文本特征,即"放弃传统叙述现实主义、人物发展",而对"话语实验、形而上的思考和巧思进行一种混合"(Lea 475)。与此同时,这部小说立足于当下英国的社会心理、阶层关系和社会共识的前景,探索可知与未知之间的张力,以实验和开放的叙事彰显出现实主义书写的多元可能。

值得一提的是,小说认为在个体和公共生活中直面真实的紧迫性与"他者"的来临不无关系,这个"他者"或许是人生无可回避的亲密关系,或许是新自由主义经济中流动的移民劳工。个体的自我反思始终是卡斯克重构公共生活的起点。作家大量关注到人们在生活中被"工具化"的感受,人物甚至直接表达自己成了他人生活欲望"红色的雾霭幻化而成的形象,一个转移的客体"(6);"爱的能力被最大化进行了利用"(175)。而对于卡斯克,小说叙事形式和人物走向的开放式选择一定程度体现了她所认可的公共生活中面对"他者"的原则,即避免那种"无所不能、创造世界、主宰命运"的预设((Ophir 355)。在此基础上,才会有群体叙述构造真实生成语境的可能。此外,小说还清晰意识到,文学叙述自身其实也已经无法逃脱与真实愈来愈复杂的关系。作品颇具自反意味地提到,昔日默默无闻的作家在当代文学场域中物质条件提升,实现了阶层跃迁,看到花园里"老猫捕鸟",一时竟不知该认同心爱的猫,还是那处于弱势、逆境逃脱、与自己相似的猎物小鸟。叙事仍要继续,因为写作并非"在一种美学现实中躲避"(7),而且责任感来自"充分意识到两个事物即将碰撞"(105)。现实主义作家的境况就是在遮蔽与去蔽的抉择中不断探索,如吉奥乔·阿甘本(Giorgio Agamben)在讨论"当代人"时所说,"正是通过这种断裂与时代错位,他们(真正的当代人)比其他人更能够感知和把握他们自己的时代";而另一方面"他无可改变地属于这个时代,无法逃离他自己的时代"(40-41)。

注解【Notes】

①本文《转折》引文均出自 Rachel Cusk, *Transit*, Faber & Faber, 2018. 以下引用随文标注页码,不再一一说明。

引用文献【Works Cited】

Agamben, Giorgio. "What is the contemporary?" *What is an Apparatus? and Other Essays*. Translated by David Kishik and Stefan Pedatella, Stanford UP, 2009, pp. 39-54.

Ali, Monica. "On Rachel Cusk's Risky, Revolutionary Novel." *The New York Times*, 23 Jan. 2017, 10 Jan. 2024, https://www.nytimes.com/2017/01/23/books/review/rachel-cusk-transit.html.

路易·阿尔都塞:《一封论艺术的信》,杜章智译,《二十世纪西方文论选》(上),朱立元、李钧主编,高等教育出版社,2002年,第665—668页。
[Althusser, Louis. "A Letter on Arts." Translated by Du Zhangzhi, *Selected*

Readings of Western Literary Theory in the Twentieth Century, vol. 1, edited by Zhu Liyuan and Li Jun, Higher Education Press, 2002, pp. 665 – 668.]

Audi, Robert, editor. *The Cambridge Dictionary of Philosophy*. Cambridge UP, 1999.

Boym, Svetlana. *The Future of Nostalgia*. Basic Books, 2001.

Cusk, Rachel. *Transit*. Faber & Faber, 2018.

Cusk, Rachel, *Kudos*. Faber & Faber, 2019.

Evans, Geoffrey and Anand Menon. *Brexit and British Politics*. Polity Press, 2017.

Ermarth, Elizabeth Deeds. *Realism and Consensus in the English Novel*. Edinburgh UP, 1998.

Garner, Dwight. "With 'Kudos,' Rachel Cusk Completes an Exceptional Trilogy." *New York Times*, 21 May 2018, 10 Jan. 2024, https://www.nytimes.com/2018/05/21/books/review-kudos-rachel-cusk.html.

James, David and Urmila Seshagiri. "Metamodernism: Narratives of Revolution and Continuity." *PMLA*, vol. 129, no. 1, Jan. 2014, pp. 87 – 100.

Lea, Danie. "The Anxieties of Authenticity in Post-2000 British Fiction." *Modern Fiction Studies*, vol. 58, no. 3, Fall 2012, pp. 459 – 76.

刘杰:《战后英国共识政治研究综述》,《世界历史》第 1 期,2000 年 2 月,第 94—101 页。

[Liu Jie. "A Survey of the Researches on Post-war Consensus Politics in Britain." *World History*, vol. 1, Feb. 2010, pp. 94 – 101.]

卢毅:《现代欲望哲学的法国演进拉康——与萨特学说中的欲望、存在与伦理》,《社会科学》第 8 期,2019 年 8 月,第 118—126 页。

[Lu Yi. "The Evolution of Desire in Modern French Philosophy: Desire, Existence and Ethics in Lacan and Satre." *Social Science*, vol. 8, Aug. 2019, pp. 118 – 126.]

McEwan, Ian. *Cockroach*. Jonathan Cape, 2019.

McGarvey, Darren. *Poverty Safari: Understanding the Anger of Britain's Underclass*. Luath Press, 2017.

McIntyre, Lee. *Post-truth*. MIT UP, 2018.

Nagi, Sianne. *Ugly Feelings*. Harvard UP, 2005.

玛莎·纳斯鲍姆:《修订版序言》,《善的脆弱性》,徐向东、陆萌译,译林出版社,2017 年,第 1—44 页。

[Nussbaum, Martha C. "Preface to the Revised Edition." *The Fragility of Goodness*, translated by Xu Xiangdong and Lu Meng, Yilin Press, 2017, pp. 1 – 44.]

Ophir, Ella. "Neomodernism and the Social Novel: Rachel Cusk's *Outline* Trilogy." *Critique: Studies in Contemporary Fiction*, vol. 64, no. 2, 2023, pp. 353 – 364.

Schwartz, Alexandra. "A Conversation with Rachel Cusk." *New Yorker*, 18 Nov. 2018, 10 Jan. 2024, https://www.newyorker.com/culture/the-new-yorker-interview/i-dont-think-character-exists-anymore-a-conversation-with-rachel-cusk.

Shields, David. *Reality Hunger: A Manifesto*. Hamish, 2010.

Smith, Zadie. "Two Directions for the Novel." *Changing My Mind: Occasional Essays*. Penguin Books, 2009, pp. 71 – 96.

王守仁等:《战后世界进程与外国文学进程研究》(一),译林出版社,2019 年。

[Wang Shouren, et al. *The Turbulence of Post-war World and the Development of Foreign Literature*, vol. 1. Yilin Press, 2019.]

汪行福:《"后真相"本质上是后共识》,《探索与争鸣》第 4 期,2017 年 4 月,第 14—16 页。

[Wang Xingfu. "'Post-truth' is in Essence 'Post-Consensus.'" *Exploration and Free Views*, vol. 4, Apr. 2017, pp. 14 – 16.]

Warren, Kathryn Hamilton. "Against Plot." *The Hopkins Review*, vol. 15, no. 4, Fall 2022, pp. 167 – 177.

Wellings, B. "'Our Island Story': England, Europe and the Anglosphere Alternative." *Political Studies Review*, vol. 14, no. 3, Aug. 2016, pp. 368 – 77.

夏莹:《后真相:一种新的真理形态——兼与吴晓明、汪行福等教授商榷》《探索与争鸣》第 6 期,2017 年 6 月,第 66—70 页。

[Xia Ying. "'Post-truth', a New Configuration of Truth: with a view on other relevant researches." *Exploration and Free Views*, vol. 6, June 2017, pp. 66 – 70.]

战争记忆与历史书写
——论石黑一雄日本二战题材小说

刘利平

内容摘要:以记忆书写历史是石黑一雄小说中最为突出的主题之一。在他的小说中,个体经历往往以回忆的形式展开,这些个体记忆一方面极具个人化和私密化色彩,另一方面又融进了很多公共历史化因素。以此,作家将个体经历从私人化领域提升至公共意识层面,通过记忆与历史书写之间的关系来揭示历史的本质。《远山淡影》,《浮世画家》和《上海孤儿》构成了石黑一雄日本战争历史记忆化书写的三个阶段,隐藏在《远山淡影》中的战争记忆,经过了《浮世画家》的自我修正,最终在《上海孤儿》中呈现出历史的真相。而小说家石黑一雄,正是借助这种以记忆书写历史的方式,对人们在战争中所遭受到的创伤,对于日本二战的历史真相不断进行增补,并在文本的留白、压抑和矛盾的缝隙中,呈现出过去史实若隐若现、无由确定的踪迹。

关键词:战争记忆 战争书写 《远山淡影》《浮世画家》《上海孤儿》

作者简介:刘利平,西北师范大学外国语学院副教授,硕士生导师,主要从事文艺学,英美文学研究。

Title: War Memory and History Writing—On Kazuo Ishiguro's Novels about Japanese History of World War II

Abstract: Writing history through memory is one of the most prominent themes in Ishiguro's novels. In his novels, individual experiences are often carried out in the form of memories. On the one hand, these individual memories are highly personalized and private, whereas on the other hand, they are integrated with many public historical factors. In this way, the writer elevates individual experience from the private realm to the level of public consciousness, and reveals the essence of history through the relationship between memory and historical writing. The three stages of Ishiguro's historical writing of Japanese WWII through memories are presented by his three novels: *A Pale View of Hills*, *An Artist of the Floating World*, and *When We Were Orphans*. The war memory hidden in *A Pale View of Hills*, after being self-corrected in *An Artist of the Floating World*, finally presents the historical truth in *When We Were Orphans*. The novelist Kazuo Ishiguro, with the help of writing history by memory, keeps adding the trauma suffered by people in the war and the historical truth of the Second World War in Japan, and presents the vague and uncertain traces of the past history in the blank space of the text, the gaps of the depression and contradiction within the text.

Key words: War memories; historical writing; *A Pale View of Hills*; *An Artist of the Floating World*; *When We Were Orphans*

Author: Liu Liping is an associate professor at College of Foreign Languages and Literature, North West Normal University, China, specializing in literary theory, British and American literature.

一直以来，记忆与历史之间一直存在着一种若即若离、暧昧含混的关系，对过去的记忆当然不能完全等同于历史，尽管它们都关乎于对过去和时间的叙事。记忆与历史之间最大的区别在于记忆可以借助想象在过去和现实之间不停往返，它是可以重复、修改甚至消失的，而历史却具有确切无疑的不可重复性。记忆是一个借助主体不断被创造,被生成的过程,历史却是已然发生的事实,代表着人类自身或是群体不可更改的过去。历史与记忆的相互关联来自于历史叙事性的凸显。新历史主义理论家海登·怀特认为历史其实像一种文学制品,必须经由"叙事"之形式表达,"事实上,叙事一直是并且继续是历史著作中的主导性模式"(White 168)。新历史主义另一位理论家蒙特鲁斯将其称为"历史的文本性"。"历史从历史事实发展至历史话语,从历史的真实性发展至历史的诗性,就是主体对历史原始经验的主观记忆化过程,也可以称为历史的记忆化过程"(Zhao 60)。历史和记忆的关系因而演化为一种共存互生的关系,构成了一种自我建构和自我论证式的封闭式循环结构:"历史的书写提供了个体记忆的可能性,决定了集体记忆的背景,而记忆的传播和接续又固化了历史知识,对世人塑造某种被期待知识体系和价值结构提供强有力的支撑。"(Zhao 6)

以记忆书写历史是石黑一雄小说中最为突出的主题之一。在他的小说中,常常通过主人公的回溯性人生经历来反映整个社会的历史变迁,但是与传统小说不同而且超越了传统小说的是作家所呈现的个体经历以回忆的形式展开。这些个体记忆一方面极具个人化和私密化色彩,另一方面又融进了很多公共历史化因素。以此,作家将个体记忆从私人化领域提升至公共意识层面,通过记忆与历史之间的关系来揭示历史的本质。这种由个人化历史体验延伸出来的所谓历史是以一个人物作为基点,以个体的视角情感立场等因素来划定范畴而记述出来的历史。因此"这里所谓的历史是作者设置的特定人物所目击和参与到的历史,是通过特定人物的个人回忆讲述出来的,特定人物通过这种方式获得对事实的主要拥有权"(Wang 86)。在石黑一雄关于日本"二战"历史的三部小说《远山淡影》,《浮世画家》和《上海孤儿》中,正是借助不同类型的记忆,日本"二战"的历史得以多面相地呈现,共同构成了一种最接近于真相的历史书写。

一、《远山淡影》:创伤记忆与历史反思

从心理学角度来看,创伤记忆是"指对生活中具有严重伤害性事件的记忆"(Yang,412)。这是一种建立在个体的创伤性体验或是经历的记忆,首先会因为记忆主体的不同而具有差异化和多元化的特点。其次创伤记忆一定是一种亲历性记忆,记忆主体在事件发生时一定是在场的,或者在空间上具有场地性,或者在时间上具有即时性以及广义上的时段性,即事件发生的当时及后来的一段时间内,记忆主体是在场的。但是这种在场性并不确保同一事件的不同经历者的记忆是完全相同的,相反,它会因为主体在认知、情感以及价值判断方面的不同反应而呈现迥异的面相。创伤记忆不是记忆主体对所经历的事件的完全还原,它是一种带有强烈主观情绪或情感的记忆,即"当某种情景或事件引起个人强烈或深刻的情绪、情感体验时,对情境、事件的感知和记忆。这类记忆的回忆过程中,只要有关的表象浮现,相应的情绪、情感就会出现"(Yang 412)。因此,创伤记忆带有鲜明的立场和倾向性。对于主体而言,这种创伤体验会一直留存在记忆深处,并不断提醒和暗示过程曾经发生的事情,与此同时,"创伤记忆的主体又会控制这部分记忆来平衡创伤性过去和现实之间的关系,通过压抑、释放、梳理或分析等多种手段来适应创伤体验对于主体日常生活的介入,并最终趋向缓解痛苦甚或治愈创伤的目的"(Zhao 94)。

《远山淡影》选择了长崎作为故事的发生地点,以"原爆"事件亲历者悦子为故事主人公,借助悦子时断时续、过去和现在交叉呈现的叙事,主要聚焦了战时及战后的日本普通民众所遭受到的战争创伤。徐贲在《人以什么理由来记忆》中写道:"经历了历史人性灾难的人们,幸运的和不幸运,都只能拥有对过去的局部的、零碎记忆……如果她不记忆,那不是因为直接记忆者已经死绝,没法再记忆,而是因为他拒绝接

受自己那一份隔代但不断代的记忆分工。放弃了直接见证者的个人记忆，就从根本上断绝了集体记忆的可能。"(11)《远山淡影》中的悦子为了逃避过往记忆，远渡重洋来到陌生的国度。但是战争的阴影如影随形，在女儿自杀之后的寂寞日子里，过往生活的记忆不断闪现，尽管她借用了另一个人的身份来讲述这段过往，但是其中呈现的却是"二战"期间以及战后日本民众的真实生活。如前所述，创伤记忆带有鲜明的个体性色彩，正是这些充满了个人印记、碎片化、零散的个体记忆，从不同方面汇聚成一种新的群体记忆，并在其中投射出最真实的历史面相。带着女儿独居木屋的单身母亲佐知子，在战争中先后失去四个儿子和丈夫的藤原太太，以及那个作为替身出现的悦子，他们的生活都因为这场战争发生了天翻复地的变化。至于在闪回中不断出现的战争期间母亲亲手溺死孩子的景象，则代表性地表现了战争期间日本民众如地狱般的生活现实。

　　对于创伤记忆而言，除了其中所涵盖的事实来源，也就是由事件、事发环境、亲历者所共同构成的已经过去的"历史"，更重要的是创伤记忆是如何讲述和流传，这代表了对"历史"的文化表征和现实化。《远山淡影》中的个体记忆往往蒙着一层虚幻的面纱，时真时假，时远时近。石黑一雄有意识地借助一种看似虚假的叙事策略，通过谎言与真相之间的博弈，旨在以一种完全个体化的视角来讲述并审视这段"历史"。对于每一个个体而言，对创伤的体验和感受都是完全不同的。有人选择沉默，以逃避的方式阻挡创伤对现实生活的侵入，也有人选择讲述，借助复述自己的故事来缓解伤痛，寻求帮助。小说中的悦子选择了第三种方式，以讲述他人的故事来缓解自己的伤痛。在这个看似第三者的故事中，她将自己一分为二，佐知子是那个深陷痛苦往事无法自拔的一半，悦子则是努力想要从过往走出来，开始新生活的另一半。当故事结尾时，悦子与佐知子合二为一，完成了创伤主体借助讲述创伤过往的自我疗愈和解脱。沉淀在个体创伤记忆深处的历史正是通过这样一种方式实现了历史的表征化和现实化。

如果说这种方式仅仅实现的是一种个体化的历史表述,那么在个体记忆中出现的对于战争的反思则成为将个体创伤深化为一个族群、民族和国家群体危机的契机。小说中的悦子以旁观者的身份,回忆了绪方先生和重夫关于"二战"的不同态度以及由此引发的师生冲突。在重夫看来,以绪方为代表的战争鼓吹派误导了年轻人对于日本发动战争的看法。绪方先生对此不能理解,在他看来,日本之所以战败的原因在于没有足够的枪和坦克,但这一点不能抹去日本人在战争期间的辛勤工作,也不能否认他认为的正确价值观。重夫反驳道:"我不怀疑您的真诚和辛勤工作。可是您的精力用在了不对的地方,罪恶的地方。"(Ishiguro, "*A Pale View of Hills*" 189)在两人的谈话中,重夫直言:"您那个时候,老师教给日本的孩子们可怕的东西。他们学到的是最具破坏力的谎言。最糟糕的是,老师教他们不能看,不能问,这就是为什么我们国家会卷入有史以来最可怕灾难的原因。"(189)石黑一雄以战后日本两代人对于战争的不同态度,一方面正面谴责了日本发动"二战"给本国以及其他侵略国带来的灾难,同时也试图将一种个体创伤上升为一种集体危机。正是由于受到军国主义思想的蛊惑,像绪方先生这样的人即使面对战败的事实,仍然无法正视日本发动侵略战争的历史真相。如果个体创伤无法形成一个民族共同的文化创伤,那么那些造成这种创伤的历史错误迟早会重蹈覆辙。

"石黑一雄小说中的主人公总是在寻求慰藉以弥补人生中的缺憾,他们重探了过往的创伤事件,讲述对于他们来说是一种精神宣泄,帮助他们重建过往,理解自己的缺失"(Wong 2)。借助个体创伤记忆的讲述,那些隐身于宏达历史叙事纵深之处的褶皱和阴影得以浮出,但更为重要的是这些个体创伤记忆将会汇聚成一种新的属于一个民族、一个国家的文化创伤。正如美国社会学家杰弗里·C.亚历山大所说:"借由建构文化创伤,各种社会群体、国族社会,有时候甚至是整个文明,不仅在认知上辨认出人类苦难的存在和根源，还会就此担负起一些重大责任。"(2)《远山淡影》中的悦子（佐知子）是无数经历过"二战"的日本民众的缩影，他们在战前和战后天壤之别的生活境遇真实再现了战争带来的巨大创伤，它不仅构成了属于整个民族、国家共有的文化创伤，同时也应肩负起对此进行反思的历史责任和使命。

二、《浮世画家》：集体记忆与历史责任

　　个体记忆这一概念是相对于哈布瓦赫的集体记忆而言的，这一概念的提出将记忆理论从原先的心理学范畴扩展至社会学范畴，"社会框架"是其中最为重要的概念。哈布瓦赫认为，个体只有将自身置于这些框架中，才能进行有效的记忆。所以说个体之所以能够记忆，是因为"无论何时，我生活的群体能提供给我重建记忆的方法"（Halbwachs 68-69），无论个体记忆存在多大的区别，都是集体记忆的一部分。人类学家玛丽·道格拉斯认为："任何机制想要维持良好状况，就必须控制其成员的记忆。"（Appleby 93）对于个体记忆的掌握，一个机制，一个国家，才能使其成员"忘记其不合乎其正义形象的经验，使他们想起能够维系自我欣赏观念的事件"（Appleby 93），而一个群体，才能"利用历史来美化自己，粉饰过去，安定人心，为所作所为正名"（Appleby 93）。在集体记忆的层面上，记忆实际上就是一种"被治理的政治"，政治的道德或记忆的德性，其核心思想就是记忆的伦理或是记忆政治，它的产生与一个国家的传统思想方式或是政治统治方式相关，它的实施效应也与后现代化的社会状态有关。从这个层面来看，记忆的本质不仅牵涉到记忆主体的个人情感，同时也暗含他人（包括个体、群体、社会）对主体的价值判断，甚至涉及到主体与历史的关系。至此，记忆不再是主体的权利问题，也是主体的义务问题。"记忆的伦理责任意味着牢记某些历史事件是人类的责任和义务，遗忘它们，无论是无意遗忘还是刻意遗

忘,都是一种违反伦理的不道德行为,而铭记过去的苦难、灾难、暴行等历史事件本身就是一种值得提倡的美德"(Li & Hu 136-140)。

关于"二战"的集体记忆可以归属为记忆的义务问题范畴,日本大学教授高桥哲哉在他反思中日关系的重要著作《战后责任论》中将其归结为日本的战后责任之一。他认为,责任的本意其实就是一种"应答可能性",是共同生活在社会现实中的人与人之间的呼应关系。日本的战后责任就是一种"应答可能性"。高桥哲哉区分了日本的战争责任和战后责任,他认为"战争责任就是日本侵略亚洲各国,把那里作为自己的殖民地和占领地,违反各种国际法,进行战争犯罪和迫害行为的责任"(Tetsuya 13),而战后责任则是作为战后一代的日本人被追究的应答可能性的责任,是指战后的日本人"从根本上克服、改变曾经使侵略战争和殖民地统治成为可能的这个社会现状"(13)的责任。"战后责任"明确指出那些没有直接参加过战争的日本人同样不得不承担记忆战争的责任。

对于日本而言,明治维新带来了本国经济的蓬勃发展,同时也导致了日本传统文化不断被西方文明价值观所改变的现实。整个社会被一种商业文明所统治,人们都以追求经济利益的最大化作为人生的价值和目标。左翼人物松山将日本的现状归结于商人和政客处于统治地位,而这些人都是自私、腐朽和堕落的。按照松山的逻辑,日本要想有所改变,必须要实行所谓的"光复",恢复天皇陛下一国之主的正当地位。已经具备强大力量的日本民族,有能力和任何西方国家抗衡。因此,"现在我们应该打造一个像英国和法国那样强大而富有的帝国。我们必须利用我们的力量向外扩张。时机已到,日本应该在世界列强中占领它应得的位置。我们必须摆脱那些商人和政客。然后,军队就只会听从天皇陛下的召唤"(Ishiguro, *An Artist of the Floating World*, 218)。这种借助对外扩张来改变日本社会现状的策略,被冠之以"新爱国主义"逐渐占据了整个日本,"二战"的侵略性被刻意抹杀和曲解,国内因为贫富差距而产生的尖锐的阶级矛盾被一种所谓的民族主义所替代。

正是由于受到这种"新爱国主义"的影响,在军国主义者的欺瞒和操控之下,小野和众多希图改变日本附庸于西方大国现状的民众一样,将对外侵略扩张看作日本的出路,成为日本侵略战争的追随者和鼓吹者。他的关于"二战"的记忆也因为受到了这种政治化因素的规约而呈现出被扭曲,被篡改的形态。在关于"二战"期间职业生涯的回忆中,小野一直保持着一种所谓的理性立场,认为自己的所作所为没有任何值得诟病之处,甚至认为自己在为一个伟大的事业而奋斗。正如他自己所言:"如果你的国家卷入战争,你只能尽你的力量去支持,这是无可厚非的。"(67)对于自己在战争中如火如荼的艺术事业,以及自己对身边人的影响,甚至对所在社区的影响,小野充满了某种自我的成就感和荣誉感。小野关于"二战"的记忆正是战后日本部分民众关于"二战"群体记忆的缩影。石黑一雄正是以此为缝隙,洞悉了日本民众如何被军国主义者蛊惑操控,并进而不自知地成为战争拥护者的历史真相。

《浮世画家》在呈现日本民众群体记忆被政治规约化的同时,也不断通过战后的一系列现实真相来展示被操控的记忆如何被打破并进而被修正的过程。战后的小野因为身边发生的一系列事件开始重新认识自己在战争中的言行。因为战争而被耽误的小女儿在战后被毫无征兆地退婚,背后的原因正在于他无意之间发表的维护战争的言论。曾经依附于他的弟子绅太郎为了保住自己的教职,希望他出面证明自己在创作那些军国主义宣传画时曾经与老师之间有过意见分歧。为了小女儿的婚事能够能够顺利进行,他被迫去拜访和自己分道扬镳的弟子黑田。黑田是小野最为出色的弟子,却因为反战思想被小野告发并被当局逮捕入狱。在黑田居所里,小野遭到黑田弟子的冷遇和训斥,并且得知黑田被捕之后被残酷虐待的事实。面对从战场归来的女婿的质问:"勇敢的青年为愚蠢的事业丢掉性命,真正的罪犯却仍然活在我们中间,不敢露出自己的真面目,不敢承担自己的责任。"(Ishiguro, *An Artist of the Floating World* 71)作为其中一员的小野必须承担作出应答可能性的责任,反思日本作为侵略者所应当承担的历史责任。借助野口先生自杀谢罪一事,小野作出了自己应有的回应:"他觉得他应该谢罪,向每一个离世的人谢罪。向那些失去像你这样的小男孩的父母谢罪。他想对所有这些人说声对不起。"(193)这里的他不仅仅是野口,也是小野本人,以及众多和小野一样曾经为日本发动侵略战争摇旗呐喊的人。至此,战后的小野逐步由军国主义的追随者成为战争历史的忏悔者和反思者。

《浮世画家》中的战争历史,一直处于一种群体记忆不断被政治规约化的同时,又试图突破这种约束呈现历史真相的矛盾性张力之中,表现为记忆中所涵盖的对于战争责任的反思往往以间接的方式加以呈现。小野的自我忏悔总是表现为对事情的评论,而且他的反思自始至终都伴随着对自我的某种辩解。玛格丽特·斯坎伦曾精当地评价了小野的这种自我辩解方式:"当直面伤痛的往事,他倾向于将它抽象化、笼统化;而在谈论他人时,他似乎常常是在谈论他自己。"(139)因此,在回忆自己的艺术生涯如何受到松田的影响并进而转向军国主义思想时,小野常常以复数的"我们"代替"我",借用集体的"我们"来掩饰战后深感内疚的"我"。对小野而言,战争成就了他作为艺术家的职业生涯,尽管他本人在目睹了战争给日本巨大的破坏之后,在周围人不断高涨地对战争的批判声中,逐渐意识到这场战争的非正义性,日本因为这场战争所付出的惨痛代价。但是这种悔恨因为羞耻而难以企口,于是他时常要借助对他人事件的描述来表达自己的态度。他借口评论野口自杀,以及为了小女儿的婚事不得不向未来的亲家表达自己的忏悔之意,都采用了这种不得已而为之的策略。他在记忆中不停地想要反证自己对于战争的不自知或是不自觉的被动姿态。在这种被动姿态中,是一个曾经怀有理想主义的艺术家被政治所裹挟,所淹没,所控制的人生历程。在这些被政治挤压而变形的记忆中,在不断被不同群体、他人的价值质询中,以小野为代表的战争拥趸者群体最终还是突破了政治规约化的逾限,承担起了反思历史的责任和使命。正如他在女儿订婚宴上所言:"我承认我做的许多事情对我们的民族极其有害,我承认在那种最后给我们人民带来数不清的痛苦的影响当中,也有我的一份。"(Ishiguro, *An Artist of the Floating World* 156)这里的"我"也是"我们"。

三、《上海孤儿》:他者记忆与历史真相

与《远山淡影》和《浮世画家》以日本视角关注"二战"不同,《上海孤儿》借助了一个从小生活在上海的英国人视角,以外在于日本的他者记忆再现了远东战场的历史真相。记忆书写视角的转化,是石黑一雄作为日裔英籍作家反思日本"二战"历史的一种书写策略,这构成了记忆书写不同视角之间的相互视角化。"相互矛盾、互为相对化的视角,在争夺记忆主导权的敌对关系中互为对手,这就挑战了一种理念,即认为存在着优势统一有约束力的记忆"(Neumann 420)。从某种意义上看,主人公班克斯身上或多或少存在着石黑一雄本人的影子,一个在各种文化中不断追寻自我主体身份的移民者。在小说中,上海是一个独特的记忆之场,这个记忆之场是一个各种文化不断碰撞又不断融合的场域,且处在战争这样一个独特的历史语境之中。因此,在班克斯自我身份的重构过程中,作为主要记忆场域的上海扮演了其中非常重要的角色,而这些记忆又与当时关于战争的历史紧密结合,自我身份的探寻之旅与关于战争的记忆互为指涉,构成了《上海孤儿》中以他者记忆再现历史真相的书写策略。

在自我的建构中,他者是其中不容忽视的参照物。他者和自我的关系往往呈现极为复杂的面相,"他者不是物质实在的人或物,从本质

上讲,他者是指一种他性,即异己性,指与自我不同的、外在于自我的或不属于自我之本性的特质"(Zhao 214),自我的特征需要在这种异己性特征的比照中得到凸显和确定。然而,他者或"他性"是一个复数概念,因此,在具体的实践活动中,所谓"他者的参照"也一定是一种多元参照,而认同也不可能只是一种关系认同。就这点而言,班克斯作为一个生活在上海租界的英国公民,关于他的身份认同就是一组建立在英国文化与租界之内的其他国家文化之间的相互关系的认同。石黑一雄在此有意识地将其聚焦于英国文化与本土的中国文化以及同为殖民者的日本文化之间的对照关系之中。站在班克斯的立场之上,他最初的文化认同来自于对自己英国身份的认同,然而这种认同随着他回到英国之后的种种经历而趋于瓦解。因为特殊的成长经历,班克斯不可避免地受到中国文化以及上海租界内其他文化(主要表现为以秋田为代表的日本文化)的影响。在回到英国之后,他反而成了一个外来者,一个无法融入英国文化的他者。班克斯终其一生都要寻找自己离奇失踪的双亲,正是因为这是他自我身份确认的唯一方式,它必须要建立在一种稳定的文化认同基础之上,这种文化认同首先来自于父母的文化认同。

关于班克斯游移的文化立场,小说还将其折射于他与日本邻居秋田的关系之中。对于班克斯而言,秋田是儿时的伙伴,在他们的童年经历中,日本和英国都是遥远陌生的所在,上海才是记忆中可以称为家乡的所在。多年之后,两人在已经成为战场的上海再次重逢,以日本兵身份出现的秋田在回忆起曾经居住的租界时,仍然将其称为他的"家乡村子",为此,班克斯也做出相应的回应:"我想这也算是我的家乡村子吧。"(Ishiguro, *When We Were Orphans* 294)在这一刻,无论是班克斯还是秋田,都成了英国或日本文化的他者,而本应是他者的中国则变成了自己的家乡。《上海孤儿》的他者与自我之间的关系因而显得混杂,模糊,充满了不确定性。正是这种不确定性造成了班克斯在回忆自己穿越战火纷飞的闸北区去寻找母亲的下落时,其记忆中所展现有关战争的面貌因为摒弃了一种单一的文化立场而呈现出历史的不同面相。

在班克斯关于战场的记忆中,他似乎在英国身份和中国立场之间游移。在穿行于闸北区的过程中,他以旁观者的视角呈现了战场的惨烈景象:到处都是被战火损毁的房子,被困在其中的中国难民,随处可见的死难者,以及濒死的伤者痛苦的哀嚎。到了日占区,地上到处都是人的肠子,按照秋田的说法,这是被刺刀捅死之后的人遗留下来的。在那所被认为有可能囚禁了母亲的房子里,旁观者的班克斯目睹了一番类似于世界末日一般的荒诞景象:"靠近屋后,在墙那边,有具女人的尸体,大概是女孩的母亲,可能爆炸让她飞过去,人就躺在落地之处。她的脸上带着震惊的表情,一只手臂齐肘折断。此时她以断臂指着天空,也许是要指示炮弹飞来的方向。几码外的瓦砾堆里,有位老太太也同样张口睁眼,对着天花板上的大洞。她脸的一侧已经焦黑,不过我没看到血或是其他明显的伤口。最后,就在最靠近我们站立之处的地方——压在倒下的架子底下,我们起先没有看到——有个男孩,只比那个带我们进来的女孩大一点。他的一条腿从臀部炸断,伤口处拖着肠子,长的出奇,有如装饰在风筝后面的长尾巴。"(312)与如此惨烈的景象相对应的是对此感到懵懂无知的小女孩,她的亲人都在轰炸中丧生,她却守在已经奄奄一息的小狗身边,哀求他们的帮助。此时的班克斯不再是一个置身其外的他者,他对小女孩说:"我对你发誓,不管是谁造成了这一切,不管是谁做了这些可怕的事情,他们会得到报应的。你也许不知道我是谁,不好我正好……呃,我正好是你需要的。我保证这些人逃不掉的。"(312)他将自己和小女孩置于同一个立场之上,自我和他者之间的界限被打破,他同样也是这场战争的亲历者和受害者。

从象征意义上看,班克斯的寻母之旅就是他的自我重构之旅,这种自我的重构首先建立在文化认同的基础之上。班克斯在穿越战场的过程中,目睹了战争的残酷,面对日军的暴行,他最初认为自己只是一个置身其外的旁观者，因此他试图以英国人的立场来批判日本的暴行，然而面对日本人对于英国侵略历史的反击，他的英国立场被轻易瓦解。石黑一雄以一个外来者班克斯的视角展现了战争的真相，但是在这一过程中，作为日本人的秋田始终在场，显性视角的班克斯和隐形视角的秋田并行存在于文本之中，所以班克斯记忆中的历史真相实是借助双重视角呈现的。双重视角的相互视角化解构了记忆的叙事盲点，呈现出记忆书写的多重面相。在以他者为参照物确认自我的过程中，班克斯的身份认同是游移不定的，他时而是英国文化的他者，时而是中国文化的他者，这种不确定性决定了他关于战争的记忆可以同时站在不同文化的立场之上，也可以完全抛弃各种文化立场。脱离了文化立场的局限，班克斯或者是借助班克斯，石黑一雄真实再现了远东战场的历史真相。

结　语

在通过记忆书写历史的过程中，石黑一雄往往要借助真实与谎言之间的博弈，以及两者之间的内在纠缠，借助小说叙事层次间的矛盾性导致一种自省式的叙事流。"在真实和谎言之间，他创造了一种语境，使叙述者们在欺骗自己的同时为自己辩护。这种通过打破时间的直线性和主题的逻辑性的叙述语言，最接近于那种无人能够精确表述的悲伤的本质"（Mei201）。无论是经历了战争创伤的日本平民，被军国主义思想所蛊惑对战争不自知的参与者，还是真正在战场上目睹战争真相的亲历者，日本发动侵略战争的历史不可磨灭，他们所应承担的历史责任也不会随着战争的远去而被历史遗忘。而小说家石黑一雄，正是借助这种以记忆书写历史的方式，对人们在战争中所遭受到的创伤，对于日本"二战"的历史真相不断进行增补，并在文本的留白、压抑和矛盾的缝隙中，呈现出过去史实若隐若现、无由确定的踪迹。

引用文献【Works Cited】

Alexander, Jeffery C. "Toward a Theory of Cultural Trauma". In Jeffery C. Alexander et. al., *Cultural Trauma and Collective Identity*. Berkeley, CA: U of California P, 2004.

Appleby, Joyce & Lynn Avery Hunt & Margaret Jacob. *Telling the Truth About History*. Trans. Liu Beicheng, Xue Xuan. Shanghai: Shanghai Renmin Press, 2011.

［乔伊斯.阿普尔比、林恩.亨特等:《历史的真相》,刘北成,薛绚译,上海:上海人民出版社,2011年。］

Halbwachs, Maurice. *On Collective Memory*. Trans. Bi Ran, Guo Jinhua. Shanghai: Shanghai Renmin Press, 2002.

［莫里斯.哈布瓦赫:《论集体记忆》,毕然,郭金华译,上海:上海人民出版社,2002年。］

Ishiguro, Kazuo. *A Pale View of Hills*. Trans. Zhang Xiaoyi. Shanghai: Shanghai Translation Publishing House, 2011.

［石黑一雄:《远山淡影》,张晓意译,上海:上海译文出版社,2011年。］

Ishiguro, Kazuo. *An Artist of the Floating World*. Trans. Ma Ainong. Shanghai: Shanghai Translation Publishing House, 2011.

［石黑一雄:《浮世画家》,马爱农译,上海:上海译文出版社,2011年。］

Ishiguro, Kazuo. *When We Were Orphans*. Trans. Lin Weizheng. Shanghai: Shanghai Translation Publishing House, 2018.

［石黑一雄:《上海孤儿》,林为正译,上海:上海译文出版社,2018年。］

Li Jingxuan, Hu Qiang. "The Ethical Concern of Historical Memory in Julian Barne's 101/2 *World History*". Journal of Xiangtan University (Social Science Edition), 2019, 43(2)。

［李婧璇,胡强:朱利安·巴恩斯《101/2章世界史》中历史记忆的伦理关怀［J］.湘潭大学学报(哲学社会科学版),2019,43(2)。］

Mei Li. "On Ishiguro's Writing of Historical Trauma". Journal of Central South University(Social Science Edition), 2016 (22 - 1).

［梅丽:论石黑一雄的历史创伤书写,《中南大学学报》(社会科学版),2016年,第22卷第1期。］

Neumann, Birgit. "The Literary Representation of Memory". From *A Companion to Cultural Memory Studies*. Astrid Erll, Ansgar Nunning eds. Trans. Li Gongzhong, Lixia. Nanjing: Nanjing UP, 2021.

［柏吉特.纽曼:《记忆的文学再现》,引自《文化记忆研究指南》,阿斯特莉特·埃尔,安斯加尔·纽宁编,李恭忠,李霞译,南京:南京大学出版社,2021年。］

Wang Ye. "Historical Subjectivity and Ideological Implications: Kazuo Ishiguro's

Resistance to Historical Authority". Journal of Shanxi Normal University (Social Science Edition), 2013(3).

[王烨:历史的主观性和意识形态蕴涵:石黑一雄对历史威权的反抗,《山西师大学报(社会科学版)》,2013年第3期。]

White, Hayden. *Literary Theory and History Writing in Figural Realism: Studies in Mimesis Effect*. Baltimore: The John Hopkins U P, 1999.

Wong, Cynthia F. *Kazuo Ishiguro*. Plymouth, England: Northcote House, with British Council, 2000.

Scanlan, Margaret. "Mistaken Identity: First-Person Narration in Kazuo Ishiguro". Journal of Narrative and Life History, 1993(3).

Takahashi Tetsuya. *On Postwar Responsibility*. Trans. Xu Man. Beijing: Social Science Academic Press, 2008.

[高桥哲哉:《战后责任论》,徐曼译,北京:社会科学文献出版社,2008年。]

Xu Ben. *For What Do Human Beings Remember*. Changchun: Jilin Publishing Group Co. Ltd, 2018.

[徐贲:《人以什么理由来记忆》,长春:吉林出版集团有限公司,2008年。]

Yang Zhiliang, eds. *Psychology of Memory* (3rd Edition). Shanghai: East China Normal UP, 2012.

[杨治良等编著:《记忆心理学》(第三版),上海:华东师范大学出版社,2012年。]

Zhao Jingrong. *Culture Memory and Identity*. Beijing: Sdx Joint Publishing Company, 2015.

[赵静蓉:《文化记忆与身份认同》,北京:生活·读书·新知三联书店,2015年。]

数字人文视阈下德国移民家庭小说《我从哪里来》中的情感研究

胡成静　庄　玮

内容摘要：2019年德国图书奖获奖小说《我从哪里来》被广泛视为德国新现实主义时期关于移民题材的代表性作品，展现了移民家庭复杂且多维的情感世界。本研究基于BERT模型，结合数字人文中的远读和细读对小说进行了分句情感极性识别，科学绘制出文学作品中的情感纹理和日常情感空间。通过探讨1990年代波黑战争难民在德国面临的移民政策、社会情感挑战和个人情感适应与身份认同问题，本文突显了复杂情感体验对移民叙事核心的构成作用，提供了洞察移民家庭在新国家生活的关键视角，以此观察文学与情感的交融和跨学科范式的进一步应用。小说通过勾勒特定地点、教育、工作、语言、生存困境等日常生活细节，揭示了移民家庭情感的链式反应和身份认同的塑造过程。这种方法使得原本难以捉摸的情感被重构和重新感知，形成了一个连贯而生动的情感世界。

关键词：《我从哪里来》　情感分析　移民家庭　身份认同

作者简介：胡成静，浙江大学外国语学院博士研究生，主要从事当代德语文学和文化研究；庄玮，浙江大学外国语学院"百人计划"研究员，主要从事德语文学和文化学相关研究。

Title: Emotional Studies of the German Immigrant Family Novel *Where You Come From* from the Perspective of Digital Humanities

Abstract: The 2019 German Book Prize-winning Novel *Where You Come From* is widely recognized as a representative work of

German New Realism on the theme of immigration, showing the complex and multidimensional emotional world of immigrant family. This study employs the BERT model, combined with distant and close reading from digital humanities, to perform sentence-level sentiment polarity identification in the novel, scientifically mapping the emotional texture and daily emotional spaces within the literary work. By examining the immigration policies, social emotional challenges, and personal emotional adaptations and identity issues faced by Bosnian War refugees in Germany during the 1990s, this paper highlights the crucial role of complex emotional experiences in the core narrative of immigration, providing key insights into the lives of immigrant family in new countries and observing the fusion of literature and emotion and the further application of interdisciplinary paradigms. Through delineating everyday life details such as specific locations, education, work, language, and survival struggles, the novel reveals the chain reactions of emotions in immigrant family and the process of identity formation. This approach allows for the reconstruction and re-perception of emotions that were once elusive, forming a coherent and vivid emotional world.

Key words: *Where You Come From*; Sentiment Analysis; Immigrant Family; Identity

Author: Hu Chengjing is a PhD candidate at School of International Studies, Zhejiang University, China. Her research interests are German contemporary literature and culture. Zhuang Wei is an associate professor at School of International Studies. Zhejiang University, China. His research interests are German Literature and culture.

家庭小说在 21 世纪的德国文学中受到广泛关注,尤其是关于移民家庭和少数族裔的作品。自2005年以来，德国图书奖及莱比锡图书奖均多次授予描绘从传统向多元和包容性家庭转变的小说。萨沙·斯坦尼西奇（Saša Stanišić，1978— ）的《我从哪里来》（*Herkunft*，2019）作为此类文学的代表，荣获2019年德国图书奖。评委会称赞"萨沙是一位出色的叙述者，以至于他不信任叙述。这部小说的每个句子背后都隐藏着不可获得的'出身'（Herkunft），并推动着叙事……作者以其广阔的想象力为读者构建了一个超越时间线、超脱于现实主义及形式桎梏的世界"（Jury des Deutschen Buchpreis,"Begründung"）。

《我从哪里来》通过碎片化和非线性叙事方式，探索了主人公斯坦尼西奇在多重时空背景中的情感历程。通过串联不同地域和历史时刻的人物经历，小说勾勒出从1978年斯坦尼西奇在波斯尼亚小镇维舍格勒出生，到2018年祖母被诊断出阿尔茨海默症的情感脉络，背景跨越前南斯拉夫至德国等多国。小说视角不断进行转变，细致描绘出移民家庭的生活群像，反映了从逃离波斯尼亚战争到适应新国家的复杂情感历程。作为移民家庭第二代的萨沙，以其真实姓名和个人经历为叙述基础，体现了勒热纳所定义的"自我虚构"——作者、叙述者和人物的同一性，通过这种同一性，作者与读者之间达成了自传契约（勒热纳 20）。萨沙以祖母患阿尔茨海默症为写作动机，将自己完全融入角色"我"中，"重新构建了一段真实历史或故事，呈现出了碎片化的记忆和人生经历"（车琳 104），不断探索自己的"出身"。这部小说为读者提供了跨文化视角，展示了一个移民作者如何看待自己在两个文化之间的位置，对移民经历、文化身份和历史记忆进行了深入探讨，具有重要的学术和文学价值。

《我从哪里来》自2019年出版以来受到学界广泛关注，学者们围绕叙事技巧、记忆书写和身份认同的塑造等多角度进行研究。例如克吕佩尔（Joscha Klueppel）以《我从哪里来》和瓦拉塔拉贾（Varatharajah）的处女作《在符号增多前》（*Vor der Zunahme der Zeichen*，2016），探讨了羞愧和负罪感两种情感在家庭和社会边界中的形成原因，并认为这两种情感构成了个体在社会道德秩序中的"社会生活语法"(grammar of social living)(7)。他认为斯坦尼西奇通过文学作品探索自我身份时,未能为自身争取一个精神家园,反而陷入了一场奇幻故事之中(17)。尽管克吕佩尔指出当前研究在将情感与移民结合方面还不够充分(7),但他的分析也只侧重于羞愧和负罪感两种负面情感。在《情感、空间、社会》杂志特刊中,博卡尼(Paolo Boccagni)和巴尔达萨尔(Loretta Baldassar)曾强调,情感分析能够提供"对移民融合更为细腻和多维的理解"(76)。据此,本文旨在探讨《我从哪里来》中非线性叙事框架下情感线索的构建和表现及其所隐含的、尚未充分识别的情感特征。文章还将分析小说情感随叙事发展的动态变化,尤其是在移民经历和跨文化交流背景下,主要人物的情感轨迹如何随故事进展和空间背景的转换而演变,以及其情感表达如何映射出身份认同和文化适应的议题。

一、研究方法

文学情感研究与神经科学在方法论上存在显著差异。神经科学依赖大脑扫描技术观察情感反应,文学研究则通过语言艺术探索情感的社会文化维度。文学的情感表达不单是精确的语言活动,更关注于情感在社会互动中的作用(金雯 44)。梅尔曼(Katja Mellmann)强调,文学能如同自然界的刺激一般激发读者情感,读者将这些情感归因于文本,进而在内心激发相应的情感反应("Bindung")。自"情感转向"和文学情感研究兴起以来,依然存在两个难题:一是忽视对作者和读者真实情感的分析,二是在情感分析时忽略文本本身(Anz, "Gefühlsforschung")。金雯进一步指出,情感研究促进了学术创新与跨学科交流,同时也带来了跨学科研究的挑战(50)。有鉴于此,本文采用数字人文中的情感分析方法,深入探索文学作品中的情感表达。情感分析作为计算技术,可以帮助评估文本中的情感信息,进一步揭示文学作品的情感结构。本文基于 BERT 模型，结合文本分析，量化考察《我从哪里来》中的情感特征，探索其情感分布、变化趋势及其与情节的关联，为理解文学作品中的情感表达及移民文学叙事提供新视角。

BERT(Bidirectional Encoder Representations from Transformers)是2018年由谷歌推出的自然语言处理的预训练技术。它可以利用双向 Transformer 编码器和注意力机制，有效捕捉上下文中的语义关联。其特色在于能够捕捉常见的语义差异(如多义词问题)并根据上下文调整词项的词嵌入，从而获得更精确的语言特征表示(McCormick and Ryan, "BERT")。它通过组合词向量(Token embeddings)、分段向量(Segment embeddings)与位置向量(Positions embeddings)实现对句子深层双向语义信息的提取(McCormick and Ryan, "BERT")。词向量负责捕捉词的语义信息，分段向量用于区分不同的句子，而位置向量则给出词在句中的位置信息。经 BERT 编码器处理后，利用 Encode 特征提取器获得双向语义信息的词向量(McCormick and Ryan, "BERT")。与传统情感分析方法不同，BERT 能够全面考虑上下文信息，有效处理文学作品中的一词多义现象。它能从无标签文本中训练出深层双向表示，在多个自然语言处理(NLP, Natural Language Processing)任务中都已经实现了前沿的性能("Open Sourcing")。

情感极性识别作为研究的关键步骤，旨在判断文本中的主观情感色彩，即正面/积极(positive)、负面/消极(negative)和中性(neutral)三种倾向。研究选取《我从哪里来》德语原版为语料，按句子粒度将语句划分为积极、中性和消极三种情感极性。如表1所示，积极情感包括高兴、满意、希望等，消极情感包括伤心、失望、愤怒等，中性情感则指无明显情感倾向的语句。鉴于目前缺乏针对德语文学文本的情感分析语料库，本研究采用了古尔、舒曼等人开发的预训练德语情感分析模型[①]。如图1所示，该模型基于 BERT 架构，在超过535.5万个样本上接受了训练，覆盖 Twitter、Facebook 及电影、应用的评论等多领域文本，兼容了多种现有数据集以及原创数据集,该数据集也在不断更新,并在多个数据集上取得了高 F1 得分[②],表明其具有良好的性能和处理不同类型数据集时的鲁棒性[③]。为准确捕捉小说非线性叙事中各角色和场景的情感变化,研究将小说文本按照现有标题手动划分为 65 个独立章节,每个样本都被视为一个独立变量,按章节序号编列。通过人工标注与 BERT 模型的协同,对未标注数据进行深度词嵌入和情感极性分类,最终共整理得到 7 414 条有效数据。

Data Set	Positive Samples	Neutral Samples	Negative Samples	Total Samples
Emotions	188	28	1,090	1,306
filmstarts	40,049	0	15,610	55,659
GermEval-2017	1,371	16,309	5,845	23,525
holidaycheck	3,135,449	0	388,744	3,524,193
Leipzig Wikipedia Corpus 2016	0	1,000,000	0	1,000,000
PotTS	3,448	2,487	1,569	7,504
SB10k	1,716	4,628	1,130	7,474
SCARE	538,103	0	197,279	735,382
Sam	3,720,324	1,023,452	611,267	5,355,043

图 1 本研究所采用数据集情况

表 1 数据标注规则及示例

情感极性	积极/正面	高兴、希望、希望、鼓舞、满意等
	消极/负面	害怕、悲伤、生气、失望等
	中性	没有体现清楚的情感倾向,例如好奇、描述、阐释
遴选规则	词类	形容词、动词、连词等
	语境	根据句子所处位置
	标点符号	感叹号、问号等

续 表

标注示例	积极/正面	Die Antwort entlockte ihm ein anerkennedes Nicken. （我的回答博得他赞许地点点头。）(Stanišić 61) Mit dem Umzug nach Heidelberg wurde einiges leichter. （搬到海德堡以后，日子变得稍微轻松了些。） (Stanišić 69)
	消极/负面	Ich empand sie in Deutschland oft ehr als Hindernis. （可我在德国常常觉得它们很碍事。）(Stanišić 61) Mutter darf nicht arbeiten, und ihr habt wenig Geld. （母亲不被允许去工作，而你们又没什么钱。） (Stanišić 132)
	中性	Großmutter hat ein Mädchen auf der Straße gesehen. （奶奶看到大街上站着一个小姑娘。）(Stanišić 5)

　　由于文学文本中情感表达的复杂性，例如"这是一项荣耀，我们感到自豪，我们也感到恐惧"（斯坦尼西奇 270）同时包含了积极情感"自豪"和消极情感"恐惧"。在此情境下，尽管 BERT 模型将此类句子归为消极类别，但文学作品的多维情感表达要求通过人工进行上下文分析，实现对同一句子的复合情感识别。此外，小说的最后一章（第 65 章）通过叙述视角的不断变换及现实与神话的结合，营造了一个冒险色彩的虚构世界，其中祖母几乎化身为神话般的人物。作者构建了一个让读者自行决定故事走向的多重选择空间，提供了不同选择路径，如"你接受了她的好意，喝起水。接着看第 397 页。你直接去喝泉水，趴在菜地上。接着看第 393 页"（335）。他为"我"和祖母提供了在有限的记忆与生命中寻求情感满足的不同可能性。因其独特叙事结构，该章节未纳入情感分析范围。

　　经过对小说前 64 个章节的 6 253 条有效数据进行预测、计算机处理和人工校验，结果显示积极情感语句 332 条，消极情感 665 条。这些情感语句覆盖了小说中跨越的三个关键时空维度：与前南斯拉夫背景相关的情感、波黑战争相关的情感以及移民德国后的情感体验。其中，与前南斯拉夫背景相关的积极与消极情感分别为148条与260条；波黑战争相关情感积极2条，消极79条；移民德国后的情感体验中，积极情感182条，消极326条。本文聚焦移民德国这一关键阶段，揭示移民在新环境中的适应过程、面对文化差异的挑战以及在建立新的身份认同过程中所经历的情感波折。通过综合分句情感极性识别和分析，本研究旨在探讨1990年代战争难民在德国面临的政策、社会互动的情感挑战以及个人情感适应与身份认同。正是这些丰富且复杂的情感体验构成了移民故事的核心，为我们提供了理解移民家庭在新国家生活的关键视角。深入探讨这些情感体验及其在小说中的呈现，有助于深化对移民家庭情感动态的理解，展现文学在传递移民经验和情感层面的独特价值，进而全面把握移民在德国生活的挑战与情感经历。

二、移民德国后的情感体验

1992年，波黑战争在巴尔干半岛爆发，给前南斯拉夫人民带来巨大创伤和不确定性，迫使他们离开家园，从而面临生活的巨大转变。这一历史背景为《我从哪里来》提供了丰富的叙事土壤，尤其反映在移民在德国的复杂情感体验上。在新环境中，叙述者及家庭不仅重建生活，还需适应新文化并处理战争和逃难遗留的心理创伤。小说通过个人、社会和国家三个层面，深入探讨了移民的情感世界，涵盖了身份认同、社会排外、语言障碍、移民政策、社交互动等多个方面，以及具体的地点如海德堡、埃默茨格伦德和奥尔滕瑙大街等，这些元素共同构成了叙述者及其家庭在新环境中的社交互动与情感历程。统计显示，在国家层面，移民政策相关情感语句有34条；社会层面中的社交互动被提及124次、生存困境43次、社会排外41次、特定地点40次、语言障碍39次、工作挑战30次、代际关系25次、文化适应20次；在个人层面，身份认同被提及36次、适应性30次、归属感15次。

2.1 移民政策下的国家视角与情感反响

通过34条关于德国移民政策的情感语句可以深入理解90年代德国针对战争难民和移民的政策环境。这些语句普遍渗透着负面情绪色彩,展现了叙述者对德国移民政策的不满和担忧。通过小说这一叙事媒介,叙述者及其家庭成员、朋友在面对遣返威胁的复杂情境中的困境与挣扎被细腻地展现。小说中有6个章节都提及了父母从逃离原籍国到德国再到不得不离开德国的艰辛旅程。他们在1992年抵达德国,但到了1998年,却因担心被遣返回曾经遭受种族清洗的维舍格勒,被迫再次迁移,小说中4次提到在1992年到1998年间,他们的命运由于德国移民政策的影响而发生了剧烈变化:

> 1998年,他们又不得不离开这个国家。(80)
> 1998年,父母不得不离开这个国度。(245)
> 六个月后,对他们来说,德国这一章彻底画上了句号。(244)
> 那是1998年冬天,一个冰天雪地的日子。几个星期后,父母就不得不离开德国。(274)

这种"不得不(mussten)"在情感上强烈反映了一种被迫离别的悲剧性质,强调了离别的艰难,象征性地表现出他们在德国生活的冰冷终结。最终,父母"为了抢在被遣送回遭到种族清洗的维舍格勒之先,他们移民去了佛罗里达"(80),此后以美国退休人员的身份在克罗地亚定居。这一转变不仅体现了他们在德国生活的结束,更深层地反映了国家层面移民政策对个人命运和情感体验的深刻影响。

这一地理与情感层面的转变对于移民而言预示着生活新篇章的艰

难开启,同时伴随着被遣返阴影下的不断挣扎。正如文中所指出,"摆脱依赖的出路常常是走不通的,或者为时已晚——而遣返却来得太快"(211),反映出移民在面对国家机制与政策时的深切无力感与绝望。叙述者自身的遭遇进一步印证了这一点,在他和母亲抵达慕尼黑机场时,仅仅是因为姨妈以劳工身份作担保,她们才得以在德国境内暂时留下。这一细节揭露了移民面临的不确定性,突显出他们对于稳定生活的迫切渴望。遗憾的是,并非所有移民都有机会获得这样的"幸运"。在遣返阴影下生活成为许多人不得不接受的现实:

> 当母亲和我在慕尼黑机场被扣留,并且要被遣返回去时,他们出具了担保书,表明必要时他们会承担我们的生活费用。然后我们才被允许入境。别的一些人就没有这样幸运的担保了。(82)

此种情形对移民的日常生活和心态产生了深远的影响,"由于面临被遣返的危险,我这里接二连三地出状况,哪里还有心思去观赏阿尔卑斯山山路赛段的冲刺呢?"(185)。叙述者表达出个体在压力下的心理状态,也间接指出了生活在不确定性中的移民如何逐渐失去对生活美好事物的感知与欣赏能力。

此外,通过对情感语句定量分析,我们可以追踪叙述者在德国长达三十年的人生轨迹,从最初获得居留许可到三十年后成为德国公民。该过程见证了个体奋斗和自我实现的历程,映射出德国移民政策的复杂性与多变性,如叙述者所述:

> 我获准继续留在德国。起先,只要我上大学就能待在这里。之后我需要得到一个与我的学业紧密相关的工作。我想成为作家。这就是说,我必须出具证明,文学与作家息息相

关。接下来还需要证明,作家真的是一个职业。最终要证明的是,这个职业可以养活一个成年人。(246)

叙述者最初能够留在德国是因为其学生身份,前提是必须从事与学业相关的工作。然而,作为一名梦想成为作家的人,他必须向移民局证明文学创作是一项合法且可持续的职业。这个过程充满挑战,因为即使他获得作家身份,移民局仍对他的生计来源持怀疑态度。一位移民局官员甚至表示:"自由职业艺术家,尤其是作家和小丑,几乎不可能持续地养家糊口。"(246)尽管遭遇质疑和障碍,叙述者通过签订小说合同和获得稿酬,最终在莱比锡移民局成功获得了以作家身份的居留许可:"在作家这个自由职业以及相关活动结束时自动失效。"(247)但这也伴随着严格的工作限制,仅限于作家职业,"除此之外,我不能够干任何别的工作"(247)。

在经过三十年的居留后,叙述者于2008年获得申请德国国籍的资格。这标志着一个重要的转变,他需要向移民局提交一份亲笔书写的简历(12),这不仅是满足行政程序的必要环节,也象征着他与德国这个国家之间的深度融合。在描述这一过程时,叙述者对德国移民政策的复杂感受是,"这是怎样的煎熬啊!德国人喜欢各种各样的表格"(12)。

叙述者的经历和感受揭示了德国社会中对文化多样性和身份认同的复杂态度,以及移民在适应和融入过程中的艰辛和努力。通过叙述者朋友德多的故事,小说进一步展现了德国移民法的另一面。当德多面临被遣返的风险时,他的朋友们建议他寻求精神科医生的帮助,以识别其精神创伤,为其争取留在德国的可能性:

当我们获悉他面临被遣返的危险时,大家都恳求德多去看医生。每个精神科医生恐怕都会看出他的精神创伤。如此一来,德多可能就不会被遣返了。(192)

这个情节则揭示了移民可能利用的法律漏洞，也反映了战争创伤对难民的持续影响。

因此，通过以叙述者为代表的战争难民的生命旅程，我们得以洞察1990年代移民的集体命运，呈现了他们如候鸟般未定的命运——"有可能命运多舛……不是英勇献身，就是命运悲惨"(259)。

2.2 社会互动背景下的情感挑战

在社会层面，情感语句深刻展示了移民在德国所面临的多样化挑战。通过参与各类社会活动，移民群体展现了伊恩·伯基特（Ian Burkitt）所论述的"隐藏的"自我。伯基特认为，个体的自我塑造过程不是"向内"探察以找到自身，而是在与他人的互动及共同活动中"向外"探索的，"我们寻找自身的地方基本上就是与他人共享的世界，而不是我们通过反思自己的所思所感为自己创造的那个世界"(11)。这一观点与移民在德国的身份重构过程相呼应，虽然他们面临诸多生存挑战和社会排外，但通过社交、教育和工作等活动，以及对新环境中地点的感知，他们不断重塑自我认同。此过程揭示移民自我认同构建的核心论点：这不是孤立的自我中心过程，而是一个动态的、与他人及社会环境紧密相连的过程。

值得注意的是，在《我从哪里来》描绘的移民世界中，社交互动和地点感知普遍呈现出积极色彩。在涉及社交互动的124条情感语句中，有80条展现出积极的情感色彩，占比65%。这一数据凸显了积极社交关系在构建移民幸福感和满足感中的重要性，突出了社交互动在其生活中的核心地位。积极的社交关系为移民提供了支持、认同感和归属感，对于他们在新国家的适应和融入至关重要。在移民的艰难旅程中，这些积极的社交关系成为他们面对生存困境、文化障碍和身份认同挑战的重要支撑。例如，"在德国，第一次有人邀请你去干什么"(155)看似简单的互动实际上标志着移民融入新社会的重要一步。这一互动不仅促成了基于共同回忆和经历的深厚友谊,"我们成了朋友,因为我们共同错过了一些令人向往的东西,这种情况把我们联结在了一起"(186),而且反映了移民在新环境中寻求共鸣和连接的内在需求。

不同的社交经历丰富了叙述者在异国他乡的生活,帮助他在新文化环境中找到了自己的位置,成为其在新国家中找到方向的关键。文中提到了3次对朋友的积极情感,展现了叙述者通过与他人的交流和共同活动探索自我定位的过程,凸显了积极社交关系在其移民生活中的核心价值:

> 我享受阿拉尔团伙的放荡无忌、时而为之的冒险行为和友谊。我也享受拉希姆家按照主题分门别类的书架、宽敞而令人舒适的客厅和彼此让对方说完话的氛围。(206)
> 一天结束时彼此倾听对方的心声,即使有我这个地地道道的外人在场,我觉得这让人感到惬意;我仿佛不在那里,因为这是一场只属于他们两人的对话。(213)
> 在埃默茨格伦德和海德堡,正是和他们在一起,也正是因为有他们,我才没有迷失方向。(249)

特定地点对叙述者情感的影响同样显著。在提及特定地点的40条情感表述中,有26条呈现出积极情感,占比65%,表明德国和海德堡作为新生活的开端,对叙述者及其家庭的过去经历转折扮演了重要角色:

> 搬到海德堡以后,日子变得稍微轻松了些。(82)
> 对我来说,观看这座城堡,永远都会带来巧克力的味道。(145)

对于逃离动乱的移民而言,这些地点代表了安全和新生活的希望,因此海德堡的描绘主要以积极情感为主:

> 雨后的海德堡,一切都变得清澈明亮,如此美丽,只有一些生长橄榄树的城市才可以与之媲美。(146)
> 在奥尔滕瑙大街上,你从来没有遭到过辱骂。在奥尔滕瑙大街上,你从来没有感到过饥肠辘辘。(158)

这些叙述勾勒出一个和谐且宜居的环境,为逃离不安和动荡的移民家庭供了梦寐以求的避风港。即便在面临父母可能被遣返的情况下,海德堡在他们心中依然占据着特别的地位:

> 时至今日,海德堡仍是他们所钟爱的城市之一,因为在他们的想象中,要是他们有可能过上一种正常的生活,海德堡似乎就是他们梦寐以求的地方。(245)

虽然社交活动和特定地点对叙述者及其家人产生了积极影响,但小说同时也揭示了他们在德国所面临的生存困境和工作挑战。这些经历不仅涉及经济上,还包括心理和情感上的考验,突出了移民在经济和社会适应方面的双重挑战。在经济方面,叙述者描述了家庭在物质匮乏中的生存挣扎:

> 人人都等待着好消息,等待着生存条件得以改善,当然肯定不会抱有什么奢望。(81)
> 可是我们没家具,也没钱,毫无选择。(81)
> 沙发是人家扔掉的旧货。恐慌的苍蝇弄得你拳头里痒痒的。(156)

在社会适应的语境下,叙述者对父母在德国生活和社会地位变迁的反思尤为深刻:

> 我明白了他们在30多岁之前一直过着安稳的生活,如今却要与房东讨价还价能不能在花园里栽种西红柿,明白这对他们到底意味着什么。(210)
> 他们俩不得不放弃熟悉和喜欢的职业。(210)
> 父母只能忍气吞声,敢怒不敢言。(210)

父母被迫放弃他们熟悉和热爱的职业而面对新的文化和语言的障碍,这不仅是职业生涯的重大转变,也是对他们个人身份和自尊的挑战。这种工作变化体现了非技术类移民在新国家必须面临的艰难选择和适应过程,即"不得不放弃熟悉和喜欢的职业":"身为政治学家的母亲落脚到一家洗衣厂里。她和滚烫的毛巾打了五年半交道。身为企业经济学家的父亲流落到建筑工地上。"(80)这种"不得不耗费绝大部分时间"来挣薪水的工作被吕西安·塞夫(Lucien Sève)称为"第二类行为"(sector II acts),它们涉及"单调重复、令人厌烦的活动",利用而非发展个体能力,无法促进个人发展或提供满足(伯基特257)。伯基特进一步指出这种工作是"伤及灵魂"的,因为它剥夺了工人的自我实现和成长潜能(258):

> 母亲在洗衣房里热得不知"死"过多少次。作为非德国籍的女人,而且是来自巴尔干的女人,她处在工作阶梯的最底层,人家也会让她感受到这一点。(179)
> 父亲和母亲一天到晚辛勤劳作,让人心痛。1994年,父亲在一家康复医院里干了整整一个月,腰背都累坏了。(210)

这些挑战对第二代移民子女影响深远，塑造了家庭的情感氛围和子女的未来展望。对叙述者来说，母亲作为"马克思主义者，本来算是一位研究剥削的专家，现在却受人剥削"(210)。

父母虽然在个人层面上作出巨大牺牲，他们"不爱惜自己"(210)，但仍然"很照顾我"(210)，努力为子女创造机会，"他们通过鼓励、关爱和一点零花钱为我创造了一个个机会，让我在一定程度上克服移民身份的种种障碍，成了一个正常的青年"(211)。第一代移民在融入新的国家和社会过程中，面临着"社会起点低下，接纳社会也有封闭倾向"(Apitsch 15)的双重困境，但他们仍努力为后代创造良好的生活条件和教育机会。一方面，小说中提及为子女购买新裤子以确保其在学校中得到良好对待的举动，突显了移民家庭对教育的高度重视和对子女融入新环境的深切关怀：

> 这是1992年9月20日。你来德国一个月了。这扇门属于你的学校，今天是你上学的第一天。你穿着新牛仔裤。它是母亲专为你买的，因为她不忍心看到你穿着一条破破烂烂的裤子去德国学校上学。(153)

母亲为"我"购买新裤子的行为，彰显了她希望"我"在新学校中得到良好对待和融入的愿景。这种努力体现了他们对子女未来的乐观追求及对适应新环境的积极态度。另一方面，"海德堡国际小学(IGH)非常国际化，很好地适应了学生的多元化"(176)，"种族歧视在这里零容忍"(176)，进一步为移民青少年的融入和成长提供了安全港湾。因此，对移民青少年来说，"海德堡国际小学是遮风挡雨之地，是学习语言之地，是日常生活之地，是学生食堂的塑料盘子，上面总是放着太软的炸薯条"(177)。

但家庭和学校的积极努力并不能完全消解外界对移民的结构性歧

视和社会排外现象。文中引述了1993年德国新纳粹主义复兴背景下的恐惧和威胁实例。一个土耳其家庭在索林根遭到极端右翼青年的纵火袭击("Brandenanschlag"),"1993年5月29日,在索林根一次极右分子实施的纵火案中,有五个人失去了生命"(165),至"2017年,攻击难民住地的事件在264起到1387起之间(数据由于来源不同而有差异)"(165)。因此,新一代移民"从自己这个幸运的例子看得出,这种对难民的结构性歧视在当时有多么广泛,而如今一如既往"(211)。这些事件反映了移民家庭在德国社会中遭遇的歧视和恐惧是持续且深刻的。对移民家庭而言,这些生存威胁给他们带来了巨大的心理压力,被迫学会在偏见中生存,同时积累起一系列被歧视的经验:

在公共场合,父母用塞尔维亚-克罗地亚语交谈时,声音会变得很小,怕惹来麻烦。(179)

随着时间的推移,我们对一个个偏见了如指掌,学会了你说你的,我做我的。(179)

我们积累着被歧视的经历,如同徒步旅行者收集徒步戳记一样。(248)

此外,这种歧视经历使得叙述者在语言使用上感到矛盾和困惑,对母语产生羞耻,对德语也抱有畏惧。为了适应新环境,叙述者不得不在身份和文化之间做出妥协,揭示了移民生活中的困境,也反映了移民如何在他人的期待与个人情感之间寻求平衡。在与语言学习相关的39条情感叙述中,负面情感语句有27条,占比高达69%:

但我看了20次房子,还是没能成为备选,后来,我只好把我的名字 Saša 写成 Sascha。(75)

我深有感触,想要表述一些东西而没有合适的语言,会让

人从心底里感到难以忍受的苦涩。(75)

在德语学习过程中,叙述者特别记录了那些与移民命运紧密相关的排外性词汇,例如 aufgebracht(愤怒的),Bürgerwehr(市民抵抗),Krawal(暴动),Sprengsatz(炸药),ersticken(窒息)……(163)这一选择非偶然,而是深刻反映了移民在新国家面临的社会挑战与文化障碍。词汇学习过程中的经历,尤其是那些与排外和歧视有关的词汇,更加凸显了他们在新国家的复杂心理状态和社会处境。

2.3 个体情感适应与身份认同

社会维度上的情感表达揭示了叙述者在重新理解出身的过程中,如何将这种理解投射到自身在社会层面的建构,形成一种充斥着他人能量和声音的自我意识(伯基特 75)。以叙述者为代表的第二代移民在探索"我是谁"这一问题的过程中,实际上是在通过"我在做什么"的方式向外来塑造和实现自我。正如伯基特所指出,"我们如何领会我们的自我,取决于我们如何对世界起作用,如何使整个社会生活或我们与之互动的他人的生活有所不同"(163-164)。这表明,自我认同的构建不是孤立的内省过程,而是与个体所处的社会环境和其参与的活动密切相关。在琐碎的生活和叙述片段中,情感语句为我们提供了线索,帮助我们串联起叙述者追求的身份认同。在此过程中,个体的情感适应和身份认同成为相互交织的主题。叙述者通过与社会的互动、文化的适应以及生活琐事的处理,逐渐塑造了自己的身份认同。这一过程不仅涉及对外部世界的适应,亦涵盖了对内在自我归属感的反思和身份的重构。身份构建是一个动态过程,它涉及个体与社会环境的持续互动及情感的演变和自我意识的发展。

小说中涉及身份认同的情感语句共 36 条,其中负面情感有 32 条,占比高达89%，这一数据突出显示了移民在异乡身份认同过程中所体验到的深刻负面情绪。这些情感主要源于对前南斯拉夫身份的否认和对德国社会中经历的排外和歧视的直接反应：

> 不言而喻，这些南斯拉夫人，彼此混战不断，行为举止恶劣。(175)
>
> 在德国初期，我不愿当两种人：南斯拉夫人和难民。(175)
>
> 在学校之外，很长一段时间里我仍然以为自己会被认作移民，也会因此受到攻击。(178)

叙述者在德国的经历进一步加剧了这种负面情感。他们遭遇的社会排外和歧视加深对自我认同的消极看法和在新环境中的身份困惑：

> 你从巴尔干来，逃亡到这里，不说这个国家的语言，这些就是你本来的属性和证明。(80)
>
> 我们是犯罪率、失业率、外国人的一分子。(148)

这种从他人视角构建的自我形象不仅展示了个体与社会之间的深层裂痕，也反映了身份认同过程中的内在矛盾和挑战。在努力融入德国生活的过程中，叙述者采取了逃避现实的策略，试图通过迎合德国人的期待来塑造自己的身份。他"宁可让人把我看作滑雪者，而不是牺牲品"(175)，这种适应策略揭示了身份认同过程中的复杂性和挑战。在家庭生活中，叙述者的自我认知同样充满负面情感。他认为自己"是一个自私的碎片……更多关心的是自己，而不是家庭和团聚"(245)，凸显了个人与家庭关系中的紧张，也揭示了移民个体在新社会中寻求认同和地位时所遇到的内心斗争。这场斗争既关乎如何在新文化中找到归属感,也涉及如何在家庭和社会的期望之间找到平衡。

由消极的身份认同过程也带来了以负面情感为主的归属感和适应性方面的情感体验,在涉及归属感的15条情感语句中,有11条负面情感,占比73%;与适应性有关的30条情感语句中,负面情感有16条,占比53%。在小说中,消极的归属感在叙述者的父母和外祖父身上尤为明显,反映了成年移民在社会地位、工作和语言方面的巨大转变所带来的挑战。"他们俩在德国幸福吗?幸福,有时候;幸福,太少见了"(80),这种感受不仅来源于个人移民经历的直接反应,也是对德国社会中排外和歧视的间接体验。外祖父则"是我们当中在德国最少感到幸福的人,但他为人友善,知恩图报,不愿意说出心里的不快"(202)。由此叙述者也将这种上一代对德国的消极归属感投射到自己书写的人物中。他的"人物几乎没有一个留在原处。有一些人去了他们本来要去的地方。他们定居在那里却很少感到幸福"(77),进一步强调了移民家庭对幸福感的稀缺体验和对新环境的复杂适应过程。在适应性方面,这种负面情感同样在叙述者的父母和外祖父母身上显现。外祖父母在德国的生活受到语言障碍的限制,导致他们"大多数时间都守在家里"(89)。母亲在带孩子从波黑战争逃亡至德国时,内心充满了混乱和焦虑,"她自己同样也被折腾得不知所措,可她竭尽全力掩饰着,不让这种情绪暴露出来"(144)。

相比之下,第二代移民如叙述者,一方面"获得了接受高等教育和上大学期间打工的机会"(211),另一方面"没有承受过父母所承受的生存压力"(211),因而能更积极地适应德国生活,表现出更积极的适应性。这种积极情感让叙述者有了更多的思考空间,对自身的出身起源和民族认同进行深刻反思:

> 我的反抗就是适应。不是适应一种在德国作为移民必须要怎样的期待,但也不是自觉地与之对抗。我反抗的是对出

身起源的神化和民族认同的幻象。我赞成其中的归属感。无论我在哪里，无论我愿意待在哪儿，那里都应该让人有归属感。找到最低限度的共同点，这就足够了。(250)

叙述者的反抗态度实际上是对出身起源的神化和民族认同的幻象的适应，他追求的是一种超越具体地理和文化界限的普遍归属感。因此，第一代移民经历了社会地位和文化环境的巨大变化，遭遇深刻的归属感和适应性困境。相比之下，第二代移民在享受更好教育机会的同时，也面临着自己的身份认同和文化适应的挑战。这些情感体验不仅构成了家庭成员间的情感动态，也塑造了他们在新社会中的身份认同和文化适应策略。

三、结论和反思

本文基于 BERT 模型，结合数字人文的远读和近读对《我从哪里来》进行分句情感极性识别，通过深入分析揭示了文本中的丰富情感空间及人物在不同事件中的情感倾向。此方法不仅为当代移民文学提供了新的解读路径，而且展示了数字技术在文学分析中的创新潜力。《我从哪里来》的叙事结构虽然分散为 65 个看似独立的章节，但通过细腻的情感线索紧密相连，形成了一种独特的凝聚力。萨沙在叙述战争、移民等宏大主题之外，还通过日常生活细节，如特定地点、教育、工作、语言、生存困境等微妙细节，构筑了一个立体且复杂的移民身份认同图景，如同"欧班夫人的晴雨表"，悄无声息地透露出深层的情感和认同的问题。利用 BERT 模型等工具，我们得以捕捉这些看似零散的情感动态，理解它们之间的内在联系。通过统计和分析，原本难以捉摸的情感被重构和重新感知，形成了一个连贯而生动的情感世界。这些情感碎片汇聚成一个平等的情感展现空间，打破了传统叙事的界限，提供了全新的审美体验。这样的叙事方式赋予读者更加积极的角色,能够在不同情感节点间自由导航,深入理解和感知文本的情感深度和广度。

　　这部作品突显了文学在情感教育方面的独特价值,无论是通过传统阅读还是现代技术的辅助,都能够为我们提供一种深刻的生活体验,让我们在理解文本的同时体验生活本身,并在这个过程中寻找人性的共通之处。这不仅是对身份和经历的叙述,更是对情感和存在的深刻反思。本研究展示了数字人文技术在分析现代碎片化叙事文本中的潜力,但同时也揭示了一些局限性。例如,我们采用的预训练德语情感分析模型虽然覆盖了广泛的样本,但在文学文本的具体应用中仍存在提升空间。未来的研究可以考虑构建更专注于当代文学领域的语料数据集,并持续完善样本,以期在降低人工投入的同时,提高模型的准确性和应用效果。

注解【Notes】

① https://github.com/oliverguhr/german-sentiment.
② F1 得分是精确度和召回率的调和平均数,常用于评估分类模型的性能,尤其是在数据集类别分布不均时。这里的"平衡"指的是数据集中各类别的样本数量相同或接近,而"不平衡"指的是某些类别的样本数量远多于其他类别。
③ 鲁棒性是指一个系统、模型或函数在面对错误、变化或干扰时,仍能维持其性能不受影响的能力。在机器学习和统计学中,一个鲁棒的模型能够处理不同类型的输入数据和潜在的异常值,同时仍能产生准确可靠的结果。鲁棒性是衡量模型可靠性和稳定性的重要指标,尤其是在实际应用中,它有助于确保模型在现实世界的复杂和不可预测环境下仍能正常工作。

引用文献【Works Cited】

Anz, Thomas. "Emotional Turn? Beobachtungen zur Gefühlsforschung." *Literaturkritik*, no. 12, Dec. 2006, 28 August 2023, https://literaturkritik.de/id/10267.

Apitzsch, Ursula. "Transnationale Familienkooperation." *Migration, Familie, Gesellschaft*, edited by Thomas Geisen, Tobias Studer and Erol Yildiz, Springer Fachmedien, 2014, pp. 13 – 26.

Boccagni, Paolo, Loretta Baldassar. "Emotions on the move: Mapping the emergent field of emotion and migration." *Emotion, Space and Society*, vol. 16, 2015, pp. 73–80.

bpb: "29. Mai 1993: Brandanschlag in Solingen." 26 May 2023, 15 Dec. 2023, https://www.bpb.de/kurz-knapp/hintergrund-aktuell/161980/29-mai-1993-brandanschlag-in-solingen/.

伊恩·伯基特:《社会性自我》,李康译,上海文艺出版社,2023年。

[Burkitt, Ian. *Social Selves: Theories of Self and Society*. Translated by Li Kang, Literature and Art Publishing House, 2023.]

车琳:《西方文论关键词:自我虚构》,《外国文学》第1期,2019年1月,第97—107页。

[Che, Lin. "Autofiction: A Keyword in Critical Theory." *Foreign Literature*, no. 1, Jan. 2019, pp. 97–107.]

Deutscher Buchpreis. "Begründung der Jury." 28 Aug. 2023, https://www.deutscher-buchpreis.de/archiv/jahr/2019.

金雯:《情动与情感:文学情感研究及其方法论启示》,《文化艺术研究》第15卷第1期,2022年1月,第44—45页。

[Jin, Wen. "Affect and Emotion: A Study on Literary Emotions and Its Methodology." *Studies in Culture & Art*, vol. 15, no. 1, Jan. 2022, pp. 44–55.]

Klueppel, Joscha. "Emotionale Landschaften der Migration: Von unsichtbaren Grenzen, Nicht-Ankommen und dem Tod in Stanišićs *Herkunft* und Varatharajahs *Vor der Zunahme der Zeichen*". TRANSIT, vol. 12, no. 2, 2020, pp. 1–21.

菲力浦·勒热纳:《自传契约》,杨国政译,北京大学出版社,2013年。

[Lejeune, Philippe. *Le Pacte Autobiographique*, Translated by Yang Guozheng, Beijing UP, 2013.]

Mellmann, Katja. "Lust, Attrappenwirkung und affektive Bindung. Literarische Ästhetik im Zeichen der Evolutionspsychologie." *Literaturkritik*, no. 12, Dec. 12, 28 Aug. 2023, https://literaturkritik.de/public/rezension.php?rez_id=10266&ausgabe=200612.

McCormick, Chris and Nick Ryan. "BERT Word Embeddings Tutorial." 14 May 2019, 11 Jul. 2023, https://mccormickml.com/2019/05/14/BERT-word-embeddings-tutorial/.

Stanišić, Saša. *Herkunft*. Luchterhand Literaturverlag, 2019.

萨沙·斯坦尼西奇:《我从哪里来》,韩瑞祥译,上海人民出版社,2021年。

[Stanišić, Saša. *Herkunft*. Translated by Han Ruixiang. Shanghai People's Publishing House, 2021.]

两个世界间的调停者
——达维德·迪奥普及其"世界性"书写

陶 沙 高 方

内容摘要:达维德·迪奥普是塞内加尔法国混血作家,他迄今所创作的三部小说关注法国和塞内加尔之间的历史互动与文化关系。法属马提尼克思想家格里桑用"世界性"指涉多元文化共生、彼此尊重的状态,以抵抗"全球化"的同化力量。通过书写越界人物的身份困境和时代洪流中人类的共同命运,迪奥普构建起个体间和民族间的对话关系,尝试调停文化间的矛盾,恢复被扭曲的"世界性"。本文对迪奥普作品中的空间、历史和互文关系进行考察,揭示其"世界性"书写的创作路径和跨文化意义。

关键词:迪奥普 世界性 空间 历史 互文

作者简介:陶沙,南京大学外国语学院博士研究生,南京传媒学院讲师,研究方向为法语文学、翻译学。高方,南京大学外国语学院教授,博士生导师,研究方向为比较文学、翻译学。

Title: Mediator between two worlds—David Diop and the "mondialité" in his writings

Abstract: David Diop is a biracial writer of Senegalese and French descent. His three novels focus on the historical interactions and cultural relations between France and Senegal. The Martiniquais thinker Édouard Glissant referred to "mondialité" as a state of multicultural coexistence and mutual respect, a stance against the assimilating forces of globalization. By writing about the identity crises of characters who cross boundaries and the common fate of humanity in the torrent of the times, Diop constructs dialogues between individuals and nations, attempting to mediate cultural contradictions and restore the distorted "mondialité". This article examines the spaces, history, and intertextual relationships in Diop's works, revealing his path of "mondialité" writing and its cross-cultural significance.

Key words: David Diop; mondialité; space; history; intertextuality

Author: Tao Sha is a Ph. D. candidate at the School of Foreign Sudies, Nanjing University, China. Her research interests are French literature and translation studies. Gao Fang is a professor at the School of Foreign Sudies, Nanjing University, China. Her research interests are comparative literature and translation studies.

2021年，塞内加尔裔法国作家达维德·迪奥普凭借小说《灵魂兄弟》(*Frère d'âme*)英译本当选布克国际奖，成为首位获得该奖项的法语作者和非洲裔小说家。此前,《灵魂兄弟》曾摘得2018年龚古尔中学生奖。小说随后被译成十几种语言，为作家赢得国际声誉。丹穆若什在《什么是世界文学?》中指出,"如果一个塞内加尔人用法语写成的小说在巴黎、魁北克、马提尼克被阅读，它在实际意义上可以进入世界文学范畴；而翻译只是它在世界范围传播的下一步"(237)。这一论述表明身份、语言、流通以及翻译对世界文学的外部建构功能。宏观来看，这些因素在迪奥普小说的传播路径中得到了印证。除了《灵魂兄弟》，作家还有两部作品面世，分别是《1889，万国博览会》(1889, *l'Attraction universelle*, 2012)和《不归路之门或米歇尔·阿当松的秘密笔记》(*La porte du voyage sans retour ou les cahiers secrets de Michel Adanson*,

2021，以下简称《不归路之门》）。微观上看，三部作品有其共性：作者关注欧洲与非洲间的历史关系，以空间、人种、文化间的跨越性为创作主题。因此，他被法国《十字架报》(La Croix)称为"两个世界间的作家"。借用法属马提尼克思想家爱德华·格里桑(Édouard Glissant)的术语，迪奥普的文学创作路径或可归纳为一种"世界性"书写。

何谓"世界性"？我们常用以描述超越民族、具有普世意义的事物。"世界性"似乎成了"国际化"和"全球化"的同义反复。在法语语境中，"世界性"(mondialité)被名词化，继而获哲学化和理论化。正如它的词根——比较文学研究者艾普特(Emily Apter)指出"世界"(monde)一词具有概念上的密度和哲学上的不可译性(101)——"世界性"作为术语具有丰富的阐释空间。法国哲学家让-吕克·南希(Jean-Luc Nancy)认为，"世界性"是世界的符号化(symbolisation)，是世界自我象征的方式，它使意义流通成为可能而不必指向世界外(59)。因此，"世界性"反映出世界的特征。格里桑认为世界本质上具有整体性、混杂性和空时性等属性，由此提出了"世界性"的理论构想。他在《外围与您对话》(Les périphériques vous parlent)杂志的访谈中阐述了"世界性"与"全球化"的差异："'全球化'是经济和历史演变的事实状态，源于竞相逐低的同质化；相反，'世界性'是文化多元共生、彼此尊重的状态。"简言之，"世界性"是一种文化混响的共同体意识，促成交流和改变，且在走近他者时不失去自我。

空间、时间、文化是世界的三个维度。文学作为世界的符号化与意义流通手段，在这三个层次展现出世界性和文学性的共生关系。格里桑从加勒比海独特的群岛面貌出发，关注文学与场所的关系，倡导通过"克里奥尔化"(créolisation)让文学摆脱单一场所的束缚，走向多元关系的呈现（高方，《法语语境中"世界文学"概念的移译与构建》69）。法国作家米歇尔·乐彼(Michel Le Bris)提出旅行文学和世界写作的概念，认为"世界文学"意味着一种向世界开放的文学，或者说，一种谈论真实和生活而非在自恋意识中自我封闭的文学(25)。格里桑和乐彼的设想促使"法语世界文学"(littérature-monde en français)概念生成,对法国中心的法语文学观发起挑战,呼唤一种丰富的、多元的、去中心的法语世界文学。迪奥普的小说创作是这一写作潮流的例证。本文认为,其"世界性"书写经由以下路径实现:① 通过人物的流动,讲述异质文化空间的联系和越界者的身份迷思;② 通过历史虚构,展现人类命运共同的现实性与复杂性;③ 通过缔结欧洲和非洲文学间的关系,践行"和解"和"跨文化"的文学使命。

一、空间的越界:跨文化流动的困境

迪奥普父亲是塞内加尔人,母亲是法国人。他生于巴黎,五岁前往塞内加尔并在那里度过童年和青少年时期,后回法国接受高等教育,博士毕业后获大学教职。和同为塞内加尔裔,但从小在法国长大、欧洲化了的法国女作家玛丽·恩迪亚耶(Marie NDiaye)相比,达维德·迪奥普拥有非洲生活经历,会说沃洛夫语,并不是一个徒有其表的混血儿。和勒克莱齐奥(Le Clézio)一样,迪奥普很早就开始写作(四岁写诗),而且,他的童年记忆也同样对其日后的文学创作产生了不可磨灭的影响。在接受《读书》(Lire)杂志采访时,迪奥普谈及童年往事:和堂兄弟去达喀尔的祖母家,一起坐船去恩格尔,熬夜在屋顶看星星,听姆巴拉科斯音乐(Mbalax)和歌剧《奥菲欧与尤丽迪丝》(Orphée et Eurydice),"我的童年真是一种音响、喧哗、聚会和阅读的混合。某些属于我的双重文化的东西,它们在我身上和解"(Marivat 51)。迪奥普的双重文化背景不可避免地塑造了他的志趣,其学术视野聚焦于欧洲对非洲的表述,这后来也成了他文学创作的领域。

塞内加尔和法国成为小说故事发生的场所。圣路易、佛得角、巴黎、波尔多……不同坐标通过虚构被串连起来,呈现在作家的文学地图上,形成空间的交错。地域界限被打破,作者搭起一座文学之桥,凭栏而望,一面是塞内加尔河畔的独木舟和鱼鹰,一面是矗立在塞纳河边的巴黎铁塔。于是,不同时期东西方世界的人文景观通过小说人物跨越大西洋的流动被并置在虚拟的文学空间之中,呈现出一种混杂的状态:猴面包树、乌木树、棕榈树与橡树、山毛榉、杨树、白桦树交相辉映;塞内加尔人的舞蹈、歌声、音乐与巴黎博览会机器展馆的钟表异曲同工;"一战"欧洲战场的黑暗血腥与西非乡村的田园牧歌形成鲜明对比。两个世界看似格格不入,却通过某些方式(往往是剥削)保持着联系和互动:"曾经遍布在佛得角半岛与圣路易岛之间六十里海岸线上的乌木林如今已所剩无几。在我去塞内加尔之前的两个世纪里,欧洲人大量砍伐这些树木,现在它们装饰着我们的镶木写字台、珍品收藏柜和大键琴琴键。"(Diop, *La porte du voyage sans retour* 89 - 90)作为法国与塞内加尔文化的交汇点,圣路易是迪奥普作品中重要的文学地标,是多元和模糊的空间。这里是流动的起点,亦是旅途的终点,是越界发生的场所。一定程度上,它甚至具有文化符号的意义。这个以法国国王名字命名、带有空间殖民主义色彩的西非海滨城市不仅指涉历史上真实的殖民地理空间,同时还隐喻了法国和塞内加尔在人种、语言、文化上的交杂与冲突。这座充满矛盾与融合的城市就像是讲法语的非洲人——"圣路易之美是因为其居民之美……只有当黑、白和混种的圣路易人为了某一盛事齐聚圣路易岛上之时,才算是戴上了最好的庆典面具"(Diop, 1889, *L'Attraction universelle* 108)。

  流动与越界是迪奥普小说共同的主题,是所有主角所共享的行动:《1889,万国博览会》讲述了法国大革命一百周年之际,来自塞内加尔圣路易岛的黑人代表团前往巴黎参加"万国博览会"的遭遇;《灵魂兄弟》是关于"一战"期间塞内加尔土著兵赴欧洲战场作战的故事;而《不归路之门》则描述了十八世纪五十年代,法国植物学家米歇尔·阿当松在塞内加尔的旅行。这种行动具有两个方向,从塞内加尔到法国(从东方到西方)或相反(从西方到东方)。空间上反向的流动,其文化含义截然不同。萨义德在《东方学》中指出,欧洲在东西方关系中处于强势地位,掌握自由交流的特权,"不仅在欧洲五花八门的印度公司这些庞大的机构中,就是在旅行家的故事中,殖民地也得到创造,民族中心的视角得到保护"(157)。因此,迪奥普使笔下的人物往返于法国和塞内加尔之间具有象征意义:越界的双向流动意在消解欧洲中心的观点。

然而,往返于两个世界之间的旅行并不简单,人物从家乡进入异域,成为异乡人,这意味着地理空间和文化空间的双重跨越。迪奥普小说中的人物在流动中面临着文化冲击和身份危机。尤其当来自边缘世界(非洲)的人进入所谓的"中心"(métropole)世界(欧洲)时,他必然会经历考验和痛苦。一方面,他可能由于语言和宗教文化的差异,无法完成自我表达与双向交流,这是《灵魂兄弟》中塞内加尔土著兵阿尔法的困境,他不会说法语,信奉伊斯兰教,失去好友马丹巴后,在战争中陷入了疯狂;另一方面,当边缘群体试图发出不同的声音,中心世界就会剥夺他们的话语权,并施以惩戒。比如《1889,万国博览会》中圣路易代表团团长巴希胡,他对塞内加尔总督营私舞弊的举报不仅毫无结果,还招致法国当局的报复和羞辱。当然,跨文化流动的困境不单存在于从非洲到欧洲的越界行为之中,来自西方的越界者也往往受到历史情境的限制和困扰。

米歇尔·阿当松是历史上真实存在的人物,这个启蒙时期的博物学家——按照萨义德的说法——算得上一位不折不扣的东方学者。无可避免地,他带有所处时代的烙印,受到西方优势的心理暗示,对于殖民主义和奴隶制秉持暧昧的态度。因此,作为启蒙学者的真实阿当松和小说人物之间存在着差异,后者从某种意义上来说是迪奥普本人的化身。作者在小说中努力协调真实与虚构之间的关系,对于历史的局限,既有所突破又有所保留。这种突破和保留构成一种矛盾,其本质与跨文化的矛盾一致。青年学者为编写百科全书来到塞内加尔。当他听说从美洲回来的"幽灵"的故事后,毅然出发寻找这个叫玛哈姆的黑人女性并且爱上了她。其间他的理性观念与非洲的神秘主义相碰撞，泛灵论的思想深刻影响了他的世界观。本来，他的思维对于时代而言就具有超前性："天主教（我险些儿成为它的仆役）教导世人说，黑人是天生的奴隶。然而，我很清楚地知道，如果说黑人是奴隶，并不是上帝的意旨如此，而是因为这种想法有助于人们继续毫无悔意地卖掉他们。"他赞美黑人的智慧，认为"黑人不像我们一样，不假思索地把贪婪当作一种美德，甚至觉得自己的行为是如此自然。他们也不像我们一样，受笛卡尔鼓动，认为应当使自己成为整个自然界的主宰和拥有者"（Diop, *La porte du voyage sans retour* 54,55）。由于旅行中的经历和见闻，尤其是通过使用沃洛夫语，他文化身份的同一性被打破。小说里多次写到晚年的阿当松"用塞内加尔黑人的方式蹲着"，他成为精神上的塞内加尔人，白人中的"异类"。如他自己所说，"在塞内加尔生活了三年后，我觉得自己似乎成为了一个黑人，所有的口味都是如此。这不仅是由于习惯的力量，像人们轻易相信的那样，而是因为，由于说沃洛夫语，我忘了自己是白人"（189）。然而，对黑人文化的认同并未使阿当松进一步做出超越时代局限的政治选择。作为塞内加尔事务专家，他为殖民地办公室起草文件鼓吹戈雷奴隶贸易，其学术创新性也仅局限于在出版的游记中写下符合殖民利益的建议："成千上万被塞内加尔租界送往美洲的黑人本可以被更好地用于耕种非洲的可耕地。甘蔗在塞内加尔长得毫不费力，从中产出法国亟需的糖比从安的列斯群岛获取更为有利可图。"（233-234）这一选择是造成他晚年心灵煎熬的一个直接原因，他将此视为对玛哈姆的背叛。由此我们注意到，虚构主要集中在人物的思维和情感范畴，迪奥普通过将虚构情节与关键史实适配，强调了人物精神层面的越界和现实层面的妥协，继而获得一种合理性。阿当松的流动与越界，一方面是对历史现实的突破，另一方面又受到客观条件的制约。他试图打破西方世界的秩序，却无法逃脱世界中心的引力。

二、历史的引力：人类命运交织

迪奥普在第一部小说的题目中玩了个文字游戏——法语"attraction universelle"一词具有双重涵义，一指"万国博览会（Exposition universelle）"，二指万有引力定律（loi de la gravitation）。这一表述后来再度出现在了《不归路之门》中，"我（阿当松）被戈雷总督打败了，被他的世界打败了，这世界的力量就像强大的万有引力定律一样不可阻挡，它把黑人同白人的身体以及灵魂都拖在身后"（Diop, *La porte du voyage sans retour* 207-208）。"万有引力"的隐喻，是迪奥普写作的原点，是关于普遍性的思考。"万有引力"是现实世界的重力，是两种文化间的张力，也是历史的引力。基于此，迪奥普认为个体的命运无法脱离集体的命运，人永远存在于和世界的关系之中。文化间总是存在相互作用，不同民族的命运交织在人类共同的历史之中。他笔下的人物生活在两种文化的交界处，往往体现出时代的悲剧性，反映了特定历史背景下边缘群体的集体宿命。

在《1889，万国博览会》中，由于团长巴希胡的"叛逆"和其他成员的罢工，参加1889年巴黎"万国博览会"的圣路易代表团被送往波尔多的马戏团。法国当局逼迫他们和动物一起进行屈辱的"黑人表演"。在欧洲中心主义语境下，非洲人作为彻头彻尾的他者，在"自我"的凝视中被异化成了动物。他们幻想通过"万国博览会"改善自己的身份和地位，却最终被现实的重量压得粉碎。故事取材于真实事件，是对欧洲殖民历史的回溯。十九世纪后半叶，伴随着工业革命的发展和殖民帝国的崛起，欧洲人统治了世界大部分地区并发现了居于其间的"他者"。西方人类学基于外形、体力、智力等标准对种族进行分类，假定白人具有原始的优越性，将黑人归入人类底层，其他种族则是中间人，以此捍卫达尔文的进化论："人类社会的历史是按照连续但统一的线性进化模式构成的,每个社会都应该经历一定数量的阶段,从残暴的动物阶段经过未开化和野蛮的中间阶段,再到理性和技术的文明阶段。"(Girardet 90)这一价值体系在当时足以证明殖民主义的合理性,使欧洲人心安理得将殖民地土著居民作为物品进行展示和欣赏。自十九世纪七十年代初以来,在伦敦,然后在德国、法国和意大利,土著人被陈列在真正的人类动物园中(Abbal 23)。"万国博览会"象征扭曲的世界主义,彻底沦为殖民压迫的工具。此外,迪奥普也在小说中谈及法国的犹太人群体,指出他们和非洲人同命相连。反对"黑人表演"的年轻犹太医生拉斐尔向他的父亲发问:"阿扎姆教授,你知道吗?对于一部分法国人来说,我们不仅是弑神的人,还是边缘的种族。在法国,有些'科学家'想要对我们实行测颅法,就像上世纪以来他们对非洲人和美洲印第安人所做的那样。同样的动机,同样的惩罚。而你要我沉默吗?"(1889, *L'Attraction universelle* 204-205)

在《灵魂兄弟》中,作者试图突破欧洲中心主义,将话语权还给历史上长期沉默的塞内加尔土著步兵(tirailleurs sénégalais),进而解构殖民语境下自我与他者的关系。全书是黑人士兵阿尔法和马丹巴的独白,以意识流的方式讲述了"我"对战争的感知、对故乡的怀念、对友情和爱情的体验。视角的切换,导致了身份的互换。"自我"与"他者"的位置颠倒过来,黑人成了观察者,而白人成了被观察的对象。这里,作者借人物之口讲述了战争的黑暗和殖民主义的残酷。阿尔法和马丹巴有着共同的名字,是法国人口中的"巧克力兵",他们一方面被殖民帝国宣传成天真烂漫的服从者形象,另一方面被配以砍刀、在战场上被迫发出野兽般的叫喊以震慑敌人。"一战"期间,共有二十万塞内加尔土著步兵为法国作战,其中十三万五千人奔赴欧洲战场,三万多客死他乡。然而这一群体并未得到应有的重视,他们几乎被历史遗忘。黑人性运动的代表人物、塞内加尔诗人和总统桑戈尔(Léopold Sédar Senghor)"二战"期间曾在塞内加尔步兵团中服役,写下了悲壮的诗句:"塞内加尔的步兵们,我的黑人兄弟,你们的手在冰与死亡之下依旧滚烫。若非你们的战友(frère d'armes),你们浴血的弟兄(frère de sang),谁将为你们歌唱?"(7)"灵魂兄弟"和"战友"的法语音近形似,迪奥普或许也受到了桑戈尔的启发。他在小说中"巧妙地营造了'一战'欧洲战场和战前西非故乡的时空交叠,构建了善与恶、美与丑、生与死、文明与野蛮、和平与战乱等多重对比。这些矛盾的两极相互碰撞、交织,融为一体,难解难分,呈现出塞内加尔人的生命张力"(陶沙 33)。

通过《不归路之门》,迪奥普揭开了西方奴隶贸易的伤疤,揭示了三角贸易和奴隶制下非洲黑人的悲惨命运。戈雷岛是西非重要的贸易站,在持续三个世纪的奴隶贸易中,数以百万计的非洲黑人从这里被贩运到安的列斯群岛,沦为甘蔗种植园里的奴隶。玛哈姆的形象集中体现了黑人女性所遭受的暴力和奴役。美貌和黑人女性身份导致她悲惨的命运。她受到男性的觊觎,无论黑人还是白人。她的舅舅试图对她施以强奸和谋杀,租界主管用步枪交换她为奴并意欲侵犯她,戈雷总督打算将她卖给好色的路易斯安那总督。玛哈姆最终死在了戈雷岛的码头边。如果说玛哈姆最终并没有穿越大西洋被卖到美洲,那么小说结尾出现的玛德莱娜则补充说明了离散的黑人女性在糖岛种植园和法国的可悲境遇。如格里桑所言,"非洲人赤条条地抵达(美洲),被剥夺了所有可能性,甚至他们的语言:贩奴船的船舱是非洲语言消失的地方,因为在贩奴船上,和在种植园里一样,说相同语言的人永远不会被安置在一起"(16)。这个酷似玛哈姆的黑人女仆幼年时就被卖到瓜德鲁普,遗失了原本的语言、种族和关于故乡的全部记忆,她接受了自己的奴隶身份,在白人世界饱受男性的骚扰。在故事最后一章,迪奥普巧妙地让一个名叫玛库的老黑奴出场。这个玛库就是阿当松当年在塞内加尔乡村抱过的婴儿,他一直坚信是因为自己扯了白人(阿当松)的头发,才导致他和姐姐沦为奴隶。作者用寓言的手法,表现了黑人命运的悲剧性和荒诞性。

值得一提的是,迪奥普不单谴责了西方在三角贸易和奴隶制中所扮演的角色,他同时清醒地认识到非洲民族自身并非毫无责任。奴隶制在西方人到达之前就存在于非洲,奴隶贸易是非洲部落和西方殖民者共谋的结果。在他的笔下,塞内加尔的瓦洛国王和卡约尔国王都是导致非洲悲惨命运的帮凶,他们贪得无厌,发动奴隶战争,从和西方人的贸易中谋取私利。此外,迪奥普也塑造了恩迪亚克这样忠诚、善良的黑人角色。作为瓦洛王子,他为了朋友奋起抗争,却无力改变现实,只能放弃王位,去往这个国家唯一禁止奴隶买卖的地方潜心研习《古兰经》。

历史对文学具有引力。通过写作穿梭于历史之间,迪奥普为长期失语的边缘群体发声:十九世纪的圣路易黑人、塞内加尔土著兵、奴隶制下的塞内加尔黑人女性、法国社会中的犹太人群体……作家对他们在殖民历史中的他者地位及其集体命运的悲剧性进行反思,让他们从历史的边缘回归文学舞台之上。需要注意的是,迪奥普对黑人世界的关注并不意味着自身文化认同的单向选择,而是一种站在两个世界之间的、冷静的历史回望。在今天的英美语境中,黑人人权被过度政治化,导致出现矫枉过正的倾向。迪奥普对此表达了自己的看法:"在我身上没有对立,这可能对一些美国人来说难以理解……我们不该害怕说出'黑人'有可能是个怪物,杀人犯,就像'白人'一样。从我们对此避而不谈开始,我们便陷入一种完全的异化。"(Lestavel)迪奥普没有在虚构中刻意回避黑人世界中人性的恶,比如《不归路之门》中试图强奸及杀死自己外甥女的黑人首领,《1889,万国博览会》中土库勒人和颇尔人之间的种族仇杀,等等。他(以阿当松的身份)写道,"他们是和我们一样的人。像所有人类一样,他们的心灵和思想会渴求荣耀与财富。在他们当中,也有一些贪婪的人,随时准备牺牲他人的利益来中饱私囊,准备着掠夺,为了黄金而杀戮。我想到他们的国王,和我们直到拿破仑一世皇帝的历代君主一样,为了获得或保持权力,毫不犹豫地推行奴隶制"(Diop, *La porte du voyage sans retour* 56)。在迪奥普的小说中,总是存在多个民族和多种文化在场,存在复杂而多元的人性。但无论是非洲民族还是欧洲民族,黑人或白人,本质上都是人类,有着共同的焦虑。文化间彼此牵连,人类命运息息相关,共同汇入历史的洪流,就像这世上一切都受万有引力作用一样。

三、互文的世界:通过对话走向和解

迪奥普的小说建立在两种文化对话的基础之上,创造出一个互文的世界。在他的作品中,总是存在着来自不同时空的声音,欧洲和非洲文学的记忆碎片杂陈交织。正如萨莫瓦约(Tiphaine Samoyault)在《互文性研究:文学的记忆》中指出的,"互文性首先呈现的是混合的一面,这也是它的一个基本特色,它将若干种言语、语境和声音罗列于前"(79)。在迪奥普构建的文学世界中,文本间的互文促成了文明间的交流与对话,是传承的方式,也是和解的手段。这正回应了迪奥普"它们(双重文化)在我身上和解"的自述。

二十世纪八十年代初,迪奥普从塞内加尔回到法国,进入图卢兹大学学习,他最初研究狄德罗《百科全书》中的政治哲学思想、孟德斯鸠和十八世纪的政治文本。1998年,他在巴黎四大完成了题为《〈狄德罗和达朗贝尔百科全书中政治哲学的思想渊源:自然法则中自我保护优先思想之嬗变〉的博士论文。迪奥普对植物学家米歇尔·阿当松的关注始于2006年,他在阅读后者的《塞内加尔行纪》时深受感动。这位百科全书作者在回忆录中讲述了自己对非洲大陆的亲身体验,并保留了大量沃洛夫语表达。迪奥普对《读书》杂志做出了如下表述,"他品尝了鲨鱼肉古斯古斯,他对我说他一点也不喜欢"(Marivat 53)。"他对我说"——显然,通过阅读阿当松的笔记,迪奥普和三个世纪前的启蒙学者间建立起一种对话关系,并且从中发现了进行文学虚构的空间。正是基于这种联系,迪奥普想象了米歇尔·阿当松不为人知的隐秘生活,创作了《不归路之门》。迪奥普巧妙地借鉴了十八世纪小说中常用的桥段:阿当松的女儿阿格莱在父亲遗物的抽屉暗格中发现了留给她的笔记,从而开启了画中画、曲中曲。自小说第十一章开始,阿当松透过笔记向女儿讲述自己在塞内加尔的往事,坦陈自己年轻时的爱情故事。他通过传承性的亲子间对话,消解了父女间的隔阂,也完成了与自我的和解。迪奥普在小说中多次提到格鲁克的歌剧《奥菲欧与尤丽迪丝》,源于希腊神话的故事隐喻了主人公的爱情悲剧。阿当松和玛哈姆在戈雷码头的出逃可以视为是对奥菲欧(希腊神话中的诗人和音乐家)前往冥界拯救爱人尤丽迪丝的改写。小说末章谈到种植园主给黑奴马库取名"奥菲欧",让人不禁联想到萨特(Jean-Paul Sartre)为桑戈尔《黑人和马尔加什法语新诗选》(*Anthologie de la nouvelle poésie nègre et malgache de langue française*)所作序文《黑奥菲欧》(*Orphée Noir*)。它歌颂了黑人性运动(la Négritude)中的黑人和马达加斯加诗人。通过神话的永恒回归,作者编织了文本间纵横交错的互文网络,同时将个人记忆融入小说叙事,在自身和人物之间建立了紧密联系。

在迪奥普的小说中,这种互文现象十分普遍。读者在阅读过程中往往能够发现一些指向文本外部的线索,进而开启新的阅读和对话的可能。在《灵魂兄弟》中,我们可以发现三个隐迹文本:一是法国超现实主义诗人阿波利奈尔(Apollinaire)的一首图形诗《蓝色矢车菊》(*Bleuet*),二是塞利纳(Louis-Ferdinand Céline)的代表作《茫茫黑夜漫游》(*Voyage au bout de la nuit*)(主要是前九章军队生活场景的描述),三是瑞裔法国诗人布莱斯·桑德拉(Blaise Cendrars)的小说《断手》(*La Main coupée*)。小说在叙述方式、人物形象塑造、故事情节与隐喻构造方面均受到了以上三个文本的影响(王天宇、高方 55)。高方指出,"断手"是小说家达维德·迪奥普布下的一个重要的符号,是他在文本中设下的一个互文游戏。桑德拉之外,桑戈尔也曾在《白雪笼罩着巴黎》这首诗中列举了欧洲人以"教化"和"拯救文明"的名义,用他们的白手所犯下的累累罪行。在《灵魂兄弟》结尾处,迪奥普通过一个关于伤疤和身份的巫狮寓言点出马丹巴的灵魂在阿尔法的肉身上重生。这一诗意的表达打破了传统"一体二魂"的二元对立,丰富了十八世纪以来西方文学史中复身(double)母题的创作(《"我们通过名字而相互拥抱"——〈灵魂兄弟〉的关联阅读》52,54)。

此外,《1889,万国博览会》中描述的圣路易黑人代表团的遭遇使人想起迪迪埃·达尼尼科斯(Didier Daeninckx)《食人族》(*Cannibale*)里参加1931年殖民博览会的卡纳克人(Kanaks)——他们在人类动物园里被迫扮演原始的食人族并被用来交换德国马戏团的鳄鱼。与此同时,小说中几度出现的马拉美诗歌则把我们引向了象征主义的隐喻世界。可以说,与超现实主义、象征主义等文学流派之间的互文交织体现了欧洲文学对达维德·迪奥普的深刻影响,是他双重身份中欧洲部分的集中体现。而在迪奥普的小说中,欧洲文化的声音并不是独白式的自我言说,它拥有来自异域的对话者。

迪奥普在《灵魂兄弟》的扉页引用了三位作家的格言。前两句是法国文学家蒙田(Montaigne)的"我们通过名字而相互拥抱"和帕斯卡尔·基尼亚尔(Pascal Quignard)的"思考即背叛"。第三句则出自塞内加尔作家谢赫·哈米杜·卡纳(Cheikh Hamidou Kane),"我是同时奏响的两个声音,一个远去另一个升起"。这句话正是小说寓言性的起点,它暗和了故事结尾马丹巴的灵魂在阿尔法的肉身上重生,他们成为真正的灵魂兄弟。同时,这句话也是一个链接,将我们引向卡纳的半自传小说《模棱境遇》(*L'Aventure ambiguë*)。作为非洲最重要的哲理小说之一,《模棱境遇》通过描写主人公身处非洲和西方文明之间所产生的精神和文化上的撕裂,隐喻了时代背景下黑人知识分子的心灵之旅和身份困惑。小说的结尾耐人寻味,主人公在他古兰经导师的墓前陷入和神灵的对话,疯子将他说的"不"理解为对祈祷的拒绝,于是将他刺死。卡纳认为,主人公之死代表了一种和解的可能,因为"伟大的和解正在发生"(189),"你进入了无歧义之境"(190)。这里,卡纳谈到了信仰和理性的关系,其本质是精神世界和物质世界的二元对立,从这个角度看,作者试图摆脱时间和政治的藩篱,超越"身为黑人之焦虑"的主题,进而思考永恒的存在问题,一种生而为人的焦虑。

卡纳对迪奥普的影响显而易见,人类的"焦虑"与"和解"在后者的作品中留下了痕迹。对迪奥普而言,"焦虑"是现实层面的,其根源是现实的重力或所谓"万有引力"般的世界秩序(西方主导的)。殖民主义、奴隶制、战争和生态问题都是这一力量的恶果。而"和解"在精神层面发生,其前提是对话与认同,尊重文化间差异。如果说"西方世界的秩序"是万有引力消极的一面,那么文化间的张力则是万有引力内部消解自身消极性的一种方式。比如《不归路之门》中阿当松与玛哈姆跨越种族的爱情神话,实质隐喻了两种文化间的相互吸引、相互作用,软化了两种文明间冲突的关系。玛哈姆身上散发出非洲自然、宗教、哲学神秘的美与智慧,相形之下,白人世界的科学、理性、价值反倒显得苍白与鄙俗。针对西方所引发的问题,迪奥普在作品中展示了从非洲文化中寻求解法的可能性。他在小说中多次提及存在于非洲大陆的戏虐关系(parenté à plaisenterie),一种通过玩笑来链接家族成员或不同族群的社会习俗,是缓解争端、促进和解的有效手段。他也从非洲世界的神秘主义中汲取了灵感,意识到理性主义和神秘主义对于自然奥秘同样敏感,差别在于前者渴望洞悉自然规律,进而驯服自然,而后者则渴望依靠自然之力因而敬畏自然。他谈到塞内加尔的拉奥贝人(Laobés):"尽管我信奉笛卡尔主义,信仰那些我推崇的哲学家们所颂扬的理性的上帝,但想象在这片大地上有一群男人和女人知道如何与树木交谈,在砍伐前请求它们原谅,这使我感到欣慰。"在万物有灵论的诱惑下,阿当松思索"如果对于每一棵被砍伐的树木,智慧的异教徒拉奥贝人的祈祷都是必须的,那么巨大的乌木林可能还没有从塞内加尔消失",于是,他

"跪在半明半暗的教堂里,被它们上了清漆、布满钉子的尸体所包围,开始请求乌木树宽恕他们的罪过,宽恕那些砍伐它们,把它们锯开并运到另一片天空下,远离其非洲母亲的人"(Diop, *La porte du voyage sans retour* 89,90)。假借人物之口,迪奥普描述了两个维度的和解:一是人与人之间,二是人与自然之间。

四、结　语

2018年《灵魂兄弟》获得龚古尔中学生奖后,迪奥普坦言,"这种媒体曝光,或许一项文学奖,这一切使我能够与更多读者相遇。而每一次相遇都为我的小说增添了一层意义"(Félix)。迪奥普将作品视为开放的文本,认为文学的价值是由作者和读者所共同创造的。作品通过被阅读来影响甚至改变世界,同时也丰富了自身的价值。文学在与世界的双向互动中获得了一种当代性。

近些年,战争、疫情、生态等问题卷土重来,国家、民族间矛盾加剧。迪奥普小说中对于人类焦虑的历史书写有其现实意义。勒克莱齐奥指出,"文学有助于消弭民族和文化间的冲突,推动文化间性的到来,推动跨文化实践,而跨文化会成为解决种种问题、获得世界和平的途径"(高方、施雪莹 9)。文学是一条纽带,将两个世界、两种文化串联起来。通过文学想象,迪奥普让读者往返于欧洲和非洲之间,探索历史记忆的隐秘角落,感受现实重力下的人类命运交织。他因此成为两个世界间的调停者。写作中,作家的语言策略同样承载了他"和解"与"跨文化"的文学观。对迪奥普而言,沃洛夫语中蕴藏着"黑人人性的宝藏:他们好客的信仰、兄弟情谊、他们的诗歌、他们的历史、他们对植物的知识、他们的谚语和他们关于世界的哲学"(*La porte du voyage sans retour* 55-56)。而法语是他面向世界写作、表达的语言。迪奥普选择将沃洛夫语词汇保留在法语表达中,用法语解释沃洛夫谚语,并尝试在法语中引入塞内加尔口语的节奏感。他的小说中总是存在一个不在场的翻译，即作者本人，写作亦是自我翻译的过程。这让我们想起分别将克里奥尔语和马林凯语移植到法语中的马提尼克作家帕特里克·夏莫瓦佐（Patrick Chamoiseau）和科特迪瓦作家阿玛杜·库鲁马（Ahmadou Kourouma）。语言移植的尝试让不同文化得以通过法语传播，同时丰富了法语自身，是民族和文化间交流、互鉴、和解的途径，也是"世界性"在语言层面的体现。

引用文献【Works Cited】

Abbal, Odon. *L'Exposition coloniale de 1889: la Guyane présentée aux Français*. Matoury: Ibis Rouge, 2010.

Apter, Emily. "Le mot 'monde' est un intraduisible." *Relief*, N°6(2012), p.98-112.

Damrosch, David. *What Is World Literature?* Trans. Zha Mingjian and Song Mingwei, et al. Beijing: Peking UP, 2014.

［丹穆若什：《什么是世界文学？》，查明建、宋明炜等译。北京：北京大学出版社，2014。］

Diop, David. *Frère d'Âme*. Trans. Gao Fang. Beijing: People's Literature, 2008.

［迪奥普：《灵魂兄弟》，高方译。北京：人民文学出版社，2008。］

Diop, David. 1889, *L'Attraction universelle*. Paris: L'Harmattan, 2018.

Diop, David. *La porte du voyage sans retour ou les cahiers secrets de Michel Adanson*. Paris: Seuil, 2021.

Félix, Jean-Marie. "La pensée d'un tirailleur sénégalais dans *Frère d'âme* de David Diop", *RTS Culture*, le 4 octobre, 2018. Web. 30 Oct 2022 ⟨https://www.rts.ch/info/culture/livres/9892189-la-pensee-dun-tirailleur-senegalais-dans-frere-dame-de-david-diop.html⟩.

Gao, Fang. "The Conceptual Development of Weltliteratur and Its Transplantation via Translation in French Context." *Journal of Northwestern Polytechnical U (Social Sciences)* 4 (2022): 65-72.

［高方：《法语语境中"世界文学"概念的移译与构建》，载《西北工业大学学报（社会科学版）》，2022年第4期，第65—70页。］

Gao, Fang. "We embrace each other through our names: a connected reading of *Frère d'Âme*." *Foreign Literature and Art* 5 (2021): 48-55.

[高方:《"我们通过名字而相互拥抱"——〈灵魂兄弟〉的关联阅读》,载《外国文艺》,2021年第5期,第48—55页。]

Gao, Fang, and Shi Xueying. "Understanding Literature from Both Conventional and Evolutionary Perspectives: An Interview with Nobel Laureate Jean-Marie Gustave Le Clézio." *Journal of SJTU (Philosophy and Social Sciences)* 2 (2023): 1 - 13.

[高方、施雪莹:《文学的守常与流变——访谈诺贝尔文学奖得主勒克莱齐奥》,载《上海交通大学学报(哲学社会科学版)》2023年第2期,第1—13页。]

Girardet, Raoul. *L'idée coloniale en France*, Paris: la table Ronde, 1972.

Glissant, Édouard. *Introduction à une Poétique du Divers*, Paris: Gallimard, 1996.

Kane, Cheikh Hamidou. *L'Aventure ambiguë*. Paris: Éditions Julliard, 1961.

Le Bris, Michel, et al., eds. *Pour une littérature-monde*. Paris: Gallimard, 2007.

Lestavel, François. "David Diop aux âmes, etc." *Paris Match*, le 23 août, 2021. Web. 30 Oct. 2022
⟨https://www.parismatch.com/Culture/Livres/David-Diop-aux-ames-etc-1753848⟩.

Marivat, Gladys. "Un pont entre deux rives." *Lire—Magazine littéraire*, N°499 (2021), p. 50 - 54.

Nancy, Jean-Luc. *La création du monde ou la mondialisation*. Paris: Galilée, 2002.

Said, Edward. W. *Orientalism*. Trans. Wang Yugen. Beijing: SDX Joint, 2019.

[萨义德:《东方学》,王宇根译。北京:生活·读书·新知三联书店,2019。]

Samoyault, Tiphaine. *L'Intertextualité. Mémoire de la littérature*. Paris: Nathan/HER, 2001.

Senghor, Léopold Sédar. *Hosties noires*, Paris, Edition du Seuil, 1948.

Tao, Sha. "A Neglected Group in World War I: The Senegalese Tirailleurs." *World Culture* 2 (2021): 33 - 35.

[陶沙:《"一战"中被忽视的群体——塞内加尔土著步兵形象》,《世界文化》,2021年第2期第33—35页。]

Wang, Tianyu, and Gao Fang. "The Cross-cultural Writing of Metaphors in *Frère d'Âme*." *Contemporary Foreign Literature* 3 (2020): 52 - 59.

[王天宇、高方:《〈灵魂兄弟〉中隐喻的跨文化书写》,《当代外国文学》,2020年第3期,第52—58页。]

论中上健次《十九岁的地图》动物化书写的现实主义内涵

宁 宇　王奕红

内容摘要：中上健次（1946—1992）是日本首位出生于"二战"之后的芥川奖获奖作家，于创作初期即怀有与大江健三郎文学创作的对话意识，专注于捕捉战后出生者眼中的新型现实。其中，短篇小说《十九岁的地图》(1973)以动物化的书写策略重新演绎了大江《奇妙的工作》《十七岁》的"监禁状态"、天皇制批判等主题，进而揭露繁荣的社会表象背后底层群体如动物般失语的生存困境，反映出1970年代初日本社会去历史化、去政治化乃至趋向动物化的时代走向，并进一步剖解了伴有歧视意义的动物化话语在社会话语空间中的运作机制，是充分展现早期中上现实主义书写特色的代表性作品。

关键词：中上健次　《十九岁的地图》　动物化书写　现实主义　大江健三郎

作者简介：宁宇，南京大学外国语学院博士研究生，主要从事现代日本文学研究。王奕红，南京大学外国语学院教授、博士生导师，主要从事日本文学与文化研究。

Title: The Realistic Connotations of Animalization Writing in Kenji Nakagami's *The Nineteen-Year-Old's Map*

Abstract: Kenji Nakagami (1946—1992) was the first Japanese author born after World War II to win the Akutagawa Prize. In the early stages of his career, he held a conscious dialogue with the literary creations of Kenzaburo Oe, focusing on capturing the new reality as seen through the eyes of those born after the war. In particular, his short story *The Nineteen-Year-Old's Map* (1973) employs an animalization writing strategy to reinterpret themes such as the "Confinement" and criticism of the Mikado system, echoing Oe's *An Odd Job* and *Seventeen*. Through this approach, Nakagami exposes the silenced existence of marginalized groups, akin to animals, concealed behind the facade of a prosperous society, reflecting the trend of Japanese society towards dehistoricization, depoliticization, and even animalization in the early 1970s. The story also dissected the mechanisms of animalization discourse with discriminatory undertones in the social discourse space, making *The Nineteen-Year-Old's Map* a representative work showcasing the distinctive features of Nakagami's early realism writing.

Key words: Kenji Nakagami; *The Nineteen-Year-Old's Map*; Animalization Writing; Realism; Kenzaburo Oe

Author: Ning Yu is a PhD Candidate at School of Foreign Studies, Nanjing University, China. His research interest is modern Japanese literature. Wang Yihong is a professor at School of Foreign Studies, Nanjing University, China. Her research interests are Japanese literature and culture.

1976年,中上健次(1946—1992)历经四次芥川奖候补后终于以《岬》(1975)斩获奖项,成为日本首位"二战"后出生的芥川奖获奖作家,并与此后登上文坛的村上龙、三田诚广等战后出生的作家共同"引领日本文学的时代浪潮"①(川村凑 340)。与其他同一代作家相比,中上的初期创作尤其呈现出大江健三郎文学的影响。究其所以,正如大江以继承日本战后文学为己任(《大江健三郎同时代论集》第1卷110),拓宽了战后日本文学的现实主义书写维度，中上对大江同样并未止于某种被动的接受，而是呈现出一种演绎与对话的姿态。大江出生、登上文坛约早于中上十年，作为文坛先驱固然是中上需要攀越的一座高峰[②]，更为重要的是，与大江文学的对话为中上审视自身所处现实提供了一条切实的途径。换言之，中上的初期创作从战后出生者的视角出发，并辅以自觉的历史意识探索、把握其所处的现实时，同样关注战后日本的现实状况的大江文学作为中上文学创作的参照物，具有不可或缺的功能和意义，这也正可谓中上将自己比作大江以后的战后第二代[③]的意义所在。据此而言，与大江文学的互文性为理解中上初期创作的现实主义书写特色提供了关键的切入点，1973年中上所作《十九岁的地图》（后文简称《地图》）则是典型地呈现出这种现实主义书写特色的作品。《地图》讲述了一名亦人亦狗的穷苦青年频繁拨打恐吓电话排解内心苦闷的故事，并以这一青年的视角揭露日本社会繁荣表象背后的种种问题。一方面，《地图》动物化的书写策略延续了早期大江《奇妙的工作》（1957）、《十七岁》（1961）等作品中动物意象内含的社会批判色彩；另一方面，《地图》与这些作品间的差异则再现了十年之间日本时代状况的变迁，同时反映出中上独特的反歧视问题意识。本文拟以动物化书写为切入点，关注《地图》如何依据1970年代初的日本社会现实重新演绎早期大江文学中"监禁状态"、天皇制批判等主题，并进一步考察这种现实表象背后中上独特的现实关怀和批判理路，明确《地图》现实主义书写的时代价值。

一、动物化书写对日本社会的去历史化批判

动物是贯穿《地图》始终的重要意象，《地图》主人公生活贫苦，于是自比徘徊在社会边缘的野狗，屡屡拨打恐吓电话报复社会，主人公的背后更有数名生活在社会底层、始终失语的"动物"角色，与主人公共同构

成了作品中底层群体的现实书写维度。无论是主人公自暴自弃意欲主动化作动物的举措，抑或作品中被动以动物形象示以读者的底层群体，在《地图》的动物化书写的背后，暗藏着边缘群体在日益繁荣的日本社会中被强制失语的压抑结构。这一压抑结构包含日本国内社会环境和国际社会关系的双重位相，根植于高速成长期的时代动向，呈现出1970年代日本社会的另一种"监禁状态"。

《地图》的主人公"我"是一名唾弃升学就业，感到未来无望的"上京青年"[④]，为了生计兼职送报。每日拂晓"我"便要起床摸黑送报，途中需要爬上一段长长的坡道，这条坡道空无一人，却多有野狗。由此，主人公为自己与家家户户中熟睡的人们间的落差而愤懑不已，路上野狗的丧家之犬形象更唤起孤身上京的"我"的自我认知，催发主人公主动宣称"我就是条狗。是一有破绽我就狠狠咬向你们的软肋的野兽"[⑤]（388）。自觉身处社会边缘的主人公要化身为趁"人"不备反咬一口的"狗"，这与主人公自觉并非社会意义上的"人"是同一回事，而主人公"哪能让你们活得那么惬意，这世间还有许多被你们忘了的家伙，等着趁机收拾你们呢"（387）的心理活动更暗示着《地图》中被社会所遗忘者不只主人公一人。事实上，隔壁公寓频频遭受家暴的女人、疑似暗娼的"疮疤玛丽亚"等角色都可谓被遗忘的社会"动物"。前者时不时与丈夫口角、曾开窗大喊"让世上的人都听听！"（407）却立马被强制关上窗户，希望世上的人倾听自己的境遇却以失败告终，屋内传出的只有"狗嚎叫一般的声音"（408）；后者被形容为浑身疮疤、营养不良、体态浮肿如河马一般，虽然一直哭诉自己求死不得，却对自身暗娼的生存境遇钳口不言。正如动物不具备人类的语言，二者在社会话语空间中隐形，其困境首先表征为某种失语症候。

包括集居在老旧公寓"鹤声庄"的孤寡老人、落魄的中年送报员室友绀野在内，《地图》所描绘的这些"动物"可谓一一对应着1970年，由日本经济白书官方规定的"贫困户"（貧困世帯）：其中包括"因事故灾害导致的单亲母亲家庭""因老龄化、身体精神障碍无法适应社会变化的阶层""被经济成长抛下的阶层"(岩田正美 194)等等。从 1970 年前后日本国内的社会环境来看,《地图》中失语的"动物"们生活在"一亿总中流"(也译全民中产)社会的阴翳之中,被排除在战后日本的经济神话之外。日本社会学者佐藤俊树就曾指出所谓的全民中产暗示着人人都平等地拥有攀升至上级阶层的可能性(89),这意味着全民中产更像是某种类似于起跑线的概念,尚不及起跑线的社会底层在这种言说中并无容身之处,难免被排除到目所不及的无意识层面,橄榄型的社会构造更加剧了他/她们的失语状态。上述吞噬弱者声音的社会压迫结构在这一时期的中上的文学表达中也被称作"以社会为名的软体动物"(《中上健次全集》第 1 卷 85),这不仅与大江所言"我们在黏液质的厚厚墙壁中规矩地活着"(《大江健三郎自选短篇》79)的"监禁状态"遥相呼应,《地图》主人公的野狗形象更可谓对大江《奇妙的工作》中处于"监禁状态"下的"狗"的戏仿。关于两部作品动物表象的异与同,可以结合两部作品的时代背景加以分析。

  作为早期大江文学表现"监禁状态"主题的代表作品之一,《奇妙的工作》围绕三名大学生处理医院实验用狗的"奇妙工作"展开,这些待宰的实验用狗被锁在柱子上"丧失了见人就咬的习性""连叫都不叫"(《奇妙的工作》2),这些实验用狗的形象在小说刊行时被平野谦、荒正人等批评家普遍视作同时代日本人精神状态的隐喻。与之相对,《地图》的主人公的野狗形象呈现出明显的攻击性,可谓截然不同。究其所以,《奇妙的工作》的"狗"的意象背后始终潜藏着日本"二战"战败后受美国占领、支配的权力关系,但在《地图》中这种权力关系在 1970 年代美国霸权衰退和多极化的时代背景下已逐渐失去了现实感。不仅如此,从《地图》主人公送的一份报纸上印有"国会解散"(380)的字样来看,可以确认故事时间处于 1972 年田中内阁解散前后,这意味着 1972 年的冲绳"返还"和中日复交同样是小说的重要时代背景。就前者而言,这一时间段处于越南战争后期，此时在美方的战争越南化政策下，冲绳逐渐摆脱美军后方基地的身份，并于1972年如期"返还"，日本社会层面的反美情绪渐趋消弭。而与后者相对应的是，主人公的室友绀野虽然自称"伪满洲"出身，在大连长大，他却被描述为说谎成性、没一句真话的男人；主人公更对教科书上的历史知识嗤之以鼻。这隐蔽地涉及了中日战争的历史，但无疑已经失去了其应有的厚重。

上述作品细节彰显着看似和平的高度成长社会中所隐藏的战争痕迹，也同时表现了时代条件制约下，战争的现实和历史所受到的遮蔽。进而言之，中美两国这两个对日本而言的巨大他者在《地图》中不仅丧失了存在感，连第二次世界大战的历史本身似乎都成了虚构，那么主人公在社会内部受到的压抑在社会外部缺乏投射或转移的对象，进而自认"见谁咬谁"的野狗也就绝非偶然。据此而言，未体验过太平洋战争乃至1968年的大学斗争，就连同时代的战争记忆都遭受着遗忘和遮蔽的《地图》主人公看似摆脱了《奇妙的工作》中"实验用狗"般完全无力的状态，事实上《地图》主人公的攻击欲只是国内的社会压迫结构与（战争）历史意识的消弭的双重压抑下的产物。不仅如此，这一双重压抑下的产物最终又以恐吓电话的形式，作为被压抑之物的回归（弗洛伊德116）对表面和平繁荣的社会形成反噬，在这层意义上，主人公野狗般的人物形象实为日本社会压迫和遗忘机制的倒影。如此，《地图》以压迫、遗忘和社会暴力之间的恶性循环结构，尝试呈现1970年代初，趋向均质的日本社会对少数受压抑者的新型"监禁状态"，准确地捕捉到了日本社会去历史化动向背后隐藏的现实症结。

二、动物化书写对日本社会的去政治化批判

如前所述，就野狗的形象和"监禁状态"的主题性而言，可以将《奇妙的工作》视作《地图》的前文本。在此基础上，《地图》进一步使主人公

具有右翼、天皇崇拜的倾向,这种将动物意象与天皇崇拜相结合的情节设定更与大江健三郎的《十七岁》(1961)⑥相呼应。确实,日本批评家渡部直已就曾提及《地图》与《十七岁》在"右翼"表象上呈现出了互文关系(174),但仍有必要从两部作品动物形象的关联性入手,进一步明确两部作品中"右翼"表象的异同及其意义所在。

《十七岁》以现实中的"浅沼稻次郎刺杀事件"为原型,描述了一名沉溺于自渎的17岁少年在加入右翼组织后逐渐偏激,妄想与"神"(天皇)合一,最终公然行凶乃至自我毁灭的故事。《十七岁》的主人公本就对自己孱弱的身心怀有自卑感,常常想象他人将自己视作软弱而不知羞耻的可鄙动物,在日常生活中像"刚刚脱换上软壳的螃蟹,孤独不安,极易受伤,弱小无力"(27)。而在主人公加入右翼组织后,他摇身一变将组织制服视作"甲虫一样的铠甲"(47),更幻想成为天皇这"永恒的大树上的一片嫩叶"(51)。与之相对,《地图》同样将主人公设定为沉溺于自渎的,"没有伟大的精神,只有性器官"(375)的动物化形象,并使主人公在右翼的名号下越陷越深,同样不甘于自居孱弱的动物,而是主动成为野兽来获得某种自我认同。在这层意义上,《地图》与《十七岁》都刻画了未曾实际经历战争时期日本的皇国体制,而是成长于象征天皇制的战后青年因天皇崇拜的蛊惑而误入歧途的问题。

然而,两部作品同中有异之处无疑更值得关注。具体而言,右翼身份在《地图》中不过是主人公动物化冲动的副产物,不再像《十七岁》一般能够充当主人公的精神支柱。《地图》主人公自称右翼是某次电话中的临时起意,只不过在挂掉电话后"如同呼唤恋人的名字一般"(387)对右翼一词的音响感到亢奋,久久不能忘怀。由此可见,右翼标签为"我"带来的只是联想"恋人的名字"一般的动物化(性)冲动。喃喃自语"我就是右翼"(388)之后,主人公紧接着又脱口而出一句"我就是条狗。是冷不防就要反咬你们一口的野兽"(388),更是无意间反讽了所谓的右翼,也使所谓的"神"彻底失去了超越性意义。换言之,《地图》颠倒了

《十七岁》中天皇崇拜与动物意象间的从属关系，这具体表现在两个层面：其一是《地图》主人公的右翼崇拜只是徒托空言，其二是《地图》主人公的动物化冲动更加占据其思考的支配性地位。

无论是政治思想的空洞，抑或是动物化冲动的强化，都可以基于1970年代初日本去政治化的时代背景进一步加以阐释，这也是《十七岁》与《地图》间的十年之差的具体表征。首先，与《十七岁》中描绘的左右翼针锋相对的图示不同，《地图》中所谓左、右翼的关系已经伴随着"政治的季节"的结束丧失了原有的张力关系。全共斗(1968)之后日美安保条约自动延长(1970)乃至浅间山庄事件(1972)等事件宣告了日本"政治的季节"结束，此后日本的新左翼运动逐渐失去群众基础，日本全共斗时期的"左翼国士"的形象逐渐转型成为"消费主体"。疋田雅昭指出，在这一过程中，右翼的形象仍无需与"暴力"的形象切割，由此右翼才毫无阻碍地成了《地图》主人公自我认同的道具(206)。如此，《地图》主人公的天皇崇拜只是主人公动物化表征的副产物，不再如《十七岁》一般，充当作品展开所需的核心矛盾。但与此同时，正如大江认为象征天皇制因其象征性质反而可以具有无比巨大的能量(《大江健三郎同时代论集》第1卷10)，《地图》中右翼、天皇观念即便空洞虚无却依然一度能够赋予主人公畸形的驱力，这也再次印证了《十七岁》所描绘的"普遍而深入地存在于日本人的外部和内部的天皇制及其阴影"(《作家能够绝对地反政治吗？》381)，由此延续了大江天皇制批判的脉络。

在此基础上，《地图》主人公表现出的动物化冲动同样可置于"政治的季节"结束的背景下加以把握。日本批评家东浩纪认为，在1970年之后日本的大叙事消解呈现出一种后历史的状态，对此，人们只有"动物化回归"或"清高主义化"两种进路。于此，东浩纪采取的是科耶夫对黑格尔哲学的阐释，其背景在于"二战"以后快餐化的美国式生活迅速扩散，在性产业与速食产业的高速发展下大众的生存不再需要与他者斗争乃至接触，而是陷入动物般"需要——满足"的封闭循环。所谓的"历史的终结"论固然有其局限性，但《地图》主人公平日吃泡面度日、为性冲动支配、沉溺于自慰的即时满足的行为模式，确实呈现出一种明显的动物化回归倾向。与之相应，主人公表现出的野狗般的攻击欲，看似是某种（黑格尔/科耶夫语境下）"人"之为"人"所必须的"斗争"，但主人公的"斗争"实则同样为动物化冲动所裹挟。如此，《地图》主人公的矛盾性形象一方面可谓1970年代前后日本社会去政治化转型的象征，另一方面则预示了日本社会的动物化倾向。而在1970年代初日本左翼退潮与去政治化的双重背景下，《地图》在延续早期大江文学的天皇制批判的同时展现出对同时代社会现实的精确把握，并以动物化书写在衍生出现实寓言的深层内涵。

三、动物化书写对日本社会的话语空间批判

上文探讨了《地图》的动物化书写如何在与大江文学的对话中相对化地捕捉、批判时代状况。但不仅如此，《地图》的动物化书写以"人为何要主动成为动物"这一问题切入了社会歧视话语的双向运作机制，可谓呈现出了中上文学独有的特色，开拓了《奇妙的工作》和《十七岁》的动物意象所展现的视野。《地图》的结局更描绘了社会"动物"间的共鸣，表露出反歧视的积极愿景和伦理关怀。《地图》的双向视野与现实关怀与中上出身被歧视部落的个人经历息息相关，于探究中上文学现实主义书写的特色而言不可或缺。

《地图》采取了动物化的书写策略，而与动物化有关的话语往往强调动物非人的等级观念，源自一种人类中心主义的物种主义（Speciesism）思考，伴有歧视意识。对此，阿甘本曾追溯历史，指出西欧文化中"支配着所有其他冲突的最关键的政治冲突就是人的动物性和人性之间的冲突"（96），在这种强调人与非人（动物）的区别的"人类机

制"(一译人类学机器)中,一些人可以比另一些人更像人,并在人种、宗教、性别等领域中逆向生产人的动物化(非人化)话语。值得注意的是,上述动物与人的关系在出身被歧视部落的中上的文学语境中同样重要。日本的部落歧视问题有着较为深远的文化背景,且至今仍然根深蒂固。日语中的"非人"一词乃至暗指四肢行走的动物的"四",都是对部落民的歧视语,这种歧视又与部落民曾专职牲畜屠宰业的历史息息相关。事实上,《地图》主人公也曾自称"畜生"(376,日语原文"人非人"),又时时在电话中恐吓要像肉店屠夫一般"处理"对方,这不仅隐蔽地涉及了歧视问题的历史记忆,其中也不乏被歧视者自白的意味,可谓与主人公声称自己就是狗的行为逻辑如出一辙。在这一点上,中上可谓在歧视/反歧视的论域中通过主人公的自我动物化别出心裁地提出了"人为何要主动成为动物"的问题。

为明确《地图》中"人主动成为动物"的批判意义所在,《地图》刊行两年后日本发生的"东亚反日武装战线"事件是一个无法绕过的参照物。在这起被戏称这正是"《十九岁的地图》作者引起的"(松本健一,202)的事件中,主谋"东亚反日武装战线"不仅重申日本于国内外推行殖民压迫的历史,将所谓的"市民社会"[②]和大企业视作日本帝国主义和殖民主义的帮凶,呼吁社会底层的劳动者奋起对抗(《腹腹时钟》2-4),并以"狼"为代号展开恐怖行动,对三菱重工等大企业进行爆破造成三百余人伤亡。于此,从动物与人的对立到底层群体与市民社会的对立,再到爆破的行径,"东亚反日武装战线"事件都可谓与《地图》的结构呈现出高度的相似性,正可谓"人主动成为动物"的典型现实案例。值得关注的是,中上围绕这起事件作出了一篇名为《愤怒与饥饿》的随笔,这篇随笔作为《地图》的副文本,其重要性在于中上补充了《地图》中所缺乏的"人类",或者说"市民"的视角。

具体而言,在这篇随笔里,中上关注的并非"动物"一方的行动逻辑,反而是市民社会中所流通社会言论的形态,其中尤以一篇新闻报道的标题《市民的假面,狼的心》使中上感到格外刺眼(《中上健次全集》第14卷196)。无疑,中上一眼看破了"假面"或"心"等用词所隐藏的叙事逻辑,取自清高之意的"狼"代号在世间看来只是狼子野心,在这种言说中狼小队被排除到了人类社会以外,成了潜藏在人类社会的动物、搅乱繁荣清梦的敌人,也是破坏社会契约、使他的个人利益与其他所有人的利益相对立的"社会成立以前的林中野人"(Foucault 91)。换言之,上述社会言论意味着恐怖事件中绝非只存有"狼"对"人"的单方向敌意或暴力,在市民假面、动物内心的叙事框架中,社会大众将边缘群体视作刻意隐藏本性的野兽,再次正当化了自身对边缘群体的避讳和遗忘。然而,也正是在这一叙事框架中,社会大众的忽视和遗忘反而也是底层"动物"趁其不备反击与报复社会的有利条件,狼小队与所谓的"市民社会"必然在某种程度上共享同一叙事框架,二者共同创造着社会中动物与市民相对立的故事,成为歧视意识滋生的温床。从这种视角回望《地图》可见,主人公同样遵循着这一叙事框架报复社会,这既意味着主人公深深地内面化了这种人与动物的歧视性叙事框架,也意味着主人公的报复行为绝非反抗社会歧视和社会不公平的举措,毋宁说主人公正是依据着同一种歧视框架变相地行使着社会歧视。由此可见,如果说《奇妙的工作》《十七岁》等早期大江文学作品所描绘的人对动物的暴力,本身即映射人对人暴力的手段(村上克尚129),那么《地图》的动物化书写则通过主人公"主动成为动物"的举措,讲述了人同样可以借动物的名号对他者施以暴力,反向地暴露出歧视意识的危害所在。

就此而言,从《地图》的动物叙事已经能够窥见中上数年后所谓"歧视就是结构"(《中上健次全》第14卷678)观点的萌芽,但不应忽视的是,《地图》仍为主人公留存了摆脱这一歧视框架的希望。小说尾声,主人公在向东京火车站拨打恐吓电话并遭到冷嘲之后,终于开始直面自身的境遇。此时,放下电话的"我"已不再是狗或右翼或神中的任何一方,只是涕泗横流地自觉又变回了那个"白痴送报员"。此时,主人公不仅发觉自身对"市民社会"的报复荒唐而徒劳,更在涕泗横流中开始不受控地幻听疮疤玛利亚的哭喊声。于此,由凌驾于"我"的"人"、企图成为凶猛野兽的"我"、"我"所鄙夷的弱小"动物"这三项关系所组成的认知结构已经倾覆。而主人公的幻听更展现了,即使主人公"我"在文本全篇始终只是对隔壁女人和疮疤玛利亚持鄙夷态度,实际上却仍未丧失与她们相互感知、相互接纳的能力。进而言之,正因为这种相互感知并非"我"有意而为,反而使其超越了基于主观移情机制的自我感伤式同情,可谓达成了酒井直树所言能够突破现代社会中人与人之间异化关系的"'相互触摸'的政治"(3)。据此,部分既往观点认为《地图》的结尾只是批判或讥嘲了主人公,恐怕并不完全妥当。正相反,《地图》看似压抑讽刺的作品基调中不时闪烁着中上含蓄而切实的社会关怀,"我"与隔壁女人、疮疤玛丽亚等社会弱者在不自知间构成的连带关系中暗含中上对跨越歧视、暴力的瞩望。正是小说尾声中主人公的"身体中心的结晶溶解后从眼窝流淌出的热泪"(414),为早期中上文学的现实主义书写注入了一股真挚的暖流。

结　语

均质社会趋向封闭、社会生活去政治化、现实认知去历史化,《地图》继承大江健三郎文学中社会批判的文脉,以动物化的书写策略反映和剖析1970年代初的日本社会的上述问题,并进一步尝试揭露日本社会对边缘群体的遗忘、压抑,以及普遍存在于这种遗忘与压抑背后的社会歧视意识。当然,上述批判理路不仅限于早期中上的文学创作,也延续到了中上此后以被歧视部落为主体的"路地"书写之中,在这层意义上,早期中上文学的现实关怀于中上的创作生涯贯彻始终,同时为中上文学带来了时代证言和时代批判的双重底蕴。

注解【Notes】

① 本文引用的外文文本均为笔者所译。
② 一般的文学史观点认为中上登场于"内向一代"之后。但需要注意的是,"内向一代"的命名基于1970年川村二郎的论文《内部季节的丰饶》,经由1971年小田切秀雄命名"内向一代"后固定化。而早期中上的文学活动在时间上与"内向一代"的前后关系其实并不明显。相较而言,早期中上自我定位时始终以大江为参照,而此后则对"内向一代"持批判态度较多。
③ 中上生于1946年,大江生于1935年;二者的亮相作品分别为1969年的《最开头的事》和1957年的《奇妙的工作》。此外,大江自命为战后文学的继承者,中上则曾在和村上龙的对谈《我们的航船在静止的雾霭中解开缆绳》(1976)中表明大江是第一代战后,自己是第二代战后,村上属于第三代。
④ 上京指从日本的其他地区来到东京。
⑤ 本文引用的小说文本采用中上健次著《十九岁的地图》,收入《中上健次全集第1卷》(1995)。此后的文本引用只随文标注页码。
⑥ 本文将《十七岁》及其续作《政治少年之死》(1961)两部作品统称为《十七岁》。
⑦ 战后日本语境下的"市民社会"一词,可以定义为伴随1960年代日本高度成长期成立的消费社会。参见拓植光彦:《日常与非日常的夹缝》,《讲座昭和文学史》第4卷。东京:有精堂,1989年,第9页。

引用文献【Works Cited】

Alexandre, Kojève. *Introduction to the Reading of Hegel*. Trans. Jiang Zhihui. Nanjing: Yilin Press, 2005.

[科耶夫:《黑格尔导读》,姜志辉译,南京:译林出版社,2005年。]

Azuma, Hiroki. *Animalizing Postmodernity*. Trans. Zhu Xuanchu. Taipei: BIG ART co, 2012.

[东浩纪:《动物化的后现代》,褚炫初译,台北:大鸿芸术股份有限公司,2012年。]

Hikita, Masaaki: "Struggle of Words and Flight from Words: Exploring Kenji Nakagami's 'The Nineteen-Year-Old's Map'" *Bulletin of Tokyo Gakugei University. Humanities and Social Sciences*. Ⅰ. 69(2018): 198 - 212.

[疋田雅昭:《话语的"斗争"与从"话语"处逃遁:以中上健次〈十九岁的地图〉为中心》,载《东京学艺大学纪要.人文社会科学系.Ⅰ69》2018年,第198—212页。]

Iwata, Masami. *Aftermath History of Poverty: How Has the 'Shape' of Poverty Changed Post-War?* Tokyo: Chikuma Shobo, 2018.

[岩田正美:《贫困的战后史——贫困的"形态"是如何变化的?》,东京:筑摩书房,2018年。]

Kawamura, Minato. "Commentary a Chronicle of Modern Novels: *1975～1979*"

Japanese Literature Association, eds. *A Chronicle of Modern Novels: 1975~ 1979*. Tokyo: Kodansha, 2014: 340 - 345.

［川村凑:《解说现代小说年代记——1975～1979》,日本文艺家协会编:《现代小说年代记 1975～1979》,东京:讲谈社,2014 年,第 340—345 页。］

Matsumoto, Kenichi. "Contemporary Bombs" Kenji, Nakagami. *The Nineteen-Year-Old's Map*. Tokyo: Kawade Shobo Shinsha, 1994: 216 - 222.

［松本健一:《同时代的炸弹》,中上健次:《十九岁的地图》,东京:河出书房新社,1994 年,第 216—222 页。］

Michel, Foucault. *Abnormal Lectures at The Collège De France* 1974 - 1975. Trans. Graham Burchell. London: VERSO, 2003.

Murakami, Katsunao. *The Voice of The Animal, The Voice of The Other: The Ethics of Postwar Japanese Literature*. Tokyo: Shinyosha, 2017.

［村上克尚:《动物之声,他者之声:日本战后文学的伦理》,东京:新曜社,2017 年。］

Nakagami, Kenji. *The Complete Works of Kenji Nakagami 1*. Tokyo: Shueisha, 1995.

［中上健次:《中上健次全集》第 1 卷,东京:集英社,1995 年。］

---. *Compilation of Statements by Kenji Nakagami 1*. Tokyo: Daisan Bunmei-Sha, 1995.

［中上健次:《中上健次发言集成》第 1 卷,东京:第三文明社,1995 年。］

---. *The Complete Works of Kenji Nakagami 14*. Tokyo: Shueisha, 1996.

［中上健次:《中上健次全集》第 14 卷,东京:集英社,1996 年。］

Naoki, Sakai. *Hikikomori Nationalism*. Tokyo: Iwanami Shoten, 2017.

［酒井直树:《蛰居式的民族主义》,东京:岩波书店,2017 年。］

Oe, Kenzaburo. "Can a Writer Remain Absolutely Anti-political?" *Complete Works of Oe Kenzaburo 3*. Tokyo: Shinchosha, 1966: 372 - 86.

［大江健三郎:《作家能够绝对地反政治吗?》,《大江健三郎全作品》第 3 卷,东京:新潮社,1966 年,第 371—86 页。］

---. *Collection of Contemporary Essays of Kenzaburo Oe 1*. Tokyo: Iwanami Shoten, 1980.

［大江健三郎:《大江健三郎同时代论集》第 1 卷,东京:岩波书店,1980 年。］

---. "An Odd Job" Trans. Si Hai. *Lavish Are the Dead*. Beijing: Guangming Daily Press, 1995.

［大江健三郎:《奇妙的工作》,斯海译,大江健三郎著:《死者的奢华》,北京:光明日报出版社,1995 年。］

---. *Self-Selected Stories of Kenzaburo Oe*. Tokyo: Iwanami Bunko, 2014.

［大江健三郎:《大江健三郎自选短篇小说》,东京:岩波文库,2014 年。］

Sato, Toshiki. *Japan as an Unequal Society*. Tokyo: Chuokoron Shinsha, 2000.

［佐藤俊树:《不平等的日本》,东京:中央公论新社,2000年。］

Sigmund, Freud. *Moses and Monotheism*. Trans. Li Zhankai. Beijing: SDX Joint Publishing Company, 1992.

［弗洛伊德:《摩西与一神教》,李展开译,北京:生活・读书・新知三联书店,1992年。］

The East Asia Anti-Japan Armed Front "Wolf" Soldier Reader Compiled by the Editorial Committee. *Hara Hara Tokei*. Tokyo: East Asia Anti-Japan Armed Front "Wolf" Information Department, Propaganda Bureau, 1974.

［东亚反日武装战线"狼"士兵读本编纂委员会:《腹腹时钟》,东京:东亚反日武装战线"狼"情报部情宣局,1974年。］

Watanabe, Naomi. *So Delicate a Tyranny: A Literary Analysis of Japanese Novels from 1968*. Tokyo: Kodansha, 2003.

［渡部直己:《如此细腻的凶暴:日本"六八年"小说论》,东京:讲谈社,2003年。］

藏原惟人"新写实主义"理论在中国左翼文坛的译介与运用
——以"太阳社"为中心

顾宇玥

内容摘要：在 1928 年中国左翼文坛爆发的"革命文学"论争中，太阳社率先译介了日本左翼理论家藏原惟人的"新写实主义"论，以此作为"新兴文学"重要的理论支柱。太阳社关注"藏原理论"，既是缘于新兴文学实践过程中自然产生的文艺理论诉求，又存在与创造社"理论竞备"的现实契机。而"新写实主义"在中国左翼文坛的批评实践及其演变轨迹，实际与太阳、创造二社同茅盾有关"革命文学"的论争相伴相生。在茅盾与钱杏邨的对话关系中，正是对于"新写实主义"之无意/有意的误读，部分造成了论争的错位、激化，并实质上影响了这一理论在中国的阐释路径及走向，"钱杏邨理论"与"藏原理论"之差异亦由此呈现。钱杏邨的理论取舍与得失并非孤例，而是折射出早期中国左翼文艺理论实践的普泛性困境。

关键词：新写实主义　革命文学　钱杏邨　茅盾　误读

作者简介：顾宇玥，江苏开放大学外国语学院教师，主要从事中国现代文学研究。

Title: The Translation and Utilization of Kurahara Korehito's Theory of "New Realism" in the Chinese Left-Wing Literary Sphere—Centering on the Sun Society

Abstract: During the "revolutionary literature" controversy that broke out in the left-wing literary circles in China in 1928, the Sun Society took the lead in translating and introducing Japanese left-wing theorist Kurahara Korehito's theory of "new realism" as an important theoretical pillar of the "emerging literature". The Sun Society's concern for the Kurahara's theory is not only due to the demand for literary theory that naturally arises in the process of emerging literary practice, but also due to the realistic opportunity of "theoretical competition" with the Creation Society. The critical practice of "New Realism" and its evolution in the left-wing literary circles in China actually accompanied by the debates on "revolutionary literature" between the Sun Society, the Creation Society, and Mao Dun. In the dialogue between Mao Dun and Qian Xingcun, it is the unintentional/intentional misinterpretation of "New Realism" that partly causes the misplacement and intensification of the debate, and substantially affects the path of interpretation and direction of this theory in China, and the difference between "Qian Xingcun's Theory" and "Kurahara's theory" is also presented as a result. Qian Xingcun's theoretical trade-offs and gains and losses are not an isolated case, but reflect the generalized dilemma of early Chinese left-wing literary theory and practice.

Key words: new realism; revolutionary literature; Qian Xingcun; Mao Dun; misreading

Author: GU Yuyue is a lecturer at School of Foreign Languages, Jiangsu Open University, China. Her research interest is modern Chinese literature.

在1928年爆发的"革命文学"论争中,随着茅盾《从牯岭到东京》一文的发表,继鲁迅、郁达夫之后,太阳社、创造社又与茅盾之间,围绕"革命""现实""小资产阶级"等一系列问题展开了激烈的争论。其中,太阳、创造二社所援引的关键理论资源,就是日本藏原惟人在同期所提出的"普罗列塔利亚写实主义"论(即"新写实主义"论)。同样是在这场论争中,钱杏邨作为"革命文学"初期的代表性左翼理论家登上了历史舞台,而"钱杏邨理论"与"藏原理论"间也存在密切的承袭与关联。可见"藏原理论"是我们深入理解"革命文学"论争所不可绕开的重要一环。此外,虽然"藏原理论"之核心——"新写实主义"论在风靡一阵之后很快又为"社会主义现实主义"的新理论所取代,但其中的一些内核观念却在左翼文坛之中长久的遗存。因此,"新写实主义"并非"革命文学"风潮中"昙花一现"的舶来品和理论工具,而是深刻影响了中国左翼文学的走向与进程。

一、"理论竞备"与"文学本位"
——"新写实主义"理论的引介契机

藏原惟人是近现代日本左翼文坛重要的文艺理论家和批评家。作为日本共产党的文化方面负责人,在日本无产阶级文艺运动的"纳普"至"克普"阶段,藏原的理论活动深刻影响了运动的方向与进程,并最终决定了其走向与成败。1928年5月,藏原惟人在《战旗》杂志创刊号发表著名文章《普罗列塔利亚写实主义的路》,正式提出和阐发了"普罗列塔利亚写实主义"的理论主张。同年7月,林伯修将该文翻译为中文,并将题名改译为《到新写实主义之路》,发表于《太阳月刊》的停刊号上。相较于"普罗列塔利亚写实主义","新写实主义"的译名既有规避国民党书报审查制度的考量,亦有在"新——旧"对比中凸显理论新锐之意,自此起"新写实主义"也成为这一理论的主流指称而在国内广泛传播。

太阳社对于藏原惟人的译介,既是出于对世界左翼文坛,尤其是日本左翼文坛情势的及时关注和深切的理论洞察,也与当时中国文坛所活跃的另一大"革命文学"团体创造社的动向密切相关。1927年底,后期创造社成员李初梨、冯乃超、朱镜我等甫一归国登上文坛,就展现出了极强的理论意识和新锐视野。成仿吾为《文化批判》创刊号所作《祝词》,开篇就引列宁的名言"没有革命的理论,没有革命的行动",并宣言"'文化批判'将贡献全部的革命的理论,将给予革命的全战线以郎朗的光火"(1-2)。而《文化批判》杂志也正以理论之纷繁,名词之驳杂晦涩著称。相较之下,前期太阳社则更加注重文学创作而相对忽视理论活动。蒋光慈就曾言:"我不爱空谈理论,我以为与其空谈什么空空洞洞的理论,不如为事实的表现,因为革命文学是实际的艺术的创作,而不是几篇不可捉摸的论文所能建设出来的。"(《蒋光慈文集》第4卷166)钱杏邨也曾暗讽创造社"没有外国书可抄,没有革命文学的理论",呼唤文坛应"抛弃了一味只相信理论的迷梦",回归社会实际与现实实践(《批评与抄书》1-4)。

然而,理论素养的匮乏很快就让太阳社在与创造社争夺"革命文学"话语权的过程中感到力不从心。在双方停止论争而统一战线后,太阳社最终自我检讨道:"过去的本刊没有注意系统的理论的建设,缺乏重要的理论与翻译,描写的范围狭小单调。"(《编后》1)当然,太阳、创造二社从交锋到休战的个中因素错综复杂,也绝非"理论与创作"分歧之单一向度可以概括[1]。但与创造社的论争无疑促使太阳社意识到理论资源之重要性,同时其所一贯注重的新兴文学实践(即"革命文学")也需要新的文学理论来促进发展。正是基于此,太阳社开始了对日本左翼文坛新兴的"藏原理论"之全面关注。

在译介理论的同时,太阳社同人与藏原惟人亦有过一段宝贵的交游经历。1929年8月,蒋光慈因病赴日修养。在此期间,经由当时的"中国通"——日本作家藤枝丈夫的引介,拜访结识了藏原惟人。蒋光慈并不擅于日语,但他与藏原惟人都有在莫斯科东方大学留学的经历,

---

[1] 有关太阳社与创造社二社内部"革命文学"论争情况始末,详见张广海:《"革命文学"论争与阶级文学理论的兴起》,北京大学博士学位论文,2011年。

因此二人的交流"少见"的以俄语形式展开，对话的内容也以双方所熟悉的苏俄文坛为开端。据蒋光慈《异邦与故国》记载，在日期间他一共四次拜访藏原惟人，在藏原的藏书中借阅了不少俄文批评集和长篇小说。其间二人又以友人漫谈的形式，交流了有关"俄文坛的现状，中国的普洛文学，日本的作家""文学家与实际工作""未来主义与新写实主义"以及中日文坛翻译现状等众多现实议题（《蒋光慈文集》第2卷462、476、479、487）。

这其中10月22日二人的第三次会面及长谈尤为值得关注。据蒋光慈记录，他与藏原就"新写实主义"的问题交换了不同意见。双方都赞同"新写实主义"在形式上的新特点是"动性"和"节势"，分歧则在于其究竟是受到俄国"未来主义"还是现代工业生活的影响（479）。事实上，藏原的观念在其随后发表的《向新艺术形式的探求去》（载1929年12月《改造》）中有更为系统的阐发。文章将未来派和无产阶级文学等现代文艺思潮都放置在大都会与机械时代的资本主义大背景下进行考察，从而发现无产艺术部分继承了未来派关于"美"的见解，同时也发扬了其"力学的，敏捷的"特征（12-46）。虽然没有明确的材料证明该文的写作受到此前与蒋光慈对谈的触动与启发，但藏原的这一论断实然又构成了谈话之中双方观念的综合。

如果说林伯修和吴之本的主要贡献是向国内文坛译介——引入了"藏原理论"；蒋光慈凭借文学家阅读与创作的"实感"而与藏原产生了共鸣，又在对话与交流之中加深了对于"新写实主义"的理解；那么钱杏邨就是系统性地将"藏原理论"运用于国内"革命文学"理论建设与批评实践的"第一人"。钱杏邨的《"动摇"》（书评）与林伯修译《到新写实主义之路》一同刊载于《太阳月刊》停刊号，在这篇文章中他已经率先开始运用"新/旧写实主义"的二元概念对茅盾的创作进行定性。而1930年出版的《怎样研究新兴文学》一书，则是钱氏综合运用"藏原理论"的代表性著述。据统计，该书所引述的藏原文论不下八篇，囊括了其同期对于"新写实主义"理论、意识形态论、内容与形式关系、俄罗斯文艺等多方问题的重要思考,且钱杏邨的观点也基本延续了藏原的论断和认知。书稿特别以介绍藏原"新写实主义"论"作为全书的总结"(118),亦可以证明钱杏邨将"新写实主义"的理论主张视作"新兴文学"思潮之核心与关键所在。

二、从"时代题材"到"阶级立场"
——太阳社与茅盾的对话和论争

旷新年曾提出:"在中国,作为'新写实主义'译介的重要背景和'潜对话'是1928年底创造社、太阳社和茅盾之间的争论。"(136)鲁迅也曾讥讽在"革命文学"论战中,钱杏邨是"挽着藏原惟人,一段又一段的,在和茅盾扭结"(246)。因此,当我们试图追踪"新写实主义"理论在中国左翼文坛的批评实践及其演变时,就有必要将其放置在太阳社,尤其是其中的主将钱杏邨与茅盾对话、论争之结构关系中加以考察。

太阳社与茅盾之间的关系,以茅盾《从牯岭到东京》一文的发表为分水岭。此前,双方基本保持着较为友好的互动、交流。蒋光慈曾多次表示茅盾"是我们的友人"(《蒋光慈文集》第4卷175)。《太阳月刊》创刊后,茅盾也立刻写作《欢迎〈太阳〉》,向文艺界"郑重介绍"了这一刊物,且尤为推介小将钱杏邨的文学批评。这篇批评之所以能获得茅盾的青睐,关键在于其始终紧扣"创作"与"时代"的关系命题:"伟大的创作是没有一部离开了它的时代的。不但不离开时代,有时还要超越时代,创造时代,永远的站在时代前面。"(《阿英全集》第1卷233)"时代"正是钱杏邨早期文艺批评中的一个重要概念。在对《幻灭》的书评中,钱杏邨亦从"时代"的维度给予小说很高的评价,认为茅盾"认清了文学的社会的使命,在创作中把整个的时代色彩表现了出来"(《"幻灭"》1)。可以说,对于文学"时代性"的强调,恰恰构成了前期太阳社与茅盾得以

"对话",甚至相互"欣赏"的基础。

然而,双方之间的友好"对话"随着《从牯岭到东京》的发表而中止,并即刻转为紧张的论战。在这篇关键性的文章中,茅盾首先宣称了自我由左拉——托尔斯泰,由自然主义——写实主义之文学理念的转变,在此基础上自陈了《蚀》三部曲之创作心路,认为这三篇创作只是"忠实的时代描写",而并非积极指引"出路"的"革命小说";再者,茅盾又对于当下国内文坛兴盛的"革命文艺"提出了异议,指出其中存在着"标语口号文学"倾向,"读者对象"认识局限以及文艺描写技巧的三方面问题,尤其呼唤推动"新文艺走到小资产阶级市民的队伍去"(《茅盾全集》第19卷176-194)。目前学界对于《从牯岭到东京》一文的细读,包括对于由此引发的"革命文学"论争的阐释已不胜枚举。而本文则希望能从"新写实主义"的特定视角,重新对这一问题进行梳理分析。

可以说,茅盾对于"革命文艺"的发难,一个重要原因即他对太阳社所倡导的"新写实主义"理论存在"误读"。据茅盾晚年回忆:"我讲到文艺的技巧问题,还因为我曾在广告上看见《太阳》七月号(后来成为终刊号)上有一篇评论《到新写实主义的路》,但未见原文,不知是什么主张。"(《我走过的道路》24)而他所联想到的是自己在1924年《小说月报》发表的《俄国的新写实主义及其他》一文中曾提到的"新写实主义",由是认为:

> 新写实主义起于实际的逼迫;当时俄国承白党内乱之后,纸张非常缺乏,定期刊物或报纸的文艺栏都只有极小的地位,又因那时的生活是紧张的疾变的,不宜于弛缓迂迥的调子,那就自然而然产生了一种适合于此种精神律奏和实际困难的文体,那就是把文学作品的章段句字都简练起来,省去不必要的环境描写和心理描写,使成为短小精悍,紧张,有刺激性的一种文体,因为用字是愈省愈好,仿佛打电报,所以最初有人戏

称为"电报体",后来就发展成为新写实主义。(《茅盾全集》第19卷191-192)

茅盾所介绍的"新写实主义"显然不是指太阳社新近引入的"藏原理论",而是苏俄革命时期一种特殊的文学产物。但在茅盾的理解中,这种"短小精悍,紧张,有刺激性"的文体追求正恰恰为"革命文艺""不能摆脱'标语口号文学'的拘囿",缺失"文艺的价值"而找到了"理论根源";同时他认为,不理解中苏两国国情之差异而盲目"移植"新的文艺技巧,也必然会造成理论倡导与时代、社会现实的脱节,造成了"革命文艺"对其事实上的广大读者"小资产阶级"群体的漠视。因此,对于"新写实主义"理论的"误读"实际构成了茅盾批判"革命文艺"逻辑理路的核心一环。

茅盾的檄文发表后,钱杏邨一反此前对其小说书写"革命的实际",表现"时代性"的赞许,而与创造社达成了立场的一致。钱氏随后发表《从东京回到武汉》,严厉批判了茅盾"信仰"之"叛变"。该文最后一节取名为《从东京回到武汉——关于新写实主义问题》,专题对比分析了藏原与茅盾所提的两种"新写实主义"之间的差异,并彻底否定了"茅盾先生关于新写实主义技巧的两个问题,根本上是没有讨论的可能性的"(《阿英全集》第1卷367)。茅盾自言"从牯岭到东京",以空间之腾挪暗示自我身份、观念之转换;钱杏邨反用这一隐喻,由东京(日本左翼思潮兴盛之地)而至武汉(大革命落潮之所),暗示了茅盾革命态度的"回转"与"倒退";在与"新写实主义"的对照之中呈现了茅盾"资产阶级旧写实主义"创作理念之"落伍"与"错误"。

一则容易被忽视的材料,是茅盾本人在《读〈倪焕之〉》这篇回驳文章中的这段表述:

所谓时代性,我以为,在表现了时代空气而外,还应该有两个要义：一是时代给与人们以怎样的影响，二是人们的集团的活力又怎样地将时代推进了新方向，换言之，即是怎样地催促历史进入了必然的新时代，再换一句说，即是怎样地<u>由于人们的集团的活动而及早实现了历史的必然</u>。在这样的意义下，<u>方是现代的新写实派文学所要表现的时代性</u>！（《茅盾全集》第 19 卷 165）

这里茅盾以肯定"新写实派文学"存在之合理性为前提的论述，其实已然隐晦表达了他对于"新写实主义"理论的部分认同，只不过这种微妙的认同往往淹没在他对于"革命文学"派的回击，尤其是对创造社由"艺术"——"革命"转向之快的指摘中而不易被察觉。显然在此前论战中，太阳、创造二社对于"新写实主义"的不断"正名释义"，促成了茅盾对于这一理论的正视和理解。因而他也开始尝试在对小说"时代性"的一贯文学倡导之中，融入"藏原理论"所强调的"集团"之观点和意识，以达成自身对于"新写实主义"的诠释和求同。换言之，随着"误读"的消解，茅盾的立场已经向"革命文学"派有所靠拢。

但是，茅盾立场的松动并没有提前结束这场论争。正相反的是，作为太阳社的理论干将，钱杏邨对于茅盾的攻讦反而愈演愈烈。当我们试图理解钱杏邨对茅盾由"引为同道"到"铲除异己"的姿态转变时，也必须结合其对于"新写实主义"理论的"接受——理解"历程来进行解读。《茅盾与现实》一文由钱杏邨将其不同时期对于茅盾小说的四篇评论整合汇集而成。在这篇长文的序引中，钱杏邨清晰表述了自我在写作过程中批评立场的巨大转变：

我的考察是分为四部分的，一是他的《幻灭》的考察，二是他的《动摇》的考察，这一部分自己认为是最不满意的，<u>我没有站在新兴阶级文学的立场上去考察</u>，差不多把精神完全注在创作与时代的关系的一点上去了。重作既在事实上为不可能，只好把它们留在这里了。第三是对他的《追求》的考察，四是关于他的《野蔷薇》的考察。这二篇，在立场上自信是没有错误的，可是仍旧不是我满意的东西。(《阿英全集》第 2 卷 168-169)

钱杏邨态度逆转的实质是其"批评标准"由反映"创作与时代的关系"到呈现"新兴阶级文学的立场"的转变，是由"时代文艺"到"阶级文艺"的方向转换。四篇评论中，第二篇《动摇》的书评写作于 1928 年 5 月 29 日，而第三篇考察《追求》的书信则写作于 1928 年 10 月 18 日，在这两篇文章写作的间隔期间，影响钱杏邨态度转变的文坛动向，一则是茅盾的檄文《从牯岭到东京》的发表，二则是藏原的译作《到新写实主义之路》的引入。

日本学者芦田肇指出，藏原惟人的"新写实主义"论正是造成"钱杏邨的批评原理发生质变"的"直接原因"，钱杏邨选择接受了"藏原理论"之中"'用无产阶级前卫的眼睛'观察世界"的"第一命题"，而相对忽视了"以严正的现实主义者的态度进行描写"的"第二命题"，这就造成其关注的重心由"时代"转向作者的"立场"和"思想"。至于他为何在两项命题中专注前者而忽略后者，芦田肇认为这是缺失"现实的基础"就"从日本机械地输入"而发生的理论"错位"(24-52)。芦田肇对于钱杏邨接受藏原理论之脉络的现象梳理基本正确，但对于其中原因的归纳则有待商榷。值得追问的是，如果仅仅是简单的机械输入理论，那么为何又在其中有所选择偏重？这种选择究竟是源于"现实基础"的缺失，还是因为钱杏邨与藏原在论战之中所面对的"现实"并不相同呢？

藏原惟人在《到新写实主义之路》中曾提出过一个重要论断："普罗列搭利亚作家，决不单以战斗的普罗列搭利亚特为他的题材"，"他只是在那时候，将用其阶级的观点——用现在的唯一的客观的观点——去描写牠吧。问题只在作家的观点,不必在其题材"(16)。藏原这句话所针对的现状,是当时日本普罗文学只以"工人""劳动者"为描写对象而导致的题材单一化倾向;他将判定标准由"题材"转换为"观点",目的是在保证立场正确的同时"拓展"左翼文艺的题材和视野。而在中国文坛,"革命文学"论战状况则反其道而行之。前文提到,太阳社与茅盾最初在"文学反映时代"这一认知上达成共识,因此即使描写的对象是"小资产阶级",只要其反映了时代的一种面向,依旧可以被视为"革命文学"创作。换言之,"时代题材"构成了钱杏邨早期文学批评的"标准",这一标准实则也是相对包容且开放的。

然而,自《从牯岭到东京》起,茅盾在创作小资产阶级"题材"的基础上,进一步宣扬了"新文艺"应当为"小资产阶级"而非"无产阶级"而作的"观点"。在钱杏邨看来,这也就是茅盾公然宣布了自身作为小资产阶级的"态度"与"立场",借高举"小资产阶级革命文艺"的大纛以消解二社"无产阶级革命文学"命题之合法性,这无疑展现了他从"我们的友人"而站在了"革命文学"对立一面的姿态。依据"藏原理论",正是"观点"而非"题材"决定了作家及文学创作的根本"性质"。因此就钱杏邨而言,也正是茅盾的"发难"首先宣布了他与"革命文学"派在"阶级立场"上的"对立",钱氏亦由此发现此前自身以"时代题材"评判"革命文学"之"标准"的"失效"。"一个革命的作家,他不能把握得革命的内在的精神,虽然作品上抹着极浓厚的时代色彩,虽然尽了'表现'的能事,可是,这种作品我们是不需要的,是不革命的。"(《"追求"——一封信》111)所以,正是批判茅盾的现实需求,促使了钱杏邨在"藏原理论"的两个命题中"发现"了"写正确"(对应阶级立场)之重要,并有意淡化"写真实"(对应时代题材)的另一面。然而从结果来说,与日本语境相较,对"观点"而非"题材"的强化,反而造成了中国"革命文学"文艺视野的"收缩"。

综上所述,以"新写实主义"为线索重审"革命文学"论争,可以发现既往"二元对立"思维模式所遮蔽的历史现场之复杂性。事实上,钱杏邨对于"新写实主义"的阐释,也未尝不可视作另一种策略性的"误读"。在钱杏邨与茅盾论争的关系结构中,正是对于"新写实主义"之无意/有意的误读,部分造成了论争的错位、激化,并实质上影响了"新写实主义"在中国的阐释路径及走向。

三、"误读"的"新写实主义"——"钱杏邨理论"与"藏原理论"之差异

在《从东京回到武汉》中,钱杏邨将"新写实主义"的特质概括为四点;其中,仅有第一点是对"写实性"的阐释,且仍附加了有关阶级立场的限定(《阿英全集》第1卷366-367)。可以说,"钱杏邨理论"之要素虽然均取自藏原惟人,但相较"藏原理论"试图在"文学"与"政治","写真实"与"写正确"之间调和、折中的态度,钱杏邨显然更为凸显其中政治的、"阶级正确"的一面。前文提到,正是与茅盾的论战促使钱杏邨对于"藏原理论"进行偏重和取舍,生成了钱杏邨对于"新写实主义"的策略性"误读"。也正是在"误读"这一特定视角中,"钱杏邨理论"与"藏原理论"之差异得以呈现。

首先关涉的问题是对"现实"这一概念的理解与阐释。"藏原理论"大力倡导写实主义的复归,所针对的事实对象是日本左翼文坛"主观主义""观念主义"盛行的积习。因此,藏原所呼唤的"现实"首要是与"客观"同调,而与"主观"相对的一种概念。与此同时,为了与日本近代强大的自然主义文艺传统相抗衡,凸显普罗列塔利亚的阶级立场,他又要求艺术在"客观现实"中发现于无产阶级所"必要的""典型的"一面,书写"现实以上的现实",这又提出了对于"现实"有选择的,甚至"超验"的认知。由此,"现实"和"现实以上的现实"这一对概念,在藏原文论中就产生了一定的理论裂隙与张力。

当"藏原理论""旅行"到中国文坛时,钱杏邨对于"新写实主义"之"现实"的介绍基本延续了藏原的理路,而在"革命文学"的论争实践中,"现实"这一概念则成为双方交锋的一大焦点。茅盾"以'现实'作为自我证明的手段","'合于现实'是茅盾证明自己创作的重要途径"(张广海 26)。在《从牯岭到东京》中,他反复强调《蚀》三部曲的创作是完全排除了主观因素,"老实""忠实""客观"的表现"现实"。"茅盾之所以要亲自对《蚀》三部曲的'客观'性做权威性的论证,其用意在于通过强化三部曲纯粹的'客观的真实'来淡化它在美学上的意识形态性,即所谓的'倾向''立场'。"(李跃力 58)与之相对的,为了破除茅盾"客观性"的"假象",揭示其中小资产阶级意识形态及立场的"反革命"性,钱杏邨就必须召唤"新写实主义"文论中,"客观性"之外的,"现实"之"意识形态性"的另一种面影。这就进一步扩张了"藏原理论"的裂隙,强化了对于"现实以上的现实"之追求。

在《中国新兴文学中的几个具体的问题》中,钱杏邨直截了当指明了"革命文学"派与茅盾在何为"现实"问题上观念的分歧:

> 普罗列塔利亚作家所要描写的"现实"……决不是像那旧的写实主义,像茅盾所主张的,仅止是"描写""现实","暴露"黑暗与丑恶;而是要把"现实"扬弃一下,把那动的,力学的,向前的"现实"提取出来,作为描写的题材。(《阿英全集》第 1 卷 449–450)

在另一篇名为《茅盾与现实》的文章中,钱杏邨曾借茅盾的言述提出,当下实际存在两种维度的"现实":一种是"大勇者,真正的革命者",另一种是"幻灭动摇的没落人物"。这两种"现实"既然都作为"事实"而存在,关键就在于何者"真正的代表着时代""完成这时代的作家的任务",何者就成为应当被发扬的"现实"(《阿英全集》第 2 卷 195–

197)。结合这两篇文章来看,以钱杏邨为代表的"革命文学"派并不将"现实"真正等同于"客观事实",而认为其中内含着强烈的意识形态及价值导向。对于"现实"概念的层层切割、包装让其仿佛成为又一个"任人打扮的小姑娘"——"现实"必须被"提取""扬弃",成为"向上的""向前的"的题材,方才成为"真正"的"现实"。这种对于"现实"过于"先验"的约束只能造成"观念的""虚假的"的遮蔽,最终导向一种"非现实"的艺术论。虽然理论的拆解并不困难,但值得反思的是这种"非现实"的艺术论,尤其是其"拆解——重塑""现实"的逻辑理路,并未随着"钱杏邨理论"之批判以及"新写实主义"热的消散而结束,反而长久遗存下来,成为日后革命现实主义美学中主流的思维范式和支配性原则。

再者,藏原惟人与钱杏邨理论的又一个显著差异体现在对"小资产阶级"这一阶级群体的认知之上。藏原的态度总体而言是积极的,他认为小资产阶级作家及其创作虽然呈现出摇摆的、阶级协调主义的倾向,但仍具有一定的革命性与进步性。对于小布尔乔亚写实主义的创作成果,应当在批判其"个人主义"的基础上有所继承发展。在有关"文艺大众化"问题的讨论中,藏原的一个核心构想就是将普罗文艺的创作以其读者大众"自身的文化的水准"为标准进行分层分类:一类是"作为艺术的,有着社会底价值的作品的大众化",另一类则是"没有艺术性,但在大众的教化和宣传的意味上有着价值的大众的作品的制作"(《新写实主义论文集》78)。前者以"已经获得了相当的文化的水准的读者(观者)"(79)为对象,后者以广大工厂、农村的大众为读者群。这里藏原虽没有明确提出"小资产阶级"的概念,但在具有相当文化水准的读者中,小资产阶级知识分子显然就占有很大的比重。因此,在藏原的观念体系中,小资产阶级文艺创作既有值得取法之处,小资产阶级读者群亦是文艺大众化的重要对象,这一群体自然也成为革命文艺构想所不可忽略的一环。

而在中国"革命文学"论争的语境中,"小资产阶级"则成为话语交锋的焦点。也可以说,正是茅盾对于"小资产阶级"作家立场、作品创作以及读者群的全面宣扬,"应激"了"革命文学"派对于这一概念的集中声讨和批判。在论争开始前,钱杏邨对于"小资产阶级"的态度甚至是友善且宽容的。在《批评的建设》中,他特意强调对小资产阶级的批评要注意"维持他们的革命情绪",要以"友谊的态度"处之(15-16)。而在论争开始后,他却公开表态了自己态度的转向:"我的态度较之批评'幻灭'与'动摇'时变了一点,这是对的,因为在我最近的经验之中,觉得批评的态度要严整,不能太宽容。无论对于敌人,抑是自己阵营里的同道者。"(《"追求"——一封信》111)钱杏邨调整姿态的直接原因是有感于论争情势之迫切。在他看来,作为小资产阶级代言人的茅盾已经率先于政治领域强调了该阶级之于中国革命的重要性,在文学领域又尤其将对于"小资产阶级"及其文学的宣扬建立在对"革命文学"的批判之上;而在论敌如此主动出击的情况下,己方对于小资产阶级的批评教育自然也不待徐徐图之。因此,钱杏邨等一众"革命文学"派同人才会聚集火力,短时间内针对这一阶级展开集中批判,包括在文学上否认"小资产阶级革命文学"存在之合法性,同时在意识形态上指认其"妥协""动摇""不长进"的阶级特性。应该说,"革命文学"派对于"小资产阶级"之性质的认知基本符合马克思主义阶级学说的一贯论述(包括并非全然否认其革命性),但显然与茅盾的论争更加激化了其中批判性的一面。

结　语

从日本共运的自身发展脉络来说,藏原惟人作为福本和夫的后继者,批判并扬弃了"福本学说"对于日本无产阶级文艺运动的负面影响,从而确立了"藏原理论"新的指导地位。而在中国的"革命文学"论争中,"福本学说"和"藏原理论"却分别经由创造社和太阳社之引介,几乎"共时性"地对中国的左翼文艺运动产生了显著的影响。

后期创造社主要通过效仿"福本主义"的话语模式,先发制人地开展"理论斗争"和"文化批判",以确证"革命文学"的合法性并迅速抢占主导和话语权。相较之下,太阳社对于"藏原理论"的引介和运用过程,则更加呈现出历史现场的复杂面貌。就理论本身而言,"藏原理论"之所以吸引太阳社,最初源于其对普罗文艺和文学创作"本体"之注重。然而,中国左翼对于"新写实主义"的现实运用,实际却与太阳、创造二社同茅盾有关"革命文学"的论争相伴相生。尤其就茅盾和钱杏邨二者而言,正是对于"新写实主义"之无意/有意的误读,部分造成了论争的错位、激化,并实质上影响了这一理论在中国的阐释路径及走向,最终造成了钱杏邨理论偏重"阶级立场"而轻视"现实书写"的"左倾"面貌。此外,本文虽然论证了钱杏邨对于"藏原理论"的运用——偏重——取舍也存在现实基础,但这一"现实"更多指向论战之中的"现实语境",而非对于中国左翼文艺之"文学现场"与未来发展更为长远及深度之思考。因此,以钱杏邨为代表的早期中国左翼文艺实践,在学习、借鉴国际共运理论过程中的经验与得失,依然值得我们当下持续的注重和反思。

引用文献【Works Cited】

"Post-Edited." *Sun Monthly* 5(1928): 1-5.

［《编后》,《太阳月刊》1928 年第 5 期,第 1—5 页。］

Kurahara Korehito. "The Road to Neorealism." Trans. Lin Boxiu. *Sun Monthly* stoppage issue(1928): 1-18.

［藏原惟人:《到新写实主义之路》,林伯修译,《太阳月刊》1928 年停刊号,第 1—18 页。］

Kurahara Korehito. "The Quest for New Art Forms." Trans. Shao Shui. *Gregarious* 12(1929): 12-46.

［藏原惟人:《向新艺术形式的探求去》,勺水译,《乐群》1929 年第 12 期,第 12—46

页。]

Kurahara Korehito. *Essays on New Realism*. Trans. Zhi Ben. Shanghai: Modern Bookstore, 1930.

[藏原惟人:《新写实主义论文集》,之本译,上海:现代书局,1930 年。]

Cheng Fangwu. "Toasts." *Cultural Critique* 1(1928): 1-2.

[成仿吾:《祝词》,《文化批判》1928 年第 1 期,第 1—2 页。]

Ji Mingxue and Sun Luqian, eds. *Materials on "Literary and Artistic Freedom Debate" in the Thirties*. Shanghai: Shanghai Literature and Art Publishing House, 1990.

[吉明学、孙露茜编:《三十年代"文艺自由论辩"资料》,上海:上海文艺出版社,1990 年。]

Jiang Guangci. *The Collected Writings of Jiang Guangci* vols. 2 and 4. Shanghai: Shanghai Literature and Art Publishing House, 1983 and 1988.

[蒋光慈:《蒋光慈文集》第 2 卷、第 4 卷,上海:上海文艺出版社,1983、1988 年。]

Kuang Xinnian. *1928: Revolutionary Literature*. Beijing: People's Literature Publishing House, 1998.

[旷新年:《1928:革命文学》,北京:人民文学出版社,1998 年。]

Li Yueli. "The Avoidance and Exile of 'Reality'-Revisiting 'New Realism'." *Modern Chinese Culture and Literature* 1(2012): 55-66.

[李跃力:《对"现实"的规避与放逐——再论"新写实主义"》,《现代中国文化与文学》2012 年第 1 辑,第 55—66 页。]

Ashida Hajime. "Qian Xingcun's 'New Realism': Relationship with Kurahara Korehito's 'Proletarian-Realism' and Beyond." Trans. Li Xuan. *The Era of Left-Wing Literature: Selected Papers from "The Society for the Study of Chinese Literature of the 1930s" in Japan*. Ed. Wang Feng and Shigenori Shirai. Beijing: Peking University Press, 2011.24-52.

[芦田肇:《钱杏邨的"新写实主义"——与藏原惟人"无产阶级・现实主义"的关系及其他》,见王风、白井重范编:《左翼文学的时代:日本"中国三十年代文学研究会"论文选》,李选译,北京:北京大学出版社,2011 年,第 24—52 页。]

Lu Xun. *The Complete Works of Lu Xun* vol. 4. Beijing: People's Literature Publishing House, 2005.

[鲁迅:《鲁迅全集》第 4 卷,北京:人民文学出版社,2005 年。]

Mao Dun. *The Complete Works of Mao Dun* vol. 19. Beijing: People's Literature Publishing House, 1991.

[茅盾:《茅盾全集》第 19 卷,北京:人民文学出版社,1991 年。]

Mao Dun. *The Road I Traveled* (middle). Beijing: People's Literature Publishing House, 1984.

[茅盾:《我走过的道路》(中),北京:人民文学出版社,1984年。]

Qian Xingcun. *The Complete Works of Ah Ying Vol. 1 and Vol. 2*. Hefei: Anhui Education Publishing House, 2003.

[钱杏邨:《阿英全集》第1卷、第2卷,合肥:安徽教育出版社,2003年。]

Qian Xingcun. "Disillusionment." *Sun Monthly* 3(1928):1-9.

[钱杏邨:《"幻灭"》,《太阳月刊》1928年第3期,第1—9页。]

Qian Xingcun. "'The Quest'—A Letter." *Taito Monthly* 4(1928): 105-112.

[钱杏邨:《"追求"——一封信》,《泰东月刊》1928年第4期,第105—112页。]

Qian Xingcun. "Criticism and Copybook." *Sun Monthly* 4(1928): 1-24.

[钱杏邨:《批评与抄书》,《太阳月刊》1928年第4期,第1—24页。]

Qian Xingcun. "The Construction of Criticism." *Sun Monthly* 5(1928): 1-21.

[钱杏邨:《批评的建设》,《太阳月刊》1928年第5期,第1—21页。]

Qian Xingcun. "Shaken." *Sun Monthly* stoppage issue(1928): 1-19.

[钱杏邨:《"动摇"》,《太阳月刊》1928年停刊号,第1—19页。]

Qian Xingcun, ed. *How to Study Emerging Literature*. Shanghai: Nanqiang Bookstore, 1930.

[钱杏邨编:《怎样研究新兴文学》,上海:南强书局,1930年。]

Zhang Guanghai. "Mao Dun and the Revolutionary Literary School's Dispute over the View of 'Reality'". *Modern Chinese Literature Research Series* 1(2012): 16-31.

[张广海:《茅盾与革命文学派的"现实"观之争》,《中国现代文学研究丛刊》2012年第1期,第16—31页。]

现实主义的回归与开拓
——以新时代乡土书写为中心

周 倩

内容摘要：新世纪以来，乡土现实书写面临困境，阎连科长篇小说《受活》的后记《寻找超越主义的现实》一度引发学界关于乡土文学中"现实主义传统的失落"的争论。乡土书写中"现实"向"现代"的转型，"写实"到"象征"的变迁，在一定程度上导致对故事叙述的过度偏重，由此产生失真、浅薄等问题与弊病。进入新时代的乡土写作力求突破这一困境，重构乡土文学与乡村现实之间的有效关系，重振乡土文学介入现实的能动效应。作家通过如盐入水地走近乡村，深入肌理地采风与考察，探知与体认当下真实的中国乡村。他们的创作经由风土人情与民风民俗的融入，乡村日常生活的刻画，贴近真实、贴近自然、贴近土地的书写姿态，使得民间文化资源与现实主义风格互构，赋予乡土写作新生意义与审美特质，开拓乡土书写与现实主义创作的新路径。

关键词：乡土文学 现实主义 新时代

作者简介：周倩，兰州大学文学院博士研究生，主要从事中国现当代文学研究。

Title: The Return and Development of Realism—Focusing on Local Writing in the New Era

Abstract: Since the new century, the writing of local reality has been faced with difficulties. Yan Lianke's postscript "In Search of the Reality of Transcendence" in his novel *Lenin's Kisses* once triggered a debate about the "loss of the realistic tradition" in local literature. The transition from "reality" to "modern" and from "realism" to "symbolism" in local writing, to a certain extent, lead to excessive emphasis on story narration, resulting in distortion, superficiality and other problems and drawbacks. Local writing in the new era strives to break through this dilemma, reconstruct the effective relationship between local literature and rural reality, and revive the dynamic effect of local literature intervening in reality. The writer approaches the countryside like salt into the water, and goes deep into the texture of the sampling and investigation, to explore and understand the real Chinese countryside. Through the integration of local customs and folk customs, the depiction of rural daily life, and the writing attitude close to reality, nature and land, their creation makes the folk cultural resources and realistic style mutually construct, endows local writing with new meaning and aesthetic characteristics, and opens up a new path for local writing and realistic creation.

Key words: local literature; Realism; New era

Author: Zhou Qian is a PhD candidate at School of Literature, Lanzhou University, China. Her research interests are modern and contemporary Chinese literature.

阎连科在长篇小说《受活》的后记《寻找超越主义的现实》(阎连科,《受活后记》297)以及与李陀的对谈中,指斥现实主义是"谋杀文学的元凶",宣称要实现对现实主义的突破与超越,提出"超现实写作"这一新路径,由此引发了关于乡土文学中"现实主义传统的失落"的争议与讨论。

新世纪以来,乡土现实书写的进一步发展曾一度遭遇瓶颈,阎连科、贾平凹等重要乡土作家都曾表露出他们所面临的叙事焦虑与言说困境。如何在现代性的冲击之下延续写实主义传统,如何开拓适应当下时代的创作模式,如何展现新时代山乡巨变、乡村多元发展的社会现实,这一系列问题成为乡土文学中现实主义写作发展的关注重点。

新时代的乡土写作力求对这些书写困境与难题做出突破与回应,作家通过更加深入地贴近乡土自然与乡村真实,以求真的笔触如实记录、还原和呈现当下中国乡村的真实样貌,并对乡村的未来发展提出建设性思考,尝试开拓乡土文学与现实主义创作发展的新路径。

一、失落抑或回归？——乡土文学现实主义书写的困境与新尝试

《受活》扉页上的题词"现实主义——我的兄弟姐妹哦,请你离我再近些。现实主义——我的墓地哦,请你离我再远些"揭示了阎连科个人文学经验的某种本质,其作家自我塑成与文学世界的建构源于长期的现实主义接受、认知与训练。与此同时,这句题词也明确表露了他在当下个人创作体验中遭遇的困境,即他所面临的某种叙事焦虑。阎连科敬仰20世纪30年代的作家对"劳苦人的命运"的书写,排斥"庸俗的现实主义,粉饰的现实主义,私欲的现实主义",但他又不愿回到"简单、概念、教条,甚至庸俗"(李陀48–49)的传统文学手段及现实主义的正剧模式创作之路上。因此他将创作的困境、叙事的无力归结于现实主义创作范式的限制,决意突破和超越现实主义的窠臼,通过"解除叙事的成规","解放文学视域"(南帆66),开辟出新的乡土小说写作路径。从《日光流年》中荒诞的神话宿命式结构,到《坚硬如水》中奇异的政治隐喻怪像,再到《受活》狂想式的超现实写作,如同学者南帆所言,到达《年月日》这一临界点之后,缓慢的故事节奏无法承载和抑制强烈的叙事压力与表达动力,最终这一创作冲动冲破了现实主义形式的躯壳。阎连科开始用超现实想象构建起高于逻辑、超出现实的乡村世界,借由种种

怪诞、奇诡的文学构想去言说与展现他心目中真实的乡村居民的生存形态。

阎连科固然做出了凸显个性化的新尝试，而他的写作观念也引发诸多争论。在持经典现实主义观的学者与评论家看来，阎连科怪诞的狂想损伤了现实主义性，以恣意的虚构取代了对现实的描摹，只将自我的狂想当做真实，他的创作嬗变可被视作乡土文学现实主义传统失落的标志，而路遥的《平凡的世界》才可称作是现实主义的真正典范（邵燕君 5）。另一方面，也有评论家持相反的观点，认为阎连科回到了对乡土中国生存困境的关照，以融入后现代写作思维及表达手段的方式，使传统现实主义呈现出开放姿态，实现了对乡土文学写作范式的新的开创（陈晓明 67-69）。更有学者提出，阎连科并未背离书写乡土现实的根本目的，他所标榜的"超越主义"或是一种"反现实主义的现实主义"（梁鸿 95）。

从某种意义上来说，阎连科的创作的确并未背离书写乡土现实的初衷和关切农民命运、为劳苦大众发声的立场，他认为"只能用超现实的方法，才能够接近现实的核心，才有可能揭示生活的内心"，否则他的写作将难以为继（李陀 49）。事实上，阎连科所经受的叙事焦虑也折射出当代乡土文学发展所面临的共同困境，尤其是乡土现实书写中，写实的写作传统与现实主义边界拓展之间的不协调与不契合之处，持续引发着文学创作与理论批评的相关争议。

从 19 世纪的批判现实主义，到 20 世纪的社会主义现实主义，再到兼容现代派的无边的现实主义，抑或以《百年孤独》的风行与影响为代表的魔幻现实主义等流派、定义的盛行，伴随着现代性观念意识、思维方式的涌入与流行，似乎传统的"现实"所能承载与蕴含的表现力在逐渐衰弱，而寻求更为多元化、更富文本张力、更具美学意蕴的表达方式成为更为主流的创作趋向。随着社会现代化发展深入，商品经济、消费主义的热潮涌动，一方面文学具有了更多市场化价值追求，另一方面，传统乡村的边缘化，使得乡土文学的现实书写总体偏向对逝去的田园牧歌的哀婉叹息，流露出对乡土现实感到无望的消极态度。

在这种发展态势下，乡村逐渐成为某种寓言的载体，或者一种文化符号的象征，乡土世界一度成为与现代社会相背而行、渐行渐远的世外桃源，成为由文学话语与构想搭建起来的封闭式的小世界，而真实的乡村样貌却日渐模糊。"作为现实主义的'叛逆之子'，现代主义对现实主义的超越具有反抗性质，同时也是有代价的"，"现代主义将人类具体的苦难放置到人类历史的深远背景中进行形而上的哲学思考，从而具有了超历史性、神秘性和荒诞性"。（邵燕君 5-6）但由此苦难被抽象化，历史被神秘化，现实被荒诞化，失去了其原有的意义的厚度。乡土写作中"现实"向"现代"的转型，"写实"到"象征"的变迁，引导了对故事叙述方式与结构的过度偏重，对写作手段与技巧的过分倚重，使得形式逐渐大于内容，最终产生失真、浅薄等问题与弊病。

有关乡土文学中的现实主义的争论，以及乡土现实书写的叙事困境成为笼罩着当代乡土写作的一个整体背景。在面临诸多相悖的观念意见、创作与批评的相关问题和困惑的情况下，新时代的乡土写作又出现了回归现实主义的趋向，这也是当下的乡土作家对乡土书写困境的一个回应和新的尝试。面对观念和写法上的争论，他们不再沉湎于对逝去的传统乡土的过分哀叹，而试图真正地回归到当下乡土中的真实。

乡土文学中回归现实这一创作趋向的出现，与社会现实发展的总体进程与历史背景息息相关。新世纪以来，随着脱贫攻坚、乡村振兴等国家重要战略的推行与落实，乡村社会由内而外发生新的变化，对这一变革加以关注、观察、记录和书写成为乡土作家创作的应有之义，从而促使乡土文学作品也呈现出一种新的面向，如周大新的《湖光山色》（2006）、关仁山的《金谷银山》（2017）、老藤（滕贞甫）的《战国红》（2019）、赵德发的《经山海》（2019）以及乔叶的《宝水》（2022）等作品，不仅如实反映乡村的风土人情、发展困境，以及乡民的真实内心与诉求，不只停留于对传统乡土中国的渐渐消弭与逝去的慨叹,而是"以建设性姿态思考着中国乡村的未来,并试图提出乡村重建的方案"(雷鸣 92)。正如乔叶所宣言的那样:"我想写有新特质的乡村",对"牧歌式的,悲歌式的,审判式的,或者是隔着遥远的时间距离而把相对静止状态的乡村记忆放在过去时中去感叹的写作"缺乏兴致(乔叶)。

当下中国乡村转型与变革的实况给予乡土写作以现实支撑,促使乡土现实书写在乡村思考路径方面实现突破。不同于鲁迅及"五四"时期乡土文学群体,以及 1980 年代以来高晓声、韩少功等对乡村的批判性思考,主要以客观中立的视角与立场进行冷峻揭露、审视、剖析;也不同于 20 年代的废名、30 年代的沈从文,以及 90 年代以来迟子建、阿来、贾平凹、张炜等对乡村传统文化的考察、寻根,对现代文明的批判,以期寻找精神家园、发掘原始的自然的理想人性;当下的乡土书写提出对乡村的建设性思考,呈现乡村现代化发展新形态,展现对乡村未来图景的设想与展望,从而为乡土现实的新的生长与发展谋求文学建构与文化意义上的新出路。

二、贴近现实的创作诉求与路径

在乡土书写中出现回归现实主义的创作诉求是一种必然的趋势,事实上中国的乡土书写从未远离对乡村社会历史真实的描摹、反映与回应。乡土写作的现实主义传统可以追溯到鲁迅那里,从鲁迅批判国民性的启蒙之作以及在他的旗帜下形成的乡土小说流派,茅盾主张贴近现实的社会剖析小说为代表的批判现实主义,到以左翼文学作家和中华人民共和国成立后柳青、周立波等作家的创作为主的革命现实主义/社会主义现实主义,再到被认为接续了批判现实主义传统的 80 年代路遥、高晓声、李佩甫等乡土作家的创作,现实主义的写作范式与时俱进,乡土书写的创作模式也随之改变。

乡土写作对现实主义的回归是必然会产生的诉求与趋向,而对现实主义的开拓则成为当下乡土作家所面临的历史难题。正如学者丁帆所指出的"'柳青模式'和'路遥模式'这两种书写模式,是被认可的乡村书写典范。但是,我们不能不说,这样的模式已经不适合当下乡村巨变的历史语境了。如何面对当代巨变下的乡村书写?写什么?怎么写?这是这一世纪文学给作家提出的历史诘问"(张清俐)。在新时代的历史进程中,伴随着中国式现代化的深入发展,在脱贫攻坚、乡村振兴的宏大时代背景笼罩下,为回应时代的需求与召唤,新时代乡土文学理当以乡村革新、时代巨变为关注焦点,书写山乡巨变、伟大事业、改革进程成为个人化情感诉求与时代性任务感召相结合统一的创作目的与动机。

在此基础上,创作路径的选择成为新时代乡土文学作家所共同面临的难题,其中有相当一部分作家选择了与阎连科秉持的超越现实之道相反的方向,抑制了向"现代性""超写实"的转型这一"自然"的"进步之途"(邵燕君9),而是萌生了更加深入、全面贴近乡土现实的创作诉求。比起鲁迅站在知识分子立场对国民性进行审视与剖析,以启蒙主题与文化批判为主要内容的主观现实主义,这类作家的创作诉求与理想似乎更贴近赵树理、柳青式的对某一历史时段乡村具体发展、现实变革进程的如实还原与书写。他们聚焦乡土社会现实及其历史变迁,延续客观展现乡村社会现实本身的赵树理传统。例如,王跃文的《家山》以百年家族史为聚焦点,沙湾地区的沧桑历变与几代父老乡亲的生活变迁为叙事轴心,几乎涉及近百年中国历史进程中的所有重大事件,书写"沙湾巨变"的乡村史诗,与柳青《创业史》的史诗性建构如出一脉。但与彼时宏大叙事的建构不同,当下的乡土小说更倾向以日常生活为本位,如乔叶的《宝水》以"极小事"、碎片化的日常生活叙事来还原乡村生活,并提出面向未来的乡村建设性思考。

中国式现代化进程中乡村社会的多元发展与重大转型,对乡土现实书写提出了空前的巨大挑战。《秦腔》问世之后,贾平凹在与郜元宝的对谈中,坦言随着农村的巨大变化与个人认知的嬗变,他没办法再把握对故乡的书写,"我所目睹的农村情况太复杂,不知道如何处理,确实无能为力,也很痛苦。实际上我并非不想找出理念来提升,但实在寻找不到"(郜元宝)。由此贾平凹一直以来面对乡土时的"回去"姿态,转变为了"告别"的情绪,并以此构成了这部作品的情感基调和意义旨归——贾平凹宣言写下《秦腔》是在为故乡立碑,"为了忘却的纪念"。在当代作家的创作视域中,传统的乡土认知已然发生根本性的改变,他们无法再遵循和贯彻传统的、经典的写作模式,面对传统村庄不可避免的、日渐消逝的最终宿命,以及正在新生的现代化乡村日新月异的陌生面貌,他们不得不开拓新的思考路径,探寻新的写作方法。

"在中国当前的社会背景和文学背景下,继续走现实主义的路,重续'庄重、严肃、深刻'的现实主义传统不是一条因循的坦途,而是一条充满挑战、'费力不讨好'的畏途,其中有些困境是许多作家难以跨越的。这样的困境首先在于,继续现实主义传统必须对瞬息万变的新社会现实有着敏感深入的了解,对于写苦难的作家而言,必须一直与广大'受苦人'站在一起,对于他们现实的痛苦有着感同身受的体验。这一点看似简单,但对于许多深陷于'名利场'的作家来说,却是'不现实'的要求。"(邵燕君 11)面对乡土世界中正在进行中的宏大的社会转型与疾速的多元变革,当下的乡土作家或是缺乏足够深入、全面、切身、长期的生活体验,或是缺乏足以囊括和阐释这一社会变革历程的思想资源的知识储备,传统的写作范式已然过时,过去建构的理性判断和美学原则都已失效。"当作家们面对在第三次文化裂变中变得陌生的乡村社会时,他们既已建立起来的现实认知和艺术表现能力渐渐不足","在这种情况下,'真实记录'似乎成了一种可靠的叙事策略"。(李震 95)作家缺乏深入的主体体验,难以对当下多元的变革作出整体的把握和鞭辟入里的剖析与书写,难以把控对完整的乡土故事的叙述,所以选择将如实记录作为一种可行的有效路径,口述实录、纪实文学开始在乡土写作中盛行,整体的价值取向也不再固化于此前对美和善的过度强调,而是出现了求真的趋向。

进入新时代,乡土作家群体开始顺应时代潮流的号召,或自觉自发地履行记录、反映乡村社会真实与变革的使命,产生贴近现实的创作诉求,并将采风与考察,田野调查与实地采访作为触及真实、探知本质的必由之路,走近并深入乡村,积淀真实的生活经验,力求做到对当地大量地方性知识的全面掌握。赵德发在他的现实主义题材长篇小说《经山海》中呈现出一个依山傍水、半农半渔的海边乡镇之前,已在日照有了近30年的生活体验,而为了更好地完成反映新时代乡村振兴历程的写作任务,为了更加生动、真实地反映这一变革过程,他在2018年走过山东多地的村落进行采风、调查,采访了众多基层乡镇干部,最终花费一年时间写下这部书写新时代中国乡村振兴伟业的现实主义小说力作,聚焦海边乡镇的时代新人经山历海、振兴乡村的历程。乔叶自言在个人诉求与时代感召两相呼应之下,通过长期的"跑村"与"泡村",观察乡村新面貌、新人物、新现象,积累大量的写作素材,试图在创作中与新时代同频共振,在新作《宝水》中描摹出当下中国的新山乡,展现一个处于传统与现代这一历史嬗变阶段中的寻常普通的豫北山村,力求实现对乡土中国现代化的文学书写。王跃文在《家山》的创作中,贯彻朴实的现实主义创作方法,坚持"史笔为文"的创作态度,"对小说中写到的岁月,从烟火日常到家国大事都下过一番考证功夫。他认为,文学从来都是人类的共同记忆,与其说是自己创作了《家山》,不如说是生养他的那一方父老乡亲创作了这部小说,创作者只是替同胞在言说。"(中国评协)杨志军在写下《雪山大地》之前,已在青海藏区有过相当漫长的生存经历,对藏民、牧民生活环境的深入了解与体验,让他能够深入肌理地书写青海藏区数十年来改天换地的沧桑巨变,当地藏汉民众生产生活方式、身份地位及价值追求的嬗变,草原牧人的生活变迁以及青藏高原上的父辈故事和家族历史。俯下身紧贴现实土壤的姿态,近距离的细致观察,切身的生活体验,切实的走访、考察与实践,作家们所采取的这一系列实际行动,为真正回归乡村的真实,消弭远离群众、偏离现实的失真弊病提供了可行方案。

三、"非虚构"策略借鉴与内容形式的现实指向

出于回归真实的乡土,贴近现实的土壤这一创作诉求,乡土作家愈加青睐纪实文学的形式和现实描摹的笔触,新世纪以来的乡土写作中涌现出大量报告文学和非虚构写作的创作现象。相当一部分作家抵达近年来脱贫攻坚和乡村振兴战略在乡村中推行实施的前线阵地,以记者的立场与视角,如实反映和记录这一宏大的社会转型与变革历程,观察和描摹当下中国乡村脱胎换骨、日新月异的革新与发展。例如王华的《海雀,海雀》就记述了"时代楷模"海雀村的村支书文朝荣带领村民改善石漠化地貌、退耕还林、保护生态、强化教育、摆脱贫困和共同富裕奔小康的事迹。为了写好这部报告文学,王华住进了海雀村文老支书儿子的家里,与海雀人同吃同住,最终在作品中呈现出这一怀揣朴素的信仰,吃苦耐劳、热爱家国、为民奉献、朴实亲切的活生生的农村老干部形象。顾长虹的《被星星围住的阿丽玛》,何永飞的《奔腾的独龙江》,何炬学的《太阳出来喜洋洋》,次仁罗布的《鲁甸:废墟上开出的花》,黄伟的《悬崖之上》,刘晓平的《遥远的故土》,彭学明的《人间正是艳阳天》,罗大佺的《石头开花的故事》,侯健飞的《石竹花开》,徐一洛、冯昱的《山那边,有光》,林超俊的《红土地上的秀美人生》等诸多作品都是集文学性与新闻性为一体的报告文学作品。即便其中不乏受命之作,但大量报告文学的产生也构成了顺应时代感召、记录社会变革、关注民生问题、回应社会关切的文艺创作潮流,不少作品的诞生都建立在切身的走访、调研、考察的基础之上,真切地反映了这一历史阶段乡村转型与革

新的社会真实。

另一部分作家则由文艺创作者的采风深入到社会学层面的田野调查，显示出更具专业性的严谨考量和对中国乡村发展过程更加深入的理性思考。梁鸿的《中国在梁庄》和《出梁庄记》即其中的典型之作，通过广泛的走访与真实的记录，走过从梁庄起始，经西安—南阳—内蒙古—北京—郑州—南方（主要指广东深圳）—青岛，最后再回到梁庄的人物采访路线，以非虚构写作的方式还原一个乡村的变迁史，直击农民最真实的生存境况，感受他们在新时期的悲欢离合。孙惠芬的《生死十日谈》以作家在辽南农村的实地社会调研为写作基础背景，聚焦农村的自杀事件，记述"我"对死亡者亲属与邻人的采访过程，由此还原事件的本来面目，揭露造成村民心态失衡的社会问题。林白的《妇女闲聊录》则采用了口述实录这一非虚构写作中的主要方式，小说中明确标注了"闲聊"发生的时间、地点和讲述人的姓名，用真实性的拼贴来结构文学叙事，打破了过去乡土文学中农民失声或只能由他人代言的尴尬处境，尤其是让作为社会中弱势群体的底层女性也能够开口发声，言说自己真实的人生。林白在后记中表明，"我听到的和写下的，都是真人的声音，是口语，它们粗糙、拖沓、重复、单调，同时也生动朴素、眉飞色舞，是人的声音和神的声音交织在一起，没有受到文人更多的伤害"（林白，《妇女闲聊录后记》226）。她在创作中有意摒弃了文学性的加工，只强调原生态的如实还原。

20世纪70年代末80年代初，美国六七十年代的非虚构小说（Nonfiction Novel）和新新闻报道（New Journalism）逐渐引入国内并产生影响，"非虚构"的概念由此传入中国，并在八九十年代和21世纪初先后掀起纪实文学和非虚构写作的热潮（刘栋39）。学者张文东指出"非虚构是一种创新的叙事策略或模式，这种写作在模糊了文学（小说）与历史、记实之间界限的意义上，生成了一种具有'中间性'的新的叙事方式"（张文东44）。学者杨庆祥在论及非虚构写作的当下与可能时提出其"以在场的方式再次勾连起文学与社会的有机关联","试图在'个人性'与'公共性'之间找到一种平衡,以这种方式激活并拓展现实主义写作的广度和深度","'非虚构'成为现实主义作家一种应对激变社会的主流叙述方式"(杨庆祥 81)。

新世纪以来,非虚构写作在作家在场、行动意识、真实记录、日常生活书写等方面的策略意识与现实主义书写深化与拓展的发展趋向相吻合,贴近现实、记录现实、反映现实的这一共通的创作意图,使得非虚构写作与现实主义创作显示出类似的创作心理,而非虚构写作在叙事策略、写法取径上对现实主义的乡土小说创作显现出示范性。

《人民文学》设置《非虚构》这一栏目,"特别注重作者的'行动'和'在场',鼓励对特定现象、事件的深入考察和体验"(《人民文学》208)。这一走出书斋、回到文学现场的"行动"与"在场"意识,在当下的乡土文学现实主义创作中也多有体现,尤其是以新时代脱贫攻坚、山乡巨变为题材的小说,作家在采风与写作过程中也展现出和报告文学相似的社会调查的广泛性与深入性。口述实录的表现方法也在现实主义乡土小说中日常化、通俗化、地方化的语言运用中多有借鉴,不少作家会将民间采风、走访考察过程中实地采访的对谈内容作为叙事片段,原汁原味地呈现在文本中。

以乔叶的《宝水》为例,文本跟随主人公地青萍的视角展开,地青萍的身份背景不仅具有传统乡土叙事中较为经典的返乡的知识分子这一属性,还具备退休的记者这一设定,因此她的观察角度、思考路径在一定意义上具有社会调查的专业性,她对乡村人像物象的观察,对民风民俗民情的体察,对乡民观念意识的体认,对乡村社会规则、人情世态的理解,也都与文本之外、现实世界中作家乔叶本人"跑村"和"泡村"的主体实践经验相融通。以地青萍的视角面向宝水村所作的参与性观察,对乡村社会中的乡建工作、基层治理、人情往来等社会现象,以及留守儿童教育、空巢老人赡养、传统文化传承乃至家暴与出轨等社会问题都进行了集中且持续的关注与反馈。回到乡土现场让写作具有一种在场感和参与性，梁鸿曾在《中国在梁庄》的前言中言及"不以偶然的归乡者的距离观察，而以一个亲人的情感进入村庄"，才有可能真正发现与理解乡村"存在的复杂性"（梁鸿，《中国在梁庄前言》2)，这一点与《宝水》的创作路径非常一致。在表现方法层面，乔叶在语言上应用了大量原生态的豫北方言，不少叙事情节都是在"扯云话"这一叙事场景中展开，对原始自然的村庄闲话进行了还原。同时，考虑到读者接受问题，乔叶也对极度简洁的地方方言进行艺术改造与创化，使其更易于为读者所理解，例如将教育孩子的俗语"该娇娇，该敲敲"改为"该娇就娇，该敲就敲"，既保留方言的原味，又避免误读的困惑。

  同样采用真实记录的叙事策略，另一部分作家选择从志人志怪等传统古典文学中汲取营养，选取地方志、史传体的文体形式为故乡立传，将地方风物风俗、人文传统全都纳入文学观照的视域，使自己的创作不单具有文学层面的审美性，还具备了包罗万象的百科全书式的博物属性。例如贾平凹用《秦腔》来为故乡立碑，此后又在原定名为《秦岭》和《秦岭志》的《山本》以及《秦岭记》中广纳秦岭地区在地理环境、生物特征、人文景观等方方面面的知识内容，希望整理出一部秦岭的动物记和草木记。他在《秦岭记》的后记中自陈："几十年过去了，我一直在写秦岭。写它历史的光荣和苦难，写它现实的振兴和忧患，写它山水草木和飞禽走兽的形胜，写它儒释道加红色革命的精神。"（贾平凹，《秦岭记后记》263)他将秦岭视作中华大地的"龙脉"，亦是中国乡土的中心，对秦岭的地方志书写和树碑立传，也蕴含着记录乡土的根源与原乡，传承悠久的历史记忆与厚重的文化底蕴的意味。海男的《乡村传》副标题为"一个国家的乡村史"，也是从标题的命名上就表明了为乡村立传编史的写作意图，她在书中勾勒乡村的形象，描写普通平凡的乡村人物，呈现粮食、牲畜、风沙等乡村物象，记述置身于乡村之中的身体体验。孙惠芬的《上塘书》同样是以编纂史书的态度，记录一个小村落地理、政治、交通、通讯、教育、贸易、文化、婚姻、历史的方方面面,深入乡村生活内层,把握乡村现实,实现对乡村凡俗世界的还原与建构。付秀莹也坦言自己怀有"为我的村庄立传"的野心,她所推出的《陌上》与《野望》都旨在绘出芳村这一华北平原上一个普通乡村的精神地图。

现实主义创作在作家在场、行动意识、真实记录、日常生活书写等方面的策略意识,以及文体样式、创作技巧、结构模式、表现方法上对"非虚构"的借鉴,体现了当下的现实主义创作对先验性的超越和对实践理性的坚持。

总体而言,在叙事内容与主题上,当代乡土现实主义作家逐渐倾向于将宏大时代叙事的背景框架与日常生活叙事的具体笔触相结合,呈现乡土中国的新形态,讲述返乡的情感体验与精神之旅,在新时代传承与延续家园意识和寻根情结。日常化、碎片化的叙事使得乡土文学作品不再仅仅聚焦于尖锐的社会矛盾,而偏向于描摹静水流深的乡村日常生活,不再固化于概念化的乡村故事模式,而是追求对原生态的、自然、真实的乡村形态与面貌的呈现。

以贾平凹为例,自《废都》起始,他的现实主义叙事转向了"日常生活流动的书写",与"新写实主义"所提倡的"生活流"书写相暗合,他从《秦腔》(2005)起,包括《高兴》(2006)《古炉》(2011)《带灯》(2013)《老生》(2014)在内的一系列长篇小说,被称为"微写实主义"(李遇春 44)小说,从强烈、尖锐、犀利的精英立场的社会与文化批判视角,慢慢转向冷静、客观、写实的叙事姿态,采用"闲聊体""慢叙事"的艺术策略加强小说的真实性。贾平凹的这一叙事观念的嬗变,也代表着整个乡土文学创作的新面向与新路径。

通过客观写实的叙事姿态,当下的乡土文学展现当下真实的中国乡村图景,揭示处于传统与现代之间的乡村,对传统文化根基的延续,与其现代化的转型、革新与发展,并对这一变革过程进行深入体验与忠实记录,对未来乡村蓝图作出文学性展望。

一方面,在真实的乡村生活描写中,融入大量地方性知识,广纳风土人情、民风民俗、方言俚语、民谣民谚等民间文化资源。其中在叙事语体的选用方面,对方言的广泛采纳显得尤为突出,例如王跃文《家山》中的语言是典型的湘西溆浦方言,文本中大量采用口语化的俚语,林白的《北流》则是对广西粤语的展现。

另一方面,当下的乡土现实写作注重对乡村主体性、内生力的发掘,表明在传统乡村融入现代化发展的进程中,并非只有对消逝的记忆中的故乡的惋惜与哀叹,更多的是对未来乡村建构与发展的乐观想象,以及自发投入乡村建设的积极心态。作品广泛展现乡村农业新业态,弘扬乡村精神新面貌,塑造新乡村人物形象,书写现代化进程中智慧乡村的多元化发展,新型农民的多样化身份。在对新乡村人物形象长廊的建设中,新时代背景下的基层乡村干部和坚持创新创业的新型农民这两类人物形象最具典型性,如周大新《湖光山色》中楚王庄的楚暖暖,关仁山的《金谷银山》中白羊峪的范少山,《天高地厚》中蝙蝠村的女青年鲍真,《麦河》中鹦鹉村的曹双羊,老藤的《战国红》中柳城的会写诗的杏儿、网红李青,赵德发的《经山海》中的吴小蒿等。

在叙事结构和形式上,当下的乡土写作出现再次启用线性叙事的现象,体现出对现代性写作的反拨。较之以往的乡土文学创作,叙事主体意识也在发生嬗变,视角的设定、观察的角度、共情的体验等方面都呈现新变,主角往往拥有新农民或外来者(不同于传统乡土小说)的身份属性,由此具备了超越性的意识与视角。

作品通常具备时间与空间上的真实性。主体意识经由个体存在介入乡村空间,以这一乡村空间为聚焦中心与主要舞台,兼顾城市与乡村之间链接/对立的空间关系,体现传统与现代的碰撞与融合。以一户农家、一个村庄为点,由点及面,通过这一乡村空间隐喻乡土中国的整个演变历程。

在这一文学世界中所建构起来的真实的乡村空间中,作家往往依据时间的流动架构整个故事的框架,引导叙事的推进。贾平凹在《秦腔》中用"密实的流年式的书写方式"(贾平凹,《秦腔》518)书写清风街近二十年来的发展演变和芸芸众生生老病死、悲欢爱恨的真实生活。王跃文的《家山》细致描绘沙湾村春种秋收的四季日常,展现湘西大地二十多年的历史风云。同样是对乡村改革发展历史演变的观照,在时间上对乡村现代化进程时间轴的截取则存在不同,比起《家山》偏向史诗形态的,时间跨度较大的宏大框架,《宝水》则选择聚焦并记录一年之间宝水村的革新与变化。

值得一提的是,包含《宝水》在内,有多部作品在结构编排上采取了依照时序的设计,回归到简单朴实的线性叙事,使故事内容的日常性与叙事结构的秩序性两相交融。"实际上叙事内容上的日常性和叙事结构上的秩序性,更考验作者对现实生活的洞察力,以及将其转化为洗练语句和动人故事的讲述能力。"(谢乔羽 150)叶炜的《后土》以二十四节气的时序来结构整个叙事,以惊蛰作序曲,又以惊蛰为尾声,使整个故事套入循环轮回的农业时间观,节气的更替、推移与农民生产劳作的日常作息相互呼应、融合,从而将三十年乡土中国的历史演变、线性发展融汇于平实的叙事之中。付秀莹的《野望》也采用二十四节气来谋篇布局,以节气的推移和流转作为出发点,聚焦一户农家的岁时纪事,以线性叙事的形式,由点及面折射出一个村庄在新时代的沧桑巨变。

小说中一年四季十二月二十四节气的时序流转,使得文本在自然秩序的支配下,与现实世界相贴近。这类小说创作从讲求充满波折起伏、戏剧冲突的故事性的叙事套路中脱离,转而寻求一种紧贴现实的日常性记述。当代作家在乡土叙事中不约而同地选取依照传统乡土观念与知识资源来结构故事,建立一种有别于现代性追求下的非线性叙事的新的叙事结构与秩序,亦可窥见本土性、地方性写作对现代化潮流的反拨与对抗。

总之,新时代以来的乡土文学直面现实写作的困境,坚守贴近现实的初衷,忠实履行关注、反映、记录乡土世界变革、乡村社会转型、农民身份转变等社会现象及民生问题的文学责任。在文体样式的选择、叙事结构的架设、写作方法的创新等方面作出新的尝试,彰显对现代性叙事的反拨与对抗,对写实传统的继承与开拓。对乡土文学中现实主义写作路径的新尝试与新突破,力求重构乡土文学与乡村现实之间的有效关系,试图重振乡土文学介入现实的能动效应,不仅深化了文学反映现实的功能,还发挥了文学具有前瞻性的想象力,不但立于当下,而且指向未来,对乡村的未来建设与发展提出了文学性的想象与展望。

引用文献【Works Cited】

阎连科:《寻找超越主义的现实——代后记》,《受活》,春风文艺出版社,2004年。
[Yan Lianke, "In Search of the Reality of Transcendence." *Lenin's Kisses*. Chunfeng Literature and Art Publishing House, 2004, pp.297-299.]

李陀,阎连科:《〈受活〉超现实写作的新尝试》,《读书》第3期,2004年,第44—54页。
[Li Tuo, Yan Lianke. "*Lenin's Kisses* A New Attempt at Surrealist Writing." *Reading*, no.3, 2004, pp.44-54.]

南帆:《〈受活〉:怪诞及其美学谱系》,《上海文学》第6期,2004年,第66—73页。
[Nan Fan. "*Lenin's Kisses* The Grotesque and its Aesthetic Pedigree." *Shanghai Literature*, no.6, 2004, pp.66-73.]

邵燕君:《与大地上的苦难擦肩而过——由阎连科〈受活〉看当代乡土文学现实主义传统的失落》,《文艺理论与批评》第6期,2004年,第4—17页。
[Shao Yanjun. "Brush with the Suffering on the Earth—The Loss of the Realistic Tradition of Contemporary Local Literature Judging from Yan Lianke's *Lenin's Kisses*." *Literary Theory and Criticism*, no.6, 2004, pp.4-17.]

陈晓明:《他引来鬼火,他横扫一切》,《当代作家评论》第5期,2007年,第62—69页。
[Chen Xiaoming. "He Attracted the Ghost Fire, He Swept Everything." *Contemporary Writers Review*, no.5, 2007, pp.62-69.]

梁鸿:《阎连科长篇小说的叙事模式与美学策略——兼谈乡土文学的"现实主义之争"》,《当代作家评论》第5期,2007年,第92—99页。
[Liang Hong. "Narrative Mode and Aesthetic Strategy of Yan Lianke's Novels: A Discussion on the 'Realism Debate' of Local Literature." *Contemporary Writers Review*, no.5, 2007, pp.92-99.

雷鸣:《乡村建设之寻路与中国乡土小说的变调——以长篇小说〈湖光山色〉〈金谷银山〉为例》,《小说评论》第 1 期,2022 年,第 89—97 页。

[Lei Ming. "Finding the Way of Rural Construction and the Change of Tone of Chinese Local Novels: A Case Study of the Novel *Lakes and Mountains, Golden Valley Silver Mountain*." *Novel Review*, no.1, 2022, pp.89-97.]

乔叶:《贴合乡村的骨骼去生长》,《文学报》2022 年 10 月 18 日。

[Qiao Ye. "Fit the bones of the countryside to grow." *Literary Newspaper* October 18, 2022.]

张清俐,张杰:《书写新时代的乡土文学》,《中国社会科学报》2022 年 12 月 9 日。

[Zhang Qingli, Zhang Jie. "Writing Local Literature in the New Era." *Chinese Journal of Social Science* December 9, 2022.]

贾平凹,郜元宝:《关于〈秦腔〉和乡土文学的对谈》,《河北日报》2005 年 4 月 29 日。

[Jia Pingwa, Gao Yuanbao. "On the Dialogue Between *Qin Opera* and Local Literature." *Hebei Daily* April 29, 2005.]

李震:《新乡村叙事及其文化逻辑》,《中国社会科学》第 7 期,2023 年,第 80—99+205—206 页。

[Li Zhen. "New Village Narrative and Its Cultural Logic." *Chinese Social Sciences*, no.7, 2023, pp.80-99+205-206.]

中国评协:《书写南方乡村"沙湾巨变"读懂〈家山〉就读懂乡土中国——王跃文长篇小说〈家山〉学术研讨会综述》,《中国文艺评论网》2023 年 4 月 24 日。https://www.zgwypl.com/content/details32_439664.html

[China Critics Association. "Writing the 'Shawan Great Change' in the Southern Countryside, Read the *Home Mountain* to Understand the Local China: Summary of academic seminar on Wang Yuewen's novel *Home Mountain*." *China Literature and Art Review Network* April 24, 2023.]

林白:《后记——世界如此辽阔》,《妇女闲聊录》,新星出版社,2005 年。

[Lin Bai. "Postscript: The World Is So Vast." *Women's Gossip*. Xinxing Publishing House, 2005.]

刘栋:《非虚构写作的相关概念界定及策略意识——从纪实文学的概念出发》,《文艺评论》第 5 期,2023 年,第 38—47 页。

[Liu Dong. "The Definition of Related Concepts and Srategic Awareness of Nonfiction Writing: Starting from the Concept of Non-fiction Literature." *Literature Review*, no.5, 2023, pp.38-47.]

张文东:《"非虚构"写作:新的文学可能性?——从《人民文学》的"非虚构"说起》,《文艺争鸣》第 3 期,2011 年,第 43—47 页。

[Zhang Wendong. "'Non-fiction' Writing: New Literary Possibilities—Starting from the 'Non-fiction' of People's Literature." *Literature and Art Contention*, no.3, 2011, pp.43-47.]

杨庆祥:《"非虚构写作"的历史、当下与可能》,《中国现代文学研究丛刊》第 7 期,2021 年,第 79—89 页。

[Yang Qingxiang. "The History, Present and Possibility of 'Nonfiction Writing'." *Modern Chinese Literature Research Series*, no. 7, 2021, pp. 79 - 89.]

《人民文学》杂志社:《"人民大地·行动者"非虚构写作计划启事》,《人民文学》第 11 期,2010 年,第 208—208 页。

[People's Literature Magazine. "'People's Land · Actors' Nonfiction Writing Project Announcement." *People's Literature*, no. 11, 2010, pp. 208.]

梁鸿:《前言》,《中国在梁庄》,台海出版社,2016 年。

[Liang Hong. "Preface." *China in Liangzhuang*. Taihai Publishing House, 2016.]

贾平凹:《后记》,《秦岭记》,人民文学出版社,2022 年。

[Jia Pingwa. "Postscript." *The Tale of Qinling Mountains*. People's Literature Publishing House, 2022.]

李遇春:《贾平凹:走向"微写实主义"》,《当代作家评论》第 6 期,2016 年,第 41—51 页。

[Li Yuchun. "Jia Pingwa: 'Towards Microrealism'." *Contemporary Writers Review*, no. 6, 2016, pp. 41 - 51.]

贾平凹:《秦腔》,作家出版社,2018 年。

[Jia Pingwa. *Qin Opera*. Writers Publishing House, 2018.]

谢乔羽,蒋述卓:《〈野望〉的节气美学》,《中国当代文学研究》第 3 期,2023 年,第 146—153 页。

[Xie Qiaoyu, Jiang Shuzhuo. "The aesthetics of the solar term of *A Field View*." *Chinese Contemporary Literature Studies*, no. 3, 2023, pp. 146 - 153.]

从"可能世界"到"实在世界":
科幻小说与现实

杨湃湃

内容摘要:本文运用可能世界(Possible World)理论观照科幻小说与"现实"的关系。科幻小说的概念蕴含着内在张力,它一方面是基于"幻想"的虚构作品,一方面又与"科学"紧密相关,需要遵循现实世界的认知逻辑。依据可能世界理论,科幻小说构建的文本世界虽然不"摹仿"外部客观世界,却与现实有着内在联系:推想未来的科幻小说构建的"可能世界"与社会现实存在"对应"(Counterpart)关系,既反映了科技对人类生活的深刻改造,又显示了人类对科技由"片面乐观"到"全面反思"的认知变化。通过"可能世界"与"实在世界"之间的"互惠反馈"(Reciprocal Feedback),科幻小说既为技术发明提供了灵感,又预警了技术应用催生的社会危机、伦理困境等问题。科幻小说的诗学是对"虚构"与"现实"二元关系的解构,通过对可能世界的虚构,优秀的科幻作品既能反映和批判当下的社会现实,又能对未来世界的现实进行展望,显示出与现实主义文学作品相似的思想深度、批判精神与历史责任感。

关键词:科幻小说　可能世界　现实　虚构

作者简介:杨湃湃,南京大学英语语言文学专业博士研究生,主要研究方向为科幻小说、鲍勃·迪伦、现实主义理论。

Title: From "Possible World" to "Actual World": Science Fiction and Reality

Abstract: This paper employs the Possible World theory to examine the relationship between science fiction and "reality". The connotation of science fiction suggests inherent tension, as it is both a work of fiction based on "fantasy" and closely related to "science", requiring to be consistent with cognitive logic in the actual world. In the light of Possible World theory, science fiction, although not "imitating" the real world, has an inner connection with reality: the "possible world" in the future envisioned by science fiction is "counterpart" of social reality, showcasing the profound impact of technology on human life and the shift in human's perception of technology from "reckless optimism" to "comprehensive reflection". Through "Reciprocal Feedback" between the "possible world" and the "actual world," science fiction not only inspires technological invention but also warns of the social crises and ethical dilemmas arising from the application of technology. The poetics of science fiction deconstruct the binary relationship between "fiction" and "reality". Through the extrapolation of possible worlds, excellent science fiction can reflect the current social reality as well as anticipate the reality of the future world, demonstrating similar intellectual depth, critical spirit, and sense of historical responsibility as literary works of realism.

Key words: Science fiction; Possible World; Reality; Fiction

Author: Yang Paipai (18851822126@163.com) is a PhD candidate in English Language and Literature at Nanjing University, specializing in the research of science fiction, Bob Dylan, and realism theory.

科幻小说与现实的关系紧密而充满张力。当今世界,许多曾经的科幻小说情节都已成为现实,《皮格马利翁的眼镜》(*Pygmalion's Spectacles* 1935)中戴上就可进入异想世界(Paracosma)的眼镜与如今的头戴式虚拟现实设备十分相似;随着 ChatGPT、Sora 等 AI 技术的发展和应用,《我,机器人》(*I, Robot* 1950)中人类与人工智能之间的深度互动和内在矛盾正在融入日常生活;《神经漫游者》(*Neuromancer* 1984)中的赛博空间也由于元宇宙概念的出现引发了更多关注和讨论。然而,科幻小说真的能"预测现实"吗? 中国科幻作家刘慈欣认为,科幻小说可以"把未来的各种可能性排列出来……但这无数个可能的未来哪一个会成为现实,科幻小说并不能告诉我们"(47)。的确,科幻小说无法直接预测未来,甚至可能包含大量科学谬误,但即使是与事实相悖的科幻情节,仍旧可能深刻影响现实世界,比如《弗兰肯斯坦》(*Frankenstein* 1818)中拼凑尸体造人的情节完全不符合实际,却遇见了人造生命带来的安全隐患和伦理问题,在现当代,人们使用"弗兰肯斯坦"来形容核武器、生化武器等威力巨大的技术发明对人类社会的威胁,"弗兰肯斯坦的怪物"也经常被援引警告克隆人和基因工程等技术可能引发的伦理困境(Mellor 525)。可见,科幻小说虽然也是人类想象力的产物,却与奇幻小说、童话、寓言等文类中纯粹脱离现实的奇想有明显的区别。

　　托多罗夫(Tzvetan Todorov)在《荒诞:一种文学体裁的结构方法》(*The Fantastic: A Structural Approach to a Literary Genre* 1973)中区分了多种类型的"超现实"(supernatural):"怪诞奇幻"(hyperbolic marvelous)和"神异奇幻"(exotic marvelous)完全违背现实,其中情节只能诉诸梦境、幻觉或超自然力量;"工具性奇幻"(instrumental marvelous)作品中的事物是"在所描述的时期尚未实现的……技术发展,但从某种程度上说,它们是完全可能的";还有一种"科学奇幻"(scientific marvelous),其中的"超自然现象以一种理性的方式解释,但依据的是当代科学不承认的规律"(54-57)。托多罗夫对"科学奇幻"的界定实际上已经借鉴了"科幻小说"的概念。1926 年,根斯巴克(Hugo Gernsback)在《惊奇故事》(*Amazing Stories*)杂志第 1 期上首创"科幻小说"的说法:"我用科学的小说(scientifiction)来指代儒勒·凡尔纳、H.G.威尔斯和埃德加·爱伦·坡这一类故事",还确立了科幻作品的三个基本要素,"浪漫传奇"(charming romance)的叙事架构,"科学事实(scientific fact)"的阐释和"预言式愿景(prophetic vision)",即对可能的新科学发现或发明进行细节性描述(崴斯特福208)。从根斯巴克的说明中可以看出,科幻小说的概念从形成之初就与"现实"有内在关联:它一方面是"浪漫传奇",是作者主观的幻想;一方面又要基于"科学事实",通过严密的逻辑"外推"(extrapolation),构建符合现实世界认知规律的"预言式愿景"。后来,苏恩文(Darko Suvin)把科幻小说蕴含的这种"幻想与现实"之间的张力总结为"认知陌生化"(cognitive estrangement)(4),"认知"指向经验现实,"陌生化"描述文学效果,在科幻研究界获得了广泛认同。同时,苏恩文还把科幻小说的"外推"创作过程界定为"从虚构('文学')的假设出发,以总体性(totalizing)('科学')的严谨态度加以展开"(6)。

谈及科幻小说基于现实进行逻辑"外推"的写作方式,塑造了美国"科幻小说黄金时代"的科幻作家、编辑坎贝尔(John W. Campbell)曾说,通过"对过去和当前的形势进行想象性的反思……科幻小说将能够成为一条道路……让我们以一个不同以往的视角去思考过去、现在和将来"(转引自崴斯特福214),这说明科幻小说虽然不像传统现实主义作品一样"摹仿""实在世界",却同样可以反思"当前的形势",构建"过去、现在和将来"之间的连续性,触达深层次的社会现实。中国科幻作家是观照科幻与现实关系的理论先行者之一。1981年,科幻作家郑文光首次提出"科幻现实主义"概念,指出科幻小说也是"反映现实生活的小说",如果说现实主义小说是"平面镜",科幻小说就是"折光镜"。当代科幻作家陈楸帆指出,科幻小说和现实主义作品都追求"真实性",科幻小说"基于我们对现有世界运行规律的认知和理解设置规则,然后引入一些变量……引发链式反应……整个世界都将为之产生改变,但这一切都是可理解、可推敲的，符合逻辑的，我们的故事便会在这样的具有'真实性'的舞台上演"（"对'科幻现实主义'的再思考" 39）①。

坎贝尔和陈楸帆实际上都把科幻小说的"真实性"归之于其"外推"的写作方式，而"外推"的实质则是构建"可能世界"。可能世界理论"把世界分为真实世界，即已经实现的可能世界；可能世界，即可能实现但尚未实现的世界；不可能世界，即尚未实现且永远不会实现的世界"（邱蓓 78）。科幻小说即通过"外推"，构建"可能实现但尚未实现的世界"。"一些事项例如'飞船'（air-ship）和穿越空间航行的可能性——必须是已得到承认的；而另一些构思则主要来自已知事实和对科学数据的逻辑演绎或合理推论"（Wicks x-xi）。背景宏大的科幻作品还往往"关注世界建构的复杂性，在（小说）中科幻作家设计出自洽的或然世界。世界建构现在已经成为科幻小说所提供给读者的最可称赞之物"（罗伯茨 3）。"外推"已经成为作家和学者们讨论科幻小说与现实关系的一个关键词，但"可能世界"与现实之间的关系实际上十分复杂，远非"外推"这一单一概念可以概括，哲学上的"可能世界"理论系统为进一步分析科幻小说与现实之间的关系提供了丰富的理论资源。

本文运用可能世界理论观照科幻小说与现实的关系，指出科幻小说构建的文本世界虽然不"摹仿"外部客观世界，却以"可能世界"为虚构的参照域，与现实世界互动密切：依据现实推想未来的科幻小说以"逻辑上的可能世界"为参照域，反映技术对人类生活方式与认知角度的改造过程，反思科技可能催生的伦理和社会问题；而来自不同背景的读者对科幻小说的阅读和评价则通过科幻"可能世界"与"实在世界"之间的"互惠反馈"，推动科幻小说的文学品质与思想深度不断提升，越来越成为人们审视现实的重要视角。科幻小说的诗学是对"虚构"与"现实"二元关系的解构，通过对可能世界的虚构，优秀科幻作品既能反映和批判当下的社会现实，又能对未来世界的现实进行预测和警示，显示出与"现实主义文学"相似的思想深度、批判精神与历史责任感。

一、可能世界视阈下的科幻小说：虚构何以"通达"现实

"可能世界"在哲学上可以追溯到亚里士多德（Aristotle），《诗学》中论及：历史"叙述已经发生过的事"，而诗人的职责"不在于描述发生过的事情，而在于描述可能发生的事，即根据可然或必然的原则可能的事"(81)。莱布尼茨在《神正论》(*Theodicy*)中正式提出该概念："现存世界是偶然的，无数其他的可能世界同样有权要求存在……在无数可能的世界中，上帝选择了最好的一个（使之成为现实）。"(130 - 131)二十世纪七八十年代，"可能世界"概念被引入文艺理论，通过托多罗夫、帕维尔（Thomas Pavel）、多勒泽尔、迈特尔（Doreen Maitre）和瑞恩（Marie-Laure Ryan）等人的阐释与扩充，为文学作品的分类和叙事学解读提供了新视角[②]，也重构了现实主义诗学。

传统的现实主义文学艺术以"摹仿"为核心，"现实主义"作品被认为是摹仿实在世界的虚构作品。在"摹仿"的理论框架下，虚构与现实之间形成了笛卡尔式的二元关系：虚构无论如何与现实相似，都只是一个"摹本"，形而上学上无法通达现实本身。为了跨越"虚构"与"现实"之间的"鸿沟"，理论家们各展其能，有人提出"虚构的特殊性"（fictional particulars）能够表征"事实的普遍性"（actual universals），此论的典型代表是奥尔巴赫（Erich Auerbach）和卢卡奇（György Lukács），还有人以"形式现实主义"（Formal Realism）的写作技巧制造"伪摹仿"（pseudomimetic）效果，此论的典型代表是伊恩·瓦特（Ian Watt）[③]。总而言之，"虚构实体须与事实原型相匹配"（Dolezel 9），也就是说传统的现实主义虚构"只有一个合法的参照域，即现实世界"(2)。在可能世界理论视域下，虚构并不依附于现实，现实主义文本也不是在"摹仿"或"指涉"现实，而是创造或者说召唤了一个独立的文本世界——可能世界，而非现实世界，是现实主义作品的参照域（Dolezel 24 - 26）。虚构作品的

"现实程度",不体现在它对现实世界的摹仿"像不像""典不典型",即"似真性"(verisimilitude)或"普遍性"(universality)上,而是体现在它构建的文本世界与"实在世界"之间的"可通达"(accessibility)关系上。

"可通达性"是可能世界理论视阈下测量文本"现实程度"的指标。虚构的文本世界是否具有"可通达性"取决于它对现实世界规则的改变情况,符合现实世界基本规则的文本即可通达。"利用虚构世界与真实世界的可通达关系,学者们能够界定文学作品的体裁类型,建立可能世界文类理论"(邱蓓 81)。迈特尔在《文学与可能世界》中根据可通达的程度把虚构文本分为四类:一、包含高精确指称真实历史事件的作品;二、包含通过想象产生但是仍可以成为真实事态的作品;三、涉及在可以真实与永远不可能真实之间波动的事态的作品;四、关于永远不可能实现的事态的作品(转引自邱蓓 81)。瑞恩依据文本世界对实在世界规则的改变情况,建构了不同文类系统与实在世界之间可通达关系的量表,将文本世界的"可通达程度"标准进一步细化。该量表从九个方面标识文本世界是否"可通达"现实世界:A. 属性同一性、B. 存品同一性、C. 扩充存品兼容性、D. 编年兼容性、E. 物理兼容性、F. 分类兼容性、G. 逻辑兼容性、H. 分析兼容性、I. 语言兼容性[④]。若九个方面皆为"真"(在图表中以"+"表示),则该文本世界完全可通达现实世界,若九个方面皆为"假"(在图表中以"-"表示),则该文本世界无法通达现实世界。图表中"+"与"-"的数量直观地显示了不同文类的"可通达程度",而"+"与"-"的位置则标明了文本世界对现实世界规则的改变情况。在此量表中,"精确的非虚构作品"(Accurate nonfiction)九个方面皆为"真","象形诗"(concrete poetry)九个方面皆为"假",它们之间不同文类的可通达程度依次降低。现实主义小说(Realistic Historical Fiction)除了 A. 属性同一性、B. 存品同一性、C. 扩充存品兼容性以外,所有的指标都是"+",说明现实主义作品构建的文本世界包含的事物与现实世界并非一一对应,但在时序(D)、物理规律(E)、物种分类(F)、逻辑(G)、分析真理性(H)、语言(I)这些维度上都可以通达现实。

瑞恩的量表为分析"科幻小说"的"现实程度"提供了具象的指标。整体来看,科幻小说位于量表中间,说明其"现实程度"的确处在描摹现实的"精确的非虚构作品"与纯粹为文字游戏和"胡言乱语"的"象形诗"之间,印证了内在于科幻小说概念中的"幻想与现实"之间的张力。据表可知,科幻小说构建的文本世界逻辑上是"可通达"的(E, G, H, I指标都是"+"),但涉及现实世界的具体情况时,不一定具有"可通达性"(A, B, C, D, F指标要么不一定,要么是"□")。也就是说,科幻小说进行虚构的参照域是"逻辑上的可能世界"(logical possible world),却不一定是"实际上的可能世界"(actual possible world),这种不稳定的"可通达性"再次显示了科幻世界与现实世界之间紧密而充满张力的关系,科幻小说中的"可能世界"既是实际上"超现实"的,又是逻辑上"可通达"现实的。使用"可能世界"与"实在世界"之间关系的哲学框架,可以分析科幻小说构建的文本世界与现实的关系。

关于可能世界的哲学理论分为温和实在论与激进实在论。温和实在论的代表人物克里普克(Saul A. Kripke)认为,可能世界是"世界的可能状态"或者"事物的可能存在方式",这个概念描述人们设想出来的"非真实情形",而非实际存在的"不同维度的世界"(Kripke 15)。也就是说,只有"实在世界"具有本体论上的"真实性",所谓"可能世界"即探索"实在世界"的"替代情形"(alternative),而非有意构造改变实在世界规则的平行世界。然而,大部分科幻小说在推想未来时都改变了实在世界的规则,"可以引用不曾存在过的学术权威,并虚构子虚乌有的重量级理论"来"营造必须的逼真氛围"(艾文斯 193)。因此,大多数科幻小说构建的文本世界完全依据自身独有的规则运行,与实在世界在本体论上相互独立。这种具有独立本体论地位的逻辑上的"可能世界"符合激进实在论观点。

二、"逻辑上的可能世界":科幻与现实的"对应关系"

关于"可能世界"的激进实在论以刘易斯(David Lewis)为代表人物,他认为"存在不同于我们碰巧所居住的这个世界的其他一些可能世界……事物除了现在的实际存在方式之外还可能会具有其他许多种存在方式"(Lewis, *On the Plurality of Worlds* 2)。刘易斯定义下的"可能世界"是一种逻辑上可能的"实存",它并不因可通达"现实"而成立,而是与"实在世界"具有同样的本体论地位:论及"实在世界"与众多"可能世界"之间的关系,刘易斯认为,"我们只把这个世界称为现实世界,并不是因为它在性质上与所有其他世界不同,只是因为它是我们所居住的世界。其他世界的居民也可以真实地把他们自己的世界称作现实的"(转引自陈波 第331页)。

在激进实在论框架下观照科幻小说与社会现实之间的关系,需要注意的关键是主体的"认知维度"和虚构文本与现实情况的"对应关系"。激进实在论者纵然认为每个可能世界都与实在世界一样是真实存在的,但也只能基于自己的"生活世界"去认知其他世界。对此,古德曼(Nelson Goodman)的见解很有代表性。古德曼的基本观点符合激进实在论,即现实世界与可能世界不存在"先后","许多不同的世界版本具有彼此独立的价值和重要性,不存在任何要求或假设可以把它们还原为单一基础"(4)。古德曼指出,无论是现实世界还是可能世界,都是主体思想建构的产物(20),他用"版本"(version)一词来描述这些对现实世界的个体描述或感知,并声称"这些版本——有些相互冲突,有些相差悬殊,以至于它们之间的冲突或兼容性无法确定——都同样正确(Raghunath 53)。瑞恩对古德曼的评论揭示了这些"版本"与现实的关系:"版本,顾名思义,就是某物的版本"("The Text as World" 148),所以每个独立的"可能世界"实质上都是主体对"原初之物"(也就是现实世界)的认知图像。因此,尽管在激进实在论下"可能世界""之间的冲突或兼容性无法确定",而且未必"通达"现实,它们却与现实存在千丝万缕的"对应关系"。刘易斯这样描述不同世界中的"对应物":"你的对应物(counterparts)在内容(content)和背景(context)等重要方面都与你非常相似。它们比它们世界中的任何其他事物都更像你"("Counterpart Theory" 114)。由于激进实在论下每个可能世界都与实在世界一样是"确实存在"的,独立的不同世界之间不存在"同一性",只能讨论"相似性"。这种基于相似的"对应物理论"被克里普克批判为模糊不清,却比较准确地描述了科幻小说构建的文本世界与现实世界之间的关系。在科幻文学的创作中,"对应"不是落在具体的"对应物"上(现实主义小说与现实世界存在许多具体的"对应物"),而是科幻作品对未来的想象整体上"对应"和反映了现实情况。理解科幻构造的"可能世界",要从作为建构主体的作者如何认知科技、写作科幻小说入手,分析科幻文本中的"可能世界"与不同时期的现实世界之间的"对应关系"。

  世界上最早的科幻小说之一——开普勒(Johannes Kepler)的《梦》(*Somnium, The Dream* 1634)就是科幻小说的内容与现实"对应"的生动例子。故事的主人公在经过一次月球之旅后讲述了从月球看到的地球外观和天体运动,从而为地动说提供了直观的说明。在故事的注释中,开普勒直言"我写《梦》的目的在于以月球为例建立起一个支持地动说的论证"(艾文斯 169),因为在当时的社会"科学的探究在可能的宗教迫害面前蒙受着危险"(170),可见这篇科幻作品本身就颇具现实意义,旨在推动科学在现实世界确立自身的合法性。19 世纪,电气时代到来,科技发展带来了许多新发明,也激发了科幻作家对未来的美好愿景,"对应"在科幻小说中,爱伦·坡的作品是其中典例。"随着(爱伦·坡)对'科学发现的美学'的欣赏与日俱增,他试图通过文学手段来传播和赞美科学奇迹的尝试也变得更加多样和富有创造性"(Stableford 18)。在坡的小说中，主人公乘坐热气球进行月球之旅［《汉斯·普法尔无与伦比的冒险》("The Unparalleled Adventure of One Hans Pfaall")］，气球在三日内横越大西洋［《气球骗局》("The Balloon Hoax")］，还出现了"能战胜几乎所有人类棋手的自动下棋机器人"和"智力远超越其创造者，能在1秒内完成5万人一年计算量的生物"［《一千零二夜的故事》("The Thousand-and-Second Tale of Scheherazad")］。在此时期，科幻作家对科技的认知根植于启蒙思想，认为奇妙的技术发明会使未来生活更美好。

进入20世纪中后期，科幻写作形成了两条不同的"外推"逻辑："60年代许多'实验'科幻是暗色调的，而持续的商业科幻主流则是鲜明的积极乐观，他们相信通过努力，人类能够建立一个技术拯救一切的世界"(Broderick 55)。科幻作家对技术态度的分化也与当时的现实情况密不可分。二十世纪六七十年代科技成果颇丰，出现了激光(1960)、LED、核潜艇(1960)、集成电路(1961)、个人电脑(1971)等影响深远的发明，阿姆斯特朗(Neil Armstrong)还在1969年成功登月。与此同时，科技的迅猛发展也催生了一些难以解决的问题，作为全球科技发展最快的国家，20世纪60年代的美国甚至一度笼罩着"末日氛围"：1962年的古巴导弹危机使全美人民生活在对核战的恐惧中；60年代末，洛杉矶和纽约的雾霾问题严重到可能致人死亡；1969年1月，联合石油公司的一个钻井平台在加利福尼亚州圣巴巴拉海岸发生爆炸，约10万桶原油倾倒入海，导致大量生物死亡；1969年6月，美国水道的工业石油污染引起凯霍加河火灾。"对应"在科幻小说中，有些作品依旧高唱科技的赞歌，但推测科技将带来问题，甚至毁灭世界的科幻作品也开始出现。比如，舒特(Nevil Shute)的《海滩》(*On the Bcach*, 1957)和霍班(Russell Hoban)的《漫步者雷德利》(*Riddley Walker*, 1980)以核战争和世界末日为背景，布林(David Brin)的《地球》(*Earth*, 1990)预测全球环境即将崩溃。

随着科幻小说新浪潮运动的开展，科幻作家开始有意识地超越启

425

蒙叙事,对技术发明进行全面的反思,形成了不同于"技术创造美好未来"的全新叙事。在潘辛(Alexei Panshin)的《成年仪式》(*Rite of Passage*, 1968)和斯科特(Ridley Scott)的电影《异形》(*Alien*)中,火箭和飞船不再是逃离地球、进军太空的希望之舟,而是"脆弱而且环境极其封闭",飞行器内部的生存和权力争斗成为科幻作品的叙事核心,"通过技术应用摆脱人类环境的想法已经转变为不同的形式"(Jones 165);机器人也不再是阿西莫夫(Isaac Asimov)笔下忠实于人类的"好仆人"[⑤],在《类人生物》(*The Humanoids*, 1949)中,类人生物取代人类,主宰地球;《与机器人的战争》(*War with the Robots: Science Fiction Stories*, 1962)的封面上写着"人类制造了机器,当发现危险,为时已晚";在《仿生人会梦见电子羊吗?》(*Do Androids Dream of Electric Sheep?*, 1968)中,仿生人具有高度复杂的思想和情感,与人类之间的区别难以界定。时至今日,关于机器人取代人类,引起伦理危机的叙事依旧备受关注,近年出现了《机器人末日》(*Robopocalypse*, 2011)、《克拉拉与太阳》(*Klara and the Sun*, 2022)等科幻新作。

詹明信(Fredric Jameson)曾指出"在社会层面上……我们的想象力受制于我们自己的生产方式(或许还受制于它所保留的过去生产方式的残余)"(*Archaeologies of the Future* xiii),科幻作家对可能世界的想象亦如是,不同时期的科幻作者推想未来、构思"可能世界"的不同逻辑受制于各自时代的社会现实,科幻小说叙事模式的发展史也是科技与现实关系的嬗变史。

三、"可能世界"与"实在世界"的互动:互惠反馈机制

通过分析科幻作家建构可能世界的逻辑可以发现,科幻小说描绘的"可能世界"在本体论上是独立的,但实际上是"现实的寄生虫"(Eco 63),作为可能世界的认知主体,读者如何阅读科幻小说,也揭示了科幻

作品与现实世界之间的彼此影响和相互塑造。读者在阅读过程中本能地依据他们自己生活的世界来体认虚构世界,因此,他们对文本世界的想象本来就与现实世界尽可能相似,只有在文本的提示下才会出现偏差。更确切地说,读者通过与现实世界的类比来弥补虚构世界不可避免的不完整性(Doležel 22)——除非文本本身明确规定了某些从现实世界的偏离,比如,在勒奎恩(Ursula K. Le Guin)的"海恩斯宇宙"(Hainish universe)系列小说中,格森星球上的人被规定为雌雄同体人,艾斯珊星球上的人被规定具有通过做梦洞察潜意识的能力。瑞恩将这一基本规则称为"最小化偏差原则"(The Principle of Minimal Departure)(*Artificial Intelligence* 48-5)。读者依据自己在现实世界的经验来理解科幻小说构建的可能世界,"这种世界之间的流动使读者能够在现实世界的领域内对文本世界进行语境分析和评价,同时也在文本世界的领域内对现实世界进行语境分析和评价"(Raghunath 89),拉古纳特(Riyukta Raghunath)把这个过程称为"可能世界"与"实在世界"之间的"互惠反馈机制"(Reciprocal Feedback)(Raghunath 68)。"互惠反馈"生动体现在科幻小说的创作史和接受史中,科幻作品从被视为商业导向的流行文化到渐渐为文学批评界认可,走入严肃文学的"大雅之堂",其实也是科幻构建的可能世界与现实世界之间"互惠反馈"的结果,在这一过程中,科技对人类生活的影响越来越大,科幻作品反映现实的深度与艺术水平也不断提高。

  在其发展的初期阶段,科幻小说令读者感到兴奋的原因是其对技术应用场景的展望。读者"在文本世界的领域内对现实世界进行语境分析和评价",倾向于认为科幻小说中出现的技术,未来将变为现实。为技术创新提供灵感也是科幻小说作为一种文本类型最初的指向,世界上第一本科幻小说杂志《惊奇故事》的创始人根斯巴克本人既是发明家又是科幻作家,他认为,科幻小说可以"通过教育公众认识科学的可能性和科学对生活的影响,使世界成为人类更美好的家园"。根斯巴克希望科幻小说能够"预言新的科学发现和技术发明",并提供"能实际指导青少年读者如何尝试科学的故事,来激发他们从事科学的兴趣"(Landon 140)。由于它为大众提供了畅想未来世界的窗口,"科幻小说在电影业和出版业中都占有重要地位……一直畅销不衰,在所有主要工业国家都很受欢迎"(Travis 244)。然而,作为"文学作品",科幻小说最初却未得到广泛承认,因为作家和批评家们"在现实世界的领域内对文本世界进行语境分析和评价",认为科幻小说情节程式化,缺乏思想内涵,只是"低俗的消遣,缺乏任何于事有补的社会价值"(艾文斯 199)。谈到著名科幻小说家 H. G. 威尔斯的作品,作家切斯特顿(G. K. Chesterton)说"(威尔斯先生)凭着相对狭隘的科学观点,无法看清楚,有些事情事实上不应是科学的。他仍然受到科学谬误的影响……不从人的灵魂开始(写起),却从细胞质开始"。《奇幻与科幻》杂志评论员阿尔弗雷德·贝斯特(Alfred Bester)说,"许多科幻作家在作品中反映出自己是多么的愚蠢和幼稚,他们把科幻视作避难所,在这里他们可以无视现实,随意制定规则以适应自己的无能"(Broderick 50)。

20 世纪中期以来,反思技术应用之隐患的科幻作品大量涌现,读者通过阅读科幻小说"对现实世界进行语境分析和评价",更加关注科技催生的伦理和社会问题,得到了关于未来世界的警示。例如,"在公共管理实践方面,科幻小说《神经漫游者》成了一段时期内世界各国规划未来网络发展的参考读物"(吴岩 2),科幻电影《物种》(*Species*, 1995)影响了 2008 年英国《人类受精和胚胎学法案》的修订⑥,法律上对复杂的案件进行裁决,还会参考科幻小说:在 Rank Hovis McDougall 有限公司诉专利、设计和商标局局长案([1978] F. S. R. 588)中,法官认为"尽管目前的科幻小说显示,有朝一日人类可能会制造出生物,因此根据 1964 年法案可以申请专利,但这并不意味着,人类制造出的东西就一定是成文法意义上的制造品"。Re A Ward of Court,[1995] Nos. 167、171、175、177 案的裁决指出"医疗技术的进步模糊了生死之间的界限——从前,这些进步是儒勒·凡尔纳和 H. G. 威尔斯等科幻小说家的构想"。医疗技术有效地创造了一个悬浮的"黄昏地带",在那里,死亡开始了,而生命却以某种形式延续着。然而,"有些病人并不希望仅靠医疗技术维持生命,他们更愿意选择一种顺其自然的医疗方案,让自己死得有尊严"(Travis 259)。

与此同时,由于文人学者们亲眼见证社会现实在科幻中得到了生动的预演和深刻的反思,文学界越来越关注科幻小说。20 世纪 70 年代中期,科幻作品"拥有了学术关注和深度",以苏恩文为代表的学者"已经确信这种文学应该与探讨作品、社会和历史之间的关联的结构主义理论以及……马克思主义理论家放在一起研究",因为科幻小说与现实世界紧密相关,体现出"庞杂的物质性"(哈斯勒 260)。随着科幻小说触及的议题愈加复杂而有现实参考价值,科幻小说的读者也更有素养和批判思维能力,会对小说写作进行一系列颇具见地的批评。哈罗德·布鲁姆(Harold Bloom)曾评价获得雨果奖与星云奖的作品《黑暗的左手》(*The Left Hand of Darkness*),是一本"值得多次重读的书",因为"它具有伟大之作(a great representation)的关键品质,即为我们所谓的现实提供了新的视角"(Bloom 6-7),而即使是这样具有现实参考价值的佳作也收到了一些读者的批评,因为他们认为其中描写的"雌雄同体人"太像男人,而非男性与女性生理特征与社会角色的结合,影响了小说对性别塑造与社会结构的有效探究(Le Guin 169-171)。

学界的关注和读者层次的提升同时"反哺"了科幻小说的创作,更多优秀的科幻作品问世,通过推想未来有力地表征现实。比如,赛博朋克小说"将诸多重大议题,如人与科技、资本、阶层、代际等社会问题,总体性地纳入其设想的多元空间之内,具象地展开了对当代社会境况及其前景的反思与批判"(王一平 129),被詹明信称为"对晚期资本主义的……最佳文学表达"(*Postmodernism* 419)。以现在的视角反观科幻小说的发展史,会发现曾经仅在科幻小说中出现的技术和社会问题许多都已经成为事实,科幻小说建构的可能世界或许不能真正从"实在世界""通达",但它与现实的内在"对应"与"互惠反馈"关系为反映现实提供了独特而具有洞察力的视角。

结　语

刘慈欣曾表示,"我最初创作科幻小说的目的,是为了逃离平淡的生活,用想象力去接触那些我永远无法到达的神奇时空。但后来我发现,周围的世界变得越来越像科幻小说了"(46),其实,当代科幻小说持续受到广大读者的欢迎,科幻小说研究也越来越被学术界关注,从根本上讲就是因为"世界越来越像科幻小说","科技已成为我们当今社会不可分割的一部分,你无法想象如何剥离了科技成分去讨论我们的日常生活经验"(陈楸帆,"'超真实'时代" 46-47)。

通过在可能世界的理论视阈下分析科幻小说的叙事模式和发展历程,我们可以发现,从其诞生之初,科幻小说对可能世界的构建就深受现实世界的影响,包含着对社会现象的反思与潜在危机的预判。科幻小说不仅"已经成为今天的'现实主义文学'"(韩松,丁杨 2),而且始终与其他现实主义文学作品一样,是"来源于现实却又高于现实的艺术现实"(王守仁 132)。

注解【Notes】

① 许多中国当代学者与科幻作家都对科幻小说与现实主义的关系提出过富有见地的论述,见丁杨,韩松.《在今天,科幻小说其实是"现实主义"文学》,《中华读书报》2019-01-30,011,书评周刊·文学;陈楸帆,胡勇.《专访陈楸帆:科幻是人类最大的现实主义》,2015.09.10.(https://www.tmtpost.com/1430551.html);姜振宇.《贡献与误区:郑文光与"科幻现实主义"》,《中国现代文学研究丛刊》.08(2017):78-92。

② 见托多罗夫《荒诞:一种文学体裁的结构方法》、帕维尔《虚构世界》(*Fictional Worlds* 1986)、多勒泽尔《异宇宙:虚构与可能世界》(*Heterocosmica: Fiction and Possible Worlds* 1998)、迈特尔《文学与可能世界》(*Literature and Possible*

Worlds 1983)、和瑞恩《可能世界、人工智能与叙述研究》(*Possible Worlds, Artificial Intelligence and Narrative Theory* 1991)。

③ 见多勒泽尔(Lubomir Dolezel)在《异宇宙：虚构与可能世界》第7—9页对奥尔巴赫的《摹仿说》(*Mimesis: The Representation of Reality in Western Literature*, 1957)和瓦特的《小说的兴起》(*Rise of the Novel*)的分析。对"伪摹仿"(pseudomimetic)概念更加详细的解析见多勒泽尔"摹仿与可能世界"(Mimesis and Possible World)第479—480页。笔者认为，卢卡奇的"典型人物论"也是以"虚构的特殊性"表征"事实的普遍性"的理论代表。

④ 参看瑞恩的"Possible Worlds and Accessibility Relations: A Semantic Typology of Fiction"第558—559页，对九个指标的含义有详细的说明。第560页的"文类与可通达关系"量表如下：

	Genre and Accessibility Relations									
	A	B	C	D	E	F	G	H	I
Accurate nonfiction	+	+	+	+	+	+	+	+	+
Ture fiction	+	+	+	+	+	+	+	+	+
Realistic & historical fiction	+	−	+	+	+	+	+	+	+
Historical confabulation	−	−	+	+	+	+	+	+	+
Realistic ahistorical fiction	*	−	+	+	+	+	+	+	+
Anticipation	+	−	+	−	+	+	+	+	+
Science fiction	+ / *	−	+ / −	−	+	+ / −	+	+	+
Fairy tale	*	−	−	+	−	−	+	+	+
Legend	−	−	+	+	−	−	+	+	+
Fantastic realism	+ / *	−	+ / −	+	−	+	+	+	+
Nonsense rhymes	−	−	− / +	#	−	− / +	−	+ / −	+
Jabberwockyism	−	−	#	−	−	−	?	+	−
Concrete poetry	−	−	#	−	−	−	−	−	−

431

＊: nonapplicable because of a "−" on C

♯: nonapplicable because of a "−" or "?" on G: when the laws of logic no longer hold, the concept of time loses any meaning.

A = identity of properties F = taxonomic compatibility

B = identity of inventory G = logical compatibility

C = compatibility of inventory H = analytical compatibility

D = chronological compatibility I = linguistic compatibility

E = physical compatibility

⑤ 阿西莫夫1950年前后提出了"机器人三定律",作为机器人的"道德原则":一、机器人不可伤害人类,或者通过不作为方式使人类受到伤害;二、机器人必须遵守人类下达的命令,但如果这些命令有违第一条准则,机器人可以不服从;三、机器人必须保护其自身存在,条件是不得与第一条和第二条准则相冲突。(Jones 166)

⑥ Mitchell Travis. "Making Space: Law and Science Fiction". *Law and Literature*. Vol. 23, No. 2 (Summer 2011), pp. 241–261. 对这个问题做了说明。

引用文献【Works Cited】

亚里士多德.《诗学》,陈忠梅译。北京:商务印书馆,1996。

[Aristotle. *Poetics*. Trans. Chen Zhongmei. The Commercial Press, 1996.]

Bloom, Harold. "Introduction." *Ursula K. Le Guin's The Left Hand of Darkness*. Chelsea House Publishers, 1987.

Broderick, Damien. "New Wave and Backwash: 1960–1980", in *The Cambridge Companion to Science Fiction*. Eds. Edward James, Farah Mendelsohn. Cambridge University Press, 2003.

陈波.《逻辑哲学》. 北京:北京大学出版社,2005年。

[Chen Bo. *Philosophy of Logic*. Beijing: Peking University Press, 2005.]

陈楸帆.《对"科幻现实主义"的再思考》.《名作欣赏》. 28(2013): 38–39.

[Chen Qiufan. "Rethink Science Fiction Realism." *Masterpieces Review*. 28 (2013): 38–39.]

——.《"超真实"时代的科幻文学创作》.《中国比较文学》. 02(2020): 36–49.

[---. "Science Fiction Writing in Hyper-reality Era." *Comparative Literature in China*. 02(2020): 36–49.]

Chesterton, G. K. *Heretics*, in *The Complete Works of G. K. Chesterton*, Delphi Classics, 2014.

丁杨.韩松.《在今天,科幻小说其实是"现实主义"》.《文学中华读书报》2019-01-30,011,书评周刊·文学.

[Ding Yang and Han Song. "Today, Science Fiction is Realistic." *China Reading Weekly*, 2019-01-30, 011, Book Review/Literature.]

Dolezel, Lubomir. *Heterocosmica: Fiction and Possible Worlds*. The Johns Hopkins University Press, 1998.

---. "Mimesis and Possible World." *Poetics Today*, 1988, Vol.9, No.3, *Aspects of Literary Theory* (1988), pp.475–496.

Eco, Umberto. "Small Worlds." *Versus* 52/53: 53–70, 1989.

阿瑟 B. 艾文斯.《科幻批评的起源:从开普勒到威尔斯》.《科幻文学的评与建构》,(美)詹姆逊等著,王逢振等译. 合肥:安徽文艺出版社,2011,第 165 页至第 203 页.

[Euans. Arthur B. "The Origins of Science Fiction Criticism: From Kepler to Wells" in *Criticism and Construction of Science Fiction Literature* by Robert Scholes and Fredric Jameson, with Arthur B. Evans etc. Trans. Wang Fengzhen ect. Hefei: Anhui Literature and Art Publishing House, 2011, pp. 165–203.]

Ferreira, Rachel Haywood. "Ciencia Ficción / Ficção Científica from Latin America" in *The Cambridge History of Science Fiction*. Eds. Gerry Canavan, and Eric Carl Link. Cambridge University Press, 2018.

Goodman, Nelson. *Ways of Worldmaking*. Indianapolis: Hackett Publishing, 1978.

唐纳德·M. 哈斯勒.《科幻批评的学术先驱 1940-1980》.《科幻文学的批评与建构》,(美)詹姆逊等著,王逢振等译. 合肥:安徽文艺出版社,2011,第 239—303 页。

[Hassler, Donald M. "Academic Pioneer of Science Fiction Criticism 1940–1980" in *Criticism and Construction of Science Fiction Literature* by Robert Scholes and Fredric Jameson, with Arthur B. Evans etc. Trans. Wang Fengzhen ect. Hefei: Anhui Literature and Art Publishing House, 2011, pp.239–303.]

Jameson, Fredric. *Archaeologies of the Future: The Desire Called Utopia and Other Science Fictions*. Verso, 2005.

---. *Postmodernism, or, The Cultural Logic of Late Capitalism*. Duke University Press, 1991.

Jones, Gwyneth. "The Icons of Science Fiction", in *The Cambridge Companion to Science Fiction*. Eds. Edward James, Farah Mendelsohn. Cambridge: Cambridge University Press, 2003.

Kepler, Johannes. *Kepler's Somnium; the Dream, or Posthumous Work on Lunar Astronomy.* University of Wisconsin Press, 1967.

Kripke, Saul A. *Naming and Necessity.* Harvard University Press, 1980.

Landon, Brooks. "The Gernsback Years: Science Fiction and the Pulps in the 1920s and 1930s", in *The Cambridge History of Science Fiction*, Gerry Canavan and Eric Carl ed., Cambridge University Press, 2019.

Leibniz, Gottfried Wilhelm. *Theodicy: Essays on the Goodness of God the Freedom of Man and the Origin of Evil.* Trans. E. M. Huggard. BiblioBazaar, 2007.

Le Guin, Ursula K. *The Language of the Night.* Harper Perennial, 1993.

Lewis, David K. "Truth in Fiction." *American Philosophical Quarterly* 15: 37 – 46, 1978.

---. *On the Plurality of Worlds.* Basil Blackwell, 1987.

---. "Counterpart Theory and Quantified Modal Logic." *The Journal of Philosophy*, Vol. 65, No. 5. (Mar. 7, 1968), pp. 113 – 12.

刘慈欣.《我写科幻小说,但是我不预测未来》.《少先队研究》.02(2019): 46 – 47.

[Liu Cixin. "I Write Science Fiction, But I Don't Predict the Future." *Young Pioneer Review.* 02(2019): 46 – 47.]

Mellor, Anne K. "Mary Wollstonecraft Shelley." *The Oxford Encyclopedia of British Literature,* Shanghai Foreign Language Education Press, 2009.

Maitre, Doreen. *Literature and Possible Worlds.* Hendon: Middlesex Polytechnic, 1983.

Poe, Edgar Allan. *The Science Fiction of Edgar Allan Poe.* Penguin Books, 1976.

邱蓓.《可能世界理论》.《外国文学》. 02(2018): 77 – 86.

[Qiu Bei. "Possible World Theory." *Foreign Literature.* 02(2018): 77 – 86.]

亚当·罗伯茨.《科幻小说史》. 马小悟译,北京:北京大学出版社,2010.

[Roberts, Adam. *The History of Science Fiction.* Trans. Ma Xiaowu. Beijing: Peking University Press, 2010.]

Ryan, Marie-Laure. "Possible Worlds and Accessibility Relations: A Semantic Typology of Fiction". *Poetics Today*, Autumn, 1991, Vol. 12, No. 3 (Autumn, 1991), pp. 553 – 576.

---. *Possible Worlds, Artificial Intelligence, and Narrative Theory.* Bloomington: Indiana University Press, 1991.

---. "The Text as World Versus the Text as Game: Possible Worlds Semantics and Postmodern Theory". *Journal of Literary Semantics,* 27(3), 137 – 163, 1998.

Stableford, Brian. "Science Fiction Before the Genre", in *The Cambridge Companion to Science Fiction.* Eds. Edward James, Farah Mendelsohn.

Cambridge University Press, 2003.

Suvin, Darko. *Metamorphoses of Science Fiction: On the Poetics and History of a Literary Genre*. Yale University Press, 1979.

Todorov, Tzvetan. *The Fantastic a Structural Approach to a Literary Genre*. Press of Case Western Reserve University, 1973.

Travis, Mitchell. "Making Space: Law and Science Fiction". *Law and Literature*, Vol. 23, No. 2 (Summer 2011), pp. 241 - 261.

王守仁."现实主义文学研究的勃勃生机".《浙江社会科学》(10): 129 - 142, 2021.

[Wang Shouren. On the New Developments of Literary Realism Studies. Zhejiang Social Sciences. (10): 129 - 142, 2021.]

王一平."《神经漫游者》的三重空间书写与批判".《外国文学研究》43.02(2021): 128 - 139.

[Wang Yiping. "The Representation and Criticism of the Three Spaces in Neuromancer." *Foreign Literature Studies*. 43.02(2021): 128 - 139.]

格雷·崴斯特福."科幻批评的通俗传统 1926—1980".《科幻文学的批评与建构》,(美)詹姆逊等著,王逢振等译. 合肥:安徽文艺出版社,2011,第 204 页至第 238 页。

[Westfahl, Gary. "The Popular Tradition of Science Fiction Criticism 1926 - 1980" in *Criticism and Construction of Science Fiction Literature* by Robert Scholes and Fredric Jameson, with Arthur B. Evans etc. Trans. Wang Fengzhen ect. Hefei: Anhui Literature and Art Publishing House, 2011, pp. 204 - 238.]

Wicks, Mark. "Preface". *To Mars via the Moon: An Astronomical Story*. Ballantyne Press, 1911.

吴岩."总序".《亿万年大狂欢:西方科幻小说史》,布赖恩·奥尔迪斯、戴维·温格罗著,舒伟、孙法理、孙丹丁译,合肥:安徽文艺出版社,2011.

[Wu Yan. "General Preface" of *Trillion Year Spree: The History of Science Fiction* by Brian Aldiss with David Wingrove. Trans. Shu Wei, Sun Fali, and Sun Danding. Hefei: Anhui Literature and Art Publishing House, 2011.]

郑文光."在文学创作座谈会上关于科幻小说的发言",《科幻小说创作参考资料》,中国科普创作协会科学文艺委员会编,1982 年 5 月,总第 4 期。

[Zheng Wenguang. "Speech at the Forum of Literature Creation on Science Fiction" in *References of Science Fiction Writing*. Edited by the Science and Art Committee of China Popular Science Creation Association. May 1982, Issue 4.]

科幻与现实主义文学的距离与张力

林 叶

内容摘要：波粒二象性的光学实验表明，人类的主观实验观察方式可以改变客观现实世界。以时间轴、技术发展为移动坐标，同一文艺作品表现出科幻/现实的二象性，由此科幻与现实主义文学亦产生了距离与张力。本文选取的分析样本有：现实主义经典风格的1974年北岛《波动》的加速度开头叙事、1982年铁凝《哦，香雪》的火车停留一分钟以及电视剧《狂飙》中1996年开始的"小灵通热"；近期热议的科幻议题，如2022年詹姆斯·卡梅隆的《阿凡达2：水之道》"家"的集体意识、2023年《三体》电视剧的大众化传播模式以及《瞬息全宇宙》的中年大妈伊芙琳（杨紫琼饰）在亚裔社区的平凡生活轨迹。前者在现实主义中带有科幻性；后者的科幻作品体现了现实风格。而刘慈欣与赵树理"个体群像化"的人物描写共同形成了"物化"的人物张力。科幻文学具有破除本质论和二元对立思维的不确定性特质，对于现实主义文学具有跨学科、多视角的启发性。

关键词：量子思维　不确定性　加速度　平行宇宙　跨学科

作者简介：林叶，天涯杂志社编辑，博士，主要从事科幻文学与中国现当代文学研究。

Title: The Wave-Particle Duality of Science Fiction and Reality

Abstract: The optical experiments of wave-particle duality shows that human observation can change the objective world. Taking time axis and technological development as moving coordinates, the same literary works manifest the duality of science fiction or reality. The samples of the double-slit experiment extracted in this paper are as follows: the acceleration beginning narration of Bei Dao's *Wave* in 1974, the one-minute train stopover in *Oh, Xiangxue* by Tie Ning in 1982, and the "*PHS fever*" in the TV drama *Storm* from 1996. In 2022, the collective consciousness of "Home" in James Cameron's *Avatar 2: The Way of Water*, the popular communication mode of TV series *Three-Body* in 2023, and the ordinary life trajectory of Evelyn (Michelle Yeoh), the middle-aged woman in *Everything Everywhere ALL at Once* in the Asian community. The former is sci-fi in realism; The latter's sci-fi works reflect the realistic style. And Liu Cixin and Zhao Shuli's "individual group image" character description together formed a "materialized" character tension. Wave-particle duality, which breaks the uncertainty of essentialism and binary opposition thinking, has inspired comparative perspectives and interdisciplinary cultural studies, including the humanities.

Key words: quantum thinking; uncertainty; acceleration; parallel universe; interdisciplinary

Author: Lin Ye is an editor at *Frontiers*, Hainan, China. His research interests are science fiction and Chinese modern and contemporary literature.

文学的本质是什么？从经典光学的双缝实验视角看，文学不一定是人的文学，钱谷融提出的"文学是人学"是20世纪80年代的社会文化氛围倡导和召唤的强调"人的主体性"的经典文学观念。而在21世纪的人工智能浪潮下，文学更可能是接近于去人类中心主义的物理学和文学跨界融合的科幻文学。运用光学的波粒二象性进行思想实验,我们可以发现内涵丰富的经典文艺作品是多个双缝实验装置,既是现实的也是科幻的。当故事中人的行为和新技术趋势相悖时,通常面临阻力和失败;而应用新技术进行同频共振则可能产生现象级的轰动效应。不过在此之前总是要克服旧思维、旧习俗的固有惯性和羁绊。新发明的技术就像一块磁石,周围环绕着不同的人物和事件,情节的起承转合在环形轨道上或远或近地运行,在地球的不同片场演绎出人世间的悲欢离合,拉伸出各自专属的张力。缘于"距离"不同,"这不是物理的距离,而是指想象和幻想的力度和自由度……科幻小说中的想象世界肯定不能与现实太近,否则就会失去其魅力甚至存在的意义。但想象世界与现实的距离也不能太远,否则读者无法把握。创造想象世界如同发射一颗卫星,速度太小则坠回地面,速度太大则逃逸到虚空中。科幻的想象世界,只有找准其在现实和想象之间的平衡点,才真正具有生命力。"(刘慈欣 104)文学即"光",有光的地方就有文学。文学和光一样古老,为不同时代不同的人观察思考。

一、科幻的牵引力:加速度的火车站叙事

当82岁高龄的托尔斯泰在晚年离家出走,还来不及前往高加索或西欧就最终病逝于阿斯塔波沃火车站。这一事件充满了隐喻,似乎象征着十九世纪现实主义文学告一段落,也宣告了二十世纪文学开启。当与此相关的人物、时间顺新技术而为时,科学与文学的相互交织和碰撞产生了独特的科幻特质。"新作家的产生也许还得归因于一系列环境因素:新编辑、新杂志、科幻小说的演化、相互激励、科学和社会学投入、不断变化的社会条件——比如我们经常提到的'蒸汽机时代'。"(冈恩 235)

> 车站到了,缓冲器吱吱嘎嘎地响着。窗外闪过路灯、树影和一排跳动的栅栏。列车员打开车门,拉起翻板,含糊不清地

嚷了句什么。一股清爽的空气迎面扑来,我深深地吸了一口,走下车厢。站台上空荡荡的。远处,机车喷着汽,一盏白惨惨的聚光灯在升腾的雾气中摇曳。从列车狭长的阴影里传来小锤叮当的敲击声。(北岛 45)

这是《波动》的开头,也是很多读者喜欢的句词类型。这是北岛于 1974 年 10 月前后动笔并完成初稿的小说,这种"快"的叙事速度奠定了整个小说的"现代化"叙事调子。这在当时说不清、道不明的叙事产生的令当时的读者所着迷的现代意识是通过火车的缓冲器、翻板、机车和小锤叮当的敲击声等波动传递的。确切地说,是火车的动力加速了小说的叙事速度,由此产生了一种类似达科·苏恩文所说的陌生化的文学类型。当时间轴停留在中国火车发展史和第一次工业革命上,这是用科幻的视角对火车的描述。1974 年,东风 4 型机车正式出厂,转入批量生产,时速突破 120 km/h,标志着我国新一代内燃机车登场。① 刘慈欣曾说:"当自己第一次看到轰鸣的大型火力发电机组,第一次看到高速歼击机在头顶呼啸而过时,那种心灵的震颤,这震颤只能来自对一种巨大的强有力的美的深切感受。"(刘慈欣 3)从移动时间轴和交通迭代的视角看火车已经由此诞生了数不胜数的经典文艺作品,文学表现出了丰富的波粒性。以今日之眼光看绿皮火车已是认为是落后的技术,而站在 1982 年的时间轴上,在铁凝的《哦,香雪》中,这可能是改变命运的新事物。

> 如果不是有人发明了火车,如果不是有人把铁轨铺进深山,你怎么也不会发现台儿沟这个小村。它和它的十几户乡亲,一心一意掩藏在大山那深深的皱褶里,从春到夏,从秋到冬,默默的接受着大山任意给予的温存和粗暴。
> 然而,两根纤细、闪亮的铁轨延伸过来了。它勇敢地盘旋

在山腰,又悄悄的试探着前进,弯弯曲曲,曲曲弯弯,终于绕到台儿沟脚下,然后钻进幽暗的隧道,冲向又一道山梁,朝着神秘的远方奔去。(铁凝)

这个开头多么像科幻小说!铁凝曾自述:"1985年在纽约一次同美国作家的座谈会上,曾经有一位美国青年要我讲一讲香雪的故事,我毫不犹豫地拒绝了他。因为在我内心深处,觉得一个美国青年是无法懂得中国贫穷的山沟里一个女孩子的世界的。但是拗不过他们的一再要求,我用三言两语讲述了小说梗概,我说这是一个女孩和火车的故事,我写一群从未出过大山的女孩子,每天晚上是怎样像等待情人一样地等待在她们村口只停留一分钟的一列火车。出乎我意料,在场的人理解了这小说。他们告诉我,因为你表达了一种人类的心灵能够同感受到的东西。也许这是真实的。"(於可训 79)铁凝的这篇成名作具有技术乐观主义的基调,现在读来仍然耳目一新。谢有顺、贺绍俊和戴锦华等众多学者,曾围绕人性、社会的人类社会学维度去解读,折射出了1980年代中国社会特殊的文化症候。而程光炜从知青经历和观察香雪等千千万万个农村少女们的"劳动人民意识"(程光炜 58),这些解读是有阅历且犀利的。笔者认为这些角度总体上看是以人类的情感叙事表达的,如果以火车的视角进行观察,解读将变得具有科幻风格。这和张爱玲的"电车回家"萌发的现代意识是异曲同工的。"城里人的思想,背景是条纹布的幔子,淡淡的白条子便是行驶着的电车——平行的,匀净的,声响的河流,汩汩流入下意识里去……'电车回家'这句子仿佛不很合适——大家公认电车为没有灵魂的机械,而'回家'两个字有着无数的情感洋溢的联系……有时候,电车全进了厂了,单剩下一辆,神秘地,像被遗弃了似的,停在街心。"(张爱玲 24)荒凉,好像是无情感的,但是却埋着一种被遗弃的隐秘的情感,"荒凉的手势"就像"电车回家",明明是回家,这个手势想表现的是温暖、有归属感,但回家的是电车,这电车冰冷、机械,骨子里透着荒凉。或许,这也是人们从农村走向城市的内心感受。具体来说,是火车改变了香雪的世界观。1990年代的颇具现实主义风格的《外来妹》可能就是成年后的香雪们的故事,当然也有可能是沦为被物质所困的"小黄米"们的故事。在火车没有出现之前的时间轴上,《哦,香雪》就是科幻文学。而在火车出现后,成为了现实主义文学。如果没有科幻想象,没有第一次工业革命,也就没有火车的出现,也就不会有海子、安娜卡列尼娜的卧轨自杀,世界上将少一种富有决绝的文艺气息的死亡方式。海子的卧轨自杀象征着90年代大转型时期、全球化背景下诗歌的边缘与失落。回望80年代,当诗歌乘着时代的火车头,迎来的是爱情和成名。顾城在一次乘坐火车时邂逅了妻子谢烨,同时把握住了成名与走红。可惜在90年代隐居激流岛过着闭塞的生活,诗人没有拥抱新技术,顾城抗拒学习驾驶和外语这两项走向国际化的生存技能,长期依靠妻子谢烨作为对外交流的拐杖,同时在岛上以自我意志过一夫两妻的非现代的生活方式。当妻子选择离开时,诗人无法在世界上站立和生存,从而酿成了玉石俱焚的杀妻惨剧。

  在火车上,发生了多少爱恨离别的人类情感。技术会思考,火车是有生命的小说主角,它感受得到丰富而剧烈的人类情感波动。"火车带来了外边的一切新奇,对少女来说,它是物质的,更是精神的,那是山外和山里空气的对流,经济的活泛,物质的流通,时装的变迁,乃至爱情的幻想……都因这火车的停留而变成可以触摸的具体。"(於可训 80)在这个意义上,《波动》和《哦,香雪》都属于科幻类型的火车文学。这样的物质感、技术感强烈的文学更加体现了作家对人类的体贴和爱。铁凝说:"我愿意拥抱高科技带给人类的所有的进步和幸福,哪怕它天生具有一种不由分说的暴力色彩。但我还是要说,巨大的物质力量最终并不是我们生存的全部依据,它从来都该是巨大精神力量的预示和陪衬。而这两种力量会长久地纠缠在一起,互相依存难解难分,交替作战滚动向前。"(於可训 81)这充分体现了物质与精神的波粒转化、量子纠缠。"从蒸汽机到内燃机、电气机车,还有计划中的高速干线,不管怎样,火车至今仍是与中国人的生活联系最紧密的交通工具,从数代领导人的考察巡视到大小商品的推广销售,从出差公干到旅游探亲,火车虽说已不是唯一的老大,但还是老大的一员。由此也可以解释为什么青海和西藏早已有飞机起降,这么多人流血流汗战天斗地却还要建造青藏铁路。"(王福春 90)为争取 1991 年世界科幻大会在成都的主办权,《科幻世界》杂志社主编杨潇一行从中国坐了八天八夜的火车假道俄罗斯到荷兰海牙。(董仁威 340)这是真正的科幻现实主义文学。1980 年代的文学是以人为本的波动的主体性,而在 90 年代乃至新世纪可能就是原子化的个人叙事。文学的波粒转化之快足以让人惊叹。时代精神和新技术更新迭代同样迅速。

二、支撑与阻力:平行宇宙的多重变奏

当现实主义文学与新技术应用脱离的时候,就会被抛出运行轨道,人物命运多舛,在时代的边缘徘徊不前。与持续乐观的现代交通工具带给人类的形成鲜明对比的是更新换代迅速的通信技术。选取的样本来自热播电视剧《狂飙》。在第二次工业革命,科技发展迎来了电磁学的发展成熟,人类的通信技术由此狂飙迭代。1996 年是 2G 时代"小灵通"上线的年代。1990 年代出现的"小灵通"来自科幻作家叶永烈《小灵通漫游未来》的无偿授权,暗含着信息革命和财富的密码。《狂飙》中高启强兄弟在 2000 年抓住了"小灵通热",在市场中占住商机快速致富,而在 2006 年前后随着小灵通热潮后的衰落而一泻千里。高启盛因错判形势,囤积了几十万的小灵通通信设备导致只能通过贩毒来填补资金,从此走上黑社会的不归途。以时间轴和技术发展为移动坐标,《狂飙》的剧情是发生在九十年代的商人因"小灵通热"的风口而获利后又

因技术迭代而破产的故事。《狂飙》的关键剧情变化缘于小灵通的通信技术迭代。2000年,在开启的千禧年,中国开始开门红,2008年奥运会期间展现的上升的国力和友好形象得到了国际社会的瞩目。国内观众对国际市场和资本的仰望则通过2009年放映的现象级科幻电影《阿凡达》体现得淋漓尽致。作家文珍的《安翔路情事》(2011年)出现了看《阿凡达》的情节,美式科幻《阿凡达》与日料寿司在作家笔下并置为强大的外来资本符号,而符号化的《阿凡达》是小说剧情的关键变量,是人物产生情感波动的相关变量,人的物化由此发生,小说读来隐约有对逝去的田园爱情的惆怅和对资本入侵的抵抗。然而,如果没有《阿凡达》,卖麻辣烫的豆腐西施只有和卖灌饼的小胡一同回乡过男耕女织的田园生活这一种可能。这部现实主义小说也被众多学者归为底层文学的小说。值得注意的是:豆腐西施在经历心理斗争后最终选择了留在城市,豆腐西施做选择的驱动力不在具体的"人",而是对以《阿凡达》为象征的财富和技术的城市生活的向往。谈到写作的全部动因,是文珍在出租车上的一瞥,促成了这篇小说诞生。这现实一瞥充满了悲悯的色彩。卖灌饼的小胡是让人心疼的,"这么热的天,在那么狭小的不到五平方米的一个小门面里,他一天到晚哪里都不去,一直站着在那里摊饼,只要有顾客过来买,他就一刻也不能休息,就像希腊神话里那个不断要把石头推上山的西西弗一样"①。小胡的生活是那么单一枯燥,这和带给当时观众巨大震撼的《阿凡达》的丰富感受形成鲜明对比。而从科技发展和女性发展的双重角度来看,对于拼命想在城市立足的女性,科技的进步推动了智慧城市的发展,让女性有可能摆脱体力劳动过上更文明的生活方式,运用金钱和技术去置换劳动力,在大城市生活更适合女性生存。从人类进化角度上看,生物意义上的女性明显在体力上是弱势的,在数字化浪潮的影响下或许有一定转机。因此,从科幻的视角看文珍的《安翔路情事》,在这个双缝实验中,可以看到科技掠夺同时也看到女性在城市生活的更多可能性。2022年上映的詹姆斯·卡梅隆的《阿凡达2：水之道》与2009年的《阿凡达》相比，中国观众似乎不再惊讶于美式科幻的技术和构建，因为中国经济实力和科技发展在稳步增强。面对中国这个有着庞大人口基数的市场，卡梅隆迎合中国观众集体主义的"家"的价值观，在其电影热播后于B站连线热门的科普UP主毕导等年轻科幻爱好者，期待来自中国科幻和青年观众的反馈。拥有优越感和压迫感的美式科幻从天空回归海洋，从个人连接集体，似乎更接地气了，似乎也更接近于科幻现实主义风格。

科幻现实主义风格的传播媒介不是电影，而是大众化的传媒电视剧，切入科幻与现实的文艺形式更为平易近人，最能深入千家万户的仍然是电视剧。这种传播模式不仅适用于典型的现实主义风格的《人世间》，也能把科幻现实主义元素融入大众化的日常精神文化生活。电视的发明本身就是科技的魔法诞生，电视长期以来一直是一个传播文化的有效宣传窗口。2023年《三体》电视剧的推出不仅是国家文化战略部署，而且承载科普功能。这个时代的中国主流观众，可以从内心接受科幻，《三体》电视剧可以实现中国式的《生活大爆炸》。同样在全球热映的《瞬息全宇宙》，中年大妈伊芙琳在亚裔社区的平凡生活轨迹与杨紫琼产生了一种奇妙的连接，是多重宇宙的拼接和碰撞。杨紫琼本人出身于优越的马来西亚拿督家庭，但想为亚裔社区的华人发声，又练习了少有女演员走的功夫路线，杨紫琼的人生之路在演艺生涯没有越走越窄，反而是在60岁还有更多的可能。杨紫琼的从影实践作为现实积累为她争取到了与之生活轨迹截然不同的伊芙琳这一角色，而伊芙琳这个角色的家庭矛盾和报税纠纷的现实又成为了科幻风格的多重宇宙的编码，开源出现实之外的多重可能性。伊芙琳一地鸡毛的现实生活和杨紫琼功成名就的演绎生涯形成了科幻/现实二象性，勾勒了华裔在海外生活的双重轨迹。"光子似乎在根据观测者选择进行的实验来决定它自己是粒子或是波。"（麦肯齐165）勇于探索、敢于冒险、亲和力强、共情他人的综合素质让杨紫琼在国际上大放异彩。

新技术的发明和应用处于上升繁荣期,人物和事件刚好又能够趋于无限接近达到零阻力的情况下,就会涌现出一种现象级的文学潮流或文学类型。比如金庸武侠小说和香港报业、印刷术的繁荣以及多元文化的交叉融合分不开。再比如网络文学的兴起是文学与互联网自《第一次亲密接触》开始后一骑绝尘,在文坛占据了一席之地。再到短视频平台papi酱的爆火和直播带货的媒介化实践。近期,以严肃文学著称的国刊《人民文学》主动"与辉同行",把握住了上升风口,经由主播董宇辉带货创下了可能是中国乃至世界上杂志发行量最高的成交额记录1 785万元。纸质媒介时代的衰落不由个人意志而改变,但是积极拥抱新生的媒体技术并进行融合跨界,就可能形成轰动效应,再创辉煌。主动求新求变,应用新技术的能力,其间的人与物就会充分体现出一种生机勃勃的张力之美。在科幻和现实主义文学形成的交错世界的子集中,更易诞生现象级的文艺作品。足够丰富、巧妙融合、独特元素叠加新技术应用,或许这是诞生像《三体》这样的作品的时代密码。刘慈欣在第一次接触克拉克的科幻世界时,是通过父亲收藏的纸质图书。书籍是古典的、成熟的,但确实是和时代逐渐脱离的纸媒。在1950年代的美国,印刷业使得杂志繁荣发展,科幻处于黄金时代,诞生了一批主流的科幻作家,比如阿西莫夫、雨果·根斯巴克,相当于美国的科技启蒙导师,贝佐斯、马斯克这些在黄金时代成长起来的一代人,他们青少年时代的现实主义文学就是科幻文学。爱伦·坡对凡尔纳产生影响、凡尔纳对克拉克产生影响、克拉克对刘慈欣产生影响,不断传承。当下科幻对科技大佬产生了影响,阿西莫夫对马斯克的影响、刘慈欣和尼尔·斯蒂芬森对扎瓦伯格的影响正在改变当下世界。"新一代伴随着原子弹、电视和航天长大,随之而来的还有变化带来的不确定性,他们发现传统文学并不关注自己日常生活中的这些基本事实,哪怕关注了,也只是为了表达哀叹和绝望的情绪。他们的父母基本上都对科幻小说嗤之以鼻,认为这类小说太不真实,或是真实得令人不快,而孩子们却认为科幻小说就是他们的文学。"(詹姆斯·冈恩:《交错的世界——世界科幻图史》,姜倩译,上海人民出版社2020年版,第295—296页。)已经成年的人容易认同传统文学的审美习惯,认为眼前的悲欢离合、日常的消费、世俗的交际才是生活的现实。公认的传统的现实主义文学容易囿于封闭的文学圈子,创作的作品隔靴搔痒,消遣性强,远不如时事新闻精彩,并不真切关注科技发展带来的真正变化及不确定性,哪怕关注了也只为表达作家个人的牢骚和情绪。强调文学是人学,将人视为情感动物,这低估了人类。面临世界末日,纯文学作家或许只能哀嚎。离日常生活更近的、关注五分钟后"近未来"的巴拉德可能会拥有更多受众,不过科幻的理想是创造新的生存环境,这是未来人类最大的希望和温暖。

三、跨界与平衡:"物化"的人物张力

"物化"在科幻文学的语境下不是贬义词,从万物的本质和发源来看,人类是在复杂系统中堆叠进化的产物。物的立体性表达需要平面的人更好地表现。相对于稳定的物来说,人性随着时间轴的移动更加千变万化。刘慈欣的长篇小说《球状闪电》的叙事主角就是物本身——球状闪电。这是刘慈欣认为自己写得最像科幻的科幻小说。球状闪电是少年刘慈欣看到的令他惊奇不已、记忆深刻的自然奇象,也是触发他写作科幻的驱动力之一。与不同时间、相似时空的山西作家赵树理的创作异曲同工。"赵树理小说的最大争议,源自其人物描写。除却《孟祥英翻身》《套不住的手》《实干家潘永福》等纪实性人物故事,赵树理很少创造出一种作为个体的典型人物形象……更为重要的是,他的小说很少涉及人物的内心活动,仅仅从人物在事件发展中的功能、人物的语言和外在行为上来表现人物。"(贺桂梅:《人文学的想象力——当代中国思想文化与文学问题》,开封:河南出版社2005年版,第353页。)正如竹内好在《新颖的赵树理文学》中指出,人物是背景化的扁平人物,作

品中的人物在完成其典型的同时与背景溶为一体。一个人物代表的是一个群体。"在赵树理的构想中,他的读者不是孤独地面对作品的个体,而是一种群体性的场景。人们是以'读'和'听'的方式建立起与小说世界的认同关系。也可以说,就其消费和阅读方式而言,赵树理取消了那种个人主义的主体,而试图建立起一种群众性主体。"(354页)这正是赵树理文学的新颖性和现代性。站在冷漠的宇宙视角维度上,真正的"硬"科幻不以人类的情感和主观感受为转移,不关心个人的生死,也不在乎人类的存亡。在新冠病毒长期与人类共存的事实、不可抗力的环境气候大变化面前,人类不得不树立在太空生存的意识。向外求,才能获得更高维的生存发展空间。科幻是难以定义的:布鲁斯·富兰克林认为科幻小说描摹的是可能发生的事情;海因莱因认为科幻小说最好更名为"推测小说";约翰·坎贝尔说科幻小说就是科幻编辑出版的东西;克拉克认为科幻小说写的可能发生但你却不希望它发生的事情;达科·苏恩文倾向于"认知疏离的文学"这个定义;詹姆斯·冈恩则称科幻小说是"变化的文学"或"全人类的文学"。科幻作家的文学理念十分开放、多元。未来学家阿尔文·托夫勒认为:科幻小说是一种拓展思维的力量,可以用来培养人们预测未来的习惯。我们的儿童应当学习克拉克、海因莱因等科幻作家的小说,不是因为这些作家能够让他们了解宇宙飞船和时间机器,而是因为他们能够引领那些年轻的心灵去探索政治、社会、心理、伦理事务的丛林,这些是他们长大成人之后必须面对的。科幻小说将是"未来学初级课程"的必读书目。威尔斯曾预言:假如未来型头脑能够自由表达自己,将会创造出巨大的成就。西方科幻和西方科学技术同步在美苏争霸的航空竞赛阶段开启了"奥德赛"赛道。克拉克的《2001:太空漫游》直接影响了2001年在肯尼迪发射中心火星"奥德赛"探测器的成功发射,直接影响了现实的科学进程。苏联人造卫星、肯尼迪登月计划、阿姆斯特朗的一小步让人类见证了太空科学不是幻想,是肉眼可见的科学现实。科幻小说的力量就在让人们相信科幻是关于现实而非梦想的文学。马斯克在发射"重型猎鹰"火箭的特斯拉跑车中放上了一套微缩版的《银河帝国》,因为阿西莫夫在年少的马斯克心中埋下了太空梦。美国大部分 NASA 员工更是受《银河帝国》启发而走上了科研道路。科学需要渗入日常的场景,霍金、马斯克都曾客串《生活大爆炸》,这部美剧相当于物理版的《老友记》。当你突然穿着绿巨人或者蝙蝠侠的着装出现在朋友家门口,不会被当作怪物,而是稀松平常之事。科普能产生更广泛的影响,发展起一大批热爱科学的青少年群体,在此基础向上进阶攀登科学高峰,入门非常关键,多少人因为科学看起来高冷深奥的面孔望而却步。对于当时九岁的男孩阿西莫夫来说,科幻小说始于 1926 年 4 月,它的缔造者是雨果·根斯巴克。因为世界上最早的科幻杂志《惊奇故事》创办了。自 11 世纪中国发明活字印刷到约翰·谷森堡发明了铅字印刷,杂志成为了信息传播的重要载体和媒介。美国科幻文学的衰落也被归结于杂志的式微。中国发明的造纸、火药在全世界范围内被更广泛地应用,西方的科学技术发明可追根溯源到古老的中华文明的发明创造中。在全球化背景下,中国在世界格局中迅速崛起,成为世界第二大经济体,中国科学技术发展进入新纪元,文明周而复始。还是回到铁凝的经典成名作《哦,香雪》:一个农村小女孩向往外面的世界,对技术产生的惊奇感。《哦,香雪》回应着时代对文学的召唤,让大众对作家个人的文学创作更为肯定。

结　语

量子力学以一种完全矛盾的形式解决了"粒子与波动之争"的百年疑案:光既是一种粒子也是一种波。它看上去'像什么'取决于你如何审视它。如果你测量它的频率与波长,光

看上去像波；如果你通过光电效应来为光子计数，那时候的光看上去像粒子。（麦肯齐 156）

文艺作品可以承载科幻/现实二象性的双重共振。波粒二象性具有破除本质论和二元对立思维的不确定性，启发了包括人文学科在内的比较视角、跨学科文化研究。人类在 Chat-GPT 更新迭代的数字浪潮中，对人工智能的认知还有很长的路要走，在马斯克思考人类命运和火星移民时，多少人认为这和自己没有关系，甚至从现实层面，大多数人的认知还停留在第二次工业革命的燃油车时代，而人工智能已经不分日夜，甚至不受人类意志完全控制地指数迭代。光学基础科学的微观世界不再像牛顿时代的宏观世界肉眼可见，微观世界变得不易观察和难以理解。"科学的美感被禁锢在冷酷的方程式中，普通人需要经过巨大的努力，才能窥见她的一线光芒。"（刘慈欣 3）技术进步主义者容易在新技术还在概念层面还没有投入量产应用前，超前推进；保守主义者一般不屑一顾，被技术推搡前进，可一旦形成应用规模后又往往反应不及时。因此，灵活掌握科幻与现实主义文学的距离才能形成独特的张力美学。新的想法和发明总会实现。在现实世界和虚拟世界交错的"元宇宙"，以科学技术作为创作动力的跨界作家更有可能为人类社会开拓出新的思维空间和生存空间。

注解【Notes】

① 参见文珍在 2018 创意写作国际论坛上的讲座内容。

引用文献【Works Cited】

Liu, Cixin. *"The Worst Universe, The Best Earth" Science Fiction Review Essay Collection.* Chengdu: Sichuan Science and Technology Literature Publishing House, 2015.
［刘慈欣：《最糟的宇宙，最好的地球》科幻评论随笔集，成都：四川科学技术文献出

版社,2015年。]

James, Gunn. *Interlaced Worlds—A History of World Science Fiction* . trans. Jiang Qian. Shanghai: Shanghai People's Publishing House, 2020.

[詹姆斯·冈恩:《交错的世界——世界科幻图史》,姜倩译,上海:上海人民出版社,2020年。]

Bei, Dao. *Volatility*, Beijing: Life, Reading, New Knowledge Sanlian Bookstore, 2015.

[北岛:《波动》,北京:生活·读书·新知三联书店,2015年。]

Tie, Ning. *Oh, Xiangxue* . People's Daily, June 16, 2018.

[铁凝:《哦,香雪》,《人民日报》2018年6月16日。]

Yu, Kexun, ed. *Novelist Archives*. Zhengzhou: Zhengzhou University Press, 2005.

[於可训主编:《小说家档案》,郑州:郑州大学出版社,2005年。]

Cheng, Guangwei. "The Fragrant Snow's '1980s'—A Corner of the Countryside Reflected from the Novel *Oh, Fragrant Snow* and Literary Criticism." *Shanghai Literature*, 2(2011): 52-58.

[程光炜:《香雪们的"1980年代"——从小说〈哦,香雪〉和文学批评中折射的当时农村之一角》,《上海文学》2011年第2期,第52—58页。]

Zhang, Ailing. *Rumors* . Beijing: Beijing October Literature and Art Publishing House, 2012.

[张爱玲:《流言》,北京:北京十月文艺出版社,2012年。]

Wang, Fuchun: *The Chinese on the Train* . Shanghai: Shanghai Jinxiu Article Publishing House, 2007.

[王福春:《火车上的中国人》,上海:上海锦绣文章出版社,2007年。]

Dong, Renwei. *A Century of Science Fiction History in China*. Beijing: Tsinghua University Press, 2017.

[董仁威:《中国百年科幻史话》,北京:清华大学出版社,2017年。]

Dana, Mackenzie. *The Wordless Universe*. trans. Li Yongxue. Beijing: Beijing United Publishing Company, 2018.

[达纳·麦肯齐:《无言的宇宙》,李永学译,北京:北京联合出版公司,2018年。]

论张纯如非虚构类作品《南京大屠杀》的现实主义文学价值

葛雅纯

内容摘要：1997年，美籍华裔作家张纯如出版了《南京大屠杀：第二次世界大战中被遗忘的大浩劫》一书，该书出版后盘踞《纽约时报》非虚构类畅销书榜长达三个月，售出50万余册，引发了国际社会对于南京大屠杀史实的重新关注与讨论。作为史学作品，该书遭受了诸如考据不够严谨、论断过于主观等诸多批评，但若将该书界定为纪实文学作品，其可读性与多重叙事价值是毋庸置疑的。本文将基于艾布拉姆斯提出的文学四要素（作者、作品、读者、世界）说明《南京大屠杀》一书的文学性；也将基于卢卡奇总结的现实主义文学典型特征（即真实性、典型性和历史性），深入分析文本以揭示该书被长期忽视的现实主义文学价值。作为结论，本文认为体裁分类不应成为判定作品文学价值的唯一标准；学界应推动文学史的重新梳理，将传记、日记、历史纪实等非虚构类作品也纳入现实主义文学的研究视野中，不断丰富现实主义文学研究的内涵。

关键词：张纯如 《南京大屠杀：第二次世界大战中被遗忘的大浩劫》 现实主义 文学四要素

作者简介：葛雅纯，国防科技大学博士研究生，主要研究叙事学、话语分析和认知语言学。

Title: On the Literary Value of Iris Chang's Non-fiction *The Rape of Nanking* in Terms of Realism

Abstract: Iris Chang, a Chinese-American author, published her book *The Rape of Nanking: The Forgotten Holocaust of World War II* in 1997. Since its publication, the book has been sold more than 500,000 copies and stayed on the *New York Times* bestseller list for three months. The Nanjing Massacre sparked intense debates and captured the interest of the global community due to its portrayal in the book. Recognized as a piece of historical work, the book has faced intense criticism for its insufficient rigor and objectivity. However, if we redefine the book as a form of documentary literature, its exceptional readability and diverse narrative are undoubtedly remarkable. Hence, the purpose of this article is to examine the literary aspects of *The Rape of Nanking*, using Abrams' four elements of literature (artist, work, audience, and universe) and the three key traits of Realism (namely authenticity, typicality, and historicity) summarized by Lukacs. The book will be further analyzed to reveal its literary value in terms of Realism, which has been neglected for such a long time. In essence, this article suggests that genre classification should not be the sole measure when appraising a piece. To continuously enrich the exploration of realistic literature, researchers should prioritize the re-examination of literary history and the integration of non-fiction works such as biography, diary and historical documentary into the research scope.

Key words: Iris Chang, *The Rape of Nanking: The Forgotten Holocaust of the World War II*; Realism; Four elements of literature

Author: Ge Yachun is a PhD candidate at National University of Defense Technology. Her research interests are narratology, discourse analysis and cognitive linguistics.

张纯如(Iris Chang, 1968—2004),出生于美国新泽西州,作为一名华裔作家,曾为《纽约时报》《芝加哥论坛报》等期刊报社供稿,并著有多部纪实作品,致力于展现在美华人真实生活或揭示鲜为人知的中国历史。《南京大屠杀:第二次世界大战中被遗忘的大浩劫》(后简称《南京大屠杀》)是第一部全面介绍南京大屠杀史实的英文著作(Zagoria 163)。该书出版于1997年暨南京大屠杀60周年之际,自出版后盘踞《纽约时报》非虚构类畅销书榜长达三个月,售出50万余册,引发了国际社会对南京大屠杀史实的重新关注与讨论。1995年,张纯如便开始在美国国家档案馆和华盛顿国会图书馆等地完成了写作资料的初步准备,并前往中国北京、上海、南京等多地调研、探寻相关史料。因此,该书出版后长期被视为史学著作,早期评价褒贬不一。牛津大学的历史学者Christian Jessen Klingenberga的高度赞扬:"这是一部杰出的史学作品。"("Praise for *THE RAPE OF NANKING*" 7)学者Joshua Fogel则认为该书数倍夸大了南京大屠杀的恐怖程度,批评张纯如在史料考据方面不够严谨:"[她]不假思索地采信了一些资料,作出了一些无端的断言,作品中的观点表达情绪化、过激、充满愤怒。"(818)

　　文学史的书写往往决定了文学研究的范畴以及文学作品的价值。《南京大屠杀》取材于真实的一手史料,采用了不同视角、全面介绍了南京大屠杀史实。因此,《南京大屠杀》长期被定性为史学著作,国内外针对于此的学术研究也集中在史学界,相关研究侧重于其国际影响力、史实考据与表述客观性,却并未充分关注到该部作品在揭露历史真相外的其他价值,如现实主义文学价值。该作出版后的二十余年间,该书都未能顺利进入文学研究的视野中,该部作品的文学价值被严重低估,在文学评论领域颇受忽视。虽然早在《南京大屠杀》出版时,普利策奖得主Dale Maharidge就盛赞其"可读性强"("Praise for *THE RAPE OF NANKING*" 6);《南京大屠杀》也成为多部南京大屠杀主题的小说与诗歌的素材与灵感来源,例如严歌苓的《金陵十三钗》、林永得的《南京大屠杀:诗歌》、哈金的《南京安魂曲》等(张小玲 106),但直至2018年,郭

453

英剑主编的《美国华裔文学作品选》才首次将张纯如的《南京大屠杀》正式纳入文学作品的范畴内(178)。随后,逐渐有学者认可该书的文学艺术价值(李良 33),但相关研究仍停留在分析该书对华裔文学的影响,或分析该作与其他南京大屠杀小说之间的互文关系(张小玲 112),却并未聚焦作品本身的文学性或对作品开展深入的文本细读以揭示其文学价值。

一、《南京大屠杀》的叙事特点

不同于戏剧、小说等经典的虚构文学体裁,非虚构类作品并非文学研究中的典型性对象。因此,本文将《南京大屠杀》这部长期被归类为历史纪实的作品纳入文学范畴进行探讨的尝试,本身就是一项颇具挑战性的任务。然而,由于张纯如并不是一位训练有素的历史学者,却是一名出色的职业作家,《南京大屠杀》一书在出版后虽遭到不少史学家的挑战,却也因受大众读者的喜爱而广为传播,连历史学者 William Kirby 在批判该作"民族主义情感偏向"的同时,也忍不住称赞"张纯如对南京大屠杀的描述生动、可读性强。写作是她的强项,她用简洁有力的语言描述了大屠杀,带领读者经历残暴和毁灭,让读者感受大屠杀的真相,并用个体故事让读者会感到恐惧、震惊、难以忘怀"(433)。

《南京大屠杀》全书分为两个部分:第一部分主要讲述真实发生的南京大屠杀的经过,第二部分则主要论述南京大屠杀结束后在国际社会惨遭遗忘的现实境遇。该书在叙事视角、人物塑造等方面都同一般历史著作存在明显差异,并呈现出高度文学化的叙事特点。

在叙事视角方面,张纯如直言在写作第一部分时,曾受芥川龙之介小说《竹林中》改编电影《罗生门》的影响,因而采取了日方、中方以及南京沦陷后安全区的西方人士这三方视角来共同讲述南京大屠杀(XXXII)。不同于一般史学著作惯于通篇使用第三人称全知视角,采取多视角叙事是因为张纯如写作的主要目的不是纯粹的历史考据,而是合理运用各方资料,以更加客观地向读者呈现南京大屠杀的原貌。例如:在讲述日军强奸妇女的残暴行径时,作者便同时采用了日本老兵东史郎的回忆录(32-33)、田所耕三的自述(33)、幸存者的回忆(79-81),以及安全区欧美传教士的证言(74-75),从加害者和受害者视角共同讲述日军对中国女性惨无人道的蹂躏与杀害。采用多立场、多视角的叙事使得文本呈现出一种"复调小说"的效果(Bakhtin 27)。

这种复调的效果不仅由作品中援引的日、中、西这三方的话语与声音来呈现,也与作者在书写中提供的评价资源与展露的情感态度紧密相关。例如,张纯如在书写围攻南京的三支日本军队(即在白茆口登陆的第十六师团、上海派遣军和第十军)的指挥员,便基于已掌握的史料分别调用了不同的评价资源,其中暗含了作者对不同人物的情感态度。在描述第十六师团的总指挥中岛今朝吾时,张纯如称与之相关的书面资料十分有限,且发现的记录相当负面,并引用了作家戴维·伯格米尼(David Bergamini)及其他人的评语,称中岛是"一个小希姆莱,一个思想控制、恐吓和酷刑专家""一头野兽"和"一个暴力的人"(19-20)。在描述日军司令松井石根时,张纯如不仅花费笔墨形容了他的外貌"他体质虚弱,身材矮小,留着小胡子"(21),成长背景"出身于书香门第,是一个虔诚的佛教徒"(21),还介绍了他的现实处境:因患有肺结核被调离担任华中方面军(由上海派遣军与第十军合并而成)司令,转由裕仁天皇的姑父朝香宫鸠彦接任原上海派遣军司令,接替松井成为日军入侵南京的一线指挥(22-23)。在东京审判中,松井石根因纵容下属实施各种暴行而不加阻止的"不作为"被认定有罪,作为甲级战犯被处以绞刑。

可以发现,尽管中岛今朝吾与松井石根同为日军入侵南京的指挥官,但作者在刻画不同人物时,其用词的情感态度明显相距甚远,甚至让部分读者认为"作者显然对松井寄予了某种同情"。这或许因为彼时美苏冷战刚结束,南京大屠杀的公开史料十分有限,作者的态度很大程度上受到东京审判案卷的影响,其中记录了松井石根本人及其下属在法庭上的辩护词。暂且不论这种情感态度的差异缘何而来,作者调用不同评价资源的行为,也是其叙事声音的一种体现。在历史情节发展的明线之下,作者基于史料刻画不同历史人物,允许其作为叙事者传递不同的声音与立场,同时也凭借着评价资源暗自传达了独立于笔下人物的叙事声音与情感态度。作品中的多种叙事声音碰撞在一起,读者必须将作品中所有叙事者的回忆拼凑在一起,鉴别每一个人声音的真伪,在这一过程中对抗自我的主观与自信,去伪存真,对所发生之事得出更为客观的结论(ⅩⅩⅩⅡ)。最终,作品的"复调"叙事得以由作者、读者及参与叙事的历史人物共同完成。

  由此可见,《南京大屠杀》中塑造的历史人物颇具主体性,不同于一般史学作品的人物塑造。史学作品中通常会介绍历史人物的生平信息,有时为讲述人物事迹才描述其行为、言语。但无论刻画得多细致,史书中塑造的人物通常是绝对的客体,是被书写、被阅读、被评判的对象。反观文学作品中的人物塑造则不尽然。小说人物不仅能够去扁平化,随着情节推进动态成长,甚至能够发展出独立于作者写作意图、情感价值导向的人物主体性。同样以《南京大屠杀》中对松井石根的刻画为例,在讲述松井石根因病暂退,朝香宫鸠彦接掌指挥权时,作者写道:"当时,这似乎是一个微不足道的人事异动,但后来的事实证明,这对成千上万中国人的性命产生了决定性影响。"(23)同时写道:"松井石根对这个新来的皇室成员存有戒心,也担心部队滥用权力,于是对进攻南京的部队发布了一系列道德命令。"(23)在此处,作者运用了预叙(foreshadowing)的手法暗示未来的惨剧,调动读者对朝香宫担任指挥官的负面情绪,再通过刻画松井石根的心理活动与行动,对比说明松井与朝香宫在行事间的"不同",间接衬托出松井石根颇为正面的形象。正因如此,即便作者特地说明当时的具体细节并不可考,文中援引的证据主要源于东京审判中松井石根及其下属的证词,可能属于不可靠叙事,在阅读时需谨慎对待,但该人物的"正面"形象早已摆脱作者的束缚,在字里行间形成了。作为南京大屠杀幸存者后代的张纯如,在写作时绝无心为任何日本战犯进行"洗白",却在自身未察觉时将笔下人物刻画地颇为立体鲜活,以至其独立于作者的创作意图而存在,令读者不免产生"作者对松井寄予了同情"的"误读"。

《南京大屠杀》在叙事特点上颇具文学色彩,但这不足以扭转对作品分类的刻板认识。要让这部作品正式进入文学研究的视野,也许还须以更加普适的文学批评标准加以审视。

二、《南京大屠杀》的文学性

"文学性"问题的讨论起始于二十世纪初期的俄国形式主义,学者周海波指出"文学性"与文学批评关系密切,当文学批评活动中的非文学性现象泛滥之时,有关"文学性"问题的讨论便自觉浮现出来。在讨论这一问题时,洪子诚曾提出:"最好的文学,都是认真思考和呈现人类的生存处境,关怀人的灵魂和感情,呈现人的希望和恐惧的本真的文学。"(吴晓东 1-2)从这个意义上来看,《南京大屠杀》无疑是属于"最好的文学"这一范畴的,但以此作为文学价值评判标准的权威性与普适性尚待检校。缘于此,本小节中将借用艾布拉姆斯在《镜与灯》中提出的文学批评四要素,即作品(work)、作者(artist)、世界(universe)与读者(audience),以探讨《南京大屠杀》的文学内涵。将艺术作品置于这四个维度来进行分析,有助于揭示作品的本质与价值(Abrams 6-7)。

在四个要素中,作品是文学批评当之无愧的核心。无论是以文本细读为重点的俄国形式主义和欧美新批评一派,还是着重关注作品背后社会现实与意识形态的西方马克思主义一派,在阐释文学意义与价值时都是高度聚焦作品本身的。评论家们或将作品视为自足的整体,基于叙事、修辞、美学等方面评价作品本身的文学价值;或将作品视作对现实世界和客观事实的摹仿,反映出特定时代的真实,以此探讨作品与世界之间的关系;或将作品视为作者生活经验与灵感想象的外在表现,以此讨论作品与作者之间的关系;或将作品视作供读者的阅读、欣赏,以丰富其情感体验与认知的工具,基于读者的评价反馈衡量作品的价值意义。可以说,艾布拉姆斯提出的四要素对此后的文学批评产生了巨大的影响。因此,下文中将围绕着作者、世界、读者与作品之间的关系,进一步探讨《南京大屠杀》一书的文学性。

就作者而言,张纯如身为第二代美籍华裔,她外公一家是大屠杀前逃离南京的幸存者。幼时就曾听父母讲述过南京大屠杀的残酷,小学时遍寻当地公共图书馆查找相关资料却一无所获,内心疑惑若南京大屠杀真如传闻中残酷,为何无人为其书写(XXV-XXVI)。这是张纯如父母在她内心埋下的一粒种子,但此事很快被抛诸脑后,并未成为张纯如生活的主旋律。她随后为《纽约时报》等报刊供稿,成为了一名职业作家。童年埋下的种子被孵化在其成年后,张纯如从其他华裔朋友处重新听说有人制作了南京大屠杀的记录片,但发行时遇到资金困难,由此接触到在美华人团体举办的一个草根活动,活动主旨是促进南京大屠杀史料公开于世。她留心到美国人对于纳粹屠犹、奥斯维辛、广岛长崎这部分"二战"史烂熟于心,却对南京大屠杀一无所觉,加之彼时许多日本政客、学者和行业领袖矢口否认南京大屠杀的行径,这些事激励着张纯如决心写作《南京大屠杀》,告知世人这一段长期被忽视与遗忘的历史,同时警醒世人铭记历史教训,不要重蹈覆辙。作者创作此书之前并未受过专业的史学训练,故此在史料考据等方面或许不够严谨,不符合相关学术规范,这也成为作品出版后备受指摘之处。作者本人并非对作品可能存在的纰漏毫无察觉,与之相反,张纯如是一个相当自觉的写作者,她在书中多次借由尾注等方式告知读者文中引用的某段史料或某个推论的不可靠。张纯如所从事的是一种明知不可为而为之的书写。2011年完成出版的《南京大屠杀史料集》长达78卷、4 000万余字、耗时共10年,而张纯如从1995年开始相关史料的收集整理工作,走访了美、中、德等多个国家寻访幸存者,于1997年便完成作品写作并付梓。她的创作意图并不是历史考证,而是广而告知,将她所知晓的、被长期遗忘的这段历史告之世人。她也仅把自己的作品当作"抛砖引玉"的工具(XIV),希望能唤起更多人对于这段历史的兴趣。同样,张纯如也是一名高度敏感的写作者,她在书写过程中通过所掌握的史料洞悉到事件背后隐藏着一个可怖真相:日军在南京犯下惨无人道的罪行背后,存在一种能够使所有人都变成魔鬼的文化影响力(the power of cultural forces to make devils of us all),这种力量既能够剥夺使人之为人的那一层单薄的社会约束,也可以增强这一约束(XXXI)。这种力量就是教育。因此,作者创作此书的核心目的是警醒世人:错误的文化教育足以扭曲人性。这一创作主旨符合"文学实用论"的主张,即文学的最终目的是愉悦和教育(to teach and delight)而进行模仿(Abrams 14-15)。为实现上述创作目的,作者采用了多视角化的叙事鼓励读者参与真相的探寻与文本阐释。然而,日本右翼及其资助的学者对此并不买账。鉴于她美籍华裔的身份,右翼学者批评她的作品偏激、不客观,其所有"真诚地要求日本正视历史并承担相应责任的努力往往被贴上'打击日本'的标签"(张纯如 XXXI)。

十分遗憾,作者自我陈述的创作意图并未得到所有读者的认可。面对复杂多变的国际环境和数量庞大的读者群体,当时的社会环境、时代背景,以及不同读者群体的立场等因素势必会影响对作者创作意图和作品内涵的解读。

在世界维度,《南京大屠杀》的创作与当时美国社会的三件大事关系密切:由苏联解体标志的冷战结束、美国身份政治运动的兴起(包括纳粹大屠杀记忆的"美国化")、二十世纪九十年代日本经济腾飞。东京审判后,美苏冷战正式拉开序幕,美国为应对苏联和中国的共产主义"威胁",为拉拢昔日敌人日本,对南京大屠杀搁置不提(21),主导了国际社会对南京大屠杀的遗忘。1991年冷战结束,国际政治环境愈加宽松,使南京大屠杀有了重提的可能性,美国军方也解密了一批档案,使相关研究有了新的史料证据。同一时期,美国的黑人寻根运动和女性身份政治运动也带动了美国国内少数群体的自我身份探寻。"二战"期间美国接收了大量犹太难民,幸存者们书写的以《安妮日记》《大屠杀》为代表的大众文化作品在民众中引发激烈的情感共振。美国民众(尤其是犹太移民)对于彼时未能切实援助其欧洲同胞而深感内疚,在大屠杀真相浮出水面后,逐步转变为关注大屠杀,勿让悲剧重演的警钟。1993年4月22日,坐落于华盛顿核心纪念区的美国大屠杀纪念馆正式开馆,犹太大屠杀记忆美国化,美国社会出现了"大屠杀热"(诺维克43)。与此同时,日本经济自二十世纪八十年代迅猛发展,到1995年,日本经济总量仅次于美国,位世界第二,人均GDP位居全球第一,隐有威胁美国世界霸主地位之嫌。冷战的结束为张纯如写作《南京大屠杀》一书营造了良好的社会氛围与客观条件;身份政治运动的兴起也促使她思考自身作为二代华裔的自我认同与使命责任;在美国对犹太大屠杀的高度关注的衬托下,南京大屠杀的无人问津更令她下定决心要将这段历史告之世人。可以发现,张纯如的创作反映出她所处时代的部分社会现实,客观政治环境的宽松友好,社会氛围对大屠杀的天然关注,为张纯如的写作创造了得天独厚的有利土壤,而她的作品也进一步助推了彼时美国社会中弥漫的"大屠杀热"。

  作为一本备受争议的畅销书,《南京大屠杀》拥有非常庞大的读者群体,不同经验、立场的群体势必会从作品中解读出不同的主旨内涵。该作的典型读者大致可以分为三类:第一类是此前不曾听闻过南京大屠杀的普通西方读者;第二类是各国从事历史研究的学者;第三类是意图否认和抹杀南京大屠杀的部分人群,其中以日本右翼政客为典型。大众读者对于该部作品的态度比较积极,在美国社会大屠杀热的影响下,多数读者对该书称赞有加,认为它将南京大图杀史实传播到西方世界,读者们震惊于日本军队的残酷暴行,也同情中国人民的不幸遭遇。历史研究者们的态度则大相径庭:既有学者称赞张纯如女士向世界公布南京大屠杀真相的勇气,认可该书填补了相关空白,全面介绍了有关史实,并给予作品高度赞誉;也有学者批评该作存在引用了来源存疑、事件归因与结论存在争议的史料证据,指责她全盘否认了日本普通学者为研究南京大屠杀所做出的努力(Fogel 818-819)。不可否认,部分中立的日本学者的确长期从事并为南京大屠杀研究并做出了突出贡献。但作者母亲张盈盈女士也指出:有些在美国从事中国或亚洲研究的所谓"历史专家"其实是在日本资助下为日本说话的,甚至有些美国大学里中日历史研究的经费也出自日本,因此这些研究很难保持客观(XIV)。读者群体中对《南京大屠杀》批判得最为狠厉的是某些日本右翼政客。为实现其否认和淡化南京大屠杀的目的,日本右翼政客几乎是不遗余力地抨击、抹黑该部作品。例如,1998年4月,日本驻美大使齐藤邦彦在华盛顿举行记者招待会,他攻击张纯如的书是一本"歪曲历史的书",但他也无法说出该书究竟扭曲了何种事实。

总之,《南京大屠杀》出版后因在国际社会引发巨大反响而备受瞩目。但与其说这部作品的完成仅仅源于作者个人的国仇家恨和民族情怀,又或是说受到某种意图打击日本的政治目的驱使,不如说是天时地利人和的多种因素共同作用下的水到渠成。在一个恰如其分的时间,一位颇具正义感的女作家,勇敢地、义无反顾地讲述了一段值得铭记却被人遗忘的历史。同时,《南京大屠杀》是一部颇具开放性的作品,给读者留有充足的阐释空间。作者坚信"一个人的力量"能改变世界,也在书中给出了自身对于当时社会热点问题的思考,呼应时代主题,紧扣社会现实。

三、《南京大屠杀》的现实主义文学价值

按照文学实用论的观点,西德尼指出:文学应具有某种目的和功

能,能对读者产生影响(Abrams 14-15)。《南京大屠杀》无疑对许多读者产生了深远影响。它的影响不仅在于让许多不曾知晓此事的读者了解、认识到这段历史的残酷,也实实在在激励了许多历史研究者关注和研究南京大屠杀相关问题。据统计,1997年之后国际学术期刊上发表的南京大屠杀主题论文逐年增加,学科方向也从历史学拓展到国际政治、文化艺术研究等多个学科领域,更是成为了东亚政治(尤其是中日关系)研究中避不开的一个重点议题。值得注意的是,该部作品对于文学领域的影响或许要远胜过对历史学界的影响。《南京大屠杀》出版后,不仅成为许多相关主题小说、诗歌的灵感来源,其多视角的叙事方式更是俨然成为了新世纪南京大屠杀主题作品的叙事蓝本。二十一世纪以来,国内外的南京大屠杀主题的小说与影视作品都不再囿于中方视角来进行苦难叙事,而是灵活采用多方视角(如电影《金陵十三钗》中同时借用南京安全区的西方传教士视角)来呈现这一事件(Shang 63),响应"铭记历史 珍爱和平"的新时代号召。

现实主义文学的表现对象是客观世界,日常生活经验也告诉我们"现实主义所模仿的现实确实存在"(Lodge 26)。王守仁指出:"现实主义文学在其发展演变中,逐渐形成了具有辨识度的创作特征,卢卡奇将其总结为真实性、典型性和历史性。"(130)基于卢卡奇的观点,现实主义的真实是对现实存在的认同,"真实"并非是绝对客观的,而同样是经过意识形态处理的。正如学者Andrea Hanson在艾布拉姆斯"镜"与"灯"隐喻基础上指出的:镜面反射所呈现的真实是糅合了作者视角的"真实",而并非绝对的客观现实。因此,现实主义文学中的"真实"仅仅是一个相对概念,势必要受到作者主观性与时代背景的调和。典型性意味着对现实主义文学并非对现实生活的照搬全抄,而是在大量生活素材中挑选具有代表性的案例,又或是从众多相似案例中抽象概括出事件背后的真相,予以摹仿再现,进而揭示生活的本质特征。历史性则意味着现实主义文学立足于历史语境,并随历史进程而变化,所反映的是与时俱进的开放、动态的现实世界,而并非陈旧、固化的历史切片。复杂的社会生活为现实主义文学提供了大量创作素材与表现主题,不同的时间地域内反映真实生活的作品也将呈现出差异化的表达,丰富现实主义的内涵。

就真实性而言,《南京大屠杀》取材于大量一手史料。作者在美国国家档案馆和华盛顿国会图书馆等地调阅了大量相关档案,并亲身前往中国北京、上海、南京等多地调研,采访幸存者并通过访谈收集口述证据,发掘了《拉贝日记》这样被埋没的宝贵史料。作者基于掌握的大量资料,借由多名幸存者、施暴者、旁观者的证言和口述,拼凑出南京大屠杀的真实过往。同时在写作过程中,作者格外注重细节描写,以细腻的文字勾勒出鲜活的画面,如摄影技术般还原事件场景。例如,在描述南京陷落后日军搜索战俘的场面时,作者根据《东史郎日记》写道:"战俘们衣衫褴褛,有的穿着蓝色棉军服,蓝色棉大衣,戴着帽子;有的用毯子裹着头,拎着粗布袋子;有的还背着床垫子。日本人让俘虏排成四队,队伍前面是那面白旗。……他们成群地走着,就像是地上爬的蚂蚁。他们看上去就像是一群无家可归的人,脸上带着愚昧无知的表情。他们就像一群羊,毫无规矩和秩序,在黑暗中前行,并相互耳语着。"(张纯如 26-27)从此处的描述来看,南京被俘人数众多,并且懦弱无序、全然没有反抗的能力与意图,然而此处的"真实"仅是东史郎视角里的真实。事实上,由于南京驻守军队很快便脱去制服,乔装混入平民之中,我们无法确认这些"看上去就像是一群无家可归"的所谓"战俘"是否真的只是无辜百姓,而他们"脸上带着愚昧无知的表情"和"毫无规矩和秩序"或许并不如东史郎所认为的那般,是对军人身份的折辱(尤其是在日本武士道精神的审视下)。如前文所言,《南京大屠杀》是一本具有多重声音叙事的作品,因此作品中的"真实"往往是各个叙事者的视角与意识形作用下的"真实",作者基于自己的判断将不同信源的史料梭织在一处,她对史料的挑选与编排本身也体现出作者对南京大屠杀有关过往"真实"的认知与理解。也无怪乎许多抨击者要从作者的主观性与立场站位来抨击作品的客观真实性。

从典型性来看,张纯如在海量的南京大屠杀史料中,选取了其中最具代表性和说服力的材料,以完成这部作品。在创作第一部作品《蚕丝》时,张纯如曾遇到资料不足的问题。与之相对,在写作《南京大屠杀》时,她面临的是史料过于庞杂的问题。她从美国国家档案馆等地查找当年的日记、信函、照片、政府报告等原始资料,并通过调查走访南京、通过书信联系日本"二战"老兵、联系拉贝后人等渠道又获取了中、日、德和英四种语言来源的大量史料。她曾花费大量时间来阅读整理这些资料,却并未在作品中只简单地对史料进行罗列,而是在抽象的事实概括和数据总结之外,选取了若干施暴者与幸存者的日记、信件和口述回忆作为典型案例,以揭示南京大屠杀的残酷本质。例如,在讲述日军惨无人道屠杀中国平民时,作者选取了日军杀人比赛的幸存者唐顺山的口述回忆作为证明:唐顺山由于好奇日本人与中国人外貌是否相似,离开了原本的藏身之处,没多久就被一支八九人组成的日本小队发现踪迹并带走,亲眼经历了日军以人头计数的杀人游戏,目睹日本企图强暴怀孕的妇女,遭到反抗后将人开膛破肚,借前排被斩头同胞的尸体掩护掉入埋尸的坑洞里,被刺了五刀后侥幸存活了下来。唐顺山是当天被杀死的数百人中唯一的幸存者(张纯如 65-69)。在南京大屠杀中,相比于数十万死难同胞而言,幸存者其实是非典型的。但作者借由幸存者的视角,揭露那些将永远沉默的死难者们的现实遭遇却是尤为典型的,通过个体的叙事来呈现群体的故事,以小见大、以点带面地再现历史真实。

《南京大屠杀》一书的历史性则恰如其分地由作品的两个部分得以呈现。第一部分立足于1937年的历史语境,从三方视角讲述南京大屠杀事实;第二部分则是立足于1990年代的历史语境,讲述南京大屠杀从公共意识中消失半个多世纪,被别有用心之人扭曲的现实境遇。在第一部分讲述南京大屠杀历史时,作者引用的大量材料都源于事件亲历者的日记、信件或口述,真实地反映出事件发生当下的历史真相。在第二部分讲述世人因遗忘而造成二次屠杀时,张纯如广泛地考察了日本社会对于南京大屠杀的刻意扭曲和否认,西方社会对于成堆史料与证据的冷漠与无视,巧妙地应和美国当时社会环境中萌生的"大屠杀热"这一时代背景,在书中将南京大屠杀与犹太大屠杀并置讨论,从多个维度对比二者之间的异同:许多日本战犯不仅没有如同德国战犯一般受到应有的惩罚,其后代还堂而皇之地重新步入政治舞台,从未真诚地认识到自身错误,从未向曾经的受害者们道歉,反而厚颜无耻地参拜靖国神社。《南京大屠杀》两个部分的内容反映出不同时代的人们对南京大屠杀认识的动态变化,作者也有意通过自身写作改变其所处时代的社会现实,终结因遗忘而带来的二次屠杀。事实证明,张纯如成功做到了这一点。不同于世纪之交,由历史学界带头形成了对《南京大屠杀》一书的刻板印象,时代发展令二十一世纪的读者能够立足于新的社会现实与时代背景,更加多元地来评价这部作品。经过时间的检验,可以发现《南京大屠杀》不仅扩大了南京大屠杀史实在国际社会的知晓范围,引发了学界对相关问题的广泛关注与思考,启发了南京大屠杀主题文学的创作,也助推了南京大屠杀记忆成为世界集体记忆的组成部分。《南京大屠杀》从取材于历史现实,回应特定历史时期的社会现实号召,最终成功影响并改变现实、创造历史,其历史性正是在时代前进的过程中得以彰显。

结　语

诚然,若仅从严苛的历史学科规范出发,《南京大屠杀》不得不时刻直面那些因"严谨性不足""存在诸多偏误"而招致的质疑与挑战,从而导致该部作品的真正价值遭到贬损。一旦挣脱这一桎梏,将该部作品置于现实主义文学作品的语境下来审视,这的确是一部颇为难得的佳作。张纯如凭借自己绝佳的写作功底,将一段鲜为人知的中日历史说予西方读者,触动了无数读者的内心,造成巨大的社会反响。若从对外讲好中国故事,传播中国文化,加强国家软实力的层面来看,这更是一张值得深入研究的高分答卷。

必须承认,文学史在很大程度上决定了哪些作品能够进入主流的文学研究视野中。《南京大屠杀》的叙事特点不同于一般史学著作,反倒颇具文学色彩,作品高度吻合现实主义文学作品的三大特征,即便将其置于严肃的文学批评体系下进行审视,仍旧可算作一本不俗的现实主义文学著作。然而,由于作品分类的缘故,《南京大屠杀》长期被剔除在文学研究的范畴之外。因此,本文认为应该拓宽现实主义文学研究的视野,将小说、诗歌等虚构类作品之外的非虚构类文学体裁(如日记、传记、历史纪实等)也纳入文学研究的范畴中,不断丰富现实主义文学研究的内涵。

引用文献【Works Cited】

Abrams, Meyer H. *The Mirror and the Lamp.* London: Oxford UP, 1958.

Bakhtin, Mikhail. "Polyphonic discourse in the novel". *The Discourse Studies Reader: Main currents in theory and analysis* (2014): 27-35.

Chang, Iris. *The Rape of Nanking: The Forgotten Holocaust of World War II.* Trans. Tan Chunxia & Jiao Guolin. Beijing: Citic Press, 2012.

[张纯如:《南京大屠杀:第二次世界大战中被遗忘的大浩劫》,谭春霞、焦国林译,北京:中信出版社,2012年。]

Fogel, Joshua A. "Book Review of *The Rape of Nanking: The Forgotten Holocaust of World War II* / Japan's War Memories: Amnesia or Concealment?" *The Journal of Asian Studies* 57:3(1998):818-20.

Guo, Yingjian et al. *An Anthology of Chinese American Literature.* Beijing: China Renmin UP, 2018.

[郭英剑等:《美国华裔文学作品选》,北京:中国人民大学出版社,2018年。]

Hanson, Andrea J. "The Window, the Mirror, and the Stone: A reassessment of the roles of mimesis and opsis in critical theory". Las Vegas: U of Nevada, 1992.

Kirby, William C. "The Internationalization of China: Foreign Relations at Home and Abroad in the Republican Era". *The China Quarterly*, 150(1997):433.

Li, Liang. "Between Disenchantment and Re-enchantment: the narrative of 'Nanjing Massacre' from the perspective of new immigrant literature". *Contemporary Writers' Review* 6(2018):33-40.

[李良:《祛魅与复魅之间——新移民文学视域中的'南京大屠杀'叙事》,《当代作家评论》2018年第6期,第33-40页。]

Lodge, David. "The Novelist at the Cross Road". *The Novelist at the Cross Road*. London: Routledge, 1971.

Maharidge, Dale et al. "Praise for *The Rape of Nanking*". *The Rape of Nanking: The Forgotten Holocaust of World War* II. By Iris Chang. New York: Basic Books, 1997. 6-7.

Novick, Peter. *The Holocaust and Collective Memory*. Tran. by Wang Zhihua. Nanjing: Yilin Publishing House, 2019.

[彼得·诺维克:《大屠杀与集体记忆》,王志华译,南京:译林出版社,2019年。]

Shang Biwu. "Memory/ Postmemory, Ethics and Ideology: Toward a Historiographic Narratology in Film". *Primerjalna Knjizevnost*. 38:1(2015): 63-85.

Wang Shouren. "The Vitality of Realistic Literature Research". *Zhejiang Social Sciences* 10 (2021): 129-134 + 142 + 159-160.

[王守仁:《现实主义文学研究的勃勃生机》,《浙江社会科学》2021年第10期,第129-134、142、159-160页。]

Wu, Xiaodong. "Literary Classics, Criticism, Reading and Interpretation: A Dialogue with Mr. Hong Zicheng". *The Fate of Literary Nature*, Guangzhou: Guangdong People's Publishing House, 2014.

[吴晓东:《文学性·文学经典·批评、阅读 和阐释——与洪子诚先生对话》,《文学性的命运》,广州:广东人民出版社,2014年。]

Zagoria, Donald. Book Review of "The Rape of Nanking: The Forgotten Holocaust of World War II." *Foreign Affairs* 77:2(1998):163.

Zhang, Xiaolin. "The Origin of the Nanjing Massacre in Contemporary Chinese American Literature". *Foreign Language Teaching* 43:04(2022):106-112.

[张小玲:《当代美国华裔文学南京大屠杀书写探源》,《外语教学》2022年第43卷第4期,第106-112页。]

Zhang, Yingying. "Preface to Chinese Version." *The Rape of Nanking: The Forgotten Holocaust of World War* II. By Iris Chang. Trans. Tan Chunxia & Jiao Guolin. Beijing: Citic Press, 2012. XI-XVI.

[张盈盈:"中文版序",《南京大屠杀:第二次世界大战中被遗忘的大浩劫》张纯如著,谭春霞、焦国林译,北京:中信出版社,2012年,第XI—XVI页。]

图书在版编目(CIP)数据

历史·记忆·世界：新时代现实主义文学研究 / 徐蕾，王守仁主编. -- 南京：南京大学出版社，2024.6.
ISBN 978-7-305-28209-6

Ⅰ. I206.6

中国国家版本馆 CIP 数据核字第 2024J0D673 号

出版发行	南京大学出版社		
社　　址	南京市汉口路 22 号	邮　编	210093

书　　名　历史·记忆·世界：新时代现实主义文学研究
　　　　　LISHI JIYI SHIJIE: XINSHIDAI XIANSHI ZHUYI WENXUE YANJIU
主　　编　徐　蕾　王守仁
责任编辑　刁晓静　　　　　　　　　　编辑热线　025-83596997
照　　排　南京开卷文化传媒有限公司
印　　刷　苏州市古得堡数码印刷有限公司
开　　本　718 mm×1000 mm　1/16　印张 30　字数 390 千
版　　次　2024 年 6 月第 1 版　2024 年 6 月第 1 次印刷
ISBN　978-7-305-28209-6
定　　价　148.00 元

网　　址：http://www.njupco.com
官方微博：http://weibo.com/njupco
官方微信号：njupress
销售咨询热线：(025)83594756

＊版权所有，侵权必究
＊凡购买南大版图书，如有印装质量问题，请与所购
　图书销售部门联系调换